WILLIAM GOLDING: Three Novels

also by William Golding

THE INHERITORS
THE BRASS BUTTERFLY
FREE FALL
THE SPIRE
THE HOT GATES
THE PYRAMID
THE SCORPION GOD
DARKNESS VISIBLE
A MOVING TARGET
THE PAPER MEN

WILLIAM GOLDING

Lord of the Flies

Pincher Martin

Rites of Passage

faber and faber
LONDON·BOSTON

*This collection first published in 1984
by Faber and Faber Limited
3 Queen Square London WC1N 3AU
Printed in Great Britain by
Richard Clay (The Chaucer Press) Ltd,
Bungay, Suffolk*

Lord of the Flies © William Golding, 1954
Pincher Martin © William Golding, 1956
Rites of Passage © William Golding, 1980

British Library Cataloguing in Publication Data

Golding, William
Lord of the flies; Pincher Martin; Rites of passage.
I. Title II. Golding, William. Pincher Martin
III. Golding, William. Rites of passage
823'.914[F]   PR6013.035

ISBN 0-571-13368-1

CONTENTS

LORD OF

THE FLIES

For my mother and father

Contents

CHAPTER ONE

The Sound of the Shell

The boy with fair hair lowered himself down the last few feet of rock and began to pick his way towards the lagoon. Though he had taken off his school sweater and trailed it now from one hand, his grey shirt stuck to him and his hair was plastered to his forehead. All round him the long scar smashed into the jungle was a bath of heat. He was clambering heavily among the creepers and broken trunks when a bird, a vision of red and yellow, flashed upwards with a witch-like cry; and this cry was echoed by another.

'Hi!' it said, 'wait a minute!'

The undergrowth at the side of the scar was shaken and a multitude of raindrops fell pattering.

'Wait a minute,' the voice said, 'I got caught up.'

The fair boy stopped and jerked his stockings with an automatic gesture that made the jungle seem for a moment like the Home Counties.

The voice spoke again.

'I can't hardly move with all these creeper things.'

The owner of the voice came backing out of the undergrowth so that twigs scratched on a greasy wind-breaker. The naked crooks of his knees were plump, caught and scratched by thorns. He bent down, removed the thorns carefully, and turned round. He was shorter than the fair boy and very fat. He came forward, searching out safe lodgements for his feet, and then looked up through thick spectacles.

'Where's the man with the megaphone?'

The fair boy shook his head.

'This is an island. At least I think it's an island. That's a reef out in the sea. Perhaps there aren't any grown-ups anywhere.'

The fat boy looked startled.

'There was that pilot. But he wasn't in the passenger tube, he was up in the cabin in front.'

The fair boy was peering at the reef through screwed-up eyes.

'All them other kids,' the fat boy went on. 'Some of them must have got out. They must have, mustn't they?'

The fair boy began to pick his way as casually as possible towards the water. He tried to be offhand and not too obviously uninterested, but the fat boy hurried after him.

'Aren't there any grown-ups at all?'

'I don't think so.'

The fair boy said this solemnly; but then the delight of a realized ambition overcame him. In the middle of the scar he stood on his head and grinned at the reversed fat boy.

'No grown-ups!'

The fat boy thought for a moment.

'That pilot.'

The fair boy allowed his feet to come down and sat on the steamy earth.

'He must have flown off after he dropped us. He couldn't land here. Not in a plane with wheels.'

'We was attacked!'

'He'll be back all right.'

The fat boy shook his head.

'When we was coming down I looked through one of them windows. I saw the other part of the plane. There were flames coming out of it.'

He looked up and down the scar.

'And this is what the tube done.'

The fair boy reached out and touched the jagged end of a trunk. For a moment he looked interested.

'What happened to it?' he asked. 'Where's it got to now?'

'That storm dragged it out to sea. It wasn't half dangerous with all them tree trunks falling. There must have been some kids still in it.'

He hesitated for a moment then spoke again.

'What's your name?'

'Ralph.'

The fat boy waited to be asked his name in turn but this proffer of acquaintance was not made; the fair boy called Ralph smiled vaguely, stood up, and began to make his way once more towards the lagoon. The fat boy hung steadily at his shoulder.

'I expect there's a lot more of us scattered about. You haven't seen any others have you?'

Ralph shook his head and increased his speed. Then he tripped over a branch and came down with a crash.

The fat boy stood by him, breathing hard.

'My auntie told me not to run,' he explained, 'on account of my asthma.'

'Ass-mar?'

'That's right. Can't catch me breath. I was the only boy in our school what had asthma,' said the fat boy with a touch of pride. 'And I've been wearing specs since I was three.'

He took off his glasses and held them out to Ralph, blinking and smiling, and then started to wipe them against his grubby wind-breaker. An expression of pain and inward concentration altered the pale contours of his face. He smeared the sweat from his cheeks and quickly adjusted the spectacles on his nose.

'Them fruit.'

He glanced round the scar.

'Them fruit,' he said, 'I expect——'

He put on his glasses, waded away from Ralph, and crouched down among the tangled foliage.

'I'll be out again in just a minute——'

Ralph disentangled himself cautiously and stole away through the branches. In a few seconds the fat boy's grunts were behind him and he was hurrying towards the screen that still lay between him and the lagoon. He climbed over a broken trunk and was out of the jungle.

The shore was fledged with palm trees. These stood or leaned or reclined against the light and their green feathers were a hundred feet up in the air. The ground beneath them was a bank covered with coarse grass, torn everywhere by the upheavals of fallen trees, scattered with decaying coco-nuts and palm saplings. Behind this was the darkness of the forest proper and the open space of the scar. Ralph stood, one hand against a grey trunk, and screwed up his eyes against the shimmering water. Out there, perhaps a mile away, the white surf flinked on a coral reef, and beyond that the open sea was dark blue. Within the irregular arc of coral the lagoon was still as a mountain lake—blue of all shades and shadowy green and purple. The beach between the palm terrace and the water was a thin bowstave, endless apparently, for to Ralph's left the perspectives of palm and beach and water drew to a point at infinity; and always, almost visible, was the heat.

He jumped down from the terrace. The sand was thick over his black shoes and the heat hit him. He became conscious of the weight of his clothes, kicked his shoes off fiercely and ripped off each stocking with its elastic garter in a single movement. Then he leapt back on the terrace, pulled off his shirt, and stood there among the skull-like coco-nuts with green shadows from the palms and the forest sliding over his skin. He undid the snake-clasp of his belt, lugged off his shorts and pants, and stood there naked, looking at the dazzling beach and the water.

He was old enough, twelve years and a few months, to have lost the prominent tummy of childhood; and not yet old enough for adolescence to have made him awkward. You could see now that he might make a boxer, as far as width and heaviness of shoulders went, but there was a mildness about his mouth and eyes that proclaimed no devil. He patted the palm trunk softly; and, forced at last to believe in the reality of the island, laughed delightedly again and stood on his head. He turned neatly on to his feet, jumped down to the beach, knelt and swept a double armful of sand into a pile against his chest. Then he sat back and looked at the water with bright, excited eyes.

'Ralph——'

The fat boy lowered himself over the terrace and sat down carefully, using the edge as a seat.

'I'm sorry I been such a time. Them fruit——'

He wiped his glasses and adjusted them on his button nose. The frame had made a deep, pink 'V' on the bridge. He looked critically at Ralph's golden body and then down at his own clothes. He laid a hand on the end of a zipper that extended down his chest.

'My auntie——'

Then he opened the zipper with decision and pulled the whole wind-breaker over his head.

'There!'

Ralph looked at him side-long and said nothing.

'I expect we'll want to know all their names,' said the fat boy, 'and make a list. We ought to have a meeting.'

Ralph did not take the hint so the fat boy was forced to continue.

'I don't care what they call me,' he said confidentially, 'so long as they don't call me what they used to call me at school.'

Ralph was faintly interested.

'What was that?'

The fat boy glanced over his shoulder, then leaned towards Ralph.

He whispered.

'They used to call me "Piggy".'

Ralph shrieked with laughter. He jumped up.

'Piggy! Piggy!'

'Ralph—please!'

Piggy clasped his hands in apprehension.

'I said I didn't want——'

'Piggy! Piggy!'

Ralph danced out into the hot air of the beach and then returned as a fighter-plane, with wings swept back, and machine-gunned Piggy.

'Sche-aa-ow!'

He dived in the sand at Piggy's feet and lay there laughing.

'Piggy!'

Piggy grinned reluctantly, pleased despite himself at even this much recognition.

'So long as you don't tell the others——'

Ralph giggled into the sand. The expression of pain and concentration returned to Piggy's face.

'Half a sec'.'

He hastened back into the forest. Ralph stood up and trotted along to the right.

Here the beach was interrupted abruptly by the square motif of the landscape; a great platform of pink granite thrust up uncompromisingly through forest and terrace and sand and lagoon to make a raised jetty four feet high. The top of this was covered with a thin layer of soil and coarse grass and shaded with young palm trees. There was not enough soil for them to grow to any height and when they reached perhaps twenty feet they fell and dried, forming a criss-cross pattern of trunks, very convenient to sit on. The palms that still stood made a green roof, covered on the underside with a quivering tangle of reflections from the lagoon. Ralph hauled himself on to this platform, noted the coolness and shade, shut one eye, and decided that the shadows on his body were really green. He picked his way to the seaward edge of the platform and stood looking down into the water. It was clear to the bottom and bright with the efflorescence of tropical weed and coral. A school of tiny, glittering fish flicked hither and thither. Ralph spoke to himself, sounding the bass strings of delight.

'Whizzoh!'

Beyond the platform there was more enchantment. Some act of
God—a typhoon perhaps, or the storm that had accompanied his
own arrival—had banked sand inside the lagoon so that there
was a long, deep pool in the beach with a high ledge of pink
granite at the further end. Ralph had been deceived before now
by the specious appearance of depth in a beach pool and he
approached this one preparing to be disappointed. But the island
ran true to form and the incredible pool, which clearly was only
invaded by the sea at high tide, was so deep at one end as to be
dark green. Ralph inspected the whole thirty yards carefully and
then plunged in. The water was warmer than his blood and he
might have been swimming in a huge bath.

Piggy appeared again, sat on the rocky ledge, and watched
Ralph's green and white body enviously.

'You can't half swim.'

'Piggy.'

Piggy took off his shoes and socks, ranged them carefully on
the ledge, and tested the water with one toe.

'It's hot!'

'What did you expect?'

'I didn't expect nothing. My auntie——'

'Sucks to your auntie!'

Ralph did a surface dive and swam under water with his eyes
open; the sandy edge of the pool loomed up like a hillside. He
turned over, holding his nose, and a golden light danced and
shattered just over his face. Piggy was looking determined and
began to take off his shorts. Presently he was pale and fatly
naked. He tip-toed down the sandy side of the pool, and sat there
up to his neck in water smiling proudly at Ralph.

'Aren't you going to swim?'

Piggy shook his head.

'I can't swim. I wasn't allowed. My asthma——'

'Sucks to your ass-mar!'

Piggy bore this with a sort of humble patience.

'You can't half swim well.'

Ralph paddled backwards down the slope, immersed his mouth
and blew a jet of water into the air. Then he lifted his chin and
spoke.

'I could swim when I was five. Daddy taught me. He's a
commander in the Navy. When he gets leave he'll come and
rescue us. What's your father?'

Piggy flushed suddenly.

'My dad's dead,' he said quickly, 'and my mum——'

He took off his glasses and looked vainly for something with which to clean them.

'I used to live with my auntie. She kept a sweet-shop. I used to get ever so many sweets. As many as I liked. When'll your dad rescue us?'

'Soon as he can.'

Piggy rose dripping from the water and stood naked, cleaning his glasses with a sock. The only sound that reached them now through the heat of the morning was the long, grinding roar of the breakers on the reef.

'How does he know we're here?'

Ralph lolled in the water. Sleep enveloped him like the swathing mirages that were wrestling with the brilliance of the lagoon.

'How does he know we're here?'

Because, thought Ralph, because, because. The roar from the reef became very distant.

'They'd tell him at the airport.'

Piggy shook his head, put on his flashing glasses and looked down at Ralph.

'Not them. Didn't you hear what the pilot said? About the atom bomb? They're all dead.'

Ralph pulled himself out of the water, stood facing Piggy, and considered this unusual problem.

Piggy persisted.

'This an island, isn't it?'

'I climbed a rock,' said Ralph slowly, 'and I think this is an island.'

'They're all dead,' said Piggy, 'an' this is an island. Nobody don't know we're here. Your dad don't know, nobody don't know——'

His lips quivered and the spectacles were dimmed with mist.

'We may stay here till we die.'

With that word the heat seemed to increase till it became a threatening weight and the lagoon attacked them with a blinding effulgence.

'Get my clothes,' muttered Ralph. 'Along there.'

He trotted through the sand, enduring the sun's enmity, crossed the platform and found his scattered clothes. To put on a

grey shirt once more was strangely pleasing. Then he climbed the
edge of the platform and sat in the green shade on a convenient
trunk. Piggy hauled himself up, carrying most of his clothes
under his arms. Then he sat carefully on a fallen trunk near the
little cliff that fronted the lagoon; and the tangled reflections
quivered over him.

Presently he spoke.

'We got to find the others. We got to do something.'

Ralph said nothing. Here was a coral island. Protected from
the sun, ignoring Piggy's ill-omened talk, he dreamed pleasantly.

Piggy insisted.

'How many of us are there?'

Ralph came forward and stood by Piggy.

'I don't know.'

Here and there, little breezes crept over the polished waters
beneath the haze of heat. When these breezes reached the platform
the palm-fronds would whisper, so that spots of blurred sunlight
slid over their bodies or moved like bright, winged things in the
shade.

Piggy looked up at Ralph. All the shadows on Ralph's face
were reversed; green above, bright below from the lagoon. A
blur of sunlight was crawling across his hair.

'We got to do something.'

Ralph looked through him. Here at last was the imagined but
never fully realized place leaping into real life. Ralph's lips parted
in a delighted smile and Piggy, taking this smile to himself as a
mark of recognition, laughed with pleasure.

'If it really is an island——'

'What's that?'

Ralph had stopped smiling and was pointing into the lagoon.
Something creamy lay among the ferny weeds.

'A stone.'

'No. A shell.'

Suddenly Piggy was a-bubble with decorous excitement.

'S'right. It's a shell. I seen one like that before. On someone's
back wall. A conch he called it. He used to blow it and then his
mum would come. It's ever so valuable——'

Near to Ralph's elbow, a palm sapling leaned out over he
lagoon. Indeed, the weight was already pulling a lump from the
poor soil and soon it would fall. He tore out the stem and began
to poke about in the water, while the brilliant fish flicked away

on this side and that. Piggy leaned dangerously.

'Careful! You'll break it——'

'Shut up.'

Ralph spoke absently. The shell was interesting and pretty and a worthy plaything: but the vivid phantoms of his daydream still interposed between him and Piggy, who in this context was an irrelevance. The palm sapling, bending, pushed the shell across the weeds. Ralph used one hand as a fulcrum and pressed down with the other till the shell rose, dripping, and Piggy could make a grab.

Now the shell was no longer a thing seen but not to be touched, Ralph too became excited. Piggy babbled:

'—a conch; ever so expensive. I bet if you wanted to buy one, you'd have to pay pounds and pounds and pounds—he had it on his garden wall, and my auntie——'

Ralph took the shell from Piggy and a little water ran down his arm. In colour the shell was deep cream, touched here and there with fading pink. Between the point, worn away into a little hole, and the pink lips of the mouth, lay eighteen inches of shell with a slight spiral twist and covered with a delicate, embossed pattern. Ralph shook sand out of the deep tube.

'—moo-ed like a cow,' he said. 'He had some white stones too, an' a bird cage with a green parrot. He didn't blow the white stones, of course, an' he said——'

Piggy paused for breath and stroked the glistening thing that lay in Ralph's hands.

'Ralph!'

Ralph looked up.

'We can use this to call the others. Have a meeting. They'll come when they hear us——'

He beamed at Ralph.

'That was what you meant, didn't you? That's why you got the conch out of the water?'

Ralph pushed back his fair hair.

'How did your friend blow the conch?'

'He kind of spat,' said Piggy. 'My auntie wouldn't let me blow on account of my asthma. He said you blew from down here.' Piggy laid a hand on his jutting abdomen. 'You try, Ralph. You'll call the others.'

Doubtfully, Ralph laid the small end of the shell against his mouth and blew. There came a rushing sound from its mouth but nothing more. Ralph wiped the salt water off his lips and tried again, but the shell remained silent.

'He kind of spat.'

Ralph pursed his lips and squirted air into the shell, which emitted a low, farting noise. This amused both boys so much that Ralph went on squirting for some minutes, between bouts of laughter.

'He blew from down here.'

Ralph grasped the idea and hit the shell with air from his diaphragm. Immediately the thing sounded. A deep, harsh note boomed under the palms, spread through the intricacies of the forest and echoed back from the pink granite of the mountain. Clouds of birds rose from the tree-tops, and something squealed and ran in the undergrowth.

Ralph took the shell away from his lips.

'Gosh!'

His ordinary voice sounded like a whisper after the harsh note of the conch. He laid the conch against his lips, took a deep breath and blew once more. The note boomed again: and then at his firmer pressure, the note, fluking up an octave, became a strident blare more penetrating than before. Piggy was shouting something, his face pleased, his glasses flashing. The birds cried, small animals scuttered. Ralph's breath failed; the note dropped the octave, became a low wubber, was a rush of air.

The conch was silent, a gleaming tusk; Ralph's face was dark with breathlessness and the air over the island was full of bird-clamour and echoes ringing.

'I bet you can hear that for miles.'

Ralph found his breath and blew a series of short blasts.

Piggy exclaimed: 'There's one!'

A child had appeared among the palms, about a hundred yards along the beach. He was a boy of perhaps six years, sturdy and fair, his clothes torn, his face covered with a sticky mess of fruit. His trousers had been lowered for an obvious purpose and had only been pulled back half-way. He jumped off the palm terrace into the sand and his trousers fell about his ankles; he stepped out of them and trotted to the platform. Piggy helped him up. Meanwhile Ralph continued to blow till voices shouted in the forest. The small boy squatted in front of Ralph, looking up brightly and vertically. As he received the reassurance of something pur-

poseful being done he began to look satisfied, and his only clean
digit, a pink thumb, slid into his mouth.

Piggy leaned down to him.

'What's yer name?'

'Johnny.'

Piggy muttered the name to himself and then shouted it to
Ralph, who was not interested because he was still blowing. His
face was dark with the violent pleasure of making this stupendous
noise, and his heart was making the stretched shirt shake. The
shouting in the forest was nearer.

Signs of life were visible now on the beach. The sand, trembling
beneath the heat-haze, concealed many figures in its miles of
length; boys were making their way towards the platform through
the hot, dumb sand. Three small children, no older than Johnny,
appeared from startlingiy close at hand where they had been
gorging fruit in the forest. A dark little boy, not much younger
than Piggy, parted a tangle of undergrowth, walked on to the
platform, and smiled cheerfully at everybody. More and more of
them came. Taking their cue from the innocent Johnny, they sat
down on the fallen palm trunks and waited. Ralph continued to
blow short, penetrating blasts. Piggy moved among the crowd,
asking names and frowning to remember them. The children
gave him the same simple obedience that they had given to the
men with megaphones. Some were naked and carrying their
clothes: others half-naked, or more-or-less dressed, in school uni-
forms; grey, blue, fawn, jacketed or jerseyed. There were badges,
mottoes even, stripes of colour in stockings and pullovers. Their
heads clustered above the trunks in the green shade; heads brown,
fair, black, chestnut, sandy, mouse-coloured; heads muttering,
whispering, heads full of eyes that watched Ralph and speculated.
Something was being done.

The children who came along the beach, singly or in twos,
leapt into visibility when they crossed the line from heat-haze to
nearer sand. Here, the eye was first attracted to a black, bat-like
creature that danced on the sand, and only later perceived the
body above it. The bat was the child's shadow, shrunk by the
vertical sun to a patch between the hurrying feet. Even while he
blew, Ralph noticed the last pair of bodies that reached the platform above a fluttering patch of black. The two boys, bullet-
headed and with hair like tow, flung themselves down and lay
grinning and panting at Ralph like dogs. They were twins, and

the eye was shocked and incredulous at such cheery duplication. They breathed together, they grinned together, they were chunky and vital. They raised wet lips at Ralph, for they seemed provided with not quite enough skin, so that their profiles were blurred and their mouths pulled open. Piggy bent his flashing glasses to them and could be heard between the blasts, repeating their names.

'Sam, Eric, Sam, Eric.'

Then he got muddled; the twins shook their heads and pointed at each other and the crowd laughed.

At last Ralph ceased to blow and sat there, the conch trailing from one hand, his head bowed on his knees. As the echoes died away so did the laughter, and there was silence.

Within the diamond haze of the beach something dark was fumbling along. Ralph saw it first, and watched till the intentness of his gaze drew all eyes that way. Then the creature stepped from mirage on to clear sand, and they saw that the darkness was not all shadow but mostly clothing. The creature was a party of boys, marching approximately in step in two parallel lines and dressed in strangely eccentric clothing. Shorts, shirts, and different garments they carried in their hands: but each boy wore a square black cap with a silver badge in it. Their bodies, from throat to ankle, were hidden by black cloaks which bore a long silver cross on the left breast and each neck was finished off with a hambone frill. The heat of the tropics, the descent, the search for food, and now this sweaty march along the blazing beach had given them the complexions of newly washed plums. The boy who controlled them was dressed in the same way though his cap badge was golden. When his party was about ten yards from the platform he shouted an order and they halted, gasping, sweating, swaying in the fierce light. The boy himself came forward, vaulted on to the platform with his cloak flying, and peered into what to him was almost complete darkness.

'Where's the man with the trumpet?'

Ralph, sensing his sun-blindness, answered him.

'There's no man with a trumpet. Only me.'

The boy came close and peered down at Ralph, screwing up his face as he did so. What he saw of the fair-haired boy with the creamy shell on his knees did not seem to satisfy him. He turned quickly, his black cloak circling.

'Isn't there a ship, then?'

Inside the floating cloak he was tall, thin, and bony: and his hair was red beneath the black cap. His face was crumpled and freckled, and ugly without silliness. Out of this face stared two light blue eyes, frustrated now, and turning, or ready to turn, to anger.

'Isn't there a man here?'

Ralph spoke to his back.

'No, we're having a meeting. Come and join in.'

The group of cloaked boys began to scatter from close line. The tall boy shouted at them.

'Choir! Stand still!'

Wearily obedient, the choir huddled into line and stood there swaying in the sun. None the less, some began to protest faintly.

'But, Merridew. Please, Merridew . . . can't we?'

Then one of the boys flopped on his face in the sand and the line broke up. They heaved the fallen boy to the platform and let him lie. Merridew, his eyes staring, made the best of a bad job.

'All right then. Sit down. Let him alone.'

'But Merridew.'

'He's always throwing a faint,' said Merridew. 'He did in Gib.; and Addis; and at matins over the precentor.'

This last piece of shop brought sniggers from the choir, who perched like black birds on the criss-cross trunks and examined Ralph with interest. Piggy asked no names. He was intimidated by this uniformed superiority and the offhand authority in Merridew's voice. He shrank to the other side of Ralph and busied himself with his glasses.

Merridew turned to Ralph.

'Aren't there any grown-ups?'

'No.'

Merridew sat down on a trunk and looked round the circle.

'Then we'll have to look after ourselves.'

Secure on the other side of Ralph, Piggy spoke timidly.

'That's why Ralph made a meeting. So as we can decide what to do. We've heard names. That's Johnny. Those two— they're twins, Sam 'n Eric. Which is Eric—? You? No—you're Sam——'

'I'm Sam——'

''n I'm Eric.'

'We'd better all have names,' said Ralph, 'so I'm Ralph.'

'We got most names,' said Piggy. 'Got 'em just now.'

'Kids' names,' said Merridew. 'Why should I be Jack? I'm Merridew.'

Ralph turned to him quickly. This was the voice of one who knew his own mind.

'Then,' went on Piggy, 'that boy—I forget——'

'You're talking too much,' said Jack Merridew. 'Shut up, Fatty.'

Laughter arose.

'He's not Fatty,' cried Ralph, 'his real name's Piggy!'

'Piggy!'

'Piggy!'

'Oh, Piggy!'

A storm of laughter arose and even the tiniest child joined in. For the moment the boys were a closed circuit of sympathy with Piggy outside: he went very pink, bowed his head and cleaned his glasses again.

Finally the laughter died away and the naming continued. There was Maurice, next in size among the choir boys to Jack, but broad and grinning all the time. There was a slight, furtive boy whom no one knew, who kept to himself with an inner intensity of avoidance and secrecy. He muttered that his name was Roger and was silent again. Bill, Robert, Harold, Henry; the choir boy who had fainted sat up against a palm trunk, smiled pallidly at Ralph and said that his name was Simon.

Jack spoke.

'We've got to decide about being rescued.'

There was a buzz. One of the small boys, Henry, said that he wanted to go home.

'Shut up,' said Ralph absently. He lifted the conch. 'Seems to me we ought to have a chief to decide things.'

'A chief! A chief!'

'I ought to be chief,' said Jack with simple arrogance, 'because I'm chapter chorister and head boy. I can sing C sharp.'

Another buzz.

'Well then,' said Jack, 'I——'

He hesitated. The dark boy, Roger, stirred at last and spoke up.

'Let's have a vote.'

'Yes!'

'Vote for a chief!'

'Let's vote——'

This toy of voting was almost as pleasing as the conch. Jack started to protest but the clamour changed from the general wish for a chief to an election by acclaim of Ralph himself. None of the boys could have found good reason for this; what intelligence had been shown was traceable to Piggy while the most obvious leader was Jack. But there was a stillness about Ralph as he sat that marked him out: there was his size, and attractive appearance; and most obscurely, yet most powerfully, there was the conch. The being that had blown that, had sat waiting for them on the platform with the delicate thing balanced on his knees, was set apart.

'Him with the shell.'

'Ralph! Ralph!'

'Let him be chief with the trumpet-thing.'

Ralph raised a hand for silence.

'All right. Who wants Jack for chief?'

With dreary obedience the choir raised their hands.

'Who wants me?'

Every hand outside the choir except Piggy's was raised immediately. Then Piggy, too, raised his hand grudgingly into the air.

Ralph counted.

'I'm chief then.'

The circle of boys broke into applause. Even the choir applauded; and the freckles on Jack's face disappeared under a blush of mortification. He started up, then changed his mind and sat down again while the air rang. Ralph looked at him, eager to offer something.

'The choir belongs to you, of course.'

'They could be the army——'

'Or hunters——'

'They could be——'

The suffusion drained away from Jack's face. Ralph waved again for silence.

'Jack's in charge of the choir. They can be—what do you want them to be?'

'Hunters.'

Jack and Ralph smiled at each other with shy liking. The rest began to talk eagerly.

Jack stood up.

'All right choir. Take off your togs.'

As if released from class, the choir boys stood up, chattered, piled their black cloaks on the grass. Jack laid his on the trunk by Ralph. His grey shorts were sticking to him with sweat. Ralph glanced at them admiringly, and when Jack saw his glance he explained.

'I tried to get over that hill to see if there was water all round. But your shell called us.'

Ralph smiled and held up the conch for silence.

'Listen, everybody. I've got to have time to think things out. I can't decide what to do straight off. If this isn't an island we might be rescued straight away. So we've got to decide if this is an island. Everybody must stay round here and wait and not go away. Three of us—if we take more we'd get all mixed, and lose each other—three of us will go on an expedition and find out. I'll go, and Jack, and, and. . . .'

He looked round the circle of eager faces. There was no lack of boys to choose from.

'And Simon.'

The boys round Simon giggled, and he stood up, laughing a little. Now that the pallor of his faint was over, he was a skinny, vivid little boy, with a glance coming up from under a hut of straight hair that hung down, black and coarse.

He nodded at Ralph.

'I'll come.'

'And I——'

Jack snatched from behind him a sizable sheath-knife and clouted it into a trunk. The buzz rose and died away.

Piggy stirred.

'I'll come.'

Ralph turned to him.

'You're no good on a job like this.'

'All the same——'

'We don't want you,' said Jack, flatly. 'Three's enough.'

Piggy's glasses flashed.

'I was with him when he found the conch. I was with him before anyone else was.'

Jack and the others paid no attention. There was a general dispersal. Ralph, Jack and Simon jumped off the platform and walked along the sand past the bathing-pool. Piggy hung bumbling behind them.

'If Simon walks in the middle of us,' said Ralph, 'then we could talk over his head.'

The three of them fell into step. This meant that every now and then Simon had to do a double shuffle to catch up with the others. Presently Ralph stopped and turned back to Piggy.

'Look.'

Jack and Simon pretended to notice nothing. They walked on.

'You can't come.'

Piggy's glasses were misted again—this time with humiliation.

'You told 'em. After what I said.'

His face flushed, his mouth trembled.

'After I said I didn't want——'

'What on earth are you talking about?'

'About being called Piggy. I said I didn't care as long as they didn't call me Piggy; an' I said not to tell and then you went an' said straight out——'

Stillness descended on them. Ralph, looking with more understanding at Piggy, saw that he was hurt and crushed. He hovered between the two courses of apology or further insult.

'Better Piggy than Fatty,' he said at last, with the directness of genuine leadership, 'and anyway, I'm sorry if you feel like that. Now go back, Piggy, and take names. That's your job. So long.'

He turned and raced after the other two. Piggy stood and the rose of indignation faded slowly from his cheeks. He went back to the platform.

The three boys walked briskly on the sand. The tide was low and there was a strip of weed-strewn beach that was almost as firm as a road. A kind of glamour was spread over them and the scene and they were conscious of the glamour and made happy by it. They turned to each other, laughing excitedly, talking, not listening. The air was bright. Ralph, faced by the task of translating all this into an explanation, stood on his head and fell over. When they had done laughing, Simon stroked Ralph's arm shyly; and they had to laugh again.

'Come on,' said Jack presently, 'we're explorers.'

'We'll go to the end of the island,' said Ralph, 'and look round the corner.'

'If it is an island——'

Now, towards the end of the afternoon, the mirages were settling a little. They found the end of the island, quite distinct and not magicked out of shape or sense. There was a jumble of the usual squareness, with one great block sitting out in the lagoon. Sea birds were nesting there.

'Like icing,' said Ralph, 'on a pink cake.'

'We shan't see round this corner,' said Jack, 'because there isn't one. Only a slow curve—and you can see, the rocks get worse——'

Ralph shaded his eyes and followed the jagged outline of the crags up towards the mountain. This part of the beach was nearer the mountain than any other that they had seen.

'We'll try climbing the mountain from here,' he said. 'I should think this is the easiest way. There's less of that jungly stuff; and more pink rock. Come on.'

The three boys began to scramble up. Some unknown force had wrenched and shattered these cubes so that they lay askew, often piled diminishingly on each other. The most usual feature of the rock was a pink cliff surmounted by a skewed block; and that again surmounted, and that again, till the pinkness became a stack of balanced rock projecting through the looped fantasy of the forest creepers. Where the pink cliffs rose out of the ground there were often narrow tracks winding upwards. They could edge along them, deep in the plant world, their faces to the rock.

'What made this track?'

Jack paused, wiping the sweat from his face. Ralph stood by him, breathless.

'Men?'

Jack shook his head.

'Animals.'

Ralph peered into the darkness under the trees. The forest minutely vibrated.

'Come on.'

The difficulty was not the steep ascent round the shoulders of rock, but the occasional plunges through the undergrowth to get to the next path. Here, the roots and stems of creepers were in such tangles that the boys had to thread through them like pliant needles. Their only guide, apart from the brown ground and occasional flashes of light through the foliage, was the tendency of slope: whether this hole, laced as it was with cables of creeper, stood higher than that.

Somehow, they moved up.

Immured in these tangles, at perhaps their most difficult moment, Ralph turned with shining eyes to the others.

'Wacco.'

'Wizard.'

'Smashing.'

The cause of their pleasure was not obvious. All three were hot, dirty and exhausted. Ralph was badly scratched. The creepers were as thick as their thighs and left little but tunnels for further penetration. Ralph shouted experimentally and they listened to the muted echoes.

'This is real exploring,' said Jack. 'I bet nobody's been here before.'

'We ought to draw a map,' said Ralph, 'only we haven't any paper.'

'We could make scratches on bark,' said Simon, 'and rub black stuff in.'

Again came the solemn communion of shining eyes in the gloom.

'Wacco.'

'Wizard.'

There was no place for standing on one's head. This time Ralph expressed the intensity of his emotion by pretending to knock Simon down; and soon they were a happy, heaving pile in the under-dusk.

When they had fallen apart Ralph spoke first.

'Got to get on.'

The pink granite of the next cliff was further back from the creepers and trees so that they could trot up the path. This again led into more open forest so that they had a glimpse of the spread sea. With openness came the sun; it dried the sweat that had soaked their clothes in the dark, damp heat. At last the way to the top looked like a scramble over pink rock, with no more plunging through darkness. The boys chose their way through defiles and over screes of sharp stone.

'Look! Look!'

High over this end of the island, the shattered rocks lifted up their stacks and chimneys. This one, against which Jack leaned, moved with a grating sound when they pushed.

'Come on——'

But not 'Come on' to the top. The assault on the summit must wait while the three boys accepted this challenge. The rock was as large as a small motor car.

'Heave!'

Sway back and forth, catch the rhythm.

'Heave!'

Increase the swing of the pendulum, increase, increase, come up and bear against that point of further balance—increase—increase——

'Heave!'

The great rock loitered, poised on one toe, decided not to return, moved through the air, fell, struck, turned over, leapt droning through the air and smashed a deep hole in the canopy of the forest. Echoes and birds flew, white and pink dust floated, the forest further down shook as with the passage of an enraged monster: and then the island was still.

'Wacco!'

'Like a bomb!'

'Whee-aa-oo!'

Not for five minutes could they drag themselves away from this triumph. But they left at last.

The way to the top was easy after that. As they reached the last stretch Ralph stopped.

'Golly!'

They were on the lip of a cirque, or a half-cirque, in the side of the mountain. This was filled with a blue flower, a rock plant of some sort; and the overflow hung down the vent and spilled lavishly among the canopy of the forest. The air was thick with butterflies, lifting, fluttering, settling.

Beyond the cirque was the square top of the mountain and soon they were standing on it.

They had guessed before that this was an island: clambering among the pink rocks, with the sea on either side, and the crystal heights of air, they had known by some instinct that the sea lay on every side. But there seemed something more fitting in leaving the last word till they stood on the top, and could see a circular horizon of water.

Ralph turned to the others.

'This belongs to us.'

It was roughly boat-shaped: humped near this end with behind them the jumbled descent to the shore. On either side rocks, cliffs, tree-tops and a steep slope: forward there, the length of the boat, a tamer descent, tree-clad, with hints of pink: and then the jungly flat of the island, dense green, but drawn at the end to a pink tail. There, where the island petered out in water, was another island; a rock, almost detached, standing like a fort, facing them across the green with one bold, pink bastion.

The boys surveyed all this, then looked out to sea. They were high up and the afternoon had advanced; the view was not robbed of sharpness by mirage.

'That's a reef. A coral reef. I've seen pictures like that.'

The reef enclosed more than one side of the island, lying perhaps a mile out and parallel to what they now thought of as their beach. The coral was scribbled in the sea as though a giant had bent down to reproduce the shape of the island in a flowing, chalk line but tired before he had finished. Inside was peacock water, rocks and weed showing as in an aquarium; outside was the dark blue of the sea. The tide was running so that long streaks of foam tailed away from the reef and for a moment they felt that the boat was moving steadily astern.

Jack pointed down.

'That's where we landed.'

Beyond falls and cliffs there was a gash visible in the trees; there were the splintered trunks and then the drag, leaving only a fringe of palm between the scar and the sea. There, too, jutting into the lagoon, was the platform, with insect-like figures moving near it.

Ralph sketched a twining line from the bald spot on which they stood down a slope, a gully, through flowers, round and down to the rock where the scar started.

'That's the quickest way back.'

Eyes shining, mouths open, triumphant, they savoured the right of domination. They were lifted up: were friends.

'There's no village smoke, and no boats,' said Ralph wisely. 'We'll make sure later; but I think it's uninhabited.'

'We'll get food,' cried Jack. 'Hunt. Catch things . . . until they fetch us.'

Simon looked at them both, saying nothing but nodding till his black hair flopped backwards and forwards: his face was glowing.

Ralph looked down the other way where there was no reef.

'Steeper,' said Jack.

Ralph made a cupping gesture.

'That bit of forest down there . . . the mountain holds it up.'

Every coign of the mountain held up trees—flowers and trees. Now the forest stirred, roared, flailed. The nearer acres of rock flowers fluttered and for half a minute the breeze blew cool on their faces.

Ralph spread his arms.

'All ours.'

They laughed and tumbled and shouted on the mountain.

'I'm hungry.'

When Simon mentioned his hunger the others became aware of theirs.

'Come on,' said Ralph. 'We've found out what we wanted to know.'

They scrambled down a rock slope, dropped among flowers and made their way under the trees. Here they paused and examined the bushes round them curiously.

Simon spoke first.

'Like candles. Candle bushes. Candle buds.'

The bushes were dark evergreen and aromatic and the many buds were waxen green and folded up against the light. Jack slashed at one with his knife and the scent spilled over them.

'Candle buds.'

'You couldn't light them,' said Ralph. 'They just look like candles.'

'Green candles,' said Jack contemptuously, 'we can't eat them. Come on.'

They were in the beginnings of the thick forest, plonking with weary feet on a track, when they heard the noises—squeakings— and the hard strike of hoofs on a path. As they pushed forward the squeaking increased till it became a frenzy. They found a piglet caught in a curtain of creepers, throwing itself at the elastic traces in all the madness of extreme terror. Its voice was thin, needle-sharp and insistent. The three boys rushed forward and Jack drew his knife again with a flourish. He raised his arm in the air. There came a pause, a hiatus, the pig continued to scream and the creepers to jerk, and the blade continued to flash at the end of a bony arm. The pause was only long enough for them to understand what an enormity the downward stroke would be. Then the piglet tore loose from the creepers and scurried into the undergrowth. They were left looking at each other and the place of terror. Jack's face was white under the freckles. He noticed that he still held the knife aloft and brought his arm down replacing the blade in the sheath. Then they all three laughed ashamedly and began to climb back to the track.

'I was choosing a place,' said Jack. 'I was just waiting for a moment to decide where to stab him.'

'You should stick a pig,' said Ralph fiercely. 'They always talk about sticking a pig.'

'You cut a pig's throat to let the blood out,' said Jack, 'otherwise you can't eat the meat.'

'Why didn't you——?'

They knew very well why he hadn't: because of the enormity of the knife descending and cutting into living flesh; because of the unbearable blood.

'I was going to,' said Jack. He was ahead of them and they could not see his face. 'I was choosing a place. Next time——!'

He snatched his knife out of the sheath and slammed it into a tree trunk. Next time there would be no mercy. He looked round fiercely, daring them to contradict. Then they broke out into the sunlight and for a while they were busy finding and devouring food as they moved down the scar towards the platform and the meeting.

CHAPTER TWO

Fire on the Mountain

By the time Ralph finished blowing the conch the platform was crowded. There were differences between this meeting and the one held in the morning. The afternoon sun slanted in from the other side of the platform and most of the children, feeling too late the smart of sunburn, had put their clothes on. The choir, noticeably less of a group, had discarded their cloaks.

Ralph sat on a fallen trunk, his left side to the sun. On his right were most of the choir; on his left the larger boys who had not known each other before the evacuation; before him small children squatted in the grass.

Silence now. Ralph lifted the cream and pink shell to his knees and a sudden breeze scattered light over the platform. He was uncertain whether to stand up or remain sitting. He looked sideways to his left, towards the bathing-pool. Piggy was sitting near but giving no help.

Ralph cleared his throat.

'Well then.'

All at once he found he could talk fluently and explain what he had to say. He passed a hand through his fair hair and spoke.

'We're on an island. We've been on the mountain-top and seen water all round. We saw no houses, no smoke, no footprints, no boats, no people. We're on an uninhabited island with no other people on it.'

Jack broke in.

'All the same you need an army—for hunting. Hunting pigs——'

'Yes. There are pigs on the island.'

All three of them tried to convey the sense of the pink live thing struggling in the creepers.

'We saw——'

'Squealing——'

'It broke away——'

'Before I could kill it—but—next time!'

Jack slammed his knife into a trunk and looked round chal-lengingly.

The meeting settled down again.

'So you see,' said Ralph, 'we need hunters to get us meat. And another thing.'

He lifted the shell on his knees and looked round the sun-slashed faces.

'There aren't any grown-ups. We shall have to look after our-selves.'

The meeting hummed and was silent.

'And another thing. We can't have everybody talking at once. We'll have to have "Hands up" like at school.'

He held the conch before his face and glanced round the mouth.

'Then I'll give him the conch.'

'Conch?'

'That's what this shell's called. I'll give the conch to the next person to speak. He can hold it when he's speaking.'

'But——'

'Look——'

'And he won't be interrupted. Except by me.'

Jack was on his feet.

'We'll have rules!' he cried excitedly. 'Lots of rules! Then when anyone breaks 'em——'

'Whee-oh!'

'Wacco!'

'Bong!'

'Doink!'

Ralph felt the conch lifted from his lap. Then Piggy was stand-ing cradling the great cream shell and the shouting died down. Jack, left on his feet, looked uncertainly at Ralph who smiled and patted the log. Jack sat down. Piggy took off his glasses and blinked at the assembly while he wiped them on his shirt.

'You're hindering Ralph. You're not letting him get to the most important thing.'

He paused effectively.

'Who knows we're here? Eh?'

'They knew at the airport.'

'The man with a trumpet-thing——'

'My dad.'

Piggy put on his glasses.

'Nobody knows where we are,' said Piggy. He was paler than before and breathless. 'Perhaps they knew where we was going to; and perhaps not. But they don't know where we are 'cos we never got there.' He gaped at them for a moment, then swayed and sat down. Ralph took the conch from his hands.

'That's what I was going to say,' he went on, 'when you all, all. . . .' He gazed at their intent faces. 'The plane was shot down in flames. Nobody knows where we are. We may be here a long time.'

The silence was so complete that they could hear the fetch and miss of Piggy's breathing. The sun slanted in and lay golden over half the platform. The breezes that on the lagoon had chased their tails like kittens were finding their way across the platform and into the forest. Ralph pushed back the tangle of fair hair that hung on his forehead.

'So we may be here a long time.'

Nobody said anything. He grinned suddenly.

'But this is a good island. We—Jack, Simon and me—we climbed the mountain. It's wizard. There's food and drink, and——'

'Rocks——'

'Blue flowers——'

Piggy, partly recovered, pointed to the conch in Ralph's hands, and Jack and Simon fell silent. Ralph went on.

'While we're waiting we can have a good time on this island.'

He gesticulated widely.

'It's like in a book.'

At once there was a clamour.

'Treasure Island——'

'Swallows and Amazons——'

'Coral Island——'

Ralph waved the conch.

'This is our island. It's a good island. Until the grown-ups come to fetch us we'll have fun.'

Jack held out his hand for the conch.

'There's pigs,' he said. 'There's food; and bathing-water in that little stream along there—and everything. Didn't anyone find anything else?'

He handed the conch back to Ralph and sat down. Apparently no one had found anything.

The older boys first noticed the child when he resisted. There was a group of little boys urging him forward and he did not want to go. He was a shrimp of a boy, about six years old, and one side of his face was blotted out by a mulberry-coloured birthmark. He stood now, warped out of the perpendicular by the fierce light of publicity, and he bored into the coarse grass with one toe. He was muttering and about to cry.

The other little boys, whispering but serious, pushed him towards Ralph.

'All right,' said Ralph, 'come on then.'

The small boy looked round in panic.

'Speak up!'

The small boy held out his hands for the conch and the assembly shouted with laughter; at once he snatched back his hands and started to cry.

'Let him have the conch!' shouted Piggy. 'Let him have it!'

At last Ralph induced him to hold the shell but by then the blow of laughter had taken away the child's voice. Piggy knelt by him, one hand on the great shell, listening and interpreting to the assembly.

'He wants to know what you're going to do about the snake-thing.'

Ralph laughed, and the other boys laughed with him. The small boy twisted further into himself.

'Tell us about the snake-thing.'

'Now he says it was a beastie.'

'Beastie?'

'A snake-thing. Ever so big. He saw it.'

'Where?'

'In the woods.'

Either the wandering breezes or perhaps the decline of the sun allowed a little coolness to lie under the trees. The boys felt it and stirred restlessly.

'You couldn't have a beastie, a snake-thing, on an island this size,' Ralph explained kindly. 'You only get them in big countries, like Africa, or India.'

Murmur; and the grave nodding of heads.

'He says the beastie came in the dark.'

'Then he couldn't see it!'

Laughter and cheers.

'Did you hear that? Says he saw the thing in the dark——'

'He still says he saw the beastie. It came and went away again an' came back and wanted to eat him——'

'He was dreaming.'

Laughing, Ralph looked for confirmation round the ring of faces. The older boys agreed; but here and there among the little ones was the dubiety that required more than rational assurance.

'He must have had a nightmare. Stumbling about among all those creepers.'

More grave nodding; they knew about nightmares.

'He says he saw the beastie, the snake-thing, and will it come back tonight?'

'But there isn't a beastie!'

'He says in the morning it turned into them things like ropes in the trees and hung in the branches. He says will it come back to-night?'

'But there isn't a beastie!'

There was no laughter at all now and more grave watching. Ralph pushed both hands through his hair and looked at the little boy in mixed amusement and exasperation.

Jack seized the conch.

'Ralph's right of course. There isn't a snake-thing. But if there was a snake we'd hunt it and kill it. We're going to hunt pigs and get meat for everybody. And we'll look for the snake too——'

'But there isn't a snake!'

'We'll make sure when we go hunting.'

Ralph was annoyed and, for the moment, defeated. He felt himself facing something ungraspable. The eyes that looked so intently at him were without humour.

'But there isn't a beast!'

Something he had not known was there rose in him and compelled him to make the point, loudly and again.

'But I tell you there isn't a beast!'

The assembly was silent.

Ralph lifted the conch again and his good humour came back as he thought of what he had to say next.

'Now we come to the most important thing. I've been thinking. I was thinking while we were climbing the mountain.' He flashed a conspiratorial grin at the other two. 'And on the beach just now. This is what I thought. We want to have fun. And we want to be rescued.'

The passionate noise of agreement from the assembly hit him like a wave and he lost his thread. He thought again.

'We want to be rescued; and of course we shall be rescued.'

Voices babbled. The simple statement, unbacked by any proof but the weight of Ralph's new authority, brought light and happiness. He had to wave the conch before he could make them hear him.

'My father's in the Navy. He said there aren't any unknown islands left. He says the Queen has a big room full of maps and all the islands in the world are drawn there. So the Queen's got a picture of this island.'

Again came the sounds of cheerfulness and better heart.

'And sooner or later a ship will put in here. It might even be daddy's ship. So you see, sooner or later, we shall be rescued.'

He paused, with the point made. The assembly was lifted towards safety by his words. They liked and now respected him. Spontaneously they began to clap and presently the platform was loud with applause. Ralph flushed, looking sideways at Piggy's open admiration, and then the other way at Jack who was smirking and showing that he too knew how to clap.

Ralph waved the conch.

'Shut up! Wait! Listen!'

He went on in the silence, borne on his triumph.

'There's another thing. We can help them to find us. If a ship comes near the island they may not notice us. Se we must make smoke on top of the mountain. We must make a fire.'

'A fire! Make a fire!'

At once half the boys were on their feet. Jack clamoured among them, the conch forgotten.

'Come on! Follow me!'

The space under the palm trees was full of noise and movement. Ralph was on his feet too, shouting for quiet, but no one heard him. All at once the crowd swayed towards the island and were gone—following Jack. Even the tiny children went and did their best among the leaves and broken branches. Ralph was left, holding the conch, with no one but Piggy.

Piggy's breathing was quite restored.

'Like kids!' he said scornfully. 'Acting like a crowd of kids!'

Ralph looked at him doubtfully and laid the conch on the tree trunk.

'I bet it's gone tea-time,' said Piggy. 'What do they think they're going to do on that mountain?'

He caressed the shell respectfully, then stopped and looked up.

'Ralph! Hey! Where you going?'

Ralph was already clambering over the first smashed swathes
of the scar. A long way ahead of him was crashing and laughter.
Piggy watched him in disgust.

'Like a crowd of kids——'

He sighed, bent, and laced up his shoes. The noise of the errant
assembly faded up the mountain. Then, with the martyred expression of a parent who has to keep up with the senseless ebulli-
ence of the children, he picked up the conch, turned towards the
forest, and began to pick his way over the tumbled scar.

Below the other side of the mountain-top was a platform of
forest. Once more Ralph found himself making the cupping gesture.

'Down there we could get as much wood as we want.'

Jack nodded and pulled at his underlip. Starting perhaps a
hundred feet below them on the steeper side of the mountain, the
patch might have been designed expressly for fuel. Trees, forced
by the damp heat, found too little soil for full growth, fell early
and decayed: creepers cradled them, and new saplings searched a
way up.

Jack turned to the choir, who stood ready. Their black caps of
maintenance were slid over one ear like berets.

'We'll build a pile. Come on.'

They found the likeliest path down and began tugging at the
dead wood. And the small boys who had reached the top came
sliding too till everyone but Piggy was busy. Most of the wood
was so rotten that when they pulled it broke up into a shower of
fragments and woodlice and decay; but some trunks came out in
one piece. The twins, Sam 'n Eric, were the first to get a likely
log but they could do nothing till Ralph, Jack, Simon, Roger and
Maurice found room for a hand-hold. Then they inched the grotesque dead thing up the rock and toppled it over on top. Each
party of boys added a quota, less or more, and the pile grew. At
the return Ralph found himself alone on a limb with Jack and
they grinned at each other, sharing this burden. Once more, amid
the breeze, the shouting, the slanting sunlight on the high mountain, was shed that glamour, that strange invisible light of friendship, adventure, and content.

'Almost too heavy.'

Jack grinned back.

'Not for the two of us.'

Together, joined in effort by the burden, they staggered up the last steep of the mountain. Together, they chanted One! Two! Three! and crashed the log on to the great pile. Then they stepped back, laughing with triumphant pleasure, so that immediately Ralph had to stand on his head. Below them, boys were still labouring, though some of the small ones had lost interest and were searching this new forest for fruit. Now the twins, with unsuspected intelligence, came up the mountain with armfuls of dried leaves and dumped them against the pile. One by one, as they sensed that the pile was complete the boys stopped going back for more and stood, with the pink, shattered top of the mountain around them. Breath came even by now, and sweat dried.

Ralph and Jack looked at each other while society paused about them. The shameful knowledge grew in them and they did not know how to begin confession.

Ralph spoke first, crimson in the face.

'Will you?'

He cleared his throat and went on.

'Will you light the fire?'

Now the absurd situation was open, Jack blushed too. He began to mutter vaguely.

'You rub two sticks. You rub——'

He glanced at Ralph, who blurted out the last confession of incompetence.

'Has anyone got any matches?'

'You make a bow and spin the arrow,' said Roger. He rubbed his hands in mime. 'Psss. Psss.'

A little air was moving over the mountain. Piggy came with it, in shorts and shirt, labouring cautiously out of the forest with the evening sunlight gleaming from his glasses. He held the conch under his arm.

Ralph shouted at him.

'Piggy! Have you got any matches?'

The other boys took up the cry till the mountain rang. Piggy shook his head and came to the pile.

'My! You've made a big heap, haven't you?'

Jack pointed suddenly.

'His specs—use them as burning glasses!'

Piggy was surrounded before he could back away.

'Here—Let me go!' His voice rose to a shriek of terror as Jack snatched the glasses off his face. 'Mind out! Give 'em back! I can hardly see! You'll break the conch!'

Ralph elbowed him to one side and knelt by the pile.

'Stand out of the light.'

There was pushing and pulling and officious cries. Ralph moved the lenses back and forth, this way and that, till a glossy white image of the declining sun lay on a piece of rotten wood. Almost at once a thin trickle of smoke rose up and made him cough. Jack knelt too and blew gently, so that the smoke drifted away, thickening, and a tiny flame appeared. The flame, nearly invisible at first in that bright sunlight, enveloped a small twig, grew, was enriched with colour and reached up to a branch which exploded with a sharp crack. The flame flapped higher and the boys broke into a cheer.

'My specs!' howled Piggy. 'Give me my specs!'

Ralph stood away from the pile and put the glasses into Piggy's groping hands. His voice subsided to a mutter.

'Jus' blurs, that's all. Hardly see my hand——'

The boys were dancing. The pile was so rotten, and now so tinder-dry, that whole limbs yielded passionately to the yellow flames that poured upwards and shook a great beard of flame twenty feet in the air. For yards round the fire the heat was like a blow, and the breeze was a river of sparks. Trunks crumbled to white dust.

Ralph shouted.

'More wood! All of you get more wood!'

Life became a race with the fire and the boys scattered through the upper forest. To keep a clean flag of flame flying on the mountain was the immediate end and no one looked further. Even the smallest boys, unless fruit claimed them, brought little pieces of wood and threw them in. The air moved a little faster and became a light wind, so that leeward and windward side were clearly differentiated. On one side the air was cool, but on the other the fire thrust out a savage arm of heat that crinkled hair on the instant. Boys who felt the evening wind on their damp faces paused to enjoy the freshness of it and then found they were exhausted. They flung themselves down in the shadows that lay among the shattered rocks. The beard of flame diminished quickly; then the pile fell inwards with a soft, cindery sound, and sent a great tree of sparks upwards that leaned away and drifted downwind. The boys lay, panting like dogs.

Ralph raised his head off his forearms.

'That was no good.'

Roger spat efficiently into the hot dust.

'What d'you mean?'

'There wasn't any smoke. Only flame.'

Piggy had settled himself in a coign between two rocks, and sat with the conch on his knees.

'We haven't made a fire,' he said, 'what's any use. We couldn't keep a fire like that going, not if we tried.'

'A fat lot you tried,' said Jack contemptuously. 'You just sat.'

'We used his specs,' said Simon, smearing a black cheek with his forearm. 'He helped that way.'

'I got the conch,' said Piggy indignantly. 'You let me speak!'

'The conch doesn't count on top of the mountain,' said Jack, 'so you shut up.'

'I got the conch in my hand.'

'Put on green branches,' said Maurice. 'That's the best way to make smoke.'

'I got the conch——'

Jack turned fiercely.

'You shut up!'

Piggy wilted. Ralph took the conch from him and looked round the circle of boys.

'We've got to have special people for looking after the fire. Any day there may be a ship out there'—he waved his arm at the taut wire of the horizon—'and if we have a signal going they'll come and take us off. And another thing. We ought to have more rules. Where the conch is, that's a meeting. The same up here as down there.'

They assented. Piggy opened his mouth to speak, caught Jack's eye and shut it again. Jack held out his hands for the conch and stood up, holding the delicate thing carefully in his sooty hands.

'I agree with Ralph. We've got to have rules and obey them. After all, we're not savages. We're English; and the English are best at everything. So we've got to do the right things.'

He turned to Ralph.

'Ralph—I'll split up the choir—my hunters, that is—into groups, and we'll be responsible for keeping the fire going——'

This generosity brought a spatter of applause from the boys, so that Jack grinned at them, then waved the conch for silence.

'We'll let the fire burn out now. Who would see smoke at

night-time anyway? And we can start the fire again whenever we
like. Altos—you can keep the fire going this week; and trebles
the next——'

The assembly assented gravely.

'And we'll be responsible for keeping a lookout too. If we see
a ship out there'—they followed the direction of his bony arm
with their eyes—'we'll put green branches on. Then there'll be
more smoke.'

They gazed intently at the dense blue of the horizon, as if a
little silhouette might appear there at any moment.

The sun in the west was a drop of burning gold that slid nearer
and nearer the sill of the world. All at once they were aware of
the evening as the end of light and warmth.

Roger took the conch and looked round at them gloomily.

'I've been watching the sea. There hasn't been the trace of a
ship. Perhaps we'll never be rescued.'

A murmur rose and swept away. Ralph took back the conch.

'I said before we'll be rescued sometime. We've just got to
wait; that's all.'

Daring, indignant, Piggy took the conch.

'That's what I said! I said about our meetings and things and
then you said shut up——'

His voice lifted into the whine of virtuous recrimination. They
stirred and began to shout him down.

'You said you wanted a small fire and you been and built a pile
like a hayrick. If I say anything,' cried Piggy, with bitter realism,
'you say shut up; but if Jack or Maurice or Simon——'

He paused in the tumult, standing, looking beyond them and
down the unfriendly side of the mountain to the great patch
where they had found dead wood. Then he laughed so strangely
that they were hushed, looking at the flash of his spectacles in
astonishment. They followed his gaze to find the sour joke.

'You got your small fire all right.'

Smoke was rising here and there among the creepers that festooned the dead or dying trees. As they watched, a flash of fire
appeared at the root of one wisp, and then the smoke thickened.
Small flames stirred at the bole of a tree and crawled away through
leaves and brushwood, dividing and increasing. One patch
touched a tree trunk and scrambled up like a bright squirrel. The
smoke increased, sifted, rolled outwards. The squirrel leapt on
the wings of the wind and clung to another standing tree, eating

downwards. Beneath the dark canopy of leaves and smoke the fire laid hold on the forest and began to gnaw. Acres of black and yellow smoke rolled steadily towards the sea. At the sight of the flames and the irresistible course of the fire, the boys broke into shrill, excited cheering. The flames, as though they were a kind of wild life, crept as a jaguar creeps on its belly towards a line of birch-like saplings that fledged an outcrop of the pink rock. They flapped at the first of the trees, and the branches grew a brief foliage of fire. The heart of flame leapt nimbly across the gap between the trees and then went swinging and flaring along the whole row of them. Beneath the capering boys a quarter of a mile square of forest was savage with smoke and flame. The separate noises of the fire merged into a drum-roll that seemed to shake the mountain.

'You got your small fire all right.'

Startled, Ralph realized that the boys were falling still and silent, feeling the beginnings of awe at the power set free below them. The knowledge and the awe made him savage.

'Oh, shut up!'

'I got the conch,' said Piggy, in a hurt voice. 'I got a right to speak.'

They looked at him with eyes that lacked interest in what they saw, and cocked ears at the drum-roll of the fire. Piggy glanced nervously into hell and cradled the conch.

'We got to let that burn out now. And that was our firewood.'

He licked his lips.

'There ain't nothing we can do. We ought to be more careful. I'm scared——'

Jack dragged his eyes away from the fire.

'You're always scared. Yah—Fatty!'

'I got the conch,' said Piggy bleakly. He turned to Ralph. 'I got the conch, ain't I Ralph?'

Unwillingly Ralph turned away from the splendid, awful sight.

'What's that?'

'The conch. I got a right to speak.'

The twins giggled together.

'We wanted smoke——'

'Now look——'

A pall stretched for miles away from the island. All the boys except Piggy started to giggle; presently they were shrieking with laughter.

Piggy lost his temper.

'I got the conch! Just you listen! The first thing we ought to have made was shelters down there by the beach. It wasn't half cold down there in the night. But the first time Ralph says "fire" you goes howling and screaming up this here mountain. Like a pack of kids!'

By now they were listening to the tirade.

'How can you expect to be rescued if you don't put first things first and act proper?'

He took off his glasses and made as if to put down the conch; but the sudden motion towards it of most of the older boys changed his mind. He tucked the shell under his arm, and crouched back on a rock.

'Then when you get here you build a bonfire that isn't no use. Now you been and set the whole island on fire. Won't we look funny if the whole island burns up? Cooked fruit, that's what we'll have to eat, and roast pork. And that's nothing to laugh at! You said Ralph was chief and you don't give him time to think. Then when he says something you rush off, like, like——'

He paused for breath, and the fire growled at them.

'And that's not all. Them kids. The little 'uns. Who took any notice of 'em? Who knows how many we got?'

Ralph took a sudden step forward.

'I told you to. I told you to get a list of names!'

'How could I,' cried Piggy indignantly, 'all by myself? They waited for two minutes, then they fell in the sea; they went into the forest; they just scattered everywhere. How was I to know which was which?'

Ralph licked pale lips.

'Then you don't know how many of us there ought to be?'

'How could I with them little 'uns running round like insects? Then when you three came back, as soon as you said make a fire, they all ran away, and I never had a chance——'

'That's enough!' said Ralph sharply, and snatched back the conch. 'If you didn't you didn't.'

'——then you come up here an' pinch my specs——'

Jack turned on him.

'You shut up!'

'——and them little 'uns was wandering about down there where the fire is. How d'you know they aren't still there?'

Piggy stood up and pointed to the smoke and flames. A murmur rose among the boys and died away. Something strange was happening to Piggy, for he was gasping for breath.

'That little 'un——' gasped Piggy—'him with the mark on his face, I don't see him. Where is he now?'

The crowd was as silent as death.

'Him that talked about the snakes. He was down there——'

A tree exploded in the fire like a bomb. Tall swathes of creepers rose for a moment into view, agonized, and went down again. The little boys screamed at them.

'Snakes! Snakes! Look at the snakes!'

In the west, and unheeded, the sun lay only an inch or two above the sea. Their faces were lit redly from beneath. Piggy fell against a rock and clutched it with both hands.

'That little 'un that had a mark on his—face—where is—he now? I tell you I don't see him.'

The boys looked at each other fearfully, unbelieving.

'—where is he now?'

Ralph muttered the reply as if in shame.

'Perhaps he went back to the, the——'

Beneath them, on the unfriendly side of the mountain, the drum-roll continued.

CHAPTER THREE

Huts on the Beach

Jack was bent double. He was down like a sprinter, his nose only a few inches from the humid earth. The tree trunks and the creepers that festooned them lost themselves in a green dusk thirty feet above him; and all about was the undergrowth. There was only the faintest indication of a trail here; a cracked twig and what might be the impression of one side of a hoof. He lowered his chin and stared at the traces as though he would force them to speak to him. Then dog-like, uncomfortably on all fours yet unheeding his discomfort, he stole forward five yards and stopped. Here was a loop of creeper with a tendril pendant from a node. The tendril was polished on the underside; pigs, passing through the loop, brushed it with their bristly hide.

Jack crouched with his face a few inches away from this clue, then stared forward into the semi-darkness of the undergrowth. His sandy hair, considerably longer than it had been when they dropped in, was lighter now; and his bare back was a mass of dark freckles and peeling sunburn. A sharpened stick about five feet long trailed from his right hand; and except for a pair of tattered shorts held up by his knife-belt he was naked. He closed his eyes, raised his head and breathed in gently with flared nostrils, assessing the current of warm air for information. The forest and he were very still.

At length he let out his breath in a long sigh and opened his eyes. They were bright blue, eyes that in this frustration seemed bolting and nearly mad. He passed his tongue across dry lips and scanned the uncommunicative forest. Then again he stole forward and cast this way and that over the ground.

The silence of the forest was more oppressive than the heat, and at this hour of the day there was not even the whine of insects. Only when Jack himself roused a gaudy bird from a primitive nest of sticks was the silence shattered and echoes set ringing by a harsh cry that seemed to come out of the abyss of ages. Jack himself shrank at this cry with a hiss of indrawn breath; and for a minute became less a hunter than a furtive thing, ape-like among the tangle of trees. Then the trail, the frustration, claimed him again and he searched the ground avidly. By the bole of a vast tree that grew pale flowers on a grey trunk he checked, closed his eyes, and once more drew in the warm air; and this time his breath came short, there was even a passing pallor in his face, and then the surge of blood again. He passed like a shadow under the darkness of the tree and crouched, looking down at the trodden ground at his feet.

The droppings were warm. They lay piled among turned earth. They were olive green, smooth, and they steamed a little. Jack lifted his head and stared at the inscrutable masses of creeper that lay across the trail. Then he raised his spear and sneaked forward. Beyond the creeper, the trail joined a pig-run that was wide enough and trodden enough to be a path. The ground was hardened by an accustomed tread and as Jack rose to his full height he heard something moving on it. He swung back his right arm and hurled the spear with all his strength. From the pig-run came the quick, hard patter of hoofs, a castanet sound, seductive, maddening—the promise of meat. He rushed out of the undergrowth and snatched up his spear. The pattering of pig's trotters died away in the distance.

Jack stood there, streaming with sweat, streaked with brown earth, stained by all the vicissitudes of a day's hunting. Swearing, he turned off the trail and pushed his way through until the forest opened a little and instead of bald trunks supporting a dark roof there were light grey trunks and crowns of feathery palms. Beyond these was the glitter of the sea and he could hear voices. Ralph was standing by a contraption of palm trunks and leaves, a rude shelter that faced the lagoon, and seemed very near to falling down. He did not notice when Jack spoke.

'Got any water?'

Ralph looked up, frowning, from the complication of leaves. He did not notice Jack even when he saw him.

'I said have you got any water? I'm thirsty.'

Ralph withdrew his attention from the shelter and realized Jack with a start.

'Oh, hullo. Water? There by the tree. Ought to be some left.'

Jack took up a coco-nut shell that brimmed with fresh water from among a group that were arranged in the shade, and drank. The water splashed over his chin and neck and chest. He breathed noisily when he had finished.

'Needed that.'

Simon spoke from inside the shelter.

'Up a bit.'

Ralph turned to the shelter and lifted a branch with a whole tiling of leaves.

The leaves came apart and fluttered down. Simon's contrite face appeared in the hole.

'Sorry.'

Ralph surveyed the wreck with distaste.

'Never get it done.'

He flung himself down at Jack's feet. Simon remained, looking out of the hole in the shelter. Once down, Ralph explained.

'Been working for days now. And look!'

Two shelters were in position, but shaky. This one was a ruin.

'And they keep running off. You remember the meeting? How everyone was going to work hard until the shelters were finished?'

'Except me and my hunters——'

'Except the hunters. Well, the littluns are——'

He gesticulated, sought for a word.

'They're hopeless. The older ones aren't much better. D'you see? All day I've been working with Simon. No one else. They're off bathing, or eating, or playing.'

Simon poked his head out carefully.

'You're chief. You tell 'em off.'

Ralph lay flat and looked up at the palm trees and the sky.

'Meetings. Don't we love meetings? Every day. Twice a day. We talk.' He got on one elbow. 'I bet if I blew the conch this minute, they'd come running. Then we'd be, you know, very solemn, and someone would say we ought to build a jet, or a submarine, or a TV set. When the meeting was over they'd work for five minutes then wander off or go hunting.'

Jack flushed.

'We want meat.'

'Well, we haven't got any yet. And we want shelters. Besides, the rest of your hunters came back hours ago. They've been swimming.'

'I went on,' said Jack. 'I let them go. I had to go on. I——'

He tried to convey the compulsion to track down and kill that was swallowing him up.

'I went on. I thought, by myself——'

The madness came into his eyes again.
'I thought I might kill.'
'But you didn't.'
'I thought I might.'
Some hidden passion vibrated in Ralph's voice.
'But you haven't yet.'
His invitation might have passed as casual, were it not for the undertone.
'You wouldn't care to help with the shelters, I suppose?'
'We want meat——'
'And we don't get it.'
Now the antagonism was audible.
'But I shall! Next time! I've got to get a barb on this spear! We wounded a pig and the spear fell out. If we could only make barbs——'
'We need shelters.'
Suddenly Jack shouted in rage.
'Are you accusing——?'
'All I'm saying is we've worked dashed hard. That's all.'
They were both red in the face and found looking at each other difficult. Ralph rolled on his stomach and began to play with the grass.
'If it rains like when we dropped in we'll need shelters all right. And then another thing. We need shelters because of the——'
He paused for a moment and they both pushed their anger away. Then he went on with the safe, changed subject.
'You've noticed, haven't you?'
Jack put down his spear and squatted.
'Noticed what?'
'Well. They're frightened.'
He rolled over and peered into Jack's fierce, dirty face.
'I mean the way things are. They dream. You can hear 'em. Have you been awake at night?'
Jack shook his head.
'They all talk and scream. The littluns. Even some of the others. As if——'
'As if it wasn't a good island.'
Astonished at the interruption, they looked up at Simon's serious face.
'As if,' said Simon, 'the beastie, the beastie or the snake-thing, was real. Remember?'

The two older boys flinched when they heard the shameful syllable. Snakes were not mentioned now, were not mentionable.

'As if this wasn't a good island,' said Ralph slowly. 'Yes, that's right.'

Jack sat up and stretched out his legs.

'They're batty.'

'Crackers. Remember when we went exploring?'

They grinned at each other, remembering the glamour of the first day. Ralph went on.

'So we need shelters as a sort of——'

'Home.'

'That's right.'

Jack drew up his legs, clasped his knees, and frowned in an effort to attain clarity.

'All the same—in the forest. I mean when you're hunting—not when you're getting fruit, of course, but when you're on your own——'

He paused for a moment, not sure if Ralph would take him seriously.

'Go on.'

'If you're hunting sometimes you catch yourself feeling as if——' He flushed suddenly.

'There's nothing in it of course. Just a feeling. But you can feel as if you're not hunting, but—being hunted; as if something's behind you all the time in the jungle.'

They were silent again: Simon intent, Ralph incredulous and faintly indignant. He sat up, rubbing one shoulder with a dirty hand.

'Well, I don't know.'

Jack leapt to his feet and spoke very quickly.

'That's how you can feel in the forest. Of course there's nothing in it. Only—only——'

He took a few rapid steps towards the beach, then came back.

'Only I know how they feel. See? That's all.'

'The best thing we can do is get ourselves rescued.'

Jack had to think for a moment before he could remember what rescue was.

'Rescue? Yes, of course! All the same, I'd like to catch a pig first——' He snatched up his spear and dashed it into the ground. The opaque, mad look came into his eyes again. Ralph looked at him critically through his tangle of fair hair.

'So long as your hunters remember the fire——'

'You and your fire!'

The two boys trotted down the beach and turning at the water's edge, looked back at the pink mountain. The trickle of smoke sketched a chalky line up the solid blue of the sky, wavered high up and faded. Ralph frowned.

'I wonder how far off you could see that.'

'Miles.'

'We don't make enough smoke.'

The bottom part of the trickle, as though conscious of their gaze, thickened to a creamy blue which crept up the feeble column.

'They've put on green branches,' muttered Ralph. 'I wonder!' He screwed up his eyes and swung round to search the horizon.

'Got it!'

Jack shouted so loudly that Ralph jumped.

'What? Where? Is it a ship?'

But Jack was pointing to the high declivities that led down from the mountain to the flatter part of the island.

'Of course! They'll lie up there—they must do, when the sun's too hot——'

Ralph gazed bewildered at his rapt face.

'——they get up high. High up and in the shade, resting during the heat, like cows at home——'

'I thought you saw a ship!'

'We could steal up on one—paint our faces so they wouldn't see—perhaps surround them and then——'

Indignation took away Ralph's control.

'I was talking about smoke! Don't you want to be rescued? All you can talk about is pig, pig, pig!'

'But we want meat!'

'And I work all day with nothing but Simon and you come back and don't even notice the huts!'

'I was working too——'

'But you like it!' shouted Ralph. 'You want to hunt! While I——'

They faced each other on the bright beach, astonished at the rub of feeling. Ralph looked away first, pretending interest in a group of littluns on the sand. From beyond the platform came the shouting of the hunters in the swimming pool. On the end of the platform Piggy was lying flat, looking down into the brilliant water.

'People don't help much.'

He wanted to explain how people were never quite what you thought they were.

'Simon. He helps.' He pointed at the shelters.

'All the rest rushed off. He's done as much as I have. Only——'

'Simon's always about.'

Ralph started back to the shelters with Jack by his side.

'Do a bit for you,' muttered Jack, 'before I have a bathe.'

'Don't bother.'

But when they reached the shelters Simon was not to be seen. Ralph put his head in the hole, withdrew it, and turned to Jack.

'He's buzzed off.'

'Got fed up,' said Jack, 'and gone for a bathe.'

Ralph frowned.

'He's queer. He's funny.'

Jack nodded, as much for the sake of agreeing as anything, and by tacit consent they left the shelter and went towards the bathing-pool.

'And then,' said Jack, 'when I've had a bathe and something to eat, I'll just trek over to the other side of the mountain and see if I can see any traces. Coming?'

'But the sun's nearly set!'

'I might have time——'

They walked along, two continents of experience and feeling, unable to communicate.

'If I could only get a pig!'

'I'll come back and go on with the shelter.'

They looked at each other, baffled, in love and hate. All the warm salt water of the bathing-pool and the shouting and splashing and laughing were only just sufficient to bring them together again.

Simon, whom they expected to find there, was not in the bathing-pool.

When the other two had trotted down the beach to look back at the mountain he had followed them for a few yards and then stopped. He had stood frowning down at a pile of sand on the beach where somebody had been trying to build a little house or hut. Then he turned his back on this and walked into the forest with an air of purpose. He was a small, skinny boy, his chin pointed, and his eyes so bright they had deceived Ralph into thinking him delightfully gay and wicked. The coarse mop of black hair was long and swung down, almost concealing a low, broad forehead. He wore the remains of shorts and his feet were bare like Jack's. Always darkish in colour, Simon was burned by the sun to a deep tan that glistened with sweat.

He picked his way up the scar, passed the great rock where Ralph had climbed on the first morning, then turned off to his right among the trees. He walked with an accustomed tread through the acres of fruit trees, where the least energetic could find an easy if unsatisfying meal. Flower and fruit grew together on the same tree and everywhere was the scent of ripeness and the booming of a million bees at pasture. Here the littluns who had run after him caught up with him. They talked, cried out unintelligibly, lugged him towards the trees. Then, amid the roar of bees in the afternoon sunlight, Simon found for them the fruit they could not reach, pulled off the choicest from up in the foliage, passed them back down to the endless outstretched hands. When he had satisfied them he paused and looked round. The littluns watched him inscrutably over double handfuls of ripe fruit.

Simon turned away from them and went where the just perceptible path led him. Soon high jungle closed in. Tall trunks bore unexpected pale flowers all the way up the dark canopy where life went on clamorously. The air here was dark too, and the creepers dropped their ropes like the rigging of foundered ships. His feet left prints on the soft soil and the creepers shivered throughout their lengths when he bumped them.

He came at last to a place where more sunshine fell. Since they had not so far to go for light the creepers had woven a great mat that hung at the side of an open space in the jungle; for here a patch of rock came close to the surface and would not allow more than little plants and ferns to grow. The whole space was walled with dark aromatic bushes, and was a bowl of heat and light. A great tree, fallen across one corner, leaned against the trees that still stood and a rapid climber flaunted red and yellow sprays right to the top.

Simon paused. He looked over his shoulder as Jack had done at the close ways behind him and glanced swiftly round to confirm that he was utterly alone. For a moment his movements were almost furtive. Then he bent down and wormed his way into the centre of the mat. The creepers and the bushes were so close that he left his sweat on them and they pulled together behind him. When he was secure in the middle he was in a little cabin screened off from the open space by a few leaves. He squatted down, parted the leaves and looked out into the clearing. Nothing moved but a pair of gaudy butterflies that danced round each other in the hot air. Holding his breath he cocked a critical ear at the sounds of the island. Evening was advancing towards the island; the sounds of the bright fantastic birds, the bee-sounds, even the crying of the gulls that were returning to their roosts among the square rocks, were fainter. The deep sea breaking miles away on the reef made an undertone less perceptible than the susurration of the blood.

Simon dropped the screen of leaves back into place. The slope of the bars of honey-coloured sunlight decreased; they slid up the bushes, passed over the green candle-like buds, moved up towards the canopy, and darkness thickened under the trees. With the fading of the light the riotous colours died and the heat and urgency cooled away. The candle-buds stirred. Their green sepals drew back a little and the white tips of the flowers rose delicately to meet the open air.

Now the sunlight had lifted clear of the open space and with-drawn from the sky. Darkness poured out, submerging the ways between the trees till they were dim and strange as the bottom of the sea. The candle-buds opened their wide white flowers glimmering under the light that pricked down from the first stars. Their scent spilled out into the air and took possession of the island.

CHAPTER FOUR

Painted Faces and Long Hair

The first rhythm that they became used to was the slow swing from dawn to quick dusk. They accepted the pleasures of morning, the bright sun, the whelming sea and sweet air, as a time when play was good and life so full that hope was not necessary and therefore forgotten. Towards noon, as the floods of light fell more nearly to the perpendicular, the stark colours of the morning were smoothed in pearl and opalescence; and the heat—as though the impending sun's height gave it momentum—became a blow that they ducked, running to the shade and lying there, perhaps even sleeping.

Strange things happened at midday. The glittering sea rose up, moved apart in planes of blatant impossibility; the coral reef and the few, stunted palms that clung to the more elevated parts would float up into the sky, would quiver, be plucked apart, run like rain-drops on a wire or be repeated as in an odd succession of mirrors. Sometimes land loomed where there was no land and flicked out like a bubble as the children watched. Piggy discounted all this learnedly as a 'mirage'; and since no boy could reach even the reef over the stretch of water where the snapping sharks waited, they grew accustomed to these mysteries and ignored them, just as they ignored the miraculous, throbbing stars. At midday the illusions merged into the sky and there the sun gazed down like an angry eye. Then, at the end of the afternoon, the mirage subsided and the horizon became level and blue and clipped as the sun declined. That was another time of comparative coolness but menaced by the coming of the dark. When the sun sank, darkness dropped on the island like an extinguisher and soon the shelters were full of restlessness, under the remote stars.

Nevertheless, the northern European tradition of work, play, and food right through the day, made it impossible for them to adjust themselves wholly to this new rhythm. The littlun Percival had early crawled into a shelter and stayed there for two days, talking, singing, and crying, till they thought him batty and were faintly amused. Ever since then he had been peaked, red-eyed, and miserable; a littlun who played little and cried often.

The smaller boys were known now by the generic title of 'littluns'. The decrease in size, from Ralph down, was gradual; and though there was a dubious region inhabited by Simon and Robert and Maurice, nevertheless no one had any difficulty in recognizing biguns at one end and littluns at the other. The undoubted littluns, those aged about six, led a quite distinct, and at the same time intense, life of their own. They ate most of the day, picking fruit where they could reach it and not particular about ripeness and quality. They were used now to stomach-aches and a sort of chronic diarrhoea. They suffered untold terrors in the dark and huddled together for comfort. Apart from food and sleep, they found time for play, aimless and trivial, among the white sand by the bright water. They cried for their mothers much less often than might have been expected; they were very brown, and filthily dirty. They obeyed the summons of the conch, partly because Ralph blew it, and he was big enough to be a link with the adult world of authority; and partly because they enjoyed the entertainment of the assemblies. But otherwise they seldom bothered with the biguns and their passionately emotional and corporate life was their own.

They had built castles in the sand at the bar of the little river. These castles were about one foot high and were decorated with shells, withered flowers, and interesting stones. Round the castles was a complex of marks, tracks, walls, railway lines, that were of significance only if inspected with the eye at beach-level. The littluns played here, if not happily at least with absorbed attention; and often as many as three of them would play the same game together.

Three were playing here now—Henry was the biggest of them. He was also a distant relative of that other boy whose mulberry marked face had not been seen since the evening of the great fire; but he was not old enough to understand this, and if he had been told that the other boy had gone home in an aircraft, he would have accepted the statement without fuss or disbelief.

Henry was a bit of a leader this afternoon, because the other two were Percival and Johnny, the smallest boys on the island. Percival was mouse-coloured and had not been very attractive even to his mother; Johnny was well built, with fair hair and a natural belligerence. Just now he was being obedient because he was interested; and the three children, kneeling in the sand, were at peace.

Roger and Maurice came out of the forest. They were relieved from duty at the fire and had come down for a swim. Roger led the way straight through the castles, kicking them over, burying the flowers, scattering the chosen stones. Maurice followed, laughing, and added to the destruction. The three littluns paused in their game and looked up. As it happened, the particular marks in which they were interested had not been touched, so they made no protest. Only Percival began to whimper with an eyeful of sand and Maurice hurried away. In his other life Maurice had received chastisement for filling a younger eye with sand. Now, though there was no parent to let fall a heavy hand, Maurice still felt the unease of wrong-doing. At the back of his mind formed the uncertain outlines of an excuse. He muttered something about a swim and broke into a trot.

Roger remained, watching the littluns. He was not noticeably darker than when he had dropped in, but the shock of black hair, down his nape and low on his forehead, seemed to suit his gloomy face and made what seemed at first an unsociable remoteness into something forbidding. Percival finished his whimper and went on playing, for the tears had washed the sand away. Johnny watched him with china-blue eyes; then began to fling up sand in a shower, and presently Percival was crying again.

When Henry tired of his play and wandered off along the beach, Roger followed him, keeping beneath the palms and drifting casually in the same direction. Henry walked at a distance from the palms and the shade because he was too young to keep himself out of the sun. He went down the beach and busied himself at the water's edge. The great Pacific tide was coming in and every few seconds the relatively still water of the lagoon heaved forwards an inch. There were creatures that lived in this last fling of the sea, tiny transparencies that came questing in with the water over the hot, dry sand. With impalpable organs of sense they examined this new field. Perhaps food had appeared where the last incursion there had been none; bird droppings, insects perhaps, any of the strewn detritus of landward life. Like a myriad of tiny teeth in a saw, the transparencies came scavenging over the beach.

This was fascinating to Henry. He poked about with a bit of stick, that itself was wave-worn and whitened and a vagrant, and tried to control the motions of the scavengers. He made little runnels that the tide filled and tried to crowd them with creatures. He became absorbed beyond mere happiness as he felt himself exercising control over living things. He talked to them, urging them, ordering them. Driven back by the tide, his footprints became bays in which they were trapped and gave him the illusion of mastery. He squatted on his hams at the water's edge, bowed, with a shock of hair falling over his forehead and past his eyes, and the afternoon sun emptied down invisible arrows.

Roger waited too. At first he had hidden behind a great palm bole; but Henry's absorption with the transparencies was so obvious that at last he stood out in full view. He looked along the beach. Percival had gone off, crying, and Johnny was left in triumphant possession of the castles. He sat there, crooning to himself and throwing sand at an imaginary Percival. Beyond him, Roger could see the platform and the glints of spray where Ralph and Simon and Piggy and Maurice were diving in the pool. He listened carefully but could only just hear them.

A sudden breeze shook the fringe of palm trees, so that the fronds tossed and fluttered. Sixty feet above Roger, a cluster of nuts, fibrous lumps as big as rugby balls, were loosed from their stems. They fell about him with a series of hard thumps and he was not touched. Roger did not consider his escape, but looked from the nuts to Henry and back again.

The subsoil beneath the palm trees was a raised beach; and generations of palms had worked loose in this the stones that had lain on the sands of another shore. Roger stooped, picked up a stone, aimed, and threw it at Henry—threw it to miss. The stone, that token of preposterous time, bounced five yards to Henry's right and fell in the water. Roger gathered a handful of stones and began to throw them. Yet there was a space round Henry, perhaps six yards in diameter, into which he dare not throw. Here, invisible yet strong, was the taboo of the old life. Round the squatting child was the protection of parents and school and policemen and the law. Roger's arm was conditioned by a civilization that knew nothing of him and was in ruins.

Henry was surprised by the plopping sounds in the water. He abandoned the noiseless transparencies and pointed at the centre of the spreading rings like a setter. This side and that the stones fell, and Henry turned obediently but always too late to see the stones in the air. At last he saw one and laughed, looking for the friend who was teasing him. But Roger had whipped behind the palm bole again, was leaning against it breathing quickly, his eyelids fluttering. Then Henry lost interest in stones and wandered off.

'Roger.'

Jack was standing under a tree about ten yards away. When Roger opened his eyes and saw him, a darker shadow crept beneath the swarthiness of his skin; but Jack noticed nothing. He was eager, impatient, beckoning, so that Roger went to him.

There was a pool at the end of the river, a tiny mere dammed back by sand and full of white water-lilies and needle-like reeds. Here Sam and Eric were waiting, and Bill. Jack, concealed from the sun, knelt by the pool and opened the two large leaves that he carried. One of them contained white clay, and the other red. By them lay a stick of charcoal brought down from the fire.

Jack explained to Roger as he worked.

'They don't smell me. They see me, I think. Something pink under the trees.'

He smeared on the clay.

'If only I'd some green!'

He turned a half-concealed face up to Roger and answered the comprehension of his gaze.

'For hunting. Like in the war. You know—dazzle paint. Like things trying to look like something else——'

He twisted in the urgency of telling.

'—like moths on a tree trunk.'

Roger understood and nodded gravely. The twins moved towards Jack and began to protest timidly about something. Jack waved them away.

'Shut up.'

He rubbed the charcoal stick between the patches of red and white on his face.

'No. You two come with me.'

He peered at his reflection and disliked it. He bent down, took up a double handful of lukewarm water and rubbed the mess from his face. Freckles and sandy eyebrows appeared.

Roger smiled, unwillingly.

'You don't half look a mess.'

Jack planned his new face. He made one cheek and one eye-socket white, then rubbed red over the other half of his face and slashed a black bar of charcoal across from right ear to left jaw. He looked in the mere for his reflection, but his breathing troubled the mirror.

'Samneric. Get me a coco-nut. An empty one.'

He knelt, holding the shell of water. A rounded patch of sun-light fell on his face and a brightness appeared in the depths of the water. He looked in astonishment, no longer at himself but at an awesome stranger. He spilt the water and leapt to his feet, laughing excitedly. Beside the mere, his sinewy body held up a mask that drew their eyes and appalled them. He began to dance and his laughter became a bloodthirsty snarling. He capered to-wards Bill and the mask was a thing on its own, behind which Jack hid, liberated from shame and self-consciousness. The face of red and white and black, swung through the air and jigged towards Bill. Bill started up laughing; then suddenly he fell silent and blundered away through the bushes.

Jack rushed towards the twins.

'The rest are making a line. Come on!'

'But——'

'—we——'

'Come on! I'll creep up and stab——'

The mask compelled them.

Ralph climbed out of the bathing-pool and trotted up the beach and sat in the shade beneath the palms. His fair hair was plastered over his eyebrows and he pushed it back. Simon was floating in the water and kicking with his feet, and Maurice was practising diving. Piggy was mooning about, aimlessly picking up things and discar-ding them. The rock-pools which so fascinated him were covered by the tide, so he was without an interest until the tide went back. Presently, seeing Ralph under the palms, he came and sat by him.

Piggy wore the remainders of a pair of shorts, his fat body was golden brown, and the glasses still flashed when he looked at anything. He was the only boy on the island whose hair never seemed to grow. The rest were shock-headed, but Piggy's hair still lay in wisps over his head as though baldness were his natural state, and this imperfect covering would soon go, like the velvet on a young stag's antlers.

'I've been thinking,' he said, 'about a clock. We could make a sundial. We could put a stick in the sand, and then——'

The effort to express the mathematical processes involved was too great. He made a few passes instead.

'And an airplane, and a TV set,' said Ralph sourly, 'and a steam engine.'

Piggy shook his head.

'You have to have a lot of metal things for that,' he said, 'and we haven't got no metal. But we got a stick.'

Ralph turned and smiled involuntarily. Piggy was a bore; his fat, his ass-mar and his matter-of-fact ideas were dull: but there was always a little pleasure to be got out of pulling his leg, even if one did it by accident.

Piggy saw the smile and misinterpreted it as friendliness. There had grown up tacitly among the biguns the opinion that Piggy was an outsider, not only by accent, which did not matter, but by fat, and ass-mar, and specs, and a certain disinclination for manual labour. Now, finding that something he had said made Ralph smile, he rejoiced and pressed his advantage.

'We got a lot of sticks. We could have a sundial each. Then we should know what the time was.'

'A fat lot of good that would be.'

'You said you wanted things done. So as we could be rescued.'

'Oh, shut up.'

He leapt to his feet and trotted back to the pool, just as Maurice did a rather poor dive. Ralph was glad of a chance to change the subject. He shouted as Maurice came to the surface.

'Belly flop! Belly flop!'

Maurice flashed a smile at Ralph who slid easily into the water. Of all the boys, he was the most at home there; but today, irked by the mention of rescue, the useless, footling mention of rescue, even the green depths of water and the shattered, golden sun held no balm. Instead of remaining and playing, he swam with steady strokes under Simon and crawled out of the other side of the pool to lie there, sleek and streaming like a seal. Piggy, always clumsy, stood up and came to stand by him, so that Ralph rolled on his stomach and pretended not to see. The mirages had died away and gloomily he ran his eye along the taut blue line of the horizon.

The next moment he was on his feet and shouting.

'Smoke! Smoke!'

Simon tried to sit up in the water and got a mouthful. Maurice, who had been standing ready to dive, swayed back on his heels, made a bolt for the platform, then swerved back to the grass under the palms. There he started to pull on his tattered shorts, to be ready for anything.

Ralph stood, one hand holding back his hair, the other

clenched. Simon was climbing out of the water. Piggy was rubbing his glasses on his shorts and squinting at the sea. Maurice
had got both legs through one leg of his shorts—of all the boys,
only Ralph was still.

'I can't see no smoke,' said Piggy incredulously. 'I can't see no
smoke, Ralph—where is it?'

Ralph said nothing. Now both his hands were clenched over
his forehead so that the fair hair was kept out of his eyes. He was
leaning forward and already the salt was whitening his body.

'Ralph—where's the ship?'

Simon stood by, looking from Ralph to the horizon. Maurice's trousers gave way with a sigh and he abandoned them as a
wreck, rushed towards the forest, and then came back again.

The smoke was a tight little knot on the horizon and was
uncoiling slowly. Beneath the smoke was a dot that might be a
funnel. Ralph's face was pale as he spoke to himself.

'They'll see our smoke.'

Piggy was looking in the right direction now.

'It don't look much.'

He turned round and peered up at the mountain. Ralph continued to watch the ship, ravenously. Colour was coming back
into his face. Simon stood by him, silent.

'I know I can't see very much,' said Piggy, 'but have we got
any smoke?'

Ralph moved impatiently, still watching the ship.

'The smoke on the mountain.'

Maurice came running, and stared out to sea. Both Simon and
Piggy were looking up at the mountain. Piggy screwed up his
face but Simon cried out as though he had hurt himself.

'Ralph! Ralph!'

The quality of his speech slewed Ralph on the sand.

'You tell me,' said Piggy anxiously. 'Is there a signal?'

Ralph looked back at the dispersing smoke on the horizon,
then up at the mountain.

'Ralph—please! Is there a signal?'

Simon put out his hand, timidly, to touch Ralph; but Ralph
started to run, splashing through the shallow end of the bathing-
pool, across the hot, white sand and under the palms. A moment
later, he was battling with the complex undergrowth that was
already engulfing the scar. Simon ran after him, then Maurice.
Piggy shouted.

'Ralph! Please—Ralph!'

Then he too started to run, stumbling over Maurice's discarded shorts before he was across the terrace. Behind the four boys, the smoke moved gently along the horizon; and on the beach, Henry and Johnny were throwing sand at Percival who was crying quietly again; and all three were in complete ignorance of the excitement.

By the time Ralph had reached the landward end of the scar he was using precious breath to swear. He did desperate violence to his naked body among the rasping creepers so that blood was sliding over him. Just where the steep ascent of the mountain began, he stopped. Maurice was only a few yards behind him.

'Piggy's specs!' shouted Ralph, 'if the fire's right out, we'll need them——'

He stopped shouting and swayed on his feet. Piggy was only just visible, bumbling up from the beach. Ralph looked at the horizon, then up to the mountain. Was it better to fetch Piggy's glasses, or would the ship have gone? Or if they climbed on, supposing the fire was right out, and they had to watch Piggy crawling nearer and the ship sinking under the horizon? Balanced on a high peak of need, agonized by indecision, Ralph cried out:

'Oh God, oh God!'

Simon, struggling with bushes, caught his breath. His face was twisted. Ralph blundered on, savaging himself, as the wisp of smoke moved on.

The fire was dead. They saw that straight away; saw what they had really known down on the beach when the smoke of home had beckoned. The fire was right out, smokeless and dead; the watchers were gone. A pile of unused fuel lay ready.

Ralph turned to the sea. The horizon stretched, impersonal once more, barren of all but the faintest trace of smoke. Ralph ran stumbling along the rocks, saved himself on the edge of the pink cliff, and screamed at the ship.

'Come back! Come back!'

He ran backwards and forwards along the cliff, his face always to the sea, and his voice rose insanely.

'Come back! Come back!'

Simon and Maurice arrived. Ralph looked at them with unwinking eyes. Simon turned away, smearing the water from his cheeks. Ralph reached inside himself for the worst word he knew.

'They let the bloody fire out.'

He looked down the unfriendly side of the mountain. Piggy arrived, out of breath and whimpering like a littlun. Ralph clenched his fist and went very red. The intentness of his gaze, the bitterness of his voice pointed for him.

'There they are.'

A procession had appeared, far down among the pink screes that lay near the water's edge. Some of the boys wore black caps but otherwise they were almost naked. They lifted sticks in the air together, whenever they came to an easy patch. They were chanting, something to do with the bundle that the errant twins carried so carefully. Ralph picked out Jack easily, even at that distance, tall, red-haired, and inevitably leading the procession.

Simon looked now, from Ralph to Jack, as he had looked from Ralph to the horizon, and what he saw seemed to make him afraid. Ralph said nothing more, but waited while the procession came nearer. The chant was audible but at that distance still wordless. Behind Jack walked the twins, carrying a great stake on their shoulders. The gutted carcass of a pig swung from the stake, swinging heavily as the twins toiled over the uneven ground. The pig's head hung down with gaping neck and seemed to search for something on the ground. At last the words of the chant floated up to them, across the bowl of blackened wood and ashes.

'*Kill the pig. Cut her throat. Spill her blood.*'

Yet as the words became audible, the procession reached the steepest part of the mountain, and in a minute or two the chant had died away. Piggy snivelled and Simon shushed him quickly as though he had spoken too loudly in church.

Jack, his face smeared with clays, reached the top first and hailed Ralph excitedly, with lifted spear.

'Look! We've killed a pig—we stole up on them—we got in a circle——'

Voices broke from the hunters.

'We got in a circle——'

'We crept up——'

'The pig squealed——'

The twins stood with the pig swinging between them, dropping black gouts on the rock. They seemed to share one wide, ecstatic grin. Jack had too many things to tell Ralph at once. Instead, he danced a step or two, then remembered his dignity and stood still, grinning. He noticed blood on his hands and grimaced distastefully, looked for something on which to clean them, then wiped them on his shorts and laughed.

Ralph spoke.

'You let the fire out.'

Jack checked, vaguely irritated by this irrelevance but too happy to let it worry him.

'We can light the fire again. You should have been with us, Ralph. We had a smashing time. The twins got knocked over——'

'We hit the pig——'

'—I fell on top——'

'I cut the pig's throat,' said Jack, proudly, and yet twitched as he said it. 'Can I borrow yours, Ralph, to make a nick in the hilt?'

The boys chattered and danced. The twins continued to grin.

'There was lashings of blood,' said Jack, laughing and shuddering, 'you should have seen it!'

'We'll go hunting every day——'

Ralph spoke again, hoarsely. He had not moved.

'You let the fire out.'

This repetition made Jack uneasy. He looked at the twins and then back at Ralph.

'We had to have them in the hunt,' he said, 'or there wouldn't have been enough for a ring.'

He flushed, conscious of a fault.

'The fire's only been out an hour or two. We can light up again——'

He noticed Ralph's scarred nakedness, and the sombre silence of all four of them. He sought, charitable in his happiness, to include them in the thing that had happened. His mind was crowded with memories; memories of the knowledge that had come to them when they closed in on the struggling pig, knowledge that they had outwitted a living thing, imposed their will upon it, taken away its life like a long satisfying drink.

He spread his arms wide.

'You should have seen the blood!'

The hunters were more silent now, but at this they buzzed again. Ralph flung back his hair. One arm pointed at the empty horizon. His voice was loud and savage, and struck them into silence.

'There was a ship.'

Jack, faced at once with too many awful implications, ducked away from them. He laid a hand on the pig and drew his knife. Ralph brought his arm down, fist clenched, and his voice shook.

'There was a ship. Out there. You said you'd keep the fire going and you let it out!' He took a step towards Jack who turned and faced him.

'They might have seen us. We might have gone home——'

This was too bitter for Piggy, who forgot his timidity in the agony of his loss. He began to cry out, shrilly:

'You and your blood, Jack Merridew! You and your hunting! We might have gone home——'

Ralph pushed Piggy on one side.

'I was chief; and you were going to do what I said. You talk. But you can't even build huts—then you go off hunting and let out the fire——'

He turned away, silent for a moment. Then his voice came again on a peak of feeling.

'There was a ship——'

One of the smaller hunters began to wail. The dismal truth was filtering through to everybody. Jack went very red as he hacked and pulled at the pig.

'The job was too much. We needed everyone.'

Ralph turned.

'You could have had everyone when the shelters were finished. But you had to hunt——'

'We needed meat.'

Jack stood up as he said this, the bloodied knife in his hand. The two boys faced each other. There was the brilliant world of hunting, tactics, fierce exhilaration, skill; and there was the world of longing and baffled common-sense. Jack transferred the knife to his left hand and smudged blood over his forehead as he pushed down the plastered hair.

Piggy began again.

'You didn't ought to have let that fire out. You said you'd keep the smoke going——'

This from Piggy, and the wails of agreement from some of the hunters drove Jack to violence. The bolting look came into his blue eyes. He took a step, and able at last to hit someone, stuck his fist into Piggy's stomach. Piggy sat down with a grunt. Jack stood over him. His voice was vicious with humiliation.

'You would, would you? Fatty!'

Ralph made a step forward and Jack smacked Piggy's head. Piggy's glasses flew off and tinkled on the rocks. Piggy cried out in terror:

'My specs!'

He went crouching and feeling over the rocks but Simon, who got there first, found them for him. Passions beat about Simon on the mountain-top with awful wings.

'One side's broken.'

Piggy grabbed and put on the glasses. He looked malevolently at Jack.

'I got to have them specs. Now I only got one eye. Jus' you wait——'

Jack made a move towards Piggy who scrambled away till a great rock lay between them. He thrust his head over the top and glared at Jack through his one flashing glass.

'Now I only got one eye. Just you wait——'

Jack mimicked the whine and scramble.

'Jus' you wait—yah!'

Piggy and the parody were so funny that the hunters began to laugh. Jack felt encouraged. He went on scrambling and the laughter rose to a gale of hysteria. Unwillingly Ralph felt his lips twitch; he was angry with himself for giving way.

He muttered.

'That was a dirty trick.'

Jack broke out of his gyration and stood facing Ralph. His words came in a shout.

'All right, all right!'

He looked at Piggy, at the hunters, at Ralph.

'I'm sorry. About the fire, I mean. There. I——'

He drew himself up.

'—I apologize.'

The buzz from the hunters was one of admiration at this handsome behaviour. Clearly they were of the opinion that Jack had done the right thing, had put himself in the right by his generous apology and Ralph, obscurely, in the wrong. They waited for an appropriately decent answer.

Yet Ralph's throat refused to pass one. He resented, as an addition to Jack's misbehaviour, this verbal trick. The fire was dead, the ship was gone. Could they not see? Anger instead of decency passed his throat.

'That was a dirty trick.'

They were silent on the mountain-top while the opaque look appeared in Jack's eyes and passed away.

Ralph's final word was an ungracious mutter.

'All right. Light the fire.'

With some positive action before them, a little of the tension died. Ralph said no more, did nothing, stood looking down at the ashes round his feet. Jack was loud and active. He gave orders, sang, whistled, threw remarks at the silent Ralph—remarks that did not need an answer, and therefore could not invite a snub; and still Ralph was silent. No one, not even Jack, would ask him to move and in the end they had to build the fire three yards away and in a place not really as convenient. So Ralph asserted his chieftainship and could not have chosen a better way if he had thought for days. Against this weapon, so indefinable and so effective, Jack was powerless and raged without knowing why. By the time the pile was built, they were on different sides of a high barrier.

When they had dealt with the fire another crisis arose. Jack had no means of lighting it. Then to his surprise, Ralph went to Piggy and took the glasses from him. Not even Ralph knew how a link between him and Jack had been snapped and fastened elsewhere.

'I'll bring 'em back.'

'I'll come too.'

Piggy stood behind him, islanded in a sea of meaningless colour, while Ralph knelt and focused the glossy spot. Instantly the fire was alight Piggy held out his hands and grabbed the glasses back.

Before these fantastically attractive flowers of violet and red and yellow, unkindness melted away. They became a circle of boys round a camp fire and even Piggy and Ralph were half-drawn in. Soon some of the boys were rushing down the slope for more wood while Jack hacked the pig. They tried holding the whole carcass on a stake over the fire, but the stake burnt more quickly than the pig roasted. In the end they skewered bits of meat on branches and held them in the flames: and even then almost as much boy was roasted as meat.

Ralph dribbled. He meant to refuse meat but his past diet of fruit and nuts, with an odd crab or fish, gave him too little resistance. He accepted a piece of half-raw meat and gnawed it like a wolf.

Piggy spoke, also dribbling.

'Aren't I having none?'

Jack had meant to leave him in doubt, as an assertion of power; but Piggy by advertising his omission made more cruelty necessary.

'You didn't hunt.'

'No more did Ralph,' said Piggy wetly, 'nor Simon.' He amplified. 'There isn't more than a ha'porth of meat in a crab.'

Ralph stirred uneasily. Simon, sitting between the twins and Piggy, wiped his mouth and shoved his piece of meat over the rocks to Piggy, who grabbed it. The twins giggled and Simon lowered his face in shame.

Then Jack leapt to his feet, slashed off a great hunk of meat, and flung it down at Simon's feet.

'Eat! Damn you!'

He glared at Simon.

'Take it!'

He spun on his heel, centre of a bewildered circle of boys.

'I got you meat!'

Numberless and inexpressible frustrations combined to make his rage elemental and awe-inspiring.

'I painted my face—I stole up. Now you eat—all of you—and I——'

Slowly the silence on the mountain-top deepened till the click of the fire and the soft hiss of roasting meat could be heard clearly. Jack looked round for understanding but found only respect. Ralph stood among the ashes of the signal fire, his hands full of meat, saying nothing.

Then at last Maurice broke the silence. He changed the subject to the only one that could bring the majority of them together.

'Where did you find the pig?'

Roger pointed down the unfriendly side.

'They were there—by the sea.'

Jack, recovering, could not bear to have his story told. He broke in quickly.

'We spread round. I crept, on hands and knees. The spears fell out because they hadn't barbs on. The pig ran away and made an awful noise——'

'It turned back and ran into the circle, bleeding——'

All the boys were talking at once, relieved and excited.

'We closed in——'

The first blow had paralysed its hind quarters, so then the circle could close in and beat and beat——

'I cut the pig's throat——'

The twins, still sharing their identical grin, jumped up and ran round each other. Then the rest joined in, making pig-dying noises and shouting.

'One for his nob!'

'Give him a fourpenny one!'

Then Maurice pretended to be the pig and ran squealing into the centre, and the hunters, circling still, pretended to beat him. As they danced, they sang.

'*Kill the pig. Cut her throat. Bash her in.*'

Ralph watched them, envious and resentful. Not till they flagged and the chant died away, did he speak.

'I'm calling an assembly.'

One by one, they halted, and stood watching him.

'With the conch. I'm calling a meeting even if we have to go on into the dark. Down on the platform. When I blow it. Now.'

He turned away and walked off, down the mountain.

CHAPTER FIVE

Beast from Water

The tide was coming in and there was only a narrow strip of firm beach between the water and the white, stumbling stuff near the palm terrace. Ralph chose the firm strip as a path because he needed to think; and only here could he allow his feet to move without having to watch them. Suddenly, pacing by the water, he was overcome with astonishment. He found himself understanding the wearisomeness of this life, where every path was an improvisation and a considerable part of one's waking life was spent watching one's feet. He stopped, facing the strip; and remembering that first enthusiastic exploration as though it were part of a brighter childhood, he smiled jeeringly. He turned then and walked back towards the platform with the sun in his face. The time had come for the assembly and as he walked into the concealing splendours of the sunlight he went carefully over the points of his speech. There must be no mistake about this assembly, no chasing imaginary. . . .

He lost himself in a maze of thoughts that were rendered vague by his lack of words to express them. Frowning, he tried again.

This meeting must not be fun, but business.

At that he walked faster, aware all at once of urgency and the declining sun and a little wind created by his speed that breathed about his face. This wind pressed his grey shirt against his chest so that he noticed—in this new mood of comprehension—how the folds were stiff like cardboard, and unpleasant; noticed too how the frayed edges of his shorts were making an uncomfortable, pink area on the front of his thighs. With a convulsion of the mind, Ralph discovered dirt and decay; understood how much he disliked perpetually flicking the tangled hair out of his eyes, and at last, when the sun was gone, rolling noisily to rest among dry leaves. At that, he began to trot.

The beach near the bathing-pool was dotted with groups of boys waiting for the assembly. They made way for him silently, conscious of his grim mood and the fault at the fire.

The place of assembly in which he stood was roughly a tri-angle; but irregular and sketchy, like everything they made. First there was the log on which he himself sat; a dead tree that must have been quite exceptionally big for the platform. Perhaps one of those legendary storm of the Pacific had shifted it here. This palm trunk lay parallel to the beach, so that when Ralph sat he faced the island but to the boys was a darkish figure against the shimmer of the lagoon. The two sides of the triangle of which the log was base were less evenly defined. On the right was a log polished by restless seats along the top, but not so large as the chief's and not so comfortable. On the left were four small logs, one of them—the furthest—lamentably springy. Assembly after assembly had broken up in laughter when someone had leaned too far back and the log had whipped and thrown half a dozen boys backwards into the grass. Yet now, he saw, no one had had the wit—not himself nor Jack, nor Piggy—to bring a stone and wedge the thing. So they would continue enduring the ill-balanced twister, because, because. . . . Again he lost himself in deep waters.

Grass was worn away in front of each trunk but grew tall and untrodden in the centre of the triangle. Then, at the apex, the grass was thick again because no one sat there. All round the place of assembly the grey trunks rose, straight or leaning, and supported the low roof of leaves. On two sides was the beach; behind, the lagoon; in front, the darkness of the island.

Ralph turned to the chief's seat. They had never had an assembly as late before. That was why the place looked so differ-ent. Normally the underside of the green roof was lit by a tangle of golden reflections, and their faces were lit upside down, like—thought Ralph, when you hold an electric torch in your hands. But now the sun was slanting in at one side, so that the shadows were where they ought to be.

Again he fell into that strange mood of speculation that was so foreign to him. If faces were different when lit from above or below—what was a face? What was anything?

Ralph moved impatiently. The trouble was, if you were a chief you had to think, you had to be wise. And then the occasion slipped by so that you had to grab at a decision. This made you think; because thought was a valuable thing, that got results. . . .

Only, decided Ralph as he faced the chief's seat, I can't think. Not like Piggy.

Once more that evening Ralph had to adjust his values. Piggy could think. He could go step by step inside that fat head of his, only Piggy was no chief. But Piggy, for all his ludicrous body, had brains. Ralph was a specialist in thought now, and could recognize thought in another.

The sun in his eyes reminded him how time was passing, so he took the conch down from the tree and examined the surface. Exposure to the air had bleached the yellow and pink to near-white, and transparency. Ralph felt a kind of affectionate reverence for the conch, even though he had fished the thing out of the lagoon himself. He faced the place of assembly and put the conch to his lips.

The others were waiting for this and came straight away. Those who were aware that a ship had passed the island while the fire was out were subdued by the thought of Ralph's anger; while those, including the littluns who did not know, were impressed by the general air of solemnity. The place of assembly filled quickly; Jack, Simon, Maurice, most of the hunters, on Ralph's right; the rest on the left, under the sun. Piggy came and stood outside the triangle. This indicated that he wished to listen, but would not speak; and Piggy intended it as a gesture of disapproval.

'The thing is: we need an assembly.'

No one said anything but the faces turned to Ralph were intent. He flourished the conch. He had learnt as a practical business that fundamental statements like this had to be said at least twice, before everyone understood them. One had to sit, attracting all eyes to the conch, and drop words like heavy round stones among the little groups that crouched or squatted. He was searching his mind for simple words so that even the littluns would understand what the assembly was about. Later perhaps, practised debators—Jack, Maurice, Piggy—would use their whole art to twist the meeting: but now at the beginning the subject of the debate must be laid out clearly.

'We need an assembly. Not for fun. Not for laughing and falling off the log'—the group of littluns on the twister giggled and looked at each other—'not for making jokes, or for'—he lifted the conch in an effort to find the compelling word—'for cleverness. Not for these things. But to put things straight.'

He paused for a moment.

'I've been along. By myself I went, thinking what's what. I

know what we need. An assembly to put things straight. And first of all, I'm speaking.'

He paused for a moment and automatically pushed back his hair. Piggy tiptoed to the triangle, his ineffectual protest made, and joined the others.

Ralph went on.

'We have lots of assemblies. Everybody enjoys speaking and being together. We decide things. But they don't get done. We were going to have water brought from the stream and left in those coco-nut shells under fresh leaves. So it was, for a few days. Now there's no water. The shells are dry. People drink from the river.'

There was a murmur of assent.

'Not that there's anything wrong with drinking from the river. I mean I'd sooner have water from that place—you know—the pool where the waterfall is—than out of an old coco-nut shell. Only we said we'd have the water brought. And now not. There were only two full shells there this afternoon.'

He licked his lips.

'Then there's huts. Shelters.'

The murmur swelled again and died away.

'You mostly sleep in shelters. Tonight, except for Samneric up by the fire, you'll all sleep there. Who built the shelters?'

Clamour rose at once. Everyone had built the shelters. Ralph had to wave the conch once more.

'Wait a minute! I mean, who built all three? We all built the first one, four of us the second, and me 'n Simon built the last one over there. That's why it's so tottery. No. Don't laugh. That shelter might fall down if the rain comes back. We'll need those shelters then.'

He paused and cleared his throat.

'There's another thing. We chose those rocks right along beyond the bathing-pool as a lavatory. That was sensible too. The tide cleans the place up. You littluns know about that.'

There were sniggers here and there and swift glances.

'Now people seem to use anywhere. Even near the shelters and the platform. You littluns, when you're getting fruit; if you're taken short——'

The assembly roared.

'I said if you're taken short you keep away from the fruit. That's dirty.'

Laughter rose again.

'I said that's dirty!'

He plucked at his stiff, grey shirt.

'That's really dirty. If you're taken short you go right along the beach to the rocks. See?'

Piggy held out his hands for the conch but Ralph shook his head. This speech was planned, point by point.

'We've all got to use the rocks again. This place is getting dirty.' He paused. The assembly, sensing a crisis, was tensely expectant. 'And then: about the fire.'

Ralph let out his spare breath with a little gasp that was echoed by his audience. Jack started to chip a piece of wood with his knife and whispered something to Robert, who looked away.

'The fire is the most important thing on the island. How can we ever be rescued except by luck, if we don't keep a fire going? Is a fire too much for us to make?'

He flung out an arm.

'Look at us! How many are we? And yet we can't keep a fire going to make smoke. Don't you understand? Can't you see we ought to—ought to die before we let the fire out?'

There was a self-conscious giggling among the hunters. Ralph turned on them passionately.

'You hunters! You can laugh! But I tell you the smoke is more important than the pig, however often you kill one. Do all of you see?' He spread his arms wide and turned to the whole triangle.

'We've got to make smoke up there—or die.'

He paused, feeling for his next point.

'And another thing.'

Someone called out.

'Too many things.'

There came mutters of agreement. Ralph overrode them.

'And another thing. We nearly set the whole island on fire. And we waste time, rolling rocks, and making little cooking fires. Now I say this and make it a rule, because I'm chief. We won't have a fire anywhere but on the mountain. Ever.'

There was a row immediately. Boys stood up and shouted and Ralph shouted back.

'Because if you want a fire to cook fish or crab, you can jolly well go up the mountain. That way we'll be certain.'

Hands were reaching for the conch in the light of the setting sun. He held on and leapt on the trunk.

'All this I meant to say. Now I've said it. You voted me for chief. Now you do what I say.'

They quietened, slowly, and at last were seated again. Ralph dropped down and spoke in his ordinary voice.

'So remember. The rocks for a lavatory. Keep the fire going and smoke showing as a signal. Don't take fire from the mountain. Take your food up there.'

Jack stood up, scowling in the gloom, and held out his hands.

'I haven't finished yet.'

'But you've talked and talked!'

'I've got the conch.'

Jack sat down, grumbling.

'Then the last thing. This is what people can talk about.'

He waited till the platform was very still.

'Things are breaking up. I don't understand why. We began well; we were happy. And then——'

He moved the conch gently, looking beyond them at nothing, remembering the beastie, the snake, the fire, the talk of fear.

'Then people started getting frightened.'

A murmur, almost a moan, rose and passed away. Jack had stopped whittling. Ralph went on, abruptly.

'But that's littluns' talk. We'll get that straight. So the last part, the bit we can all talk about, is kind of deciding on the fear.'

The hair was creeping into his eyes again.

'We've got to talk about this fear and decide there's nothing in it. I'm frightened myself, sometimes; only that's nonsense! Like bogies. Then, when we've decided, we can start again and be careful about things like the fire.' A picture of three boys walking along the bright beach flitted through his mind. 'And be happy.'

Ceremonially, Ralph laid the conch on the trunk beside him as a sign that the speech was over. What sunlight reached them was level.

Jack stood up and took the conch.

'So this is a meeting to find out what's what. I'll tell you what's what. You littluns started all this with the fear talk. Beasts! Where from? Of course we're frightened sometimes but we put up with being frightened. Only Ralph says you scream in the night. What does that mean but nightmares? Anyway, you don't hunt or build or help——you're a lot of cry-babies and sissies. That's what. And as for the fear——you'll have to put up with that like the rest of us.'

Ralph looked at Jack open-mouthed, but Jack took no notice.

'The thing is—fear can't hurt you any more than a dream. There aren't any beasts to be afraid of on this island.' He looked along the row of whispering littluns. 'Serve you right if something did get you, you useless lot of cry-babies! But there *is* no animal——'

Ralph interrupted him testily.

'What is all this? Who said anything about an animal?'

'You did the other day. You said they dream and cry out. Now they talk—not only the littluns, but my hunters sometimes—talk of a thing, a dark thing, a beast, some sort of animal. I've heard. You thought not, didn't you? Now listen. You don't get big animals on small islands. Only pigs. You only get lions and tigers in big countries like Africa and India——'

'And the Zoo——'

'I've got the conch. I'm not talking about the fear. I'm talking about the beast. Be frightened if you like. But as for the beast——'

Jack paused, cradling the conch, and turned to his hunters with their dirty black caps.

'Am I a hunter or am I not?'

They nodded, simply. He was a hunter all right. No one doubted that.

'Well then—I've been all over this island. By myself. If there were a beast I'd have seen it. Be frightened because you're like that—but there is no beast in the forest.'

Jack handed back the conch and sat down. The whole assembly applauded him with relief. Then Piggy held out his hand.

'I don't agree with all Jack said, but with some. 'Course there isn't a beast in the forest. How could there be? What would a beast eat?'

'Pig.'

'We eat pig.'

'Piggy!'

'I got the conch!' said Piggy indignantly. 'Ralph—they ought to shut up, oughtn't they? You shut up, you littluns! What I mean is that I don't agree about this here fear. Of course there isn't nothing to be afraid of in the forest. Why—I been there myself! You'll be talking about ghosts and such things next. We know what goes on and if there's something wrong, there's someone to put it right.'

He took off his glasses and blinked at them. The sun had gone as if the light had been turned off.

He proceeded to explain.

'If you get a pain in your stomach, whether it's a little one or a big one——'

'Yours is a big one.'

'When you done laughing perhaps we can get on with the meeting. And if them littluns climb back on the twister again they'll only fall off in a sec. So they might as well sit on the ground and listen. No. You have doctors for everything, even the inside of your mind. You don't really mean that we got to be frightened all the time of nothing? Life,' said Piggy expansively, 'is scientific, that's what it is. In a year or two when the war's over they'll be travelling to Mars and back. I know there isn't no beast—not with claws and all that, I mean—but I know there isn't no fear, either.'

Piggy paused.

'Unless——'

Ralph moved restlessly.

'Unless what?'

'Unless we get frightened of people.'

A sound, half-laugh, half-jeer, rose among the seated boys. Piggy ducked his head and went on hastily.

'So let's hear from the littlun who talked about a beast and perhaps we can show him how silly he is.'

The littluns began to jabber among themselves, then one stood forward.

'What's your name?'

'Phil.'

For a littlun he was self-confident, holding out his hands, cradling the conch as Ralph did, looking round at them to collect their attention before he spoke.

'Last night I had a dream, a horrid dream, fighting with things. I was outside the shelter by myself, fighting with things, those twisty things in the trees.'

He paused, and the other littluns laughed in horrified sympathy.

'Then I was frightened and I woke up. And I was outside the shelter by myself in the dark and the twisty things had gone away.'

The vivid horror of this, so possible and so nakedly terrifying, held them all silent. The child's voice went piping on from behind the white conch.

'And I was frightened and started to call out for Ralph and then I saw something moving among the trees, something big and horrid.'

He paused, half-frightened by the recollection yet proud of the sensation he was creating.

'That was a nightmare,' said Ralph, 'he was walking in his sleep.'

The assembly murmured in subdued agreement.

The littlun shook his head stubbornly.

'I was asleep when the twisty things were fighting and when they went away I was awake, and I saw something big and horrid moving in the trees.'

Ralph held out his hands for the conch and the littlun sat down.

'You were asleep. There wasn't anyone there. How could anyone be wandering about in the forest at night? Was anyone? Did anyone go out?'

There was a long pause while the assembly grinned at the thought of anyone going out in the darkness. Then Simon stood up and Ralph looked at him in astonishment.

'You! What were you mucking about in the dark for?'

Simon grabbed the conch convulsively.

'I wanted—to go to a place—a place I know.'

'What place?'

'Just a place I know. A place in the jungle.'

He hesitated.

Jack settled the question for them with that contempt in his voice that could sound so funny and so final.

'He was taken short.'

With a feeling of humiliation on Simon's behalf, Ralph took back the conch, looking Simon sternly in the face as he did so.

'Well, don't do it again. Understand? Not at night. There's enough silly talk about beasts, without the littluns seeing you gliding about like a——'

The derisive laughter that rose had fear in it and condemnation. Simon opened his mouth to speak but Ralph had the conch, so he backed to his seat.

When the assembly was silent Ralph turned to Piggy.

'Well, Piggy?'

'There was another one. Him.'

The littluns pushed Percival forward then left him by himself. He stood knee-deep in the central grass, looking at his hidden feet, trying to pretend he was in a tent. Ralph remembered another small boy who had stood like this and he flinched away from the memory. He had pushed the thought down and out of sight, where only some positive reminder like this could bring it to the surface. There had been no further numberings of the littluns, partly because there was no means of ensuring that all of them were accounted for and partly because Ralph knew the answer to at least one question Piggy had asked on the mountain-top. There were little boys, fair, dark, freckled, and all dirty, but their faces were all dreadfully free of major blemishes. No one had seen the mulberry-coloured birthmark again. But that time Piggy had coaxed and bullied. Tacitly admitting that he remembered the unmentionable, Ralph nodded to Piggy.

'Go on. Ask him.'

Piggy knelt, holding the conch.

'Now then. What's your name?'

The small boy twisted away into his tent. Piggy turned helplessly to Ralph, who spoke sharply.

'What's your name?'

Tormented by the silence and the refusal the assembly broke into a chant.

'What's your name? What's your name?'

'Quiet!'

Ralph peered at the child in the twilight.

'Now tell us. What's your name?'

'Percival Wemys Madison, The Vicarage, Harcourt St Anthony, Hants, telephone, telephone, tele——'

As if this information was rooted far down in the springs of sorrow, the littlun wept. His face puckered, the tears leapt from his eyes, his mouth opened till they could see a square black hole. At first he was a silent effigy of sorrow; but then the lamentation rose out of him, loud and sustained as the conch.

'Shut up, you! Shut up!'

Percival Wemys Madison would not shut up. A spring had been tapped, far beyond the reach of authority or even physical intimidation. The crying went on, breath after breath, and seemed to sustain him upright as if he were nailed to it.

'Shut up! Shut up!'

For now the littluns were no longer silent. They were reminded of their personal sorrows; and perhaps felt themselves to share in a sorrow that was universal. They began to cry in sympathy, two of them almost as loud as Percival.

Maurice saved them. He cried out.

'Look at me!'

He pretended to fall over. He rubbed his rump and sat on the twister so that he fell in the grass. He clowned badly; but Percival and the others noticed and sniffed and laughed. Presently they were all laughing so absurdly that the biguns joined in.

Jack was the first to make himself heard. He had not got the conch and thus spoke against the rules; but nobody minded.

'And what about the beast?'

Something strange was happening to Percival. He yawned and staggered, so that Jack seized and shook him.

'Where does the beast live?'

Percival sagged in Jack's grip.

'That's a clever beast,' said Piggy jeering, 'if it can hide on this island.'

'Jack's been everywhere——'

'Where could a beast live?'

'Beast my foot!'

Percival muttered something and the assembly laughed again. Ralph leaned forward.

'What does he say?'

Jack listened to Percival's answer and then let go of him. Percival, released, surrounded by the comfortable presence of humans, fell in the long grass and went to sleep.

Jack cleared his throat, then reported casually.

'He says the beast comes out of the sea.'

The last laugh died away. Ralph turned involuntarily, a black, humped figure against the lagoon. The assembly looked with him; considered the vast stretches of water, the high sea beyond, unknown indigo of infinite possibility; heard silently the sough and whisper from the reef.

Maurice spoke—so loudly that they jumped.

'Daddy said they haven't found all the animals in the sea yet.'

Argument started again. Ralph held out the glimmering conch and Maurice took it obediently. The meeting subsided.

'I mean when Jack says you can be frightened because people are frightened anyway that's all right. But when he says there's only pigs on this island I expect he's right but he doesn't know, not really, not certainly I mean'—Maurice took a breath—'My

daddy says there's things, what d'you call'em that make ink—
squids—that are hundreds of yards long and eat whales whole.'
He paused again and laughed gaily. 'I don't believe in the beast of
course. As Piggy says, life's scientific, but we don't know, do we?
Not certainly, I mean——'

Someone shouted.

'A squid couldn't come up out of the water!'

'Could!'

'Couldn't!'

In a moment the platform was full of arguing, gesticulating
shadows. To Ralph, seated, this seemed the breaking-up of sanity.
Fear, beasts, no general agreement that the fire was all-important:
and when one tried to get the thing straight the argument sheered
off, bringing up fresh, unpleasant matter.

He could see a whiteness in the gloom near him so he grabbed
it from Maurice and blew as loudly as he could. The assembly
was shocked into silence. Simon was close to him, laying hands
on the conch. Simon felt a perilous necessity to speak; but to
speak in assembly was a terrible thing to him.

'Maybe,' he said hesitantly, 'maybe there is a beast.'

The assembly cried out savagely and Ralph stood up in amazement.

'You, Simon You believe in this?'

'I don't know,' said Simon. His heartbeats were choking him.
'But. . . .'

The storm broke.

'Sit down!'

'Shut up!'

'Take the conch!'

'Sod you!'

'Shut up!'

Ralph shouted.

'Hear him! He's got the conch!'

'What I mean is . . . maybe it's only us.'

'Nuts!'

That was from Piggy, shocked out of decorum. Simon went
on.

'We could be sort of. . . .'

Simon became inarticulate in his effort to express mankind's
essential illness. Inspiration came to him.

'What's the dirtiest thing there is?'

As an answer Jack dropped into the uncomprehending silence that followed it the one crude expressive syllable. Release was like an orgasm. Those littluns who had climbed back on the twister fell off again and did not mind. The hunters were screaming with delight.

Simon's effort fell about him in ruins; the laughter beat him cruelly and he shrank away defenceless to his seat.

At last the assembly was silent again. Someone spoke out of turn.

'Maybe he means it's some sort of ghost.'

Ralph lifted the conch and peered into the gloom. The lightest thing was the pale beach. Surely the littluns were nearer? Yes— there was no doubt about it, they were huddled into a tight knot of bodies in the central grass. A flurry of wind made the palms talk and the noise seemed very loud now that darkness and silence made it so noticeable. Two grey trunks rubbed each other with an evil squeaking that no one had noticed by day.

Piggy took the conch out of his hands. His voice was indignant.

'I don't believe in no ghosts—ever!'

Jack was up too, unaccountably angry.

'Who cares what you believe—Fatty!'

'I got the conch!'

There was the sound of a brief tussle and the conch moved to and fro.

'You gimme the conch back!'

Ralph pushed between them and got a thump on the chest. He wrested the conch from someone and sat down breathlessly.

'There's too much talk about ghosts. We ought to have left all this for daylight.'

A hushed and anonymous voice broke in.

'Perhaps that's what the beast is—a ghost.'

The assembly was shaken as by a wind.

'There's too much talking out of turn,' Ralph said, 'because we can't have proper assemblies if you don't stick to the rules.'

He stopped again. The careful plan of this assembly had broken down.

'What d'you want me to say then? I was wrong to call this assembly so late. We'll have a vote on them; on ghosts I mean; and then go to the shelters because we're all tired. No—Jack is it?—wait a minute. I'll say here and now that I don't believe in ghosts. Or I don't think I do. But I don't like the thought of them. Not now that is, in the dark. But we were going to decide what's wrong.'

He raised the conch for a moment.

'Very well then. I suppose what's what is whether there are ghosts or not——'

He thought for a moment, formulating the question.

'Who thinks there may be ghosts?'

For a long time there was silence and no apparent movement. Then Ralph peered into the gloom and made out the hands. He spoke flatly.

'I see.'

The world, that understandable and lawful world, was slipping away. Once there was this and that; and now—and the ship had gone.

The conch was snatched from his hands and Piggy's voice shrilled.

'I didn't vote for no ghosts!'

He whirled round on the assembly.

'Remember that all of you!'

They heard him stamp.

'What are we? Humans? Or animals? Or savages? What's grown-ups going to think? Going off—hunting pigs—letting fires out—and now!'

A shadow fronted him tempestuously.

'You shut up, you fat slug!'

There was a moment's struggle and the glimmering conch jigged up and down. Ralph leapt to his feet.

'Jack! Jack! You haven't got the conch! Let him speak.'

Jack's face swam near him.

'And you shut up! Who are you, anyway? Sitting there—telling people what to do. You can't hunt, you can't sing——'

'I'm chief. I was chosen.'

'Why should choosing make any difference? Just giving orders that don't make any sense——'

'Piggy's got the conch.'

'That's right—favour Piggy as you always do——'

'Jack!'

Jack's voice sounded in bitter mimicry.

'Jack! Jack!'

'The rules!' shouted Ralph, 'you're breaking the rules!'

'Who cares?'

Ralph summoned his wits.

'Because the rules are the only thing we've got!'

But Jack was shouting against him.

'Bollocks to the rules! We're strong—we hunt! If there's a beast, we'll hunt it down! We'll close in and beat and beat and beat——'

He gave a wild whoop and leapt down to the pale sand. At once the platform was full of noise and excitement, scramblings, screams and laughter. The assembly shredded away and became a discursive and random scatter from the palms to the water and away along the beach, beyond night-sight. Ralph found his cheek touching the conch and took it from Piggy.

'What's grown-ups going to say?' cried Piggy again. 'Look at 'em!'

The sound of mock hunting, hysterical laughter and real terror came from the beach.

'Blow the conch, Ralph.'

Piggy was so close that Ralph could see the glint of his one glass.

'There's the fire. Can't they see?'

'You got to be tough now. Make 'em do what you want.'

Ralph answered in the cautious voice of one who rehearses a theorem.

'If I blow the conch and they don't come back; then we've had it. We shan't keep the fire going. We'll be like animals. We'll never be rescued.'

'If you don't blow, we'll soon be animals anyway. I can't see what they're doing but I can hear.'

The dispersed figures had come together on the sand and were a dense black mass that revolved. They were chanting something and littluns that had had enough were staggering away, howling. Ralph raised the conch to his lips and then lowered it.

'The trouble is: Are there ghosts, Piggy? Or beasts?'

'Course there aren't.'

'Why not?'

''Cos things wouldn't make sense. Houses an' streets, an'—TV—they wouldn't work.'

The dancing, chanting boys had worked themselves away till their sound was nothing but a wordless rhythm.

'But s'pose they don't make sense? Not here, on this island? Supposing things are watching us and waiting?'

Ralph shuddered violently and moved closer to Piggy, so that they bumped frighteningly.

'You stop talking like that! We got enough trouble, Ralph, an' I've had as much as I can stand. If there is ghosts——'

'I ought to give up being chief. Hear 'em.'

'Oh lord! Oh no!'

Piggy gripped Ralph's arm.

'If Jack was chief he'd have all hunting and no fire. We'd be here till we died.'

His voice ran up to a squeak.

'Who's that sitting there?'

'Me. Simon.'

'Fat lot of good we are,' said Ralph. 'Three blind mice. I'll give up.'

'If you give up,' said Piggy, in an appalled whisper, 'what'ud happen to me?'

'Nothing.'

'He hates me. I dunno why. If he could do what he wanted—you're all right, he respects you. Besides—you'd hit him.'

'You were having a nice fight with him just now.'

'I had the conch,' said Piggy simply. 'I had a right to speak.'

Simon stirred in the dark.

'Go on being chief.'

'You shut up, young Simon! Why couldn't you say there wasn't a beast?'

'I'm scared of him,' said Piggy, 'and that's why I know him. If you're scared of someone you hate him but you can't stop thinking about him. You kid yourself he's all right really, an' then when you see him again; it's like asthma an' you can't breathe. I tell you what. He hates you too, Ralph——'

'Me? Why me?'

'I dunno. You got him over the fire; an' you're chief an' he isn't.'

'But he's, he's, Jack Merridew!'

'I been in bed so much I done some thinking. I know about people. I know about me. And him. He can't hurt you: but if you stand out of the way he'd hurt the next thing. And that's me.'

'Piggy's right, Ralph. There's you and Jack. Go on being chief.'

'We're all drifting and things are going rotten. At home there was always a grown-up. Please, sir; please, miss; and then you got an answer. How I wish!'

'I wish my auntie was here.'

'I wish my father . . . O, what's the use?'

'Keep the fire going.'

The dance was over and the hunters were going back to the shelters.

'Grown-ups know things,' said Piggy. 'They ain't afraid of the dark. They'd meet and have tea and discuss. Then things 'ud be all right——'

'They wouldn't set fire to the island. Or lose——'

'They'd build a ship——'

The three boys stood in the darkness, striving unsuccessfully to convey the majesty of adult life.

'They wouldn't quarrel——'

'Or break my specs——'

'Or talk about a beast——'

'If only they could get a message to us,' cried Ralph desperately. 'If they could send us something grown-up . . . a sign or something.'

A thin wail out of the darkness chilled them and set them grabbing for each other. Then the wail rose, remote and unearthly, and turned to an inarticulate gibbering. Percival Wemys Madison, of the Vicarage, Harcourt St Anthony, lying in the long grass, was living through circumstances in which the incantation of his address was powerless to help him.

CHAPTER SIX

Beast from Air

There was no light left save that of the stars. When they had understood what made this ghostly noise and Percival was quiet again, Ralph and Simon picked him up unhandily and carried him to a shelter. Piggy hung about near for all his brave words, and the three bigger boys went together to the next shelter. They lay restlessly and noisily among the dry leaves, watching the patch of stars that was the opening towards the lagoon. Sometimes a littlun cried out from the other shelters and once a bigun spoke in the dark. Then they too fell asleep.

A sliver of moon rose over the horizon, hardly large enough to make a path of light even when it sat right down on the water; but there were other lights in the sky, that moved fast, winked, or went out, though not even a faint popping came down from the battle fought at ten miles' height. But a sign came down from the world of grown-ups, though at the time there was no child awake to read it. There was a sudden bright explosion and a corkscrew trail across the sky; then darkness again and stars. There was a speck above the island, a figure dropping swiftly beneath a parachute, a figure that hung with dangling limbs. The changing winds of various altitudes took the figure where they would. Then, three miles up, the wind steadied and bore it in a descending curve round the sky and swept it in a great slant across the reef and the lagoon towards the mountain. The figure fell and crumpled among the blue flowers of the mountain-side, but now there was a gentle breeze at this height too and the parachute flopped and banged and pulled. So the figure, with feet that dragged behind it, slid up the mountain. Yard by yard, puff by puff, the breeze hauled the figure through the blue flowers, over the boulders and red stones, till it lay huddled among the shattered rocks of the mountain-top. Here the breeze was fitful and allowed the strings of the parachute to tangle and festoon; and the figure sat, its helmeted head between its knees, held by a complication of lines. When the breeze blew the lines would strain taut and some accident of this pull lifted the head and chest upright so that the figure seemed to peer across the brow of the mountain. Then, each time the wind dropped, the lines would slacken and the figure bow forward again, sinking its head between its knees. So as the stars moved across the sky, the figure sat on the mountain-top and bowed and sank and bowed again.

In the darkness of early morning there were noises by a rock a little way down the side of the mountain. Two boys rolled out of a pile of brushwood and dead leaves, two dim shadows talking sleepily to each other. They were the twins, on duty at the fire. In theory one should have been asleep and one on watch. But they could never manage to do things sensibly if that meant acting independently, and since staying awake all night was impossible, they had both gone to sleep. Now they approached the dark smudge that had been the signal fire, yawning, rubbing their eyes, treading with practised feet. When they reached it they stopped yawning, and one ran quickly back for brushwood and leaves.

The other knelt down.

'I believe it's out.'

He fiddled with the sticks that were pushed into his hands.

'No.'

He lay down and put his lips close to the smudge and blew softly. His face appeared, lit redly. He stopped blowing for a moment.

'Sam—give us——'

'—tinder wood.'

Eric bent down and blew softly again till the patch was bright. Sam poked the piece of tinder wood into the hot spot, then a branch. The glow increased and the branch took fire. Sam piled on more branches.

'Don't burn the lot,' said Eric, 'you're putting on too much.'

'Let's warm up.'

'We'll only have to fetch more wood.'

'I'm cold.'

'So'm I.'

'Besides, it's——'

'—dark. All right, then.'

Eric squatted back and watched Sam make up the fire. He built a little tent of dead wood and the fire was safely alight.

'That was near.'

'He'd have been——'

'Waxy.'

'Huh.'

For a few moments the twins watched the fire in silence. Then Eric sniggered.

'Wasn't he waxy?'

'About the——'

'Fire and the pig.'

'Lucky he went for Jack, 'stead of us.'

'Huh. Remember old Waxy at school?'

'"Boy—you-are-driving-me-slowly-insane!"'

The twins shared their identical laughter, then remembered the darkness and other things and glanced round uneasily. The flames, busy about the tent, drew their eyes back again. Eric watched the scurrying wood-lice that were so frantically unable to avoid the flames, and thought of the first fire—just down there, on the steeper side of the mountain, where now was complete darkness. He did not like to remember it, and looked away at the mountain-top.

Warmth radiated now, and beat pleasantly on them. Sam amused himself by fitting branches into the fire as closely as possible. Eric spread out his hands, searching for the distance at which the heat was just bearable. Idly looking beyond the fire, he resettled the scattered rocks from their flat shadows into daylight contours. Just there was the big rock, and the three stones there, that split rock, and there beyond, was a gap—just there——

'Sam.'

'Huh?'

'Nothing.'

The flames were mastering the branches, the bark was curling and falling away, the wood exploding. The tent fell inwards and flung a wide circle of light over the mountain-top.

'Sam——'

'Huh?'

'Sam! Sam!'

Sam looked at Eric irritably. The intensity of Eric's gaze made the direction in which he looked terrible, for Sam had his back to it. He scrambled round the fire, squatted by Eric and looked to see. They became motionless, gripped in each other's arms, four unwinking eyes aimed and two mouths open.

Far beneath them, the trees of the forest sighed, then roared.

The hair on their foreheads fluttered and flames blew out sideways from the fire. Fifteen yards away from them came the plopping noise of fabric blown open.

Neither of the boys screamed but the grip of their arms tightend and their mouths grew peaked. For perhaps ten seconds they crouched like that while the flailing fire sent smoke and sparks and waves of inconstant light over the top of the mountain.

Then as though they had but one terrified mind between them they scrambled away over the rocks and fled.

Ralph was dreaming. He had fallen asleep after what seemed hours of tossing and turning noisily among the dry leaves. Even the sounds of nightmare from the other shelters no longer reached him, for he was back from where he came from, feeding the ponies with sugar over the garden wall. Then someone was shaking his arm, telling him that it was time for tea.

'Ralph! Wake up!'

The leaves were roaring like the sea.

'Ralph, wake up!'

'What's the matter?'

'We saw——'

'——the beast——'

'——plain!'

'Who are you? The twins?'

'We saw the beast——'

'Quiet. Piggy!'

The leaves were roaring still. Piggy bumped into him and a twin grabbed him as he made for the oblong of paling stars.

'You can't go out—it's horrible!'

'Piggy—where are the spears?'

'I can hear the——'

'Quiet then. Lie still.'

They lay there listening, at first with doubt but then with terror to the description the twins breathed at them between bouts of extreme silence. Soon the darkness was full of claws, full of the awful unknown and menace. An interminable dawn faded the stars out, and at last light, sad and grey, filtered into the shelter. They began to stir though still the world outside the shelter was impossibly dangerous. The maze of the darkness sorted into near and far, and at the high point of the sky the cloudlets were warmed with colour. A single sea bird flapped upwards with a hoarse cry that was echoed presently, and something squawked in the forest. Now streaks of cloud near the horizon began to glow rosily, and the feathery tops of the palms were green.

Ralph knelt in the entrance to the shelter and peered cautiously round him.

'Sam'n Eric. Call them to an assembly. Quietly. Go on.'

The twins, holding tremulously to each other, dared the few yards to the next shelter and spread the dreadful news. Ralph stood up and walked for the sake of dignity, though with his back pricking, to the platform. Piggy and Simon followed him and the other boys came sneaking after.

Ralph took the conch from where it lay on the polished seat and held it to his lips; but then he hesitated and did not blow. He held the shell up instead and showed it to them and they understood.

The rays of the sun that were fanning upwards from below the horizon, swung downwards to eye-level. Ralph looked for a moment at the growing slice of gold that lit them from the right hand and seemed to make speech possible. The circle of boys before him bristled with hunting spears.

He handed the conch to Eric, the nearest of the twins.

'We've seen the beast with our own eyes. No—we weren't asleep——'

Sam took up the story. By custom now one conch did for both twins, for their substantial unity was recognized.

'It was furry. There was something moving behind its head—wings. The beast moved too——'

'That was awful. It kind of sat up——'

'The fire was bright——'

'We'd just made it up——'

'—more sticks on——'

'There were eyes——'

'Teeth——'

'Claws——'

'We ran as fast as we could——'

'Bashed into things——'

'The beast followed us——'

'I saw it slinking behind the trees——'

'Nearly touched me——'

Ralph pointed fearfully at Eric's face, which was striped with scars where the bushes had torn him.

'How did you do that?'

Eric felt his face.

'I'm all rough. Am I bleeding?'

The circle of boys shrank away in horror. Johnny, yawning still, burst into noisy tears and was slapped by Bill till he choked on them. The bright morning was full of threats and the circle began to change. It faced out, rather than in, and the spears of sharpened wood were like a fence. Jack called them back to the centre.

'This'll be a real hunt! Who'll come?'

Ralph moved impatiently.

'These spears are made of wood. Don't be silly.'

Jack sneered at him.

'Frightened?'

'Course I'm frightened. Who wouldn't be?'

He turned to the twins, yearning but hopeless.

'I suppose you aren't pulling our legs?'

The reply was too emphatic for anyone to doubt them.

Piggy took the conch.

'Couldn't we—kind of—stay here? Maybe the beast won't come near us.'

But for the sense of something watching them, Ralph would have shouted at him.

'Stay here? And be cramped into this bit of the island, always on the lookout? How should we get our food? And what about the fire?'

'Let's be moving,' said Jack restlessly, 'we're wasting time.'

'No we're not. What about the littluns?'

'Sucks to the littluns!'

'Someone's got to look after them.'

'Nobody has so far.'

'There was no need! Now there is. Piggy'll look after them.'

'That's right. Keep Piggy out of danger.'

'Have some sense. What can Piggy do with only one eye?'

The rest of the boys were looking from Jack to Ralph, curiously.

'And another thing. You can't have an ordinary hunt because the beast doesn't leave tracks. If it did you'd have seen them. For all we know, the beast may swing through the trees like what's its name.'

They nodded.

'So we've got to think.'

Piggy took off his damaged glasses and cleaned the remaining lens.

'How about us, Ralph?'

'You haven't got the conch. Here.'

'I mean—how about us? Suppose the beast comes when you're all away. I can't see proper, and if I get scared——'

Jack broke in, contemptuously.

'You're always scared.'

'I got the conch——'

'Conch! Conch!' shouted Jack, 'we don't need the conch any more. We know who ought to say things. What good did Simon do speaking, or Bill, or Walter? It's time some people knew they've got to keep quiet and leave deciding things to the rest of us——'

Ralph could no longer ignore his speech. The blood was hot in his cheeks.

'You haven't got the conch,' he said. 'Sit down.'

Jack's face went so white that the freckles showed as clear, brown flecks. He licked his lips and remained standing.

'This is a hunter's job.'

The rest of the boys watched intently. Piggy, finding himself uncomfortably embroiled, slid the conch to Ralph's knees and sat down. The silence grew oppressive and Piggy held his breath.

'This is more than a hunter's job,' said Ralph at last, 'because you can't track the beast. And don't you want to be rescued?'

He turned to the assembly.

'Don't you all want to be rescued?'

He looked back at Jack.

'I said before, the fire is the main thing. Now the fire must be out——'

The old exasperation saved him and gave him the energy to attack.

'Hasn't anyone got any sense? We've got to re-light that fire. You never thought of that, Jack, did you? Or don't any of you want to be rescued?'

Yes, they wanted to be rescued, there was no doubt about that; and with a violent swing to Ralph's side, the crisis passed. Piggy let out his breath with a gasp, reached for it again and failed. He lay against a log, his mouth gaping, blue shadows creeping round his lips. Nobody minded him.

'Now think, Jack. Is there anywhere on the island you haven't been?'

Unwillingly Jack answered.

'There's only—but of course! You remember? The tail-end part, where the rocks are all piled up. I've been near there. The rock makes a sort of bridge. There's only one way up.'

'And the thing might live there.'

All the assembly talked at once.

'Quiet! All right. That's where we'll look. If the beast isn't there we'll go up the mountain and look; and light the fire.'

'Let's go.'

'We'll eat first. Then go.' Ralph paused. 'We'd better take spears.'

After they had eaten Ralph and the biguns set out along the beach. They left Piggy propped up on the platform. This day promised, like the others, to be a sunbath under a blue dome. The beach stretched away before them in a gentle curve till perspective drew it into one with the forest; for the day was not advanced enough to be obscured by the shifting veils of mirage. Under Ralph's direction, they picked a careful way along the palm terrace, rather than dare the hot sand down by the water. He let Jack lead the way; and Jack trod with theatrical caution though they could have seen an enemy twenty yards away. Ralph walked in the rear, thankful to have escaped responsibility for a time.

Simon, walking in front of Ralph, felt a flicker of incredulity—a beast with claws that scratched, that sat on a mountain-top, that left no tracks and yet was not fast enough to catch Samneric. However Simon thought of the beast, there rose before his inward sight the picture of a human at once heroic and sick.

He sighed. Other people could stand up and speak to an assembly, apparently, without that dreadful feeling of the pressure of personality; could say what they would as though they were speaking to only one person. He stepped aside and looked back. Ralph was coming along, holding his spear over his shoulder. Diffidently, Simon allowed his pace to slacken until he was walking side by side with Ralph and looking up at him through the coarse black hair that fell now to his eyes. Ralph glanced sideways, smiled constrainedly as though he had forgotten that Simon had made a fool of himself, then looked away again at nothing. For a moment or two Simon was happy to be accepted and then he ceased to think about himself. When he bashed into a tree Ralph looked sideways impatiently and Robert sniggered. Simon reeled and a white spot on his forehead turned red and trickled. Ralph dismissed Simon and returned to his personal hell. They would reach the castle some time; and the chief would have to go forward.

Jack came trotting back.

'We're in sight now.'

'All right. We'll get as close as we can.'

He followed Jack towards the castle where the ground rose slightly. On their left was an impenetrable tangle of creepers and trees.

'Why couldn't there be something in that?'

'Because you can see. Nothing goes in or out.'

'What about the castle then?'

'Look.'

Ralph parted the screen of grass and looked out. There were only a few more yards of stony ground and then the two sides of the island came almost together so that one expected a peak of headland. But instead of this a narrow ledge of rock, a few yards wide and perhaps fifteen long, continued the island out into the sea. There lay another of those pieces of pink squareness that underlay the structure of the island. This side of the castle, perhaps a hundred feet high, was the pink bastion they had seen from the mountain-top. The rock of the cliff was split and the top littered with great lumps that seemed to totter.

Behind Ralph the tall grass had filled with silent hunters. Ralph looked at Jack.

'You're a hunter.'

Jack went red.

'I know. All right.'

Something deep in Ralph spoke for him.

'I'm chief. I'll go. Don't argue.'

He turned to the others.

'You. Hide here. Wait for me.'

He found his voice tended either to disappear or to come out too loud. He looked at Jack.

'Do you—think?'

Jack muttered.

'I've been all over. It must be here.'

'I see.'

Simon mumbled confusedly: 'I don't believe in the beast.'

Ralph answered him politely, as if agreeing about the weather.

'No. I suppose not.'

His mouth was tight and pale. He put back his hair very slowly.

'Well. So long.'

He forced his feet to move until they had carried him out on to the neck of land.

He was surrounded on all sides by chasms of empty air. There was nowhere to hide, even if one did not have to go on. He paused on the narrow neck and looked down. Soon, in a matter of centuries, the sea would make an island of the castle. On the right hand was the lagoon, troubled by the open sea; and on the left——

Ralph shuddered. The lagoon had protected them from the Pacific: and for some reason only Jack had gone right down to the water on the other side. Now he saw the landsman's view of the swell and it seemed like the breathing of some stupendous creature. Slowly the waters sank among the rocks, revealing pink tables of granite, strange growths of coral, polyp, and weed. Down, down, the waters went, whispering like the wind among the heads of the forest. There was one flat rock there, spread like a table, and the waters sucking down on the four weedy sides made them seem like cliffs. Then the sleeping leviathan breathed out—the waters rose, the weed streamed, and the water boiled over the table rock with a roar. There was no sense of the passage of waves; only this minute-long fall and rise and fall.

Ralph turned away to the red cliff. They were waiting behind him in the long grass, waiting to see what he would do. He noticed that the sweat in his palm was cool now; realized with surprise that he did not really expect to meet any beast and didn't know what he would do about it if he did.

He saw that he could climb the cliff but this was not necessary. The squareness of the rock allowed a sort of plinth round it, so that to the right, over the lagoon, one could inch along a ledge and turn the corner out of sight. It was easy going, and soon he was peering round the rock.

Nothing but what you might expect: pink, tumbled boulders with guano layered on them like icing; and a steep slope up to the shattered rocks that crowned the bastion.

A sound behind him made him turn. Jack was edging along the ledge.

'Couldn't let you do it on your own.'

Ralph said nothing. He led the way over the rocks, inspected a sort of half-cave that held nothing more terrible than a clutch of rotten eggs and at last sat down, looking round him and tapping the rock with the butt of his spear.

Jack was excited.

'What a place for a fort!'

A column of spray wetted them.

'No fresh water.'

'What's that then?'

There was indeed a long green smudge half-way up the rock. They climbed up and tasted the trickle of water.

'You could keep a coco-nut shell there, filling all the time.'

'Not me. This is a rotten place.'

Side by side they scaled the last height to where the diminishing pile was crowned by the last broken rock. Jack struck the near one with his fist and it grated slightly.

'Do you remember——?'

Consciousness of the bad times in between came to them both. Jack talked quickly.

'Shove a palm trunk under that and if an enemy came—look!'

A hundred feet below them was the narrow causeway, then the stony ground, then the grass dotted with heads, and behind that the forest.

'One heave,' cried Jack, exulting, 'and—wheee——!'

He made a swooping movement with his hand. Ralph looked towards the mountain.

'What's the matter?'

Ralph turned.

'Why?'

'You were looking—I don't know how.'

'There's no signal now. Nothing to show.'

'You're nuts on the signal.'

The taut blue horizon encircled them, broken only by the mountain-top.

'That's all we've got.'

He leaned his spear against the rocking stone and pushed back two handfuls of hair.

'We'll have to go back and climb the mountain. That's where they saw the beast.'

'The beast won't be there.'

'What else can we do?'

The others, waiting in the grass, saw Jack and Ralph unharmed and broke cover into the sunlight. They forgot the beast in the excitement of exploration. They swarmed across the bridge and soon were climbing and shouting. Ralph stood now, one hand against an enormous red block, a block large as a millwheel that had been split off and hung, tottering. Sombrely he watched the mountain. He clenched his fist and beat hammer-wise on the red wall at his right. His lips were tightly compressed and his eyes yearned beneath the fringe of hair.

'Smoke.'

He sucked his bruised fist.

'Jack! Come on.'

But Jack was not there. A knot of boys, making a great noise that he had not noticed, were heaving and pushing at a rock. As he turned, the base cracked and the whole mass toppled into the sea so that a thunderous plume of spray leapt half-way up the cliff.

'Stop it! Stop it!'

His voice struck a silence among them.

'Smoke.'

A strange thing happened in his head. Something flittered there in front of his mind like a bat's wing, obscuring his idea.

'Smoke.'

At once the ideas were back, and the anger.

'We want smoke. And you go wasting your time. You roll rocks.'

Roger shouted.

'We've got plenty of time!'

Ralph shook his head.

'We'll go to the mountain.'

The clamour broke out. Some of the boys wanted to go back to the beach. Some wanted to roll more rocks. The sun was bright and danger had faded with the darkness.

'Jack. The beast might be on the other side. You can lead again. You've been.'

'We could go by the shore. There's fruit.'

Bill came up to Ralph.

'Why can't we stay here for a bit?'

'That's right.'

'Let's have a fort——'

'There's no food here,' said Ralph, 'and no shelter. Not much fresh water.'

'This would make a wizard fort.'

'We can roll rocks——'

'Right on to the bridge——'

'I say we'll go on!' shouted Ralph furiously. 'We've got to make certain. We'll go now.'

'Let's stay here——'

'Back to the shelter——'

'I'm tired——'

'No!'

Ralph struck the skin off his knuckles. They did not seem to hurt.

'I'm chief. We've got to make certain. Can't you see the mountain? There's no signal showing. There may be a ship out there. Are you all off your rockers?'

Mutinously, the boys fell silent or muttering.

Jack led the way down the rock and across the bridge.

CHAPTER SEVEN

Shadows and Tall Trees

The pig-run kept close to the jumble of rocks that lay down by the water on the other side and Ralph was content to follow Jack along it. If you could shut your ears to the slow suck down of the sea and boil of the return, if you could forget how dun and unvisited were the ferny coverts on either side, then there was a chance that you might put the beast out of mind and dream for a while. The sun had swung over the vertical and the afternoon heat was closing in on the island. Ralph passed a message forward to Jack and when they next came to fruit the whole party stopped and ate.

Sitting, Ralph was aware of the heat for the first time that day. He pulled distastefully at his grey shirt and wondered whether he might undertake the adventure of washing it. Sitting under what seemed an unusual heat, even for this island, Ralph planned his toilet. He would like to have a pair of scissors and cut his hair—he flung the mass back—cut this filthy hair right back to half an inch. He would like to have a bath, a proper wallow with soap. He passed his tongue experimentally over his teeth and decided that a toothbrush would come in handy too. Then there were his nails——

Ralph turned his hand over and examined them. They were bitten down to the quick though he could not remember when he had restarted this habit nor any time when he indulged it.

'Be sucking my thumb next——'

He looked round, furtively. Apparently no one had heard. The hunters sat, stuffing themselves with this easy meal, trying to convince themselves that they got sufficient kick out of bananas and that other olive-grey, jelly-like fruit. With the memory of his sometime clean self as a standard, Ralph looked them over. They were dirty, not with the spectacular dirt of boys who have fallen into mud or been brought down hard on a rainy day. Not one of them was an obvious subject for a shower, and yet—hair, much too long, tangled here and there, knotted round a dead leaf or a twig; faces cleaned fairly well by the process of eating and sweating but marked in the less accessible angles with a kind of shadow; clothes, worn away, stiff like his own with sweat, put on, not for decorum or comfort but out of custom; the skin of the body, scurfy with brine——

He discovered with a little fall of the heart that these were the conditions he took as normal now and that he did not mind. He sighed and pushed away the stalk from which he had stripped the fruit. Already the hunters were stealing away to do their business in the woods or down by the rocks. He turned and looked out to sea.

Here, on the other side of the island, the view was utterly different. The filmy enchantments of mirage could not endure the cold ocean water and the horizon was hard, clipped blue. Ralph wandered down to the rocks. Down here, almost on a level with the sea, you could follow with your eye the ceaseless bulging passage of the deep sea waves. They were miles wide, apparently not breakers or the banked ridges of shallow water. They travelled the length of the island with an air of disregarding it and being set on other business; they were less a progress than a momentous rise and fall of the whole ocean. Now the sea would suck down, making cascades and waterfalls of retreating water, would sink past the rocks and plaster down the seaweed like shining hair: then, pausing, gather and rise with a roar, irresistibly swelling over point and outcrop, climbing the little cliff, sending at last an arm of surf up a gully to end a yard or so from him in fingers of spray.

Wave after wave, Ralph followed the rise and fall until something of the remoteness of the sea numbed his brain. Then gradually the almost infinite size of this water forced itself on his attention. This was the divider, the barrier. On the other side of the island, swathed at midday with mirage, defended by the shield of the quiet lagoon, one might dream of rescue; but here, faced by the brute obtuseness of the ocean, the miles of division, one was clamped down, one was helpless, one was condemned, one was——

Simon was speaking almost in his ear. Ralph found that he had rock painfully gripped in both hands, found his body arched, the muscles of his neck stiff, his mouth strained open.

'You'll get back to where you came from.'

Simon nodded as he spoke. He was kneeling on one knee,

looking down from a higher rock which he held with both hands; his other leg stretched down to Ralph's level.

Ralph was puzzled and searched Simon's face for a clue.

'It's so big, I mean——'

Simon nodded.

'All the same. You'll get back all right. I think so, anyway.'

Some of the strain had gone from Ralph's body. He glanced at the sea and then smiled bitterly at Simon.

'Got a ship in your pocket?'

Simon grinned and shook his head.

'How do you know, then?'

When Simon was still silent Ralph said curtly, 'You're batty.'

Simon shook his head violently till the coarse black hair flew backwards and forward across his face.

'No, I'm not. I just *think you'll get back all right.*'

For a moment nothing more was said. And then they suddenly smiled at each other.

Roger called from the coverts.

'Come and see!'

The ground was turned over near the pig-run and there were droppings that steamed. Jack bent down to them as though he loved them.

'Ralph—we need meat even if we are hunting the other thing.'

'If you mean going the right way, we'll hunt.'

They set off again, the hunters bunched a little by fear of the mentioned beast, while Jack quested ahead. They went more slowly than Ralph had bargained for; yet in a way he was glad to loiter, cradling his spear. Jack came up against some emergency of his craft and soon the procession stopped. Ralph leaned against a tree and at once the day-dreams came swarming up. Jack was in charge of the hunt and there would be time to get to the mountain——

Once, following his father from Chatham to Devonport, they had lived in a cottage on the edge of the moors. In the succession of houses that Ralph had known, this one stood out with particular clarity because after that house he had been sent away to school. Mummy had still been with them and Daddy had come home every day. Wild ponies came to the stone wall at the bottom of the garden, and it had snowed. Just behind the cottage there was a sort of shed and you could lie up there, watching the flakes swirl past. You could see the damp spot where each flake died; then you could mark the first flake that lay down without melting and watch the whole ground turn white. You could go indoors when you were cold and look out of the window, past that bright copper kettle and the plate with the little blue men——

When you went to bed there was a bowl of cornflakes with sugar and cream. And the books—they stood on the shelf by the bed, leaning together with always two or three laid flat on top because he had not bothered to put them back properly. They were dog-eared and scratched. There was the bright, shining one about Topsy and Mopsy that he never read because it was about two girls; there was the one about the Magician which you read with a kind of tied-down terror, skipping page twenty-seven with the awful picture of the spider; there was a book about people who had dug things up, Egyptian things; there was the *Boy's Book of Trains*, *The Boy's Book of Ships*. Vividly they came before him; he could have reached up and touched them, could feel the weight and slow slide with which the *Mammoth Book for Boys* would come out and slither down. . . . Everything was all right; everything was good-humoured and friendly.

The bushes crashed ahead of them. Boys flung themselves wildly from the pig track and scrabbled in the creepers, screaming. Ralph saw Jack nudged aside and fall. Then there was a creature bounding along the pig track towards him, with tusks gleaming and an intimidating grunt. Ralph found he was able to measure the distance coldly and take aim. With the boar only five yards away, he flung the foolish wooden stick that he carried, saw it hit the great snout and hang there for a moment. The boar's note changed to a squeal and it swerved aside into the covert. The pig-run filled with shouting boys again. Jack came running back, and poked about in the undergrowth.

'Through here——'

'But he'd do us!'

'Through here, I said——'

The boar was floundering away from them. They found another pig-run parallel to the first and Jack raced away. Ralph was full of fright and apprehension and pride.

'I hit him! The spear stuck in——'

Now they came, unexpectedly, to an open space by the sea. Jack cast about on the bare rock and looked anxious.

'He's gone.'

'I hit him,' said Ralph again, 'and the spear stuck in a bit.'

He felt the need of witnesses.

'Didn't you see me?'

Maurice nodded.

'I saw you. Right bang on his snout—Whee!'

Ralph talked on, excitedly.

'I hit him all right. The spear stuck in. I wounded him!'

He sunned himself in their new respect and felt that hunting was good after all.

'I walloped him properly. That was the beast, I think!'

Jack came back.

'That wasn't the beast. That was a boar.'

'I hit him.'

'Why didn't you grab him? I tried——'

Ralph's voice ran up.

'But a boar!'

Jack flushed suddenly.

'You said he'd do us. What did you want to throw for? Why didn't you wait?'

He held out his arm.

'Look.'

He turned his left forearm for them all to see. On the outside was a rip; not much, but bloody.

'He did that with his tusks. I couldn't get my spear down in time.'

Attention focused on Jack.

'That's a wound,' said Simon, 'and you ought to suck it. Like Berengaria.'

Jack sucked.

'I hit him,' said Ralph indignantly. 'I hit him with my spear, I wounded him.'

He tried for their attention.

'He was coming along the path. I threw, like this——'

Robert snarled at him. Ralph entered into the play and everybody laughed. Presently they were all jabbing at Robert who made mock rushes.

Jack shouted.

'Make a ring!'

The circle moved in and round. Robert squealed in mock terror, then in real pain.

'Ow! Stop it! You're hurting!'

The butt end of a spear fell on his back as he blundered among them.

'Hold him!'

They got his arms and legs. Ralph, carried away by a sudden thick excitement, grabbed Eric's spear and jabbed at Robert with it.

'Kill him! Kill him!'

All at once, Robert was screaming and struggling with the strength of frenzy. Jack had him by the hair and was brandishing his knife. Behind him was Roger, fighting to get close. The chant rose ritually, as at the last moment of a dance or a hunt.

'*Kill the pig! Cut his throat! Kill the pig! Bash him in!*'

Ralph too was fighting to get near, to get a handful of that brown, vulnerable flesh. The desire to squeeze and hurt was over-mastering.

Jack's arm came down; the heaving circle cheered and made pig-dying noises. Then they lay quiet, panting, listening to Robert's frightened snivels. He wiped his face with a dirty arm, and made an effort to retrieve his status.

'Oh, my bum!'

He rubbed his rump ruefully, Jack rolled over.

'That was a good game.'

'Just a game,' said Ralph uneasily. 'I got jolly badly hurt at rugger once.'

'We ought to have a drum,' said Maurice, 'then we could do it properly.'

Ralph looked at him.

'How properly?'

'I dunno. You want a fire, I think, and a drum, and you keep time to the drum.'

'You want a pig,' said Roger, 'like in a real hunt.'

'Or someone to pretend.' said Jack. 'You could get someone to dress up as a pig and then he could act—you know, pretend to knock me over and all that——'

'You want a real pig,' said Robert, still caressing his rump, 'because you've got to kill him.'

'Use a littlun,' said Jack, and everybody laughed.

Ralph sat up.

'Well. We shan't find what we're looking for at this rate.'

One by one they stood up, twitching rags into place.

Ralph looked at Jack.

'Now for the mountain.'

'Shouldn't we go back to Piggy,' said Maurice, 'before dark?'

The twins nodded like one boy.

'Yes, that's right. Let's go up there in the morning.'

Ralph looked out and saw the sea.

'We've got to start the fire again.'

'You haven't got Piggy's specs,' said Jack, 'so you can't.'

'Then we'll find out if the mountain's clear.'

Maurice spoke, hesitating, not wanting to seem a funk.

'Supposing the beast's up there?'

Jack brandished his spear.

'We'll kill it.'

The sun seemed a little cooler. He slashed with the spear.

'What are we waiting for?'

'I suppose,' said Ralph, 'if we keep on by the sea this way, we'll come out below the burnt bit and then we can climb the mountain.'

Once more Jack led them along by the suck and heave of the blinding sea.

Once more Ralph dreamed, letting his skilful feet deal with the difficulties of the path. Yet here his feet seemed less skilful than before. For most of the way they were forced right down to the bare rock by the water and had to edge along between that and the dark luxuriance of the forest. There were little cliffs to be scaled, some to be used as paths, lengthy traverses where one used hands as well as feet. Here and there they could clamber over wave-wet rock, leaping across clear pools that the tide had left. They came to a gully that split the narrow foreshore like a defence. This seemed to have no bottom and they peered awe-stricken into the gloomy crack where water gurgled. Then the wave came back, the gully boiled before them and spray dashed up to the very creeper so that the boys were wet and shrieking. They tried the forest but it was thick and woven like a bird's nest. In the end they had to jump one by one, waiting till the water sank; and even so, some of them got a second drenching. After that the rocks seemed to be growing impassable so they sat for a time, letting their rags dry and watching the clipped outlines of the rollers that moved so slowly past the island. They found fruit in a haunt of bright little birds that hovered like insects. Then

Ralph said they were going too slowly. He himself climbed a tree and parted the canopy, and saw the square head of the mountain seeming still a great way off. Then they tried to hurry along the rocks and Robert cut his knee quite badly and they had to recognize that this path must be taken slowly if they were to be safe. So they proceeded after that as if they were climbing a dangerous mountain, until the rocks became an uncompromising cliff, overhung with impossible jungle and falling sheer into the sea.

Ralph looked at the sun critically.

'Early evening. After tea-time, at any rate.'

'I don't remember this cliff,' said Jack, crest-fallen, 'so this must be the bit of the coast I missed.'

Ralph nodded.

'Let me think.'

By now, Ralph had no self-consciousness in public thinking but would treat the day's decisions as though he were playing chess. The only trouble was that he would never be a very good chess player. He thought of the littluns and Piggy. Vividly he imagined Piggy by himself, huddled in a shelter that was silent except for the sounds of nightmare.

'We can't leave the littluns alone with Piggy. Not all night.'

The other boys said nothing but stood round, watching him.

'If we went back we should take hours.'

Jack cleared his throat and spoke in a queer, tight voice.

'We mustn't let anything happen to Piggy, must we?'

Ralph tapped his teeth with the dirty point of Eric's spear.

'If we go across——'

He glanced round him.

'Someone's got to go across the island and tell Piggy we'll be back after dark.'

Bill spoke, unbelieving.

'Through the forest by himself? Now?'

'We can't spare more than one.'

Simon pushed his way to Ralph's elbow.

'I'll go if you like. I don't mind, honestly.'

Before Ralph had time to reply, he smiled quickly, turned and climbed into the forest.

Ralph looked back at Jack, seeing him, infuriatingly, for the first time.

'Jack—that time you went the whole way to the castle rock.'

Jack glowered.

'Yes?'

'You came along part of this shore—below the mountain, beyond there.'

'Yes.'

'And then?'

'I found a pig-run. It went for miles.'

Ralph nodded. He pointed at the forest.

'So the pig-run must be somewhere in there.'

Everybody agreed, sagely.

'All right then. We'll smash a way through till we find the pig-run.'

He took a step and halted.

'Wait a minute though! Where does the pig-run go to?'

'The mountain,' said Jack. 'I told you.' He sneered. 'Don't you want to go to the mountain?'

Ralph sighed, sensing the rising antagonism, understanding that this was how Jack felt as soon as he ceased to lead.

'I was thinking of the light. We'll be stumbling about.'

'We were going to look for the beast——'

'There won't be enough light.'

'I don't mind going,' said Jack hotly. 'I'll go when we get there. Won't you? Would you rather go back to the shelters and tell Piggy?'

Now it was Ralph's turn to flush but he spoke despairingly, out of the new understanding that Piggy had given him.

'Why do you hate me?'

The boys stirred uneasily, as though something indecent had been said. The silence lengthened.

Ralph, still hot and hurt, turned away first.

'Come on.'

He led the way and set himself as by right to hack at the tangles. Jack brought up the rear, displaced and brooding.

The pig-track was a dark tunnel, for the sun was sliding quickly towards the edge of the world and in the forest shadows were never far to seek. The track was broad and beaten and they ran along at a swift trot. Then the roof of leaves broke up and they halted, breathing quickly, looking at the few stars that pricked round the head of the mountain.

'There you are.'

The boys peered at each other doubtfully. Ralph made a decision.

'We'll go straight across to the platform and climb tomorrow.'

They murmured agreement; but Jack was standing by his shoulder.

'If you're frightened of course——'

Ralph turned on him.

'Who went first on the castle rock?'

'I went too. And that was daylight.'

'All right. Who wants to climb the mountain now?'

Silence was the only answer.

'Samneric? What about you?'

'We ought to go an' tell Piggy——'

'—yes, tell Piggy that——'

'But Simon went!'

'We ought to tell Piggy—in case——'

'Robert? Bill?'

They were going straight back to the platform now. Not, of course, that they were afraid—but tired.

Ralph turned back to Jack.

'You see?'

'I'm going up the mountain.'

The words came from Jack viciously, as though they were a curse. He looked at Ralph, his thin body tensed, his spear held as if he threatened him.

'I'm going up the mountain to look for the beast—now.'

Then the supreme sting, the casual, bitter word.

'Coming?'

At that word the other boys forgot their urge to be gone and turned back to sample this fresh rub of two spirits in the dark. The word was too good, too bitter, too successfully daunting to be repeated. It took Ralph at low water when his nerve was relaxed for the return to the shelter and the still, friendly waters of the lagoon.

'I don't mind.'

Astonished, he heard his voice come out, cool and casual, so that the bitterness of Jack's taunt fell powerless.

'If you don't mind, of course.'

'Oh, not at all.'

Jack took a step.

'Well then——'

Side by side, watched by silent boys, the two started up the mountain.

Ralph stopped.

'We're silly. Why should only two go? If we find anything, two won't be enough——'

There came the sound of boys scuttling away. Astonishingly, a dark figure moved against the tide.

'Roger?'

'Yes.'

'That's three, then.'

Once more they set out to climb the slope of the mountain. The darkness seemed to flow round them like a tide. Jack, who had said nothing, began to choke and cough; and a gust of wind set all three spluttering. Ralph's eyes were blinded with tears.

'Ashes. We're on the edge of the burnt patch.'

Their footsteps and the occasional breeze were stirring up small devils of dust. Now that they stopped again, Ralph had time while he coughed to remember how silly they were. If there was no beast—and almost certainly there was no beast—in that case, well and good; but if there was something waiting on top of the mountain—what was the use of three of them, handicapped by the darkness and carrying only sticks?

'We're being fools.'

Out of the darkness came the answer.

'Windy?'

Irritably Ralph shook himself. This was all Jack's fault.

'Course I am. But we're still being fools.'

'If you don't want to go on,' said the voice sarcastically, 'I'll go up by myself.'

Ralph heard the mockery and hated Jack. The sting of ashes in his eyes, tiredness, fear, enraged him.

'Go on then! We'll wait here.'

There was silence.

'Why don't you go? Are you frightened!'

A stain in the darkness, a stain that was Jack, detached itself and began to draw away.

'All right. So long.'

The stain vanished. Another took its place.

Ralph felt his knee against something hard and rocked a charred trunk that was edgy to the touch. He felt the sharp cinders that had been bark push against the back of his knee and knew that Roger had sat down. He felt with his hands and lowered himself beside Roger, while the trunk rocked among invisible ashes.

Roger, uncommunicative by nature, said nothing. He offered no opinion on the beast nor told Ralph why he had chosen to come on this mad expedition. He simply sat and rocked the trunk gently. Ralph noticed a rapid and infuriating tapping noise and realized that Roger was banging his silly wooden stick against something.

So they sat, the rocking, tapping, impervious Roger and Ralph, fuming; round them the close sky was loaded with stars, save where the mountain punched up a hole of blackness.

There was a slithering noise high above them, the sound of someone taking giant and dangerous strides on rock or ash. Then Jack found them, and was shivering and croaking in a voice they could just recognize as his.

'I saw a thing on top.'

They heard him blunder against the trunk which rocked violently. He lay silent for a moment, then muttered.

'Keep a good lookout. It may be following.'

A shower of ash pattered round them. Jack sat up.

'I saw a thing bulge on the mountain.'

'You only imagined it,' said Ralph shakily, 'because nothing would bulge. Not any sort of creature.'

Roger spoke; they jumped for they had forgotten him.

'A frog.'

Jack giggled and shuddered.

'Some frog. There was a noise too. A kind of "plop" noise. Then the thing bulged.'

Ralph surprised himself, not so much by the quality of his voice, which was even, but by the bravado of its intention.

'We'll go and look.'

For the first time since he had first known Jack, Ralph could feel him hesitate.

'Now——?'

His voice spoke for him.

'Of course.'

He got off the trunk and led the way across the clinking cinders up into the dark, and the others followed.

Now that his physical voice was silent the inner voice of reason, and other voices too, made themselves heard. Piggy was calling him a kid. Another voice told him not to be a fool; and the darkness and desperate enterprise gave the night a kind of dentist's chair unreality.

As they came to the last slope, Jack and Roger drew near, changed from ink-stains to distinguishable figures. By common consent they stopped and crouched together. Behind them, on the horizon, was a patch of lighter sky where in a moment the moon would rise. The wind soared once in the forest and pushed their rags against them.

Ralph stirred.

'Come on.'

They crept forward, Roger lagging a little. Jack and Ralph turned the shoulder of the mountain together. The glittering lengths of the lagoon lay below them and beyond that a long white smudge that was the reef. Roger joined them.

Jack whispered.

'Let's creep forward on hands and knees. Maybe it's asleep.'

Roger and Ralph moved on, this time leaving Jack in the rear, for all his brave words. They came to the flat top where the rock was hard to hands and knees.

A creature that bulged.

Ralph put his hand in the cold, soft ashes of the fire and smothered a cry. His hand and shoulder were twitching from the unlooked-for contact. Green lights of nausea appeared for a moment and ate into the darkness. Roger lay behind him and Jack's mouth was at his ear.

'Over there, where there used to be a gap in the rock. A sort of hump—see?'

Ashes blew into Ralph's face from the dead fire. He could not see the gap or anything else, because the green lights were opening again and growing, and the top of the mountain was sliding sideways.

Once more, from a distance, he heard Jack's whisper.

'Scared?'

Not scared so much as paralysed; hung up here immovable on the top of a diminishing, moving mountain. Jack slid away from him, Roger bumped, fumbled with a hiss of breath, and passed onwards. He heard them whispering.

'Can you see anything?'

'There——'

In front of them, only three or four yards away, was a rock-like hump where no rock should be. Ralph could hear a tiny chattering noise coming from somewhere—perhaps from his own mouth. He bound himself together with his will, fused his fear and loathing into a hatred, and stood up. He took two leaden steps forward.

Behind them the silver of moon had drawn clear of the horizon. Before them, something like a great ape was sitting asleep with its head between its knees. Then the wind roared in the forest, there was confusion in the darkness and the creature lifted its head, holding towards them the ruin of a face.

Ralph found himself taking giant strides among the ashes, heard other creatures crying out and leaping and dared the impossible on the dark slope; presently the mountain was deserted, save for the three abandoned sticks and the thing that bowed.

CHAPTER EIGHT

Gift for the Darkness

Piggy looked up miserably from the dawn-pale beach to the dark mountain.

'Are you sure? Really sure, I mean?'

'I told you a dozen times now,' said Ralph, 'we saw it.'

'D'you think we're safe down here?'

'How the hell should I know?'

Ralph jerked away from him and walked a few paces along the beach. Jack was kneeling and drawing a circular pattern in the sand with his forefinger. Piggy's voice came to them, hushed.

'Are you sure? Really?'

'Go up and see,' said Jack contemptuously, 'and good riddance.'

'No fear.'

'The beast had teeth,' said Ralph, 'and big black eyes.'

He shuddered violently. Piggy took off his one round of glass and polished the surface.

'What are we going to do?'

Ralph turned towards the platform. The conch glimmered among the trees, a white blob against the place where the sun would rise. He pushed back his mop.

'I don't know.'

He remembered the panic flight down the mountain-side.

'I don't think we'd ever fight a thing that size, honestly, you know. We'd talk, but we wouldn't fight a tiger. We'd hide. Even Jack'ud hide.'

Jack still looked at the sand.

'What about my hunters?'

Simon came stealing out of the shadows by the shelters. Ralph ignored Jack's question. He pointed to the touch of yellow above the sea.

'As long as there's light we're brave enough. But then? And now that thing squats by the fire as though it didn't want us to be rescued——'

He was twisting his hands now, unconsciously. His voice rose.

'So we can't have a signal fire. . . . We're beaten.'

A point of gold appeared above the sea and at once all the sky lightened.

'What about my hunters?'

'Boys armed with sticks.'

Jack got to his feet. His face was red as he marched away. Piggy put on his one glass and looked at Ralph.

'Now you done it. You been rude about his hunters.'

'Oh shut up!'

The sound of the inexpertly blown conch interrupted them. As though he were serenading the rising sun, Jack went on blowing till the shelters were astir and the hunters crept to the platform and the littluns whimpered as now they so frequently did. Ralph rose obediently, and Piggy and they went to the platform.

'Talk,' said Ralph bitterly, 'talk, talk, talk.'

He took the conch from Jack.

'This meeting——'

Jack interrupted him.

'I called it.'

'If you hadn't called it I should have. You just blew the conch.'

'Well isn't that?'

'Oh, take it! Go on—talk!'

Ralph thrust the conch into Jack's arms and sat down on the trunk.

'I've called an assembly,' said Jack, 'because of a lot of things. First—you know now, we've seen the beast. We crawled up. We were only a few feet away. The beast sat up and looked at us. I don't know what it does. We don't even know what it is——'

'The beast comes out of the sea——'

'Out of the dark——'

'Trees——'

'Quiet!' shouted Jack. 'You listen. The beast is sitting up there, whatever it is——'

'Perhaps it's waiting——'

'Hunting——'

'Yes, hunting.'

'Hunting,' said Jack. He remembered his age-old tremors in the forest. 'Yes. The beast is a hunter. Only—shut up! The next thing is that we couldn't kill it. And the next thing is that Ralph said my hunters are no good.'

'I never said that!'

'I've got the conch. Ralph thinks you're cowards, running away from the boar and the beast. And that's not all.'

There was a kind of sigh on the platform as if everyone knew what was coming. Jack's voice went on, tremulous yet determined, pushing against the unco-operative silence.

'He's like Piggy. He says things like Piggy. He isn't a proper chief.' Jack clutched the conch to him.

'He's a coward himself.'

For a moment he paused and then went on.

'On top, when Roger and me went on—he stayed back.'

'I went too!'

'After.'

The two boys glared at each other through screens of hair.

'I went on too,' said Ralph, 'then I ran away. So did you.'

'Call me a coward then.'

Jack turned to the hunters.

'He's not a hunter. He'd never have got us meat. He isn't a prefect and we don't know anything about him. He just gives orders and expects people to obey for nothing. All this talk——'

'All this talk!' shouted Ralph. 'Talk, talk! Who wanted it? Who called the meeting?'

Jack turned, red in the face, his chin sunk back. He glowered up under his eyebrows.

'All right then,' he said in tones of deep meaning, and menace, 'all right.'

He held the conch against his chest with one hand and stabbed the air with his index finger.

'Who thinks Ralph oughtn't to be chief?'

He looked expectantly at the boys ranged round, who had frozen. Under the palms there was deadly silence.

'Hands up,' said Jack strongly, 'whoever wants Ralph not to be chief?'

The silence continued, breathless and heavy and full of shame. Slowly the red drained from Jack's cheeks, then came back with a painful rush. He licked his lips and turned his head at an angle, so that his gaze avoided the embarrassment of linking with another's eye.

'How many think——'

His voice tailed off. The hands that held the conch shook. He cleared his throat, and spoke loudly.

'All right then.'

He laid the conch with great care in the grass at his feet. The humiliating tears were running from the corner of each eye.

'I'm not going to play any longer. Not with you.'

Most of the boys were looking down now, at the grass or their feet. Jack cleared his throat again.

'I'm not going to be part of Ralph's lot——'

He looked along the right-hand logs, numbering the hunters that had been a choir.

'I'm going off by myself. He can catch his own pigs. Anyone who wants to hunt when I do can come too.'

He blundered out of the triangle towards the drop to the white sand.

'Jack!'

Jack turned and looked back at Ralph. For a moment he paused and then cried out, high-pitched, enraged.

'—No!'

He leapt down from the platform and ran along the beach, paying no heed to the steady fall of his tears; and until he dived into the forest Ralph watched him.

Piggy was indignant.

'I been talking Ralph, and you just stood there like——'

Softly, looking at Piggy and not seeing him, Ralph spoke to himself.

'He'll come back. When the sun goes down he'll come.' He looked at the conch in Piggy's hand.

'What?'

'Well there!'

Piggy gave up the attempt to rebuke Ralph. He polished his glass again and went back to his subject.

'We can do without Jack Merridew. There's others besides him on this island. But now we really got a beast, though I can't hardly believe it, we'll need to stay close to the platform; there'll be less need of him and his hunting. So now we can really decide on what's what.'

'There's no help. Piggy. Nothing to be done.'

For a while they sat in depressed silence. Then Simon stood up and took the conch from Piggy, who was so astonished that he remained on his feet. Ralph looked up at Simon.

'Simon? What is it this time?'

A half-sound of jeering ran round the circle and Simon shrank from it.

'I thought there might be something to do. Something we——'

Again the pressure of the assembly took his voice away. He sought for help and sympathy and chose Piggy. He turned half towards him, clutching the conch to his brown chest.

'I think we ought to climb the mountain.'

The circle shivered with dread. Simon broke off and turned to Piggy who was looking at him with an expression of derisive incomprehension.

'What's the good of climbing up to this here beast when Ralph and the other two couldn't do nothing?'

Simon whispered his answer.

'What else is there to do?'

His speech made, he allowed Piggy to lift the conch out of his hands. Then he retired and sat as far away from the others as possible.

Piggy was speaking now with more assurance and with what, if the circumstances had not been so serious, the others would have recognized as pleasure.

'I said we could all do without a certain person. Now I say we got to decide on what can be done. And I think I could tell you what Ralph's going to say next. The most important thing on the island is the smoke and you can't have no smoke without a fire.'

Ralph made a restless movement.

'No go, Piggy. We've got no fire. That thing sits up there— we'll have to stay here.'

Piggy lifted the conch as though to add power to his next words.

'We got no fire on the mountain. But what's wrong with a fire down here? A fire could be built on them rocks. On the sand, even. We'd make smoke just the same.'

'That's right!'

'Smoke!'

'By the bathing-pool!'

The boys began to babble. Only Piggy could have the intellectual daring to suggest moving the fire from the mountain.

'So we'll have the fire down here,' said Ralph. He looked about him. 'We can build it just here between the bathing-pool and the platform. Of course——'

He broke off, frowning, thinking the thing out, unconsciously tugging at the stub of a nail with his teeth.

'Of course the smoke won't show so much, not be seen so far away. But we needn't go near; near the——'

The others nodded in perfect comprehension. There would be no need to go near.

'We'll build the fire now.'

The greatest ideas are the simplest. Now there was something to be done they worked with passion. Piggy was so full of delight and expanding liberty in Jack's departure, so full of pride in his contribution to the good of society, that he helped to fetch wood. The wood he fetched was close at hand, a fallen tree on the platform that they did not need for the assembly; yet to the others the sanctity of the platform had protected even what was useless there. Then the twins realized they would have a fire near them as a comfort in the night and this set a few littluns dancing and clapping hands.

The wood was not so dry as the fuel they had used on the mountain. Much of it was damply rotten and full of insects that scurried; logs had to be lifted from the soil with care or they crumbled into sodden powder. More than this, in order to avoid going deep into the forest the boys worked near at hand on any fallen wood no matter how tangled with new growth. The skirts of the forest and the scar were familiar, near the conch and the shelters and sufficiently friendly in daylight. What they might become in darkness nobody cared to think. They worked therefore with great energy and cheerfulness, though as time crept by there was a suggestion of panic in the energy and hysteria in the cheerfulness. They built a pyramid of leaves and twigs, branches and logs, on the bare sand by the platform. For the first time on the island, Piggy himself removed his one glass, knelt down and focused the sun on tinder. Soon there was a ceiling of smoke and a bush of yellow fire.

The littluns who had seen few fires since the first catastrophe became wildly excited. They danced and sang and there was a partyish air about the gathering.

At last Ralph stopped work and stood up, smudging the sweat from his face with a dirty forearm.

'We'll have to have a small fire. This one's too big to keep up.'

Piggy sat down carefully on the sand and began to polish his glass.

'We could experiment. We could find out how to make a small hot fire and then put green branches on to make smoke. Some of them leaves must be better for that than the others.'

As the fire died down so did the excitement. The littluns stopped singing and dancing and drifted away towards the sea or the fruit trees or the shelters.

Ralph flopped down in the sand.

'We'll have to make a new list of who's to look after the fire.'

'If you can find 'em.'

He looked round. Then for the first time he saw how few biguns there were and understood why the work had been so hard.

'Where's Maurice?'

Piggy wiped his glass again.

'I expect . . . no, he wouldn't go into the forest by himself, would he?'

Ralph jumped up, ran swiftly round the fire and stood by Piggy, holding up his hair.

'But we've got to have a list! There's you and me and Samneric and——'

He would not look at Piggy but spoke casually.

'Where's Bill and Roger?'

Piggy leaned forward and put a fragment of wood on the fire.

'I expect they've gone. I expect they won't play either.'

Ralph sat down and began to poke little holes in the sand. He was surprised to see that one had a drop of blood by it. He examined his bitten nail closely and watched the little globe of blood that gathered where the quick was gnawed away.

Piggy went on speaking.

'I seen them stealing off when we was gathering wood. They went that way. The same way as he went himself.'

Ralph finished his inspection and looked up into the air. The sky, as if in sympathy with the great things among them, was different to-day and so misty that in some places the hot air seemed white. The disc of the sun was dull silver as though it were nearer and not so hot, yet the air stifled.

'They always been making trouble, haven't they?'

The voice came near his shoulder and sounded anxious.

'We can do without 'em. We'll be happier now, won't we?'

Ralph sat. The twins came, dragging a great log and grinning in their triumph. They dumped the log among the embers so that sparks flew.

'We can do all right on our own can't we?'

For a long time while the log dried, caught fire and turned red hot, Ralph sat in the sand and said nothing. He did not see Piggy go to the twins and whisper with them, nor how the three boys went together into the forest.

'Here you are.'

He came to himself with a jolt. Piggy and the other two were by him. They were laden with fruit.

'I thought perhaps,' said Piggy, 'we ought to have a feast kind of.'

The three boys sat down. They had a great mass of the fruit with them and all of it properly ripe. They grinned at Ralph as he took some and began to eat.

'Thanks,' he said. Then with an accent of pleased surprise— 'Thanks!'

'Do all right on our own,' said Piggy. 'It's them that haven't no common sense that make trouble on this island. We'll make a little hot fire——'

Ralph remembered what had been worrying him.

'Where's Simon?'

'I don't know.'

'You don't think he's climbing the mountain?'

Piggy broke into noisy laughter and took more fruit.

'He might be.' He gulped his mouthful. 'He's cracked.'

Simon had passed through the area of fruit trees but today the littluns had been too busy with the fire on the beach and they had not pursued him there. He went on among the creepers until he reached the great mat that was woven by the open space and crawled inside. Beyond the screen of leaves the sunlight pelted down and the butterflies danced in the middle their unending dance. He knelt down and the arrow of the sun fell on him. That other time the air had seemed to vibrate with heat; but now it threatened. Soon the sweat was running from his long coarse hair. He shifted restlessly but there was no avoiding the sun. Presently he was thirsty, and then very thirsty.

He continued to sit.

Far off along the beach, Jack was standing before a small group of boys. He was looking brilliantly happy.

'Hunting,' he said. He sized them up. Each of them wore the

remains of a black cap and ages ago they had stood in two demure rows and their voices had been the song of angels.

'We'll hunt. I'm going to be chief.'

They nodded, and the crisis passed easily.

'And then—about the beast.'

They moved, looked at the forest.

'I say this. We aren't going to bother about the beast.'

He nodded at them.

'We're going to forget the beast.'

'That's right!'

'Yes!'

'Forget the beast!'

If Jack was astonished by their fervour he did not show it.

'And another thing. We shan't dream so much down here. This is near the end of the island.'

They agreed passionately out of the depths of their tormented private lives.

'Now listen. We might go later to the castle rock. But now I'm going to get more of the biguns away from the conch and all that. We'll kill a pig and give a feast.' He paused and went on more slowly. 'And about the beast. When we kill we'll leave some of the kill for it. Then it won't bother us, maybe.'

He stood up abruptly.

'We'll go into the forest now and hunt.'

He turned and trotted away and after a moment they followed him obediently.

They spread out, nervously, in the forest. Almost at once Jack found the dug and scattered roots that told of pig and soon the track was fresh. Jack signalled the rest of the hunt to be quiet and went forward by himself. He was happy and wore the damp darkness of the forest like his old clothes. He crept down a slope to rocks and scattered trees by the sea.

The pigs lay, bloated bags of fat, sensuously enjoying the shadows under the trees. There was no wind and they were unsuspicious; and practice had made Jack silent as the shadows. He stole away again and instructed his hidden hunters. Presently they all began to inch forward sweating in the silence and heat. Under the trees an ear flapped idly. A little apart from the rest sunk in deep maternal bliss, lay the largest sow of the lot. She was black and pink; and the great bladder of her belly was fringed with a row of piglets that slept or burrowed and squeaked.

Fifteen yards from the drove Jack stopped; and his arm straightening, pointed at the sow. He looked round in inquiry to make sure that everyone understood and the other boys nodded at him. The row of right arms slid back.

'Now!'

The drove of pigs started up; and at a range of only ten yards the wooden spears with fire-hardened points flew towards the chosen pig. One piglet, with a demented shriek, rushed into the sea trailing Roger's spear behind it. The sow gave a gasping squeal and staggered up, with two spears sticking in her fat flank. The boys shouted and rushed forward, the piglets scattered and the sow burst the advancing line and went crashing away through the forest.

'After her!'

They raced along the pig-track, but the forest was too dark and tangled so that Jack, cursing, stopped them and cast among the trees. Then he said nothing for a time but breathed fiercely so that they were awed by him and looked at each other in uneasy admiration. Presently he stabbed down at the ground with his finger.

'There——'

Before the others could examine the drop of blood, Jack had swerved off, judging a trace, touching a bough that gave. So he followed, mysteriously right and assured; and the hunters trod behind him.

He stopped before a covert.

'In there.'

They surrounded the covert but the sow got away with the sting of another spear in her flank. The trailing butts hindered her and the sharp, cross-cut points were a torment. She blundered into a tree, forcing a spear still deeper; and after that any of the hunters could follow her easily by the drops of vivid blood. The afternoon wore on, hazy and dreadful with damp heat; the sow staggered her way ahead of them, bleeding and mad, and the hunters followed, wedded to her in lust, excited by the long chase and the dropped blood. They could see her now, nearly got up with her, but she spurted with her last strength and held ahead of them again. They were just behind her when she staggered into an open space where bright flowers grew and butterflies danced round each other and the air was hot and still.

Here, struck down by the heat, the sow fell and the hunters

hurled themselves at her. This dreadful eruption from an unknown world made her frantic; she squealed and bucked and the
air was full of sweat and noise and blood and terror. Roger ran
round the heap, prodding with his spear whenever pigflesh
appeared. Jack was on top of the sow, stabbing downward with
his knife. Roger found a lodgment for his point and began to
push till he was leaning with his whole weight. The spear moved
forward inch by inch and the terrified squealing became a high-
pitched scream. Then Jack found the throat and the hot blood
spouted over his hands. The sow collapsed under them and they
were heavy and fulfilled upon her. The butterflies still danced,
preoccupied in the centre of the clearing.

At last the immediacy of the kill subsided. The boys drew
back, and Jack stood up, holding out his hands.

'Look.'

He giggled and flinked them while the boys laughed at his
reeking palms. Then Jack grabbed Maurice and rubbed the stuff
over his cheeks. Roger began to withdraw his spear and the boys
noticed it for the first time. Robert stabilized the thing in a phrase
which was received uproariously.

'Right up her ass!'

'Did you hear?'

'Did you hear what he said?'

'Right up her ass!'

This time Robert and Maurice acted the two parts; and Maurice's acting of the pig's efforts to avoid the advancing spear was
so funny that the boys cried with laughter.

At length even this palled. Jack began to clean his bloody
hands on the rock. Then he started work on the sow and paunched
her, lugging out the hot bags of coloured guts, pushing them
into a pile on the rock while the others watched him. He talked as
he worked.

'We'll take the meat along the beach. I'll go back to the platform
and invite them to a feast. That should give us time.'

Roger spoke.

'Chief——'

'Uh——?'

'How can we make a fire?'

Jack squatted back and frowned at the pig.

'We'll raid them and take fire. There must be four of you;
Henry and you, Bill and Maurice. We'll put on paint and sneak

up; Roger can snatch a branch while I say what I want. The rest of you can get this back to where we were. We'll build the fire there. And after that——'

He paused and stood up, looking at the shadows under the trees. His voice was lower when he spoke again.

'But we'll leave part of the kill for . . .'

He knelt down again and was busy with his knife. The boys crowded round him. He spoke over his shoulder to Roger.

'Sharpen a stick at both ends.'

Presently he stood up, holding the dripping sow's head in his hands.

'Where's that stick?'

'Here.'

'Ram one end in the earth. Oh—it's rock. Jam it in that crack. There.'

Jack held up the head and jammed the soft throat down on the pointed end of the stick which pierced through into the mouth. He stood back and the head hung there, a little blood dribbling down the stick.

Instinctively the boys drew back too; and the forest was very still. They listened, and the loudest noise was the buzzing of flies over the spilled guts.

Jack spoke in a whisper.

'Pick up the pig.'

Maurice and Robert skewered the carcass, lifted the dead weight, and stood ready. In the silence, and standing over the dry blood, they looked suddenly furtive.

Jack spoke loudly.

'This head is for the beast. It's a gift.'

The silence accepted the gift and awed them. The head remained there, dim-eyed, grinning faintly, blood blackening between the teeth. All at once they were running away, as fast as they could, through the forest towards the open beach.

Simon stayed where he was, a small brown image, concealed by the leaves. Even if he shut his eyes the sow's head still remained like an after-image. The half-shut eyes were dim with the infinite cynicism of adult life. They assured Simon that everything was a bad business.

'I know that.'

Simon discovered that he had spoken aloud. He opened his

eyes quickly and there was the head grinning amusedly in the strange daylight, ignoring the flies, the spilled guts, even ignoring the indignity of being spiked on a stick.

He looked away, licking his dry lips.

A gift for the beast. Might not the beast come for it? The head, he thought, appeared to agree with him. Run away, said the head silently, go back to the others. It was a joke really—why should you bother? You were just wrong, that's all. A little headache, something you ate, perhaps. Go back, child, said the head silently.

Simon looked up, feeling the weight of his wet hair, and gazed at the sky. Up there, for once, were clouds, great bulging towers that sprouted away over the island, grey and cream and copper-coloured. The clouds were sitting on the land; they squeezed, produced moment by moment, this close, tormenting heat. Even the butterflies deserted the open space where the obscene thing grinned and dripped. Simon lowered his head, carefully keeping his eyes shut, then sheltered them with his hand. There were no shadows under the trees but everywhere a pearly stillness, so that what was real seemed illusive and without definition. The pile of guts was a black blob of flies that buzzed like a saw. After a while these flies found Simon. Gorged, they alighted by his runnels of sweat and drank. They tickled under his nostrils and played leap-frog on his thighs. They were black and iridescent green and without number; and in front of Simon, the Lord of the Flies hung on his stick and grinned. At last Simon gave up and looked back; saw the white teeth and dim eyes, the blood—and his gaze was held by that ancient, inescapable recognition. In Simon's right temple, a pulse began to beat on the brain.

Ralph and Piggy lay in the sand, gazing at the fire and idly flicking pebbles into its smokeless heart.

'That branch is gone.'

'Where's Samneric?'

'We ought to get some more wood. We're out of green branches.'

Ralph sighed and stood up. There were no shadows under the palms on the platform; only this strange light that seemed to come from everywhere at once. High up among the bulging clouds thunder went off like a gun.

'We're going to get buckets of rain.'

'What about the fire?'

Ralph trotted into the forest and returned with a wide spray of green which he dumped on the fire. The branch crackled, the leaves curled and the yellow smoke expanded.

Piggy made an aimless little pattern in the sand with his fingers.

'Trouble is, we haven't got enough people for a fire. You got to treat Samneric as one turn. They do everything together——'

'Of course.'

'Well, that isn't fair. Don't you see? They ought to do two turns.'

Ralph considered this and understood. He was vexed to find how little he thought like a grown-up and sighed again. The island was getting worse and worse.

Piggy looked at the fire.

'You'll want another green branch soon.'

Ralph rolled over.

'Piggy. What are we going to do?'

'Just have to get on without 'em.'

'But—the fire.'

He frowned at the black and white mess in which lay the unburnt ends of branches. He tried to formulate.

'I'm scared.'

He saw Piggy look up; and blundered on.

'Not of the beast. I mean I'm scared of that too. But nobody else understands about the fire. If someone threw you a rope when you were drowning. If a doctor said take this because if you don't take it you'll die—you would, wouldn't you? I mean?'

'Course I would.'

'Can't they see? Can't they understand? Without the smoke signal we'll die here? Look at that!'

A wave of heated air trembled above the ashes but without a trace of smoke.

'We can't keep one fire going. And they don't care. And what's more——' He looked intensely into Piggy's streaming face.

'What's more, *I* don't sometimes. Supposing I got like the others—not caring. What'ud become of us?'

Piggy took off his glasses, deeply troubled.

'I dunno, Ralph. We just got to go on, that's all. That's what grown-ups would do.'

Ralph, having begun the business of unburdening himself, continued.

'Piggy, what's wrong?'

Piggy looked at him in astonishment.

'Do you mean the———?'

'No, not it . . . I mean . . . what makes things break up like they do?'

Piggy rubbed his glasses slowly and thought. When he understood how far Ralph had gone towards accepting him he flushed pinkly with pride.

'I dunno, Ralph. I expect it's him.'

'Jack?'

'Jack.' A taboo was evolving round that word too.

Ralph nodded solemnly.

'Yes,' he said, 'I suppose it must be.'

The forest near them burst into uproar. Demoniac figures with faces of white and red and green rushed out howling, so that the littluns fled screaming. Out of the corner of his eye, Ralph saw Piggy running. Two figures rushed at the fire and he prepared to defend himself but they grabbed half-burnt branches and raced away along the beach. The three others stood still, watching Ralph; and he saw that the tallest of them, stark naked save for paint and a belt, was Jack.

Ralph had his breath back and spoke.

'Well?'

Jack ignored him, lifted his spear and began to shout.

'Listen all of you. Me and my hunters, we're living along the beach by a flat rock. We hunt and feast and have fun. If you want to join my tribe come and see us. Perhaps I'll let you join. Perhaps not.'

He paused and looked round. He was safe from shame or self-consciousness behind the mask of his paint and could look at each of them in turn. Ralph was kneeling by the remains of the fire like a sprinter at his mark and his face was half-hidden by hair and smut. Samneric peered together round a palm tree at the edge of the forest. A littlun howled, creased and crimson, by the bathing-pool and Piggy stood on the platform, the white conch gripped in his hands.

'To-night we're having a feast. We've killed a pig and we've got meat. You can come and eat with us if you like.'

Up in the cloud canyons the thunder boomed again. Jack and the two anonymous savages with him swayed, looked up, and then recovered. The littlun went on howling. Jack was waiting for something. He whispered urgently to the others.

'Go on—now!'

The two savages murmured. Jack spoke sharply.

'Go on!'

The two savages looked at each other, raised their spears together and spoke in time.

'The Chief has spoken.'

Then the three of them turned and trotted away.

Presently Ralph rose to his feet, looking at the place where the savages had vanished. Samneric came, talking in an awed whisper.

'I thought it was——'

'—and I was——'

'—scared.'

Piggy stood above them on the platform, still holding the conch.

'That was Jack and Maurice and Robert,' said Ralph. 'Aren't they having fun?'

'I thought I was going to have asthma.'

'Sucks to your ass-mar.'

'When I saw Jack I was sure he'd go for the conch. Can't think why.'

The group of boys looked at the white shell with affectionate respect. Piggy placed it in Ralph's hands and the littluns, seeing the familiar symbol, started to come back.

'Not here.'

He turned towards the platform, feeling the need for ritual. First went Ralph, the white conch cradled, then Piggy very grave, then the twins, then the littluns and the others.

'Sit down all of you. They raided us for fire. They're having fun. But the——'

Ralph was puzzled by the shutter that flickered in his brain. There was something he wanted to say; then the shutter had come down.

'But the——'

They were regarding him gravely, not yet troubled by any doubts about his sufficiency. Ralph pushed the idiot hair out of his eyes and looked at Piggy.

'But the . . . oh . . . the fire! Of course, the fire!'

He started to laugh, then stopped and became fluent instead.

'The fire's the most important thing. Without the fire we can't be rescued. I'd like to put on war-paint and be a savage. But we must keep the fire burning. The fire's the most important thing on the island, because, because——'

He paused again and the silence became full of doubt and wonder.

Piggy whispered urgently.

'Rescue.'

'Oh yes. Without the fire we can't be rescued. So we must stay by the fire and make smoke.'

When he stopped no one said anything. After the many brilliant speeches that had been made on this very spot Ralph's remarks seemed lame, even to the littluns.

At last Bill held out his hands for the conch.

'Now we can't have the fire up there—because we can't have the fire up there—we need more people to keep it going. Let's go to this feast and tell them the fire's hard on the rest of us. And then hunting and all that—being savages I mean—it must be jolly good fun.'

Samneric took the conch.

'That must be fun like Bill says—and as he's invited us——'

'—to a feast——'

'—meat——'

'crackling——'

'—I could do with some meat——'

Ralph held up his hand.

'Why shouldn't we get our own meat?'

The twins looked at each other. Bill answered.

'We don't want to go in the jungle.'

Ralph grimaced.

'He—you know—goes.'

'He's a hunter. They're all hunters. That's different.'

No one spoke for a moment, then Piggy muttered to the sand.

'Meat——'

The littluns sat, solemnly thinking of meat and dribbling. Overhead the cannon boomed again and the dry palm-fronds clattered in a sudden gust of hot wind.

'You are a silly little boy,' said the Lord of the Flies, 'just an ignorant, silly little boy.'

Simon moved his swollen tongue but said nothing.

'Don't you agree?' said the Lord of the Flies. 'Aren't you just a silly little boy?'

Simon answered him in the same silent voice.

'Well then,' said the Lord of the Flies, 'you'd better run off and play with the others. They think you're batty. You don't want Ralph to think you're batty, do you? You like Ralph a lot, don't you? And Piggy, and Jack?'

Simon's head was tilted slightly up. His eyes could not break away and the Lord of the Flies hung in space before him.

'What are you doing out here all alone? Aren't you afraid of me?'

Simon shook.

'There isn't anyone to help you. Only me. And I'm the Beast.'

Simon's mouth laboured, brought forth audible words.

'Pig's head on a stick.'

'Fancy thinking the Beast was something you could hunt and kill!' said the head. For a moment or two the forest and all the other dimly appreciated places echoed with the parody of laughter. 'You knew, didn't you? I'm part of you? Close, close, close! I'm the reason why it's no go? Why things are what they are?'

The laughter shivered again.

'Come now,' said the Lord of the Flies. 'Get back to the others and we'll forget the whole thing.'

Simon's head wobbled. His eyes were half-closed as though he were imitating the obscene thing on the stick. He knew that one of his times was coming on. The Lord of the Flies was expanding like a balloon.

'This is ridiculous. You know perfectly well you'll only meet me down there—so don't try to escape!'

Simon's body was arched and stiff. The Lord of the Flies spoke in the voice of a schoolmaster.

'This has gone quite far enough. My poor, misguided child, do you think you know better than I do?'

There was a pause.

'I'm warning you. I'm going to get waxy. D'you see? You're not wanted. Understand? We are going to have fun on this island. Understand? We are going to have fun on this island! So don't try it on, my poor misguided boy, or else——'

Simon found he was looking into a vast mouth. There was blackness within, a blackness that spread.

'—Or else,' said the Lord of the Flies, 'we shall do you. See?

Jack and Roger and Maurice and Robert and Bill and Piggy and Ralph. Do you. See?'

Simon was inside the mouth. He fell down and lost consciousness.

CHAPTER NINE

A View to a Death

Over the island the build-up of clouds continued. A steady current of heated air rose all day from the mountain and was thrust to ten thousand feet; revolving masses of gas piled up the static until the air was ready to explode. By early evening the sun had gone and a brassy glare had taken the place of clear daylight. Even the air that pushed in from the sea was hot and held no refreshment. Colours drained from water and trees and pink surfaces of rock, and the white and brown clouds brooded. Nothing prospered but the flies who blackened their lord and made the spilt guts look like a heap of glistening coal. Even when the vessel broke in Simon's nose and the blood gushed out they left him alone, preferring the pig's high flavour.

With the running of the blood Simon's fit passed into the weariness of sleep. He lay in the mat of creepers while the evening advanced and the cannon continued to play. At last he woke and saw dimly the dark earth close by his cheek. Still he did not move but lay there, his face sideways on the earth, his eyes looking dully before him. Then he turned over, drew his feet under him and laid hold of the creepers to pull himself up. When the creepers shook the flies exploded from the guts with a vicious note and clamped back on again. Simon got to his feet. The light was unearthly. The Lord of the Flies hung on his stick like a black ball.

Simon spoke aloud to the clearing.

'What else is there to do?'

Nothing replied. Simon turned away from the open space and crawled through the creepers till he was in the dusk of the forest. He walked drearily between the trunks, his face empty of expression, and the blood was dry round his mouth and chin. Only sometimes as he lifted the ropes of creeper aside and chose his direction from the trend of the land, he mouthed words that did not reach the air.

Presently the creepers festooned the trees less frequently and there was a scatter of pearly light from the sky down through the trees. This was the backbone of the island, the slightly higher land that lay beneath the mountain where the forest was no longer deep jungle. Here there were wide spaces interspersed with thickets and huge trees and the trend of the ground led him up as the forest opened. He pushed on, staggering sometimes with his weariness but never stopping. The usual brightness was gone from his eyes and he walked with a sort of glum determination like an old man.

A buffet of wind made him stagger and he saw that he was out in the open, on rock, under a brassy sky. He found his legs were weak and his tongue gave him pain all the time. When the wind reached the mountain-top he could see something happen, a flicker of blue stuff against brown clouds. He pushed himself forward and the wind came again, stronger now, cuffing the forest heads till they ducked and roared. Simon saw a humped thing suddenly sit up on the top and look down at him. He hid his face, and toiled on.

The flies had found the figure too. The life-like movement would scare them off for a moment so that they made a dark cloud round the head. Then as the blue material of the parachute collapsed the corpulent figure would bow forward, sighing, and the flies settle once more.

Simon felt his knees smack the rock. He crawled forward and soon he understood. The tangle of lines showed him the mechanics of this parody; he examined the white nasal bones, the teeth, the colours of corruption. He saw how pitilessly the layers of rubber and canvas held together the poor body that should be rotting away. Then the wind blew again and the figure lifted, bowed, and breathed foully at him. Simon knelt on all fours and was sick till his stomach was empty. Then he took the lines in his hands; he freed them from the rocks and the figure from the wind's indignity.

At last he turned away and looked down at the beaches. The fire by the platform appeared to be out, or at least making no smoke. Further along the beach, beyond the little river and near a great slab of rock, a thin trickle of smoke was climbing into the sky. Simon forgetful of the flies, shaded his eyes with both hands and peered at the smoke. Even at that distance it was possible to see that most of the boys—perhaps all the boys—were there. So they had shifted camp then, away from the beast. As Simon thought this, he turned to the poor broken thing that sat stinking by his side. The beast was harmless and horrible; and the news must reach the others as soon as possible. He started down the mountain and his legs gave beneath him. Even with great care the best he could do was a stagger.

'Bathing,' said Ralph, 'that's the only thing to do.'

Piggy was inspecting the looming sky through his glass.

'I don't like them clouds. Remember how it rained just after we landed?'

'Going to rain again.'

Ralph dived into the pool. A couple of littluns were playing at the edge, trying to extract comfort from a wetness warmer than blood. Piggy took off his glasses, stepped primly into the water and then put them on again. Ralph came to the surface and squirted a jet of water at him.

'Mind my specs,' said Piggy. 'If I get water on the glass I got to get out and clean 'em.'

Ralph squirted again and missed. He laughed at Piggy, expecting him to retire meekly as usual and in pained silence. Instead, Piggy beat the water with his hands.

'Stop it!' he shouted, 'd'you hear?'

Furiously he drove the water into Ralph's face.

'All right, all right,' said Ralph. 'Keep your hair on.'

Piggy stopped beating the water.

'I got a pain in my head. I wish the air was cooler.'

'I wish the rain would come.'

'I wish we could go home.'

Piggy lay back against the sloping sand-side of the pool. His stomach protruded and the water dried on it. Ralph squirted up at the sky. One could guess at the movement of the sun by the progress of a light patch among the clouds. He knelt in the water and looked round.

'Where's everybody?'

Piggy sat up.

'P'raps they're lying in the shelter.'

'Where's Samneric?'

'And Bill?'

Piggy pointed beyond the platform.

'That's where they've gone. Jack's party.'

'Let them go,' said Ralph, uneasily, 'I don't care.'

'Just for some meat——'

'And for hunting,' said Ralph, wisely, 'and for pretending to be a tribe, and putting on war-paint.'

Piggy stirred the sand under water and did not look at Ralph.

'P'raps we ought to go too.'

Ralph looked at him quickly and Piggy blushed.

'I mean—to make sure nothing happens.'

Ralph squirted water again.

Long before Ralph and Piggy came up with Jack's lot, they could hear the party. There was a stretch of grass in a place where the palms left a wide band of turf between the forest and the shore. Just one step down from the edge of the turf was the white, blown sand of above high water, warm, dry, trodden. Below that again was a rock that stretched away towards the lagoon. Beyond was a short stretch of sand and then the edge of the water. A fire burned on a rock and fat dripped from the roasting pig-meat into the invisible flames. All the boys of the island, except Piggy, Ralph, Simon, and the two tending the pig, were grouped on the turf. They were laughing, singing, lying, squatting, or standing on the grass, holding food in their hands. But to judge by the greasy faces, the meat-eating was almost done; and some held coco-nut shells in their hands and were drinking from them. Before the party had started a great log had been dragged into the centre of the lawn and Jack, painted and garlanded, sat there like an idol. There were piles of meat on green leaves near him, and fruit, and coco-nut shells full of drink.

Piggy and Ralph came to the edge of the grassy platform; and the boys, as they noticed them, fell silent one by one till only the boy next to Jack was talking. Then the silence intruded even there and Jack turned where he sat. For a time he looked at them and the crackle of the fire was the loudest noise over the bourdon of the reef. Ralph looked away; and Sam, thinking that Ralph had turned to him accusingly, put down his gnawed bone with a nervous giggle. Ralph took an uncertain step, pointed to a palm tree, and whispered something inaudible to Piggy; and they both giggled like Sam. Lifting his feet high out of the sand, Ralph started to stroll past. Piggy tried to whistle.

At this moment the boys who were cooking at the fire suddenly hauled off a great chunk of meat and ran with it towards the grass. They bumped Piggy who was burnt, and yelled and danced. Immediately, Ralph and the crowd of boys were united and relieved by a storm of laughter. Piggy once more was the centre of social derision so that everyone felt cheerful and normal.

Jack stood up and waved his spear.

'Take them some meat.'

The boys with the spit gave Ralph and Piggy each a succulent chunk. They took the gift, dribbling. So they stood and ate beneath a sky of thunderous brass that rang with the storm-coming.

Jack waved his spear again.

'Has everybody eaten as much as they want?'

There was still food left, sizzling on the wooden spits, heaped on the green platters. Betrayed by his stomach, Piggy threw a picked bone down on the beach and stooped for more.

Jack spoke again, impatiently.

'Has everybody eaten as much as they want?'

His tone conveyed a warning, given out of the pride of ownership, and the boys ate faster while there was still time. Seeing there was no immediate likelihood of a pause, Jack rose from the log that was his throne and sauntered to the edge of the grass. He looked down from behind his paint at Ralph and Piggy. They moved a little further off over the sand and Ralph watched the fire as he ate. He noticed, without understanding, how the flames were visible now against the dull light. Evening was come, not with calm beauty but with the threat of violence.

Jack spoke.

'Give me a drink.'

Henry brought him a shell and he drank, watching Piggy and Ralph over the jagged rim. Power lay in the brown swell of his forearms; authority sat on his shoulder and chattered in his ear like an ape.

'All sit down.'

The boys ranged themselves in rows on the grass before him but Ralph and Piggy stayed a foot lower, standing on the soft sand. Jack ignored them for the moment, turned his mask down to the seated boys and pointed at them with the spear.

'Who is going to join my tribe?'

Ralph made a sudden movement that became a stumble. Some of the boys turned towards him.

'I gave you food,' said Jack, 'and my hunters will protect you from the beast. Who will join my tribe?'

'I'm chief,' said Ralph, 'because you chose me. And we were going to keep the fire going. Now you run after food——'

'You ran yourself!' shouted Jack. 'Look at that bone in your hands!'

Ralph went crimson.

'I said you were hunters. That was your job.'

Jack ignored him again.

'Who'll join my tribe and have fun?'

'I'm chief,' said Ralph tremulously. 'And what about the fire? And I've got the conch——'

'You haven't got it with you,' said Jack, sneering. 'You left it behind. See, clever? And the conch doesn't count at this end of the island——'

All at once the thunder struck. Instead of the dull boom there was a point of impact in the explosion.

'The conch counts here too,' said Ralph, 'and all over the island.'

'What are you going to do about it then?'

Ralph examined the ranks of boys. There was no help in them and he looked away, confused and sweating. Piggy whispered.

'The fire—rescue.'

'Who'll join my tribe?'

'I will.'

'Me.'

'I will.'

'I'll blow the conch,' said Ralph breathlessly, 'and call an assembly.'

'We shan't hear it.'

Piggy touched Ralph's wrist.

'Come away. There's going to be trouble. And we've had our meat.'

There was a blink of bright light beyond the forest and the thunder exploded again so that a littlun started to whine. Big drops of rain fell among them making individual sounds when they struck.

'Going to be a storm,' said Ralph, 'and you'll have rain like when we dropped here. Who's clever now? Where are your shelters? What are you going to do about that?'

The hunters were looking uneasily at the sky, flinching from the stroke of the drops. A wave of restlessness set the boys swaying and moving aimlessly. The flickering light became brighter and the blows of the thunder were only just bearable. The littluns began to run about, screaming.

Jack leapt on to the sand.

'Do our dance! Come on! Dance!'

He ran stumbling through the thick sand to the open space of rock beyond the fire. Between the flashes of lightning the air was dark and terrible; and the boys followed him, clamorously. Roger became the pig, grunting and charging at Jack, who side-stepped. The hunters took their spears, the cooks took spits, and the rest clubs of fire-wood. A circling movement developed and a chant. While Roger mimed the terror of the pig, the littluns ran and jumped on the outside of the circle. Piggy and Ralph, under the threat of the sky, found themselves eager to take a place in this demented but partly secure society. They were glad to touch the brown backs of the fence that hemmed in the terror and made it governable.

'*Kill the beast! Cut his throat! Spill his blood!*'

The movement became regular while the chant lost its first superficial excitement and began to beat like a steady pulse. Roger ceased to be a pig and became a hunter, so that the centre of the ring yawned emptily. Some of the littluns started a ring on their own; and the complementary circles went round and round as though repetition would achieve safety of itself. There was the throb and stamp of a single organism.

The dark sky was shattered by a blue-white scar. An instant later the noise was on them like the blow of a gigantic whip. The chant rose a tone in agony.

'*Kill the beast! Cut his throat! Spill his blood!*'

Now out of the terror rose another desire, thick, urgent, blind.

'*Kill the beast! Cut his throat! Spill his blood!*'

Again the blue-white scar jagged above them and the sulphurous explosion beat down. The littluns screamed and blundered about, fleeing from the edge of the forest, and one of them broke the ring of biguns in his terror.

'Him! Him!'

The circle became a horseshoe. A thing was crawling out of the forest. It came darkly, uncertainly. The shrill screaming that rose before the beast was like a pain. The beast stumbled into the horseshoe.

'*Kill the beast! Cut his throat! Spill his blood!*'

The blue-white scar was constant, the noise unendurable. Simon was crying out something about a dead man on a hill.

'*Kill the beast! Cut his throat! Spill his blood! Do him in!*'

The sticks fell and the mouth of the new circle crunched and screamed. The beast was on its knees in the centre, its arms folded over its face. It was crying out against the abominable noise something about a body on the hill. The beast struggled forward, broke the ring and fell over the steep edge of the rock to the sand by the water. At once the crowd surged after it, poured down the rock, leapt on to the beast, screamed, struck, bit, tore. There were no words, and no movements but the tearing of teeth and claws.

Then the clouds opened and let down the rain like a waterfall. The water bounded from the mountain-top, tore leaves and branches from the trees, poured like a cold shower over the struggling heap on the sand. Presently the heap broke up and figures staggered away. Only the beast lay still, a few yards from the sea. Even in the rain they could see how small a beast it was; and already its blood was staining the sand.

Now a great wind blew the rain sideways, cascading the water from the forest trees. On the mountain-top the parachute filled and moved; the figure slid, rose to its feet, spun, swayed down through a vastness of wet air and trod with ungainly feet the tops of the high trees; falling, still falling, it sank towards the beach and the boys rushed screaming into the darkness. The parachute took the figure forward, furrowing the lagoon, and bumped it over the reef and out to sea.

Towards midnight the rain ceased and the clouds drifted away, so that the sky was scattered once more with the incredible lamps of stars. Then the breeze died too and there was no noise save the drip and trickle of water that ran out of clefts and spilled down, leaf by leaf, to the brown earth of the island. The air was cool, moist, and clear; and presently even the sound of the water was still. The beast lay huddled on the pale beach and the stains spread, inch by inch.

The edge of the lagoon became a streak of phosphorescence which advanced minutely, as the great wave of the tide flowed. The clear water mirrored the clear sky and the angular bright constellations. The line of phosphorescence bulged about the sand grains and little pebbles; it held them each in a dimple of tension, then suddenly accepted them with an inaudible syllable and moved on.

Along the shoreward edge of the shallows the advancing clearness was full of strange, moonbeam-bodied creatures with fiery eyes. Here and there a larger pebble clung to its own air and was covered with a coat of pearls. The tide swelled in over the rain-pitted sand and smoothed everything with a layer of silver. Now it touched the first of the stains that seeped from the broken body and the creatures made a moving patch of light as they gathered at the edge. The water rose further and dressed Simon's coarse hair with brightness. The line of his cheek silvered and the turn of his shoulder became sculptured marble. The strange, attendant creatures, with their fiery eyes and trailing vapours, busied themselves round his head. The body lifted a fraction of an inch from the sand and a bubble of air escaped from the mouth with a wet plop. Then it turned gently in the water.

Somewhere over the darkened curve of the world the sun and moon were pulling; and the film of water on the earth planet was held, bulging slightly on one side while the solid core turned. The great wave of the tide moved further along the island and the water lifted. Softly, surrounded by a fringe of inquisitive bright creatures, itself a silver shape beneath the steadfast constellations, Simon's dead body moved out towards the open sea.

CHAPTER TEN

The Shell and the Glasses

Piggy eyed the advancing figure carefully. Nowadays he some-times found that he saw more clearly if he removed his glasses and shifted the one lens to the other eye; but even through the good eye, after what had happened, Ralph remained unmistakably Ralph. He came now out of the coco-nut trees, limping, dirty, with dead leaves hanging from his shock of yellow hair. One eye was a slit in his puffy cheek and a great scab had formed on his right knee. He paused for a moment and peered at the figure on the platform.

'Piggy? Are you the only one left?'

'There's some littluns.'

'They don't count. No biguns?'

'Oh—Samneric. They're collecting wood.'

'Nobody else?'

'Not that I know of.'

Ralph climbed on to the platform carefully. The coarse grass was still worn away where the assembly used to sit; the fragile white conch still gleamed by the polished seat. Ralph sat down in the grass facing the chief's seat and the conch. Piggy knelt at his left, and for a long minute there was silence.

At last Ralph cleared his throat and whispered something.

Piggy whispered back.

'What you say?'

Ralph spoke up.

'Simon.'

Piggy said nothing but nodded, solemnly. They continued to sit, gazing with impaired sight at the chief's seat and the glittering lagoon. The green light and the glossy patches of sunshine played over their befouled bodies.

At length Ralph got up and went to the conch. He took the shell caressingly with both hands and knelt, leaning against the trunk.

'Piggy.'

'Uh?'

'What we going to do?'

Piggy nodded at the conch.

'You could——'

'Call an assembly?'

Ralph laughed sharply as he said the word and Piggy frowned.

'You're still Chief.'

Ralph laughed again.

'You are. Over us.'

'I got the conch.'

'Ralph! Stop laughing like that. Look there ain't no need, Ralph! What's the others going to think?'

At last Ralph stopped. He was shivering.

'Piggy.'

'Oh?'

'That was Simon.'

'You said that before.'

'Piggy.'

'Oh?'

'That was murder.'

'You stop it!' said Piggy, shrilly. 'What good're you doing talking like that?'

He jumped to his feet and stood over Ralph.

'It was dark. There was that—that bloody dance. There was lightning and thunder and rain. We was scared!'

'I wasn't scared,' said Ralph slowly, 'I was—I don't know what I was.'

'We was scared!' said Piggy excitedly. 'Anything might have happened. It wasn't—what you said.'

He was gesticulating, searching for a formula.

'Oh Piggy!'

Ralph's voice, low and stricken, stopped Piggy's gestures. He bent down and waited. Ralph, cradling the conch, rocked himself to and fro.

'Don't you understand, Piggy? The things we did——'

'He may still be——'

'No.'

'P'raps he was only pretending——'

Piggy's voice tailed off at the sight of Ralph's face.

'You were outside. Outside the circle. You never really came in. Didn't you see what we—what they did?'

There was loathing, and at the same time a kind of feverish excitement in his voice.

'Didn't you see, Piggy?'

'Not all that well. I only got one eye now. You ought to know that, Ralph.'

Ralph continued to rock to and fro.

'It was an accident,' said Piggy suddenly, 'that's what it was. An accident.' His voice shrilled again. 'Coming in the dark—he had no business crawling like that out of the dark. He was batty. He asked for it.' He gesticulated widely again.

'It was an accident.'

'You didn't see what they did——'

'Look, Ralph. We got to forget this. We can't do no good thinking about it, see?'

'I'm frightened. Of us. I want to go home. O God I want to go home.'

'It was an accident,' said Piggy stubbornly, 'and that's that.'

He touched Ralph's bare shoulder and Ralph shuddered at the human contact.

'And look, Ralph,' Piggy glanced round quickly, then leaned close—'don't let on we was in that dance. Not to Samneric.'

'But we were! All of us!'

Piggy shook his head.

'Not us till last. They never noticed in the dark. Anyway you said I was only on the outside——'

'So was I,' muttered Ralph, 'I was on the outside too.'

Piggy nodded eagerly.

'That's right. We was on the outside. We never done nothing, we never seen nothing.'

Piggy paused, then went on.

'We'll live on our own, the four of us——'

'Four of us. We aren't enough to keep the fire burning.'

'We'll try. See? I lit it.'

Samneric came dragging a great log out of the forest. They dumped it by the fire and turned to the pool. Ralph jumped to his feet.

'Hi! You two!'

The twins checked a moment, then walked on.

'They're going to bathe, Ralph.'

'Better get it over.'

The twins were very surprised to see Ralph. They flushed and looked past him into the air.

'Hullo. Fancy meeting you, Ralph.'

'We just been in the forest——'

'—to get wood for the fire——'

'—we got lost last night.'

Ralph examined his toes.

'You got lost after the . . .'

Piggy cleaned his lens.

'After the feast,' said Sam in a stifled voice. Eric nodded. 'Yes, after the feast.'

'We left early,' said Piggy quickly, 'because we were tired.'

'So did we——'

'—very early——'

'—we were very tired.'

Sam touched a scratch on his forehead and then hurriedly took his hand away. Eric fingered his split lip.

'Yes. We were very tired,' repeated Sam, 'so we left early. Was it a good——'

The air was heavy with unspoken knowledge. Sam twisted and the obscene word shot out of him. '—dance?'

Memory of the dance that none of them had attended shook all four boys convulsively.

'We left early.'

When Roger came to the neck of land that joined the Castle Rock to the mainland he was not surprised to be challenged. He had reckoned, during the terrible night, on finding at least some of the tribe holding out against the horrors of the island in the safest place.

The voice rang out sharply from on high, where the diminishing crags were balanced one on another.

'Halt! Who goes there?'

'Roger.'

'Advance, friend.'

Roger advanced.

'You could see who I was.'

'The Chief said we got to challenge everyone.'

Roger peered up.

'You couldn't stop me coming if I wanted.'

'Couldn't I! Climb up and see.'

Roger clambered up the ladder-like cliff.

'Look at this.'

A log had been jammed under the topmost rock and another lever under that. Robert leaned lightly on the lever and the rock groaned. A full effort would send the rock thundering down to the neck of land. Roger admired.

'He's a proper Chief, isn't he?'

Robert nodded.

'He's going to take us hunting.'

He jerked his head in the direction of the distant shelters where a thread of white smoke climbed up the sky. Roger, sitting on the very edge of the cliff, looked sombrely back at the island as he worked with his fingers at a loose tooth. His gaze settled on the top of the distant mountain and Robert changed the unspoken subject.

'He's going to beat Wilfred.'

'What for?'

Robert shook his head doubtfully.

'I don't know. He didn't say. He got angry and made us tie Wilfred up. He's been'—he giggled excitedly—'he's been tied for hours, waiting——'.

'But didn't the Chief say why?'

'I never heard him.'

Sitting on the tremendous rocks in the torrid sun, Roger received this news as an illumination. He ceased to work at his tooth and sat still, assimilating the possibilities of irresponsible authority. Then, without another word, he climbed down the back of the rocks towards the cave and the rest of the tribe.

The Chief was sitting there, naked to the waist, his face blocked out in white and red. The tribe lay in a semicircle before him. The newly beaten and untied Wilfred was sniffing noisily in the background. Roger squatted with the rest.

'Tomorrow,' went on the Chief, 'we shall hunt again.'

He pointed at this savage and that with his spear.

'Some of you will stay here to improve the cave and defend the gate. I shall take a few hunters with me and bring back meat. The defenders of the gate will see that the others don't sneak in——'

A savage raised his hand and the Chief turned a bleak, painted faced towards him.

'Why should they try to sneak in, Chief?'

The Chief was vague but earnest.

'They will. They'll try to spoil things we do. So the watchers at the gate must be careful. And then——'

The Chief paused. They saw a triangle of startling pink dart out, pass along his lips and vanish again.

'—and then; the beast might try to come in. You remember how he crawled——'

The semicircle shuddered and muttered in agreement.

'He came—disguised. He may come again even though we gave him the head of our kill to eat. So watch; and be careful.'

Stanley lifted his forearm off the rock and held up an interrogative finger.

'Well?'

'But didn't we, didn't we——?'

He squirmed and looked down.

'No!'

In the silence that followed each savage flinched away from his individual memory.

'No! How could we—kill—it?'

Half-relieved, half-daunted by the implication of further terrors, the savages murmured again.

'So leave the mountain alone,' said the Chief, solemnly, 'and give it the head if you go hunting.'

Stanley flicked his finger again.

'I expect the beast disguised itself.'

'Perhaps,' said the Chief. A theological speculation presented itself. 'We'd better keep on the right side of him, anyhow. You can't tell what he might do.'

The tribe considered this; and then were shaken, as if by a flaw of wind. The Chief saw the effect of his words and stood abruptly.

'But tomorrow we'll hunt and when we've got meat we'll have a feast——'

Bill put up his hand.

'Chief.'

'Yes?'

'What'll we use for lighting the fire?'

The Chief's blush was hidden by the white and red clay. Into his uncertain silence the tribe spilled their murmur once more. Then the Chief held up his hand.

'We shall take fire from the others. Listen. Tomorrow we'll hunt and get meat. Tonight I'll go along with two hunters—who'll come?'

Maurice and Roger put up their hands.

'Maurice——'

'Yes, Chief?'

'Where was their fire?'

'Back at the old place by the fire rock.'

The Chief nodded.

'The rest of you can go to sleep as soon as the sun sets. But us three, Maurice, Roger and me, we've got work to do. We'll leave just before sunset——'

Maurice put up his hand.

'But what happens if we meet——'

The Chief waved his objection aside.

'We'll keep along by the sands. Then if he comes we'll do our, our dance again.'

'Only the three of us?'

Again the murmur swelled and died away.

Piggy handed Ralph his glasses and waited to receive back his sight. The wood was damp; and this was the third time they had lighted it. Ralph stood back, speaking to himself.

'We don't want another night without fire.'

He looked round guiltily at the three boys standing by. This was the first time he had admitted the double function of the fire. Certainly one was to send up a beckoning column of smoke; but the other was to be a hearth now and a comfort until they slept. Eric breathed on the wood till it glowed and sent out a little flame. A billow of white and yellow smoke reeked up. Piggy took back his glasses and looked at the smoke with pleasure.

'If only we could make a radio!'

'Or a plane——'

'—or a boat.'

Ralph dredged in his fading knowledge of the world.

'We might get taken prisoner by the reds.'

Eric pushed back his chair.

'They'd be better than——'

He would not name people and Sam finished the sentence for him by nodding along the beach.

Ralph remembered the ungainly figure on a parachute.

'He said something about a dead man——' He flushed painfully at this admission that he had been present at the dance. He made urging motions at the smoke with his body. 'Don't stop—go on up!'

'Smoke's getting thinner.'

'We need more wood already, even when it's wet.'

'My asthma————'

The response was mechanical.

'Sucks to your ass-mar.'

'If I pull logs about, I get my asthma bad. I wish I didn't, Ralph, but there it is.'

The three boys went into the forest and fetched armfuls of rotten wood. Once more the smoke rose, yellow and thick.

'Let's get something to eat.'

Together they went to the fruit trees, carrying their spears, saying little, cramming in haste. When they came out of the forest again the sun was setting and only embers glowed in the fire, and there was no smoke.

'I can't carry any more wood,' said Eric. 'I'm tired.'

Ralph cleared his throat.

'We kept the fire going up there.'

'Up there it was small. But this has got to be a big one.'

Ralph carried a fragment to the fire and watched the smoke that drifted into the dusk.

'We've got to keep it going.'

Eric flung himself down.

'I'm too tired. And what's the good?'

'Eric!' cried Ralph in a shocked voice. 'Don't talk like that!'

Sam knelt by Eric.

'Well—what *is* the good?'

Ralph tried indignantly to remember. There was something good about a fire. Something overwhelmingly good.

'Ralph's told you often enough,' said Piggy moodily. 'How else are we going to be rescued?'

'Of course! If we don't make smoke————'

He squatted before them in the crowding dusk.

'Don't you understand? What's the good of wishing for radios and boats?'

He held out his hand and twisted the fingers into a fist.

'There's only one thing we can do to get out of this mess. Anyone can play at hunting, anyone can get us meat————'

He looked from face to face. Then, at the moment of greatest passion and conviction, that curtain flapped in his head and he forgot what he had been driving at. He knelt there, his fist clenched, gazing solemnly from one to the other. Then the curtain whisked back.

'Oh yes. So we've got to make smoke; and more smoke——'

'But we can't keep it going! Look at that!'

The fire was dying on them.

'Two to mind the fire,' said Ralph, half to himself, 'that's twelve hours a day.'

'We can't get any more wood, Ralph——'

'—not in the dark——'

'—not at night——'

'We can light it every morning,' said Piggy. 'Nobody ain't going to see smoke in the dark.'

Sam nodded vigorously.

'It was different when the fire was——'

'—up there.'

Ralph stood up, feeling curiously defenceless with the darkness pressing in.

'Let the fire go then, for tonight.'

He led the way to the first shelter, which still stood, though battered. The bed leaves lay within, dry and noisy to the touch. In the next shelter a littlun was talking in his sleep. The four biguns crept into the shelter and burrowed under the leaves. The twins lay together and Ralph and Piggy at the other end. For a while there was the continual creak and rustle of leaves as they tried for comfort.

'Piggy.'

'Yeah?'

'All right?'

'S'pose so.'

At length, save for an occasional rustle, the shelter was silent. An oblong of blackness relieved with brilliant spangles hung before them and there was the hollow sound of surf on the reef. Ralph settled himself for his nightly game of supposing. . . .

Supposing they could be transported home by jet, then before morning they would land at that big airfield in Wiltshire. They would go by car; no, for things to be perfect they would go by train; all the way down to Devon and take that cottage again. Then at the foot of the garden the wild ponies would come and look over the wall. . . .

Ralph turned restlessly in the leaves. Dartmoor was wild and so were the ponies. But the attraction of wildness had gone.

His mind skated to a consideration of a tamed town where savagery could not set foot. What could be safer than the bus centre with its lamps and wheels?

All at once, Ralph was dancing round a lamp standard. There was a bus crawling out of the bus station, a strange bus. . . .

'Ralph! Ralph!'

'What is it?'

'Don't make a noise like that——'

'Sorry.'

From the darkness of the further end of the shelter came a dreadful moaning and they shattered the leaves in their fear. Sam and Eric, locked in an embrace, were fighting each other.

'Sam! Sam!'

'Hey—Eric!'

Presently all was quiet again.

Piggy spoke softly to Ralph.

'We got to get out of this.'

'What d'you mean?'

'Get rescued.'

For the first time that day, and despite the crowding blackness, Ralph sniggered.

'I mean it,' whispered Piggy. 'If we don't get home soon we'll be barmy.'

'Round the bend.'

'Bomb happy.'

'Crackers.'

Ralph pushed the damp tendrils of hair out of his eyes.

'You write a letter to your auntie.'

Piggy considered this solemnly.

'I don't know where she is now. And I haven't got an envelope and a stamp. An' there isn't a pillar-box. Or a postman.'

The success of his tiny joke overcame Ralph. His sniggers became uncontrollable, his body jumped and twitched.

Piggy rebuked him with dignity.

'I haven't said anything all that funny——'

Ralph continued to snigger though his chest hurt. His twitchings exhausted him till he lay, breathless and woebegone, waiting for the next spasm. During one of these pauses he was ambushed by sleep.

'—Ralph! You been making a noise again. Do be quiet, Ralph—because.'

Ralph heaved over among the leaves. He had reason to be thankful that his dream was broken, for the bus had been nearer and more distinct.

'Why—because?'

'Be quiet—and listen.'

Ralph lay down carefully, to the accompaniment of a long sigh from the leaves. Eric moaned something and then lay still. The darkness, save for the useless oblong of stars, was blanket-thick.

'I can't hear anything.'

'There's something moving outside.'

Ralph's head prickled. The sound of his blood drowned all else and then subsided.

'I still can't hear anything.'

'Listen. Listen for a long time.'

Quite clearly and emphatically, and only a yard or so away from the back of the shelter, a stick cracked. The blood roared again in Ralph's ears, confused images chased each other through his mind. A composite of these things was prowling round the shelters. He could feel Piggy's head against his shoulder and the convulsive grip of a hand.

'Ralph! Ralph!'

'Shut up and listen.'

Desperately, Ralph prayed that the beast would prefer littluns.

A voice whispered horribly outside.

'Piggy—Piggy——'

'It's come!' gasped Piggy. 'It's real!'

He clung to Ralph and reached to get his breath.

'Piggy, come outside. I want you Piggy.'

Ralph's mouth was against Piggy's ear.

'Don't say anything.'

'Piggy—where are you, Piggy?'

Something brushed against the back of the shelter. Piggy kept still for a moment, then he had his asthma. He arched his back and crashed among the leaves with his legs. Ralph rolled away from him.

Then there was a vicious snarling in the mouth of the shelter and the plunge and thump of living things. Someone tripped over Ralph and Piggy's corner became a complication of snarls and crashes and flying limbs. Ralph hit out; then he and what seemed like a dozen others were rolling over and over, hitting, biting, scratching. He was torn and jolted, found fingers in his mouth and bit them. A fist withdrew and came back like a piston, so that the whole shelter exploded into light. Ralph twisted sideways on top of a writhing body and felt hot breath on his cheek. He began to pound the mouth below him, using his clenched fist as a hammer; he hit with more and more passionate hysteria as the face became slippery. A knee jerked up between his legs and he fell sideways, busying himself with his pain, and the fight rolled over him. Then the shelter collapsed with smothering finality; and the anonymous shapes fought their way out and through. Dark figures drew themselves out of the wreckage and flitted away, till the screams of the littluns and Piggy's gasps were once more audible.

Ralph called out in a quavering voice.

'All the littluns, go to sleep. We've had a fight with the others. Now go to sleep.'

Samneric came close and peered at Ralph.

'Are you two all right?'

'I think so——'

'——I got busted.'

'So did I. How's Piggy?'

They hauled Piggy clear of the wreckage and leaned him against a tree. The night was cool and purged of immediate terror. Piggy's breathing was a little easier.

'Did you get hurt, Piggy?'

'Not much.'

'That was Jack and his hunters,' said Ralph bitterly. 'Why can't they leave us alone?'

'We gave them something to think about,' said Sam. Honesty compelled him to go on. 'At least you did. I got mixed up with myself in a corner.'

'I gave one of 'em what for,' said Ralph, 'I smashed him up all right. He won't want to come and fight us again in a hurry.'

'So did I,' said Eric. 'When I woke up one was kicking me in the face. I got an awful bloody face, I think, Ralph. But I did him in the end.'

'What did you do?'

'I got my knee up,' said Eric with simple pride, 'and I hit him with it in the pills. You should have heard him holler! He won't come back in a hurry either. So we didn't do too badly.'

Ralph moved suddenly in the dark; but then he heard Eric working at his mouth.

'What's the matter?'

'Jus' a tooth loose.'

Piggy drew up his legs.

'You all right, Piggy?'

'I thought they wanted the conch.'

Ralph trotted down the pale beach and jumped on to the platform. The conch still glimmered by the chief's seat. He gazed for a moment or two, then went back to Piggy.

'They didn't take the conch.'

'I know. They didn't come for the conch. They came for something else. Ralph—what am I going to do?'

Far off along the bowstave of beach, three figures trotted towards the Castle Rock. They kept away from the forest and down by the water. Occasionally they sang softly; occasionally they turned cartwheels down by the moving streak of phosphorescence. The Chief led them, trotting steadily, exulting in his achievement. He was a chief now in truth; and he made stabbing motions with his spear. From his left hand dangled Piggy's broken glasses.

CHAPTER ELEVEN

Castle Rock

In the short chill of dawn the four boys gathered round the black smudge where the fire had been, while Ralph knelt and blew. Grey, feathery ashes scurried hither and thither at his breath but no spark shone among them. The twins watched anxiously and Piggy sat expressionless behind the luminous wall of his myopia. Ralph continued to blow till his ears were singing with the effort, but then the first breeze of dawn took the job off his hands and blinded him with ashes. He squatted back, swore, and rubbed water out of his eyes.

'No use.'

Eric looked down at him through a mask of dried blood. Piggy peered in the general direction of Ralph.

''Course it's no use, Ralph. Now we got no fire.'

Ralph brought his face within a couple of feet of Piggy's.

'Can you see me?'

'A bit.'

Ralph allowed the swollen flap of his cheek to close his eye again.

'They've got our fire.'

Rage shrilled his voice.

'They stole it!'

'That's them,' said Piggy. 'They blinded me. See? That's Jack Merridew. You call an assembly, Ralph, we got to decide what to do.'

'An assembly for only us?'

'It's all we got. Sam—let me hold on to you.'

They went towards the platform.

'Blow the conch,' said Piggy. 'Blow as loud as you can.'

The forest re-echoed; and birds lifted, crying out of the tree-tops, as on that first morning ages ago. Both ways the beach was deserted. Some littluns came from the shelters. Ralph sat down on the polished trunk and the three others stood before him. He nodded, and Samneric sat down on the right. Ralph pushed the conch into Piggy's hands. He held the shining thing carefully and blinked at Ralph.

'Go on, then.'

'I just take the conch to say this. I can't see no more and I got to get my glasses back. Awful things has been done on this island. I voted for you for chief. He's the only one who ever got anything done. So now you speak, Ralph, and tell us what—Or else——'

Piggy broke off, snivelling. Ralph took back the conch as he sat down.

'Just an ordinary fire. You'd think we could do that, wouldn't you? Just a smoke signal so we can be rescued. Are we savages or what? Only now there's no signal going up. Ships may be passing. Do you remember how he went hunting and the fire went out and a ship passed by? And they all think he's best as Chief. Then there was, there was . . . that's his fault, too. If it hadn't been for him it would never have happened. Now Piggy can't see, and they came, stealing——' Ralph's voice ran up. '—at night, in darkness, and stole our fire. They stole it. We'd have given them fire if they'd asked. But they stole it and the signal's out and we can't ever be rescued. Don't you see what I mean? We'd have given them fire for themselves only they stole it. I——'

He paused lamely as the curtain flickered in his brain. Piggy held out his hands for the conch.

'What you goin' to do, Ralph? This is jus' talk without deciding. I want my glasses.'

'I'm trying to think. Supposing we go, looking like we used to, washed and hair brushed—after all we aren't savages really and being rescued isn't a game——'

He opened the flap of his cheek and looked at the twins.

'We could smarten up a bit and then go——'

'We ought to take spears,' said Sam. 'Even Piggy.'

'—because we may need them.'

'You haven't got the conch!'

Piggy held up the shell.

'You can take spears if you want but I shan't. What's the good? I'll have to be led like a dog, anyhow. Yes, laugh. Go on, laugh. There's them on this island as would laugh at anything. And what happened? What's grown-ups goin' to think? Young Simon was murdered. And there was that other kid what had a mark on his face. Who's seen him since we first come here?'

'Piggy! Stop a minute!'

'I got the conch. I'm going to that Jack Merridew an' tell him, I am.'

'You'll get hurt.'

'What can he do more than he has? I'll tell him what's what. You let me carry the conch, Ralph. I'll show him the one thing he hasn't got.'

Piggy paused for a moment and peered round at the dim figures. The shape of the old assembly, trodden in the grass, listened to him.

'I'm going to him with this conch in my hands. I'm going to hold it out. Look, I'm goin' to say, you're stronger than I am and you haven't got asthma. You can see, I'm goin' to say, and with both eyes. But I don't ask for my glasses back, not as a favour. I don't ask you to be a sport, I'll say, not because you're strong, but because what's right's right. Give me my glasses, I'm going to say—you got to!'

Piggy ended, flushed and trembling. He pushed the conch quickly into Ralph's hands as though in a hurry to be rid of it and wiped the tears from his eyes. The green light was gentle about them and the conch lay at Ralph's feet, fragile and white. A single drop of water that had escaped Piggy's fingers now flashed on the delicate curve like a star.

At last Ralph sat up straight and drew back his hair.

'All right. I mean—you can try if you like. We'll go with you.'

'He'll be painted,' said Sam, timidly. 'You know how he'll be——'

'—he won't think much of us——'

'—if he gets waxy we've had it——'

Ralph scowled at Sam. Dimly he remembered something that Simon had said to him once, by the rocks.

'Don't be silly,' he said. And then he added quickly, 'Let's go.'

He held out the conch to Piggy who flushed, this time with pride.

'You must carry it.'

'When we're ready I'll carry it——'

Piggy sought in his mind for words to convey his passionate willingness to carry the conch against all odds.

'—I don't mind. I'll be glad, Ralph, only I'll have to be led.'

Ralph put the conch back on the shining log.

'We better eat and then get ready.'

They made their way to the devastated fruit trees. Piggy was helped to his food and found some by touch. While they ate, Ralph thought of the afternoon.

'We'll be like we were. We'll wash———'

Sam gulped down a mouthful and protested.

'But we bathe every day!'

Ralph looked at the filthy objects before him and sighed.

'We ought to comb our hair. Only it's too long.'

'I've got both socks left in the shelter,' said Eric, 'so we could pull them over our heads like caps, sort of.'

'We could find some stuff,' said Piggy, 'and tie your hair back.'

'Like a girl!'

'No. 'Course not.'

'Then we must go as we are,' said Ralph, 'and they won't be any better.'

Eric made a detaining gesture.

'But they'll be painted! You know how it is———'

The others nodded. They understood only too well the liberation into savagery that the concealing paint brought.

'Well, we won't be painted,' said Ralph, 'because we aren't savages.'

Samneric looked at each other.

'All the same———'

Ralph shouted.

'No paint!'

He tried to remember.

'Smoke,' he said, 'we want smoke.'

He turned on the twins fiercely.

'I said "smoke"! We've got to have smoke.'

There was silence, except for the multitudinous murmur of the bees. At last Piggy spoke, kindly.

''Course we have, 'Cos the smoke's a signal and we can't be rescued if we don't have smoke.'

'I knew that!' shouted Ralph. He pulled his arm away from Piggy. 'Are you suggesting———'

'I'm jus' saying what you always say,' said Piggy hastily. 'I'd thought for a moment———'

'I hadn't,' said Ralph loudly. 'I knew it all the time. I hadn't forgotten.'

Piggy nodded propitiatingly.

'You're Chief, Ralph. You remember everything.'

'I hadn't forgotten.'

''Course not.'

The twins were examining Ralph curiously, as though they were seeing him for the first time.

They set off along the beach in formation. Ralph went first, limping a little, his spear carried over one shoulder. He saw things partially through the tremble of the heat haze over the flashing sands, and his own long hair and injuries. Behind him came the twins, worried now for a while but full of unquenchable vitality. They said little but trailed the butts of their wooden spears; for Piggy had found, that looking down, shielding his tired sight from the sun, he could just see these moving along the sand. He walked between the trailing butts, therefore, the conch held carefully between his two hands. The boys made a compact little group that moved over the beach, four plate-like shadows dancing and mingling beneath them. There was no sign left of the storm, and the beach was swept clean like a blade that has been scoured. The sky and the mountain were at an immense distance, shimmering in the heat; and the reef was lifted by mirage, floating in a kind of silver pool half-way up the sky.

They passed the place where the tribe had danced. The charred sticks still lay on the rocks where the rain had quenched them but the sand by the water was smooth again. They passed this in silence. No one doubted that the tribe would be found at the Castle Rock and when they came in sight of it they stopped with one accord. The densest tangle on the island, a mass of twisted stems, black and green and impenetrable, lay on their left and tall grass swayed before them. Now Ralph went forward.

Here was the crushed grass where they had all lain when he had gone to prospect. There was the neck of land, the ledge skirting the rock, up there were the red pinnacles.

Sam touched his arm.

'Smoke.'

There was a tiny smudge of smoke wavering into the air on the other side of the rock.

'Some fire—I don't think.'

Ralph turned.

'What are we hiding for?'

He stepped through the screen of grass on to the little open space that led to the narrow neck.

'You two follow behind. I'll go first, then Piggy a pace behind me. Keep your spears ready.'

Piggy peered anxiously into the luminous veil that hung between him and the world.

'Is it safe? Ain't there a cliff? I can hear the sea.'

'You keep right close to me.'

Ralph moved forward on to the neck. He kicked a stone and it bounded into the water. Then the sea sucked down, revealing a red, weedy square forty feet beneath Ralph's left arm.

'Am I safe?' quavered Piggy. 'I feel awful——'

High above them from the pinnacles came a sudden shout and then an imitation war-cry that was answered by a dozen voices from behind the rock.

'Give me the conch and stay still.'

'Halt! Who goes there?'

Ralph bent back his head and glimpsed Roger's dark face at the top.

'You can see who I am!' he shouted. 'Stop being silly!'

He put the conch to his lips and began to blow. Savages appeared, painted out of recognition, edging round the ledge towards the neck. They carried spears and disposed themselves to defend the entrance. Ralph went on blowing and ignored Piggy's terrors.

Roger was shouting.

'You mind out—see?'

At length Ralph took his lips away and paused to get his breath back. His first words were a gasp, but audible.

'—calling an assembly.'

The savages guarding the neck muttered among themselves but made no motion. Ralph walked forwards a couple of steps. A voice whispered urgently behind him.

'Don't leave me, Ralph.'

'You kneel down,' said Ralph sideways, 'and wait till I come back.'

He stood half-way along the neck and gazed at the savages intently. Freed by the paint, they had tied their hair back and were more comfortable than he was. Ralph made a resolution to tie his own back afterwards. Indeed he felt like telling them to wait and doing it there and then; but that was impossible. The savages sniggered a bit and one gestured at Ralph with his spear. High above, Roger took his hands off the lever and leaned out to see what was going on. The boys on the neck stood in a pool of their own shadow, diminished to shaggy heads. Piggy crouched, his back shapeless as a sack.

'I'm calling an assembly.'

Silence.

Roger took up a small stone and flung it between the twins, aiming to miss. They started and Sam only just kept his footing. Some source of power began to pulse in Roger's body.

Ralph spoke again, loudly.

'I'm calling an assembly.'

He ran his eye over them.

'Where's Jack?'

The group of boys stirred and consulted. A painted face spoke with the voice of Robert.

'He's hunting. And he said we weren't to let you in.'

'I've come to see you about the fire,' said Ralph, 'and about Piggy's specs.'

The group in front of him shifted and laughter shivered outwards from among them, light, excited laughter that went echoing among the tall rocks.

A voice spoke from behind Ralph.

'What do you want?'

The twins made a bolt past Ralph and got between him and the entry. He turned quickly. Jack, identifiable by personality and red hair, was advancing from the forest. A hunter crouched on either side. All three were masked in black and green. Behind them on the grass the headless and paunched body of a sow lay where they had dropped it.

Piggy wailed.

'Ralph! Don't leave me!'

With ludicrous care he embraced the rock, pressing himself to it above the sucking sea. The sniggering of the savages became a loud derisive jeer.

Jack shouted above the noise.

'You go away, Ralph. You keep to your end. This is my end and my tribe. You leave me alone.'

The jeering died away.

'You pinched Piggy's specs,' said Ralph, breathlessly. 'You've got to give them back.'

'Got to? Who says?'

Ralph's temper blazed out.

'I say! You voted for me for Chief. Didn't you hear the conch? You played a dirty trick—we'd have given you fire if you'd asked for it——'

The blood was flowing in his cheeks and the bunged-up eye throbbed.

'You could have had fire whenever you wanted. But you didn't. You came sneaking up like a thief and stole Piggy's glasses!'

'Say that again!'

'Thief! Thief!'

Piggy screamed.

'Ralph! Mind me!'

Jack made a rush and stabbed at Ralph's chest with his spear. Ralph sensed the position of the weapon from the glimpse he caught of Jack's arm and put the thrust aside with his own butt. Then he brought the end round and caught Jack a stinger across the ear. They were chest to chest, breathing fiercely, pushing and glaring.

'Who's a thief?'

'You are!'

Jack wrenched free and swung at Ralph with his spear. By common consent they were using the spears as sabres now, no longer daring the lethal points. The blow struck Ralph's spear and slid down, to fall agonizingly on his fingers. Then they were apart once more, their positions reversed, Jack towards the Castle Rock and Ralph on the outside towards the island.

Both boys were breathing very heavily.

'Come on then——'

'Come on——'

Truculently they squared up to each other but kept just out of fighting distance.

'You come and see what you get!'

'You come on——'

Piggy clutching the ground was trying to attract Ralph's attention. Ralph moved, bent down, kept a wary eye on Jack.

'Ralph—remember what we came for. The fire. My specs.'

Raph nodded. He relaxed his fighting muscles, stood easily and grounded the butt of his spear. Jack watched him inscrutably through his paint. Ralph glanced up at the pinnacles, then towards the group of savages.

'Listen. We've come to say this. First you've got to give back

Piggy's specs. If he hasn't got them he can't see. You aren't
playing the game——'

The tribe of painted savages giggled and Ralph's mind faltered.
He pushed his hair up and gazed at the green and black mask
before him, trying to remember what Jack looked like.

Piggy whispered.

'And the fire.'

'Oh yes. Then about the fire. I say this again. I've been saying
it ever since we dropped in.'

He held out his spear and pointed at the savages.

'Your only hope is keeping a signal fire going as long as there's
light to see. Then maybe a ship 'll notice the smoke and come and
rescue us and take us home. But without that smoke we've got to
wait till some ship comes by accident. We might wait years; till
we were old——'

The shivering, silvery, unreal laughter of the savages sprayed
out and echoed away. A gust of rage shook Ralph. His voice
cracked.

'Don't you understand, you painted fools? Sam, Eric, Piggy
and me—we aren't enough. We tried to keep the fire going, but
we couldn't. And then you, playing at hunting. . . .'

He pointed past them to where the trickle of smoke dispersed
in the pearly air.

'Look at that! Call that a signal fire? That's a cooking fire.
Now you'll eat and there'll be no smoke. Don't you understand?
There may be a ship out there——'

He paused, defeated by the silence and the painted anonymity
of the group guarding the entry. The chief opened a pink mouth
and addressed Samneric who were between him and his tribe.

'You two. Get back.'

No one answered him. The twins, puzzled, looked at each
other; while Piggy, reassured by the cessation of violence, stood
up carefully. Jack glanced back at Ralph and then at the twins.

'Grab them!'

No one moved. Jack shouted angrily.

'I said "grab them"!'

The painted group moved round Samneric nervously and unhandily. Once more the silvery laughter scattered.

Samneric protested out of the heart of civilization.

'Oh, I say!'

'—honestly!'

Their spears were taken from them.

'Tie them up!'

Ralph cried out hopelessly against the black and green mask.

'Jack!'

'Go on. Tie them.'

Now the painted group felt the otherness of Samneric, felt the power in their own hands. They felled the twins clumsily and excitedly. Jack was inspired. He knew that Ralph would attempt a rescue. He struck in a humming circle behind him and Ralph only just parried the blow. Beyond them the tribe and the twins were a loud and writhing heap. Piggy crouched again. Then the twins lay, astonished, and the tribe stood round them. Jack turned to Ralph and spoke between his teeth.

'See? They do what I want.'

There was silence again. The twins lay, inexpertly tied up, and the tribe watched Ralph to see what he would do. He numbered them through his fringe, glimpsed the ineffectual smoke.

His temper broke. He screamed at Jack.

'You're a beast and a swine and bloody, bloody thief!'

He charged.

Jack, knowing this was the crisis, charged too. They met with a jolt and bounced apart. Jack swung with his fist at Ralph and caught him on the ear. Ralph hit Jack in the stomach and made him grunt. Then they were facing each other again, panting and furious, but unnerved by each other's ferocity. They became aware of the noise that was the background to this fight, the steady shrill cheering of the tribe behind them.

Piggy's voice penetrated to Ralph.

'Let me speak.'

He was standing in the dust of the fight, and as the tribe saw his intention the shrill cheer changed to a steady booing.

Piggy held up the conch and the booing sagged a little, then came up again to strength.

'I got the conch!'

He shouted.

'I tell you, I got the conch!'

Surprisingly, there was silence now; the tribe were curious to hear what amusing thing he might have to say.

Silence and pause; but in the silence a curious air-noise, close by Ralph's head. He gave it half his attention—and there it was again; a faint 'Zup!' Someone was throwing stones: Roger was dropping them, his one hand still on the lever. Below him, Ralph was a shock of hair and Piggy a bag of fat.

'I got this to say. You're acting like a crowd of kids.'

The booing rose and died again as Piggy lifted the white, magic shell.

'Which is better—to be a pack of painted niggers like you are, or to be sensible like Ralph is?'

A great clamour rose among the savages. Piggy shouted again.

'Which is better—to have rules and agree, or to hunt and kill?'

Again the clamour and again—'Zup!'

Ralph shouted against the noise.

'Which is better, law and rescue, or hunting and breaking things up?'

Now Jack was yelling too and Ralph could no longer make himself heard. Jack had backed right against the tribe and they were a solid mass of menace that bristled with spears. The intention of a charge was forming among them; they were working up to it and the neck would be swept clear. Ralph stood facing them, a little to one side, his spear ready. By him stood Piggy still holding out the talisman, the fragile, shining beauty of the shell. The storm of sound beat at them, an incantation of hatred. High overhead, Roger, with a sense of delirious abandonment, leaned all his weight on the lever.

Ralph heard the great rock long before he saw it. He was aware of a jolt in the earth that came to him through the soles of his feet, and the breaking sound of stones at the top of the cliff. Then the monstrous red thing bounded across the neck and he flung himself flat while the tribe shrieked.

The rock struck Piggy a glancing blow from chin to knee; the conch exploded into a thousand white fragments and ceased to exist. Piggy, saying nothing, with no time for even a grunt, travelled through the air sideways from the rock, turning over as he went. The rock bounded twice and was lost in the forest. Piggy fell forty feet and landed on his back across that square, red rock in the sea. His head opened and stuff came out and turned red. Piggy's arms and legs twitched a bit, like a pig's after it has been killed. Then the sea breathed again in a long slow sigh, the water boiled white and pink over the rock; and when it went, sucking back again, the body of Piggy was gone.

This time the silence was complete. Ralph's lips formed a word but no sound came.

Suddenly Jack bounded out from the tribe and began screaming wildly.

'See? See? That's what you'll get! I meant that! There isn't a
tribe for you any more! The conch is gone——'

He ran forward, stooping.

'I'm Chief!'

Viciously, with full intention, he hurled his spear at Ralph.
The point tore the skin and flesh over Ralph's ribs, then
sheared off and fell in the water. Ralph stumbled, feeling not pain
but panic, and the tribe, screaming now like the Chief, began
to advance. Another spear, a bent one that would not fly
straight, went past his face and one fell from on high where
Roger was. The twins lay hidden behind the tribe and the
anonymous devils' faces swarmed across the neck. Ralph turned
and ran. A great noise as of sea-gulls rose behind him. He
obeyed an instinct that he did not know he possessed and
swerved over the open space so that the spears went wide. He
saw the headless body of the sow and jumped in time. Then he
was crashing through foliage and small boughs and was hidden
by the forest.

The Chief stopped by the pig, turned and held up his hands.

'Back! Back to the fort!'

Presently the tribe returned noisily to the neck where Roger
joined them.

The Chief spoke to him angrily.

'Why aren't you on watch?'

Roger looked at him gravely.

'I just came down——'

The hangman's horror clung round him. The Chief said no
more to him but he looked down at Samneric.

'You got to join the tribe.'

'You lemme go——'

'—and me.'

The Chief snatched one of the few spears that were left and
poked Sam in the ribs.

'What d'you mean by it, eh?' said the Chief fiercely. 'What
d'you mean by coming with spears? What d'you mean by not
joining my tribe?'

The prodding became rhythmic. Sam yelled.

'That's not the way.'

Roger edged past the Chief, only just avoiding pushing him with his shoulder. The yelling ceased, and Samneric lay looking up in quiet terror. Roger advanced upon them as one wielding a nameless authority.

CHAPTER TWELVE

Cry of the Hunters

Ralph lay in a covert, wondering about his wounds. The bruised flesh was inches in diameter over his right ribs, with a swollen and bloody scar where the spear had hit him. His hair was full of dirt and tapped like the tendril's of a creeper. All over he was scratched and bruised from his flight through the forest. By the time his breathing was normal again, he had worked out that bathing these injuries would have to wait. How could you listen for naked feet if you were splashing in water? How could you be safe by the little stream or on the open beach?

Ralph listened. He was not really far from the Castle Rock, and during the first panic he had thought he heard sounds of pursuit. But the hunters had only sneaked into the fringes of the greenery, retrieving spears perhaps, and then had rushed back to the sunny rock as if terrified of the darkness under the leaves. He had even glimpsed one of them, striped brown, black, and red, and had judged that it was Bill. But really, thought Ralph, this was not Bill. This was a savage whose image refused to blend with that ancient picture of a boy in shorts and shirt.

The afternoon died away; the circular spots of sunlight moved steadily over green fronds and brown fibre but no sound came from behind the Rock. At last Ralph wormed out of the ferns and sneaked forward to the edge of that impenetrable thicket that fronted the neck of land. He peered with elaborate caution between branches at the edge and could see Robert sitting on guard at the top of the cliff. He held a spear in his left hand and was tossing up a pebble and catching it again with the right. Behind him a column of smoke rose thickly, so that Ralph's nostrils flared and his mouth dribbled. He wiped his nose and mouth with the back of his hand and for the first time since the morning felt hungry. The tribe must be sitting round the gutted pig, watching the fat ooze and burn among the ashes. They would be intent.

Another figure, an unrecognizable one, appeared by Robert

and gave him something, then turned and went back behind the
rock. Robert laid his spear on the rock beside him and began to
gnaw between his raised hands. So the feast was beginning and
the watchman had been given his portion.

Ralph saw that for the time being he was safe. He limped away
through the fruit trees, drawn by the thought of the poor food
yet bitter when he remembered the feast. Feast today, and then
tomorrow. . . .

He argued unconvincingly that they would let him alone; perhaps even make an outlaw of him. But then the fatal unreasoning
knowledge came to him again. The breaking of the conch and the
deaths of Piggy and Simon lay over the island like a vapour.
These painted savages would go further and further. Then there
was that indefinable connection between himself and Jack; who
therefore would never let him alone; never.

He paused, sun-flecked, holding up a bough, prepared to duck
under it. A spasm of terror set him shaking and he cried aloud.

'No. They're not as bad as that. It was an accident.'

He ducked under the bough, ran clumsily, then stopped and
listened.

He came to the smashed acres of fruit and ate greedily. He saw
two littluns and, not having any idea of his own appearance,
wondered why they screamed and ran.

When he had eaten he went towards the beach. The sunlight
was slanting now into the palms by the wrecked shelter. There
was the platform and the pool. The best thing to do was to
ignore this leaden feeling about the heart and rely on their
common sense, their daylight sanity. Now that the tribe had
eaten, the thing to do was to try again. And anyway, he couldn't
stay here all night in an empty shelter by the deserted platform.
His flesh crept and he shivered in the evening sun. No fire; no
smoke; no rescue. He turned and limped away through the forest
towards Jack's end of the island.

The slanting sticks of sunlight were lost among the branches.
At length he came to a clearing in the forest where rock prevented
vegetation from growing. Now it was a pool of shadows and
Ralph nearly flung himself behind a tree when he saw something
standing in the centre; but then he saw that the white face was
bone and that the pig's skull grinned at him from the top of a
stick. He walked slowly into the middle of the clearing and looked
steadily at the skull that gleamed as white as ever the conch had

done and seemed to jeer at him cynically. An inquisitive ant was busy in one of the eye sockets but otherwise the thing was life-less.

Or was it?

Little prickles of sensation ran up and down his back. He stood, the skull about on a level with his face, and held up his hair with two hands. The teeth grinned, the empty sockets seemed to hold his gaze masterfully and without effort.

What was it?

The skull regarded Ralph like one who knows all the answers and won't tell. A sick fear and rage swept him. Fiercely he hit out at the filthy thing in front of him that bobbed like a toy and came back, still grinning into his face, so that he lashed and cried out in loathing. Then he was licking his bruised knuckles and looking at the bare stick, while the skull lay in two pieces, its grin now six feet across. He wrenched the quivering stick from the crack and held it as a spear between him and the white pieces. Then he backed away, keeping his face to the skull that lay grinning at the sky.

When the green glow had gone from the horizon and night was fully accomplished, Ralph came again to the thicket in front of Castle Rock. Peeping through, he could see that the height was still occupied, and whoever it was up there had a spear at the ready.

He knelt among the shadows and felt his isolation bitterly. They were savages it was true; but they were human, and the ambushing fears of the deep night were coming in.

Ralph moaned faintly. Tired though he was, he could not relax and fall into a well of sleep for fear of the tribe. Might it not be possible to walk boldly into the fort, say—'I've got pax,' laugh lightly and sleep among the others? Pretend they were still boys, schoolboys who had said 'Sir, yes, Sir'—and worn caps? Daylight might have answered yes; but darkness and the horrors of death said no. Lying there in the darkness, he knew he was an outcast. ''Cos I had some sense.'

He rubbed his cheek along his forearm, smelling the acrid scent of salt and sweat and the staleness of dirt. Over to the left, the waves of ocean were breathing, sucking down, then boiling back over the rock.

There were sounds coming from behind the Castle Rock. Lis-tening carefully, detaching his mind from the swing of the sea, Ralph could make out a familiar rhythm.

'Kill the beast! Cut his throat! Spill his blood!'

The tribe was dancing. Somewhere on the other side of this rocky wall there would be a dark circle, a glowing fire, and meat. They would be savouring food and the comfort of safety.

A noise nearer at hand made him quiver. Savages were clambering up the Castle Rock, right up to the top, and he could hear voices. He sneaked forward a few yards and saw the shape at the top of the rock change and enlarge. There were only two boys on the island who moved or talked like that.

Ralph put his head down on his forearms and accepted this new fact like a wound. Samneric were part of the tribe now. They were guarding the Castle Rock against him. There was no chance of rescuing them and building up an outlaw tribe at the other end of the island. Samneric were savages like the rest; Piggy was dead, and the conch smashed to powder.

At length the guard climbed down. The two that remained seemed nothing more than a dark extension of the rock. A star appeared behind them and was momentarily eclipsed by some movement.

Ralph edged forward, feeling his way over the uneven surface as though he were blind. There were miles of vague water at his right and the restless ocean lay under his left hand, as awful as the shaft of a pit. Every minute the water breathed round the death rock and flowered into a field of whiteness. Ralph crawled until he found the ledge of the entry in his grasp. The lookouts were immediately above him and he could see the end of a spear projecting over the rock.

He called very gently.

'Samneric——'

There was no reply. To carry he must speak louder; and this would rouse those striped and inimical creatures from their feasting by the fire. He set his teeth and started to climb, finding the holds by touch. The stick that had supported a skull hampered him but he would not be parted from his only weapon. He was nearly level with the twins before he spoke again.

'Samneric——'

He heard a cry and a flurry from the rock. The twins had grabbed each other and were gibbering.

'It's me. Ralph.'

Terrified that they would run and give the alarm, he hauled himself up until his head and shoulders stuck over the top. Far below his armpit he saw the luminous flowering round the rock.

'It's only me. Ralph.'

At length they bent forward and peered in his face.

'We thought it was——'

'—we didn't know what it was——'

'—we thought——'

Memory of their new and shameful loyalty came to them. Eric was silent but Sam tried to do his duty.

'You got to go, Ralph. You go away now——'

He wagged his spear and essayed fierceness.

'You shove off. See?'

Eric nodded agreement and jabbed his spear in the air. Ralph leaned on his arms and did not go.

'I came to see you two.'

His voice was thick. His throat was hurting him now though it had received no wound.

'I came to see you two——'

Words could not express the dull pain of these things. He fell silent, while the vivid stars were spilt and danced all ways.

Sam shifted uneasily.

'Honest, Ralph, you'd better go.'

Ralph looked up again.

'You two aren't painted. How can you—? If it were light——'

If it were light shame would burn them at admitting these things. But the night was dark. Eric took up; and then the twins started their antiphonal speech.

'You got to go because it's not safe——'

'—they made us. They hurt us——'

'Who? Jack?'

'Oh no——'

They bent to him and lowered their voices.

'Push off, Ralph——'

'it's a tribe——'

'—they made us——'

'—we couldn't help it——'

When Ralph spoke again his voice was low, and seemed breathless.

'What have I done? I liked him—and I wanted us to be rescued——'

Again the stars spilled about the sky. Eric shook his head, earnestly.

'Listen, Ralph. Never mind what's sense. That's gone———'

'Never mind about the Chief———'

'———you got to go for your own good.'

'The Chief and Roger———'

'———yes, Roger———'

'They hate you, Ralph. They're going to do you.'

'They're going to hunt you tomorrow.'

'But why?'

'I dunno. And Ralph, Jack, the Chief, says it'll be dangerous———'

'———and we've got to be careful and throw our spears like at a
pig.'

'We're going to spread out in a line across the island———'

'we're going forward from this end———'

'until we find you.'

'We've got to give signals like this.'

Eric raised his head and achieved a faint ululation by beating
on his open mouth. Then he glanced behind him nervously.

'Like that———'

'———only louder, of course.'

'But I've done nothing,' whispered Ralph, urgently. 'I only
wanted to keep up a fire!'

He paused for a moment, thinking miserably of the morrow. A
matter of overwhelming importance occurred to him.

'What are you———?'

He could not bring himself to be specific at first; but then fear
and loneliness goaded him.

'When they find me, what are they going to do?'

The twins were silent. Beneath him, the death rock flowered
again.

'What are they—oh God! I'm hungry———'

The towering rock seemed to sway under him.

'Well—what———?'

The twins answered his question indirectly.

'You got to go now, Ralph.'

'For your own good.'

'Keep away. As far as you can.'

'Won't you come with me? Three of us—we'd stand a chance.'

After a moment's silence, Sam spoke in a strangled voice.

'You don't know Roger. He's a terror.'

'———And the Chief—they're both———'

'—terrors——'

'—only Roger——'

Both boys froze. Someone was climbing towards them from the tribe.

'He's coming to see if we're keeping watch. Quick, Ralph!'

As he prepared to let himself down the cliff, Ralph snatched at the last possible advantage to be wrung out of this meeting.

'I'll lie up close; in that thicket down there,' he whispered, 'so keep them away from it. They'll never think to look so close——'

The footsteps were still some distance away.

'Sam—I'm going to be all right, aren't I?'

The twins were silent again.

'Here!' said Sam suddenly. 'Take this——'

Ralph felt a chunk of meat pushed against him and grabbed it.

'But what are you going to do when you catch me?'

Silence above. He sounded silly to himself. He lowered himself down the rock.

'What are you going to do——?'

From the top of the towering rock came the incomprehensible reply.

'Roger sharpened a stick at both ends.'

Roger sharpened a stick at both ends. Ralph tried to attach a meaning to this but could not. He used all the bad words he could think of in a fit of temper that passed into yawning. How long could you go without sleep? He yearned for a bed and sheets—but the only whiteness here was the slow spilt milk, luminous round the rock forty feet below, where Piggy had fallen. Piggy was everywhere, was on his neck, was become terrible in darkness and death. If Piggy were to come back now out of the water, with his empty head—Ralph whimpered and yawned like a littlun. The stick in his hand became a crutch on which he reeled.

Then he tensed again. There were voices raised on the top of the Castle Rock. Samneric were arguing with someone. But the ferns and the grass were near. That was the place to be in, hidden, and next to the thicket that would serve for tomorrow's hideout. Here—and his hands touched grass—was a place to be in for the night, not far from the tribe, so that if the horrors of the supernatural emerged one could at least mix with humans for the time being, even if it meant . . .

What did it mean? A stick sharpened at both ends. What was
there in that? They had thrown spears and missed; all but one.
Perhaps they would miss next time, too.

He squatted down in the tall grass, remembered the meat that
Sam had given him, and began to tear at it ravenously. While he
was eating, he heard fresh noises—cries of pain from Samneric,
cries of panic, angry voices. What did it mean? Someone besides
himself was in trouble for at least one of the twins was catching
it. Then the voices passed away down the rock and he ceased to
think of them. He felt with his hands and found cool, delicate
fronds backed against the thicket. Here then was the night's lair.
At first light he would creep into the thicket, squeeze between
the twisted stems, ensconce himself so deep so that only a crawler
like himself could come through; and that crawler would be
jabbed. There he would sit, and the search would pass him by,
and the cordon waver on, ululating along the island, and he
would be free.

He pulled himself between the ferns, tunnelling in. He laid the
stick beside him, and huddled himself down in the blackness.
One must remember to wake at first light, in order to diddle the
savages—and he did not know how quickly sleep came and hurled
him down a dark interior slope.

He was awake before his eyes were open, listening to a noise
that was near. He opened an eye, found the mould an inch or so
from his face and his fingers gripped into it, light filtering between
the fronds of fern. He had just time to realize that the age-long
nightmares of falling and death were past and that the morning
was come, when he heard the sound again. It was an ululation
over by the seashore—and now the next savage answered and the
next. The cry swept by him across the narrow end of the island
from sea to lagoon, like the cry of a flying bird. He took no time
to consider but grabbed his sharp stick and wriggled back among
the ferns. Within seconds he was worming his way into the
thicket; but not before he had glimpsed the legs of a savage
coming towards him. The ferns were thumped and beaten and he
heard legs moving in the long grass. The savage, whoever he
was, ululated twice; and the cry was repeated in both directions,
then died away. Ralph crouched still, tangled in the mid-brake,
and for a time he heard nothing.

At last he examined the brake itself. Certainly no one could attack him here—and moreover he had a stroke of luck. The great rock that had killed Piggy had bounded into this thicket and bounced there, right in the centre, making a smashed space a few feet in extent each way. When Ralph had wriggled into this he felt secure, and clever. He sat down carefully among the smashed stems and waited for the hunt to pass. Looking up between the leaves he caught a glimpse of something red. That must be the top of the Castle Rock, distant and unmenacing. He composed himself triumphantly, to hear the sounds of the hunt dying away.

Yet no one made a sound; and as the minutes passed, in the green shade, his feeling of triumph faded.

At last he heard a voice—Jack's voice, but hushed.

'Are you certain?'

The savage addressed said nothing. Perhaps he made a gesture.

Roger spoke.

'If you're fooling us——'

Immediately after this, there came a gasp, and a squeal of pain. Ralph crouched instinctively. One of the twins was there, outside the thicket, with Jack and Roger.

'You're sure he meant in there?'

The twin moaned faintly and then squealed again.

'He meant he'd hide in there?'

'Yes—yes—oh——!'

Silvery laughter scattered among the trees.

So they knew.

Ralph picked up his stick and prepared for battle. But what could they do? It would take them a week to break a path through the thicket; and anyone who wormed his way in would be help-less. He felt the point of his spear with his thumb and grinned without amusement. Whoever tried that would be stuck, squeal-ing like a pig.

They were going away, back to the tower rock. He could hear feet moving and then someone sniggered. There came again that high, bird-like cry that swept along the line. So some were still watching for him; but some——?

There was a long, breathless silence. Ralph found that he had bark in his mouth from the gnawed spear. He stood and peered upwards to the Castle Rock.

As he did so, he heard Jack's voice from the top.

'Heave! Heave! Heave!'

The red rock that he could see at the top of the cliff vanished like a curtain, and he could see figures and blue sky. A moment later the earth jolted, there was a rushing sound in the air, and the top of the thicket was cuffed as with a gigantic hand. The rock bounded on, thumping and smashing towards the beach, while a shower of broken twigs and leaves fell on him. Beyond the thicket, the tribe was cheering.

Silence again.

Ralph put his fingers in his mouth and bit them. There was only one other rock up there that they might conceivably move; but that was half as big as a cottage, big as a car, a tank. He visualized its probable progress with agonizing clearness—that one would start slowly, drop from lodge to ledge, trundle across the neck like an outsize steam-roller.

'Heave! Heave! Heave!'

Ralph put down his spear, then picked it up again. He pushed his hair back irritably, took two hasty steps across the little space and then came back. He stood looking at the broken ends of branches.

Still silence.

He caught sight of the rise and fall of his diaphragm and was surprised to see how quickly he was breathing. Just left of centre, his heart-beats were visible. He put the spear down again.

'Heave! Heave! Heave!'

A shrill, prolonged cheer.

Something boomed up on the red rock, then the earth jumped and began to shake steadily, while the noise as steadily increased. Ralph was shot into the air, thrown down, dashed against branches. At his right hand, and only a few feet away, the whole thicket bent and the roots screamed as they came out of the earth together. He saw something red that turned over slowly as a mill-wheel. Then the red thing was past and the elephantine progress diminished towards the sea.

Ralph knelt on the ploughed-up soil, and waited for the earth to come back. Presently the white, broken stumps, the split sticks and the tangle of the thicket refocused. There was a kind of heavy feeling in his body where he had watched his own pulse.

Silence again.

Yet not entirely so. They were whispering out there; and suddenly the branches were shaken furiously at two places on his right. The pointed end of a stick appeared. In panic, Ralph thrust his own stick through the crack and struck with all his might.

'Aaa-ah!'

His spear twisted a little in his hands and then he withdrew it again.

'Ooh-ooh——'

Someone was moaning outside and a babble of voices rose. A fierce argument was going on and the wounded savage kept groaning. Then when there was silence, a single voice spoke and Ralph decided that it was not Jack's.

'See? I told you—he's dangerous.'

The wounded savage moaned again.

What else? What next?

Ralph fastened his hands round the chewed spear and his hair fell. Someone was muttering, only a few yards away towards the Castle Rock. He heard a savage say 'No!' in a shocked voice; and then there was suppressed laughter. He squatted back on his heels and showed his teeth at the wall of branches. He raised his spear, snarled a little, and waited.

Once more the invisible group sniggered. He heard a curious trickling sound and then a louder crepitation as if someone were unwrapping great sheets of cellophane. A stick snapped and he stifled a cough. Smoke was seeping through the branches in white and yellow wisps, the patch of blue sky over head turned to the colour of a storm cloud, and then the smoke billowed round him.

Someone laughed excitedly, and a voice shouted.

'Smoke!'

He wormed his way through the thicket towards the forest, keeping as far as possible beneath the smoke. Presently he saw open space, and the green leaves of the edge of the thicket. A smallish savage was standing between him and the rest of the forest, a savage striped red and white, and carrying a spear. He was coughing and smearing the paint about his eyes with the back of his hand as he tried to see through the increasing smoke. Ralph launched himself like a cat; stabbed, snarling, with the spear, and the savage doubled up. There was a shout from beyond the thicket and then Ralph was running with the swiftness of fear through the undergrowth. He came to a pig-run, followed it for perhaps a hundred yards, and then swerved off. Behind him the ululation swept across the island once more and a single voice shouted three times. He guessed that was the signal to advance and sped away again, till his chest was like fire. Then he flung himself down under a bush and waited for a moment till his breathing steadied. He passed his tongue tentatively over his teeth and lips and heard far off the ululation of the pursuers.

There were many things he could do. He could climb a tree— but that was putting all his eggs in one basket. If he were detected, they had nothing more difficult to do than wait.

If only one had time to think!

Another double cry at the same distance gave him a clue to their plan. Any savage baulked in the forest would utter the double shout and hold up the line till he was free again. That way they might hope to keep the cordon unbroken right across the island. Ralph thought of the boar that had broken through them with such ease. If necessary, when the chase came too close, he could charge the cordon while it was still thin, burst through, and run back. But run back where? The cordon would turn and sweep again. Sooner or later he would have to sleep or eat—and then he would awaken with hands clawing at him; and the hunt would become a running down.

What was to be done then? The tree? Burst the line like a boar? Either way the choice was terrible.

A single cry quickened his heart-beat and, leaping up, he dashed away towards the ocean side and the thick jungle till he was hung up among creepers; he stayed there for a moment with his calves quivering. If only one could have pax, a long pause, a time to think!

And there again, shrill and inevitable, was the ululation sweeping across the island. At that sound he shied like a horse among the creepers and ran once more till he was panting. He flung himself down by some ferns. The tree, or the charge? He mastered his breathing for a moment, wiped his mouth, and told himself to be calm. Samneric were somewhere in that line, and hating it. Or were they? And supposing, instead of them, he met the Chief, or Roger who carried death in his hands?

Ralph pushed back his tangled hair and wiped the sweat out of his best eye. He spoke aloud.

'Think.'

What was the sensible thing to do?

There was no Piggy to talk sense. There was no solemn assembly for debate nor dignity of the conch.

'Think.'

Most, he was beginning to dread the curtain that might waver in his brain, blacking out the sense of danger, making a simpleton of him.

A third idea would be to hide so well that the advancing line would pass without discovering him.

He jerked his head off the ground and listened. There was another noise to attend to now—a deep grumbling noise, as though the forest itself were angry with him, a sombre noise across which the ululations were scribbled excruciatingly as on slate. He knew he had heard it before somewhere, but had no time to remember.

Break the line.

A tree.

Hide, and let them pass.

A nearer cry stood him on his feet and immediately he was away again, running fast among thorns and brambles. Suddenly he blundered into the open, found himself again in that open space— and there was the fathom-wide grin of the skull, no longer ridiculing a deep blue patch of sky but jeering up into a blanket of smoke. Then Ralph was running beneath trees, with the grumble of the forest explained. They had smoked him out and set the island on fire.

Hide was better than a tree because you had a chance of breaking the line if you were discovered.

Hide, then.

He wondered if a pig would agree, and grimaced at nothing. Find the deepest thicket, the darkest hole on the island, and creep in. Now, as he ran, he peered about him. Bars and splashes of sunlight flitted over him and sweat made glistening streaks on his dirty body. The cries were far now, and faint.

At last he found what seemed to him the right place, though the decision was desperate. Here, bushes and a wild tangle of creeper made a mat that kept out all the light of the sun. Beneath it was a space, perhaps a foot high, though it was pierced everywhere by parallel and rising stems. If you wormed into the middle of that you would be five yards from the edge, and hidden, unless the savage chose to lie down and look for you; and even then, you would be in darkness—and if the worst happened and he saw you, then you had a chance to burst out at him, fling the whole line out of step and double back.

Cautiously, his stick trailing behind him, Ralph wormed between the rising stems. When he reached the middle of the mat he lay and listened.

The fire was a big one and the drum-roll that he had thought was left so far behind was nearer. Couldn't a fire out-run a gal-loping horse? He could see the sun-splashed ground over an area of perhaps fifty yards from where he lay: and as he watched, the sunlight in every patch blinked at him. This was so like the curtain that flapped in his brain that for a moment he thought the blinking was inside him. But then the patches blinked more rapidly, dulled and went out, so that he saw that a great heaviness of smoke lay between the island and the sun.

If anyone peered under the bushes and chanced to glimpse human flesh it might be Samneric who would pretend not to see and say nothing. He laid his cheek against the chocolate-coloured earth, licked his dry lips and closed his eyes. Under the thicket, the earth was vibrating very slightly; or perhaps there was a sound beneath the obvious thunder of the fire and scribbled ululations that was too low to hear.

Someone cried out. Ralph jerked his cheek off the earth and looked into the dulled light. They must be near now, he thought, and his chest began to thump. Hide, break the line, climb a tree—which was the best after all? The trouble was you only had one chance.

Now the fire was nearer; those volleying shots were great limbs, trunks even, bursting. The fools! The fools! The fire must be almost at the fruit trees—what would they eat tomorrow?

Ralph stirred restlessly in his narrow bed. One chanced nothing! What could they do? Beat him? So what? Kill him? A stick sharpened at both ends.

The cries, suddenly nearer, jerked him up. He could see a striped savage moving hastily out of a green tangle, and coming towards the mat where he hid, a savage who carried a spear. Ralph gripped his fingers into the earth. Be ready now, in case.

Ralph fumbled to hold his spear so that it was point foremost; and now he saw that the stick was sharpened at both ends.

The savage stopped fifteen yards away and uttered his cry.

Perhaps he can hear my heart over the noises of the fire. Don't scream. Get ready.

The savage moved forward so that you could only see him from the waist down. That was the butt of his spear. Now you could see him from the knee down. Don't scream.

A herd of pigs came squealing out of the greenery behind the savage and rushed away into the forest. Birds were screaming, mice shrieking, and a little hopping thing came under the mat and cowered.

Five yards away the savage stopped, standing right by the thicket, and cried out. Ralph drew his feet up and crouched. The stake was in his hands, the stake sharpened at both ends, the stake that vibrated so wildly, that grew long, short, light, heavy, light again.

The ululation spread from shore to shore. The savage knelt down by the edge of the thicket, and there were lights flickering in the forest behind him. You could see a knee disturb the mould. Now the other. Two hands. A spear.

A face.

The savage peered into the obscurity beneath the thicket. You could tell that he saw light on this side and on that, but not in the middle—there. In the middle was a blob of dark and the savage wrinkled up his face, trying to decipher the darkness.

The seconds lengthened. Ralph was looking straight into the savage's eyes.

Don't scream.

You'll get back.

Now he's seen you, he's making sure. A stick sharpened.

Ralph screamed, a scream of fright and anger and desperation. His legs straightened, the screams became continuous and foaming. He shot forward, burst the thicket, was in the open screaming, snarling, bloody. He swung the stake and the savage tumbled over; but there were others coming towards him, crying out. He swerved as a spear flew past and then was silent, running. All at once the lights flickering ahead of him merged together, the roar of the forest rose to thunder and a tall bush directly in his path burst into a great fan-shaped flame. He swung to the right, running desperately fast, with the heat beating on his left side and the fire racing forward like a tide. The ululation rose behind him and spread along, a series of short sharp cries, the sighting call. A brown figure showed up at his right and fell away. They were all running, all crying out madly. He could hear them crashing in the undergrowth and on the left was the hot, bright thunder of the fire. He forgot his wounds, his hunger and thirst, and became fear; hopeless fear on flying feet, rushing through the forest towards the open beach. Spots jumped before his eyes and turned into red circles that expanded quickly till they passed out of sight. Below him, someone's legs were getting tired and the desperate ululation advanced like a jagged fringe of menace and was almost overhead.

He stumbled over a root and the cry that pursued him rose even higher. He saw a shelter burst into flames and the fire flapped at his right shoulder and there was the glitter of water. Then he was down, rolling over and over in the warm sand, crouching with arm up to ward off, trying to cry for mercy.

He staggered to his feet, tensed for more terrors, and looked up at a huge peaked cap. It was a white-topped cap, and above the green shade of the peak was a crown, an anchor, gold foliage. He saw white drill, epaulettes, a revolver, a row of gilt buttons down the front of a uniform.

A naval officer stood on the sand, looking down at Ralph in wary astonishment. On the beach behind him was a cutter, her bows hauled up and held by two ratings. In the stern-sheets another rating held a sub-machine gun.

The ululation faltered and died away.

The officer looked at Ralph doubtfully for a moment, then took his hand away from the butt of the revolver.

'Hullo.'

Squirming a little, conscious of his filthy appearance, Ralph answered shyly.

'Hullo.'

The officer nodded, as if a question had been answered.

'Are there any adults—any grown-ups with you?'

Dumbly, Ralph shook his head. He turned a half-pace on the sand. A semicircle of little boys, their bodies streaked with coloured clay, sharp sticks in their hands, were standing on the beach making no noise at all.

'Fun and games,' said the officer.

The fire reached the coco-nut palms by the beach and swallowed them noisily. A flame, seemingly detached, swung like an acrobat and licked up the palm heads on the platform. The sky was black.

The officer grinned cheerfully at Ralph.

'We saw your smoke. What have you been doing? Having a war or something?'

Ralph nodded.

The officer inspected the little scarecrow in front of him. The kid needed a bath, a hair-cut, a nose-wipe, and a good deal of ointment.

'Nobody killed, I hope? Any dead bodies?'

'Only two. And they've gone.'

The officer leaned down and looked closely at Ralph.

'Two? Killed?'

Ralph nodded again. Behind him, the whole island was shuddering with flame. The officer knew, as a rule, when people were telling the truth. He whistled softly.

Other boys were appearing now, tiny tots some of them, brown, with the distended bellies of small savages. One of them came close to the officer and looked up.

'I'm, I'm——'

But there was no more to come. Percival Wemys Madison sought in his head for an incantation that had faded clean away.

The officer turned back to Ralph.

'We'll take you off. How many of you are there?'

Ralph shook his head. The officer looked past him to the group of painted boys.

'Who's boss here?'

'I am,' said Ralph loudly.

A little boy who wore the remains of an extraordinary black cap on his red hair and who carried the remains of a pair of spectacles at his waist, started forward, then changed his mind and stood still.

'We saw your smoke. And you don't know how many of you there are?'

'No, sir.'

'I should have thought,' said the officer as he visualized the search before him, 'I should have thought that a pack of British boys—you're all British aren't you?—would have been able to put up a better show than that—I mean——'

'It was like that at first,' said Ralph, 'before things——'

He stopped.

'We were together then——'

The officer nodded helpfully.

'I know. Jolly good show. Like the Coral Island.'

Ralph looked at him dumbly. For a moment he had a fleeting picture of the strange glamour that had once invested the beaches. But the island was scorched up like dead wood—Simon was dead—and Jack had. . . . The tears began to flow and sobs shook him. He gave himself up to them now for the first time on the island; great, shuddering spasms of grief that seemed to wrench his whole body. His voice rose under the black smoke before the burning wreckage of the island; and infected by that emotion, the other little boys began to shake and sob too. And in the middle of them, with filthy body, matted hair, and unwiped nose, Ralph wept for the end of innocence, the darkness of man's heart, and the fall through the air of the true, wise friend called Piggy.

The officer, surrounded by these noises, was moved and a little embarrassed. He turned away to give them time to pull themselves together; and waited, allowing his eyes to rest on the trim cruiser in the distance.

PINCHER
MARTIN

CHAPTER ONE

He was struggling in every direction, he was the centre of the writhing and kicking knot of his own body. There was no up or down, no light, and no air. He felt his mouth open of itself and the shrieked word burst out.

'Help!'

When the air had gone with the shriek, water came in to fill its place—burning water, hard in the throat and mouth as stones that hurt. He hutched his body towards the place where air had been but now it was gone and there was nothing but black, choking welter. His body let loose its panic and his mouth strained open till the hinges of his jaw hurt. Water thrust in, down, without mercy. Air came with it for a moment so that he fought in what might have been the right direction. But water reclaimed him and spun so that knowledge of where the air might be was erased completely. Turbines were screaming in his ears and green sparks flew out from the centre like tracer. There was a piston engine too, racing out of gear and making the whole universe shake. Then for a moment there was air like a cold mask against his face and he bit into it. Air and water mixed, dragged down into his body like gravel. Muscles, nerves, and blood, struggling lungs, a machine in the head, they worked for one moment in an ancient pattern. The lumps of hard water jerked on the gullet, the lips came together and parted, the tongue arched, the brain lit a neon track.

'Moth——'

But the man lay suspended behind the whole commotion, detached from his jerking body. The luminous pictures that were shuffled before him were drenched in light but he paid no attention to them. Could he have controlled the nerves of his face, or could a face have been fashioned to fit the attitude of his consciousness where it lay suspended between life and death that face would have worn a snarl. But the real jaw was contorted down and distant, the mouth was slopped full. The green tracer that flew from the centre began to spin into a disc. The throat at such

a distance from the snarling man vomited water and drew it in
again. The hard lumps of water no longer hurt. There was a kind
of truce, observation of the body. There was no face but there
was a snarl.

A picture steadied and the man regarded it. He had not seen
such a thing for so many years that the snarl became curious and
lost a little intensity. It examined the picture.

The jam jar was standing on a table, brightly lit from O.P. It
might have been a huge jar in the centre of a stage or a small one
almost touching the face, but it was interesting because one could
see into a little world there which was quite separate but which
one could control. The jar was nearly full of clear water and a
tiny glass figure floated upright in it. The top of the jar was
covered with a thin membrane—white rubber. He watched the
jar without moving or thinking while his distant body stilled
itself and relaxed. The pleasure of the jaw lay in the fact that the
little glass figure was so delicately balanced between opposing
forces. Lay a finger on the membrane and you would compress
the air below it which in turn would press more strongly on the
water. Then the water would force itself further up the little tube
in the figure, and it would begin to sink. By varying the pressure
on the membrane you could do anything you liked with the glass
figure which was wholly in your power. You could mutter—sink
now! And down it would go, down, down; you could steady it
and relent. You could let it struggle towards the surface, give it
almost a bit of air then send it steadily, slowly, remorselessly
down and down.

The delicate balance of the glass figure related itself to his
body. In a moment of wordless realization he saw himself touching the surface of the sea with just such a dangerous stability,
poised between floating and going down. The snarl thought
words to itself. They were not articulate, but they were there in a
luminous way as a realization.

Of course. My lifebelt.

It was bound by the tapes under that arm and that. The tapes
went over the shoulders—and now he could even feel them—
went round the chest and were fastened in front under the oilskin
and duffle. It was almost deflated as recommended by the
authorities because a tightly blown-up belt might burst when you
hit the water. Swim away from the ship then blow up your belt.

With the realization of the lifebelt a flood of connected images came back—the varnished board on which the instructions were displayed, pictures of the lifebelt itself with the tube and metal tit threaded through the tapes. Suddenly he knew who he was and where he was. He was lying suspended in the water like the glass figure; he was not struggling but limp. A swell was washing regularly over his head.

His mouth slopped full and he choked. Flashes of tracer cut the darkness. He felt a weight pulling him down. The snarl came back with a picture of heavy seaboots and he began to move his legs. He got one toe over the other and shoved but the boot would not come off. He gathered himself and there were his hands far off but serviceable. He shut his mouth and performed a grim acrobatic in the water while the tracer flashed. He felt his heart thumping and for a while it was the only point of reference in the formless darkness. He got his right leg across his left thigh and heaved with sodden hands. The seaboot slipped down his calf and he kicked it free. Once the rubber top had left his toes he felt it touch him once and then it was gone utterly. He forced his left leg up, wrestled with the second boot and got it free. Both boots had left him. He let his body uncoil and lie limply.

His mouth was clever. It opened and shut for the air and against the water. His body understood too. Every now and then it would clench its stomach into a hard knot and sea water would burst out over his tongue. He began to be frightened again—not with animal panic but with deep fear of death in isolation and long drawn out. The snarl came back but now it had a face to use and air for the throat. There was something meaningful behind the snarl which would not waste the air on noises. There was a purpose which had not yet had time and experience to discover how relentless it was. It could not use the mechanism for regular breathing but it took air in gulps between the moments of burial.

He began to think in gulps as he swallowed the air. He remembered his hands again and there they were in the darkness, far away. He brought them in and began to fumble at the hard stuff of his oilskin. The button hurt and would hardly be persuaded to go through the hole. He slipped the loop off the toggle of his duffle. Lying with little movement of his body he found that the sea ignored him, treated him as a glass figure of a sailor or as a log that was almost ready to sink but would last a few moments yet. The air was regularly in attendance between the passage of the swells.

He got the rubber tube and drew it through the tapes. He could feel the slack and uninflated rubber that was so nearly not holding him up. He got the tit of the tube between his teeth and unscrewed with two fingers while the others sealed the tube. He won a little air from between swells and fuffed it through the rubber tube. For uncounted numbers of swell and hollow he taxed the air that might have gone into his lungs until his heart was staggering in his body like a wounded man and the green tracer was flicking and spinning. The lifebelt began to firm up against his chest but so slowly that he could not tell when the change came. Then abruptly the swells were washing over his shoulders and the repeated burial beneath them had become a wet and splashing slap in the face. He found he had no need to play catch-as-catch-can for air. He blew deeply and regularly into the tube until the lifebelt rose and strained at his clothing. Yet he did not stop blowing at once. He played with the air, letting a little out and then blowing again as if frightened of stopping the one positive action he could take to help himself. His head and neck and shoulders were out of the water now for long intervals. They were colder than the rest of his body. The air stiffened them. They began to shake.

He took his mouth from the tube.

'Help! Help!'

The air escaped from the tube and he struggled with it. He twisted the tit until the air was safe. He stopped shouting and strained his eyes to see through the darkness but it lay right against his eyeballs. He put his hand before his eyes and saw nothing. Immediately the terror of blindness added itself to the terror of isolation and drowning. He began to make vague climbing motions in the water.

'Help! Is there anybody there? Help! Survivor!'

He lay shaking for a while and listened for an answer but the only sound was the hissing and puddling of the water as it washed round him. His head fell forward.

He licked salt water off his lips.

'Exercise.'

He began to tread water gently. His mouth mumbled.

'Why did I take my sea boots off? I'm no better off than I was.' His head nodded forward again.

'Cold. Mustn't get too cold. If I had those boots I could put them on and then take them off and then put them on——'

He thought suddenly of the boat sinking through water towards a bottom that was still perhaps a mile remote from them. With that, the whole wet immensity seemed to squeeze his body as though he were sunk to a great depth. His chattering teeth came together and the flesh of his face twisted. He arched in the water, drawing his feet up away from the depth, the slopping, glutinous welter.

'Help! Help——'

He began to thresh with his hands and force his body round. He stared at the darkness as he turned but there was nothing to tell him when he had completed the circle and everywhere the darkness was grainless and alike. There was no wreckage, no sinking hull, no struggling survivors but himself, there was only darkness lying close against the balls of the eyes. There was the movement of water.

He began to cry out for the others, for anyone.

'Nat! Nathaniel! For Christ's sake! Nathaniel! Help!'

His voice died and his face untwisted. He lay slackly in his lifebelt, allowing the swell to do what it would. His teeth were chattering again and sometimes this vibration would spread till it included his whole body. His legs below him were not cold so much as pressed, squeezed mercilessly by the sea so that the feeling in them was not a response to temperature but to weight that would crush and burst them. He searched for a place to put his hands but there was nowhere that kept the ache out of them. The back of his neck began to hurt and that not gradually but with a sudden stab of pain so that holding his chin away from his chest was impossible. But this put his face into the sea so that he sucked it into his nose with a snoring noise and a choke. He spat and endured the pain in his neck for a while. He wedged his hands between his lifebelt and his chin and for a swell or two this was some relief but then the pain returned. He let his hands fall away and his face dipped in the water. He lay back, forcing his head against the pain so that his eyes if they had been open would have been looking at the sky. The pressure on his legs was bearable now. They were no longer flesh, but had been transformed to some other substance, petrified and comfortable. The part of his body that had not been invaded and wholly subdued by the sea was jerking intermittently. Eternity, inseparable from pain was there to be examined and experienced. The snarl endured. He thought. The thoughts were laborious, disconnected but vital.

Presently it will be daylight.

I must move from one point to another.

Enough to see one move ahead.

Presently it will be daylight.

I shall see wreckage.

I won't die.

I can't die.

Not me——

Precious.

He roused himself with a sudden surge of feeling that had nothing to do with the touch of the sea. Salt water was coming fast out of his eyes. He snivelled and gulped.

'Help, somebody—help!'

His body lifted and fell gently.

If I'd been below I might have got to a boat even. Or a raft. But it had to be my bloody watch. Blown off the bloody bridge. She must have gone on perhaps to starboard if he got the order in time, sinking or turning over. They'll be there in the darkness somewhere where she sank asking each other if they're down-hearted, knots and stipples of heads in the water and oil and drifting stuff. When it's light I must find them. Christ I must find them. Or they'll be picked up and I'll be left to swell like a hammock. Christ!

'Help! Nathaniel! Help——!'

And I gave the right orders too. If I'd done it ten seconds earlier I'd be a bloody hero—Hard a-starboard for Christ's sake!

Must have hit us bang under the bridge. And I gave the right order. And I get blown to buggery.

The snarl fixed itself, worked on the wooden face till the upper lip was lifted and the chattering teeth bared. The little warmth of anger flushed blood back into the tops of the cheeks and behind the eyes. They opened.

Then he was jerking and splashing and looking up. There was a difference in the texture of the darkness; there were smears and patches that were not in the eye itself. For a moment and before he remembered how to use his sight the patches lay on the eyeballs as close as the darkness had been. Then he firmed the use of his eyes and he was inside his head, looking out through the arches of his skull at random formations of dim light and mist. However he blinked and squinted they remained there outside him. He bent his head forward and saw, fainter than an after-image, the scalloped and changing shape of a swell as his body was lifted in it. For a moment he caught the inconstant outline against the sky, then he was floating up and seeing dimly the black top of the next swell as it swept towards him. He began to make swimming motions. His hands were glimmering patches in the water and his movements broke up the stony weight of his legs. The thoughts continued to flicker.

We were travelling north-east. I gave the order. If he began the turn she might be anywhere over there to the east. The wind was westerly. That's the east over there where the swells are running away down hill.

His movements and his breathing became fierce. He swam a sort of clumsy breast-stroke, buoyed up on the inflated belt. He stopped and lay wallowing. He set his teeth, took the tit of the lifebelt and let out air till he was lying lower in the water. He began to swim again. His breathing laboured. He stared out of his arches intently and painfully at the back of each swell as it slunk away from him. His legs slowed and stopped; his arms fell. His mind inside the dark skull made swimming movements long after the body lay motionless in the water.

The grain of the sky was more distinct. There were vaporous changes of tone from dark to gloom, to grey. Near at hand the individual hillocks of the surface were visible. His mind made swimming movements.

Pictures invaded his mind and tried to get between him and the urgency of his motion towards the east. The jam jar came back but robbed of significance. There was a man, a brief interview, a desk-top so polished that the smile of teeth was being reflected in it. There was a row of huge masks hung up to dry and a voice from behind the teeth that had been reflected in the desk spoke softly.

'Which one do you think would suit Christopher?'

There was a binnacle-top with the compass light just visible, there was an order shouted, hung up there for all heaven and earth to see in neon lighting.

'Hard a-starboard, for Christ's sake!'

Water washed into his mouth and he jerked into consciousness with a sound that was half a snore and half a choke. The day was inexorably present in green and grey. The seas were intimate and enormous. They smoked. When he swung up a broad, hilly crest he could see two other smoking crests then nothing but a vague circle that might be mist or fine spray or rain. He peered into the circle, turning himself, judging direction by the run of the water until he had inspected every part. The slow fire of his belly, banked up to endure, was invaded. It lay defenceless in the middle of the clothing and sodden body.

'I won't die! Iwon't!'

The circle of mist was everywhere alike. Crests swung into view on that side, loomed, seized him, elevated him for a moment, let him down and slunk off, but there was another crest to take him, lift him so that he could see the last one just dimming out of the circle. Then he would go down again and another crest would loom weltering towards him.

He began to curse and beat the water with the flat of his white hands. He struggled up the swells. But even the sounds of his working mouth and body were merged unnoticed in the innumerable sounds of travelling water. He hung still in his belt, feeling the cold search his belly with its fingers. His head fell on his chest and the stuff slopped weakly, persistently over his face. Think. My last chance. Think what can be done.

She sank out in the Atlantic. Hundreds of miles from land. She was alone, sent north-east from the convoy to break WT silence. The U-boat may be hanging round to pick up a survivor or two for questioning. Or to pick off any ship that comes to rescue survivors. She may surface at any moment, breaking the swell with her heavy body like a half-tide rock. Her periscope may sear the water close by, eye of a land-creature that has defeated the rhythm and necessity of the sea. She may be passing under me now, shadowy and shark-like, she may be lying down there below my wooden feet on a bed of salty water as on a cushion while her crew sleeps. Survivors, a raft, the whaler, the dinghy, wreckage may be milling about only a swell or two away hidden in the mist and waiting for rescue with at least bully and perhaps a tot.

He began to rotate in the water again, peering blearily at the midst, he squinted at the sky that was not much higher than a roof; he searched the circle for wreckage or a head. But there was nothing. She had gone as if a hand had reached up that vertical mile and snatched her down in one motion. When he thought of the mile he arched in the water, face twisted, and began to cry out.

'Help, curse you, sod you, bugger you—Help!'

Then he was blubbering and shuddering and the cold was squeezing him like the hand that had snatched down the ship. He hiccupped slowly into silence and started to rotate once more in the smoke and green welter.

One side of the circle was lighter than the other. The swell was shouldering itself on towards the left of this vague brightness; and where the brightness spread the mist was even more impenetrable than behind him. He remained facing the brightness not because it was of any use to him but because it was a difference that broke the uniformity of the circle and because it looked a little warmer than anywhere else. He made swimming movements again without thought and as if to follow in the wake of that brightness was an inevitable thing to do. The light made the sea-smoke seem solid. It penetrated the water so that between him and the very tops of the restless hillocks it was bottle green. For a moment or two after a wave had passed he could see right into it but the waves were nothing but water—there was no weed in them, no speck of solid, nothing drifting, nothing moving but green water, cold persistent idiot water. There were hands to be sure and two forearms of black oilskin and there was the noise of breathing, gasping. There was also the noise of the idiot stuff, whispering, folding on itself, tripped ripples running tinkling by the ear like miniatures of surf on a flat beach; there were sudden hisses and spats, roars and incompleted syllables and the soft friction of wind. The hands were important under the bright side of the circle but they had nothing to seize on. There was an infinite drop of the soft, cold stuff below them and under the labouring, dying, body.

The sense of depth caught him and he drew his dead feet up to his belly as if to detach them from the whole ocean. He arched and gaped, he rose over the chasm of deep sea on a swell and his mouth opened to scream against the brightness.

It stayed open. Then it shut with a snap of teeth and his arms began to heave water out of the way. He fought his way forward.

'Ahoy—for Christ's sake! Survivor! Survivor! Fine on your starboard bow!'

He threshed with his arms and legs into a clumsy crawl. A crest overtook him and he jerked himself to the chest out of water.

'Help! Help! Survivor! For God's sake!'

The force of his return sent him under but he struggled up and shook the wave from his head. The fire of his belly had spread and his heart was thrusting the sluggish blood painfully round

his body. There was a ship in the mist to port of the bright patch.
He was on her starboard bow—or—and the thought drove him
to foam in the water—he was on her port quarter and she was
moving away. But even in his fury of movement he saw how
impossible this was since then she would have passed by him only
a few minutes ago. So she was coming towards, to cut across the
circle of visibility only a few yards from him.

Or stopped.

At that, he stopped too, and lay in the water. She was so dull a
shape, little more than a looming darkness that he could not tell
both her distance and her size. She was more nearly bows on than
when he had first seen her and now she was visible even when he
was in a trough. He began to swim again but every time he rose
on a crest he screamed.

'Help! Survivor!'

But what ship was ever so lop-sided? A carrier? A derelict carrier,
deserted and waiting to sink? But she would have been knocked
down by a salvo of torpedoes. A derelict liner? Then she must be one
of the Queens by her bulk—and why lop-sided? The sun and the
mist were balanced against each other. The sun could illumine the
midst but not pierce it. And darkly in the sun-mist loomed the shape
of a not-ship where nothing but a ship could be.

He began to swim again, feeling suddenly the desperate exhaustion of his body. The first, fierce excitement of sighting had
burned up the fuel and the fire was low again. He swam grimly,
forcing his arms through the water, reaching forward under his
arches with sight as though he could pull himself into safety with
it. The shape moved. It grew larger and not clearer. Every now
and then there was something like a bow-wave at the forefoot.
He ceased to look at her but swam and screamed alternately with
the last strength of his body. There was green force round him,
growing in strength to rob, there was mist and glitter over him;
there was a redness pulsing in front of his eyes—his body gave
up and he lay slack in the waves and the shape rose over him. He
heard through the rasp and thump of his works the sound of
waves breaking. He lifted his head and there was rock stuck up in
the sky with a sea-gull poised before it. He heaved over in the sea
and saw how each swell dipped for a moment, flung up a white
hand of foam then disappeared as if the rock had swallowed it.
He began to think swimming motions but knew now that his
body was no longer obedient. The top of the next swell between

him and the rock was blunted, smoothed curiously, then jerked up spray. He sank down, saw without comprehension that the green water was no longer empty. There was yellow and brown. He heard not the formless mad talking of uncontrolled water but a sudden roar. Then he went under into a singing world and there were hairy shapes that flitted and twisted past his face, there were sudden notable details close to of intricate rock and weed. Brown tendrils slashed across his face, then with a destroying shock he hit solidity. It was utter difference, it was under his body, against his knees and face, he could close fingers on it, for an instance he could even hold on. His mouth was needlessly open and his eyes so that he had a moment of close and intent communion with three limpets, two small and one large that were only an inch or two from his face. Yet this solidity was terrible and apocalyptic after the world of inconstant wetness. It was not vibrant as a ship's hull might be but merciless and mother of panic. It had no business to interrupt the thousands of miles of water going about their purposeless affairs and therefore the world sprang here into sudden war. He felt himself picked up and away from the limpets, reversed, tugged, thrust down into weed and darkness. Ropes held him, slipped and let him go. He saw light, got a mouthful of air and foam. He glimpsed a riven rock face with trees of spray growing up it and the sight of this rock floating in mid-Atlantic was so dreadful that he wasted his air by screaming as if it had been a wild beast. He went under into a green calm, then up and was thrust sideways. The sea no longer played with him. It stayed its wild movement and held him gently, carried him with delicate and careful motion like a retriever with a bird. Hard things touched him about the feet and knees. The sea laid him down gently and retreated. There were hard things touching his face and chest, the side of his forehead. The sea came back and fawned round his face, licked him. He thought movements that did not happen. The sea came back and he thought the movements again and this time they happened because the sea took most of his weight. They moved him forward over the hard things. Each wave and each movement moved him forward. He felt the sea run down to smell at his feet then come back and nuzzle under his arm. It no longer licked his face. There was a pattern in front of him that occupied all the space under the arches. It meant nothing. The sea nuzzled under his arm again.

He lay still.

CHAPTER TWO

The pattern was white and black but mostly white. It existed in two layers, one behind the other, one for each eye. He thought nothing, did nothing while the pattern changed a trifle and made little noises. The hardnesses under his cheek began to insist. They passed through pressure to a burning without heat, to a localized pain. They became vicious in their insistence like the nag of an aching tooth. They began to pull him back into himself and organize him again as a single being.

Yet it was not the pain nor the white and black pattern that first brought him back to life, but the noises. Though the sea had treated him so carefully, elsewhere it continued to roar and thump and collapse on itself. The wind too, given something to fight with other than obsequious water was hissing round the rock and breathing gustily in crevices. All these noises made a language which forced itself into the dark, passionless head and assured it that the head was somewhere, somewhere—and then finally with the flourish of a gull's cry over the sound of wind and water, declared to the groping consciousness: wherever you are, you are here!

Then he was there, suddenly, enduring pain but in deep communion with the solidity that held up his body. He remembered how eyes should be used and brought the two lines of sight together so that the patterns fused and made a distance. The pebbles were close to his face, pressing against his cheek and jaw. They were white quartz, dulled and rounded, a miscellany of potato-shapes. Their whiteness was qualified by yellow stains and flecks of darker material. There was a whiter thing beyond them. He examined it without curiosity, noting the bleached wrinkles, the blue roots of nails, the corrugations at the finger-tips. He did not move his head but followed the line of the hand back to an oilskin sleeve, the beginnings of a shoulder. His eyes returned to the pebbles and watched them idly as if they were about to perform some operation for which he was waiting without much interest. The hand did not move.

Water welled up among the pebbles. It stirred them slightly, paused, then sank away while the pebbles clicked and chirruped. It swilled down past his body and pulled gently at his stockinged feet. He watched the pebbles while the water came back and this time the last touch of the sea lopped into his open mouth. Without change of expression he began to shake, a deep shake that included the whole of his body. Inside his head it seemed that the pebbles were shaking because the movement of his white hand forward and back was matched by the movement of his body. Under the side of his face the pebbles nagged.

The pictures that came and went inside his head did not disturb him because they were so small and remote. There was a woman's body, white and detailed, there was a boy's body; there was a box office, the bridge of a ship, an order picked out across a far sky in neon lighting, a tall, thin man who stood aside humbly in the darkness at the top of a companion ladder; there was a man hanging in the sea like a glass sailor in a jam jar. There was nothing to choose between the pebbles and pictures. Sometimes one was uppermost, sometimes the other. The individual pebbles were no bigger than the pictures. Sometimes a pebble would be occupied entirely by a picture as though it were a window, a spy-hole into a different world or other dimension. Words and sounds were sometimes visible as shapes like the shouted order. They did not vibrate and disappear. When they were created they remained as hard enduring things like the pebbles. Some of these were inside the skull, behind the arch of the brow and the shadowy nose. They were right in the indeterminate darkness above the fire of hardnesses. If you looked out idly, you saw round them.

There was a new kind of coldness over his body. It was creeping down his back between the stuffed layers of clothing. It was air that felt like slow fire. He had hardly noticed this when a wave came back and filled his mouth so that a choke interrupted the rhythm of shaking.

He began to experiment. He found that he could haul the weight of one leg up and then the other. His hand crawled round above his head. He reasoned deeply that there was another hand on the other side somewhere and sent a message out to it. He found the hand and worked the wrist. There were still fingers on it, not because he could move them but because when he pushed he could feel the wooden tips shifting the invisible pebbles. He

moved his four limbs in close and began to make swimming
movements. The vibrations from the cold helped him. Now his
breath went in and out quickly and his heart began to race again.
The inconsequential pictures vanished and there was nothing but
pebbles and pebble noises and heart-thumps. He had a valuable
thought, not because it was of immediate physical value but because
it gave him back a bit of his personality. He made words to express
this thought, though they did not pass the barrier of his teeth.

'I should be about as heavy as this on Jupiter.'

At once he was master. He knew that his body weighed no
more than it had always done, that it was exhausted, that he was
trying to crawl up a little pebble slope. He lifted the dents in his
face away from the pebbles that had made them and pushed with
his knees. His teeth came together and ground. He timed the
expansion of his chest against the pebbles, the slow shaking of his
body till they did not hold up the leaden journey. He felt how
each wave finished farther and farther down towards his feet.
When the journey became too desperate he would wait, gasping,
until the world came back. The water no longer touched his feet.

His left hand—the hidden one—touched something that did
not click and give. He rolled his head and looked up under the
arch. There was greyish yellow stuff in front of his face. It was
pock-marked and hollowed, dotted with red lumps of jelly. The
yellow tents of limpets were pitched in every hole. Brown fronds
and green webs of weed hung over them. The white pebbles led
up into a dark angle. There was a film of water glistening over
everything, drops falling, tiny pools caught at random, lying and
shuddering or leaking down among the weed. He began to turn
on the pebbles, working his back against the rock and drawing
up his feet. He saw them now for the first time, distant projections, made thick and bear-like by the white, seaboot stockings.
They gave him back a little more of himself. He got his left hand
down beneath his ear and began to heave. His shoulder lifted a
little. He pushed with feet, pulled with hands. His back was
edging into the angle where the pools leaked down. His head was
high. He took a thigh in both hands and pulled it towards his
chest and then the other. He packed himself into the angle and
looked down at the pebbles over his knees. His mouth had fallen
open again.

And after all, as pebbles go there were not very many of them.
The length of a man or less would measure out the sides of the

triangle that they made under the shadow of the rock. They filled
the cleft and they were solid.

He took his eyes away from the pebbles and made them examine
the water. This was almost calm in comparison with the open sea;
and the reason was the rock round which the waves had whirled
him. He could see the rock out there now. It was the same stuff
as this, grey and creamy with barnacles and foam. Each wave
tripped on it so that although the water ran and thumped on
either side of the cleft, there was a few yards of green, clear water
between him and the creamy rock. Beyond the rock was nothing
but a smoking advance of sea with watery sunlight caught in it.

He let his eyes close and ignored the pictures that came and
went behind them. The slow movement of his mind settled on a
thought. There was a small fire in his body that was almost
extinguished but incredibly was still smouldering despite the
Atlantic. He folded his body consciously round that fire and
nursed it. There was not more than a spark. The formal words
and the pictures evolved themselves.

A seabird cried over him with a long sound descending down
wind. He removed his attention from the spark of fire and opened
his eyes again. This time he had got back so much of his personality that he could look out and grasp the whole of what he
saw at once. There were the dark walls of rock on either side that
framed the brighter light. There was sunlight on a rock with
spray round it and the steady march of swells that brought their
own fine mist along with them under the sun. He turned his head
sideways and peered up.

The rock was smoother above the weeds and limpets and drew
together. There was an opening at the top with daylight and the
suggestion of cloud caught in it. As he watched, a gull flicked
across the opening and cried in the wind. He found the effort of
looking up hurt him and he turned to his body, examined the
humps that were his knees under the oilskin and duffle. He looked
closely at a button.

His mouth shut then opened. Sounds came out. He readjusted
them and they were uncertain words.

'I know you. Nathaniel sewed you on. I asked him to. Said it was
an excuse to get him away from the mess-deck for a bit of peace.'

His eyes closed again and he fingered the button clumsily.

'Had this oilskin when I was a rating. Lofty sewed on the
buttons before Nathaniel.'

His head nodded on his knees.

'All the blue watch. Blue watch to muster.'

The pictures were interrupted by the solid shape of a snore. The shiverings were less dramatic but they took power from his arms so that presently they fell away from his knees and his hands lay on the pebbles. His head shook. Between the snores the pebbles were hard to the feet, harder to the backside when the heels had slid slowly from under. The pictures were so confused that there was as much danger that they would destroy the personality as that the spark of fire would go out. He forced his way among them, lifted his eyelids and looked out.

The pebbles were wavering down there where the water welled over them. Higher up, the rock that had saved him was lathered and fringed with leaping strings of foam. There was afternoon brightness outside but the cleft was dripping, dank and smelly as a dockside latrine. He made quacking sounds with his mouth. The words that had formed in his mind were: Where is this bloody rock? But that seemed to risk something by insult of the dark cleft so that he changed them in his throat.

'Where the hell am I?'

A single point of rock, peak of a mountain range, one tooth set in the ancient jaw of a sunken world, projecting through the inconceivable vastness of the whole ocean—and how many miles from dry land? An evil pervasion, not the convulsive panic of his first struggles in the water, but a deep and generalized terror set him clawing at the rock with his blunt fingers. He even got half-up and leaned or crouched against the weed and the lumps of jelly.

'Think, you bloody fool, think.'

The horizon of misty water stayed close, the water leapt from the rock and the pebbles wavered.

'Think.'

He crouched, watching the rock, not moving but trembling continually. He noted how the waves broke on the outer rock and were tamed, so that the water before the cleft was sloppily harmless. Slowly, he settled back into the angle of the cleft. The spark was alight and the heart was supplying it with what it wanted. He watched the outer rock but hardly saw it. There was a name missing. That name was written on the chart, well out in the Atlantic, eccentrically isolated so that seamen who could to a certain extent laugh at wind and weather had made a joke of the rock. Frowning, he saw the chart now in his mind's eye but not clearly. He saw the navigating commander of the cruiser bending over it with the captain, saw himself as navigator's yeoman standing ready while they grinned at each other. The captain spoke with his clipped Dartmouth accent—spoke and laughed.

'I call that name a near miss.'

Near miss whatever the name was. And now to be huddled on a near miss how many miles from the Hebrides? What was the use of the spark if it winked away in the crack of that ludicrous isolation? He spat his words at the picture of the captain.

'I am no better off than I was.'

He began to slide down the rocks as his bones bent their hinges. He slumped into the angle and his head fell. He snored.

But inside, where the snores were external, the consciousness was moving and poking about among the pictures and revelations, among the shape-sounds and the disregarded feelings like an animal ceaselessly examining its cage. It rejected the detailed bodies of women, slowly sorted the odd words, ignored the pains and the insistence of the shaking body. It was looking for a thought. It found the thought, separated it from the junk, lifted it and used the apparatus of the body to give it force and importance.

'I am intelligent.'

There was a period of black suspension behind the snores; then the right hand, so far away, obeyed a command and began to fumble and pluck at the oilskin. It raised a flap and crawled inside. The fingers found cord and shut clasp-knife. They stayed there.

The eyes blinked open so that the arch of brows was a frame to green sea. For a while the eyes looked, received impressions without seeing them. Then the whole body gave a jump. The spark became a flame, the body scrambled, crouched, the hand flicked out of the oilskin pocket and grabbed rock. The eyes stared and did not blink.

As the eyes watched, a wave went clear over the outer rock so that they could see the brown weed inside the water. The green dance beyond the pebbles was troubled. A line of foam broke and hissed up the pebbles to his feet. The foam sank away and the pebbles chattered like teeth. He watched, wave after wave as bursts of foam swallowed more and more of the pebbles and left fewer visible when they went back. The outer rock was no longer a barrier but only a gesture of defence. The cleft was being connected more and more directly with the irresistible progress

of the green, smoking seas. He jerked away from the open water
and turned towards the rock. The dark, lavatorial cleft, with its
dripping weed, with its sessile, mindless life of shell and jelly was
land only twice a day by courtesy of the moon. It felt like solidity
but it was a sea-trap, an alien to breathing life as the soft slop of
the last night and the vertical mile.

A gull screamed with him so that he came back into himself,
leaned his forehead against the rock and waited for his heart to
steady. A shot of foam went over his feet. He looked down past
them. There were fewer pebbles to stand on and those that had
met his hands when he had been washed ashore were yellow and
green beneath a foot of jumping water. He turned to the rock
again and spoke out loud.

'Climb!'

He turned round and found handholds in the cleft. There were
many to choose from. His hands were poor, sodden stuff against
their wet projections. He leaned a moment against the rock and
gathered the resources of his body together. He lifted his right
leg and dropped the foot in an opening like an ash-tray. There
was an edge to the ash-tray but not a sharp one and his foot could
feel nothing. He took his forehead away from a weedy surface
and heaved himself up until the right leg was straight. His left leg
swung and thumped. He got the toes on a shelf and stayed so,
only a few inches off the pebbles and spreadeagled. The cleft rose
by his face and he looked at the secret drops of the stillicide in the
dark angle as though he envied them their peace. Time went by
drop by drop. The two pictures drifted apart.

The pebbles rattled below him and a last lick of water flipped
into the crevice. He dropped his head and looked down over his
lifebelt, through the open skirt of the oilskin to where the wetted
pebbles lay in the angle of the cleft. He saw his seaboot stockings
and thought his feet back into them.

'I wish I had my seaboots still.'

He changed the position of his right foot cautiously and locked
his left knee stiffly upright to bear his weight without effort. His
feet were selective in a curious way. They could not feel rock
unless there was sharpness. They only became a part of him when
they were hurting him or when he could see them.

The tail end of a wave reached right into the angle and struck
in the apex with a plop. A single string of spray leapt up between
his legs, past the lifebelt and wetted his face. He made a sound

and only then found how ruinous an extension of flesh he carried round him. The sound began in the throat, bubbled and stayed there. The mouth took no part but lay open, jaw lying slack on the hard oilskin collar. The bubbling increased and he made the teeth click. Words twisted out between them and the frozen stuff of his upper lip.

'Like a dead man!'

Another wave reached in and spray ran down his face. He began to labour at climbing. He moved up the intricate rock face until there were no more limpets nor mussels and nothing clung to the rock but his own body and tiny barnacles and green smears of weed. All the time the wind pushed him into the cleft and the sea made dispersed noises.

The cleft narrowed until his head projected through an opening, not much wider than his body. He got his elbows jammed on either side and looked up.

Before his face the rock widened above the narrowest part of the cleft into a funnel. The sides of the funnel were not very smooth; but they were smooth enough to refuse to hold a body by friction. They sloped away to the top of the rock like a roof angle. The track from his face to the cliff-like edge of the funnel at the top was nearly twice the length of a man. He began to turn his head, slowly, searching for handholds, but saw none. Only at about half-way there was a depression, but too shallow for a hand-hold. Blunted fingers would never be safe on the rounded edge.

There came a thud from the bottom of the angle. Solid water shot into the angle, burst and washed down again. He peered over his lifebelt, between his two feet. The pebbles were dimmed, appeared clearly for a moment, then vanished under a surge of green water. Spray shot up between his body and the rock.

He pulled himself up until his body from the waist was leaning forward along the slope. His feet found the holds where his elbows had been. His knees straightened slowly while he breathed in gasps and his right arm reached out in front of him. Fingers closed on the blunted edge of the depression. Pulled.

He took one foot away from a hold and edged the knee up. He moved the other.

He hung, only a few inches from the top of the angle, held by one hand and the friction of his body. The fingers of his right hand quivered and gave. They slipped over the rounded edge.

His whole body slid down and he was back at the top of the crevice again. He lay still, not seeing the rock by his eyes and his right arm was stretched above him.

The sea was taking over the cleft. Every few seconds there came the thump and return of a wave below him. Heavy drops fell and trickled on the surface of the funnel before his face. Then a wave exploded and water cascaded over his legs. He lifted his face off the rock and the snarl wrestled with his stiff muscles.

'Like a limpet.'

He lay for a while, bent at the top of the crevice. The pebbles no longer appeared in the angle. They were a wavering memory of themselves between bouts of spray. Then they vanished, the rock vanished with them and with another explosion the water hit him from head to foot. He shook it from his face. He was staring down at the crevice as though the water were irrelevant.

He cried out.

'Like a limpet!'

He put his feet down and felt for folds, lowered himself resolutely, clinging each time the water hit him and went back. He held his breath and spat when each wave left him. The water was no longer cold but powerful rather. The nearer he lowered his body to the pebbles the harder he was struck and the heavier the weight that urged him down at each return. He lost his hold and fell the last few inches and immediately a wave had him, thrust him brutally into the angle then tried to tear him away. Between waves when he staggered to his feet the water was knee-deep over the pebbles and they gave beneath him. He fell on all fours and was hidden in a green heap that hit the back of the angle and climbed up in a tree-trunk of spray. He staggered round the angle then gripped with both hands. The water tore at him but he held on. He got his knife free and opened the blade. He ducked down and immediately there were visions of rock and weed in front of his eyes. The uproar of the sea sank to a singing note in the ears. Then he was up again, the knife swinging free, two limpets in his hands and the sea knocked him down and stood him on his head. He found rock and clung against the backwash. When the waves left him for a moment he opened his mouth and gasped in the air as though he were winning territory. He found holds in the angle and the sea exploded, thrust him up so that now his effort was to stay down and under control. After each blow he flattened himself to escape the descent of the water. As he rose the seas lost their quality of leaden power but became more personal and vicious. They tore at his clothing, they beat him in the crutch, they tented up his oilskin till the skirt was crumpled above his waist. If he looked down the water came straight at his face, or hit him in the guts and thrust him up.

He came to the narrowest part and was shoved through. He opened his eyes after the water gushed back and breathed wetly as the foam streamed down his face. A lock of hair was plastered just to the bridge of his nose and he saw the end of it, double. The chute struck him again, the waterfall rushed back and he was still there, wedged by his weight in the narrowest part of the crevice where the funnel began and his body was shaking. He lay forward on the slope and began to straighten his legs. His face moved up against the rock and a torrent swept back over him. He began to fumble in the crumples of his oilskin. He brought out a limpet and set it on the rock by his waist. Water came again and went. He reversed his knife and tapped the limpet on the top with the haft. The limpet gave a tiny sideways lurch and sucked itself down against the rock. A weight pressed on him and the man and the limpet firmed down against the rock together.

His legs were straight and stiff and his eyes were shut. He brought his right arm round in a circle and felt above him. He found the blunted dent that was too smooth for a handhold. His hand came back, was inundated, fumbled in oilskin. He pulled it out and when the hand crawled round and up there was a limpet in the palm. The man was looking at the rock an inch or two from his face but without interest. What life was left was concentrated in the crawling right hand. The hand found the blunted hollow, and pitched the limpet beyond the edge. The body was lifted a few inches and lay motionless waiting for the return of the water. When the chute had passed the hand came back, took the knife, moved up and tapped blindly on rock. The fingers searched stiffly, found the limpet, hit with the haft of the knife.

He turned his face, endured another wave and considered the limpet above him gravely. His hand let the knife go, which slid and clattered and hung motionless by his waist. He took the tit of the lifebelt and unscrewed the end. The air breathed out and his body flattened a little in the funnel. He laid the side of his head down and did nothing. Before his mouth the wet surface of the rock was blurred a little and regularly the blur was erased by the return of the waterfall. Sometimes the pendant knife would clatter.

Again he turned his face and looked up. His fingers closed over the limpet. Now his right leg was moving. The toes searched tremulously for the first limpet as the fingers had searched for the second. They did not find the limpet but the knee did. The hand let go, came down to the knee and lifted that part of the leg. The snarl behind the stiff face felt the limpet as a pain in the crook of the knee. The teeth set. The whole body began to wriggle; the hand went back to the higher limpet and pulled. The man moved sideways up the slope of the roof. The left leg came in and the seaboot stocking pushed the first leg away. The side of the foot was against the limpet. The leg straightened. Another torrent returned and washed down.

The man was lying with one foot on a limpet, held mostly by friction. But his foot was on one limpet and the second one was before his eyes. He reached up and there was a possible handhold that his fingers found, provided the other one still gripped the limpet by his face. He moved up, up, up and then there was an edge for his fingers. His right arm rose, seized. He pulled with both arms, thrust with both legs. He saw a trench of rock beyond the edge, glimpsed sea, saw whiteness on the rocks and jumble. He fell forward.

CHAPTER THREE

He was lying in a trench. He could see a weathered wall of rock and a long pool of water stretching away from his eye. His body was in some other place that had nothing to do with this landscape. It was splayed, scattered behind him, his legs in different worlds, neck twisted. His right arm was bent under his body and his wrist doubled. He sensed this hand and the hard pressure of the knuckles against his side but the pain was not intense enough to warrant the titanic effort of moving. His left arm stretched away along the trench and was half-covered in water. His right eye was so close to this water that he could feel a little pluck from the surface tension when he blinked and his eyelashes caught in the film. The water had flattened again by the time he saw the surface consciously but his right cheek and the corner of his mouth were under water and were causing a tremble. The other eye was above water and was looking down the trench. The inside of the trench was dirty white, strangely white with more than the glossy reflection from the sky. The corner of his mouth pricked. Sometimes the surface of the water was pitted for a moment or two and faint, interlacing circles spread over it from each pit. His left eye watched them, looking through a kind of arch of darkness where the skull swept round the socket. At the bottom and almost a straight line, was the skin colour of his nose. Filling the arch was the level of shining water.

He began to think slowly.

I have tumbled in a trench. My head is jammed against the farther side and my neck is twisted. My legs must be up in the air over the other wall. My thighs are hurting because the weight of my legs is pushing against the edge of the wall as a fulcrum. My right toes are hurt more than the rest of my leg. My hand is doubled under me and that is why I feel the localized pain in my ribs. My fingers might be made of wood. That whiter white under the water along there is my hand, hidden.

There was a descending scream in the air, a squawk and the

beating of wings. A gull was braking widely over the wall at the
end of the trench, legs and claws held out. It yelled angrily at the
trench, the wide wings gained a purchase and it hung flapping
only a foot or two above the rock. Wind chilled his cheek. The
webbed feet came up, the wings steadied and the gull side-slipped
away. The commotion of its passage made waves in the white
water that beat against his cheek, the shut eye, the corner of his
mouth. The stinging increased.

There was no pain sharp enough to compel action. Even the
stinging was outside the head. His left eye watched the whiter
white of his hand under water. Some of the memory pictures
came back. They were new ones of a man climbing up rock and
placing limpets.

The pictures stirred him more than the stinging. They made
his left hand contract under the surface and the oilskin arm roll in
the water. His breathing grew suddenly fierce so that waves
rippled away along the trench, crossed and came back. A ripple
splashed into his mouth.

Immediately he was convulsed and struggling. His legs kicked
and swung sideways. His head ground against rock and turned.
He scrabbled in the white water with both hands and heaved
himself up. He felt the too-smooth wetness running on his face
and the brilliant jab of pain at the corner of his right eye. He spat
and snarled. He glimpsed the trenches with their thick layers of
dirty white, their trapped inches of solution, a gull slipping away
over a green sea. Then he was forcing himself forward. He fell
into the next trench, hauled himself over the wall, saw a jumble
of broken rock, slid and stumbled. He was going down hill and
he fell part of the way. There was moving water round flattish
rocks, a complication of weedy life. The wind went down with
him and urged him forward. As long as he went forward the
wind was satisfied but if he stopped for a moment's caution it
thrust his unbalanced body down so that he scraped and hit. He
saw little of the open sea and sky or the whole rock but only
flashes of intimate being, a crack or point, a hand's breadth of
yellowish surface that was about to strike a blow, unavoidable
fists of rock that beat him impersonally, struck bright flashes of
light from his body. The pain in the corner of his eye went with
him too. This was the most important of all the pains because it
thrust a needle now into the dark skull where he lived. The pain
could not be avoided. His body revolved round it. Then he was

holding brown weed and the sea was washing over his head and
shoulders. He pulled himself up and lay on a flat rock with a pool
across the top. He rolled the side of his face and his eye backwards
and forwards under water. He moved his hands gently so that the
water swished. They left the water and reached round and
gathered smears of green weed.

He knelt up and held the smears of green against his eye and
the right side of his face. He slumped back against rock among
the jellies and scalloped pitches and encampments of limpets and
let the encrusted barnacles hurt him as they would. He set his left
hand gently on his thigh and squinted sideways at it. The fingers
were half-bent. The skin was white with blue showing through
and wrinkles cut the surface in regular shapes. The needle reached
after him in the skull behind the dark arch. If he moved the
eyeball the needle moved too. He opened his eye and it filled
immediately with water under the green weed.

He began to snort and make sounds deep in his chest. They
were like hard lumps of sound and they jerked him as they came
out. More salt water came out of each eye and joined the traces of
the sea and the solution on his cheeks. His whole body began to
shiver.

There was a deeper pool on a ledge farther down. He climbed
slowly and heavily down, edged himself across and put his right
cheek under again. He opened and closed his eye so that the
water flushed the needle corner. The memory pictures had gone
so far away that they could be disregarded. He felt round and
buried his hands in the pool. Now and then a hard sound jerked
his body.

The sea-gull came back with others and he heard them sounding their interlacing cries like a trace of their flight over his head.
There were noises from the sea too, wet gurgles below his ear
and the running thump of swells, blanketed by the main of the
rock but still able to sidle round and send offshoots sideways
among the rocks and into the crannies. The idea that he must
ignore pain came and sat in the centre of his darkness where he
could not avoid it. He opened his eyes for all the movement of
the needle and looked down at his bleached hands. He began to
mutter.

'Shelter. Must have shelter. Die if I don't.'

He turned his head carefully and looked up the way he had
come. The odd patches of rock that had hit him on the way down

were visible now as part of each other. His eyes took in yards at a
time, surfaces that swam as the needle pricked water out of him.
He set himself to crawl back up the rock. The wind was lighter
but dropping trails of rain still fell over him. He hauled himself
up a cliff that was no higher than a man could span with his arms
but it was an obstacle that had to be negotiated with much
arrangement and thought for separate limbs. He lay for a while
on the top of the little cliff and looked in watery snatches up the
height of the rock. The sun lay just above the high part where the
white trenches had waited for him. The light was struggling with
clouds and rain-mist and there were birds wheeling across the
rock. The sun was dull but drew more water from his eyes so that
he screwed them up and cried out suddenly against the needle.
He crawled by touch, and then with one eye through trenches
and gullies where there was no whiteness. He lifted his legs over
the broken walls of trenches as though they belonged to another
body. All at once, with the diminishing of the pain in his eye, the
cold and exhaustion came back. He fell flat in a gully and let his
body look after itself. The deep chill fitted close to him, so close
it was inside the clothes, inside the skin.

The chill and the exhaustion spoke to him clearly. Give up,
they said, lie still. Give up the thought of return, the thought of
living. Break up, leave go. Those white bodies are without attraction or excitement, the faces, the words, happened to another
man in another place. An hour on this rock is a lifetime. What
have you to lose? There is nothing here but torture. Give up.
Leave go.

His body began to crawl again. It was not that there was
muscular or nervous strength there that refused to be beaten but
rather that the voices of pain were like waves beating against the
sides of a ship. There was at the centre of all the pictures and
pains and voices a fact like a bar of steel, a thing—that which was
so nakedly the centre of everything that it could not even examine
itself. In the darkness of the skull, it existed, a darker dark, self-
existent and indestructible.

'Shelter. Must have shelter.'

The centre began to work. It endured the needle to look sideways, put thoughts together. It concluded that it must crawl this
way rather than that. It noted a dozen places and rejected them,
searched ahead of the crawling body. It lifted the luminous
window under the arch, shifted the arch of skull from side to side

like the slow shift of the head of a caterpillar trying to reach a
new leaf. When the body drew near to a possible shelter the head
still moved from side to side, moving more quickly than the slow
thoughts inside.

There was a slab of rock that had slipped and fallen sideways
from the wall of a trench. This made a triangular hole between
the rock and the side and bottom of the trench. There was no
more than a smear of rainwater in this trench and no white stuff.
The hole ran away and down at an angle following the line of the
trench and inside there was darkness. The hole even looked drier
than the rest of the rock. At last his head stopped moving and he
lay down before this hole as the sun dipped from view. He began
to turn his body in the trench, among a complication of sodden
clothing. He said nothing but breathed heavily with open mouth.
Slowly he turned until his white seaboot stockings were towards
the crevice. He backed to the triangular opening and put his feet
in. He lay flat on his stomach and began to wriggle weakly like a
snake that cannot cast its skin. His eyes were open and unfocused.
He reached back and forced the oilskin and duffle down on either
side. The oilskin was hard and he backed with innumerable separate movements like a lobster backing into a deep crevice under
water. He was in the crack up to his shoulders and rock held him
tightly. He hutched the lifebelt up till the soft rubber was across
the upper part of his chest. Ths slow thoughts waxed and waned,
the eyes were empty except for the water that ran from the needle
in the right one. His hand found the tit and he blew again slowly
until the rubber was firmed up against his chest. He folded his
arms, a white hand on either side. He let the left side of his face
fall on an oilskinned sleeve and his eyes were shut—not screwed
up but lightly closed. His mouth was still open, the jaw fallen
sideways. Now and then a shudder came up out of the crack and
set his head and arms shaking. Water ran slowly out of his sleeves,
fell from his hair and his nose, dripped from the rucked-up clothing round his neck. His eyes fell open like the mouth because the
needle was more controllable that way. Only when he had to
blink them against water did the point jab into the place where he
lived.

He could see gulls swinging over the rock, circling down.
They settled and cried with erect heads and tongues, beaks wide
open on the high point of the rock. The sky greyed down and
sea-smoke drifted over. The birds talked and shook their wings,

folded them one over the other, settled like white pebbles against the rock and tucked in their heads. The greyness thickened into a darkness in which the few birds and the splashes of their dung were visible as the patches of foam were visible on the water. The trenches were full of darkness for down by the shelter for some reason there was no dirty white. The rocks were dim shapes among them. The wind blew softly and chill over the main rock and its unseen, gentle passage made a continual and almost in-audible hiss. Every now and then a swell thumped into the angle by the safety rock. After that there would be a long pause and then the rush and scramble of falling water down the funnel.

The man lay, huddled in his crevice, left cheek pillowed on black oilskin and his hands were glimmering patches on either side. Every now and then there came a faint scratching sound of oilskin as the body shivered.

CHAPTER FOUR

The man was inside two crevices. There was first the rock, closed and not warm but at least not cold with the coldness of sea or air. The rock was negative. It confined his body so that here and there the shudders were beaten; not soothed but forced inward. He felt pain throughout most of his body but distant pain that was sometimes to be mistaken for fire. There was dull fire in his feet and a sharper sort in either knee. He could see this fire in his mind's eye because his body was a second and interior crevice which he inhabited. Under each knee, then, there was a little fire built with crossed sticks and busily flaring like the fire that is lighted under a dying camel. But the man was intelligent. He endured these fires although they gave not heat but pain. They had to be endured because to stand up or even move would mean nothing but an increase of pain—more sticks and more flame, extending under all the body. He himself was at the far end of this inner crevice of flesh. At this far end, away from the fires, there was a mass of him lying on a lifebelt that rolled backwards and forwards at every breath. Beyond the mass was the round, bone globe of the world and himself hanging inside. One half of this world burned and froze but with a steadier and bearable pain. Only towards the top half of this world there would sometimes come a jab that was like a vast needle prying after him. Then he would make seismic convulsions of whole continents on that side and the jabs would become frequent but less deep and the nature of that part of the globe would change. There would appear shapes of dark and grey in space and a patch of galactic whiteness that he knew vaguely was a hand connected to him. The other side of the globe was all dark and gave no offence. He floated in the middle of this globe like a waterlogged body. He knew as an axiom of existence that he must be content with the smallest of all small mercies as he floated there. All the extensions with which he was connected, their distant fires, their slow burning, their racks and pincers were at least far enough away. If he could hit some particular mode of inactive being, some subtlety of interior balance, he might be allowed by the nature of the second crevice to float, still and painless in the centre of the globe.

Sometimes he came near this. He became small, and the globe larger until the burning extensions were interplanetary. But this universe was subject to convulsions that began in deep space and came like a wave. Then he was larger again, filling every corner of the tunnels, sweeping with shrieking nerves over the fires, expanding in the globe until he filled it and the needle jabbed through the corner of his right eye straight into the darkness of his head. Dimly he would see one white hand while the pain stabbed. Then slowly he would sink back into the centre of the globe, shrink and float in the middle of a dark world. This became a rhythm that had obtained from all ages and would endure so.

This rhythm was qualified but not altered in essentials by pictures that happened to him and sometimes to someone else. They were brightly lit in comparison with the fires. There were waves larger than the universe and a glass sailor hanging in them. There was an order in neon lighting. There was a woman, not like the white detailed bodies but with a face. There was the gloom and hardness of a night-time ship, the lift of the deck, the slow cant and bumble. He was walking forward across the bridge to the binnacle and its dim light. He could hear Nat leaving his post as port look-out, Nat going down the ladder. He could hear that Nat had walking shoes on, not seaboots or plimsols. Nat was lowering his un-handy spider-length down the ladder with womanish care, not able now after all these months to wear the right clothes or negotiate a ladder like a seaman. Dawn had found him shivering from inadequate rig, the mess-deck would find him hurt by the language, a butt, humble, obedient, and useless.

He looked briefly at the starboard horizon then across to the convoy, bulks just coming into view in the dawn light. They interrupted the horizon like so many bleak iron walls where now the long, blurred tears of rust were nearly visible.

But Nat would be fumbling aft, to find five minutes' solitude by the rail and meet his aeons. He would be picking his diffident way towards the depth-charge thrower on the starboard side not because it was preferable to the port rail but because he always went there. He would be enduring the wind and engine stink, the peculiar dusty dirt and shabbiness of a wartime destroyer because life itself with all its touches, tastes, sights and sounds and smells had been at a distance from him. He would go on enduring until custom made him indifferent. He would never find his feet in the Navy because those great feet of his had always been away out there, attached by accident while the man inside prayed and waited to meet his aeons.

But the deck-watch was ticking on to the next leg of the zigzag. He looked carefully at the second hand.

'Starboard fifteen.'

Out on the port bow *Wildebeeste* was turning too. The grey light showed the swirl under her stern where the rudder had kicked across. As the bridge canted under him *Wildebeeste* seemed to slide astern from her position until she was lying parallel and just forrard of the beam.

'Midships.'

Wildebeeste was still turning. Connected by the soles of his feet through steel to the long waver and roll of glaucous water he could predict to himself the exact degree of her list to port as she came round. But the water was not so predictable after all. In the last few degrees of her turn he saw a mound of grey, a seventh wave slide by her bows and pass under her. The swing of her stern increased, her stern slid down the slope and for that time she had carried ten degrees beyond her course, in a sudden lurch.

'Steady.'

And curse the bloody Navy and the bloody war. He yawned sleepily and saw the swirl under *Wildebeeste*'s stern as she came back on course. The fires out there at the end of the second crevice flared up, a needle stabbed and he was back in his body. The fire died down again in the usual rhythm.

The destroyers in a V screen turned back together. Between orders he listened to the shivering ping of the Asdic and the light increased. The herd of merchantmen chugged on at six knots with the destroyers like outriders scouring the way before them, sweeping the sea clear with their invisible brooms, changing course together, all on one string.

He heard a step behind him on the ladder and busied himself to take a bearing because the captain might be coming. He checked the bearing of *Wildebeeste* with elaborate care. But no voice came with the steps.

He turned casually at last and there was Petty Officer Roberts— and now saluting.

'Good morning, Chief.'

'Good morning, sir.'

'What is it? Wangled a tot for me?'

The close eyes under their peak withdrew a little but the mouth made itself smile.

'Might, sir——'

And then, the calculation made, the advantage to self admitted, the smile widened.

'I'm a bit off me rum these days, somehow. Any time you'd care to——'

'O.K. Thanks.'

And what now? A draft chit? Recommend for commission? Something small and manageable?

But Petty Officer Roberts was playing a game too deep. Whatever it was and wherever the elaborate system of obligations might lead to, it required nothing today but a grateful opinion of his good sense and understanding.

'About Walterson, sir.'

Astonished laugh.

'My old friend Nat? What's he been doing? Not got himself in the rattle, has he?'

'Oh no, sir, nothing like that. Only——'

'What?'

'Well, just look now, sir, aft on the starboard side.'

Together they walked to the starboard wing of the bridge. Nathaniel was still engaged with his aeons, feet held by friction on the corticene, bony rump on the rail just aft of the thrower. His hands were up to his face, his improbable length swaying with the scend of the swells.

'Silly ass.'

'He'll do that once too often, sir.'

Petty Officer Roberts came close. Liar. There was rum in his breath.

'I could have put him in the rattle for it, sir, but I thought, seeing he's a friend of yours in civvy street——'

Pause.

'O.K., Chief. I'll drop him a word myself.'

'Thank you, sir.'

'Thank *you*, Chief.'

'I won't forget the tot, sir.'

'Thanks a lot.'

Petty Officer Roberts saluted and withdrew from the presence. He descended the ladder.

'Port fifteen.'

Solitude with fires under the knees and a jabbing needle. Solitude out over the deck where the muzzle of X gun was lifted over the corticene. He smiled grimly to himself and reconstructed the inside of Nathaniel's head. He must have laid aft, hopefully, seeking privacy between the crew of the gun and the depth-charge watch. But there was no solitude for a rating in a small ship unless he was knowing enough to find himself a quiet number. He must have drifted aft from the mob of the fo'castle, from utter, crowded squalor to a modified and windy form of it. He was too witless to understand that the huddled mess-deck was so dense as to ensure a form of privacy, like that a man can achieve in a London crowd. So he would endure the gloomy stare of the depth-charge watch at his prayers, not understanding that they would keep an eye on him because they had nothing else to do.

'Midships. Steady.'

Zig.

And he is praying in his time below when he ought to be turned in, swinging in his hammock, because he has been told that on watch he must keep a look-out over a sector of the sea. So he kept a look-out, dutiful and uncomprehending.

The dark centre of the head turned, saw the port look-out hutched, the swinging RDF aerial, the funnel with its tremble of hot air and trace of fume, looked down over the break of the bridge to the starboard deck.

Nathaniel was still there. His improbable height, combined with the leanness that made it seem even more incredible, had reduced the rail to an insecure parapet. His legs were splayed out and his feet held him by friction against the deck. As the dark centre watched, it saw Nathaniel take his hands down from his face, lay hold of the rail, and get himself upright. He began to work his way forrard over the deck, legs straddled, arms out for balance. He carried his absurd little naval cap exactly level on the top of his head, and his curly black hair—a trifle lank for the night's dampness—emerged from under it all round. He saw the bridge by chance and gravely brought his right hand towards the right side of his head—taking no liberties, thought the black centre, knowing his place, humble aboard as in civvy street, ludicrous, unstoppable.

But the balance of the thin figure was disturbed by this temporary exercise of the right hand; it tottered sideways, tried for
the salute again, missed, considered the problem gravely with
arms out and legs astraddle. A scend made it rock. It turned,
went to the engine casing, tried out the surface to see if the metal
was hot, steadied, turned forrard and slowly saluted the bridge.

The dark centre made itself wave cheerfully to the foreshortened figure. Nathaniel's face altered even at that distance. The
delight of recognition appeared in it, not plastered on and adjusted
as Petty Officer Roberts had smiled under his too-close eyes: but
rising spontaneously from the conjectural centre behind the face,
evidence of sheer niceness that made the breath come short with
maddened liking and rage. There was a convulsion in the substrata
of the globe at this end so that the needle came stabbing and
prying towards the centre that had floated all this while without
pain.

He seized the binnacle and the rock and cried out in an anguish
of frustration.

'Can't anyone understand how I feel?'

Then he was extended again throughout the tunnels of the
inner crevice and the fires were flaring and spitting in his flesh.

There came a new noise among the others. It was connected
with the motionless blobs of white out there. They were more
definite than they had been. Then he was aware that time had
passed. What had seemed an eternal rhythm had been hours of
darkness and now there was a faint light that consolidated his
personality, gave it bounds and sanity. The noise was a throaty
cluck from one of the roosting gulls.

He lay with the pains, considering the light and the fact of a
new day. He could inspect his wooden left hand if he was careful
about the management of the inflamed corner of his eye. He
willed the fingers to close and they quivered, then contracted.
Immediately he was back in them, he became a man who was
thrust deep into a crevice in barren rock. Knowledge and memory
flowed back in orderly succession, he remembered the funnel, the
trench. He became a castaway in broad daylight and the necessity
of his position fell on him. He began to heave at his body,
dragging himself out of the space between the rocks. As he
moved out, the gulls clamoured out of sleep and took off. They
came back, sweeping in to examine him with sharp cries then
sidling away in the air again. They were not like the man-wary

gulls of inhabited beaches and cliffs. Nor had they about them the
primal innocence of unvisited nature. They were wartime gulls
who, finding a single man with water round him, resented the
warmth of his flesh and his slow, unwarranted movements. They
told him, with their close approach, and flapping hover that he
was far better dead, floating in the sea like a burst hammock. He
staggered and struck out among them with wooden arms.

'Yah! Get away! Bugger off!'

They rose clamorously wheeling, came back till their wings
beat his face. He struck out again in panic so that one went
drooping off with a wing that made no more than a half-beat.
They retired then, circled and watched. Their heads were narrow.
They were flying reptiles. An ancient antipathy for things with
claws set him shuddering at them and thinking into their smooth
outlines all the strangeness of bats and vampires.

'Keep off! Who do you think I am?'

Their circles widened. They flew away to the open sea.

He turned his attention back to his body. His flesh seemed to
be a compound of aches and stiffnesses. Even the control system
had broken down for his legs had to be given deliberate and
separate orders as though they were some unhandy kind of stilts
that had been strapped to him. He broke the stilts in the middle,
and got upright. He discovered new fires—little islands of severer
pain in the general ache. The one at the corner of his right eye
was so near to him that he did not need to discover it. He stood
up, leaning his back against the side of a trench and looked round
him.

The morning was dull but the wind had died down and the
water was leaping rather than progressing. He became aware of a
new thing; sound of the sea that the sailor never hears in his live
ship. There was a gentle undertone compounded of countless
sloppings of wavelets, there was a constant gurgling and sucking
that ranged from a stony smack to a ruminative swallow. There
were sounds that seemed every moment to be on the point of
articulation but lapsed into a liquid slapping like appetite. Over
all this was a definable note, a singing hiss, soft touch of the air
on stone, continuous, subtle, unending friction.

A gull-cry swirled over him and he raised an arm and looked
under the elbow but the gull swung away from the rock. When
the cry had gone everything was gentle again, non-committal and
without offence.

He looked down at the horizon and passed his tongue over his upper lip. It came again, touched experimentally, vanished. He swallowed. His eyes opened wider and he paid no attention to the jab. He began to breathe quickly.

'Water!'

As in the sea at a moment of desperate crisis his body changed, became able and willing. He scrambled out of the trench on legs that were no longer wooden. He climbed across fallen buttresses that had never supported anything but their own weight; he slithered in the white pools of the trenches near the top of the rock. He came to the edge of the cliff where he had climbed and a solitary gull slipped away from under his feet. He worked himself round on his two feet but the horizon was like itself at every point. He could only tell when he had inspected every point by the lie of the rock beneath him. He went round again.

At last he turned back to the rock itself and climbed down but more slowly now from trench to trench. When he was below the level of the white bird-droppings he stopped and began to examine the rock foot by foot. He crouched in a trench, gripping the lower side and looking at every part of it with quick glances as if he were trying to follow the flight of a hover-fly. He saw water on a flat rock, went to it put his hands on either side of the puddle and stuck his tongue in. His lips contracted down round his tongue, sucked. The puddle became nothing but a patch of wetness on the rock. He crawled on. He came to a horizontal crack in the side of a trench. Beneath the crack a slab of rock was falling away and there was water caught. He put his forehead against the rock then turned sideways until his cheek rested above the crack—but still his tongue could not reach the water. He thrust and thrust, mouth ground against the stone but still the water was beyond him. He seized the cracked stone and jerked furiously until it broke away. The water spilled down and became a film in the bottom of the trench. He stood there, heart thumping and held the broken stone in his hands.

'Use your loaf, man. Use your loaf.'

He looked down the jumbled slope before him. He began to work the rock methodically. He noticed the broken stone in his hands and dropped it. He worked across the rock and back from trench to trench. He came on the mouldering bones of fish and a dead gull, its upturned breast-bone like the keel of a derelict boat. He found patches of grey and yellow lichen, traces even of earth, a button of moss. There were the empty shells of crabs, pieces of dead weed, and the claws of a lobster.

At the lower end of the rock there were pools of water but they were salt. He came back up the slope, his needle and the fires forgotten. He groped in the crevice where he had lain all night but the rock was nearly dry. He clambered over the fallen slab of stone that had sheltered him.

The slab was in two pieces. Once there must have been a huge upended layer of rock that had endured while the others weathered away. It had fallen and broken in two. The larger piece lay across the trench at the very edge of the rock. Part of it projected over the sea, and the trench led underneath like a gutter.

He lay down and inserted himself. He paused. Then he was jerking his tail like a seal and lifting himself forward with his flippers. He put his head down and made sucking noises. Then he lay still.

The place in which he had found water was like a little cave. The floor of the trench sloped down gently under water so that this end of the pool was shallow. There was room for him to lie with his elbows spread apart for the slab had smashed down the wall on the right-hand side. The roof stone lay across at an angle and the farther end of the cave was not entirely stopped up. There was a small hole high up by the roof, full of daylight and a patch of sky. The light from the sky was reflected in and from the water so that faint lines quivered over the stone roof. The water was drinkable but there was no pleasure in the taste. It tasted of things that were vaguely unpleasant though the taste were not individually indentifiable. The water did not satisfy thirst so much as allay it. There seemed to be plenty of the stuff, for the pool was yards long before him and the farther end looked deep. He lowered his head and sucked again. Now that his one and a half eyes were adjusted to the light he could see there was a deposit under the water, reddish and slimy. The deposit was not hard but easily disturbed so that where he had drunk, the slime was coiling up, drifting about, hanging, settling. He watched dully.

Presently he began to mutter.

'Rescue. See about rescue.'

He struggled back with a thump of his skull against rock. He crawled along the trench and clambered to the top of the rock and peered round and round the horizon again. He knelt and lowered himself on his hands. The thoughts began to flicker quickly in his head.

'I cannot stay up here all the time. I cannot shout to them if they pass. I must make a man to stand here for me. If they see anything like a man they will come closer.'

There was a broken rock below his hands, leaning against the wall from which the clean fracture had fallen. He climbed down and wrestled with a great weight. He made the stone rise on an angle; he quivered and the stone fell over. He collapsed and lay for a while. He left the stone and scrambled heavily down to the little cliff and the scattered rocks where he had bathed his eye. He found an encrusted boulder lying in a rock pool and pulled it up. He got the stone against his stomach, staggered for a few steps, dropped the stone, lifted and carried again. He dumped the stone on the high point above the funnel and came back. There was a stone like a suitcase balanced on the wall of a trench and he pondered what he should do. He put his back against the suitcase and his feet against the other side of the trench. The suitcase grated, moved. He got a shoulder under one end and heaved. The suitcase tumbled in the next trench and broke. He grinned without humour and lugged the larger part up into his lap. He raised the broken suitcase to the wall, turned it end over end, engineered it up slopes of fallen but unmanageable rock, pulled and hauled.

Then there were two rocks on the high part, one with a trace of blood. He looked once round the horizon and climbed down the slope again. He stopped, put a hand to his forehead, then examined the palm. But there was no blood.

He spoke out loud in a voice that was at once flat and throaty.

'I am beginning to sweat.'

He found a third stone but could not get it up the wall of the trench. He retreated with it, urged it along the bottom to a lower level until he could find an exit low enough for him to heave it up. By the time he had dragged it to the others his hands were broken. He knelt by the stones and considered the sea and sky. The sun was out wanly and there were fewer layers of cloud. He lay down across the three stones and let them hurt him. The sun shone on his left ear from the afternoon side of the rock.

He got up, put the second stone laboriously on the third and the first on the second. The three stones measured nearly two feet from top to bottom. He sat down and leaned back against them.

The horizon was empty, the sea gentle, the sun a token. A sea-gull was drifting over the water a stone's throw from the rock, and now the bird was rounded, white and harmless. He covered his aching eye with one hand to rest it but the effort of holding a hand up was too much and he let the palm fall back on his knee. He ignored his eye and tried to think.

'Food?'

He got to his feet and climbed down over the trenches. At the lower end were cliffs a few feet high and beyond them separate rocks broke the surface. He ignored these for the moment because they were inaccessible. The cliffs were very rough. They were covered with a crust of tiny barnacles that had welded their limy secretions into an extended colony that dipped down in the water as deep as his better eye could see. There were yellowish limpets and coloured sea-snails drying and drawn in against the rock. Each limpet sat in the hollow its foot had worn. There were clusters of blue mussels too, with green webs of weed caught over them. He looked back up the side of the rock—under the water-hole for he could see the roof slab projecting like a diving-board—and saw how the mussels had triumphed over the whole wall. Beneath a defined line the rock was blue with them. He lowered himself carefully and inspected the cliff. Under water the harvest of food was even thicker for the mussels were bigger down there and water-snails were crawling over them. And among the limpets, the mussels, the snails and barnacles, dotted like sucked sweets, were the red blobs of jelly, the anemones. Under water they opened their mouths in a circle of petals but up by his face, waiting for the increase of the tide they were pursed up and slumped like breasts when the milk has been drawn from them.

Hunger contracted under his clothes like a pair of hands. But as he hung there, his mouth watering, a lump rose in his throat as if he were very sad. He hung on the creamy wall and listened to the washing of water, the minute ticks and whispers that came from this abundant, but not quite vegetable, life. He felt at his waist, produced the lanyard, swung it and caught the knife with his free hand. He put the blade against his mouth, gripped with his teeth and pulled the haft away from it. He put the point under a limpet and it contracted down so that he felt its muscular strength as he turned the blade. He dropped the knife to the length of the lanyard and caught the limpet as it fell. He turned the limpet over in his hand and peered into the broad end. He saw an oval brown foot drawn in, drawn back, shutting out the light.

'Bloody hell!'

He jerked the limpet away from him and the tent made a little flip of water in the sea. As the ripples died away he watched it waver down whitely out of sight. He looked for a while at the place where the limpet had disappeared. He took his knife again and began to chisel lines among the barnacles. They wept and bled salty, uretic water. He poked an anemone with the point of the knife and the jelly screwed up tight. He pressed the top with the flat of the blade and the opening pissed in his eye. He jammed the knife against the rock and shut it. He climbed back and sat on the high rock with his back against the three stones—two broken and an encrusted one on top.

Inside, the man was aware of a kind of fit that seized his body. He drew his feet up against him and rolled sideways so that his face was on the rock. His body was jumping and shuddering beneath the sodden clothing. He whispered against stone.

'You can't give up.'

Immediately he began to crawl away down hill. The crawl became a scramble. Down by the water he found stones but they were of useless shape. He chose one from just under water and toiled back to the others. He changed the new one for the top stone, grated it into place, then put the encrusted one back. Two feet, six inches.

He muttered.

'Must. Must.'

He climbed down to the rock-side opposite the cliff of mussels. There were ledges on this side and water sucking up and down. The water was very dark and there was long weed at the bottom, straps like the stuff travellers sometimes put round suitcases when the locks are broken. This brown weed was collapsed and coiled over itself near the surface but farther out it lay upright in the water or moved slowly like tentacles or tongues. Beyond that there was nothing but the blackness of deep water going down to the bottom of the deep sea. He took his eyes away from this, climbed along one of the ledges, but everywhere the rock was firm and there were no separated pieces to be found, though in one place the solid ledge was cracked. He pushed at this part with his stockinged feet but could not move it. He turned clumsily on

the ledge and came back. At the lower end of the great rock he
found the stones with the wrong shape and took them one by one
to a trench and piled them. He pried in crevices and pulled out
blocks and rounded masses of yellowing quartz on which the
weed was draggled like green hair. He took them to the man he
was building and piled them round the bottom stone. Some were
not much bigger than potatoes and he knocked these in where
the big stones did not fit until the top one no longer rocked when
he touched it. He put one last stone on the others, one big as his
head.

Three feet.

He stood away from the pile and looked round him. The pile
reached in his view from horizon level to higher than the sun. He
was astonished when he saw this and looked carefully to establish
where west was. He saw the outlying rock that had saved him
and the sea-gulls were floating just beyond the backwash.

He climbed down the rock again to where he had prised off the
limpet. He made a wry face and pushed his doubled fists into the
damp cloth over his belly. He hung on the little cliff and began to
tear away the blobs of red jelly with his fingers. He set them on
the edge of the cliff and did not look at them for a while. Then he
turned his one and a half eyes down to them and inspected them
closely. They lay like a handful of sweets only they moved ever
so slightly and there was a little clear water trickling from the
pile. He sat by them on the edge of the cliff and no longer saw
them. His face set in a look of agony.

'Bloody hell!'

His fingers closed over a sweet. He put it quickly in his mouth,
ducked, swallowed, shuddered. He took another, swallowed, took
another as fast as he could. He bolted the pile of sweets then sat
rigid, his throat working. He subsided, grinning palely. He looked
down at his left hand and there was one last sweet lying against
his little finger in a drip of water. He clapped his hand to his
mouth, stared over the fingers and fought with his stomach. He
scrambled over the rocks to the water-hole and pulled himself in.
Again the coils of red silt and slime rose from the bottom. There
was a band of red round the nearer end of the pool that was
about half an inch across.

When he had settled his stomach with the harsh water he came
out of the hole backwards. The sea-gulls were circling the rock
now and he looked at them with hate.

'You won't get me!'

He clambered back to the top of the rock where his three-foot dwarf stood. The horizon was in sight all round and empty. He licked a trace of drinkable water from his lips.

'I have enough to drink——'

He stood, looking down at the slab over his drinking water where it projected like a diving-board. He went slowly to the cliff, got down and peered under the slab. The seaward end of the pool was held back by a jumble of broken stones that were lodged against each other. Behind the impaired window of his sight he saw the red silt rising and coiling. The stuff must lie over the inner side of these stones, sealing them lightly against the water's escape. He had a quick vision of the hidden surfaces, holes that time had furred with red till they were stopped and the incongruous fresh water held back among all the salt; but held back so delicately that the merest touch would set his life irrevocably flowing——

He backed away with staring eyes and breath that came quick.

'Forget it!'

He began to thrust himself backwards into the sleeping crevice. He got almost to his ears out of sight and filled the hole with his body and heavy clothing. He pulled the sleeves of his duffle out of the oilskin tubes until they came over the backs of his hands. After a little struggling he could grip them with his fingers and double his fists so that they were hidden in the hairy duffle. The lifebelt supported his chest and throat once more and he pillowed his left cheek on his forearm. He lay so, shivering now that the sun had gone down, while the green sky turned blue, dark blue and the gulls floated down. His body yielded to the shivers but between the bouts it lay quite still. His mouth was open and his eyes stared anxiously into the darkness. Once, he jerked and the mouth spoke.

'Forget it!'

A gull moved a little then settled down again.

CHAPTER FIVE

But he could not fall into the pit because he was extended through his body. He was aware dimly of returning strength; and this not only allowed him to savour the cold and be physically miserable but to be irritated by it. Instead of the apocalyptic visions and voices of the other night he had now nothing but ill-used and complaining flesh. The point of the needle in his eye was blunted but instead of enduring anything rather than its stab he had continually to rub one foot over the other or press with his body against the slab of rock in an effort to shut off the chill on that side, only to find that the other side required attention more and more insistently. He would heave the globe of darkness in which he most lived off a hard, wooden surface, rotate it and lay the other hemisphere down. There was another difference between this night and the last. The fires had died down but they were still there now he had the time and the strength to attend to them. The stiffness had become a settled sense of strain as if his body were being stretched mercilessly. The rock too, now that he had a little strength to spare was forcing additional discomfort on him. What the globe had taken in its extreme exhaustion for a smooth surface was in fact undulating with the suggestion of prominences here and there. These suggestions became localized discomforts that changed in turn to a dull ache. Allowed to continue, aches became pains then fires that must be avoided. So he would heave his thigh away or wriggle weakly only to find that the prominence was gone and had left nothing but an undulation. His thigh would flatten down again and wait in the darkness for the discomfort, the ache, the pain, the fire.

Up at the top end now that the window was dark the man found the intermissions of discomfort were again full of voices and things that could not be seen. He had a confused picture of the passage of the sun below him beyond the central fires of the earth. But both the sun and the fires were too far away to warm him. He saw the red silt holding back the fresh water, a double handful of red sweets, an empty horizon.

'I shall live!'

He saw the sun below him with its snail movement and was confused inside his head by the earth's revolution on its axis and its year-long journey round the sun. He saw how many months a man must endure before he was warmed by the brighter light of spring. He watched the sun for months without thought or identity. He saw it from many angles, through windows of trains or from fields. He confused its fires with other fires, on allotments, in gardens, in grates. One of these fires was most insistent that here was reality and to be watched. The fire was behind the bars of a grate. He found that the grate was in a room and then everything became familiar out of the past and he knew where he was and that the time and the words were significant. There was a tall and spider-thin figure sitting in the chair opposite. It looked up under its black curls, as if it were consulting a reference book on the other side of the ceiling.

'Take us as we are now and heaven would be sheer negation. Without form and void. You see? A sort of black lightning destroying everything that we call life.'

But he was laughing and happy in his reply.

'I don't see and I don't much care but I'll come to your lecture. My dear Nathaniel, you've no idea how glad I am to see you!'

Nathaniel looked his face over carefully.

'And I, too. About seeing you, I mean.'

'We're showing emotion, Nat. We're being un-English.'

Again the careful look.

'I think you need my lecture. You're not happy, are you?'

'I'm not really interested in heaven either. Let me get you a drink.'

'No, thanks.'

Nathaniel uncoiled from the chair and stood with his arms out on either side, hands bent up. He looked, first at nothing, then round the room. He went to the wall and perched himself absurdly high up with his bony rump on the top of a shelf. He pushed his incredible legs out and splayed them apart till he was held insecurely by the friction of the soles of his feet. He looked up at the reference book again.

'You could call it a talk on the technique of dying.'

'You'll die a long time before me. It's a cold night—and look how you're dressed!'

Nathaniel peered at the laughing window then down at himself.

'Is it? Yes. I suppose I am.'

'And I'm going to have a damned long life and get what I'm after.'

'And that is——?'

'Various things.'

'But you're not happy.'

'Why do you spill this over me, of all people?'

'There's a connection between us. Something will happen to us or perhaps we were meant to work together. You have an extraordinary capacity to endure.'

'To what end?'

'To achieve heaven.'

'Negation?'

'The technique of dying into heaven.'

'No thanks. Be your age, Nat.'

'You could, you know. And I——'

Nat's face was undergoing a change. It turned towards him again. The flush on the cheeks was painful. The eyes loomed and impended.

'—And I, have a feeling. Don't laugh, please—but I feel—you could say that I know.' Below the eyes the breath came out in a little gasp. Feet scraped.

'—You could say that I know it is important for you personally to understand about heaven—about dying—because in only a few years——'

For a while there was silence, a double shock—for the bells ceased to toll beyond the windows of the room as though they had stopped with the voice. A vicious sting from his cigarette whipped along the arm into the globe so that he flicked it away and cried out. Then he was flat on the floor, fumbling for the stub under the armchair and undulations of the floor were a discomfort to the body. Lying there, the words pursued him, made his ears buzz, set up a tumult, pushed his heart to thump with sudden, appalled understanding as though it were gasping the words that Nathaniel had not spoken.

'—because in only a few years you will be dead.'

He cried out against the unspoken words in fury and panic.

'You bloody fool, Nat! You awful bloody fool!'

The words echoed in the trench and he jerked his cheek up off the oilskin. There was much light outside, sunlight and the crying of gulls.

He shouted.

'I'm damned if I'll die!'

He hauled himself quickly out of the crevice and stood in the trench. The sea and sky were dark blue and the sun was high enough not to make a dazzle from the water. He felt the sun on his face and rubbed with both hands at the bristles. He looked quickly round the horizon then climbed down to a trench. He began to fumble with his trousers, glancing furtively behind him. Then for the first time on the rock he broke up the bristly, external face with a shout of jeering laughter. He went back to the dwarf and made water in a hosing gesture at the horizon.

'Gentlemen are requested to adjust their dress before leaving.'

He began to fumble with the buttons of his oilskin and lugged it off fiercely. He picked and pulled at the tapes that held his lifebelt inside the duffle. He slipped both off and dumped them in a heavy heap and stood there looking down. He glanced at the two wavy lines of gold braid on either arm, the gilt buttons, the black doeskin of his jacket and trousers. He peeled himself, jacket, woollen sweater, black sweater, shirt, vest; pulled off his long stockings, his socks, his pants. He stood still and examined what he could see of his body.

The feet had been so thoroughly sodden that they seemed to have lost their shape. One big toe was blue and black with bruise and drying blood. There were bruises on either knee that ended in lacerations, not cuts or jabs but places the size of a sixpence where the skin and flesh had been worn off. His right hip was blue as though someone had laid a hand dipped in paint on it.

He examined his arms. The right elbow was swollen and stiff and there were more bruises about. Here and there on his body were patches, not of raw flesh but of blood flecks under the skin. He felt the bristles on his face tenderly. His right eye was fogged and that cheek was hot and stiff.

He took his vest and tried to wring out the body but there was water held in the material that would not come free. He put his left foot on one end of the twisted cloth and screwed the other with both hands. Dampness appeared and moistened the rock. He did this in turn to each piece of clothing and spread the lot in the sun to dry. He sat down by the dwarf, fumbled in his jacket and brought out a sodden packet of papers and a small brown booklet. The colour had run from the booklet and stained the papers as if they were rusting. He spread the papers out round him and rummaged through his pockets in turn. He found two pennies and a florin. He laid them by the dwarf in a little heap. He took his knife on its lanyard from the pocket of his oilskin and hung it round his neck. When he had done that he put up his hand and tugged gently at the small brown disc that was tied round his neck by a white thread. He bent his face into a grin. He got up and scrambled over the rocks to the water-hole. He eased himself in and leaned forward. The red coils rose and reminded him of the other tamped end of the pool. He backed out carefully, holding his breath.

He climbed down over the trenches to the lower end of the rock. The water was low and tons of living jelly was spread in armour over the cliffs. Where he stood with his toes projecting over the edge the food was dry, and talked with continual tiny crepitations. The weed was transparent over the shells and only faintly green. He clambered down from handhold to handhold, wincing as he caught the sharp shells with his feet. He pulled at mussels but they would not come away. He had to twist them out as if he were breaking bones away from their tendons, screwing them out of the joints. He jerked them over his head so that they arched up and fell clattering on the rock. He worked among the sharp shells over the wavering water until his legs were trembling with strain. He climbed the cliff, rested, came back and twisted out more. There was a scattered harvest of them on the rock, some of them four inches long. He sat down, breathless in the sun and worked at them. They were not vulnerable like the red sweets; they were gripped and glued tight and there was nowhere to get the blade of the knife in. He put one on the rock and beat it with the haft of his knife until the shell fractured. He took out the complicated body and looked away over the sea.

'The Belgians do.'

He gulped the body down. He set his teeth, broke another shell. Soon he had a heap of raw flesh that lay, white and yellow on the dry rock. His jaws moved, he looked away at the horizon. The fogged side of his right eye was pulled slightly as he ate. He felt round with his hand and the heap was gone. He climbed down the cliff and got more. He opened each of these with a sudden downward jab of his knife. When they were gone he forced the red sweets from the rock and popped them in his mouth. He made no distinction between green and red. He took a wisp of green seaweed and chewed it like a leaf of lettuce. He

went back to the water-hole, inserted himself and lay for a
moment, looking down at the gleaming surface. He moistened
his lips, so that the coils of red slime only stirred a little then lay
down again. He eased himself out, clambered to the top of the
rock and looked round. The horizon was ruled straight and hard
in every part. He sat down.

The papers and booklet were still damp but he took up the
booklet and opened it. Inside the cover was a transparent guard
over a photograph. He peered through the cover and made out a
fogged portrait. He could see a carefully arranged head of hair, a
strong and smiling face, the white silk scarf round the neck. But
detail had gone for ever. The young man who smiled dimly at
him through fog and brown stains was distant as the posed por-
traits of great-grandparents in a faint, brown world.

Even so, he continued to look, searching for the details he
remembered rather than saw, touching his bristled cheek while
he divined the smiling smoothness of the one before him, re-
arranging the unkept hair, feeling tenderly the painful corner of
an eye. Opposite the photograph was writing in a slot but this
too was smeared and washed into illegibility. He put the booklet
down and felt for the brown disc hanging round his neck. He
lifted the disc as far as the string would allow until it was close to
his left eye. He strained back and got it far enough away from
him.

CHRISTOPHER

HADLEY

MARTIN

TY. LIEUT., R.N.V.R.

C. OF E.

He read the inscription again and again, cut by cut. His lips
began to move. He dropped the disc, looked down at his salted
legs with their scars, at his belly and the bush of hair over his
privates.

He spoke out loud, using his voice hoarsely and with a kind of
astonishment.

'Christopher Hadley Martin. Martin. Chris. I am what I always
was!'

All at once it seemed to him that he came out of his curious
isolation inside the globe of his head and was extended normally
through his limbs. He lived again on the surface of his eyes, he

was out in the air. Daylight crowded down on him, sunlight, there was a sparkle on the sea. The solid rock was coherent as an object, with layered guano, with fresh water and shell-fish. It was a position in a finite sea at the intersection of two lines, there were real ships passing under the horizon. He got quickly to his feet and laboured round the rock, turning his clothes in the sun. He sniffed the pants and laughed. He went back to the papers and turned them. He took up the coins, chinked them in his hand for a moment and made as if to toss them in the sea. He paused.

'That would be too cracker-motto. Too ham.'

He looked at the quiet sea.

'I don't claim to be a hero. But I've got health and education and intelligence. I'll beat you.'

The sea said nothing. He grinned a little foolishly at himself.

'What I meant was to affirm my determination to survive. And of course, I'm talking to myself.'

He looked round the rock.

'The first thing to do is to survey the estate.'

The rock had diminished from an island to a thing. In the sunlight and absence of cold the whole could be inspected not only with eyes but with understanding. He saw at once that the trenches were the worn ends of vertical strata and the walls between them, harder layers that had worn more slowly. They were the broken end of a deep bed of mud that had been compressed by weight until the mud had heated and partly fused. Some convulsion of the upper layers, an unguessable contortion, a gripe of the earth's belly had torn the deep bed and thrust this broken end up vertically through mud and clay until it erupted as the tooth bursts out of the fleshy jaw. Then the less compressed layers had worn away into trenches full of edges like the cut pages of a book. The walls too were broken in places and modified everywhere by local hazard. Some of the walls had fallen and lay jumbled in the trenches. The whole top of the rock tended down, trench by trench, from the west to the east.

The cliff sides of the rock concealed the stratification for they were water-worn and fretted into lace by the plant-animals that clustered so thickly on them. This top was concreted with whiteness under stinking water but down there the blue and shattered mussel-shells lay scattered, the rock was clean or covered with barnacles and weed. Beyond the rock was a gap of shallow water, then another smaller rock, another and another in a slightly curving line. Then there was a pock that interrupted the pattern of the water and after that, the steep climb of the sea up to the sky.

He looked solemnly at the line of rocks and found himself thinking of them as teeth. He caught himself imagining that they were emerging gradually from the jaw—but that was not the truth. They were sinking; or rather they were being worn away in infinite slow motion. They were the grinders of old age, worn away. A lifetime of the world had blunted them, was reducing them as they ground what food rocks eat.

He shook his head irritably then caught his breath at the sudden pain in his neck.

'The process is so slow it has no relevance to——'

He stopped. He looked up into the air, then round over his shoulder. He repeated the words carefully, with the same intonation and at the same strength.

'The process is so slow——'

There was something peculiar about the sound that came out of his mouth. He discounted the hoarseness as of a man recovering from a cold or a bout of violent shouting. That was explicable.

He sang loudly.

'Alouette, gentille Alouette——'

He held his nose with his right hand and tried to blow through it until the pressure rounded his cheeks. Nothing cracked in his ears. His eyes hurt and water ran round them. He bent down, put his hands on his scarred knees and turned his head sideways. He shook his head violently, ignoring the pain in his neck and hoping to feel the little wobbling weight that would tell of water caught in his ears.

He stood up, facing a whole amphitheatre of water and sang a scale.

'Lah-la, la, la, la, la, la la-lah!'

The sound ended at his mouth.

He struck an attitude and declaimed.

> *The weary moon with her lamp before*
> *Knocks even now upon dawn's grey door*——

His voice faltered and stopped. He brought his hand down, turned the wrist, held the palm about a foot in front of his mouth.

'Testing. Testing. I am receiving you, strength——'

He closed his lips, lowered his hand slowly. The blue, igloo-roof over the rock went away to a vast distance, the visible world expanded with a leap. The water lopped round a tiny rock in the middle of the Atlantic. The strain tautened his face. He took a step among the scattered papers.

'My God!'

He gripped the stone dwarf, clutched himself to the humped shoulders and stared across. His mouth was open again. His heart-beats were visible as a flutter among the ribs. The knuckles of his hands whitened.

There was a clatter from the dwarf. The head stone thumped and went knock, knock, knock down the cliff.

Flumf.

He began to curse. He scrambled down the rock, found a too heavy stone, moved it about a yard and then let go. He threw himself over the stone and went cursing to the water. But there was nothing visible within reach that he could handle. He went quickly to the top again and stood looking at the headless dwarf in terror. He scrambled back to the too heavy stone and fought with it. He moved it, end over end. He built steps to the top of a wall and worked the great stone up. He drew from his body more strength than he had got. He bled. He stood sweating among the papers at last. He dismantled the dwarf and rebuilt him on the stone that after all was not to heavy for education and intelligence and will.

Four feet.

He jammed in the dry, white potatoes.

'Out of this nettle danger——'

The air sucked up his voice like blotting-paper.

Take a grip.

Education and intelligence.

He stood by the dwarf and began to talk like a man who has an unwilling audience but who will have his say whether anyone listens to him or not.

CHAPTER SIX

'The end to be desired is rescue. For that, the bare minimum necessary is survival. I must keep this body going. I must give it drink and food and shelter. When I do that it does not matter if the job is well done or not so long as it is done at all. So long as the thread of life is unbroken it will connect a future with the past for all this ghastly interlude. Point one.

'Point two. I must expect to fall sick. I cannot expose the body to this hardship and expect the poor beast to behave as if it were in clover. I must watch for signs of sickness and doctor myself.

'Point three. I must watch my mind. I must not let madness steal up on me and take me by surprise. Already—I must expect hallucinations. That is the real battle. That is why I shall talk out loud for all the blotting-paper. In normal life to talk out loud is a sign of insanity. Here it is proof of identity.

'Point four. I must help myself to be rescued. I cannot do anything but be visible. I have not even a stick to hoist a shirt on. But no one will come within sight of this rock without turning a pair of binoculars on it. If they see the rock they will see this dwarf I have made. They will know that someone built the dwarf and they will come and take me off. All I have to do is to live and wait. I must keep my grip on reality.'

He looked firmly at the sea. All at once he found that he was seeing through a window again. He was inside himself at the top end. The window was bounded above by the mixed, superimposed skin and hair of both brows, and divided into three lights by two outlines or shadows of noses. But the noses were transparent. The right-hand light was fogged and all three drew together at the bottom. When he looked down at the rock he was seeing the surface over the scrubby hedge of his unshaven upper lip. The window was surrounded by inscrutable darkness which extended throughout his body. He leaned forward to peer round the window-frame but it went with him. He altered the frame for a moment with a frown. He turned the three lights right round the horizon. He spoke, frowning.

'That is the ordinary experience of living. There is nothing strange in that.' He shook his head and busied himself. He turned the windows on his own body and examined the skin critically. Great patches were pink over the scars and he cried out.

'Sunburn!'

He grabbed his vest and pulled it on. The material was so nearly dry that he accepted it as such and shuffled into his pants. The luminous windows became the ordinary way of seeing. He gathered his papers, put them in the identity book and stowed the whole packet in the pocket of his reefer. He padded round the top of the rock, handling his clothes and testing them for dryness. They did not feel damp so much as heavy. There was no moisture that would come off on the fingers or could be wrung out, but where he lifted them from the rock they left their shapes in darker stone that faded slowly in the sun.

He spoke flatly against the blotting-paper.

'I wish I'd kept my seaboots.'

He came to his oilskin and knelt, looking at it. Then suddenly he was rummaging through the forgotten pockets. He drew out a sou'wester from which the water ran, and a sodden balaclava. He unfolded the sou'wester and wrung out the balaclava. He spread them and dived at the other pocket. An expression of anxious concentration settled on his face. He fumbled and drew out a green ha'penny, some string and the crumpled wrapping from a bar of chocolate. He unfolded the paper with great care; but there was nothing left inside. He put his face close to the glittering paper and squinted at it. In one crease there was a single brown grain. He put out his tongue and took the grain. The chocolate stung with a piercing sweetness, momentary and agonizing, and was gone.

He leaned back against the stone dwarf, reached for his socks and pulled them on. He took his seaboot stockings, rolled down the tops and made do with them for boots.

He let his head lie against the dwarf and closed his eyes. The sun shone over his shoulder and the water washed. Inside his head the busy scenes flickered and voices spoke. He experienced all the concomitants of drowsiness but still there did not come the fall and gap of sleep. The thing in the middle of the globe was active and tireless.

'I should like a bed with sheets. I should like a pint or two and a hot meal. I should like a hot bath.'

He sat for a while, silent, while the thing jumped from thought to thought. He remembered that speech was proof of identity and his lips began to move again.

'So long as I can want these things without finding the absence of them unendurable; so long as I can tell myself that I am alone on a rock in the middle of the Atlantic and that I have to fight to survive—then I can manage. After all, I am safe compared with those silly sods in H.M. ships. They never know when they're going to be blown up. But I should like to see the brick that could shift this rock.'

The thing that could not examine itself danced on in the world behind the eyes.

'And anyway I must not sleep in the daytime. Save that for the miserable nights.'

He stood up suddenly and looked round the horizon.

'Dress and eat. Dress for dinner.'

He kicked off the seaboot stockings and got into his clothes, all but the duffle and oilskin. He pulled the stockings up over his trousers to the knees. He stood and became voluble in the flat air.

'I call this place the Look-out. That is the Dwarf. The rock out there under the sun where I came swimming is Safety Rock. The place where I get mussels and stuff is Food Cliff. Where I eat them is—The Red Lion. On the south side where the strap-weed is, I call Prospect Cliff. This cliff here to the west with the funnel in it is——'

He paused, searching for a name. A sea-gull came swinging in under the sun, saw the two figures standing on the Look-out, screamed, side-slipped crazily and wheeled away. It came straight back but at a lower level on his right hand and vanished into the cliff. He edged forward and looked down. There was a sheer, almost unbroken descent on the left and then the cleft in the middle of the cliff, and above that, the funnel. To the right the foot of the cliff was hidden for the highest corner of the Look-out leaned out. He went on hands and knees to the edge and looked down. The cliff was visible for a yard and then turned in and hid itself. The rock began again near the bottom and he could see a glint of feather.

'A lump has fallen out of the cliff.'

He searched the water carefully and thought he could make out a square shape deep under the surface. He backed away and stood up.

'Gull Cliff.'

The horizon was still empty.

He climbed down the rock to the Red Lion.

'I wish I could remember the name of the whole rock. The Captain said it was a near miss and he laughed. I have it on the tip of my tongue. And I must have a name for this habitual clamber of mine between the Look-out and the Red Lion. I shall call it the High Street.'

He saw that the rock on which he sat was dark and glanced over his shoulder. The sun was just leaving him, going down behind the Dwarf, so that the piled stones had become a giant. He got up quickly and lowered himself down the plastered Food Cliff. He hung spreadeagled, traversed a couple of yards and twisted out mussels. The deep sea tide was up now and he had much less scope. He had to lean down and work the mussels loose under water. He climbed back to the Red Lion and began to eat. The great shape of the rock had lost detail and become a blotch against the evening sky. The shadow loomed, vast as a mountain peak. He looked the other way and there were the three rocks diminishing into a dark sea.

'I name you three rocks—Oxford Circus, Piccadilly and Leicester Square.'

He went to the dark water-hole and pulled himself in. A little light still came from the hole in the jumbled stones at the other end and when he drank he could see ripples faintly but the red coils were invisible. He put his forefinger straight down into the water and felt the slimy bottom. He lay very still.

'It will rain again.'

Then he was jumping and shuddering for there was someone else in the hole with him. Or there was a voice that spoke almost with his, from the water and the slab. As his heart eased he could think coherently of the sound as a rare and forgotten thing, a resonance, an echo. Then immediately he could reason that his voice was full-sized in here so he quietened his body and spoke deliberately.

'Plenty of identity in here, Ladies and Gentlemen——'

He cut his voice off sharply and heard the rock say, '——men——'

'It will rain.'

'——ain.'

'How are you?'

'——u?'

'I am busy surviving. I am netting down this rock with names and taming it. Some people would be incapable of understanding the importance of that. What is given a name is given a seal, a chain. If this rock tries to adapt me to its ways I will refuse and adapt it to mine. I will impose my routine on it, my geography. I will tie it down with names. If it tries to annihilate me with blotting-paper, then I will speak in here where my words resound and significant sounds assure me of my own identity. I will trap rainwater and add it to this pool. I will use my brain as a delicate machine-tool to produce the results I want. Comfort. Safety. Rescue. Therefore tomorrow I declare to be a thinking day.'

He backed out of the water-hole, climbed the High Street and stood on the Look-out by the Dwarf. He dressed in everything, pulled on the damp balaclava and drew the sou'wester round his head with the chinstay down. He looked quickly round the horizon, listened to the faint movement from the invisible aery half-way down Gull Cliff. He went down the High Street, came to his crevice. He sat on the wall by the crevice, put his feet in the grey sweater and wrapped it round them. He got down and wormed his way into the crevice, pushing down his duffle and oilskin. He blew the lifebelt up tight and tied the two breast ends of the tube together with the tape. The lifebelt made a pillow big enough for his head and very soft. He lay on his back and rested his head in the sou'wester on the soft pillow. He inched his arms down on either side of him in the crevice. He spoke to the sky.

'I must dry seaweed and line this crevice. I could be as snug as a bug in a rug.'

He shut his eyes.

'Relax each muscle in turn.'

Sleep is a condition to be attained by thought like any other.

'The trouble with keeping house on a rock is that there's so much to do. But I shan't get bored, that's one thing.'

Relax the muscles of the feet.

'And what a story! A week on a rock. Lectures——'

How to Survive. By Lieutenant—but why not Lieutenant-Commander? Or Commander? Brass Hat and all.

'You men must remember——'

His eyes fell open.

'And I never remembered! Never thought of it! Haven't had a

crap for a week!' Or not since before I was blown off the bloody bridge anyway.

The flaps of his sou'wester prevented him from hearing the flatness of his voice against the sky. He lay and meditated the sluggishness of his bowels. This created pictures of chrome and porcelain and attendant circumstances. He put the toothbrush back, and stood, looking at his face in the mirror. The whole business of eating was peculiarly significant. They made a ritual of it on every level, the Fascists as a punishment, the religious as a rite, the cannibal either as a ritual or as a medicine or as a superbly direct declaration to conquest. Killed and eaten. And of course eating with the mouth was only the gross expression of what was a universal process. You could eat with your cock or with your fists, or with your voice. You could eat with hobnailed boots, or buying and selling or marrying and begetting or cuck-olding——

Cuckolding reminded him. He turned from the mirror, bound his dressing-gown with the cord and opened the bathroom door. And there, coming towards him, as if the rather antiquated ex-pression had conjured him up was Alfred. But it was a different Alfred, pale, sweating, trembling, coming at a run toward. He took the wrist as the fist came at his chest and twisted it till Alfred was gritting his teeth and hissing through them. Secure in his knowledge of the cosmic nature of eating he grinned down at him.

'Hullo, Alfred!'

'You bloody swine!'

'Nosey little man.'

'Who've you got in there? Tell me!'

'Now, now. Come along quietly Alfred, we don't want any fuss.'

'Don't pretend it's someone else! You bastard! Oh Christ——'

They were by the closed door. Alfred was crying into the lines round his mouth and struggling to get at the door handle.

'Tell me who she is, Chris. I *must* know—for God's sake!'

'Don't ham it, Alfred.'

'And don't pretend it's not Sybil, you dirty, thieving bastard!'

'Like to look, Alfred?'

Hiccups. Weak struggles.

'You mean it's someone else? You're not fooling Chris, honestly?'

'Anything to cheer you up old man. Look.'

The door opening; Sybil, giving a tiny shriek and pulling the sheet up to her mouth as if this were a bedroom-farce which, of course, in every sense, it was.

'Honestly, Alfred old man, anyone would think you'd married the girl.'

But there was a connection between eating and the Chinese box. What was a Chinese box? A coffin? Or those carved ivory ornaments, one inside the other? Yet there was a Chinese box in it somewhere——

Astonished, he lay like a stone man, open-mouthed and gazing into the sky. The furious struggle against his chest, the slobbering sobs of the weak mouth were still calling their reactions out of his stronger body when he was back in the crevice.

He cleared his throat and spoke aloud.

'Where the hell am I? Where was I?'

He heaved over and lay face downwards in the crevice, his cheeks on the lifebelt.

'Can't sleep.'

But sleep is necessary. Lack of sleep was what sent people crazy. He spoke aloud and the lifebelt wobbled under his jaw.

'I was asleep then. I was dreaming about Alfred and Sybil. Go to sleep again.'

He lay still and considered sleep. But it was a tantalizingly evasive subject.

Think about women then or eating. Think about eating women, eating men, crunching up Alfred, that other girl, that boy, that crude and unsatisfactory experiment, lie restful as a log and consider the gnawed tunnel of life right up to this uneasy intermission.

This rock.

'I shall call those three rocks out there the Teeth.'

All at once he was gripping the lifebelt with both hands and tensing his muscles to defeat the deep shudders that were sweeping through him.

'No! Not the Teeth!'

The teeth were here, inside his mouth. He felt them with his tongue, the double barrier of bone, each known and individual except the gaps—and there they persisted as a memory if one troubled to think. But to lie on a row of teeth in the middle of the sea——

He began to think desperately about sleep.

Sleep is a relaxation of the conscious guard, the sorter. Sleep is when all the unsorted stuff comes flying out as from a dustbin upset in a high wind. In sleep time was divorced from the straight line so that Alfred and Sybil were on the rock with him and that boy with his snivelling, blubbered face. Or sleep was a consenting to die, to go into complete unconsciousness, the personality defeated, acknowledging too frankly what is implicit in mortality that we are temporary structures patched up and unable to stand the pace without a daily respite from what we most think ours——

'Then why can't I sleep?'

Sleep is where we touch what is better left unexamined. There, the whole of life is bundled up, dwindled. There the carefully hoarded and enjoyed personality, our only treasure and at the same time our only defence must die into the ultimate truth of things, the black lightning that splits and destroys all, the positive, unquestionable nothingness.

And I lie here, a creature armoured in oilskin, thrust into a crack, a morsel of food on the teeth that a world's lifetime has blunted.

Oh God! Why can't I sleep?

Gripping the lifebelt in two hands, with face lifted, eyes staring straight ahead down the gloomy tunnel, he whispered the answer to his own question in a mixture of astonishment and terror.

'I am afraid to.'

CHAPTER SEVEN

The light changed before the staring eyes but so slowly that they did not notice any difference. They looked, rather, at the jumble of unsorted pictures that presented themselves at random. There was still the silent, indisputable creature that sat at the centre of things, but it seemed to have lost the knack of distinguishing between pictures and reality. Occasionally the gate in the lower part of the globe would open against the soft lifebelt and words come out, but each statement was so separated by the glossy and illuminated scenes the creature took part in that it did not know which was relevant to which.

'I said that I should be sick.'

'Drink. Food. Sanity. Rescue.'

'I shall call them the——'

But the glossy images persisted, changed, not as one cloud shape into another but with sudden and complete differences of time and place.

'Sit down, Martin.'

'Sir.'

'We're considering whether we should recommend you for a commission. Cigarette?'

'Thank you, sir.'

Sudden smile over the clicked lighter.

'Got your nickname on the lower deck yet?'

Smile in return, charming, diffident.

''Fraid so, sir. Inevitably, I believe.'

'Like Dusty Miller and Nobby Clark.'

'Yes, sir.'

'How's the life up forrard?'

'It's——endurable, sir.'

'We want men of education and intelligence; but most of all, men of character. Why did you join the Navy?'

'One felt one ought to——well, help, sir, if you see what I mean?'

Pause.

'I see you're an actor in civvy street.'

Careful.

'Yes, sir. Not a terribly good one, I'm afraid.'

'Author?'

'Nothing much, yet, sir.'

'What would you have liked to be then?'

'One felt it was—unreal. Not like this. You know, sir! Here in this ship. Here we *are* getting down to the basic business of life— something worth doing. I wish I'd been a sailor.'

Pause.

'Why would you like a commission, Martin?'

'As an ordinary seaman, sir, one's the minutest cog in a machine. As an officer one would have more chance of hitting the old Hun for six, sir, actually.'

Pause.

'Did you volunteer, Martin?'

He's got it all on those papers there if he chooses to look it up.

Frank.

'Actually, no sir.'

He's blushing, under that standard Dartmouth mask of his.

'That will be all, Martin, thank you.'

'Aye, aye, sir, thank you, sir.'

He's blushing like a virgin of sixteen.

'She's the producer's wife, old man, here where are you going?'

An exceptionally small French dictionary, looking like an exceptionally large red eraser.

A black lacquer cash-box on which the gilt was worn.

The Chinese box was evasive. Sometimes it was the fretted ivories, one inside the other, sometimes it was a single box like a cash-box. But however evasive, it was important and intrusive.

She's the producer's wife, old man. Fat. White. Like a maggot with tiny black eyes. I should like to eat you. I should love to play Danny. I should love to eat you. I should love to put you in a play. How can I put you anywhere if I haven't eaten you? He's a queer. He'd love to eat you. And I should love to eat you too. You're not a person, my sweet, you're an instrument of pleasure.

A Chinese box.

A sword is a phallus. What a huge mountain-shaking joke! A phallus is a sword. Down, dog, down. Down on all fours where you belong.

Then he was looking at a half-face and crying out. The half-face belonged to one of the feathered reptiles. The creature was perched on the slab and looking down sideways at him. As he cried out the wide wings beat and flapped away and immediately a glossy picture swept the blue sky and the stone out of sight. This was a bright patch, sometimes like a figure eight lying on its side and sometimes a circle. The circle was filled with blue sea where gulls were wheeling and settling and loving to eat and fight. He felt the swing of the ship under him, sensed the bleak stillness and silence that settled on the bridge as the destroyer slid by the thing floating in the water—a thing, humble and abused and still, among the fighting beaks, an instrument of pleasure.

He struggled out into the sun, stood up and cried flatly in the great air.

'I am awake!'

Dense blue with white flecks and diamond flashes. Foam, flowering abundantly round the three rocks.

He turned away from the night.

'Today is a thinking day.'

He undressed quickly to his trousers and sweater, spread his clothing in the sun and went down to the Red Lion. The tide was so low that mussels were in sight by the ship load.

Mussels were food but one soon tired of them. He wondered for a moment whether he should collect some sweets but his stomach did not entertain the idea. He thought of chocolate instead and the silver paper came into his mind. He sat there, chewing mechanically while his mind's eye watched silver, flashing bright.

'After all, I may be rescued today.'

He examined the thought and found that the whole idea was neutral as the mussels had become, harsh and negative as the fresh water. He climbed to the water-hole and crawled in. The red deposit lay in a band nearly two inches wide at the nearer edge.

He cried out in the echoing hole.

'It will rain again!'

Proof of identity.

'I must measure this pool. I must ration myself. I must force water to come to me if necessary. I must have water.'

A well. Boring through rock. A dew pond. Line with clay and straw. Precipitation. Education. Intelligence.

He reached out his hand and prodded down with the finger. When his hand had submerged to the knuckles his finger-tip met slime and slid. Then rock. He took a deep breath. There was darker water farther on under the window.

'A fool would waste water by crawling forward, washing this end about just to see how much there is left. But I won't. I'll wait and crawl forward as the water shrinks. And before that there will be rain.'

He went quickly to his clothes, took out the silver paper and the string and climbed back to the Dwarf.

He frowned at the Dwarf and began to talk into the blotting-paper.

'East or west is useless. If convoys appear in either of those quarters they would be moving towards the rock anyway. But they may appear to the south, or less likely, to the north. But the sun does not shine from the north. South is the best bet, then.'

He took the Dwarf's head off and laid the stone carefully on the Look-out. He knelt down and smoothed the silver paper until the sheet gleamed under his hand. He forced the foil to lie smoothly against the head and bound it in place with the string. He put the silver head back on the Dwarf, went to the southern end of the Look-out and stared at the blank face. The sun bounced at him from the paper. He bent his knees until he was looking into the paper at eye-level and still he saw a distorted sun. He shuffled round in such arc as the southern end of the Look-out would allow and still he saw the sun. He took the silver head off the Dwarf again, polished the silver on his sea-boot stockings and put it back. The sun winked at him. There stood on the Look-out a veritable man and one who carried a flashing signal on his shoulders.

'I shall be rescued today.'

He fortified and deepened the meaningless statement with three steps of a dance but stopped with a grimace.

'My feet!'

He sat down and leaned against the Dwarf on the south side.

Today is a thinking day.

'I haven't done so badly.'

He altered the arch over his window with a frown.

'Ideally of course, the stone should be a sphere. Then no matter where the ship appears in an arc of one hundred and eighty degrees the sun will bounce straight at her from the Dwarf. If a ship is under the horizon then the gleam might fetch her crow's-nest, following it along like a hand of arrest on the shoulder, persisting, nagging, till even the dullest of seamen would notice and the idea sink in.'

The horizon remained empty.

'I must get a sphere. Perhaps I could beat the nearest to it with another stone until it rounds. Stone mason as well. Who was it cut stone cannon-balls? Michael Angelo? But I must look for a very round stone. Never a dull moment. Just like Itma.'

He got up and went down to the sea. He peered over the edge of the little cliff by the mussels but saw nothing worth having. There was green weed and a mass of stone between him and the three rocks but he turned away from it. He went instead to Prospect Cliff, climbed down the ledges to low water. But here there was nothing but masses of weed that stank. His climb tired him and he clung over the water for a moment, searching the surface of the rock with his eyes for anything of value. There was a coralline substance close to his face, thin and pink like icing and then not pink as though it were for ever changing its mind to purple. He stroked the smooth stuff with one finger. They called that paint Barmaid's Blush and splashed on gallons with the inexpert and casual hand of the wartime sailor. The colour was supposed to merge a ship into the sea and air at the perilous hour of dawn. There were interminable hard acres of the pink round scuttles and on gun shields, whole fields on sides and top hamper, hanging round the hard angles, the utilitarian curves, the grudgingly conceded living quarters of ships on the Northern Patrol, like pink icing or the coral growths on a washed rock. He took his face away from the casing and turned to climb the ladders to the bridge. There must be acres of the stuff spread on the child-time rocks at Tresellyn. That was where Nat had taken her—taken her in two senses, grateful for the tip.

The ship rolled heavily and here was Nat descending the upper ladder like a daddy-longlegs, carefully placing the remote ends of the limbs for security and now faced with a crisis at the sight of the face and the cap. Here is Nat saluting as ever off balance, but this time held in position by one arm and two legs.

'Wotcher, Nat. Happy in your work?'

Dutiful Nat-smile though a little queasy. See the bright side.

'Yes, sir.'

Amble aft you drawn-out bastard.

Climb, climb. The bridge, a little wind and afternoon.

'Hallo. Mean course o-nine-o. Now on zag at one-one-o. And I may say, dead in station, not wandering all over the ocean the way you leave her. She's all yours and the Old Man is in one of his moods, so watch out for sparks.'

'Zig coming up in ten seconds? I've got her.'

'See you again at the witching hour.'

'Port fifteen. Midships. Steady.'

He looked briefly round the convoy and then aft. Nat was there, tediously in his usual place, legs wide apart, face in hands. The corticened deck lurched under him, rearranged itself and he swayed on the rail. The luminous window that looked down at him bent at the sides in a snarl that was disguised as a grin.

Christ, how I hate you. I could eat you. Because you fathomed her mystery, you have a right to handle her transmuted cheap tweed; because you both have made a place where I can't get; because in your fool innocence you've got what I had to get or go mad.

Then he found himself additionally furious with Nathaniel, not because of Mary, not because he had happened on her as he might have tripped over a ring-bolt but because he dared sit so, tilting with the sea, held by a thread, so near the end that would be at once so anguishing and restful like the bursting of a boil.

'Christ!'

Wildebeeste had turned seconds ago.

'Starboard thirty! Half-ahead together!'

Already, from the apex of the destroyer screen, a light was stabbing erratically.

'Midships! Steady. Slow ahead together.'

There was a clatter from the ladder. The Captain burst at him.

'What the bloody hell are you playing at?'

Hurried and smooth.

'I thought there was wreckage on the starboard bow, sir, and couldn't be sure so I maintained course and speed till we were clear, sir.'

The Captain stopped, one hand on the screen of the bridge and lowered at him.

'What sort of wreckage?'

'Baulks of timber, sir, floating just under the surface.'

'Starboard look-out!'

'Sir?'

'Did you see any wreckage?'

'No, sir.'

'—I may have been mistaken, sir, but I judged it better to make sure, sir.'

The Captain bored in, face to face so that his grip on the rock tightened as he remembered. The Captain's face was big, pale, and lined, the eyes red-rimmed with sleeplessness and gin. It examined for a moment what the window had to exhibit. The two shadowy noses on either side of the window caught a faint, sweet scent. Then the face changed, not dramatically, not registering, not making obvious, but changing like a Nat-face, from within. Under the pallor and moist creases, in the corners of the mouth and eyes, came the slight muscular shift of complicated tensions till the face was rearranged and bore like an open insult, the pattern of contempt and disbelief.

The mouth opened.

'Carry on.'

In a confusion too complete for answer or salute he watched the face turn away and take its understanding and contempt down the ladder.

There was heat and blood.

'Signal, sir, from Captain D. "Where are you going to my pretty maid?"'

Signalman with a wooden face. Heat and blood.

'Take it to the Captain.'

'Aye aye, sir.'

He turned back to the binnacle.

'Port fifteen. Midships. Steady.'

Looking under his arm he saw Nathaniel pass the bridge messenger in the waist. Seen thus, he was a bat hanging upside down from the roof of a cave. Nat passed on, walking and lurching till the break of the fo'castle hid him.

He found he was cursing an invisible Nat, cursing him for Mary, for the contempt in old Gin-soak's face. The centre, looking in this reversed world over the binnacle, found itself beset by a storm of emotions, acid and inky and cruel. There was a desperate amazement that anyone so good as Nat, so unwillingly loved for the face that was always rearranged from within, for the serious attention, for love given without thought, should also be so quiveringly hated as though he were the only enemy. There was amazement that to love and to hate were now one thing and one emotion. Or perhaps they could be separated. Hate was as hate had always been, and acid, the corroding venom of which could be borne only because the hater was strong.

'I am a good hater.'

He looked quickly at the deck watch, across at *Wildebeeste* and gave orders for the new course.

And love? Love for Nat? That was this sorrow dissolved through the hate so that the new solution was a deadly thing in the chest and the bowels.

He muttered over the binnacle.

'If I were that glass toy that I used to play with I could float in a bottle of acid. Nothing could touch me then.'

Zag.

'That's what it is. Ever since I met her and she interrupted the pattern coming at random, obeying no law of life, facing me with the insoluble, unbearable problem of her existence the acid's been chewing at my guts. I can't even kill her because that would be her final victory over me. Yet as long as she lives the acid will eat. She's there. In the flesh. In the not even lovely flesh. In the cheap mind. Obsession. Not love. Or if love, insanely compounded of this jealousy of her very being. *Odi et amo*. Like that thing I tried to write.'

There were lace curtains in decorous curves either side of the oak occasional table with its dusty fern. The round table in the centre of the almost unused parlour smelt of polish—might one day support a coffin in state, but until then, nothing. He looked round at the ornaments and plush, took a breath of the air that was trapped this side of the window, smelt of last year and varnish like the vilest cooking sherry. The room would suit her. She would fit it, she was the room at all points except for the mania.

He looked down at the writing-pad on his knee.

Zig.

'And that wasn't the half of it. And the acid still eats. Who could ever dream that he would fall in love—or be trapped—by a front parlour on two feet?'

He began to pace backward and forward on the bridge.

'As long as she lives the acid will eat. There's nothing that can stand that. And killing her would make it worse.'

He stopped. Looked back along the deck at the quarterdeck and the empty, starboard rail.

'Christ! Starboard twenty——'

There was a sense in which she could be—or say that the acid flow could be checked. Not to pass Petty Officer Roberts' message on was one thing—but that merely acquiesced in the pattern. But say one nudged circumstances—not in the sense that one throttled with the hands or fired a gun—but gently shepherded them the way they might go? Since it would be a suggestion to circumstances only it could not be considered what a strict moralist might call it——

'And who cares anyway?'

This was to run with a rapier at the arras without more than a hope of success.

'He may never sit there again.'

Then the officer of the watch in the execution of his duty gives a helm order to avoid floating wreckage or a drifting mine and no one is any the worse.

'But if he sits there again——'

The corrosive swamped him. A voice cried out in his belly—I do not want him to die! The sorrow and hate bit deep, went on biting. He cried out with his proper voice.

'Does no one understand how I feel?'

The look-outs had turned on their perches. He scowled at them and felt another warmth in his face. His voice came out savagely.

'Get back to your sectors.'

He leaned over the binnacle and felt how his body shook.

'I am chasing after—a kind of peace.'

Barmaid's blush with hair that was coarse even for a barmaid. He looked at the ledges of rock.

'A kind of peace.'

Coral growth.

He shook his head as though he were shaking water out of his hair.

'I came down here for something.'

But there was nothing, only weed and rock and water.

He climbed back to the Red Lion, gathered some of the uneaten mussels that he had left from the morning and went up the High Street to the Look-out. He sat under the south side of the winking Dwarf and opened them with his knife. He ate with long pauses between each mouthful. When he had finished the last one he lay back.

'Christ.'

They were no different from the mussels of yesterday but they tasted of decay.

'Perhaps I left them too long in the sun.'

But they hang in the sun between tides for hours!

'How many days have I been here?'

He thought fiercely, then made three scratches on the rock with his knife.

'I must not let anything escape that would reinforce personality. I must make decisions and carry them out. I have put a silver head on the Dwarf. I have decided not to be tricked into messing about with the water-hole. How far away is the horizon? Five miles? I could see a crow's-nest at ten miles. I can advertise myself over a circle twenty miles in diameter. That's not bad. The Atlantic is about two thousand miles wide up here. Twenty into two thousand goes a hundred.'

He knelt down and measured off a line ten inches in length as near as he could judge.

'That makes it a tenth of an inch.'

He put the blade of his knife on the line at about two inches from the end and rotated the haft slowly till the point made a white mark in the grey rock. He squatted back on his heels and looked at the diagram.

'With a really big ship I could be seen at fifteen miles.'

He put the point of the knife back on the mark and enlarged it. He paused, then went on scraping till the mark was the size of a silver threepenny-bit. He put out his foot and scuffed the seaboot stocking over the mark until it was grey and might have been there since the rock was made.

'I shall be rescued today.'

He stood up and looked into the silver face. The sun was still shining back at him. He traced mental lines from the sun to the stone, bounced them out at this part of the horizon and that. He went close to the dwarf and looked down at the head to see if he could find his face reflected there. The sunlight bounced up in his eyes. He jerked upright.

'The air! You fool! You clot! They ferry planes and they must use this place for checking the course—and Coastal Command, looking for U-boats———'

He cupped his hands at his eyes and turned slowly round, looking at the sky. The air was dense blue and interrupted by nothing but the sun over the south sea. He flung his hands away and began to walk hastily up and down by the look-out.

'A thinking day.'

The Dwarf was all right for ships—they were looking across at a silhouette. They would see the Dwarf or perhaps the gleam of the head. But to a plane, the Dwarf would be invisible, merged against the rock, and the glint from the silver might be a stray crystal of quartz. There was nothing about the rock to catch the eye. They might circle at a few thousand feet—a mile, two miles—and see nothing that was different. From above, the stone would be a tiny grey patch, that was eye-catching only by the surf that spread round in the sea.

He looked quickly and desperately up, then away at the water.

A pattern.

Men make patterns and superimpose them on nature. At ten thousand feet the rock would be a pebble; but suppose the pebble were striped? He looked at the trenches. The pebble was striped already. The upended layers would be grey with darker lines of trench between them.

He held his head in his hands.

A chequer. Stripes. Words. S.O.S.

'I cannot give up my clothes. Without them I should freeze to death. Besides if I spread them out they would still be less visible than this guano.'

He looked down the High Street between his hands.

'Pare away here and here and there. Make all smooth. Cut into a huge, shadowed S.O.S.'

He dropped his hands and grinned.

'Be your age.'

He squatted down again and considered in turn the material he had with him. Cloth. Small sheets of paper. A rubber lifebelt.

Seaweed.

He paused, lifted his hands and cried out in triumph.

'Seaweed!'

CHAPTER EIGHT

There were tons of the stuff hanging round the rock, floating or coiled down under water by Prospect Cliff.

'Men make patterns.'

Seaweed, to impose an unnatural pattern on nature, a pattern that would cry out to any rational beholder—Look! Here is thought. Here is man!

'The best form would be a single indisputable line drawn at right angles to the trenches, piled so high that it will not only show a change of colour but even throw a shadow of its own. I must make it at least a yard wide and it must be geometrically straight. Later I will fill up one of the trenches and turn the upright into a cross. Then the rock will become a hot cross bun.'

Looking down towards the three Rocks he planned the line to descend across the trenches, parallel more or less to the High Street. The line would start at the Red Lion and come up to the Dwarf. It would be an operation.

He went quickly down the High Street: and now that he had found a job with point, he was muttering without knowing why.

'Hurry! Hurry!'

Then his ears began to fill with the phantom buzzing of planes. He kept looking up and fell once, cutting himself. Only when he was already pulling at the frondy weed by Food Cliff did he pause.

'Don't be a fool. Take it easy. There's no point in looking up because you can do nothing to attract attention. Only a clot would go dancing and waving his shirt because he thought there was a plane about five miles up.'

He craned back his head and searched the sky but found nothing besides blueness and sun. He held his breath and listened and heard nothing but the inner, mingled humming of his own life, nothing outside but the lap and gurgle of water. He straightened his neck and stood there thinking. He went back to the crevice. He stripped naked and spread his clothing in the sun. He

arranged each item carefully to one side of where the line of
seaweed would lie. He went back to the Red Lion and looked
down at the space between the Red Lion and the three rocks. He
turned round and lowered himself over the edge. The water was
colder than he remembered, colder than the fresh water that he
drank. He ground his teeth and forced himself down and the rock
was so sharp against his knees that he reopened the wounds of
the first day. His waist was on the rock between his hands and he
was groaning. He could not feel bottom and the weed round his
calves was colder than the water. The cold squeezed as the water
had done in the open sea, so that he was panic-stricken at the
memory. He made a high, despairing sound, pushed himself clear
of the rock and fell. The water took him with a freezing hand. He
opened his eyes and weed was lashing before them. His head
broke the surface and he struck out frantically for the rock. He
hung there, shivering.

'Take a grip.'

There was a whiteness under the weed. He pushed off and let
his feet sink. Under the weed, caught between his own rock and
the three others were boulders, quartz perhaps, stacked and unguessable. He stood, crouched in the water, half-supporting his
weight with swimming movements of the arms and felt round
him with his feet. Carefully he found foothold and stood up. The
water reached to his chest and the weed dragged at him. He took
a breath and ducked. He seized weed and tried to tear off fronds
but they were very tough and he could win no more than a
handful before he had to surface again. He began to collect weed
without ducking, reaping the last foot of the crop. Sometimes
when he pulled there would be a stony turn and slight shock, or
the water-slowed movements of readjustment. He threw weed up
on the rock and the fronds flopped down over the edge, dripping.

Suddenly the weed between his feet tugged and something
brushed over his toes. A line of swift and erratic movement
appeared in the weed, ceased. He clawed at the cliff and hung
there, drawing his legs up.

The water lapped.

'Crab. Lobster.'

He kneed his painful way to the Red Lion and lay down by the
weed till his heart steadied.

'I loathe it.'

He crawled to the edge of the cliff and looked down. At once, as if his eye had created it, he saw the lobster among the weed, different in dragon-shape, different in colour. He knelt, looking down, mesmerized while the worms of loathing crawled over his skin.

'Beast. Filthy sea-beast.'

He picked up a mussel shell and threw it with all his strength into the water. At the smack, the lobster clenched like a fist and was gone.

'That line of seaweed's going to take a devil of a time to build.'

He shook himself free of the worms on his skin. He lowered himself over Prospect Cliff. The bottom four or five feet was covered with a hanging mass of strap-weed. At the surface of the water, weed floated out so that the sea seemed solid.

'Low water.'

He climbed along the rock and began to tug at the weed but it would not come off. The roots clung to the rock with suckers more difficult to remove than limpets or mussels. Some of the weeds were great bushes that ended in dimpled bags full of jelly. Others were long swords but with a fluted and wavered surface and edge. The rest was smooth brown leather like an assembly of sword belts for all the officers in the world. Under the weed the rock was furry with coloured growths or hard and decorative with stuff that looked like uncooked batter. There was also Barmaid's Blush. There were tiny bubblings and pips and splashes.

He tugged at a bunch of weed with one hand while he hung on to the rock with the other. He cursed and climbed back up the rock, walked up the High Street to the Look-out and stood looking at the sea and sky.

He came to with a jump.

'Don't waste time. Be quick.'

He went to the crevice, slung the knife round his neck by its lanyard and picked up the lifebelt. He unscrewed the mouth of the tit, let the air out and climbed down the rock. He slung the lifebelt over his arm and went at the weed-roots with the knife. They were not only hard as rubber but slippery. He had to find a particular angle and a particular careful sobriety of approach before he could get the edge of his knife into them. He wore the weed like firewood over his shoulder. He held the lifebelt in his teeth and drew fronds of weeds through between the lifebelt and the tape. He reversed his position, holding on with his left arm and gathering with his right. The weed made a great bundle on his shoulder that draped down and fell past his knees in a long, brown smear.

He climbed to the Red Lion, and flung down the weed. At a distance of a few feet from him it looked like a small patch. He laid out the separate blades, defining the straight line that would interrupt the trenches. In the trenches themselves the weed had no support.

'I must fill the trenches flush with the wall where the weed crosses them.'

When he had used up all the weed the load stretched from the Red Lion to the Look-out. On the average the line was two inches wide.

He went back to Prospect Cliff and got more weed. He squatted in the Red Lion with his forehead corrugated. He shut one eye and considered his handiwork. The line was hardly visible. He climbed round to the cliff again.

There was a sudden plop in the water by the farthest of the three rocks, so that he sprang round. Nothing. No foam, only a dimpled interruption in the pattern of wavelets.

'I ought to catch fish.'

He gathered himself another load of weed. The jellied bag burst when he pressed them, and he put one of the bags to his lips but the taste was neutral. He carried another load to the Red Lion and another. When he piled the weed on the first trench it did not come within a foot of the top.

He stood up in the trench, looking down at the red and brown weed and felt suddenly listless.

'Twelve loads? Twenty? And then the line to thicken after that——'

Intelligence sees so clearly what is to be done and can count the cost beforehand.

'I will rest for a while.'

He went to the Dwarf and sat down under the empty sky. The seaweed stretched away across the rock like a trail.

'Harder than ever in my life before. Worn out for today.'

He put his head on his knees and muttered to the ghost of a diagram—a line with a grey blob on it.

'I haven't had a crap since we were torpedoed.'

He sat motionless and meditated on his bowels. Presently he looked up. He saw that the sun was on the decline and made a part of the horizon particularly clear and near. Squinting at it he thought he could even see the minute distortions that the waves made in the perfect curve of the world.

There was a white dot sitting between the sun and Safety Rock. He watched closely and saw that the dot was a gull sitting in the water, letting itself drift. All at once he had a waking vision of the gull rising and flying east over the sea's shoulder. To-morrow morning it could be floating among the stacks and shields of the Hebrides or following the plough on some Irish hill-side. As an intense experience that interrupted the bright afternoon before him he saw the ploughman in his cloth cap hitting out at the squawking bird.

'Get away from me now and the bad luck go with you!'

But the bird would not perch on the boundary-stone, open its bill and speak as in all folk lore. Even if it were more than a flying machine it could not pass on news of the scarred man sitting on a rock in the middle of the sea. He got up and began to pace to and fro on the Look-out. He took the thought out and looked at it.

I may never get away from this rock at all.

Speech is identity.

'You are all a machine. I know you, wetness, hardness, move-ment. You have no mercy but you have no intelligence. I can outwit you. All I have to do is to endure. I breathe this air into my own furnace. I kill and eat. There is nothing to——'

He paused for a moment and watched the gull drifting nearer; but not so near that the reptile under the white was visible.

'There was nothing to fear.'

The gull was being carried along by the tide. Of course the tide operated here too, in mid-Atlantic, a great wave that swept round the world. It was so great that it thrust out tongues that became vast ocean currents, sweeping the water in curves that were ten thousand miles long. So there was a current that flowed past this rock, rising, pausing, reversing and flowing back again eternally and pointlessly. The current would continue to do so if life were rubbed off the skin of the world like the bloom off a grape. The rock sat immovable and the tide went sweeping past.

He watched the gull come floating by Prospect Cliff. It preened its feathers and fluttered like a duck in a pond.

He turned abruptly away and went quickly down to Prospect Cliff. Half the hanging seaweed was covered.

Tomorrow.

'Exhausted myself. Mustn't overdo it.'

Plenty to do on a rock. Never a dull moment.

He considered the mussels with positive distaste and switched his mind instead to the bags of jelly on the seaweed. He had a vague feeling that his stomach was talking to him. It disliked mussels. As for anemones—the bare thought made the bag contract and send a foul taste to his mouth.

'Overwork. Exposure. Sunburn, perhaps. I mustn't overdo it.'

He reminded himself seriously that this was the day on which he was going to be rescued but could not rediscover conviction.

'Dress.'

He put on his clothes, walked round the Dwarf then sat down again.

'I should like to turn in. But I mustn't as long as there's light. She might come close for a look, blow her siren and go away again if I didn't show myself. But I thought to some purpose today. Tomorrow I must finish the seaweed. She may be just below the horizon. Or up so high I can't see her. I must wait.'

He hunched down by the Dwarf and waited. But time had infinite resource and what at first had been a purpose became grey and endless and without hope. He began to look for hope in his mind but the warmth was gone or if he found anything it was an intellectual and bloodless ghost.

He muttered.

'I shall be rescued. I shall be rescued.'

At an end so far from the beginning that he had forgotten everything he had thought while he was there, he lifted his chin and saw that the sun was sinking. He got up heavily, went to the water-hole and drank. The stain of red round the nearer edge was wider.

He echoed.

'I must do something about water.'

He dressed as for bed and wrapped the grey sweater round his feet. It made a muffling between them and the rock like the cathedral carpets over stone. That was a particular sensation the feet never found anywhere else particularly when they wore those ridiculous medieval shoes of Michael's all fantasticated but with practically no sole. Beside the acoustics were so bad—wah, wah, wah, and then a high whine up among the barrel vault to which one added with every word one spoke as though one were giving a little periodic momentum to a pendulum——

'Can't hear you, old man, not a sausage. Up a bit. Give. I still can't hear you——'

'More? Slower?'

'Not slower for God's sake. Oh, turn it up. That's all for today boys and girls. Wait a bit, Chris. Look, George, Chris isn't coming off here at all——'

'Give him a bit more time, old man. Not your pitch is it, Chris?'

'I can manage, George.'

'He'll be better in the other part, old man. Didn't you see the rehearsal list, Chris? You're doubling—but of course——'

'Helen never said——'

'What's Helen got to do with it?'

'She never said——'

'I make out my own lists, old man.'

'Of course, Pete, naturally.'

'So you're doubling a shepherd and one of the seven deadly sins, old man. Eh, George, don't you think? Chris for one of the seven deadly sins?'

'Definitely, old man, oh, definitely.'

'Well, I do think, Pete, after the amount of work I've done for you, I shouldn't be asked to——'

'Double, old man? Everybody's doubling. I'm doubling. So you're wanted for the seven sins, Chris.'

'Which one, Pete?'

'Take your pick, old man Eh, George? We ought to let dear old Chris pick his favourite sin, don't you, think?'

'Definitely, old boy, definitely.'

'Prue's working on them in the crypt, come and look, Chris——'

'But if we've finished until tonight's house——'

'Come along, Chris. The show must go on. Eh, George? You'd like to see which mask Chris thinks would suit him?'

'Well—yes. Yes by God, Pete. I would. After you, Chris.

'I don't think I——'

'After you, Chris.'

'Curious feeling to the feet this carpet over stone, George. Something thick and costly, just allowing your senses to feel the basic stuff beneath. There they are Chris, all in a row. What about it?'

'Anything you say, old man.'

'What about Pride, George? He could play that without a mask
and just stylized make-up, couldn't he?'

'Look, Pete, if I'm doubling I'd sooner not make——'

'Malice, George?'

'Envy, Pete?'

'I don't mind playing Sloth, Pete.'

'Not Sloth. Shall we ask Helen, Chris? I value my wife's
advice.'

'Steady, Pete.'

'What about a spot of Lechery?'

'Pete! Stop it.'

'Don't mind me Chris, old man. I'm just a bit wrought-up
that's all. Now here's a fine piece of work, ladies and gentleman, guaranteed unworn. Any offers? Going to the smooth-
looking gentleman with the wavy hair and profile. Going!
Going——'

'What's it supposed to be, old man?'

'Darling, it's simply *you*! Don't you think, George?'

'Definitely, old man, definitely.'

'Chris-Greed. Greed-Chris. Know each other.'

'Anything to please you, Pete.'

'Let me make you two better acquainted. This painted bastard
here takes anything he can lay his hands on. Not food, Chris,
that's far too simple. He takes the best part, the best seat, the
most money, the best notice, the best woman. He was born with
his mouth and his flies open and both hands out to grab. He's a
cosmic case of the bugger who gets his penny and someone else's
bun. Isn't that right, George?'

'Come on, Pete. Come and lie down for a bit.'

'Think you can play Martin, Greed?'

'Come on, Pete. He doesn't mean anything, Chris. Just
wrought-up. A bit over-excited, eh, Pete?'

'That's all. Yes. Sure. That's all.'

'I haven't had a crap for a week.'

The dusk came crowding in and the sea-gulls. One sat on the
Dwarf and the silver head rocked so that the sea gull muted and
flapped away. He went down to the crevices, blew up the lifebelt,
tied the tapes and put it under his head. He got his hands tucked
in. Then his head felt unprotected, although he was wearing the
balaclava, so that he wriggled out and fetched his sou'wester

from the Red Lion. He went through the business of insertion
again.

'Good God!'

He hauled himself out.

'Where the hell's my oilskin?'

He went scrambling over the rocks to the Red Lion, the water-
hole, the Prospect Cliff——

'It can't be by the Dwarf because I never——'

In and out of the trenches, stinking seaweed, clammy, is it
underneath?

He found his oilskin where he had left it by the Dwarf. There
were white splashes on it. He put his oilskin over his duffle and
inserted himself again.

'That's what they can never tell you, never give you any idea.
Not the danger or the hardship but the niggling little idiocies, the
damnable repetitions, the days dripping away in a scrammy-
handed flurry of small mistakes you wouldn't notice if you were
at work or could drop into the Red Lion or see your popsie—
Where's my knife? Oh, Christ!'

But the knife was present, had swung round and was a rock-
like projection under his left ribs. He worked it free and cursed.

'I'd better do my thinking now. I was wrong to do it when I
could have worked. If I'd thought last night instead I could have
treated the day methodically and done everything.

Now: problems. First I must finish that line of weed. Then I
must have a place for clothes so that I never get into a panic
again. I'd better stow them here so that I never forget. Second.
No third. Clothes were second. First clothes in the crevice, then
more weed until the line is finished. Third, water. Can't dig for it.
Must catch it when it comes. Choose a trench below guano level
and above spray. Make a catchment area.'

He worked his lower jaw sideways. His bristles were very
uncomfortable in the wool of the balaclava. He could feel the
slight freezing, prickling sensation of sunburn on his arms and
legs. The unevenness of the rock were penetrating again.

'It'll soon rain. Then I'll have too much water. What shall I do
about this crack? Mustn't get my clothes wet. I must rig a tent.
Perhaps tomorrow I'll be rescued.'

He remembered that he had been certain of rescue in the
morning and that made his heart sink unaccountably as though
someone had broken his sworn word. He lay, looking up into the

stars and wondering if he could find a scrap of wood to touch. But there was no wood on the rock, not even the stub of a pencil. No salt to throw over the left shoulder. Perhaps a splash of sea-water would be just as effective.

He worked his hand down to his right thigh. The old scar must have caught the sun too, for he could feel the raised place burning gently—a not unpleasant feeling but one that took the attention. The bristles in the balaclava made a scratching sound when he grimaced.

'Four. Make the knife sharp enough to shave with. Five. Make sure I'm not egg-bound to-morrow.'

The sunburn pricked.

'I am suffering from reaction. I went through hell in the sea and in the funnel, and then I was so pleased to be safe that I went right over the top. And that is followed by a set-back. I must sleep, must keep quite still and concentrate on the business of sleeping.'

The sunburn went on pricking, the bristles scratched and scraped and the unevennesses of the rock lit their slow, smouldering fires. They stayed there like the sea. Even when consciousness was modified they insisted. They became a luminous landscape, they became a universe and he oscillated between moments of hanging in space, observing them and of being extended to every excruciating corner.

He opened his eyes and looked up. He shut them again and muttered to himself.

'I am dreaming.'

He opened his eyes and the sunlight stayed there. The light lulled the fires to a certain extent because the mind could at last look away from them. He lay, looking at the daylight sky and trying to remember the quality of this time that had suddenly foreshortened itself.

'I wasn't asleep at all!'

And the mind was very disinclined to hutch out of the crevice and face what must be done. He spoke toneless words into the height of air over him.

'I shall be rescued today.'

He hauled himself out of the crevice and the air was warm so that he undressed to trousers and sweater. He folded his clothes carefully and put them in the crevice. When he hutched forward in the water-hole the red deposit made a mark across his chest. He drank a great deal of water and when he stopped drinking he could see that there was a wider space of darkness between the water and the window.

'I must get more water.'

He lay still and tried to decide whether it was more important to arrange for catching water or to finish the line of weed. That reminded him how quickly time could pass if you let it out of your sight so he scrambled back to the Look-out. This was a day of colour. The sun burned and the water was deep blue and sparkled gaily. There was colour spilt over the rocks, shadows that were deep purple until you looked straight at them. He peered down the High Street and it was a picture. He shut his eyes and then opened them again but the rock and the sea seemed no more real. They were a pattern of colour that filled the three lights of his window.

'I am still asleep. I am shut inside my body.'

He went to the Red Lion and sat by the sea.

'What did I do that for?'

He frowned at the water.

'I mean to get food. But I'm not hungry. I must get weed.'

He fetched the lifebelt and knife from the crevice and went to Prospect Cliff. He had to climb farther along the ledges for weed because the nearer part of the cliff was stripped already. He came to a ledge that was vaguely familiar and had to think.

'I came here to get stones for the Dwarf. I tried to shift that stone there but it wouldn't move although it was cracked.'

He frowned at the stone. Then he worked his way down until he was hanging on the cliff by it with both hands and the crack was only a foot from his face. Like all the rest of the cliff where the water could reach it was cemented with layers of barnacles and enigmatic growths. But the crack was wider. The whole stone had moved and skewed perhaps an eighth of an inch. Inside the crack was a terrible darkness.

He stayed there, looking at the loose rock until he forgot what he was thinking. He was envisaging the whole rock as a thing in the water, and he was turning his head from side to side.

'How the hell is it that this rock is so familiar? I've never been here before——'

Familiar, not as a wartime acquaintance whom one knows so quickly because one is forced to live close to him for interminable

stretches of hours but familiar as a relative, seldom seen, but to
be reckoned with, year after year, familiar as a childhood friend, a
nurse, some acquaintance with a touch of eternity behind him;
familiar now, as the rocks of childhood, examined and reapprized
holiday after holiday, remembered in the darkness of bed, in
winter, imagined as a shape one's fingers can feel in the air——

There came a loud plop from the three rocks. He scrambled
quickly to the Red Lion but saw nothing.

'I ought to fish.'

The seaweed in the trenches stank. There came another plop
from the sea and he was in time to see the ripples spreading. He
put his hands on either cheek to think but the touch of hair
distracted him.

'I must have a beard pretty well. Bristles, anyway. Strange that
bristles go on growing even when the rest of you is——'

He went quickly to Prospect Cliff and got a load of weed and
dumped it in the nearest trench. He went slowly up the High
Street to the Look-out and sat down, his opened hands on either
side of him. His head sank between his knees. The lap lap of
water round Safety Rock was very quieting and a gull stood on
the Look-out like an image.

The sounds of the inside body spread. The vast darkness was
full of them as a factory is full of the sound of machinery. His
head made a tiny bobbing motion each time his heart beat.

He was jerked out of this state by a harsh scream. The gull had
advanced across the rock, its wings half-open, head lowered.

'What do you want?'

The feathered reptile took two steps sideways then shuffled its
wings shut. The beak preened under the wing.

'If I had a crap I'd feel better.'

He heaved himself round and looked at the Dwarf who winked
at him with a silver eye. The line of the horizon was hard and
near. Again he thought he could see indentations in the curve.

The trouble was there were no cushions on the rock, no tus-
socks. He thought for a moment of fetching his duffle and folding
the skirt as a seat but the effort seemed too great.

'My flesh aches inside as though it were bruised. The hardness
of the rock is wearing out my flesh. I will think about water.'

Water was insinuating, soft and yielding.

'I must arrange some kind of shelter. I must arrange to catch
water.'

He came to a little, felt stronger and worried. He frowned at the tumbled rocks that were so maddeningly and evasively familiar and followed with his eye the thin line of weed. It shone in places. Perhaps the weed would appear from the air as a shining strip.

'I could catch water in my oilskin. I could make the wall of a trench into a catchment area.'

He stopped talking and lay back until the unevenness of the Dwarf as a chair-back made him lean forward again. He sat, hunched up and frowning.

'I am aware of——'

He looked up.

'I am aware of a weight. A ponderous squeezing. Agoraphobia or anyway the opposite of claustrophobia. A pressure.'

Water catchment.

He got to his feet and climbed back down the High Street. He examined the next trench to his sleeping crevice.

'Prevailing wind. I must catch water from an area facing south west.'

He took his knife and drew a line sloping down across the leaning wall. It ended in a hollow, set back to the depth of his fist where the wall met the bottom of the trench. He went to the Dwarf, carefully extracted a white potato and brought it back. On the end of the clasp knife was a projection about a quarter of an inch long which was intended as a screwdriver. He placed this against the rock about an inch above the slanting line and tapped the other end of his knife with the stone. The rock came away in thin flakes. He put the screwdriver in the slanting line and tapped till the line sank in. Soon he had made a line perhaps an eighth of an inch deep and a foot long. He went to the bottom end of the line.

'Begin at the most important end of the line. Then no matter how soon the rain comes I can catch some of it.'

The noise of the taps was satisfactorily repeated in the trench and he felt enclosed as though he were working in a room.

'I could spread my duffle or oilskin over this trench and then I should have a roof. That ponderous feeling is not so noticeable here. That's partly because I am in a room and partly because I am working.'

His arms ached but the line rose away from the floor and he could work in an easier position. He made a dreamy calculation to see whether increasing ease would overtake tiredness and found that it would not. He sat on the floor, with his face a few inches from the rock. He leaned his forehead on stone. His hand fell open.

'I could go to the crevice and lie down for a bit. Or I could roll up in my duffle by the Dwarf.'

He jerked his head away from the rock and set to work again. The cut part of the line lengthened. This part met the part he had cut first and he sat back to examine it.

'I should have cut it back at a slant. Damn.'

He grimaced at the rock and went back over the cut so that the bottom of the groove trended inward.

'Make it deeper near the end.'

Because the amount of water in the cut—but he changed his mind and did the calculation out loud.

'The amount of water in any given length of the cut will consist of all the water collected higher up, and also will be proportional to the area of rock above.'

He tapped at the rock and the flakes fell. His hands gave out and he sat on the floor of the trench, looking at his work.

'After this I shall do a real engineering job. I shall find a complex area round a possible basin and cut a network of lines that will guide the water to it. That will be rather interesting. Like sand-castles.'

Or like Roman emperors, bringing water to the city from the hills.

'This is an aqueduct. I call it the Claudian.'

He began to flake again, imposing purpose on the senseless rock.

'I wonder how long I've been doing that?'

He lay down in the trench and felt his back bruise. The Claudian was a long, whitish scar.

'There is something venomous about the hardness of this rock. It is harder than rock should be. And—familiar.'

The ponderous weight squeezed down. He struggled up to a sitting position.

'I should have dried seaweed and lined the crevice. But there are too many things to do. I need another hand on this job of living and being rescued. Perhaps I could find another place to sleep. In the open? I feel warm enough.'

Too warm.

'My flesh is perceptible inside—as though it were bruised everywhere to the bone. And big. Tumescent.'

The globe of darkness turned a complicated window towards the sky. The voice evaporated at the gate like escaping steam on a dry day.

'I'm working too hard. If I don't watch out I shall exhaust myself. Anyway I'll hand it to you, Chris. I don't think many people would——'

He stopped suddenly, then began again.

'Chris. Christopher! Christopher Hadley Martin——'

The words dried up.

There was an instrument of examination, a point that knew it existed. There were sounds that came out of the lower part of a face. They had no meaning attached to them. They were useless as tins thrown out with the lids buckled back.

'Christopher. Christopher!'

He reached out with both arms as though to grab the words before they dried away. The arms appeared before the window and in complete unreason they filled him with terror.

'Oh, my God.'

He wrapped his arms round him, hugged himself close, rocked from side to side. He began to mutter.

'Steady. Steady. Keep calm.'

CHAPTER NINE

He got up and sat gingerly on the side of the trench. He could feel the separate leaves of rock and their edges through his trousers and pants. He shifted farther down the trench to a place where the leaves were smoothly cut but his backside seemed to fare no better.

'I am who I was.'

He examined the shape of his window and the window-box of hair that was flourishing between his two noses. He turned the window down and surveyed all that he could see of himself. The sweater was dragged out into tatters and wisps of wool. It lay in folds beneath his chest and the sleeves were concertina'd. The trousers beneath the sweater were shiny and grey instead of black and beneath them the seaboot stockings drooped like the wads of waste that a stoker wipes his hands on. There was no body to be seen, only a conjunction of worn materials. He eyed the peculiar shapes that lay across the trousers indifferently for a while until at last it occurred to him how strange it was that lobsters should sit there. Then he was suddenly seized with a terrible loathing for lobsters and flung them away so that they cracked on the rock. The dull pain of the blow extended him into them again and they became his hands, lying discarded where he had tossed them.

He cleared his throat as if about to speak in public.

'How can I have a complete identity without a mirror? That is what has changed me. Once I was a man with twenty photographs of myself—myself as this and that with the signature scrawled across the bottom right-hand corner as a stamp and seal. Even when I was in the Navy there was that photograph in my identity card so that every now and then I could look and see who I was. Or perhaps I did not even need to look, but was content to wear the card next to my heart, secure in the knowledge that it was there, proof of me in the round. There were mirrors too, triple mirrors, more separate than the three lights on this window. I could arrange the side ones so that there was a double reflection and spy myself from the side or back in the reflected mirror as

though I were watching a stranger. I could spy myself and assess
the impact of Christopher Hadley Martin on the world. I could
find assurance of my solidity in the bodies of other people by
warmth and caresses and triumphant flesh. I could be a character
in a body. But now I am this thing in here, a great many aches of
bruised flesh, a bundle of rags and those lobsters on the rock.
The three lights of my window are not enough to identify me
however sufficient they were in the world. But there were other
people to describe me to myself—they fell in love with me, they
applauded me, they caressed this body they defined it for me.
There were the people I got the better of, people who disliked
me, people who quarrelled with me. Here I have nothing to
quarrel with. I am in danger of losing definition. I am an album
of snapshots, random, a whole show of trailers of old films. The
most I know of my face is the scratch of bristles, an itch, a sense
of tingling warmth.'

He cried out angrily.

'That's no face for a man! Sight is like exploring the night with
a flashlight. I ought to be able to see all round my head——'

He climbed down to the water-hole and peered into the pool.
But his reflection was inscrutable. He backed out and went down
to the Red Lion among the littered shells. He found a pool of salt
water on one of the sea rocks. The pool was an inch deep under
the sun with one green-weeded limpet and three anemones. There
was a tiny fish, less than an inch long, sunning itself on the
bottom. He leaned over the pool, looked through the displayed
works of the fish and saw blue sky far down. But no matter how
he turned his head he could see nothing but a patch of darkness
with the wild outline of hair round the edge.

'The best photograph was the one of me as Algernon. The one
as Demetrius wasn't bad, either—and as Freddy with a pipe. The
make-up took and my eyes looked really wide apart. There was
the Night Must Fall one. And that one from The Way of the
World. Who was I? It would have been fun playing opposite
Jane. That wench was good for a tumble.'

The rock hurt the scar on the front of his right thigh. He
shifted his leg and peered back into the pool. He turned his head
sideways again, trying to catch the right angle for his profile—
the good profile, the left one, elevated a little and with a half-
smile. But first a shadowy nose and then the semicircle of an eye
socket got in the way. He turned back to inquire of his full face

but his breathing ruffled the water. He puffed down and the dark head wavered and burst. He jerked up and there was a lobster supporting his weight at the end of his right sleeve.

He made the lobster into a hand again and looked down at the pool. The little fish hung in sunshine with a steady trickle of bubbles rising by it from the oxygen tube. The bottles at the back of the bar loomed through the aquarium as cliffs of jewels and ore.

'No, thanks, old man, I've had enough.'

'He's had enough. Ju hear that, George? Ju hear?'

'Hear what, Pete?'

'Dear ol' Chris has had enough.'

'Come on, Chris.'

'Dear ol' Chris doesn't drink 'n doesn't smoke.'

'Likes company, old man.'

'Likes company. My company. I'm disgusted with myself. Yur not goin' to say "Time, Gentlemen, please", miss, are you, gentlemen? He promised his old mother. He said. She said. She said, Chris, my child, let the ten commandments look after themselves she said. But don't drink and don't smoke. Only foke, I beg your pardon, miss, had I known such an intemperate word would have escaped the barrier of my teeth I would have taken steps to have it indictated in the sex with an obelisk or employed a perifris.'

'Come on, Pete. Take his other arm, Chris.'

'Unhand me, Gentlemen. By heaven I'll make a fish of him that lets me. I am a free and liberal citizen of this company with a wife and child of indifferent sex.'

'It's a boy, old man.'

'Confidently, George, it's not the sex but the wisdom. Does it know who I am? Who we are? Do you love me, George?'

'You're the best producer we've ever had, you drunken old soak.'

'I meant soak, miss. George, you're the most divinely angelic director the bloody theatre ever had and Chris is the best bloody juvenile, aren't you, Chris?'

'Anything you say, eh, George?'

'Definitely, old man, definitely.'

'So we all owe everything to the best bloody woman in the world. I love you, Chris. Father and mother is one flesh. And so my uncle. My prophetic uncle. Shall I elect you to my club?'

'How about toddling home, now, Pete?'

'Call it the Dirty Maggot Club. You member? You speak Chinese? You open sideways or only on Sundays?'

'Come on, Pete.'

'We maggots are there all the week. Y'see when the Chinese want to prepare a very rare dish they bury a fish in a tin box. Presently all the lil' maggots peep out and start to eat. Presently no fish. Only maggots. It's no bloddy joke being a maggot. Some of 'em are phototropic. Hey, George—phototropic!'

'What of it, Pete?'

'Phototropic. I said phototropic, miss.'

'Finish your maggots, Pete and let's go.'

'Oh, the maggots. Yes, the maggots. They haven't finished yet. Only got to the fish. It's a lousy job crawling round the inside of a tin box and Denmark's one of the worst. Well, when they've finished the fish, Chris, they start on each other.'

'Cheerful thought, old man.'

'The little ones eat the tiny ones. The middle-sized ones eat the little ones. The big ones eat the middle-sized ones. Then the big ones eat each other. Then there are two and then one and where there was a fish there is now one huge, successful maggot. Rare dish.'

'Got his hat, George?'

'Come on, Pete! Now careful——'

'I love you, Chris, you lovely big hunk. Eat me.'

'Get his arm over your shoulder.'

'There's nearly half of me left'n, I'm phototropic. You eat George yet? 'N when there's only one maggot left the Chinese dig it up——'

'You can't sit down here, you silly sot!'

'Chinese dig it up——'

'For Christ's sake, stop shouting. We'll have a copper after us.'

'Chinese dig it up——'

'Snap out of it, Pete. How the hell do the Chinese know when to dig it up?'

'They know. They got X-ray eyes. Have you ever heard a spade knocking on the side of a tin box, Chris? Boom! Boom! Just like thunder. You a member?'

There was a round of ripples by the three rocks. He watched them intently. Then a brown head appeared by the rocks, another and another. One of the heads had a silver knife across its mouth.

The knife bent, flapped and he saw the blade was a fish. The seal
heaved itself on to the rock while the others dived, leaving
dimpled water and circles. The seal ate, calmly in the sun, rejected
the head and tail and lay quiet.

'I wonder if they know about men?'

He stood up slowly and the seal turned its head towards him so
that he found himself flinching from an implacable stare. He
raised his arms suddenly in the gesture of a man who points a
gun. The seal heaved round on the rock and dived. It knew about
men.

'If I could get near I could kill it and make boots and eat the
meat——'

The men lay on the open beach, wrapped in skins. They
endured the long wait and the stench. At dusk, great beasts came
out of the sea, played round them, then lay down to sleep.

'An oilskin rolled up and would look enough like a seal. When
they were used to it I should be inside.'

He examined the thought of days. They were a recession like
repeated rooms in mirrors hung face to face. All at once he
experienced a weariness so intense that it was a pain. He laboured
up to the Look-out through the pressure of the sky and all the
vast quiet. He made himself examine the empty sea in each quarter. The water was smoother today as though the dead air were
flattening it. There was shot silk in swathes, oily-looking patches
that became iridescent as he watched, like the scum in a ditch.
But the wavering of this water was miles long so that a molten
sun was elongated, pulled out to nothing here to appear there in a
different waver with a sudden blinding dazzle.

'The weather changed while I was in the Red Lion with George
and Pete.'

He saw a seal head appear for a moment beyond the three
rocks and had a sudden wild sight of himself riding a seal across
the water to the Hebrides.

'Oh, my God!'

The sound of his voice, flat, yet high and agonized, intimidated
him. He dropped his arms and huddled down in his body by the
Dwarf. A stream of muttered words began to tumble through the
hole under his window.

'It's like those nights when I was a kid, lying awake thinking
the darkness would go on for ever. And I couldn't go back to
sleep because of the dream of the whatever it was in the cellar

coming out of the corner. I'd lie in the hot, rumpled bed, hot burning hot, trying to shut myself away and know that there were three eternities before the dawn. Everything was the night world, the other world where everything but good could happen, the world of ghosts and robbers and horrors, of things harmless in the daytime coming to life, the wardrobe, the picture in the book, the story, coffins, corpses, vampires, and always squeezing, tormenting darkness, smoke thick. And I'd think of anything because if I didn't go on thinking I'd remember whatever it was in the cellar down there, and my mind would go walking away from my body and go down three stories defenceless, down the dark stairs past the tall, haunted clock, through the whining door, down the terrible steps to where the coffin ends were crushed in the walls of the cellar—and I'd be held helpless on the stone floor, trying to run back, run away, climb up——'

He was standing, crouched. The horizon came back.

'Oh, my God!'

Waiting for the dawn, the first bird cheeping in the eaves of the tree-tops. Waiting for the police by the smashed car. Waiting for the shell after the flash of the gun.

The ponderous sky settled a little more irresistibly on his shoulders.

'What's the matter with me? I'm adult. I know what's what. There's no connection between me and the kid in the cellar, none at all. I grew up. I firmed my life. I have it under control. And anyway there's nothing down there to be frightened of. Waiting for the result. Waiting for that speech—not the next one after this, I know that, but where I go across and take up the cigarette-box. There's a black hole where that speech ought to be and he said you fluffed too much last night, old man. Waiting for the wound to be dressed. This will hurt a little. Waiting for the dentist's chair.

'I don't like to hear my voice falling dead at my mouth like a shot bird.'

He put a hand up to either side of his window and watched two black lines diminish it. He could feel the roughness of bristles under either palm and the heat of cheeks.

'What's crushing me?'

He turned his sight round the horizon and the only thing that told him when he had completed the circle was the brighter waver under the sun.

'I shall be rescued any day now. I must not worry. Trailers out of the past are all right but I must be careful when I see things that never happened, like—I have water and food and intelligence and shelter.'

He paused for a moment and concentrated on the feeling in the flesh round his window. His hands and skin felt lumpy. He swivelled his eyes sideways and saw that there might indeed be a slight distortion of the semicircle of the eye-hollows.

'Heat lumps? When it rains I shall strip and have a bath. If I haven't been rescued by then.'

He pressed with the fingers of his right hand the skin round his eyes. There were heat lumps on the sides of his face, that extended down beneath the bristles. The sky pressed on them but they knew no other feeling.

'I must turn in. Go to bed. And stay awake.'

The day went grey and hot. Dreary.

'I said I should be sick. I said I must watch out for symptoms.'

He went down to the water-hole and crawled in. He drank until he could hear water washing about in his belly. He crawled out backwards and dimensions were mixed up. The surface of the rock was far too hard, far too bright, far too near. He could not gauge size at all.

There was no one else to say a word.

You're not looking too good, old man.

'How the hell can I tell how I look?'

He saw a giant impending and flinched before he could connect the silver head with his chocolate paper. He felt that to stand up would be dangerous for a reason he was not able to formulate. He crawled to the crevice and arranged the clothing. He decided that he must wear everything. Presently he lay with his head out of the crevice on an inflated lifebelt. The sky was bright blue again but very heavy. The opening under his bristles dribbled on.

'Care Charmer Sleep. Cracker mottoes. Old tags. Rag bag of a brain. But don't sleep because of the cellar. How sleep the brave. Nat's sleep. And old gin-soak. Rolled along the bottom or drifting like an old bundle. This is high adventure and anyone can have it. Lie down, rat. Accept your cage. How much rain in this month? How many convoys? How many planes? My hands are larger. All my body is larger and tenderer. Emergency. Action stations. I said I should be ill. I can feel the old scar on my leg tingling more than the rest. Salt in my trousers. Ants in my pants.'

He hutched himself sideways in the crevice and withdrew his right hand. He felt his cheek with it but the cheek was dry.

'The tingling can't be sweat, then.'

He got his hand back and scratched in his crutch. The edge of the duffle was irritating his face. He remembered that he ought to be wearing the balaclava but was too exhausted to find it. He lay still and his body burned.

He opened his eyes and the sky was violet over him. There was an irregularity in the eye sockets. He lay there, his eyes unfocused and thought of the heat lumps on his face. He wondered if they would close the sockets altogether.

Heat lumps.

The burnings and shiverings of his body succeeded each other as if they were going over him in waves. Suddenly they were waves of molten stuff, solder, melted lead, heated acid, so thick that it moved like oil. Then he was fighting and crying to get out of the crevice.

He knelt, shaking on the rock. He put his hands down and they hurt when he leaned his weight on them. He peered down at them first with one eye then the other. They swelled and diminished with a slow pulsing.

'That's not real. Thread of Life. Hang on. That's not real.'

But what was real was the mean size of the hands. They were too big even on the average, butcher's hands so full of blood that their flesh was pulpy and swollen. His elbows gave way and he fell between his hands. His cheek was against the uniquely hard rock, his mouth open and he was looking blearily back into the crevice. The waves were still in his body and he recognized them. He gritted his teeth and hung on to himself in the centre of his globe.

'That must mean I'm running a temperature of well over a hundred. I ought to be in hospital.'

Smells. Formalin. Ether. Meth. Idioform. Sweet chloroform. Iodine.

Sights. Chromium. White sheets. White bandages. High windows.

Touches. Pain, Pain, Pain.

Sounds. Forces programme drooling like a cretin in the ears from the headphones hitched under the fever chart.

Tastes. Dry lips.

He spoke again with intense solemnity and significance.

'I must go sick.'

He lugged the clothes off his body. Before he had got down to his vest and pants the burning was intolerable so that he tore off his clothes and threw them anywhere. He stood up naked and the air was hot on his body, but the action of being naked seemed to do something, for his body started to shiver. He sat painfully on the wall by the white scar of the Claudian and his teeth chattered.

'I must keep going somehow.'

But the horizon would not stay still. Like his hands, the sea pulsed. At one moment the purple line was so far away that it had no significance and the next, so close that he could stretch out his arm and lay hold.

'Think. Be intelligent.'

He held his head with both hands and shut his eyes.

'Drink plenty of water.'

He opened his eyes and the High Street pulsed below him. The rock was striped with lines of seaweed that he saw presently were black shadows cast by the sun and not seaweed at all. The sea beyond the High Street was dead flat and featureless so that he could have stepped down and walked on it, only his feet were swollen and sore. He took his body with great care to the water-hole and pulled himself in. At once he was refrigerated. He put his face in the water and half-gulped, half-ate it with chattering teeth. He crawled away to the crevice.

'The squeezing did it, the awful pressure. It was the weight of the sky and the air. How can one human body support all that weight without bruising into a pulp?'

He made a little water in the trench. The reptiles were floating back to the sea round the rock. They said nothing but sat on the flat sea with their legs hidden.

'I need a crap. I must see about that. Now I must wear everything and sweat this heat out of my body.'

By the time he had pulled on all his clothing dusk was come and he felt his way into the crevice with his legs. The crevice enlarged and became populous. There were times when it was larger than the rock, larger than the world, times when it was a tin box so huge that a spade knocking at the side sounded like distant thunder. Then after that there was a time when he was back in rock and distant thunder was sounding like the knocking of a spade against a vast tin box. All the time the opening beneath his window was dribbling on like the Forces Programme, cross-talking and singing to people whom he could not see but knew were there. For a moment or two he was home and his father was like a mountain. The thunder and lightning were playing round the mountain's head and his mother was weeping tears like acid and knitting a sock without a beginning or end. The tears were a kind of charm for after he had felt them scald him they changed the crevice into a pattern.

The opening spoke.

'She is sorry for me on this rock.'

Sybil was weeping and Alfred. Helen was crying. A bright boy face was crying. He saw half-forgotten but now clearly remembered faces and they were all weeping.

'That is because they know I am alone on a rock in the middle of a tin box.'

They wept tears that turned them to stone faces in a wall, masks hung in rows in a corridor without beginning or end. There were notices that said No Smoking, Gentlemen, Ladies, Exit and there were many uniformed attendants. Down there was the other room, to be avoided, because there the gods sat behind their terrible knees and feet of black stone, but here the stone faces wept and had wept. Their stone cheeks were furrowed, they were blurred and only recognizable by some indefinite mode of identity. Their tears made a pool on the stone floor so that his feet were burned to the ankles. He scrabbled to climb up the wall and the scalding stuff welled up his ankles to his calves, his knees. He was struggling, half-swimming, half-climbing. The wall was turning over, curving like the wall of a tunnel in the underground. The tears were no longer running down the stone to join the burning sea. They were falling freely, dropping on him. One came, a dot, a pearl, a ball, a globe, that moved on him, spread. He began to scream. He was inside the ball of water that was burning him to the bone and past. It consumed him utterly. He was dissolved and spread throughout the tear an extension of sheer, disembodied pain.

He burst the surface and grabbed a stone wall. There was hardly any light but he knew better than to waste time because of what was coming. There were projections in the wall of the tunnel so that though it was more nearly a well than a tunnel he could still climb. He laid hold, pulled himself up, projection after projection. The light was bright enough to show him the projections. They were faces, like the ones in the endless corridor. They were not weeping but they were trodden. They appeared to be made of some chalky material for when he put his weight on them they would break away so that only by constant movement upward was he able to keep up at all. He could hear his voice shouting in the well.

'I am! I am! I am!'

And all the time there was another voice that hung in his ears like the drooling of the Forces Programme. Nobody paid any attention to his voice but the nature of the cretin was to go on talking even though it said the same thing over and over again. This voice had some connection with the lower part of his own face and leaked on as he climbed and broke the chalky, convenient faces.

'Tunnels and wells and drops of water all this is old stuff. You can't tell me. I know my stuff just sexual images from the unconscious, the libido, or is it the id? All explained and known. Just sexual stuff what can you expect? Sensation, all tunnels and wells and drops of water. All old stuff, you can't tell me. I know.'

CHAPTER TEN

A tongue of summer lightning licked right inside the inner crevice so that he saw shapes there. Some were angled and massive as the corners of corridors and between them was the light falling into impenetrable distances. One shape was a woman who unfroze for that instant and lived. The lightning created or discovered her in the act of breathing in; and so nearly was that breath finished that she seemed only to check and breathe out again. He knew without thinking who she was and where she was and when, he knew why she was breathing so quickly, lifting the silk blouse with apples, the forbidden fruit, knew why there were patches of colour on either cheek-bone and why the flush had run as it so uniquely did into the nose. Therefore she presented to him the high forehead, the remote and unconquered face with the three patches of pink arranged across the middle. As for the eyes, they fired an ammunition of contempt and outrage. They were eyes that confirmed all the unworded opinions of his body and fevered head. Seen as a clothed body or listened to, she was common and undistinguished. But the eyes belonged to some other person for they had nothing to do with the irregularity of the face or the aspirations, prudish and social, of the voice. There was the individual, Mary, who was nothing but the intersection of influences from the cradle up, the Mary gloved and hatted for church, the Mary who ate with such maddening refinement, the Mary who carried, poised on her two little feet, a treasure of demoniac and musky attractiveness that was all the more terrible because she was almost unconscious of it. This intersection was so inevitably constructed that its every word and action could be predicted. The intersection would choose the ordinary rather than the exceptional; would fly to what was respectable as to a magnet. It was a fit companion for the pursed-up mouth, the too high forehead, the mousey hair. But the eyes—they had nothing in common with the mask of flesh that nature had fixed on what must surely be a real and invisible face. They were one with the

incredible smallness of the waist and the apple breasts, the transparency of the flesh. They were large and wise with a wisdom
that never reached the surface to be expressed in speech. They
gave to her many silences—so explicable in terms of the intersection—a mystery that was not there. But combined with the furious
musk, the little guarded breasts, the surely impregnable virtue,
they were the death sentence of Actaeon. They made her occupy
as by right, a cleared space in the world behind the eyes that was
lit by flickers of summer lightning. They made her a madness,
not so much in the loins as in the pride, the need to assert and
break, a blight in the growing point of life. They brought back
the nights of childhood, the hot, eternal bed with seamed sheets,
the desperation. The things she did became important though
they were trivial, the very onyx she wore became a talisman. A
thread from her tweed skirt—though she had bought it off the
hook in a shop where identical skirts hung empty and unchanged
—that same thread was magicked into power by association. Her
surname—and he thumped rock with lifted knees—her surname
now abandoned to dead Nathaniel forced him to a reference book
lest it should wind back to some distinction that would set her
even more firmly at the centre than she was. By what chance, or
worse what law of the universe was she set there in the road to
power and success, unbreakable yet tormenting with the need to
conquer and break? How could she take this place behind the eyes
as by right when she was nothing but another step on which one
must place the advancing foot? Those nights of imagined copula-
tion, when one thought not of love nor sensation nor comfort
nor triumph, but of torture rather, the very rhythm of the body
reinforced by hissed ejaculations—take that and that! That for
your pursed mouth and that for your pink patches, your closed
knees, your impregnable balance on the high, female shoes—and
that if it kills you for your magic and your isled virtue!

How can she so hold the centre of my darkness when the only
real feeling I have for her is hate?

Pale face, pink patches. The last chance and I know what she is
going to say, inevitably out of the intersection. And here it comes
quickly, with an accent immediately elevated to the top drawer.

'No.'

There are at least three vowels in the one syllable.

'Why did you agree to come here with me, then?'

Three patches.

'I thought you were a gentleman.'

Inevitably.

'You make me tired.'

'Take me home, please.'

'Do you really mean that in the twentieth century? You really feel insulted? You don't just mean "No, I'm sorry, but no"?'

'I want to go home.'

'But look——'

I must, I must, don't you understand you bloody bitch?

'Then I'll take a bus.'

One chance. Only one.

'Wait a minute. Our language is so different. Only what I'm trying to say is—well, it's difficult. Only don't you understand that I—Oh Mary, I'll do anything to prove it to you!'

'I'm sorry. I just don't care for you in that way.'

And then he, compelled about the rising fury to tread the worn path:

'Then it's still—no?'

Ultimate insult of triumph, understanding and compassion.

'I'm sorry, Chris. Genuinely sorry.'

'You'll be a sister to me, I know.'

But then the astonishing answer, serenely, brushing away the sarcasm.

'If you like.'

He got violently to his feet.

'Come on. Let's get out of here for Christ's sake.'

Wait, like a shape in the driving seat. Does she know nothing of me at all? She comes from the road house, one foot swerved in front of the other as in the photographs, walking an invisible tight-rope across the gravel, bearing proudly the invincible banner of virginity.

'That door's not properly shut. Let me.'

Subtle the scent, the touch of the cheap, transmuted tweed, hand shaking on the gear, road drawing back, hooded wartime lights, uncontrollable summer lightning ignoring the regulations from beyond that hill to away south in seven-league boots, foot hard down, fringes of leaves jagged like a painted drop, trees touched, brought into being by sidelights and bundled away to the limbo of lost chances.

'Aren't you driving rather fast?'

Tilted cheek, pursed mouth, eyes under the foolish hat, remote, blacked out. Foot hard down.

'Please drive slower, Chris!'

Tyre-scream, gear-whine, thrust and roar——

'Please——!'

Rock, sway, silk hiss of skid, scene film-flicking.

Power.

'Please! Please!'

'Let me, then. Now. Tonight, in the car.'

'Please!'

Hat awry, road unravelled, tree-tunnel drunk up——

'I'll kill us.'

'You're mad—oh, please!'

'Where the road forks at the whitewashed tree, I'll hit it with your side. You'll be burst and bitched.'

'Oh God, oh God.'

Over the verge, clout on the heap of dressing, bump, swerve back, eating macadam, drawing it in, pushing it back among the lost chances, pushing it down with time back to the cellar——

'I'm going to faint.'

'You'll let me make love to you? Love to you?'

'Please stop.'

On the verge, trodden with two feet to a stop, with dead engine and lights, grabbing a stuffed doll, plundering a doll that came to life under the summer lightning, knees clapped together over the hoarded virginity, one hand pushing down the same tweed skirt, one to ward off, finding with her voice a protection for the half-naked breast——

'I shall scream!'

'Scream away.'

'You filthly, beastly——'

Then the summer lightning over a white face with two staring eyes only a few inches away, eyes of the artificial woman, confounded in her pretences and evasion, forced to admit her own crude, human body—eyes staring now in deep and implacable hate.

Nothing out of the top drawer now. Vowels with the burr of the country on them.

'Don't you understand, you swine? You can't——'

The last chance. I must.

'I'll marry you then.'

More summer lightning.

'Chris. Stop laughing. D'you hear? Stop it! I said stop it!'

'I *loathe* you. I never want to see you or hear of you as long as I live.'

Peter was riding behind him and they were flat out. It was his new bike under him but it was not as good as Peter's new one. If Peter got past with that new gear of his he'd be uncatchable. Peter's front wheel was overlapping his back one in a perfect position. He'd never have done that if he weren't deadly excited. The road curves here to the right, here by the pile of dressing. They are built up like rock—a great pile of stones for mending the road down to Hodson's Farm. Don't turn, go straight on, keep going for the fraction of a second longer than he expects. Let him turn, with his overlapping wheel. Oh clever, clever, clever. My leg, Chris, my leg—I daren't look at my leg. Oh Christ.

The cash-box. Japanned tin, gilt lines. Open empty. What are you going to do about it, there was nothing written down. Have a drink with me some time.

She's the producer's wife, old boy.

Oh clever, clever, clever power, then you can bloody well walk home; oh clever, real tears break down triumph, clever, clever, clever.

Up stage. Up stage. Up stage. I'm a bigger maggot than you are. You can't get any further up stage because of the table, but I can go all the way up to the french window.

'No, old man. I'm sorry, but you're not essential.'
'But George—we've worked together! You know me——'
'I do, old man. Definitely.'
'I should be wasted in the Forces. You've seen my work.'
'I have, old man.'
'Well then——'
The look up under the eyebrows. The suppressed smile. The smile allowed to spread until the white teeth were reflected in the top of the desk.
'I've been waiting for something like this. That's why I didn't kick you out before. I hope they mar your profile, old man. The good one.'

There were ten thousand ways of killing a man. You could poison him and watch the smile turn into a rictus. You could hold his throat until it was like a hard bar.

She was putting on a coat.

'Helen——'

'My sweet.'

The move up, vulpine, passionate.

'It's been so long.'

Deep, shuddering breath.

'Don't be corny, dear.'

Fright.

'Help me, Helen, I must have your help.'

Black maggot eyes in a white face. Distance. Calculation. Death.

'Anything my sweet, but of course.'

'After all you're Pete's wife.'

'So crude, Chris.'

'You could persuade him.'

Down close on the settee, near.

'Helen——'

'Why don't you ask Margot, my sweet, or that little thing you took out driving?'

Panic. Black eyes in a white face with no more expression than hard, black stones.

Eaten.

Nathaniel bubbling over in a quiet way—not a bubble over, a simmer, almost a glow.

'I have wonderful news for you, Chris.'

'You've met an aeon at last.'

Nat considered this, looking up at the reference library. He identified the remark as a joke and answered it with the too profound tones he reserved for humour.

'I have been introduced to one by proxy.'

'Tell me your news. Is the war over? I can't wait.'

Nathaniel sat down in the opposite armchair but found it too low. He perched himself on the arm, then got up and rearranged the books on the table. He looked into the street between the drab black-out curtains.

'I think finally, I shall go into the Navy.'

'You!'

Nodding, still looking out of the window:

'If they'd have me, that is. I couldn't fly and I shouldn't be any use in the Army.'

'But you clot! You don't have to go, do you?'

'Not—legally.'

'I thought you objected to war.'

'So I do.'

'Conchie.'

'I don't know. I really don't know. One thinks this and that—but in the end, you know, the responsibility of deciding is too much for one man. I ought to go.'

'You've made your mind up?'

'Mary agrees with me.'

'Mary Lovell? What's she got to do with it?'

'That's my news.'

Nathaniel turned with a forgotten book in his hands. He came towards the fire, looked at the armchair, remembered the book and put it on the table. He took a chair, drew it forward and perched on the edge.

'I was telling you after the show last night. You remember? About how our lives must reach right back to the roots of time, be a trail through history?'

'I said you were probably Cleopatra.'

Nat considered this gravely.

'No, I don't think so. Nothing so famous.'

'Henry the Eighth, then. Is that your news?'

'One constantly comes across clues. One has—flashes of insight—things given. One is——' The hands began to spread sideways by the shoulders as though they were feeling an expansion of the head—'One is conscious when meeting people that they are woven in with one's secret history. Don't you think? You and I, for example. You remember?'

'You used to talk an awful lot of cock.'

Nathaniel nodded.

'I still do. But we are still interwoven and the same things hold good. Then when you introduce me to Mary—you remember? You see how we three act and re-act. There came that sudden flash, that—stab of knowledge and certainty that said, "I have known you before."'

'What on earth are you talking about?'

'She felt it too. She said so. She's so—wise, you know! And

now we are both quite certain. These things are written in the stars, of course, but under them, Chris, we have to thank you for bringing us together.'

'You and Mary Lovell?'

'Of course these things are never simple and we've meditated apart from each other and together——'

An enchantment was filling the room. Nat's head seemed to grow large and small with it.

'And I should be awfully pleased, Chris, if you'd be best man for me.'

'You're going to marry! You and——'

'That was the joyous news.'

'You can't!'

He heard how anguished his voice was, found he was standing up.

Nat looked past him into the fire.

'I know it's sudden but we've meditated. And you see, I shall be going into the Navy. She's so good and brave. And you, Chris— I knew you would bring your whole being to such a decision.'

He stood still, looking down at the tousled black hair, the length of limb. He felt the bleak recognition rising in him of the ineffable strength of these circumstances and this decision. Not where he eats but where he is eaten. Blood rose with the recognition, burning in the face, power to break. Pictures of her fell through his mind like a dropped sheaf of snapshots—Mary in the boat, carefully arranging her skirt; Mary walking to church, reeking of it, the very placing of her feet and carriage of her little bum an insolence; Mary struggling, knees clapped together over the hoarded virginity, trying with one hand to pull down her skirt, with the other to ward off, the voice finding the only protection for her half-naked breast——

'I shall scream!'

Nat looked up, his mouth open.

'I'm not being a fool this time you know. You needn't worry.'

The snapshots vanished.

'I was—I don't know what I was saying, Nat—quoting from some play or other.'

Nat spread his hands and smiled diffidently.

'The stars can't be thwarted.'

'Especially if they happen to agree with what you want.'

Nat considered this. He reddened a little and nodded gravely.

'There is that danger.'

'Be careful, Nat, for God's sake.'

But not known, not understood—what is he to be careful of? Of staying near me? Of standing with her in the lighted centre of my darkness?

'You'll be here to look after her, Chris, when I've gone.'

There is something in the stars. Or what is this obscure impulse that sets my words at variance with my heart?

'Only be careful. Of me.'

'Chris!'

Because I like you, you fool and hate you. And now I hate you.

'All right, Nat, forget it.'

'There's something the matter.'

An impulse gone, trodden down, kicked aside.

'I shall be in the Navy, too.'

'But the theatre!'

Gone down under calculation and hate.

'One has one's better feelings.'

'My dear man!' Nat was standing and beaming. 'Perhaps we can be in the same ship.'

Drearily and with the foreknowledge of a chosen road.

'I'm sure we shall be. That's in our stars.'

Nat nodded.

'We are connected in the elements. We are men for water.'

'Water. Water.'

The clothes bound him like a soggy bundle. He hauled himself out into the sun. He lay there feeling that he spread like seaweed. He got his hands up and plucked at the toggles of his duffle while the snapshots whirled and flew like a pack of cards. He got the toggles free and plucked at the rest of his clothing. When he had only vest and pants on he crawled away, yards over the rocks to the water-hole. He crawled up the High Street and lay down by the Dwarf.

'If I am not delirious this is steam rising from my clothes. Sweat.'

He propped his back against the Dwarf.

'Be intelligent.'

His legs before him were covered with white blotches. There were more on his stomach when he lifted his vest, on his arms and legs. They were deformations at the edge of the eye-sockets.

'Stay alive!'

Something fierce pushed out of his mind.

'I'll live if I have to eat everything else on this bloody box!'

He looked down at his legs.

'I know the name for you bloody blotches. Urticaria. Food poisoning.'

He lay quiet for a time. The steam rose and wavered. The blotches were well-defined and of a dead whiteness. They were raised so that even swollen fingers could feel their outline.

'I said I should be ill and I am.'

He peered hazily round the horizon but it had nothing to give. He looked back at his legs and decided that they were very thin for all the blotches. Under his vest he could feel the trickle of water that found its way down from blotch to blotch.

The pressure of the sky and air was right inside his head.

CHAPTER ELEVEN

A thought was forming like a piece of sculpture behind the eyes but in front of the unexamined centre. He watched the thought for a timeless interim while the drops of sweat trickled down from blotch to blotch. But he knew that the thought was an enemy and so although he saw it he did not consent or allow it to become attached to him in realization. If the slow centre had any activity now it brooded on its identity while the thought stayed there like an ignored monument in a park. Christopher and Hadley and Martin were separate fragments and the centre was smouldering with a dull resentment that they should have broken away and not be sealed on the centre. The window was filled with a pattern of colour but in this curious state the centre did not think of the pattern as exterior. It was the only visible thing in a dark room, like a lighted picture on the wall. Below it was the sensation of water trickling and discomfort of a hard surface. The centre for a time was sufficient. The centre knew self existed, though Christopher and Hadley and Martin were fragments far off.

A curtain of hair and flesh fell over the picture on the wall and there was nothing to be examined but the thought. It became known. The terror that swept in with the thought shocked him into the use of his body. There was a flashing of nerves, tensing of muscles, heaves, blows, vibration; and the thought became words that tumbled out of his mouth.

'I shall never get away from this rock.'

The terror did more. It straightened the hinged bones and stood him up, sent him reeling round the Look-out in the pressure of the sky till he was clinging to the Dwarf and the stone head was rocking gently, rocking gently, and the sun was swinging to and fro, up and down in the silver face.

'Get me off this rock!'

The Dwarf nodded its silver head, gently, kindly.

He crouched down by a whitish trench and the pattern of colour was sight again.

Christopher and Hadley and Martin came part way back. He forced the pattern to fit everywhere over the rock and the sea and the sky.

'Know your enemy.'

There was illness of the body, effect of exposure. There was food-poisoning that made the world a mad place. There was solitude and hope deferred. There was the thought; there were the other thoughts, unspoken and unadmitted.

'Get them out. Look at them.'

Water, the only supply, hung by a hair, held back by the slimy tamping; food that grew daily less; pressure, indescribable pressure on the body and the mind; battle with the film-trailers for sleep. There was——

'There was and is——'

He crouched on the rock.

'Take it out and look at it.

'There is a pattern emerging. I do not know what the pattern is but even my dim guess at it makes my reason falter.'

The lower half of his face moved round the mouth till the teeth were bare.

'Weapons. I have things that I can use.'

Intelligence. Will like a last ditch. Will like a monolith. Survival. Education, a key to all patterns, itself able to impose them, to create. Consciousness in a world asleep. The dark, invulnerable centre that was certain of its own sufficiency.

He began to speak against the flat air, the blotting-paper.

'Sanity is the ability to appreciate reality. What is the reality of my position? I am alone on a rock in the middle of the Atlantic. There are vast distances of swinging water round me. But the rock is solid. It goes down and joins the floor of the sea and that is joined to the floors I have known, to the coasts and cities. I must remember that the rock is solid and immovable. If the rock were to move then I should be mad.'

A flying lizard flapped overhead, and dropped down out of sight.

'I must hang on. First to my life and then to my sanity. I must take steps.'

He dropped the curtains over the window again.

'I am poisoned. I am in servitude to a coiled tube the length of a cricket pitch. All the terrors of hell can come down to nothing more than a stoppage. Why drag in good and evil when the serpent lies coiled in my own body?'

And he pictured his bowels deliberately, the slow, choked peristaltic movement, change of the soft food to a plug of poison.

'I am Atlas. I am Prometheus.'

He felt himself loom, gigantic on the rock. His jaws clenched, his chin sank. He became a hero for whom the impossible was an achievement. He knelt and crawled remorselessly down the rock. He found the lifebelt in the crevice, took his knife and sawed the metal tit away from the tube. He crawled on down towards the Red Lion and now there was background music, snatches of Tchaikovsky, Wagner, Holst. It was not really necessary to crawl but the background music underlined the heroism of a slow, undefeated advance against odds. The empty mussel shells cracked under his bones like potsherds. The music swelled and was torn apart by brass.

He came to the pool on the rock with the one weedy limpet and three prudish anemones. The tiny fish still lay in the water but on a different part of the rock. He pushed the lifebelt under the surface of the water so that the fish flicked desperately from side to side. A string of bubbles came out of the tube. He collapsed the long bladder and then began to pull it open again. Little spits of water entered the tit and worked down between more bubbles. Strings only, now, deep. He lifted the whole lifebelt out and hefted the bag. There was a washing sound from the bladder. He sank it in the pool again and went on working. The strings were working too, and woodwind was added and a note or two of brass. Presently, and soon there would come the suspended chord that would stand the whole orchestra aside for the cadenza. The weedy top of the limpet was above the surface. The tiny fish, tricked by this unnatural ebb was lying on wet rock in the sun and trying to wriggle against surface tension. The anemones had shut their mouths even tighter. The bladder of the lifebelt was two-thirds full.

He hutched himself back against a rock with his legs sprawled apart. The music rose, the sea played and the sun. The universe held its breath. Grunting and groaning he began to work the rubber tube into his backside. He folded the two halves of the long bladder together and sat on it. He began to work at the bladder with both hands, squeezing and massaging. He felt the cold trickle of the sea water in his bowels. He pumped and squeezed until the bladder was squashily flat. He extracted the tube and crept carefully to the edge of the rock while the orchestra thundered to a pause.

And the cadenza was coming—did come. It performed with explosive and triumphant completeness of technique into the sea. It was like the bursting of a dam, the smashing of all hindrance. Spasm after spasm with massive chords and sparkling arpeggios, the cadenza took of his strength till he lay straining and empty on the rock and the orchestra had gone.

He turned his face on the rock and grunted at the antagonist.

'Are you beaten yet? I'm not.'

The hand of the sky fell on him. He got up and knelt among the mussel shells.

'Now I shall be sane and no longer such a slave to my body.'

He looked down at the dead fish. He pushed the body with his finger to the mouth of an anemone. Petals emerged and tried to take hold.

'Stings. Poison. Anemones poisoned me. Perhaps mussels are all right after all.'

He felt a little stronger and no longer so heroic that he need crawl. He went slowly back to the Look-out.

'Everything is predictable. I knew I shouldn't drown and I didn't. There was a rock. I knew I could live on it and I have. I have defeated the serpent in my body. I knew I should suffer and I have. But I am winning. There is a certain sense in which life begins anew now, for all the blotting-paper and the pressure.'

He sat down by the Dwarf and drew up his knees. His sight was right on the outside and he lived in the world.

'I believe I'm hungry.'

And why not, when life begins again?

'Food on a plate. Rich food in comfort. Food in shops, butchers' shops, food, not swimming, shutting like a fist and vanishing into a crevice but dead on a slab, heaped up, all the sea's harvest——'

He examined the sea. The tide was running and glossy streaks were tailing away from the three rocks.

'Optical illusion.'

For of course the rock was fixed. If it seemed to move slowly forward in the tide that was because the eye had nothing else as a point of reference. But over the horizon was a coast and that remained at a constant distance while the water flowed. He smiled grimly.

'That wasn't a bad trick. It might have caught most people.'

Like the train that seems to move backwards when the other

one steams away from beside it. Like hatched lines with one across.

'For of course the rock is still and the water moves. Let me work it out. The tide is a great wave that sweeps round the world—or rather the world turns inside the tide, so I and the rock are——'

Hastily he looked down at the rock between his feet.

'So the rock is still.'

Food. Heaped on a slab, not swimming free but piled up, all the spoils of the sea, a lobster, not shutting like a fist and shooting back into a crevice but——

He was on his feet. He was glaring down at the place where the weed grew under water by the three rocks. He cried out.

'Whoever saw a lobster like that swimming in the sea? A red lobster?'

Something was taken away. For an instant he felt himself falling; and then there came a gap of darkness in which there was no one.

Something was coming up to the surface. It was uncertain of its identity because it had forgotten its name. It was disorganized in pieces. It struggled to get these pieces together because then it would know what it was. There was a rhythmical noise and disconnection. The pieces came shakily together and he was lying sideways on the rock and a snoring noise was coming from his mouth. There was a feeling of deep sickness further down the tunnel. There was a separation between now, whenever now was, and the instant of terror. The separation enabled him to forget what had caused that terror. The darkness of separation was deeper than that of sleep. It was deeper than any living darkness because time had stopped or come to an end. It was a gap of not-being, a well opening out of the world and now the effort of mere being was so exhausting that he could only lie sideways and live.

Presently he thought.

'Then I was dead. That was death. I have been frightened to death. Now the pieces of me have come together and I am just alive.'

The view was different too. The three rocks were nearer and there were sharp things—mussel shells, he thought, brilliantly—cutting his cheek.

'Who carried me down here?'

There came a little pain with the words which he traced to his tongue. The tip was swollen, and aching, and there was salt in his mouth. He could see a pair of empty trousers lying near him and curious marks on the rock. These marks where white and parallel. There was blood in them and traces of froth.

He attended to the rest of his body. He identified a hard, bar-like object as his right arm, twisted back. That led him to the pain in the joints. He eased over so that his arm was free and gazed at the hand on the end.

Now he saw that he was not wearing his pants because they were out there in his right hand. They were torn and there was blood on them.

'I've been in a fight.'

He lay, considering things dully.

'There is someone else on the rock with me. He crept out and slugged me.'

The face twisted.

'Don't be a fool. You're all alone. You've had a fit.'

He felt for his left hand and found it with a grunt of pain. The fingers were bitten.

'How long was I? Is it today or yesterday?'

He heaved himself up on hands and knees.

'Just when I was myself again and victorious, there came a sort of something. A Terror. There was a pattern emerging from circumstances.'

Then the gap of not-being.

'This side of the gap is different from the other. It's like when you've finished a lights rehearsal and they cut. Then where there was bright, solid scenery is now only painted stuff, grey under the pilot light. It's like chess. You've got an exultant attack moving but overlooked a check and now the game is a fight. And you're tied down.'

Bright rock and sea, hope, though deferred, heroics. Then in the moment of achievement, the knowledge, the terror like a hand falling.

'It was something I remembered. I'd better not remember it again. Remember to forget. Madness?'

Worse than madness. Sanity.

He heaved himself on his hands and knees and laboured to trace his fit, by the scattered clothing and the marks on the rock, back to where he had begun. He stopped by the Dwarf, looking down at rock with a pattern scratched on it—a pattern now crossed by the gritted mark of teeth.

'That was to be expected. Everything is to be expected. The world runs true to form. Remember that.'

He looked thoughtfully down at the streaks that the rock was leaving behind in the sea.

'I must not look at the sea. Or must I? Is it better to be sane or mad? It is better to be sane. I did not see what I thought I saw. I remembered wrongly.'

Then he had an important idea. It set him at once searching the rock, not in a casual way but inch by inch. Only after an eternity of searching, of cracks and bumps and roughnesses did he remember that he was foolish to search for a piece of wood to touch because there was none.

His pants were still trailing from his hand and he had a sudden thought that he could put them on. When he had done this his head cleared of all the mists except the pain. He put his hand up to the pain and found that there was a lump under the hair and the hair was stuck with blood. He examined his legs. The white blotches were smaller and no longer important. He remembered a custom and clambered into the water-hole. When he was in there he noticed a sudden, bright light in the opening over the far end and some deep seat of rationality drove him back to the Look-out; and he knew what the light and the noise that had come after it portended.

The sun was still shining but there was a change over a part of the horizon. He knelt to look at this change and it was divided again by a vertical jab of light. This light left a token in each eye that made seeing a divided business. He peered round the green streak that the light left and saw that the darkness made a definite line on the surface of the sea. It was coming nearer. Instantly he was in his body and knew where he was.

'Rain!'

Of course.

'I said there would be rain!'

Let there be rain and there was rain.

He scrambled down the High Street, got his sou'wester and arranged it in the lay-back under the end of the Claudian. He pulled off what clothes he was wearing and thrust them into the crevice. He was aware of bright lights and noise. He put his oilskin in a trench and ducked the body into a basin. He went almost upright to the Look-out and heard the hiss of the rain as the edge of the curtain fell on the Safety Rock. It hit him in the face sprang in foot-high leaps from the Dwarf and the surface of the look-out. He glistened and streamed from head to foot in a second.

There was a merciless flash-bang from the curtain and then he was stumbling down to the crevice and burrowing in head first while the thunder trampled overhead. Even in the depth of the crevice he saw a livid light that hurt his ears; and then there was the cessation of all noises but a high, singing note. This was so intimate to the head that it took the place of the thunder. His feet were being bastinadoed. His mouth said things but he could not hear them so did not know what they were. There was water running in the crevice, under his face, dripping from the rock, water running round his loins, water. He made his body back out of the crevice and was under a waterfall. He stumbled into a trench and found his sou'wester full and spilling. There was a tap of water running from the end of the Claudian and he took up the heavy sou'wester and poured water into his mouth. He put the sou'wester back and went to his oilskin. There was a bath ready for him but the rain was washing over him like a shower. He went back to the sou'wester, watched it fill and took it to the water-hole. He could hear the running click and trickle under the rock now—water running down, seaping through in unguessed crannies, falling with a multitudinous chattering into the hollow. Already the stretch of red clay was narrower.

'I said it would rain, and it has.'

He waited, shivering in the chilly cave, waited for the satisfaction that ought to come with the fulfilled prediction. But it would not come.

He crouched there, no longer listening to the water but frowning down at his shadow.

'What piece have I lost in my game? I had an attack, I was doing well, and then——' And then, the gap of dark, dividing that brighter time from this. On the other side of the gap was something that had happened. It was something that must not be remembered; but how could you control if you deliberately forgot? It was something about a pattern that was emerging.

'Inimical.'

He considered the word that his mouth had spoken. The word

sounded harmless unless the implications were attached. To avoid
that, he deliberately bent the process of thought and made his
mouth do as he bid.

'How can a rock be inimical?'

He crawled away quickly into a rain that fell more lightly. The
storm had hurried away over the three rocks and dulled the
motion of the water. The clouds had dulled everything. They had
left a grey, drizzly sea over which the air moved, pushed at the
rock in a perceptible wind.

'That was a subsidiary thunder-storm on the edge of a cyclone.
Cyclones revolve anti-clockwise in the northern hemisphere. The
wind is southerly. Therefore we are on the eastern edge of a
cyclone that is moving east. Since I can foretell the weather I can
be armed against it. The problem will be now to cope with too
much water, not too little.'

He paid only half-attention to his mouth. It lectured on re-
assuring nothing but itself. But the centre of the globe was
moving and flinching from isolated outcrops of knowledge. It
averted attention from one only to discover another. It attempted
to obliterate each separate outcrop when it found that they could
not be ignored.

'The whole problem of insanity is so complex that a satisfactory
definition, a norm, has never been established.'

Far out from the centre, the mouth quacked on.

'Where, for example, shall we draw the line between the man
whom we consider to be moody or excitable, and the genuine
psychopathic manic-depressive?'

The centre was thinking, with an eye lifted for the return of
the storm of terror, about how difficult it was to distinguish
between sleeping and waking when all one experienced was a
series of trailers.

'A recurrent dream, a neurosis? But surely the normal child in
its cot goes through all the symptoms of the neurotic?'

If one went step by step—ignoring the gap of dark and the
terror on the lip—back from the rock, through the Navy, the
stage, the writing, the university, the school, back to bed under
the silent eaves, one went down to the cellar. And the path led
back from the cellar to the rock.

'The solution lies in intelligence. That is what distinguishes us
from the helpless animals that are caught in their patterns of
behaviour, both mental and physical.'

But the dark centre was examining a thought like a monument
that had replaced the other in the dreary park.

Guano is insoluble.

If guano is insoluble, then the water in the upper trench could
not be a slimy wetness, the touch of which made a flaming needle
nag at the corner of an eye.

His tongue felt along the barrier of his teeth—round to the
side where the big ones were and the gap. He brought his hands
together and held his breath. He stared at the sea and saw nothing.
His tongue was remembering. It pried into the gap between the
teeth and re-created the old, aching shape. It touched the rough
edge of the cliff, traced the slope down, trench after aching trench,
down towards the smooth surface where the Red Lion was, just
above the gum—understood what was so hauntingly familiar and
painful about an isolated and decaying rock in the middle of the
sea.

CHAPTER TWELVE

Now there was nothing to do but protect normality. There was the centre wielding the exterior body as by strings. He made the body go down from the Look-out to the crevice. He found damp clothes and put them on until he could see extensions of clothing and seaboot stockings like piles of waste. The body and the clothing were ungainly as a diving dress. He went to Food Cliff and gathered mussels, made his mouth receive them. He did not look outwards but down where the water danced alongside the rock. The sea was ruffled and there were wavelets each carrying smaller wavelets on its back so that the depth was obscured and the water grave and chilly. As his jaws worked he sat still with two lobsters lying on the rock beside him. The meal went on under pricking rain, a stirring of wind and scuds of dimples across the surface of the water. He took morsels of food with one lobster and brought them to his face. The lobsters wore armour to protect them from the enormous pressure of the sky.

Between mouthfuls his voice quacked, veering in towards reason and truth and then skating away.

'I have no armour and that is why I am being squeezed thin. It has marred my profile too. My mouth sticks out such a long way and I have two noses.'

But the centre thought of other things.

'I must be careful when I look round at the wind. I don't want to die again.'

Meanwhile there were many mussels and one could make the mouth perform and obliterate the other possibilities.

'I was always two things, mind and body. Nothing has altered. Only I did not realize it before so clearly.'

The centre thought of the next move. The world could be held together by rivets driven in. Flesh could be mended by the claws of ants as in Africa. The will could resist.

And then there were no more mussels within reach. He made

the lobster mime eating but the sensations in the mouth were not the same.

'Have to do it.'

He turned himself on all fours. He held his breath and looked up and there was the old woman from the corner of the cellar standing on the skyline.

'She is the Dwarf. I gave her a silver head.'

Wind pushed in his face and a touch of rain. The old woman nodded with her face of dulled silver.

'It is lucky I put a silver mask over the other face. She is the Dwarf. That is not the next move.'

He worked his way back towards the Look-out, carried his body near the Dwarf and made it kneel down. Above him the Dwarf nodded gently with a face of dulled silver.

There was something in the topmost trench that was different. Immediately he flinched back and looked warily. The white stuff in the bottom was broken up and scattered because a chunk of rockleaf had fallen from the side of the trench. He crept forward and examined the chunk. On one edge the leaves were worn and ancient but on the other three they were white as muck and freshly broken. The chunk was about a yard each way and six inches thick. It was a considerable book and there was a strange engraving in the white cover. For a while his eye liked the engraving because it made a pattern and was not words, which would have killed him immediately. His eye followed the indented and gouged lines again and again as his mouth had eaten mussels. By the edge of the book was the recess from which it had come.

There was an engraving in the recess too. It was like a tree upside down and growing down from the old edge where the leaves were weathered by wind and rain. The trunk was a deep, perpendicular groove with flaky edges. Lower down, the trunk divided into three branches and these again into a complication of twigs like the ramifications of bookworm. The trunk and the branches and the twigs were terrible black. Round the twigs was an apple blossom of grey and silver stain. As he watched, drops of water dulled the stain and lay in the branches like tasteless fruit.

His mouth quacked.

'Lightning!'

But the dark centre was shrunk and dreadful and knowing. The knowing was so dreadful that the centre made the mouth work deliberately.

'Black lightning!'

There was still a part that could be played—there was the Bedlamite, Poor Tom, protected from knowledge of the sign of the black lightning.

He grabbed the old woman with her nodding silver head.

'Help me, my sweet, I must have your help!'

The mouth took over.

'If you let him go on doing that, my sweet, he'll knock the whole bloody rock apart and we shall be left swimming.'

Swimming in what?

The mouth went frantic.

'There was that rock round by Prospect Cliff, my sweet, that one moved, the water moved it. I wouldn't ask anyone but you because the rock is fixed and if he'll only let it alone it'll last for ever. After all, my sweet, you're his wife.'

Out of bed on the carpet with no shoes. Creep through the dark room not because you want to but because you've got to. Pass the door. The landing, huge, the grandfather clock. No safety behind me. Round the corner now to the stairs. Down, pad. Down, pad. The hall, but grown. Darkness sitting in every corner. The banisters high up, can just reach them with my hand. Not for sliding down now. Different banisters, everything different, a pattern emerging, forced to go down to meet the thing I turned my back on. Tick, tock, shadows pressing. Past the kitchen door. Draw back the bolt of the vault. Well of darkness. Down pad, down. Coffin ends crushed in the wall. Under the churchyard back through the death door to meet the master. Down, pad, down. Black lumps piled, smell damp. Shavings from coffins.

'A man must be mad when he sees a red lobster swimming in the sea. And guano is insoluble. A madman would see the gulls as flying lizards, he would connect the two things out of a book and it would come back to him when his brain turned no matter how long ago and forgotten the time when he read that—wouldn't he, my sweet? Say he would! Say he would!'

The silver face nodded on gently and the rain spattered.

Kindling from coffins, coal dust, black as black lightning. Block with the axe by it, not worn for firewood but by executions.

'Seals aren't inimical and a madman wouldn't sleep properly. He would feel the rock was too hard, too real; he would superimpose a reality, especially if he had too much imagination. He would be capable of seeing the engraving as a split into the whole nature of things—wouldn't he?'

And then fettered in the darkness by the feet, trying to lift one and finding a glue, finding a weakness where there should be strength now needed because by nature there was nothing to do but scream and try to escape. Darkness in the corner doubly dark, thing looming, feet tied, near, an unknown looming, an opening darkness, the heart and being of all imaginable terror. Pattern repeated from the beginning of time, approach of the unknown thing, a dark centre that turned its back on the thing that created it and struggled to escape.

'Wouldn't he? Say he would!'

There was a noise by his left arm and water scattered across the look-out. He made the exterior face turn into the wind and the air pushed against the cheeks. The water on the dwarf now was not rain but spray. He crept to the edge of the cliff and looked down the funnel. The water was white round Safety Rock and as he looked a dull sound in the funnel was followed by a plume of spray.

'This weather has been investigated before but from a lower level. He climbed there and the limpets held on.'

There was a gathering rhythm in the sea. The Safety Rock tripped the waves and shot them at the cleft below the funnel. Nine times out of ten these waves would meet a reflection coming back and spurt up a line of spray like a fuse burning—a fast fuse that whipped over the water. But the tenth time the wave would find the way clear because the ninth wave had been a very small one. So the tenth wave would come wheeling in, the cleft would squeeze the water so that it speeded up and hit the back of the angle—bung! and a feather of spray would flicker in the funnel. If the tenth wave was big the feather would become a plume and the wind would catch a handful from the top and sling shot across the Dwarf to go scattering down the High Street.

To watch the waves was like eating mussels. The sea was a point of an attention that could be prolonged even more than eating. The centre concentrated and left the mouth to itself.

'Of course a storm has to come after a time. That was to be expected. And who could invent all that complication of water, running true to form, obeying the laws of nature to the last drop? And of course a human brain must turn in time and the universe be muddled. But beyond the muddle there will still be actuality and a poor mad creature clinging to a rock in the middle of the sea.'

There is no centre of sanity in madness. Nothing like this 'I' sitting in here, staving off the time that must come. The last repeat of the pattern. Then the black lightning.

The centre cried out.

'I'm so alone! Christ! I'm so alone!'

Black. A familiar feeling, a heaviness round the heart, a reservoir which any moment might flood the eyes now and for so long, strangers to weeping. Black, like the winter evening through which the centre made its body walk—a young body. The window was diversified only by a perspective of lighted lamps on the top of the street lamp-posts. The centre was thinking—I am alone; so alone! The reservoir overflowed, the lights all the way along to Carfax under Big Tom broke up, put out rainbow wings. The centre felt the gulping of its throat, sent eyesight on ahead to cling desperately to the next light and then the next—anything to fasten the attention away from the interior blackness.

Because of what I did I am an outsider and alone.

The centre endured a progress through an alley, across another road, a quadrangle, climbed bare wooden stairs. It sat by a fire and all the bells of Oxford tolled for the reservoir that overflowed and the sea roared in the room.

The centre twisted the unmanliness out of its face but the ungovernable water ran and dripped down the cheeks.

'I am so alone. I am *so* alone!'

Slowly, the water dried. Time stretched out, like the passage of time on a rock in the middle of the sea.

The centre formulated a thought.

Now there is no hope. There is nothing. If they would only look at me, or speak—if I could only be a part of something——

Time stretched on, indifferently.

There was the sound of feet on the stairs, two stories down. The centre waited without hope, to hear which room they would visit. But they came on, they climbed, were louder, almost as loud as the heart-beats so that when they stopped outside the door he was standing up and his hands were by his chest. The door opened a few inches and a shock of black curls poked round by the very top.

'Nathaniel!'

Nathaniel bowed and beamed his way into the room and stood looking down at the window.

'I thought I might catch you. I'm back for the weekend.' Then as an afterthought: 'Can I come in?'

'My dear man!'

Nathaniel operated on his great-coat, peered round solemnly as though the question of where to put it was a major one.

'Here. Let me take that for you—sit down—I'm—my dear man!'

Nathaniel was grinning too.

'It's good to see you, Christopher.'

'And you can stay? You don't have to rush away?'

'I've come up to give a lecture to the——'

'But not this evening?'

'No. I can stay this evening.'

The centre sat opposite, right on the outside of its window—right out in the world.

'We'll talk. Let's talk, Nat.'

'How's the social whirl?'

'How's London?'

'Doesn't like lectures on heaven.'

'Heaven?'

Then the body was laughing, louder and louder and the water was flowing again. Nat was grinning and blushing too.

'I know. But you don't have to make it worse.'

He smeared away the water and hiccupped.

'Why heaven?'

'The sort of heaven we invented for ourselves after death, if we aren't ready for the real one.'

'You would—you curious creature!'

Nathaniel became serious. He peered upwards, raised an index finger and consulted a reference book beyond the ceiling.

'Take us as we are now and heaven would be sheer negation. Without form and void. You see? A sort of black lightning, destroying everything that we call life——'

The laughter came back.

'I don't see and I don't much care but I'll come to your lecture. My dear Nat—you've no idea how glad I am to see you!'

The burning fuse whipped through Nathaniel's face and he was gone. The centre remained looking down into the funnel. His mouth was open in astonishment and terror.

'And I liked him as much as that!'

Black and feeling one's way to the smooth steel ladder that
glinted only faintly in the cloud light. The centre tried to resist,
like a child trying to resist a descent into the midnight cellar but
its legs bore it on. Up and up, from the waist to the level of the
fo'c'sle, up past B gun. Shall I meet him? Will he stand there
tonight?

And there, sketched against the clouds in Indian ink, random
in limb and gesture, an old binder by a rick, was Nathaniel,
swaying and grabbing at a midnight salute. Wotcher, Nat, rose in
his throat and he swallowed it. Pretend not to see. Be as little
connected as possible. Fire a fuse from the bridge that will blow
him away from her body and clear the way for me. We are all past
the first course, we have eaten the fish.

And it may not work. He may not bother to lay aft and pray to
his aeons. Good-bye, Nat, I loved you and it is not in my nature
to love much. But what can the last maggot but one do? Lose his
identity?

Nathaniel stood swaying and spread-eagled in the dark, understanding obediently that he had not been seen. Instead he stood
away from the officer's approach and fumbled on down the
ladder.

Everything set, the time, the place, the loved one.

'You're early for once, thank God. Course o-four-five, speed
twenty-eight knots. Nothing in sight and we press on for another
hour.'

'Anything new?'

'Same as was. We're thirty miles north of the convoy, all on
our own, going to send off the signal in an hour's time. The old
man'll be up for that. There you are. No zig-zag. Dead easy.
Oh—the moon'll be up in ten minutes' time and we'd make quite
a target if we tripped over a U-boat. Pass it on. Nighty night.'

'Sweet dreams.'

He heard the steps descending. He crossed to the starboard
side of the bridge and looked aft. There was engine-noise, outline
of the funnel. The wake spread out dull white astern and a secon-
dary wave fanned out from midships. The starboard side of the
quarter-deck was just visible in outline but the surface was dark
by contrast and all the complications of the throwers, the depth-
charges, the sweeps and lifted gun made it very difficult to see

whether there was a figure leaning on the rail among them. He stared down and wondered whether he saw or created in his mind, the mantis shape with forelegs lifted to the face.

It is not Nathaniel leaning there, it is Mary.

I must. I must. Don't you understand, you bloody bitch?

'Messenger!'

'Sir.'

'Get me a cup of cocoa.'

'Aye aye, sir!'

'And messenger—never mind.'

Feet descending the ladder. Darkness and the wind of speed. Glow over to starboard like a distant fire from a raided city. Moonrise.

'Port look-out!'

'Sir?'

'Nip down to the wheel-house and get me the other pair of night-glasses. I think these need overhauling. You'll find them in the rack over the chart table.'

'Aye aye, sir!'

'I'll take over your sector while you're gone.'

'Aye aye, sir!'

Feet descending the ladder.

Now.

Ham it a bit. Casual saunter to the port side. Pause.

Now. Now. Now.

Scramble to the binnacle, fling yourself at the voice pipe, voice urgent, high, sharp, frightened——

'Hard a-starboard for Christ's sake!'

A destroying concussion that had no part in the play. Whiteness rising like a cloud, universe spinning. The shock of a fall somewhere, shattering, mouth filled—and he was fighting in all directions with black impervious water.

His mouth screamed in range at the whiteness that rose out of the funnel.

'And it was the right bloody order!'

Eaten.

He was no longer able to look at the waves, for every few minutes they were hidden by the rising whiteness. He made his sight creep out and look at his clothed body. The clothes were wringing wet and the seaboot stockings smeared like mops. His mouth said something mechanical.

'I wish I hadn't kicked off my seaboots when I was in the water.'

The centre told itself to pretend and keep on pretending.

The mouth had its own wisdom.

'There is always madness, a refuge like a crevice in the rock. A man who has no more defence can always creep into madness like one of those armoured things that scuttle among weed down where the mussels are.'

Find something to look at.

'Madness would account for everything, wouldn't it, my sweet?'

Do, if not look.

He got up and staggered in the wind with the rain and spray pelting him. He went down the High Street and there was his oilskin made into a basin and full of water. He took his sou'wester and began to bail out the oilskin and take the water to the water-hole. He concentrated on the laws of water, how it fell or lay, how predictable it was and manageable. Every now and then the rock shook, a white cloud rose past the look-out and there were rivulets of foam in the upper trenches. When he had emptied his oilskin he held it up, drained it and put it on. Fooling with buttons the centre could turn away from what was to come. While he did this he was facing the Claudian where the foam now hung in gobs and the oilskin thrust him against the cut. As he stood pinned, he was struck a blow in the back and bucketfuls of water fell in the trench. It washed round then settled scummily in the bottom. He felt his way along the Claudian to the crevice and backed himself in. He put on his sou'wester and laid his forehead on his arms. The world turned black and came to him through sound.

'If a madman heard it he would think it was thunder and of course it would be. There is no need to listen like that. It will only be thunder over the horizon where the ships are passing to and fro. Listen to the storm instead. It is going to flail on this rock. It is going to beat a poor wretch into madness. He does not want to go mad only he will have to. Think of it! All you people in warm beds, a British sailor isolated on a rock and going mad not because he wants to but because the sea is a terror—the worst terror there is, the worst imaginable.'

The centre co-operated but with an ear cocked. It concentrated now on the words that spilt out of the mouth because with the fringes of flesh and hair lowered over the window the words could be examined as the thoughts had been. It provided background music.

'Oh help, help! I am dying of exposure. I am starving, dying of thirst. I lie like driftwood caught in a cleft. I have done my duty for you and this is my reward. If you could only see me you would be wrung with pity. I was young and strong and handsome with an eagle profile and wavy hair; I was brilliantly clever and I went out to fight your enemies. I endured in the water, I fought the whole sea. I have fought a rock, and gulls and lobsters and seals and a storm. Now I am thin and weak. My joints are like knobs and my limbs like sticks. My face is fallen in with age and my hair is white with salt and suffering. My eyes are dull stones——'

The centre quivered and dwindled. There was another noise beyond the storm and background music and sobbed words from the mouth.

'——my chest is like the ribs of a derelict boat and every breath is an effort——'

The noise was so faint in comparison with the uproar of the wind and rain and waves that it caught and glued attention. The mouth knew this too and tried harder.

'I am going mad. There is lightning playing on the skirts of a wild sea. I am strong again——'

And the mouth sang.

The centre still attended through the singing, the background music, the uproar from outside. The noise came again. The centre could confuse it for a while with thunder.

'Hoé, hoé! Thor's lightning challenges me! Flash after flash, rippling spurts of white fire, bolts flung at Prometheus, blinding white, white, white, searing, the aim of the sky at the man on the rock——'

The noise, if one attended as the centre was forced to attend was dull and distant. It might have been thunder or gun-fire. It might have been the sound of a drum and the mouth seized on that.

'Rata tat tat tat! The soldiers come, my Emperor is taken! Rat a tat!'

It might have been the shifting of furniture in an upper room

and the mouth panicked after that thought with the automatic
flock of an insect.

'Put it down here. Roll back that corner of the carpet and then
you can get the table out. Shall we have it next to the radiogram?
Take that record off and put on something rocklike and
heroic——'

It might have been flour-sacks slid down an iron ladder to
resound on the steel deck.

'Hard a-starboard! Hard a-starboard!'

It might have been the shaking of the copper sheet in the
wings.

'I must have the lead or I shall leave the coal flat——'

The cellar door swinging to behind a small child who must go
down, down in his sleep to meet the thing he turned from when
he was created.

'Off with his head! Down on the block among the kindling
and coal-dust!'

But the centre knew. It recognized with a certainty that made
the quacking of the mouth no more help than hiccups. The noise
was the grating and thump of a spade against an enormous tin
box that had been buried.

CHAPTER THIRTEEN

'Mad,' said the mouth, 'raving mad. I can account for everything, lobsters, maggots, hardness, brilliant reality, the laws of nature, film-trailers, snapshots of sight and sound, flying lizards, enmity—how should a man not be mad? I will tell you what a man is. He goes on four legs till Necessity bends the front end upright and makes a hybrid of him. The finger-prints of those hands are about his spine and just above the rump for proof if you want it. He is a freak, an ejected foetus robbed of his natural development, thrown out in the world with a naked covering of parchment, with too little room for his teeth and a soft bulging skull like a bubble. But nature stirs a pudding there and sets a thunderstorm flickering inside the hardening globe, white, lambent lightning a constant flash and tremble. All your lobsters and film-trailers are nothing but the random intersections of instant bushes of lightning. The sane life of your belly and your cock are on a simple circuit, but how can the stirred pudding keep constant? Tugged at by the pill of the earth, infected by the white stroke that engraved the book, furrowed, lines burned through it by hardship and torment and terror-unbalanced, brain-sick, at your last gasp on a rock in the sea, the pudding has boiled over and you are no worse than raving mad.'

Sensations. Coffee. Hock. Gin. Wood. Velvet. Nylon. Mouth. Warm, wet nakedness. Caves, slack like a crevice or tight like the mouth of a red anemone. Full of stings. Domination, identity.

'You are the intersections of all the currents. You do not exist apart from me. If I have gone mad then you have gone mad. You are speaking, in there, you and I are one and mad.'

The rock shook and shook again. A sudden coldness struck his face and washed under him.

To be expected.

'Nathaniel!'

Black centre, trying to stir itself like a pudding.

The darkness was shredded by white. He tumbled over among

the sensations of the crevice. There was water everywhere and noise and his mouth welcomed both. It spat and coughed. He heaved himself out amid water that swirled to his knees and the wind knocked him down. The trench was like a little sea, like the known and now remembered extravagances of a returning tide among rocks. What had been a dry trench was half-full of moving water on which streams of foam were circling and interlacing. The wind was like an express in a tunnel and everywhere there was a trickling and washing and pouring. He scrambled up in the trench, without hearing what his mouth said and suddenly he and his mouth were one.

'You bloody great bully!'

He got his face above the level of the wall and the wind pulled the cheeks in like an airman's. Bird-shot slashed. Then the sky above the old woman jumped. It went white. An instant later the light was switched off and the sky fell on him. He collapsed under the enormous pressure and went down in the water of the trench. The weight withdrew and left him struggling. He got up and the sky fell on him again. This time he was able to lurch along the trench because the weight of water was just not suffici-ent to break him and the sea in the trench was no higher than his knees. The world came back, storm-grey and torn with flying streamers, and he gave it storm-music, crash of timpany, brass blared and a dazzle of strings. He fought a hero's way from trench to trench through water and music, his clothes shaking and plucked, tattered like the end of a windsock, hands clawing. He and his mouth shouted through the uproar.

'Ajax! Prometheus!'

The old woman was looking down at him as he struggled through bouts of white and dark. Then her head with its silver mask was taken by a whiteness and she hunched against the sky with her headless shoulders. He fell in the white trench over the book with his face against the engraving and the insoluble muck filled his mouth. There came a sudden pressure and silence. He was lifted up and thrown down again, struck against rock. For a moment as the water passed away he saw the look-out against the sky now empty of the old woman but changed in outline by scattered stones.

'She is loose on the rock. Now she is out of the cellar and in daylight. Hunt her down!'

And the knife was there among all the other sensations, jammed

against his ribs. He got it in his hands and pulled the blade open.
He began to crawl and hunt and swim from trench to trench. She
was leaning over the rail but vanished and he stole after her into
the green room. But she was out by the footlights and when he
crouched in the wings he saw that he was not dressed properly
for the part. His mouth and he were one.

'Change your clothes! Be a naked madman on a rock in the
middle of a storm!'

His claws plucked at the tatters and pulled them away. He saw
a glimpse of gold braid and an empty seaboot stocking floating
away like a handful of waste. He saw a leg, scarred, scaly and
stick thin and the music mourned for it.

He remembered the old woman and crawled after her down
the High Street to the Red Lion. The back wash of the waves was
making a welcome confusion round the three rocks and the confusion hid the place where the red lobster had been. He shouted
at the rocks but the old woman would not appear among them.
She had slipped away down to the cellar. Then he glimpsed her
lying huddled in the crevice and he struggled up to her. He fell
on her and began to slash with his knife while his mouth went on
shouting.

'That'll teach you to chase me! That'll teach you to chase me
out of the cellar through cars and beds and pubs, you at the back
and me running, running after my identity disc all the days of my
life! Bleed and die.'

But he and his voice were one. They knew the blood was sea
water and the cold, crumpling flesh that was ripped and torn
nothing but oilskin.

Now the voice became a babble, sang, swore, made meaningless
syllables, coughed and spat. It filled every tick of time with noise,
jammed the sound so that it choked; but the centre began to
know itself as other because every instant was not occupied by
noise. The mouth spat and deviated into part sense.

'And last of all, hallucination, vision, dream, delusion will haunt
you. What else can a madman expect? They will appear to you on
the solid rock, the real rock, they will fetter your attention to
them and you will be nothing worse than mad.'

And immediately the hallucination was there. He knew this
before he saw it because there was an awe in the trench, framed by
the silent spray that flew over. The hallucination sat on the rock
at the end of the trench and at last he faced it through his blurred

window. He saw the rest of the trench and crawled along through water that was gravely still unless a gust struck down with a long twitch and shudder of the foamy scum. When he was near, he looked up from the boots, past the knees, to the face and engaged himself to the mouth.

'You are a projection of my mind. But you are a point of attention for me. Stay there.'

The lips hardly moved in answer..

'You are a projection of my mind.'

He made a snorting sound.

'Infinite regression or better still, round and round the mulberry bush. We could go on like that for ever.'

'Have you had enough, Christopher?'

He looked at the lips. They were clear as the words. A tiny shred of spittle joined them near the right corner.

'I could never have invented that.'

The eye nearest the look-out was bloodshot at the outer corner. Behind it or beside it a red strip of sunset ran down out of sight behind the rock. The spray still flew over. You could look at the sunset or the eye but you could not do both. You could not look at the eye and the mouth together. He saw the nose was shiny and leathery brown and full of pores. The left cheek would need a shave soon, for he could see the individual bristles. But he could not look at the whole face together. It was a face that perhaps could be remembered later. It did not move. It merely had this quality of refusing overall inspection. One feature at a time.

'Enough of what?'

'Surviving. Hanging on.'

The clothing was difficult to pin down too so that he had to examine each piece. There was an oilskin—belted, because the buttons had fetched away. There was a woollen pullover inside it, with a roll-neck. The sou'wester was back a little. The hands were resting one on either knee, above the seaboot stockings. Then there were seaboots, good and shiny and wet and solid. They made the rock behind them seem like cardboard, like a painted flat. He bent forward until his bleared window was just above the right instep. There was no background music now and no wind, nothing but black, shiny rubber.

'I hadn't considered.'

'Consider now.'

'What's the good? I'm mad.'

'Even that crevice will crumble.'

He tried to laugh up at the bloodshot eye but heard barking noises. He threw words in the face.

'On the sixth day he created God. Therefore I permit you to use nothing but my own vocabulary. In his own image created he Him.'

'Consider now.'

He saw the eye and the sunset merge. He brought his arms across his face.

'I won't. I can't.'

'What do you believe in?'

Down to the black boot, coal black, darkness of the cellar, but now down to a forced answer.

'The thread of my life.'

'At all costs.'

Repeat after me:

'At all costs.'

'So you survived.'

'That was luck.'

'Inevitability.'

'Didn't the others want to live then?'

'There are degrees.'

He dropped the curtains of flesh and hair and blotted out the boots. He snarled.

'I have a right to live if I can!'

'Where is that written?'

'Then nothing is written.'

'Consider.'

He raged on the cardboard rock before the immovable, black feet.

'I will not consider! I have created you and I can create my own heaven.'

'You have created it.'

He glanced sideways along the twitching water, down at his skeleton legs and knees, felt the rain and spray and the savage cold on his flesh.

He began to mutter.

'I prefer it. You gave me the power to choose and all my life you led me carefully to this suffering because my choice was my own. Oh yes! I understand the pattern. All my life, whatever I had done I should have found myself in the end on that same bridge, at that same time, giving that same order—the right order, the wrong order. Yet, suppose I climbed away from the cellar over the bodies of used and defeated people, broke them to make steps on the road away from you, why should you torture me? If I ate them, who gave me a mouth?'

'There is no answer in your vocabulary.'

He squatted back and glared up at the face. He shouted.

'I have considered. I prefer it, pain and all.'

'To what?'

He began to rage weakly and strike out at the boots.

'To the black lightning! Go back! Go back!'

He was bruising skin off his hands against the streaming rock. His mouth quacked and he went with it into the last crevice of all.

'Poor mad sailor on a rock!'

He clambered up the High Street.

> *Rage, roar, spout!*
> *Let us have wind, rain, hail, gouts of blood,*
> *Storms and tornadoes . . .*

He ran about on the look-out, stumbling over scattered stones.

> *. . . hurricanes and typhoons. . . .*

There was a half-light, a storm-light. The light was ruled in lines and the sea in ridges and valleys. The monstrous waves were making their way from east to west in an interminable procession and the rock was a trifle among them. But it was charging forward, searing a white way through them, careless of sinking, it was thrusting the Safety Rock forward to burst the ridges like the prow of a ship. It would strike a ridge with the stone prow and burst water into a smother that washed over the fo'c'sle and struck beneath the bridge. Then a storm of shot would sweep over the bridge and strike sense and breath away from his body. He flung himself on a square stone that lay where the old woman had stood with her masked head. He rode it astride, facing into the wind and waves. And again there was background music and a mouth quacking.

'Faster! Faster!'

His rock bored on. He beat it with his heels as if he wore spurs.

'Faster!'

The waves were each an event in itself. A wave would come weltering and swinging in with a storm-light running and flickering along the top like the flicker in a brain. The shallow water beyond the safety rock would occur, so that the nearer part of the wave would rise up, tripped and angry, would roar, swell forward. The Safety Rock would become a pock in a whirlpool of water that spun itself into foam and chewed like a mouth. The whole top of the wave for a hundred yards would move forward and fall into acres of lathering uproar that was launched like an army at the rock.

'Faster!'

His hand found the identity disc and held it out.

The mouth screamed out away from the centre.

'I spit on your compassion!'

There was a recognizable noise away beyond the waves and in the clouds. The noise was not as loud as the sea or the music or the voice but the centre understood. The centre took the body off the slab of rock and bundled it into a trench. As it fell the eye glimpsed a black tendril of lightning that lay across the western sky and the centre screwed down the flaps of flesh and hair. Again there came the sound of the spade against the tin box.

'Hard a-starboard! I'll kill us both, I'll hit the tree with that side and you'll be burst and bitched! There was nothing in writing!'

The centre knew what to do. It was wiser than the mouth. It sent the body scrambling over the rock to the waterhole. It burrowed in among the slime and circling scum. It thrust the hands forward, tore at the water and fell flat in the pool. It wriggled like a seal on a rock with the fresh water streaming out of its mouth. It got at the tamping at the farther end and heaved at the stones. There was a scraping and breaking sound and then the cascade of falling stones and water. There was a wide space of stormlight, waves. There was a body lying in the slimy hollow where the fresh water had been.

'Mad! Proof of madness!'

It made the body wriggle back out of the hole, sent it up to the place where the Look-out had been.

There were branches of the black lightning over the sky, there were noises. One branch ran down into the sea, through the great waves, petered out. It remained there. The sea stopped moving, froze, became paper, painted paper that was torn by a black line. The rock was painted on the same paper. The whole of the

painted sea was tilted but nothing ran downhill into the black
crack which had opened in it. The crack was utter, was absolute,
was three times real.

The centre did not know if it had flung the body down or if it
had turned the world over. There was rock before its face and it
struck with lobster claws that sank in. It watched the rock between the claws.

The absolute lightning spread. There was no noise now because
noise had become irrelevant. There was no music, no sound from
the tilted, motionless sea.

The mouth quacked on for a while then dribbled into silence.
There was no mouth.

Still the centre resisted. It made the lightning do its work
according to the laws of this heaven. It perceived in some mode
of sight without eyes that pieces of the sky between the branches
of black lightning were replaced by pits of nothing. This made
the fear of the centre, the rage of the centre vomit in a mode that
required no mouth. It screamed into the pit of nothing voicelessly,
wordlessly.

'I shit on your heaven!'

The lines and tendrils felt forward through the sea. A segment
of storm dropped out like a dead leaf and there was a gap that
joined sea and sky through the horizon. Now the lightning found
reptiles floating and flying motionlessly and a tendril ran to each.
The reptiles resisted, changing shape a little, then they too,
dropped out and were gone. A valley of nothing opened up
through Safety Rock.

The centre attended to the rock between its claws. The rock
was harder than rock, brighter, firmer. It hurt the serrations of
the claws that gripped.

The sea twisted and disappeared. The fragments were not visible going away, they went into themselves, dried up, destroyed,
erased like an error.

The lines of absolute blackness felt forward into the rock and
it was proved to be as insubstantial as the painted water. Pieces
went and there was no more than an island of papery stuff round
the claws and everywhere else there was the mode that the centre
knew as nothing.

The rock between the claws was solid. It was square and there
was an engraving on the surface. The black lines sank in, went
through and joined.

The rock between the claws was gone.

There was nothing but the centre and the claws. They were huge and strong and inflamed to red. They closed on each other. They contracted. They were outlined like a night sign against the absolute nothingness and they gripped their whole strength into each other. The serrations of the claws broke. They were lambent and real and locked.

The lightning crept in. The centre was unaware of anything but the claws and the threat. It focused its awareness on the crumbled serrations and the blazing red. The lightning came forward. Some of the lines pointed to the centre, waiting for the moment when they could pierce it. Others lay against the claws, playing over them, prying for a weakness, wearing them away in a compassion that was timeless and without mercy.

CHAPTER FOURTEEN

The jetty, if the word would do for a long pile of boulders, was almost under the tide at the full. The drifter came in towards it, engine stopped, with the last of her way and the urging of the west wind. There was a wintry sunset behind her so that to the eyes on the beach she seemed soon a black shape from which the colour had all run away and been stirred into the low clouds that hung just above the horizon. There was a leaden tinge to the water except in the path of the drifter—a brighter valley of red and rose and black that led back to the dazzling horizon under the sun.

The watcher on the beach did not move. He stood, his seaboots set in the troughs of dry sand that his last steps had made, and waited. There was a cottage at his back and then the slow slope of the island.

The telegraph rang astern in the drifter and she checked her way with a sudden swirl of brighter water from the screws. A fender groaned against stone. Two men jumped on to the jetty and sought about them for the bollards that were not there. An arm gesticulated from the wheel-house. The man caught their ropes round boulders and stood, holding on.

An officer stepped on to the jetty, came quickly towards the beach and jumped down to the dry sand. The wind ruffled papers that he held in his hand so that they chattered like the dusty leaves of late summer. But here they were the only leaves. There was sand, a cottage, rocks and the sea. The officer laboured along in the dry sand with his papers chattering and came to a halt a yard from the watcher.

'Mr Campbell?'

'Aye. You'll be from the mainland about the——?'

'That's right.'

Mr Campbell removed his cloth cap and put it back again.

'You've not been over-quick.'

The officer looked at him solemnly.

'My name's Davidson, by the way. Over-quick. Do you know,
Mr Campbell, that I do this job, seven days a week?'

Mr Campbell moved his seaboots suddenly. He peered forward
into Davidson's grey and lined face. There was a faint, sweet
smell on the breath and the eyes that did not blink were just a
fraction too wide open.

Mr Campbell took off his cap and put it on again.

'Well now. Fancy that!'

The lower part of Davidson's face altered to the beginnings of
a grin without humour.

'It's quite a widespread war, you know.'

Mr Campbell nodded slowly.

'I'm sorry that I spoke. A sad harvest for you, Captain. I do
not know how you can endure it.'

The grin disappeared.

'I wouldn't change.'

Mr Campbell tilted his head sideways and peered into Davidson's face.

'No? I beg your pardon, sir. Come now and see where we
found it.'

He turned and laboured away along the sand. He stopped and
pointed down to where an arm of water was confined by a shingly
spit.

'It was there, still held by the lifebelt. You'll see, of course.
There was a broken orange-box and a tin. And the lineweed.
When we have a nor'wester the lineweed gets caught there—and
anything else that's floating.'

Davidson looked sideways at him.

'It seems important to you, Mr Campbell, but what I really
want is the identity disc. Did you remove that from the body?'

'No. No. I touched—as little as possible.'

'A brown disc about the size of a penny, probably worn round
the neck?'

'No. I touched nothing.'

Davidson's face set grim again.

'One can always hope, I suppose.'

Mr Campbell clasped his hands, rubbed them restlessly, cleared
his throat.

'You'll take it away tonight?'

Now Davidson peered in his turn.

'Dreams?'

Mr Campbell looked away at the water. He muttered.

'The wife——'

He glanced up at the too-wide eyes, the face that seemed to know more than it could bear. He no longer evaded the meeting but shrank a little and answered with sudden humility.

'Aye.'

Davidson nodded, slowly.

Now two ratings were standing on the beach before the cottage. They bore a stretcher.

Mr Campbell pointed.

'It is in the lean-to by the house, sir. I hope there is as little to offend you as possible. We used paraffin.'

'Thank you.'

Davidson toiled back along the beach and Mr Campbell followed him. Presently they stopped. Davidson turned and looked down.

'Well——'

He put his hand to the breast pocket of his battledress and brought out a flat bottle. He looked Mr Campbell in the eye, grinned with the lower part of his face, pulled out the cork and swigged, head back. The ratings watched him without comment.

'Here goes, then.'

Davidson went to the lean-to, taking a torch from his trouser pocket. He ducked through the broken door and disappeared.

The ratings stood without movement. Mr Campbell waited, silently, and contemplated the lean-to as though he were seeing it for the first time. He surveyed the mossed stones, the caved-in and lichenous roof as though they were a profound and natural language that men were privileged to read only on a unique occasion.

There was no noise from inside.

Even on the drifter there was no conversation. The only noises were the sounds of the water falling over on the little beach.

Hush. Hush.

The sun was a half-circle in a bed of crimson and slate.

Davidson came out again. He carried a small disc, swinging from a double string. His right hand went to the breast pocket. He nodded to the ratings.

'Go on, then.'

Mr Campbell watched Davidson fumble among his papers. He saw him examining the disc, peering close, transferring details carefully to a file. He saw him put the disc away, crouch, rub his hands backwards and forwards in the dry, clean sand. Mr Campbell spread his arms wide in a gesture of impotence and dropped them.

'I do not know, sir. I am older than you but I do not know.'

Davidson said nothing. He stood up again and took out his bottle.

'Don't you have second sight up here?'

Mr Campbell looked unhappily at the lean-to.

'Don't joke, sir. That was unworthy of you.'

Davidson came down from his swig. Two faces approached each other. Campbell read the face line by line as he had read the lean-to. He flinched from it again and looked away at the place where the sun was going down—seemingly for ever.

The ratings came out of the lean-to. They carried a stretcher between them that was no longer empty.

'All right, lads. There's a tot waiting for you. Carry on.'

The two sailors went cautiously away through the sand towards the jetty. Davidson turned to Mr Campbell.

'I have to thank you, Mr Campbell, in the name of this poor officer.'

Mr Campbell took his eyes away from the stretcher.

'They are wicked things, those lifebelts. They give a man hope when there is no longer any call for it. They are cruel. You do not have to thank me, Mr Davidson.'

He looked at Davidson in the gloom, carefully, eye to eye. Davidson nodded.

'Maybe. But I thank you.'

'I did nothing.'

The two men turned and watched the ratings lifting the stretcher to the low jetty.

'And you do this every day.'

'Every day.'

Mr Davidson——'

Mr Campbell paused so that Davidson turned towards him again. Mr Campbell did not immediately meet his eye.

'—we are the type of human intercourse. We meet here, apparently by chance, a meeting unpredictable and never to be repeated. Therefore I should like to ask you a question with perhaps a brutal answer.'

Davidson pushed his cap back on his head and frowned. Mr Campbell looked at the lean-to.

'Broken, defiled. Returning to the earth, the rafters rooted, the roof fallen in—a wreck. Would you believe that anything ever lived there?'

Now the frown was bewildered.

'I simply don't follow you, I'm afraid.'

'All those poor people——'

'The men I——?'

'The harvest. The sad harvest. You know nothing of my—shall I say—official beliefs, Mr Davidson; but living for all these days next to that poor derelict—Mr Davidson. Would you say there was any—surviving? Or is that all? Like the lean-to?'

'If you're worried about Martin—whether he suffered or not——'

They paused for a while. Beyond the drifter the sun sank like a burning ship, went down, left nothing for a reminder but clouds like smoke.

Mr Campbell sighed.

'Aye,' he said, 'I meant just that.'

'Then don't worry about him. You saw the body. He didn't even have time to kick off his seaboots.'

RITES OF
PASSAGE

(I)

Honoured godfather,

   With these words I begin the journal I engaged myself to keep
for you—no words could be more suitable!

   Very well then. The place: on board the ship at last. The year:
you know it. The date? Surely what matters is that it is the
first day of my passage to the other side of the world; in token
whereof I have this moment inscribed the number 'one' at the
top of this page. For what I am about to write must be a record
of our *first day*. The month or day of the week can signify little
since in our long passage from the south of Old England to
the Antipodes we shall pass through the geometry of all four
seasons!

   This very morning before I left the hall I paid a visit to my
young brothers, and they were such a trial to old Dobbie! Young
Lionel performed what he conceived to be an Aborigine's war
dance. Young Percy lay on his back and rubbed his belly, meanwhile venting horrid groans to convey the awful results of eating
me! I cuffed them both into attitudes of decent dejection, then
descended again to where my mother and father were waiting.
My mother—contrived a tear or two? Oh no, it was the genuine
article, for there was at that point a warmth in my own
bosom which might not have been thought manly. Why, even
my father—— We have, I believe, paid more attention to senti-
mental Goldsmith and Richardson than lively old Fielding and
Smollett! Your lordship would indeed have been convinced of
my worth had you heard the invocations over me, as if I were a
convict in irons rather than a young gentleman going to assist
the governor in the administration of one of His Majesty's
colonies! I felt much the better for my parents' evident feelings—and I felt the better for my own feelings too! Your
godson is a good enough fellow at bottom. Recovery took him
all the way down the drive, past the lodge and as far as the
first turning by the mill!

Well then, to resume, I am aboard. I climbed the bulging and tarry side of what once, in her young days, may have been one of Britain's formidable *wooden walls*. I stepped through a kind of low doorway into the darkness of some deck or other and gagged at my first breath. Good God, it was quite nauseous! There was much bustling and hustling about in an artificial twilight. A fellow who announced himself as my servant conducted me to a kind of hutch against the vessel's side, which he assured me was my cabin. He is a limping old fellow with a sharp face and a bunch of white hair on either side of it. These bunches are connected over his pate by a shining baldness.

'My good man,' said I, 'what is this stink?'

He stuck his sharp nose up and peered round as if he might see the stink in the darkness rather than nose it. 'Stink, sir? What stink, sir?'

'*The stink*,' said I, my hand over my nose and mouth as I gagged, 'the fetor, the stench, call it what you will!'

He is a sunny fellow, this Wheeler. He smiled at me then as if the deck, close over our heads, had opened and let in some light.

'Lord, sir!' said he. 'You'll soon get used to that!'

'I do not wish to get used to it! Where is the captain of this vessel?'

Wheeler dowsed the light of his countenance and opened the door of my hutch for me.

'There's nothing Captain Anderson could do either, sir,' said he. 'It's sand and gravel you see. The new ships has iron ballast but she's older than that. If she was betwixt and between in age, as you might say, they'd have dug it out. But not her. She's too old you see. They wouldn't want to go stirring about down there, sir.'

'It must be a graveyard then!'

Wheeler thought for a moment.

'As to that, I can't say, sir, not having been in her previous. Now you sit here for a bit and I'll bring a brandy.'

With that, he was gone before I could bear to speak again and have to inhale more of the *'tween decks* air. So there I was and here I am.

Let me describe what will be my lodging until I can secure more fitting accommodation. The hutch contains a bunk like a trough laid along the ship's side with two drawers built under it.

At one end of the hutch a flap lets down as a writing table and there is a canvas bowl with a bucket under it at the other. I must suppose the ship contains a more *commodious* area for the perform- ance of our natural functions! There is room for a mirror above the bowl and two shelves for books at the foot of the bunk. A canvas chair is the movable furniture of this noble apartment. The door has a fairly big opening in it at eye-level through which some daylight filters, and the wall on either side of it is furnished with hooks. The floor, or deck as I must call it, is rutted deep enough to twist an ankle. I suppose these ruts were made by the iron wheels of her gun trolleys in the days when she was young and frisky enough to sport a full set of weapons! The hutch is new but the ceiling—the deckhead?—and the side of the ship beyond my bunk, old, worn and splintered and hugely patched. Imagine me, asked to live in such a coop, such a sty! However, I shall put up with it good-humouredly enough until I can see the captain. Already the act of breathing has moderated my awareness of our stench and the generous glass of brandy that Wheeler brought has gone near to reconciling me to it.

But what a noisy world this wooden one is! The south-west wind that keeps us at anchor booms and whistles in the rigging and thunders over her—over *our* (for I am determined to use this long voyage in becoming wholly master of the sea affair)—over our furled canvas. Flurries of rain beat a retreat of kettledrums over every inch of her. If that were not enough, there comes from forward and on this very deck the baaing of sheep, lowing of cattle, shouts of men and yes, the shrieks of women! There is noise enough here too. My hutch, or sty, is only one on this side of the deck of a dozen such, faced by a like number on the other. A stark lobby separates the two rows and this lobby is interrupted only by the ascending and enormous cylinder of our *mizzen mast*. Aft of the lobby, Wheeler assures me, is the dining saloon for the passengers with the offices of necessity on either side of it. In the lobby dim figures pass or stand in clusters. They—we—are the passengers I must suppose; and why an ancient ship of the line such as this one has been so transformed into a travelling store- ship and farm and passenger conveyance is only to be explained by the straits my lords of the Admiralty are in with more than six hundred warships in commission.

Wheeler has told me just this minute that we dine in an hour's time at four o'clock. On my remarking that I proposed to request more ample accommodation he paused for a moment's reflection, then replied it would be a matter of some difficulty and that he advised me to wait for a while. On my expressing some indignation that such a decrepit vessel should be used for such a voyage, he, standing in the door of my hutch with a napkin over his arm, lent me as much as he could of a seaman's philosophy—as: Lord sir she'll float till she sinks, and Lord sir she was built to be sunk; with such a lecture on lying in ordinary with no one aboard but the boatswain and the carpenter, so much about the easiness of lying to a hawser *in the good old way* rather than to a nasty iron chain that rattles like a corpse on a gibbet, he has sunk my heart clear down to her filthy ballast! He had such a dismissiveness of copper bottoms! I find we are no more than *pitched within and without* like the oldest vessel of all and suppose her first commander was none other than Captain Noah! Wheeler's parting comfort to me was that he was sure she is 'safer in a blow than many a stiffer vessel'. *Safer!* 'For,' said he, 'if we get into a bit of a blow she'll render like an old boot.' To tell the truth he left me with much of the brandy's good work undone. After all that, I found it was positively required I should remove all articles that I should need on the voyage from my chests before they were *struck down below*! Such is the confusion aboard this vessel I can find no one who has the authority to countermand this singularly foolish order. I have resigned myself therefore, used Wheeler for some of this unpacking, set out my books myself, and seen my chests taken away. I should be angry if the situation were not so farcical. However, I had a certain delight in some of the talk between the fellows who took them off, the words were so perfectly nautical. I have laid Falconer's *Marine Dictionary* by my pillow; for I am determined to speak the tarry language as perfectly as any of these rolling fellows!

LATER

We have dined by the light of an ample stern window at two long tables in a great muddle. Nobody knew anything. There were no officers, the servants were harassed, the food poor, my fellow-passengers in a temper, and their ladies approaching the hysterics. But the sight of the other vessels at anchor outside the stern window was undeniably exciting. Wheeler, my staff and guide, says it is the remainder of the convoy. He assures me that the confusion aboard will diminish and that, as he phrases it, we shall *shake down*—presumably in the way the sand and gravel has shaken down, until—if I may judge by some of the passengers— we shall stink like the vessel. Your lordship may observe a certain pettishness in my words. Indeed, had it not been for a tolerable wine I should be downright angry. Our Noah, one Captain Anderson, has not chosen to appear. I shall make myself known to him at the first opportunity but now it is dark. Tomorrow morning I propose to examine the topography of the vessel and form an acquaintance with the better sort of officer if there be any. We have ladies, some young, some middling, some old. We have some oldish gentlemen, a youngish army officer and a younger parson. This last poor fellow tried to ask a blessing on our meal and fell to eating as bashful as a bride. I have not been able to see Mr Prettiman but suppose he is aboard.

Wheeler tells me the wind will *veer* during the night and we shall get a-weigh, make sail, be off, start on our vast journey when the tide turns. I have told him I am a good sailor and have observed that same peculiar light, which is not quite a smile but rather an involuntary expansiveness, flit across his face. I made an immediately resolution to teach the man a lesson in manners at the first opportunity—but as I write these very words the pattern of our wooden world changes. There is a volleying and thundering up there from what must be the loosened canvas. There is the shrilling of pipes. Good God, can human throats emit such noises? But *that* and *that* must be signal guns! Outside my hutch a passenger has fallen with many oaths and the ladies are shrieking, the cattle are lowing and the sheep baaing. All is confusion. Perhaps then the cows are baaing, the sheep lowing and the ladies damning the ship and her timbers to all hell fire? The canvas bowl into which Wheeler poured water for me has shifted in its *gimbals* and now lies at a slight angle.

Our anchor has been plucked out of the sand and gravel of Old England. I shall have no connection with my native soil for three, or it may be four or five, years. I own that even with the prospect of interesting and advantageous employment before me it is a solemn thought.

How else, since we are being solemn, should I conclude the account of my first day at sea than with an expression of my profound gratitude? You have set my foot on the ladder and however high I climb—for I must warn your lordship that my ambition is boundless!—I shall never forget whose kindly hand first helped me upwards. That he may never be found unworthy of that hand, nor *do* anything unworthy of it—is the prayer—the *intention*—of your lordship's grateful godson.

EDMUND TALBOT

(2)

I have placed the number '2' at the beginning of this entry though
I do not know how much I shall set down today. Circumstances
are all against careful composition. There has been so little
strength in my limbs—the privehouse, the loo—I beg its pardon,
I do not know what it should be called since in strict sea-language
the *heads* are at the forward end of the vessel, the young gentlemen
should have a *roundhouse* and the lieutenants should have—I do
not know what the lieutenants should have. The constant movement of the vessel and the need constantly to adjust my body to
it——

Your lordship was pleased to recommend that I should conceal
nothing. Do you not remember conducting me from the library
with a friendly arm across my shoulder, ejaculating in your jovial
way, 'Tell all, my boy! Hold nothing back! Let me live again
through you!' The devil is in it, then, I have been most confoundedly seasick and kept my bunk. After all, Seneca off Naples
was in my predicament was he not—but you will remember—
and if even a stoic philosopher is reduced by a few miles of lumpy
water, what will become of all us poor fellows on higher seas? I
must own to have been reduced already to salt tears by exhaustion
and to have been discovered in such a womanish state by Wheeler!
However, he is a worthy fellow. I explained my tears by my
exhaustion and he agreed cheerfully.

'You, sir,' said he, 'would hunt all day and dance all night at
the end of it. Now if you was to put me, or most seamen, on a
horse, our kidneys would be shook clear down to our knees.'

I groaned some sort of answer, and heard Wheeler extract the
cork from a bottle.

'Consider, sir,' said he, 'it is but learning to ride a ship. You
will do that soon enough.'

The thought comforted me; but not as much as the most
delectable odour which *came o'er my spirits like the warm south.* I
opened my eyes and lo, what had Wheeler done but produce a

huge dose of paregoric? The comfortable taste took me straight back to the nursery and *this* time with none of the melancholy attendant on memories of childhood and home! I sent Wheeler away, dozed for a while then slept. Truly, the poppy would have done more for old Seneca than his philosophy!

I woke from strange dreams and in such thick darkness that I knew not where I was but recollected all too soon and found our motion sensibly increased. I shouted at once for Wheeler. At the third shout—accompanied I admit with more oaths than I generally consider consistent with either common sense or gentlemanly conduct—he opened the door of my hutch.

'Help me out of here, Wheeler! I must get some air!'

'Now you lie still for a while, sir, and in a bit you'll be right as a trivet! I'll set out a bowl.'

Is there, can there be, anything sillier, less comforting than the prospect of imitating a trivet? I saw them in my mind's eye as smug and self-righteous as a convocation of Methodists. I cursed the fellow to his face. However, in the upshot he was being reasonable enough. He explained that we were having a *blow*. He thought my greatcoat with the triple capes too fine a garment to risk in flying salt spray. He added, mysteriously, that he did not wish me to look like a chaplain! He himself, however, had in his possession an unused suit of yellow oilskin. Ruefully enough, he said he had bought it for a gentleman who in the event had never embarked. It was just my size and I should have it for no more than he had given for it. Then at the end of the voyage I might sell it back to him at second hand if I chose. I closed there and then with this very advantageous offer, for the air was stifling me and I longed for the open. He eased and tied me into the suit, thrust India rubber boots on my feet and adjusted an oilskin hat on my head. I wish your lordship could have seen me for I must have looked a proper sailor, no matter how unsteady I felt! Wheeler assisted me into the lobby, which was running with water. He kept up his prattle as, for example, that we should learn to have one leg shorter than the other like mountain sheep. I told him testily that since I visited France during the late peace, I knew when a deck was atilt, since I had not walked across on the water. I got out into the waist and leaned against the bulwarks on the larboard, that is the downward, side of the deck. The main chains and the huge spread of the ratlines—oh Falconer, Falconer!—extended above my head, and above that a quantity of nameless ropes hummed and thrummed and whistled. There was an eye of light showing still, but spray flew over from the high, starboard side and clouds that raced past us seemed no higher than the masts. We had company, of course, the rest of the convoy being on our larboard hand and already showing lights, though spray and a smoky mist mixed with rain obscured them. I breathed with exquisite ease after the fetor of my hutch and could not but hope that this extreme, even violent, weather would blow some of the stench out of her. Somewhat restored I gazed about me, and found for the first time since the anchor was raised my intellect and interest reviving. Staring up and back, I could see two helmsmen at the wheel, black, tarpaulined figures, their faces lighted from below as they glanced alternately into the illuminated compass, then up at the set of the sails. We had few of these spread to the wind and I supposed it was due to the inclemency of the weather but learnt later from Wheeler—that walking Falconer—that it was so we should not run clear away from the rest of the convoy since we 'have the legs' of all but a few. How he knows, if indeed he knows, is a mystery, but he declares we shall speak the squadron off Ushant, detach our other ship of the line to them, take over one of theirs, be convoyed by her to the latitude of Gibraltar after which we proceed alone, secured from capture by nothing but the few guns we have left and our intimidating appearance! Is this fair or just? Do their lordships not realize what a future Secretary of State they have cast so casually on the waters? Let us hope that like the Biblical bread they get me back again! However, the die is cast and I must take my chance. I stayed there, then, my back to the bulwark, and drank the wind and rain. I concluded that most of my extraordinary weakness had been due more to the fetor of the *hutch* than to the motion of the vessel.

There were now the veriest dregs of daylight but I was rewarded for my vigil by sight of the sickness I had escaped. There emerged from our lobby into the wind and rain of the waist, a parson! I supposed he was the same fellow who had tried to ask a blessing on our first dinner and been heard by no one but the Almighty. He wore knee-beeches, a long coat and bands that beat in the wind at his throat like a trapped bird at a window! He held his hat and wig crushed on with both hands and he staggered first one way, then the other, like a drunken crab. (Of *course* your lordship has seen a drunken crab!) This parson turned, like all people unaccustomed to a tilted deck, and tried to claw his way up it rather than down. He was, I saw, about to vomit, for his complexion was the mixed pallor and greenness of mouldy cheese. Before I could shout a warning he did indeed vomit, then slid down to the deck. He got on his knees—not, I think, for the purpose of devotion!—then stood at the very moment when a *heave* from the ship gave the movement an additional impetus. The result was he came, half-running, half-flying down the deck and might well have gone clean through the larboard ratlines had I not grabbed him by the collar! I had a glimpse of a wet, green face, then the servant who performs for the starboard passengers the offices that our Wheeler performs for the larboard ones rushed out of the lobby, seized the little man under the arms, begged my pardon and lugged him back out of sight. I was damning the parson for befouling my oilskins when a heave, shudder and convenient spout of mixed rain and sea water cleaned him off me. For some reason, though the water stung my face it put me in a good humour. Philosophy and religion—what are they when the wind blows and the water gets up in lumps? I stood there, holding on with one hand, and began positively to enjoy all this confusion, lit as it was by the last lees of light. Our huge old ship with her few and shortened sails from which the rain cascaded was beating into this sea and therefore shouldering the waves at an angle, like a bully forcing his way through a dense crowd. And as the bully might encounter here and there a like spirit, so she (our ship) was hindered now and then, or dropped or lifted or, it may be, struck a blow in the face that made all her forepart, then the waist and the afterdeck to foam and wash with white water. I began, as Wheeler had put it, to *ride a ship*. Her masts leaned a little. The shrouds to windward were taut, those to leeward slack, or very near it. The huge cable of her *mainbrace* swung out to leeward between the masts; and now here is a point which I would wish to make. Comprehension of this vast engine is not to be come at gradually nor by poring over diagrams in Marine Dictionaries! It comes, when it comes, at a bound. In that semi-darkness between one wave and the next I found the ship and the sea comprehensible not merely in terms of her mechanical ingenuity but as a—a what? As a steed, a conveyance, a means working to an end. This was a pleasure that I had not anticipated. It was, I thought with perhaps a touch of complacency, quite an addition to my understanding! A single sheet, a rope attached to the lower and leeward corner of a sail, was vibrating some yards

above my head, wildly indeed, but understandably! As if to reinforce the comprehension, at the moment when I was examining
the rope and its function there came a huge thud from forward,
an explosion of water and spray, and the rope's vibration changed—
was halved at the mid-point so that for a while its length traced
out two narrow ellipses laid end to end—illustrated, in fact, the
first harmonic, like that point on a violin string which if touched
accurately enough will give the player the note an octave above
the open one.

But this ship has more strings than a violin, more than a
lute, more I think than a harp, and under the wind's tuition
she makes a ferocious music. I will own that after a while I
could have done with human company, but the Church has
succumbed and the Army too. No lady can possibly be anywhere but in her bunk. As for the Navy—well, it is literally in
its element. Its members stand here and there encased in tarpaulin, black with faces pale only by contrast. At a little distance they resemble nothing so much as rocks with the tide
washing over them.

When the light had quite faded I felt my way back to my
hutch and shouted for Wheeler, who came at once, got me out
of my oilskins, hung the suit on the hook where it at once
took up a drunken angle. I told him to bring me a lamp but
he told me it was not possible. This put me in a temper but he
explained the reason well enough. Lamps are dangerous to us
all since once overset there is no controlling them. But I might
have a candle if I cared to pay for it since a candle dowses
itself when it falls, and in any case I must take a few safety
measures in the management of it. Wheeler himself had a supply
of candles. I replied that I had thought such articles were commonly obtained from the purser. After a short pause Wheeler
agreed. He had not thought I would wish to deal directly with
the purser who lived apart and was seldom seen. Gentlemen
used not to have any traffic with him but employed their servants who ensured that the transaction was honest and above
board. 'For,' said he, 'you know what pursers are!' I agreed
with an air of simplicity which in an instant—you observe, sir,
that I was coming to myself—concealed a revised estimate of
Mr Wheeler, his fatherly concern and his willingness to serve
me! I made a mental note that I was determined always to see
round and through him farther than he supposed that he saw

round and through me. So by eleven o'clock at night—*six bells* according to the book—behold me seated at my table-flap with this journal open before me. But what pages of trivia! Here are none of the interesting events, acute observations and the, dare I say, sparks of wit with which it is my first ambition to entertain your lordship! However, our passage is but begun.

(3)

The third day has passed with even worse weather than the others. The state of our ship, or that portion of it which falls under my notice, is inexpressibly sordid. The deck, even in our lobby, streams with sea water, rain, and other fouler liquids, which find their way inexorably under the batten on which the bottom of the hutch door is supposed to close. Nothing, of course, fits. For if it did, what would happen in the next minute when this confounded vessel has changed her position from savaging the summit of a roller to plunging into the gulf on the other side of it? When this morning I had fought my way into the dining saloon—finding, by the way, nothing hot to drink there— I was unable for a while to fight my way out again. The door was jammed. I rattled the handle peevishly, tugged at it, then found myself hanging from it as she (the monstrous vessel has become 'she' as a termagant mistress) she lurched. That in itself was not so bad but what followed might have killed me. For the door snapped open so that the handle flashed in a semicircle with a radius equal to the width of the opening! I saved myself from fatal or serious injury by the same instinct that drops a cat always on its feet. This alternate stiffness then too easy compliance with one's wishes by a door—one of those necessary objects in life on which I had never before bestowed much interest—seemed to me so animated a piece of impertinence on the part of a few planks of wood I could have believed the very genii, the dryads and hamadryads of the material from which our floating box is composed, had refused to leave their ancient dwelling and come to sea with us! But no—it was merely—'merely'—dear God what a world!— the good ship doing what Wheeler called 'rendering like an old boot'.

I was on all fours, the door having been caught neatly against the transverse or thwartships bulkhead (as Falconer would have it) by a metal springhook, when a figure came through the opening that set me laughing crazily. It was one of our lieutenants and he stumped along casually at such an angle to the deck—for the deck itself was my plane of reference—that he seemed to be (albeit unconsciously) clownish and he put me in a good humour at once for all my bruises. I climbed back to the smaller and possibly more exclusive of the two dining tables—that one I mean set directly under the great stern window—and sat once more. All is firmly fixed, of course. Shall I discourse to your lordship on 'rigging screws'? I think not. Well then, observe me drinking ale at the table with this officer. He is one Mr Cumbershum, holding the King's Commission and therefore to be accounted a gentleman though he sucked his ale with as nauseating an indifference to polite usage as you would find in a carter. He is forty, I suppose, with black hair cut short but growing nearly down to his eyebrows. He has been slashed over the head and is one of our heroes, however unformed his manners. Doubtless we shall hear *that* story before we have done! At least he was a source of information. He called the weather rough but not very. He thought those passengers who were staying in their bunks—this with a meaning glance at me—and taking light refreshment there, were wise, since we have no surgeon and a broken limb, as he phrased it, could be a nuisance to everyone! We have no surgeon, it appears, because even the most inept of young sawbones can do better for himself ashore. It is a mercenary consideration that gave me a new view of what I had always considered a profession with a degree of disinterestedness about it. I remarked that in that case we must expect an unusual incidence of mortality and it was fortunate we had a chaplain to perform all the other rites, from the first to the last. At this, Cumbershum choked, took his mouth away from the pot and addressed me in tones of profound astonishment.

'A chaplain, sir? We have no chaplain!'

'Believe me, I have seen him.'

'No, sir.'

'But law requires one aboard every ship of the line does it not?'

'Captain Anderson would wish to avoid it; and since parsons are in as short supply as surgeons it is as easy to avoid the one as it is difficult to procure the other.'

'Come, come, Mr Cumbershum! Are not seamen notoriously superstitious? Do you not require the occasional invocation of Mumbo Jumbo?'

'Captain Anderson does not, sir. Nor did the great Captain

Cook, I would have you know. He was a notable atheist and would as soon have taken the plague into his ship as a parson.'

'Good God!'

'I assure you, sir.'

'But how—my dear Mr Cumbershum! How is order to be maintained? You take away the keystone and the whole arch falls!'

Mr Cumbershum did not appear to take my point. I saw that my language must not be figurative with such a man and re-phrased it.

'Your crew is not all officers! Forward there, is a crowd of individuals on whose obedience the order of the whole depends, the success of the voyage depends!'

'They are well enough.'

'But sir—just as in a state the supreme argument for the con-tinuance of a national church is the whip it holds in one hand and the—dare I say—illusory prize in the other, so here——'

But Mr Cumbershum was wiping his lips with the brown back of his fist and getting to his feet.

'I don't know about all that,' he said. 'Captain Anderson would not have a chaplain in the ship if he could avoid it—even if one was on offer. The fellow you saw was a passenger and, I believe, a very new-hatched parson.'

I remembered how the poor devil had clawed up the wrong side of the deck and spewed right in the eye of the wind.

'You must be right, sir. He is certainly a very new-hatched seaman!'

I then informed Mr Cumbershum that at a convenient time I must make myself known to the captain. When he looked sur-prised I told him who I am, mentioned your lordship's name and that of His Excellency your brother and outlined the position I should hold in the governor's entourage—or as much as it is politic to outline, since you know what other business I am charged with. I did not add what I then thought. This was that since the governor is a naval officer, if Mr Cumbershum was an average example of the breed I should give the entourage some tone it would stand in need of!

My information rendered Mr Cumbershum more expansive. He sat down again. He owned he had never been in such a ship or on such a voyage. It was all strange to him and he thought to the other officers too. We were a ship of war, store ship, a packet

boat or passenger vessel, we were all things, which amounted
to—and here I believe I detected a rigidity of mind that is to be
expected in an officer at once junior and elderly—amounted to
being nothing. He supposed that at the end of this voyage she
would moor for good, send down her top masts and be a sop to
the governor's dignity, firing nothing but salutes as he went to
and fro.

'Which,' he added darkly, 'is just as well, Mr Talbot sir, just as
well!'

'Take me with you, sir.'

Mr Cumbershum waited until the tilted servant had supplied
us again. Then he glanced through the door at the empty and
streaming lobby.

'God knows what would happen to her Mr Talbot if we was to
fire the few great guns left in her.'

'The devil is in it then!'

'I beg you will not repeat my opinion to the common sort of
passenger. We must not alarm them. I have said more than I
should.'

'I was prepared with some philosophy to risk the violence of
the enemy; but that a spirited defence on our part should do no
more than increase our danger is, is——'

'It is war, Mr Talbot; and peace or war, a ship is always in
danger. The only other vessel of our rate to undertake this enormous voyage, a converted warship I mean, converted so to speak
to general purposes—she was named the *Guardian*, I think—yes,
the *Guardian*, did not complete the journey. But now I remember
she ran on an iceberg in the Southern Ocean, so her rate and age
was not material.'

I got my breath again. I detected through the impassivity of
the man's exterior a determination to roast me, precisely because
I had made the importance of my position clear to him. I laughed
good-humouredly and turned the thing off. I thought it a moment
to try my prentice hand at the flattery which your lordship recommended to me as a possible *passe-partout*.

'With such devoted and skilful officers as we are provided
with, sir, I am sure we need fear nothing.'

Cumbershum stared at me as if he suspected my words of some
hidden and perhaps sarcastic meaning.

'Devoted, sir? Devoted?'

It was time to 'go about', as we nautical fellows say.

'Do you see this left hand of mine, sir? Yon door did it. See how scraped and bruised the palm is, you would call it my larboard hand I believe. I have a bruise on the larboard hand! Is that not perfectly nautical? But I shall follow your first advice. I shall take some food first with a glass of brandy, then turn in to keep my limbs entire. You will drink with me, sir?'

Cumbershum shook his head.

'I go on watch,' he said. 'But do you settle your stomach. However, there is one more thing. Have a care I beg you of Wheeler's paregoric. It is the very strongest stuff, and as the voyage goes on the price will increase out of all reason. Steward! A glass of brandy for Mr Talbot!'

He left me then with as courteous an inclination of the head as you would expect from a man leaning like the pitch of a roof. It was a sight to make one bosky out of hand. Indeed, the warming properties of strong drink give it a more seductive appeal at sea than it ever has ashore, I think. So I determined with that glass to regulate my use of it. I turned warily in my fastened seat and inspected the world of furious water that stretched and slanted beyond our stern window. I must own that it afforded me the scantiest consolation; the more so as I reflected that in the happiest outcome of our voyage there was not a single billow, wave, swell, *comber* that I shall cross in one direction without having, in a few years time, to cross it in the other! I sat for a great while eyeing my brandy, staring into its aromatic and tiny pool of liquid. I found little comfort in sight at that time except the evident fact that our other passengers were even more lethargic than I was. The thought at once determined me to eat. I got down some nearly fresh bread and a little mild cheese. On top of this I swallowed my brandy and gave my stomach a *dare* to misbehave; and so frightened it with the threat of an addiction to small ale, thence to brandy, then to Wheeler's paregoric and after that to the ultimate destructiveness of an habitual resource, Lord help us, to laudanum that the poor, misused organ lay as quiet as a mouse that hears a kitchen-maid rattle the fire in the morning! I *turned in* and *got my head down* and *turned out* and ate; then toiled at these very pages by the light of my candle—giving your lordship, I doubt it not, a queasy piece of 'living through' me for which I am as heartily sorry as yourself could be! I believe the whole ship, from the farm animals up or down to your humble servant, is nauseated to one degree or another—always excepting of course the leaning and streaming tarpaulins.

(4)

And how is your lordship today? In the best of health and spirits,
I trust, as I am! There is such a crowd of events at the back of my
mind, tongue, pen, what you will, that my greatest difficulty is to
know how to get them on the paper! In brief, all things about our
wooden world have altered for the better. I do not mean that I
have got my *sea legs*; for even now that I understand the physical
laws of our motion they continue to exhaust me! But the motion
itself is easier. It was some time in the hours of darkness that I
woke—a shouted order perhaps—and feeling if anything even
more stretched on the rack of our lumbering, bullying progress.
For days, as I lay, there had come at irregular intervals a kind of
impediment from our watery shoulderings that I cannot describe
except to say it was as if our carriage wheels had caught for a
moment on the drag, then released themselves. It was a movement
that as I lay in my trough, my bunk, my feet to our stern, my
head to our bows—a movement that would thrust my head more
firmly into the pillow, which being made of granite transmitted
the impulsion throughout the remainder of my person.

Even though I now understood the cause, the repetition was
unutterably wearisome. But as I awoke there were loud movements on deck, the thundering of many feet, then shouted orders
prolonged into what one might suppose to be the vociferations
of the damned. I had not known (even when crossing the Channel)
what an *aria* can be made of the simple injunction 'Ease the
sheets!' then, 'Let go and haul!' Precisely over my head, a voice—
Cumbershum's perhaps—roared, 'Light to!' and there was even
more commotion. The groaning of the yards would have made
me grind my teeth in sympathy had I had the strength; but then,
oh then! In our passage to date there has been no circumstance of
like enjoyment, bliss! The movement of my body, of the bunk, of
the whole ship changed in a moment, in the twinkling of an eye
as if—but I do not need to elaborate the allusion. I knew directly
what had brought the miracle about. We had altered course more

towards the south and in Tarpaulin language—which I confess I speak with increasing pleasure—we had brought the wind from *forrard of the starboard beam* to *large on the starboard quarter*! Our motion, ample as ever, was and is more yielding, more feminine and suitable to the sex of our conveyance. I fell healthfully asleep at once.

When I awoke there was no such folly as bounding out of my bunk or singing, but I did shout for Wheeler with a more cheerful noise than I had uttered, I believe, since the day when I was first acquainted with the splendid nature of my colonial employment——

But come! I cannot give, nor would you wish or expect, a moment by moment description of my journey! I begin to understand the limitations of such a journal as I have time to keep. I no longer credit Mistress *Pamela*'s pietistic accounts of every shift in her calculated resistance to the advances of her master! I will get myself up, relieved, shaved, breakfasted in a single sentence. Another shall see me on deck in my oilskin suit. Nor was I alone. For though the weather was in no way improved, we had it at our backs, or shoulders rather, and could stand comfortably in the shelter of our wall, that is, those *bulkheads* rising to the afterdeck and quarterdeck. I was reminded of convalescents at a spa, all up and about but wary in their new ability to walk or stagger.

Good God! Look at the time! If I am not more able to choose what I say I shall find myself describing the day before yesterday rather than writing about today for you tonight! For throughout the day I have walked, talked, eaten, drunk, explored—and here I am again, kept out of my bunk by the—I must confess—agreeable invitation of the page! I find that writing is like drinking. A man must learn to control it.

Well then. Early on, I found my oilskin suit too hot and returned to my cabin. There, since it would be in some sense an official visit, I dressed myself with care so as to make a proper impression on the captain. I was in greatcoat and beaver, though I took the precaution of securing this last on my head by means of a scarf passed over the crown and tied under my chin. I debated the propriety of sending Wheeler to announce me but thought this too formal in the circumstances. I pulled on my gloves, therefore, shook out my capes, glanced down at my boots and found them adequate. I went to climb the *ladders*—though of course they are staircases and broad at that—to the afterdeck and

quarterdeck. I passed Mr Cumbershum with an underling and
gave him good day. But he ignored my greeting in a way that
would have offended me had I not known from the previous
day's exchanges that his manners are uncouth and his temper
uncertain. I approached the captain therefore, who was to be
recognized by his elaborate if shabby uniform. He stood on the
starboard side of the quarterdeck, the wind at his back where his
hands were clasped, and he was staring at me, his face raised, as if
my appearance was a shock.

Now I have to acquaint your lordship with an unpleasant
discovery. However gallant and indeed invincible our Navy may
be, however heroic her officers and devoted her people, a ship of
war is an ignoble despotism! Captain Anderson's first remark—if
such a growl may be so described—and uttered at the very
moment when having touched my glove to the brim of my beaver
I was about to announce my name, was an unbelievably dis-
courteous one.

'Who the devil is this, Cumbershum? Have they not read my
orders?'

This remark so astonished me that I did not attend to Cumbershum's reply, if indeed he made any. My first thought was that in the
course of some quite incomprehensible misunderstanding Captain
Anderson was about to strike me. At once, and in a loud voice, I
made myself known. The man began to bluster and my anger would
have got the better of me had I not been more and more aware of the
absurdity of our position. For standing as we did, I, the captain,
Cumbershum and his satellite, we all had one leg stiff as a post while
the other flexed regularly as the deck moved under us. It made me
laugh in what must have seemed an unmannerly fashion but the
fellow deserved the rebuke even if it was accidental. It stopped his
blusters and heightened his colour, but gave me the opportunity of
producing your name and that of His Excellency your brother,
much as one might prevent the nearer approach of a highwayman by
quickly presenting a brace of pistols. Our captain squinted first—
you will forgive the figure—down your lordship's muzzle, decided
you were loaded, cast a fearful eye at the ambassador in my other
hand and reined back with his yellow teeth showing! I have seldom
seen a face at once so daunted and so atrabilious. He is a complete
argument for the sovranty of the humours. This exchange and the
following served to move me into the fringes of his local despotism
so that I felt much like an envoy at the Grande Porte who may

regard himself as reasonably safe, if uncomfortable, while all round him heads topple. I swear Captain Anderson would have shot, hanged, keel-hauled, marooned me if prudence had not in that instant got the better of his inclination. Nevertheless, if today when the French clock in the Arras room chimed ten and our ship's bell here was struck four times—at that time, I say, if your lordship experienced a sudden access of well-being and a warming satisfaction, I cannot swear that it may not have been some distant notion of what a silver-mounted and murdering piece of ordnance a noble name was proving to be among persons of a middle station!

I waited for a moment or two while Captain Anderson swallowed his bile. He had much regard for your lordship and would not be thought remiss in any attention to his, his—He hoped I was comfortable and had not at first known—The rule was that passengers came to the quarterdeck by invitation though of course in my case—He hoped (and this with a glare that would have frightened a wolf-hound), he hoped to see more of me. So we stood for a few more moments, one leg stiff, one leg flexing like reeds in the wind while the shadow of the *driver* (thank you, Falconer!) moved back and forth across us. Then, I was amused to see, he did not stand his ground, but put his hand to his hat, disguised this involuntary homage to your lordship as an attempt to adjust the set of it and turned away. He stumped off to the stern rail and stood there, his hands clasped behind his back, where they opened and shut as an unconscious betrayal of his irritation. Indeed, I was half sorry for the man, confounded as I saw him to be in the imagined security of his little kingdom. But I judged it no good time for gentling him. In politics do we not attempt to use only just sufficient force to achieve a desired end? I decided to allow the influence of this interview to work for a while and only when he has got the true state of affairs thoroughly grounded in his malevolent head shall I move towards some easiness with him. We have the whole long passage before us and it is no part of my business to make life intolerable for him, nor would I if I could. Today, as you may suppose, I am all good humour. Instead of time crawling past with a snail's gait—now *if* a crab may be said to be drunk a snail may be said to have a gait—instead of time crawling, it hurries, not to say dashes past me. I cannot get one tenth of the day down! It is late; and I must continue tomorrow.

(5)

That fourth day, then—though indeed the fifth—but to continue.

After the captain had turned to the stern rail I remained for some time endeavouring to engage Mr Cumbershum in conversation. He answered me in the fewest possible words and I began to understand that he was uneasy in the captain's presence. However, I did not wish to leave the quarterdeck as if retreating from it.

'Cumbershum,' said I, 'the motion is easier. Show me more of our ship. Or if you feel it inadvisable to interrupt the management of her, lend me this young fellow to be my conductor.'

The young fellow in question, Cumbershum's satellite, was a midshipman—not one of your ancients, stuck in his inferior position like a goat in a bush, but an example of the breed that brings a tear to every maternal eye—in a sentence, a pustular lad of fourteen or fifteen, addressed, as I soon found in pious hope, as a 'Young Gentleman'. It was some time before Cumbershum answered me, the lad looking from the one to the other of us meanwhile. At last Mr Cumbershum said the lad, Mr Willis by name, might go with me. So my object was gained. I left the Sacred Precincts with dignity and indeed had despoiled it of a votary. As we descended the ladder there was a *hail* from Mr Cumbershum.

'Mr Willis, Mr Willis! Do not omit to invite Mr Talbot to glance at the captain's Standing Orders. You may transmit to me any suggestions he has for their improvement.'

I laughed heartily at this sally though Willis did not seem to be amused by it. He is not merely pustular but pale, and he commonly lets his mouth hang open. He asked me what I would choose to see and I had no idea, having used him to get me off the quarterdeck suitably attended. I nodded towards the forward part of the vessel.

'Let us stroll thither,' said I, 'and see how the people live.'

Willis followed me with some hesitation in the shadow of the boats on the boom, across the white line at the main mast, then between the pens where our beasts are kept. He passed me then and led the way up a ladder to the front or *fo'castle*, where was the capstan, some loungers and a woman plucking a chicken. I went towards the bowsprit and looked down. I became aware of the age of this old crone of a ship for she is positively *beaked* in the manner of the last century and flimsy, I should judge, about the bow withal. I looked over her monstrous figurehead, emblem of her name and which our people as is their custom have turned colloquially into an obscenity with which I will not trouble your lordship. But the sight of the men down there squatting in the heads at their business was distasteful and some of them looked up at me with what seemed like impertinence. I turned away and gazed along her vast length and to the vaster expanse of dark blue ocean that surrounded us.

'Well sir,' said I to Willis, 'we are certainly ἐπ' εὐρέα νῶτα θαλάσσης, are we not?'

Willis replied that he did not know French.

'What do you know then, lad?'

'The rigging sir, the parts of the ship, bends and hitches, the points of the compass, the marks of the leadline to take a bearing off a point of land or a mark and to shoot the sun.'

'We are in good hands I see.'

'There is more than that, sir,' said he, 'as for example the parts of a gun, the composition of powder to sweeten the bilge and the Articles of War.'

'You must not sweeten the Articles of War,' said I solemnly. 'We must not be kinder to each other than the French are to us! It seems to me that your education is piled all on top of itself like my lady mother's sewing closet! But what is the composition of the powder that enables you to shoot the sun and should you not be careful lest you damage the source of light and put the day out?'

Willis laughed noisily.

'You are roasting me, sir,' he said. 'Even a landlubber I ask your pardon knows what shooting the sun is.'

'I forgive you that "even", sir! When shall I see you do so?'

'Take an observation, sir? Why, at noon, in a few minutes. There will be Mr Smiles, the sailing master, Mr Davies and Mr Taylor, the other two midshipmen sir, though Mr Davies does not really know how to do it for all that he is so old and Mr Taylor my friend, I beg you will not mention it to the Captain, has a sextant that does not work owing to his having pawned the one that his father gave him. So we have agreed to take turn with mine and give altitudes that are two minutes different.'

I put my hand to my forehead.

'And the safety of the whole hangs by such a spider's thread!'

'Sir?'

'Out position, my boy! Good God, we might as well be in the hands of my young brothers! Is our position to be decided by an antique midshipman and a sextant that does not work?'

'Lord, no, sir! In the first place Tommy Taylor and I believe we may persuade Mr Davies to swap his good one for Tommy's instrument. It would not really matter to Mr Davies you see. Besides, sir, Captain Anderson, Mr Smiles and some other officers are also engaged in the navigation.'

'I see. You do not merely shoot the sun. You subject him to a British Broadside! I shall watch with interest and perhaps take a hand in shooting the sun too as we roll round him.'

'You could not do that, sir,' said Willis in what seemed a kindly way. 'We wait here for the sun to climb up the sky and we measure the angle when it is greatest and take the time too.'

'Now look, lad,' said I. 'You are taking us back into the Middle Ages! You will be quoting Ptolemy at me next!'

'I do not know of him, sir. But we must wait while the sun climbs up.'

'That is no more than an apparent movement,' said I patiently. 'Do you not know of Galileo and his "Eppur si muove"? The earth goes round the sun! The motion was described by Copernicus and confirmed by Kepler!'

The lad answered me with the purest simplicity, ignorance and dignity.

'Sir, I do not know how the sun may behave among those gentlemen ashore but I know that he climbs up the sky in the Royal Navy.'

I laughed again and laid my hand on the boy's shoulder.

'And so he shall! Let him move as he chooses! To tell you the truth, Mr Willis, I am so glad to see him up there with the snowy clouds about him that he may dance a jig for all I care! Look— your companions are gathering. Be off with you and aim your instrument!'

He thanked me and dived away. I stood on the aftermost part of the fo'castle and looked back at the ceremony which, I own, pleased me. There was a number of officers on the quarterdeck. They waited on the sun, the brass triangles held to their faces. Now here was a curious and moving circumstance. All those of the ship's people who were on deck and some of the emigrants too, turned and watched this *rite* with silent attention. They could not be expected to understand the mathematics of the operation. That I have some notion of it myself is owing to education, an inveterate curiosity and a facility in learning. Even the passengers, or those of them on deck, stood at gaze. I should not have been surprised to see the gentlemen lift their hats! But the people, I mean the common sort, whose lives as much as ours depended on an accuracy of measurement beyond their comprehension and the application of formulae that would be as opaque to them as Chinese writing, these people, I say, accorded the whole operation a respect such as they might have paid to the solemnest moment of a religious service. You might be inclined to think as I did that the glittering instruments were their Mumbo Jumbo. Indeed, Mr Davies's ignorance and Mr Taylor's defective instrument were feet of clay; but I felt they might have a justifiable faith in some of the older officers! And then—their attitudes! The woman watched, the half-plucked hen in her lap. Two fellows who were carrying a sick girl up from below—why, even *they* stood and watched as if someone had said *hist*, while their burden lay helplessly between them. Then the girl, too, turned her head and watched where they watched. There was a moving and endearing pathos about their attention, as in a dog that watches a conversation it cannot possibly understand. I am not, as your lordship must be aware, a friend to those who approve the outrageous follies of democracy in this and the last century. But at the moment when I saw a number of our sailors in a posture of such intense regard I came as near as ever I have done to seeing such concepts as 'duty', 'privilege', and 'authority' in a new light. They moved out of books, out of the schoolroom and university into the broader scenes of daily life. Indeed, until I saw these fellows like Milton's hungry sheep that 'look up', I had not considered the nature of my own ambitions nor looked for the justification of them that was here presented to me. Forgive me for boring your lordship with my discovery of what you yourself must know so well.

How noble was the prospect! Our vessel was urged forward under the force of sufficient but not excessive wind, the billows sparkled, the white clouds were diversedly mirrored in the deep—*et cetera*. The sun resisted without apparent effort our naval broadside! I went down the ladder and walked back towards where our navigators were breaking from their rank and descending from the quarterdeck. Mr Smiles, the sailing master, is old, but not as old as Mr Davies, our senior midshipman, who is nearly as old as the ship! He descended not merely the ladder to the level of the waist where I was but the next one down as well—going away with a slow and broken motion for all the world like a stage apparition returning to the tomb. After leave obtained, Mr Willis, my young acquaintance, brought his companion to me with some ceremony. Mr Tommy Taylor must be a clear two years younger than Mr Willis but has the spirit and well-knit frame that his elder lacks. Mr Taylor is from a naval family. He explained at once that Mr Willis was weak in his attic and needed retiling. I was to come to him, Mr Taylor, if I wished to find out about navigation, since Mr Willis would soon have me on the rocks. Only the day before, he had informed Mr Deverel that at the latitude of sixty degrees north, a degree of longitude would be reduced to half a nautical mile. On Mr Deverel asking him—evidently a wag, Mr Deverel—what it would be reduced to at sixty degrees south, Mr Willis had replied that he had not got as far as that in the book. The memory of these cataclysmic errors sent Mr Taylor into a long peal of laughter which Mr Willis did not appear to resent. He is devoted to his young friend evidently, admires him and shows him off to the best advantage. Behold me, then, pacing to and fro between the break of the afterdeck and the mainmast, a young acolyte on either side; the younger one on my *starboard hand*, full of excitement, information, opinion, gusto; the other, silent, but smiling with open mouth and nodding at his young friend's expressions of opinion on any subject under and, indeed, including the sun!

It was from these two young hopefuls that I learnt a little about our passengers—I mean of course those who have been accommodated aft. There is the Pike family, devoted to each other, all four. There is of *course*, one Mr Prettiman, known to us all. There is, I learn from precocious Mr Taylor, in the cabin between my own hutch and the dining saloon, a portrait-painter and his wife with their daughter—a young lady characterized by

the aforesaid young gentleman as 'a regular snorter'! I found this
to be Mr Taylor's utmost in the description of female charm.
Your lordship may imagine that this news of the presence on
board of a fair *incognita* lent an added exhilaration to my animal
spirits!

Mr Taylor might have conducted me through the whole list of
passengers; but as we were returning from the mainmast for (it
may be) the twentieth time, a—or rather, the—parson who had
earlier spewed so copiously into his own face came out of the
lobby of the passenger accommodation. He was turning to ascend
the ladder to the afterdeck, but seeing me between my young
friends, and perceiving me to be of some consequence I suppose,
he paused and favoured me with a reverence. Observe I do not
call it a bow or greeting. It was a sinuous deflection of the whole
body, topped by a smile which was tempered by pallor and ser-
vility as his reverence was tempered by an uncertainty as to the
movements of our vessel. As a gesture called forth by nothing
more than the attire of a gentleman it could not but disgust. I
acknowledged it by the briefest lifting of my hand towards the
brim of my beaver and looked him through. He ascended the
ladder. His calves were in thick, worsted stockings, his heavy
shoes went up one after the other at an obtuse angle; so that I
believe his knees, though his long, black coat covered them, must
be by nature more than usually far apart. He wore a round wig
and a shovel hat and seemed, I thought, a man who would not
improve on acquaintance. He was hardly out of earshot when Mr
Taylor gave it as his opinion that the *sky pilot* was on his way to
interview Captain Anderson on the quarterdeck and that such an
approach would result in his instant destruction.

'He has not read the captain's Standing Orders,' said I, as one
deeply versed in the ways of captains and their orders and warships. 'He will be keel-hauled.'

The thought of keel-hauling a parson overcame Mr Taylor
completely. When Mr Willis had thumped him to a tear-stained
and hiccupping recovery he declared it would be the best sport of
all things and the thought set him off again. It was at this moment
that a positive roar from the quarterdeck quenched him like a
bucket of cold water. I believe—no, I am sure—the roar was
directed at the parson but the two young gentlemen leapt as one,
daunted, as it were, by no more than a ricochet or the splinters
flying from where the captain's solid shot had landed. It appeared

that Captain Anderson's ability to control his own officers, from Cumbershum down to these babes-in-arms, was not to be questioned. I must confess I did not desire more than the one engagement I had had with him as a ration *per diem*.

'Come lads,' said I. 'The transaction is private to Captain Anderson and the parson. Let us get out of earshot and under cover.'

We went with a kind of casual haste into the lobby. I was about to dismiss the lads when there came the sound of stumbling footsteps on the deck above our heads, then a clatter from the ladder outside the lobby—which turned at once to a speedier rattle as of iron-shod heels that had slipped out and deposited their wearer at the bottom with a jarring thump! Whatever my distaste for the fellow's—shall I call it—*extreme unction*, in common humanity I turned to see if he required assistance. But I had taken no more than a step in that direction when the man himself staggered in. He had his shovel hat in one hand and his wig in the other. His parsonical bands were twisted to one side. But what was of all things the most striking was—no, not the expression—but the disorder of his face. My pen falters. Imagine if you can a pale and drawn countenance to which nature has afforded no gift beyond the casual assemblage of features; a countenance moreover to which she has given little in the way of flesh but been prodigal of bone. Then open the mouth wide, furnish the hollows under the meagre forehead with staring eyes from which tears were on the point of starting—do all that, I say, and you will still come short of the comic humiliation that for a fleeting moment met me eye to eye! Then the man was fumbling at the door of his hutch, got through it, pulled it to and was scrabbling at the bolt on the other side.

Young Mr Taylor started to laugh again. I took him by the ear and twisted it until his laugh turned into a yelp.

'Allow me to tell you, Mr Taylor,' said I, but quietly as the occasion demanded, 'that one gentleman does not rejoice at the misfortune of another in public. You may make your bows and be off, the two of you. We shall take a constitutional again some day, I don't doubt.'

'Oh lord yes, sir,' said young Tommy, who seemed to think that having his ear twisted half off was a gesture of affection. 'Whenever you choose, sir.'

'Yes, sir,' said Willis with his beautiful simplicity. 'We have missed a lesson in navigation.'

They retreated down a ladder to what I am told is the Gun Room and suppose to be some sort of noisome pit. The last words I heard from them that day were spoken by Mr Taylor to Mr Willis in tones of high animation——

'Don't he hate a parson above anything?'

I returned to my cabin, called Wheeler and bade him get off my boots. He responds so readily to the demands I make on him I wonder the other passengers do not make an equal use of his services. Their loss is my gain. Another fellow—Phillips, I think—serves the other side of the lobby as Wheeler serves this one.

'Tell me, Wheeler,' said I as he fitted himself down in the narrow space, 'why does Captain Anderson so dislike a parson?'

'A little higher if you please, sir. Thank you, sir. Now the other if you would be so good.'

'Wheeler!'

'I'm sure I can't say, sir. Does he, sir? Did he say so, sir?'

'I know he does! I heard him as did the rest of the ship!'

'We do not commonly have parsons in the Navy, sir. There are not enough to go round. Or if there are, the reverend gentlemen do not choose the sea. I will give these a brush again, sir. Now the coat?'

'Not only did I hear him but one of the young gentlemen confirmed that Captain Anderson has a strong antipathy to the cloth, as did Lieutenant Cumbershum earlier, now I recollect it.'

'Did he, sir? Thank you, sir.'

'Is it not so?'

'I know nothing, Mr Talbot, sir. And now, sir, may I bring you another draught of the paregoric? I believe you found it very settling, sir.'

'No thank you, Wheeler. As you see, I have eluded the demon.'

'It *is* rather strong, sir, as Mr Cumbershum informed you. And of course as he has less left, the purser has to charge more for it. That's quite natural, sir. I believe there is a gentleman ashore as has wrote a book on it.'

I bade him leave me and lay on my bunk for a while. I cast back in memory—could not remember what day of the voyage it was—took up this book, and it seemed to be the sixth, so I have confused your lordship and myself. I cannot keep pace with the events and shall not try. I have, at a moderate estimate, already written ten thousand words and must limit myself if I am to get our voyage between the luxurious covers of your gift. Can it be that I have evaded the demon opium only to fall victim to the *furor scribendi*? But if your lordship do but leaf through the book——

A knock at the door. It is Bates, who serves in the passengers' saloon.

'Mr Summers's compliments to Mr Talbot and will Mr Talbot take a glass of wine with him in the saloon?'

'Mr Summers?'

'The first lieutenant, sir.'

'He is second in command to the captain, is he not? Tell Mr Summers I shall be happy to wait on him in ten minutes' time.'

It is not the captain, of course—but the next best thing. Come! We are beginning to move in society!

(X)

I *think* it is the seventh—or the fifth—or the eighth perhaps—let 'X' do its algebraic duty and represent the unknown quantity. Time has the habit of standing still so that as I write in the evening or night when sleep is hard to come by, my candle shortens imperceptibly as stalactites and stalagmites form in a grotto. Then all at once, time, this indefinable commodity is in short supply and a sheaf of hours has fled I know not whither!

Where was I? Ah yes! Well then——

I proceeded to the passenger saloon to keep my *rendez-vous* with the first lieutenant only to find that his invitation had been extended to every passenger in this part of the vessel and was no more than a kind of short preliminary to dinner! I have found out since, that they have heard such gatherings are customary in packets and company ships and indeed, wherever ladies and gentlemen take a sea voyage. The lieutenants have concluded to do the same in this vessel, to offset, I suspect, the peremptory and unmannerly prohibitions the captain has displayed in his 'Orders regarding the Behaviour of the Ladies and Gentlemen who have been afforded'—*afforded*, mark you, not *taken*—'Passage.'

Properly announced, then, as the door was held open, I stepped into a scene of animation that resembled more than anything else what you might find in the parlour or dining room of a coaching inn. All that distinguished the present gathering from such a *job lot* was the blue horizon a little tilted and visible above the crowded heads through the panes of the great stern window. The announcement of my name caused a silence for a moment or two and I peered at an array of pallid faces before me without being able to distinguish much between them. Then a well-built young man in uniform and two or three years my senior came forward. He introduced himself as Summers and declared I must meet Lieutenant Deverel. I did so, and thought him to be the most gentlemanlike officer I had yet found in the ship. He is slimmer than Summers, has chestnut hair and sidewhiskers but is clean-

shaven about the chin and lips like all these fellows. We made an
affable exchange of it and both determined, I don't doubt, to see
more of each other. However, Summers said I must now meet
the ladies and led me to the only one I could see. She was seated
to the starboard side of the saloon on a sort of bench; and though
surrounded or attended by some gentlemen was a severe-looking
lady of uncertain years whose bonnet was designed as a covering
for the head and as a genuine privacy for the face within it rather
than as an ambush to excite the curiosity of the observer. I
thought she had a Quakerish air about her, for her dress was
grey. She sat, her hands folded in her lap, and talked directly up
to the tall young army officer who smiled down at her. We
waited on the conclusion of her present speech.

'—have always taught them such games. It is a harmless
amusement for very young gentlemen and a knowledge of the
various rules at least appropriate in the education of a young
lady. A young lady with no gift for music may entertain her *parti*
in that way as well as another might with the harp or other
instrument.'

The young officer beamed and drew his chin back to his
collar.

'I am happy to hear you say so, ma'am. But I have seen cards
played in some queer places, I can tell you!'

'As to that, sir, of course I have no knowledge. But surely
games are not altered in themselves by the nature of the place in
which they are played? I speak of it as I must, knowing no more
of the games than as they are played in the houses of gentlefolk.
But I would expect some knowledge of—let us say—whist, as
necessary to a young lady, always provided——' and here I believe there must have been a change of expression on the invisible
face, since a curiously ironic inflection entered the voice—'always
provided she has the wit to lose prettily.'

The tall young officer crowed in the way these fellows suppose
to be *laughing* and Mr Summers took the opportunity of presenting
me to the lady, Miss Granham. I declared I had overheard part of
the conversation and felt inferior in not having a wide and deep
knowledge of the games they spoke of. Miss Granham now turned
her face on me and though I saw she could not be Mr Taylor's
'regular snorter' her features were severely pleasant enough when
lighted with the social smile. I praised the innocent hours of
enjoyment afforded by cards and hoped that at some time in our

long voyage I should have the benefit of Miss Granham's instruction.

Now there was the devil of it. The smile vanished. That word 'instruction' had a *denotation* for me and a *connotation* for the lady!

'Yes, Mr Talbot,' said she, and I saw a pink spot appear in either cheek. 'As you have discovered, I am a governess.'

Was this my fault? Had I been remiss? Her expectations in life must have been more exalted than their realization and this has rendered her tongue hair-triggered as a duelling pistol. I declare to your lordship that with such people there is nothing to be done and the only attitude to adopt with them is one of silent attention. That is how they are and one cannot detect their quality in advance any more than the poacher can see the gin. You take a step, and bang! goes the blunderbuss, or the teeth of the gin snap round your ankle. It is easy for those whose rank and position in society put them beyond the vexation of such trivial social distinctions. But we poor fellows who must work or, should I say operate, among these infinitesimal gradations find their detection in advance as difficult as what the papists call 'the discernment of spirits'.

But to return. No sooner had I heard the words 'I am a governess', or perhaps even while I was hearing them, I saw that quite unintentionally I had ruffled the lady.

'Why, ma'am,' said I soothingly as Wheeler's paregoric, 'yours is indeed the most necessary and genteel profession open to a lady. I cannot tell you what a dear friend Miss Dobson, Old Dobbie as we call her, has been to me and my young brothers. I will swear you are as secure as she in the affectionate friendship of your young ladies and gentlemen!'

Was this not handsome? I lifted the glass that had been put in my hand as if to salute the whole useful race, though really I drank to my own dexterity in avoiding the lanyard of the blunderbuss or the footplate of the gin.

But it would not do.

'If,' said Miss Granham severely, 'I am secure in the affectionate friendship of my young ladies and gentlemen it is the only thing I am secure in. A lady who is daughter of a late canon of Exeter Cathedral and who is obliged by her circumstances to take up the offer of employment among a family in the Antipodes may well set the affectionate friendship of young ladies and gentlemen at a lower value than you do.'

There was I, trapped and blunderbussed—unjustly, I think, when I remember what an effort I had made to smooth the lady's feathers. I bowed and was her servant, the army officer, Oldmeadow, drew his chin even further into his neck; and here was Bates with sherry. I gulped what I held and seized another glass in a way that it must have indicated my discomfiture, for Summers rescued me, saying he wished other people to have the pleasure of making my acquaintance. I declared I had not known there were so many of us. A large, florid and corpulent gentleman with a port-wine voice declared he would wish to *turn* a group portrait since with the exception of his good lady and his gal we were all present. A sallow young man, a Mr Weekes, who goes I believe to set up school, declared that the *emigrants* would form an admirable background to the composition.

'No, no,' said the large gentleman, 'I must not be patronized other than by the nobility and gentry.'

'The emigrants,' said I, happy to have the subject changed. 'Why, I would as soon be pictured for posterity arm in arm with a common sailor!'

'You must not have me in your picture, then,' said Summers, laughing loudly. 'I was once a "common sailor" as you put it.'

'You, sir? I cannot believe it!'

'Indeed I was.'

'But how——'

Summers looked round with an air of great cheerfulness.

'I have performed the naval operation known as "coming aft through the hawsehole". I was promoted from the lower deck, or, as you would say, from among the common sailors.'

Your lordship can have little idea of my astonishment at his words and my irritation at finding the whole of our small society waiting in silence for my reply. I fancy it was as dextrous as the occasion demanded, though perhaps spoken with a too magisterial aplomb.

'Well, Summers,' I said, 'Allow me to congratulate you on imitating to perfection the manners and speech of a somewhat higher station in life than the one you was born to.'

Summers thanked me with a possibly excessive gratitude. Then he addressed the assembly.

'Ladies and gentlemen, pray let us be seated. There must be no ceremony. Let us sit where we choose. There will, I hope, be

many such occasions in the long passage before us. Bates, bid
them strike up out there.'

At this there came the somewhat embarrassing squeak of a
fiddle and other instruments from the lobby. I did what I could
to ease what might well be called *constraint*.

'Come Summers,' I said, 'if we are not to be portrayed together,
let us take the opportunity and pleasure of seating Miss Granham
between us. Pray, ma'am, allow me.'

Was that not to risk another set-down? But I handed Miss
Granham to her seat under the great window with more ceremony
than I would have shown a peeress of the realm, and there we
were. When I exclaimed at the excellent quality of the meat Lieutenant Deverel, who had seated himself on my left hand, explained
that one of our cows had broken a leg in the late blow so we were
taking what we could while it was still there though we should
soon be short of milk. Miss Granham was now in animated
conversation with Mr Summers on her right so Mr Deverel and I
conversed for some time on the topic of seamen and their senti-
mentality over a cow with a broken leg, their ingenuity in all
manner of crafts both good and bad, their addiction to liquor,
their immorality, their furious courage and their devotion, only
half-joking, to the ship's figurehead. We agreed there were few
problems in society that would not yield to firm but perceptive
government. It was so, he said, in a ship. I replied that I had seen
the firmness but was yet to be convinced of the perception. By
now the, shall I say, animation of the whole party had risen to
such a height that nothing could be heard of the music in the
lobby. One topic leading to another, Deverel and I rapidly gained
a degree of mutual understanding. He opened himself to me. He
had wished for a proper ship of the line, not a superannuated
third-rate with a crew small in number and swept up together in a
day or two. What I had taken to be an established body of
officers and men had known each other for at most a week or two
since she came out of ordinary. It was a great shame and his
father might have done better for him. This commission would
do his own prospects no good at all let alone that the war was
running down and would soon stop like an unwound clock.
Deverel's speech and manner, indeed everything about him, is
elegant. He is an ornament to the service.

The saloon was now as noisy as a public place can well be.
Something was overset amidst shouts of laughter and some oaths.

Already a mousey little pair, Mr and Mrs Pike with the small twin daughters, had scurried away and now at a particularly loud outburst, Miss Granham started to her feet, though pressed to stay both by me and Summers. He declared she must not mind the language of naval officers which became habitual and unconscious among the greater part of them. For my part I thought the ill-behaviour came more from the passengers than the ship's officers—Good God, said I to myself, if she is like this at the after end, what is she like at the other? Miss Granham had not yet moved from her seat when the door was opened for a lady of a quite different appearance. She appeared young yet richly and frivolously dressed. She came in with such a sweep and flutter that the bonnet fell to the back of her neck, revealing a quantity of golden curls. We rose—or most of us, at least—but with an admirable presence she seated us again at a gesture, went straight to the florid gentleman, leaned over his shoulder and murmured the following sentence in accents of exquisite, far, far too exquisite, beauty.

'Oh Mr Brocklebank, at last she has contrived to retain a mouthful of consum!'

Mr Brocklebank boomed us an explanation.

'My child, my little Zenobia!'

Miss Zenobia was at once offered a choice of places at the table. Miss Granham declared she was leaving so that her place at it was free if another cushion might be brought. But the young lady, as I must call her, replied with whimsical archness that she had relied on Miss Granham to protect her virtue among so many dangerous gentlemen.

'Stuff and nonsense, ma'am,' said Miss Granham, even more severely than she had addressed your humble servant, 'stuff and nonsense! Your virtue is as safe here as anywhere in the vessel!'

'Dear Miss Granham,' cried the lady with a languishing air, 'I am sure your virtue is safe anywhere!'

This was gross, was it not? Yet I am sorry to say that from at least one part of the saloon there came a shout of laughter, for we had reached that part of dinner where ladies are better out of the way and only such as the latest arrival was proving to be can keep in countenance. Deverel, I and Summers were on our feet in a trice but it was the army officer, Oldmeadow, who escorted Miss Granham from our midst. The voice of the port-wine gentleman boomed again. 'Sit by me, Zenobia, child.'

Miss Zenobia fluttered in the full afternoon sunlight that slanted across the great stern window. She held her pretty hands up to shield her face.

'It is too bright, Mr Brocklebank, pa!'

'Lord ma'am,' said Deverel, 'can you deprive us poor fellows in the shadows of the pleasure of looking at you?'

'I must,' she said, 'I positively must and will, take the seat vacated by Miss Granham.'

She fluttered round the table like a butterfly, a painted lady perhaps. I fancy that Deveral would have been happy to have her by him but she sank into the seat between Summers and me. Her bonnet was still held loosely by a ribbon at the back of her neck so that a charming profusion of curls was visible by her cheek and ear. Yet it seemed to me even at the first sight that the very brightness of her eyes—or the one occasionally turned on me— owed a debt to the mysteries of her *toilette* and her lips were perhaps a trifle artificially coral. As for her perfume——

Does this appear tedious to your lordship? The many charmers whom I have seen to languish, perhaps in vain, near your lord- ship—devil take it, how am I to employ any flattery on my godfather when the simple truth——

To return. This bids fair to be a lengthy expatiation on the subject of a young woman's appearance. The danger here is to invent. I am, after all, no more than a young fellow! I might please myself with a rhapsody for she is the *only tolerable female object* in our company! There! Yet—and here I think the politician, the scurvy politician, as my favourite author would have it, is uppermost in my mind. I cannot get me glass eyes. I cannot rhapsodize. For Miss Zenobia is surely approaching her middle years and is defending indifferent charms before they disappear for ever by a continual animation which must surely exhaust her as much as they tire the beholder. A face that is never still cannot be subjected to detailed examination. May it not be that her parents are taking her to the Antipodes as a last resort? After all, among the convicts and Aborigines, among the emigrants and pensioned soldiers, the warders, the humbler clergy—but no. I do the lady an injustice for she is well enough. I do not doubt that the less continent of our people will find her an object of more than curiosity!

Let us have done with her for a moment. I will turn to her father and the gentleman opposite him, who became visible to me by leaping to his feet. Even in the resumed babble his voice was clearly to be heard.

'Mr Brocklebank, I would have you know that I am the inveterate foe of every superstition!'

This of course was Mr Prettiman. I have made a sad job of his introduction, have I not? You must blame Miss Zenobia. He is a short, thick, angry gentleman. You know of him. I know—it matters not how—that he takes a printing press with him to the Antipodes; and though it is a machine capable of little more than turning out handbills, yet the Lutheran Bible was produced from something not much bigger.

But Mr Brocklebank was booming back. He had not thought. It was a trifle. He would be the last person to offend the susceptibilities. Custom. Habit.

Mr Prettiman, still standing, vibrated with passion.

'I saw it distinctly, sir! You threw salt over your shoulder!'

'So I did, sir, I confess it. I will try not to spill the salt again.'

This remark with its clear indication that Mr Brocklebank had no idea at all of what Mr Prettiman meant confounded the social philosopher. His mouth still open he sank slowly into his seat, thus almost passing from my sight. Miss Zenobia turned to me with a pretty seriousness round her wide eyes. She looked, as it were, under her eyebrows and up through lashes—but no. I will not believe that unassisted Nature——

'How angry Mr Prettiman is, Mr Talbot! I declare that when roused he is quite, quite terrifying!'

Anything less terrifying than the absurd philosopher would be difficult to imagine. However, I saw that we were about to embark on a familiar set of steps in an ancient dance. She was to become more and more the unprotected female in the presence of gigantic male creatures such as Mr Prettiman and your godson. We, for our part, were to advance with a threatening good humour so that in terror she would have to throw herself on our mercy, appeal to our generosity, appeal to our chivalry perhaps: and all the time the animal spirits, the, as Dr Johnson called them, 'amorous propensities' of both sexes would be excited to that state, that *ambiance*, in which such creatures as she is or has been, have their being.

This was a distancing thought and brought me to see something else. The size, the scale, was wrong. It was too large. The lady has been at least an *habituée* of the theatre if not a performer

there! This was not a normal encounter—for now she was describing her terror in the late *blow*—but one, as it were, thrown
outwards to where Summers at her side, Oldmeadow and a Mr
Bowles across the table and indeed anyone in earshot could hear
her. We were to perform. But before act one could be said to be
well under weigh—and I must confess that I dallied with the
thought that she might to some extent relieve the tedium of the
voyage—when louder exclamations from Mr Prettiman and
louder rumbles and even thunders from Mr Brocklebank turned
her to seriousness again. She was accustomed to touch wood. I
admitted to feeling more cheerful if a black cat should cross the
road before me. Her lucky number was twenty-five. I said at once
that her twenty-fifth birthday would prove to be most fortunate
for her—a piece of nonsense which went unnoticed, for Mr
Bowles (who is connected with the law in some very junior
capacity and a thorough bore) explained that the custom of
touching wood came from a papistical habit of adoring the cruci-
fix and kissing it. I responded with my nurse's fear of crossed
knives as indication of a quarrel and horror at a loaf turned
upside-down as a presage of a disaster at sea—whereat she
shrieked and turned to Summers for protection. He assured her
she need fear nothing from the French, who were quite beat
down at this juncture; but the mere mention of the French was
enough to set her off and we had another description of her
trembling away the hours of darkness in her cabin. We were a
single ship. We were, as she said in thrilling accents,

> '—alone, alone,
> All, all alone,
> Alone on a wide, wide sea!'

Anything more crowded than the teeming confines of this ship
is not to be found, I believe, outside a debtor's gaol or a prison
hulk. But yes she had met Mr Coleridge. Mr Brocklebank—pa—
had painted his portrait and there had been talk of an illustrated
volume but it came to nothing.

At about this point, Mr Brocklebank, having presumably
caught his daughter's recitation, could be heard booming on
metrically. It was more of the poem. I suppose he knew it well if
he had intended to illustrate it. Then he and the philosopher set
to again. Suddenly the whole saloon was silent and listening to
them.

'No, sir, I would not,' boomed the painter. 'Not in any circumstances!'

'Then refrain from eating chicken, sir, or any other fowl!'

'No sir!'

'Refrain from eating that portion of cow before you! There are ten millions of Brahmans in the East who would cut your throat for eating it!'

'There are no Brahmans in this ship.'

'Integrity——'

'Once and for all, sir, I would not shoot an albatross. I am a peaceable person, Mr Prettiman, and I would shoot *you* with as much pleasure!'

'Have you a gun, sir? For I will shoot an albatross, sir, and the sailors shall see what befalls——'

'I have a gun, sir, though I have never fired it. Are you a marksman, sir?'

'I have never fired a shot in my life!'

'Permit me then, sir. I have the weapon. You may use it.'

'You, sir?'

'I, sir!'

Mr Prettiman bounced up into full view again. His eyes had a kind of icy brilliance about them.

'Thank you, sir, I will, sir, and you shall see, sir! And the common sailors shall see, sir——'

He got himself over the bench on which he had been sitting, then fairly *rushed* out of the saloon. There was some laughter and conversation resumed but at a lower level. Miss Zenobia turned to me.

'Pa is determined we shall be protected in the Antipodes!'

'He does not propose going among the natives, surely!'

'He has some thought of introducing the art of portraiture among them. He thinks it will lead to complacency among them which he says is next door to civilization. He owns, though, that a black face will present a special kind of difficulty.'

'It would be dangerous, I think. Nor would the governor allow it.'

'But Mr Brocklebank—pa—believes he may persuade the governor to employ him.'

'Good God! I am not the governor, but—dear lady, think of the danger!'

'If clergymen may go——'

'Oh yes, where is he?'

Deverel touched my arm.

'The parson keeps his cabin. We shall see little of him, I think, and thank God and the captain for that. I do not miss him, nor do you I imagine.'

I had momentarily forgotten Deverel, let alone the parson. I now endeavoured to draw him into the conversation but he stood up and spoke with a certain meaning.

'I go on watch. But you and Miss Brocklebank, I have no doubt, will be able to entertain each other.'

He bowed to the lady and went off. I turned to her again and found her to be thoughtful. Not I mean that she was solemn—no, indeed! But beyond the artificial animation of her countenance there was some expression with which I confess I was not familiar. It was—do you not remember advising me to *read* faces?—it was a directed stillness of the orbs and eyelids as if while the outer woman was employing the common wiles and archnesses of her sex, beyond them was a different and watchful person! Was it Deverel's remark about entertainment that had made the difference? What was—what is—she thinking? Does she meditate an *affaire*, as I am sure she would call it, *pour passer le temps*?

As your lordship can see by the number at the head of this section
I have not been as attentive to the journal as I could wish—nor is
the reason such as I could wish! We have had bad weather again
and the motion of the vessel augmented a colic which I trace to
the late and unlamented *Bessie*. However, the sea is now smoother.
The weather and I have improved together and by dint of resting
the book and inkstand on a tray I am able to write, though
slowly. The one thing that consoles me for my indisposition is
that during my long sufferings the ships has got on. We have
been blown below the latitudes of the Mediterranean and our
speed has been limited, according to Wheeler (that living *Falconer*), more by the ship's decrepitude than by the availability of
wind. The people have been at the pumps. I had thought that
pumps 'clanked' and that I would hear the melancholy sound
clearly but this was not so. In the worst of the weather I asked
my visitor, Lieutenant Summers, fretfully enough why they did
not pump, only to be assured the people were pumping all the
time. He said it was a delusion caused by my sickness that made
me feel the vessel to be low in the water. I believe I may be more
than ordinarily susceptible to the movement of the vessel, that is
the truth of it. Summers assures me that naval people accept the
condition as nothing to be ashamed of and invariably adduce the
example of Lord Nelson to bear them out. I cannot but think,
though, that I have lost consequence. That Mr Brocklebank and
La Belle Brocklebank were also reduced to the state in which the
unfortunate Mrs Brocklebank has been ever since we left home is
no kind of help. The condition of the two hutches in which that
family lives must be one it is better not to contemplate.

There is something more to add. Just before the nauseating
complaint struck me—I am nigh enough recovered, though
weak—a *political* event convulsed our society. The captain, having
through Mr Summers disappointed the parson's expectation that
he would be allowed to conduct some services, has also forbidden

him the quarterdeck for some infraction of the *Standing Orders*. What a little tyrant it is! Mr Prettiman, who parades the afterdeck (with a *blunderbuss*!), was our intelligencer. He, poor man, was caught between his detestation of any church at all and what he calls his *love of liberty*! The conflict between these attitudes and the emotions they roused in him was painful. He was soothed by, of all people, Miss Granham! When I heard this comical and extra-ordinary news I got out of my trough and shaved and dressed. I was aware that duty and inclination urged me forward together. The brooding captain should not dictate to me in this manner! What! Is *he* to tell *me* whether I should have a service to attend or not? I saw at once that the passenger saloon was suitable and no man unless his habit of command had become a mania could take it from our control.

The parson might easily hold a short evening service there for such of the passengers as chose to attend it. I walked as steadily as I could across the lobby and tapped on the door of the parson's hutch.

He opened the door to me and made his usual sinuous genu-flection. My dislike of the man returned.

'Mr—ah—Mr——'

'James Colley, Mr Talbot, sir. The Reverend Robert James Colley at your service, sir.'

'Service is the word, sir.'

Now there was a mighty contortion! It was as if he accepted the word as a tribute to himself and the Almighty together.

'Mr Colley, when is the Sabbath?'

'Why today, sir, Mr Talbot, sir!'

The eyes that looked up at me were so full of eagerness, of such obsequious and devoted humility you would have thought I had a brace of livings in my coat pocket! He irritated me and I came near to abandoning my purpose.

'I have been indisposed, Mr Colley, otherwise I would have made the suggestion sooner. A few ladies and gentlemen would welcome it if you was to conduct a service, a short service in the passenger saloon at seven bells in the afternoon watch or, if you prefer to remain a landsman, at half-past three o'clock.'

He grew in stature before my eyes! His own filled with tears.

'Mr Talbot, sir, this is—is—it is like you!'

My irritation increased. It was on the tip of my tongue to ask him how the devil he knew what I was like. I nodded and walked away, to hear behind my back some mumbled remark about *visiting the sick*. Good God, thought I—if he tries that, he will go off with a flea in his ear! However, I managed to get to the passenger saloon, for irritation is in part a cure for weakness in the limbs, and found Summers there. I told him what I had arranged and he greeted the information with silence. Only when I suggested that he should invite the captain to attend did he smile wryly and reply that he should have to inform the captain anyway. He would make bold to suggest a later hour. I told him the hour was a matter of indifference to me and returned to my hutch and canvas chair in which I sat and felt myself exhausted but recovered. Later in the morning, Summers came to me and said that he had altered my message somewhat and hoped I did not mind. He had made it a general request from the passengers! He hastened to add that this was more conformable to the customs of the sea service. Well. Someone who delights as I do in the strange but wholly expressive Tarpaulin language (I hope to produce some prize specimens for you) could not willingly allow the *customs of the sea service* to suffer. But when I heard that the little parson was to be allowed to address us I must own I began to regret my impulsive interference and understood how much I had enjoyed these few weeks of freedom from the whole paraphernalia of Established Religion!

However, in decency I could not back down now and I attended the service our little cleric was allowed to perform. I was disgusted by it. Just previous to the service I saw Miss Brocklebank and her face was fairly plastered with red and white! The Magdalene must have looked just so, it may be leaning against the outer wall of the temple precincts. Nor, I thought, was Colley one to bring her to a more decorous appearance. Yet later I found I had underestimated both her judgement and her experience. For when it was time for the service the candles of the saloon irradiated her face, took from it the damaging years, while what had been paint now appeared a magical youth and beauty! She looked at me. Scarcely had I recovered from the shock of having this battery play on me when I discovered what further improvement Mr Summers had made on my original proposal. He had allowed in, to share our devotions with us, a number of the more respectable emigrants—Grant, the farrier, Filton and Whitlock, who are clerks I think, and old Mr Grainger with his old wife. He is a scrivener. Of *course* any village church will exhibit just such a mixture of the orders; but here the society of the passenger saloon is so *pinchbeck*—such a shoddy example to them! I was recovering from this invasion when there entered to us—we standing in respect—five feet nothing of parson complete with surplice, cap of maintenance perched on a round wig, long gown, boots with iron-shod heels—together with a mingled air of diffidence, piety, triumph and complacency. Your lordship will protest at once that some of these attributes cannot be got together under the same cap. I would agree that in the normal face there is seldom room for them all and that one in particular generally has the mastery. It is so in most cases. When we smile, do we not do so with mouth and cheeks and eyes, indeed, with the whole face from chin to hairline! But this Colley has been dealt with by Nature with the utmost economy. Nature has pitched—no, the verb is too active. Well then, on some corner of Time's beach, or on the muddy rim of one of her more insignificant rivulets, there have been washed together casually and indifferently a number of features that Nature had tossed away as of no use to any of her creations. Some vital spark that might have gone to the animation of a sheep assumed the collection. The result is this fledgling of the church.

Your lordship may detect in the fore-going a tendency to *fine writing*: a not unsuccessful attempt, I flatter myself. Yet as I surveyed the scene the one thought uppermost in my mind was that Colley was a living proof of old Aristotle's dictum. There is after all an order to which the man belongs by nature though some mistaken quirk of patronage has elevated him beyond it. You will find that order displayed in crude medieval manuscripts where the colour has no shading and the drawing no perspective. Autumn will be illustrated by men, peasants, serfs, who are reaping in the fields and whose faces are limned with just such a skimped and jagged line under their hoods as Colley's is! His eyes were turned down in diffidence and possibly recollection. The corners of his mouth were turned up—and there was the triumph and complacency! Much bone was strewn about the rest of his countenance. Indeed, his schooling should have been the open fields, with stone-collecting and bird-scaring, his university the plough. *Then* all those features so irregularly scarred by the tropic sun might have been bronzed into a unity and one, modest expression animated the whole!

We are back with fine writing, are we not? But my restlessness

and indignation are still hot within me. He knows of my consequence. At times it was difficult to determine whether he was
addressing Edmund Talbot or the Almighty. He was theatrical as
Miss Brocklebank. The habit of respect for the clerical office was
all that prevented me from breaking into indignant laughter.
Among the respectable emigrants that attended was the poor,
pale girl, carried devotedly by strong arms and placed in a seat
behind us. I have learned that she suffered a miscarriage in our
first *blow* and her awful pallor was in contrast with the manufac-
tured allure of La Brocklebank. The decent and respectful attention of her male companions was mocked by these creatures that
were ostensibly her betters—the one in paint pretending devotion,
the other with his book surely pretending sanctity! When the
service began there also began the most ridiculous of all the circumstances of that ridiculous evening. I set aside the sound of pacing
steps from above our heads where Mr Prettiman demonstrated his
anticlericalism as noisily on the afterdeck as possible. I omit the
trampings and shouts at the changing of the watch—all done
surely at the captain's behest or with his encouragement or tacit
consent with as much rowdiness as can be procured among sky-
larking sailors. I think only of the gently swaying saloon, the pale
girl and the farce that was played out before her! For no sooner
did Mr Colley catch sight of Miss Brocklebank than he could not
take his eyes off her. She for her part—and 'part' I am very sure it
was—gave us such a picture of devotion as you might find in the
hedge theatres of the country circuits. Her eyes never left his face
but when they were turned to heaven. Her lips were always
parted in breathless ecstasy except when they opened and closed
swiftly with a passionate 'Amen!' Indeed there was one moment
when a sanctimonious remark in the course of his address from
Mr Colley, followed by an 'Amen!' from Miss Brocklebank was
underlined, as it were (well, a *snail* has a *gait*!) by a resounding fart
from that wind-machine Mr Brocklebank so as to set most of the
congregation sniggering like schoolboys on their benches.

However much I attempted to detach myself from the performance I was made deeply ashamed by it and vexed at myself for
my own feelings. Yet since that time I have discovered a sufficient
reason for my discomfort and think my feelings in this instance
wiser than my reason. For I repeat, we had a handful of the
common people with us. It is possible they had entered the after
part of the ship in much the same spirit as those visitors who

declare they wish to view your lordship's Canalettos but who are really there to see if they can how the nobility live. But I think it more probable that they had come in a simple spirit of devotion. Certainly that poor, pale girl could have no other object than to find the comforts of religion. Who would deny them to such a helpless sufferer, however illusory they be? Indeed, the trashy show of the preacher and his painted Magdalene may not have come between her and the imagined object of her supplications, but what of the honest fellows who attended her? They may well have been stricken in the tenderest regions of loyalty and subordination.

Truly Captain Anderson detests the church! His attitude has been at work on the people. He had given no orders, it is said, but would know how to esteem those officers who did not agree with him in his obsession. Only Mr Summers and the gangling army officer, Mr Oldmeadow, were present. You know why *I* was there! I do not choose to submit to tyranny!

Most of the fellow's address was over before I made the major discovery in my, as it were, diagnosis of the situation. I had thought when I first saw how the painted face of the *actrice* engaged the eye of the reverend gentleman, that he experienced disgust mingled perhaps with the involuntary excitement, the first movement of warmth—no, lust—that an evident wanton will call from the male body rather than mind, by her very pronouncement of availability. But I soon saw that this would not do. Mr Colley has never been to a theatre! Where, too, would he progress, in what must surely be one of our remoter dioceses, from a theatre to a *maison d'occasion*? His book told him of painted women and how their feet go down to hell but did not include advice on how to recognize one by candlelight! He took her to be what her performance suggested to him! A chain of tawdry linked them. There came a moment in his address when having used the word of all others 'gentlemen', he swung to her and with a swooning archness exclaimed, 'Or ladies, madam, however beautiful,' before going on with his theme. I heard a positive hiss from within Miss Granham's bonnet and Summers crossed then uncrossed his knees.

It ended at last, and I returned to my hutch, to write this entry, in, I am sorry to say, increasing discomfort though the motion of the ship is easy enough. I do not know what is the matter with me. I have written sourly and feel sour, that is the fact of the matter.

(*17*)

I think it is seventeen. What does it matter. I have suffered again—the colic. Oh Nelson, Nelson, how did you manage to live so long and die at last not from this noisome series of convulsions but by the less painful violence of the enemy?

(?)

I am up and about, pale, frail, convalescent. It seems that after all I may live to reach our destination!

I wrote that yesterday. My entries are becoming short as some of Mr Sterne's chapters! But there is one amusing circumstance that I must acquaint your lordship with. At the height of my misery and just before I succumbed to a large dose of Wheeler's paregoric there came a timid knock at my hutch door. I cried 'Who is there?' To which a faint voice replied, 'It is I, Mr Talbot, sir. Mr Colley, sir. You remember, the Reverend Mr Colley, at your service.' By some stroke of luck rather than wit I hit on the only reply that would protect me from his *visitation*.

'Leave me I beg you, Mr Colley—' a dreadful convulsion of the guts interrupted me for a moment; then—'I am at prayer!'

Either a decent respect for my privacy or Wheeler approaching with the good draught in his hand rid me of him. The paregoric—it was a stiff and justifiable dose that *knocked me out*. Yet I do have some indistinct memory of opening my eyes in stupor and seeing that curious assemblage of features, that oddity of nature, Colley, hanging over me. God knows when that happened—if it happened! But now I am *up*, if not *about*, the man surely will not have the impertinence to thrust himself on me.

The dreams of paregoric must owe something surely to its constituent opium. Many faces, after all, floated through them so it is possible his was no more than a figment of my drugged delirium. The poor, pale girl haunted me—I hope indeed she may make a good recovery. There was under her cheekbone a right-angled hollow and I do not recollect ever having seen anything so painful to behold. The hollow and the affecting darkness that lived there, and moved did she but turn her head, touched me in a way I cannot describe. Indeed I was filled with a weak kind of rage when I returned in thought to the occasion of the service and remembered how her husband had exposed her to such a miserable farce! However, today I am more myself. I have recovered from such morbid thoughts. Our progress has been as excellent as my recovery. Though the air has become humid and hot I am no longer fevered by the pacing of Mr Prettiman overhead. He walks the afterdeck with a weapon provided of all things by the sot Brocklebank and will discharge a positive shower from his antique blunderbuss to destroy an albatross in despite of Mr Brocklebank and Mr Coleridge and Superstition together! He demonstrates to the thoughtful eye how really irrational a rationalist philosopher can be!

(23)

I think it is the twenty-third day. Summers is to explain the main parts of the rigging to me. I intend to surprise him with a landsman's knowledge—most collected out of books he has never heard of! I also intend to please your lordship with some choice bits of Tarpaulin language for I begin, haltingly it is true, to *speak Tarpaulin*! What a pity this noble vehicle of expression has so small a literature!

Can a man always be counting? In this heat and humidity——

It was Zenobia. Has your lordship ever remarked—but of course you have! What am I thinking of? There is a known, true, tried and tested link between the perception of female charms and the employment of strong drink! After three glasses I have seen twenty years vanish from a face like snow in summer! A sea voyage added to that stimulant—and one that has set us to move gently through the tropics of all places—has an effect on the male constitution that *may* be noted in the more recondite volumes of the profession—I mean the medical profession—but had not come my way in the course of an ordinary education. Perhaps somewhere in Martial—but I have not got him with me—or that Theocritus—you remember, midday and summer's heat τόν Πᾶνα δεδοίκαμες. Oh yes, we may well fear Pan here or his naval equivalent whoever it may be! But sea gods, sea nymphs were chill creatures. I have to admit that the woman is most damnably, most urgently attractive, *paint* and all! We have met and met again. How should we not? And again! It is all madness, tropical madness, a delirium, if not a transport! But now, standing by the bulwarks in the tropic night, stars caught among the sails and swaying very gently all together, I find that I deepen my voice so that her name vibrates and yet I know my own madness—she meanwhile, why she heaves her scarcely covered bosom with more motion than stirs the glossy deep. It is folly, but then, how to describe——

Noble godfather, if I do you wrong, rebuke me. Once ashore and I will be sane again, I will be that wise and impartial adviser, administrator, whose foot you have set on the first rung—but did you not say 'Tell all'? You said, 'Let me live again in you!'

I am but a young fellow after all.

Well then, the problem, devil take it, was a place of assignation. To meet the lady was easy enough and indeed unavoidable. But then so was meeting everyone else! Mr Prettiman paces the afterdeck. The *Famille* Pike, father, mother and little daughters, hurry up and down the afterdeck and the waist peering on this side and that lest they should be accosted, I suppose, and subjected to some indignity or impropriety. Colley comes by in the waist; and every time nowadays he not only favours me with his *reverence* but tops it off with a smile of such understanding and sanctity he is a kind of walking invitation to *mal de mer*. What could I do? I could scarcely hand the lady into the foretop! You will ask what is wrong with my hutch or her hutch. I answer 'Everything!' Does Mr Colley but cry 'Hem!' on the other side of the lobby he wakes Miss Granham in the hutch just aft of him. Does that windbag Mr Brocklebank but break wind—as he does every morning just after seven bells—our timbers shudder clear through my hutch and into Mr Prettiman's just forrard of me. I have had to prospect farther for a place suitable to the conduct of our *amours*. I had thought of finding and introducing myself to the purser—but to my surprise I found that all the officers shied away from mention of him as if the man were holy, or indecent, I cannot tell which, and he never appears on deck. It is a subject I propose to get clear in my mind—when I have a mind again and this, this surely temporary madness——

In sheer desperation I have got Mr Tommy Taylor to take me down to the gun room which, though it has only three midshipmen instead of the more usual complement, is nevertheless so roomy it is used for the warrant officers as well, because *their* mess—I cannot go into the politics of it all—is too far forrard and has been taken over for the better sort of emigrant. These elders, the gunner, the carpenter and the sailing master, sat in a row beyond a table and watched me in a silence that seemed more *knowing* than the regard of anyone else in the ship if we except the redoubtable Miss Granham. Yet I did not pay much attention to them at first because of the extraordinary object that Mr Willis revealed as he moved his bony length towards the ladder. It was, of all things, a plant, some kind of creeper, its roots buried in a pot and the stem roped to the bulkhead for a few feet. There was never a leaf; and wherever a tendril or branch was unsupported it hung straight down like a piece of seaweed—which indeed would have been more appropriate and useful. I exclaimed at the sight. Mr Taylor burst into his usual peal and pointed to Mr Willis as the not particularly proud owner. Mr Willis vanished up the ladder. I turned from the plant to Mr Taylor.

'What the devil is that for?'

'Ah,' said the gunner. 'Gentleman Jack.'

'Always one for a joke, Mr Deverel,' said the carpenter. 'He put him up to it.'

The sailing master smiled across at me with mysterious compassion.

'Mr Deverel told him it was the way to get on.'

Tommy Taylor cried with laughter—literally cried, the tears falling from him. He choked and I beat his back more severely than he liked. But unalloyed high spirits are a nuisance anywhere. He stopped laughing.

'It's a creeper, you see!'

'Gentleman Jack,' said the carpenter again. 'I couldn't help laughing myself. God knows what sort of lark Mr Deverel will get up to in the badger bag.'

'The what, sir?'

The gunner had reached below the table and brought up a bottle.

'You'll take an observation through a glass, Mr Talbot.'

'In this heat——'

It was rum, fiery and sticky. It increased the heat in my blood and seemed to increase the oppressiveness of the air. I wished that I could shed my coat as the warrant officers had; but of course it would not do.

'This air is confoundedly close, gentlemen. I wonder you can endure it day after day.'

'Ah,' said the gunner, 'It's a hard life Mr Talbot, sir. Here today and gone tomorrow.'

'Here today and gone today,' said the carpenter. 'Do you mind that young fellow, Hawthorne I think, come aboard at the beginning of this commission? Boatswain gets him to tail on a rope with the others, only last man like and says, says he, "Don't you go leaving go no matter what happens." The boat begins to take charge on the yard and drops 'cause the rest jumps clear. Young Hawthorne, who don't know the crown of a block from its arse—he come off a farm, I shouldn't wonder—he holds on like he's been told.'

The gunners nodded and drank.

'Obeys orders.'

It seemed the story had come to an end.

'But what was wrong? What happened?'

'Why, see,' said the carpenter, 'the tail of the rope runs up to the block—swit!—just like that. Young Hawthorne he was on the end of it. He must have gone a mile.'

'We never saw him again.'

'Good God.'

'Here today and gone today, like I said.'

'I could tell you a story or two about guns if it comes to that,' said the gunner. 'Very nasty things, guns when they misbehave, which they can do so in ten thousand different ways. So if you take up to be a gunner, Mr Talbot, you need your head.'

Mr Gibbs the carpenter nudged the sailing master.

'Why, even a gunner's mate needs a head, sir,' he said. 'Did

you never hear the story of the gunner's mate who lost his head?
It was off Alicante I believe——'

'Now then George!'

'This gunner, see, was walking up and down behind his battery
with his pistol in his hand. They was swopping shot with a fort, a
foolish thing to do in my view. A red hot shot come through a
gun port and takes off the gunner's head clean as this gallantine
the Frenchies make use of. Only see the shot was red hot and
cauterizes the neck so the gunner goes on marching up and down
and nobody notices nothing until they run out of orders. Laugh!
They nigh on died until the first lieutenant wants to know why in
the name of Christ the guns had fell silent in the after starboard
maindeck battery, so they asks the gunner what to do but he had
nothing with which to tell them.'

'Really gentlemen! Oh come!'

'Another glass, Mr Talbot.'

'It's getting so *stuffy* in here——'

The carpenter nodded and knocked on a timber with his
knuckles.

'It's hard to tell whether the air sweats or her wood.'

The gunner heaved once or twice with laughter inside him like
a wave that does not break.

'We should open a winder,' he said. 'You remember the gals,
Mr Gibbs? "Couldn't we 'ave a winder open? I've come over
queer like." '

Mr Gibbs heaved like the gunner.

'Come over queer, have you? Along here, my little dear. It's
the way for some nice fresh air.'

' "Oh what was that, Mr Gibbs? Was it a rat? I can't abide rats!
I'm sure it was a rat——" '

'Just my little doggie, my dear. Here. Feel my little doggie.'

I drank some of the fiery liquid.

'And commerce can be obtained even in such a vessel as this?
Did no one see you?'

The sailing master smiled his beautiful smile.

'I saw them.'

The gunner nudged him.

'Wake up, Shiner. You wasn't even in the ship. We hadn't
hardly come out of ordinary.'

'Ordinary,' said Mr Gibbs. 'That's the life that is. No nasty sea.
Lying up a creek snug in a trot with your pick of the admirals'

cabins and a woman on the books to do the galley work. That's
the best berth there is in the Navy, Mr Talbot, sir. Seven years I
was in her before they came aboard and tried to get her out of the
mud. Then they didn't think they'd careen her what with one
thing and another so they took what weed they could off her
bottom with the drag rope. That's why she's so uncommon sluggish. It was sea water, you see. I hope this Sydney Cove or
whatever they call it has berths in fresh water.'

'If they took the weed off her,' said the gunner, 'they might
take the bottom with it.'

Clearly I was no nearer my original objective. I had but one
possible resource left me.

'Does not the purser share this commodious apartment with
you?'

Again there was that strange, uneasy silence. At last Mr Gibbs
broke it.

'He has his own place up there on planks over the water casks
among the cargo and dunnage.'

'Which is?'

'Bales and boxes,' said the gunner. 'Shot, powder, slow match,
fuse, grape and chain, and thirty twenty-four pounders, all of 'em
tompioned, greased, plugged and bowsed down.'

'Tubs,' said the carpenter. 'Tools, adzes and axes, hammers
and chisels, saws and sledges, mauls, spikes, trenails and copper
sheet, plugs, harness, gyves, wrought iron rails for the governor's
new balcony, casks, barrels, tuns, firkins, pipkins, bottles and
bins, seeds, samples, fodder, lamp oil, paper, linen.'

'And a thousand other things,' said the sailing master. 'Ten
thousand times ten thousand.'

'Why don't you show the gentleman, Mr Taylor,' said the
carpenter. 'Take the lantern. You can make believe as you're the
captain going his rounds.'

Mr Taylor obeyed and we went, or rather crept *forrard*. A
voice called behind us.

'You may even glimpse the purser.'

It was a strange and unpleasant journey where indeed rats
scurried. Mr Taylor, being accustomed, I suppose, to this kind of
journey, made short work of it. Until I ordered him back he got
so far ahead of me that I was left in complete, and need I say,
foetid, darkness. When he *did* return part way it was only to
reveal with his lantern our narrow and irregular path between

nameless bulks and shapes that seemed piled around us and indeed over us without order or any visible reason. Once I fell, and my boots trod that same noisome sand and gravel of her bilge that Wheeler had described to me on the *first day*: and it was while fumbling to extract myself from between two of her vast timbers that I had my one and only glimpse of our purser—or at least I suppose it was the purser. I glimpsed him up there through a kind of spyhole between, it may be, bales or whatnot; and since he of all people does not have to stint himself for light that hole, though it was far below deck, blazed like a sunny window. I saw a vast head with small spectacles bowed over a ledger—just that and nothing more. Yet *this* was the creature, mention of whom could produce a silence among these men so careless of life and death!

I scrambled out of the ballast and onto the planks over the *bowsed down* cannon and crawled after Mr Taylor till a quirk of our narrow passage hid the vision and we were alone with the lantern again. We reached the forepart of the ship. Mr Taylor led me up ladders, piping in his treble—'Gangway there!' You must not imagine he was ordering some mechanism to be lowered for my convenience. In Tarpaulin, a 'gangway' is a space through which one may walk and he was acting as my usher, or lictor I suppose, and ensuring that the common people would not trouble me. So we rose from the depths, through decks crowded with people of all ages and sexes and smells and noises and smoke and emerged into the crowded fo'castle whence I positively fled out into the cool, sweet air of the waist! I thanked Mr Taylor for his convoy, then went to my hutch and had Wheeler take away my boots. I stripped and rubbed myself down with perhaps a pint of water and felt more or less clean. But clearly, however freely the warrant officers obtained the favours of young women in these shadowy depths, it was of no use for your humble servant. Sitting in my canvas chair and in a mood of near desperation I came close to confiding in Wheeler but retained just enough common sense to keep my wishes to myself.

I wonder what is meant by the expression 'Badger Bag'? Falconer is silent.

(Y)

It has come to me in a flash! One's intelligence may march about and about a problem but the solution does not come gradually into view. One moment it is not. The next, and it is there. If you cannot alter the place all that is left to alter is the time! Therefore, when Summers announced that the people would provide us with an entertainment I brooded for a while, thinking nothing of it, then suddenly saw with a *political eye* that the ship was about to provide me not with a place but with an opportunity! I am happy to inform you—no, I do not think gaiety comes into it, rather a simple dignity; My lord, I have at sea emulated *one* of Lord Nelson's victories! Could the merely civil part of our country achieve more? Briefly, I let it be known that such trivial affairs as the seamen's entertainment held no attraction for me, that I had the headache and should pass the time in my cabin. I took care that Zenobia should hear me! I stood, therefore, gazing through the louvre as our passengers took their way to the afterdeck and quarterdeck, a clamorous crowd only too happy to find something out of the ordinary, and soon our lobby was empty and silent as—as it could well be. I waited, hearing the trampling of feet over my head; and soon, sure enough, Miss Zenobia came tripping down to find perhaps a shawl against the tropic night! I was out of my hutch, had her by the wrist and jerked her back in with me before she could even pretend a startled cry! But there was noise enough from other places and noise enough from the blood pounding in my ears so that I pressed my suit with positive ardour! We wrestled for a moment by the bunk, she with a nicely calculated exertion of strength that only just failed to resist me, I with mounting passion. My sword was in my hand and I boarded her! She retired in disorder to the end of the hutch where the canvas basin awaited her in its iron hoop. I attacked once more and the hoop collapsed. The bookshelf tilted. *Moll Flanders* lay open on the deck, *Gil Blas* fell on her and my aunt's parting gift to me, Hervey's *Meditations among the Tombs* (*MDCCLX*) *II vols*

London covered them both. I struck them all aside and Zenobia's tops'ls too. I called on her to yield, yet she maintained a brave if useless resistance that fired me even more. I bent for the *main course*. We flamed against the ruins of the canvas basin and among the trampled pages of my little library. We flamed upright. Ah—she did yield at last to my conquering arms, was overcome, rendered up all the tender spoils of war!

However—if your lordship follows me—although it is our male privilege to *debellare* the *superbos*—the *superbas*, if you will—it is something of a duty I think to *parcere* the *subjectis*! In a sentence, having gained the favours of *Venus* I did not wish to inflict the pains of *Lucina*! Yet her abandonment was complete and passionate. I did not think female heat could increase—but as bad luck would have it, at that very critical moment there came from the deck above our heads the sound of a veritable explosion.

She clutched me frantically.

'Mr Talbot,' she gasped, 'Edmund! The French! Save me!'

Was there ever anything more mistimed and ridiculous? Like most handsome and passionate women she is a fool; and the explosion (which I at once identified) put her, if not me, in the peril from which it had been my generous intention to protect her. Well there it is. The fault was hers and she must bear the penalties of her follies as well as the pleasures. It was—and is all the same—confoundedly provoking. Moreover she is I believe too experienced a woman not to be aware of what she has done!

'Calm yourself, my dear,' I muttered breathlessly, as my own too speedy paroxysm subsided—*confound* the woman—'It is Mr Prettiman who has at last seen an albatross. He has discharged your father's blunderbuss in its general direction. You will not be ravished by the French but by our common people if they find out what he is at.'

(In fact I found that Mr Coleridge had been mistaken. Sailors are superstitious indeed, but careless of life in any direction. The only reason why they do not shoot seabirds is first because they are not allowed weapons and second because seabirds are not pleasant to eat.)

Above us, there was trampling on the deck and much noise about the ship in general. I could only suppose the entertainment was being rowdily successful, for such as like that sort of thing or have nothing better in view.

'Now my dear,' said I, 'we must get you back to the social scene. It will never do for us to appear together.'

'Edmund!'

This with a great deal of heaving and—glowing, as it is called. Really, she was in a quite distasteful condition!

'Why—what is the matter?'

'You will not desert me?'

I paused and thought.

'Do you suppose I can step overboard into a ship of my own?'

'Cruel!'

We were now, as your lordship may observe, in about act three of an inferior drama. She was to be the deserted victim and I the heartless villain.

'Nonsense, my dear! Do you pretend that these are circumstances—even to our somewhat inelegant posture—that these are circumstances with which you are wholly unfamiliar!'

'What shall I do?'

'Fiddlesticks, woman! The danger is slight as you know very well. Or are you waiting for——'

I caught myself up. Even to pretend that there might be something about this commerce that was *commercial* seemed an unnecessary insult. To tell the truth I found there were a number of irritations combined with my natural sense of completion and victory and at the moment I wished nothing so much as that she would vanish like a soap bubble or anything evanescent.

'Waiting for what, Edmund?'

'For a reasonable moment to slip into your hutch—cabin I would say—and repair your, your toilette.'

'Edmund!'

'We have very little time, Miss Brocklebank!'

'Yet if—*if* there should be—unhappy consequences——'

'Why, my dear, we must cross that bridge when you come to it! Now go, go! I will examine the lobby—yes the coast is clear!'

I favoured her with a light salute, then leapt back into my cabin. I restored the books to their shelves and did my best to wrench the iron support of the canvas basin back into shape. I lay at last in my bunk and felt, not the Aristotelian sadness but a continuance of my previous irritation. Really the woman is *such* a fool! The French! It was her sense of theatre that had betrayed her, I could not help thinking, at my expense. But the party was breaking up on deck. I thought that I would emerge later when the light in the lobby was a concealment rather than discovery. I would take the right moment to go to the passenger saloon and drink a glass with any gentleman who might be drinking late there. I did not care to light my candle but waited—and waited in vain! Nobody descended from the upper decks! I stole into the passenger saloon therefore and was disconcerted to find Deverel there already, seated at the table under the great stern window with a glass in one hand and of all things a carnival mask in the other! He was laughing to himself. He saw me at once and called out.

'Talbot my dear fellow! A glass for Mr Talbot, steward! What a sight it was!'

Deverel was elevated. His speech was not precise and there was a carelessness about his bearing. He drank to me with grace, however exaggerated. He laughed again.

'What famous sport!'

For a moment I thought he might refer to the passage between me and Miss Zenny. But his attitude was not exactly right for that. It was something else, then.

'Why yes,' said I. 'Famous, as you say, sir.'

He returned nothing for a moment or two. Then——

'How he does hate a parson!'

I was, as we used to say in the nursery, getting warmer.

'You refer to our gallant captain.'

'Old Rumble-guts.'

'I must own, Mr Deverel, that I am no particular friend to the cloth myself; but the captain's dislike of it seems beyond anything. I have been told that he has forbidden Mr Colley the quarterdeck on account of some trivial oversight.'

Deverel laughed again.

'The quarterdeck—which Colley supposes includes the after-deck. So he is confined more or less to the waist.'

'Such *passionate* detestation is mysterious. I myself found Colley to be a, a creature of—but I would not punish the man for his nature other than to ignore him.'

Deverel rolled his empty glass on the table.

'Bates! Another brandy for Mr Deverel!'

'You are kindness itself, Talbot. I could tell you——'

He broke off, laughing.

'Tell me what, sir?'

The man, I saw too late, was deep in his cups. Only the

habitual elegance of his behaviour and bearing had concealed the fact from me. He murmured.

'Our captain. Our damned captain.'

His head fell forward on the saloon table, his glass dropped and broke. I tried to rouse him but could not. I called the steward who is accustomed enough to dealing with such situations. Now at last the audience were indeed returning from the upper decks, for I could hear feet on the ladder. I emerged from the saloon to be met by a crowd of them in the lobby. Miss Granham swept by me. Mr Prettiman hung at her shoulder and orated to what effect I know not. The Stocks were agreeing with Pike *père et mère* that the thing had gone too far. But here was Miss Zenobia, radiant among the officers as if she had made one of the audience from the beginning! She addressed me, laughing.

'Was it not diverting, Mr Talbot?'

I bowed, smiling.

'I have never been better entertained, Miss Brocklebank.'

I returned to my cabin, where it seemed to me the woman's perfume yet lingered. To tell the truth, though irritation was still uppermost in my mind, as I sat down and began to make this entry—and as the entry has progressed—irritation has been subsumed into a kind of universal sadness—Good God! Is Aristotle right in this commerce of the sexes as he is in the orders of society? I must rouse myself from too dull a view of the farmyard transaction by which our wretched species is lugged into the daylight.

It is the same night and I have recovered from what I now think a morbid view of practically everything! The truth is I am more concerned with what Wheeler may discover and pass on to his fellows than considerations of a kind of methodistical moralism! For one thing, I cannot get the iron ring back into precise shape and for another, that curst perfume lingers yet! Confound the fool of a woman! As I look back, it seems to me that what I shall ever remember is not the somewhat feverish and too brief pleasure of my *entertainment* but the occasional and astonishing recourse to the Stage which she employed whenever her feelings were more than usually roused—or perhaps when they were more than usually *definable*! Could an actress convey an emotion that is indefinable? And would she not therefore welcome with gratitude a situation where the emotion was direct and precise? And does this not account for *stagey* behaviour? In my very modest involvement with amateur theatricals at the university, those whom we had hired to be our professional advisers named for us some of the technicalities of the art, craft or *trade*. Thus, I should have said that after my remark 'Why, my dear, we must cross that bridge when you come to it!' she did not reply in words; but being half-turned away she turned wholly away and started forward away from me—would have gone much further had the hutch allowed of it—would have performed the movement we were told constituted *a break down stage right*! I laughed to remember it and was somewhat more myself again. Good God, as the captain would agree, one parson in a ship is one too many, and the stage serves as an agreeable alternative to moralism! Why, was there not a performance given us by the reverend gentleman and Miss Brocklebank in the course of the one service we have had to suffer? I am this very moment possessed by a positively and literally Shakespearean concept. *He* had found her attractive and *she* had shown herself, as women will, anxious to kneel before a male officiant—they made a pair! Should we not do them good—or, as an imp whispered to me, do us all three good? Should not this unlikely Beatrice and Benedict be brought into a mountain of affection for each other? 'I will do any modest office to help my cousin to a good husband.' I laughed aloud as I wrote that—and can only hope that the other passengers, lying in their bunks at *three bells of the middle watch* think that like Beatrice I laughed in my sleep! I shall for the future single out Mr Colley for the most, shall I say, distinguished attentions on my part—or at least until Miss Brocklebank proves to be no longer in danger from *the French*!

(Z)

Zed, you see, zed, I do not know what the day is—but here was a
to-do! What a thing!

I rose at the accustomed hour with a faint stricture about the
brows, caused I think by my somewhat liberal potations with Mr
Deverel of a rather inferior brandy. I dressed and went on deck
to blow it away—when who should emerge from our lobby but
the reverend gentleman for whom I planned to procure—the
word is unfortunate—such a pleasant future. Mindful of my determination I raised my beaver to him and gave him good day.
He bowed and smiled and raised his tricorn but with more dignity
than I had thought he had in him. Come, thought I to myself,
does Van Diemen's Land require a bishop? I watched him in
some surprise as he walked steadily up the ladder to the afterdeck.
I followed him to where Mr Prettiman still stood and cradled his
ridiculous weapon. I saluted him; for if I have a personal need,
now, of Mr Colley, as you know, Mr Prettiman must always be
an object of interest to me.

'You hit the albatross, sir?'

Mr Prettiman bounced with indignation.

'I did not, sir! The whole episode—the weapon was snatched
from my hands—the whole episode was grotesque and lamentable! Such a display of ignorance, of monstrous and savage
superstition!'

'No doubt, no doubt,' said I soothingly. 'Such a thing could
never happen in France.'

I moved on towards the quarterdeck; climbed the ladder; and
what was my astonishment to find Mr Colley there! In round
wig, tricorn and black coat he stood before Captain Anderson on
the very planks sacred to the tyrant! As I came to the top of the
ladder Captain Anderson turned abruptly away, went to the rail
and spat over the side. He was red in the face and grim as a
gargoyle. Mr Colley lifted his hat gravely, then came towards the
ladder. He saw Lieutenant Summers and went across to him.

They saluted each other with equal gravity.

'Mr Summers, I believe it was you who discharged Mr Pretti-man's weapon?'

'It was, sir.'

'I trust you injured no one?'

'I fired over the side.'

'I must thank you for it.'

'It was nothing, sir. Mr Colley——'

'Well, sir?'

'I beg of you, be advised by me.'

'In what way, sir?'

'Do not go immediately. We have not known our people long enough, sir. After yesterday—I am aware that you are no friend to intoxicants of any sort—I beg you to wait until the people have been issued with their rum. After that there will ensue a period when they will, even if they are no more than now open to reason, be at least calmer and more amiable——'

'I have armour, sir.'

'Believe me, I know of what I speak! I was once of their condition——'

'I bear the shield of the Lord.'

'Sir! Mr Colley! As a personal favour to me, since you declare yourself indebted—I beg of you, wait for one hour!'

There was a silence. Mr Colley saw me and bowed gravely. He turned back to Mr Summers.

'Very well, sir. I accept your advice.'

The gentlemen bowed once again, Mr Colley came towards me so *we* bowed to each other! Versailles could have done no better! Then the gentleman descended the ladder. It was too much! A new curiosity mingled with my *Shakespearean* purposes for him. Good God, thought I, the whole southern hemisphere has got itself an archbishop! I hurried after him and caught him as he was about to enter our lobby.

'Mr Colley!'

'Sir?'

'I have long wished to be better acquainted with you but owing to an unfortunate disposition the occasion has not presented itself——'

His *mug* split with a grin. He swept off his hat, clasped it to his stomach and bowed, or sinuously reverenced over it. The arch-bishop diminished to a country curate—no, to a hedge priest. My contempt returned and quenched my curiosity. But I remembered how much Zenobia might stand in need of his services and that I should keep him *in reserve*—or as the Navy would say—*in ordinary!*

'Mr Colley. We have been too long unacquainted. Will you not take a turn with me on deck?'

It was extraordinary. His face, burned and blistered as it was by exposure to the tropic sun, reddened even more, then as suddenly paled. I swear that tears stood in his eyes! His Adam's apple positively *danced* up and down beneath and above his hands!

'Mr Talbot, sir—words cannot—I have long desired—but at such a moment—this is worthy of you and your noble patron—this is generous—this is Christian charity in its truest meaning—God bless you, Mr Talbot!'

Once more he performed his sinuous and ducking bow, retired a yard or two backwards, ducked again as if leaving the presence, then disappeared into his hutch.

I heard a contemptuous exclamation above me, glanced up and saw Mr Prettiman gazing down at us over the forrard rail of the afterdeck. He bounced away again out of sight. But for the moment I spared him no attention. I was still confounded by the remarkable effect of my words on Colley. My appearance is that of a gentleman and I am suitably dressed. I have some height and perhaps—I say no more than perhaps—consciousness of my future employment may have added more dignity to my bearing than is customary in one of my years! In which case, sir, you are obliquely to be blamed for—but I wrote earlier did I not that I would not continue to trouble you with my gratitude? To resume then, there was nothing about me to warrant this foolish fellow treating me as a Royal! I paced between the break of the afterdeck and the mainmast for half an hour, perhaps to rid myself of that same stricture of the brows, and pondered this ridiculous circumstance. Something had happened and I did not know what it was—something, I saw, during the ship's entertainment while I was so closely engaged with the Delicious Enemy! What it was, I could not tell, nor why it should make my recognition of Mr Colley more than ordinarily delightful to him. And Lieutenant Summers had discharged Mr Prettiman's blunderbuss without injuring anyone! That seemed like an extraordinary failure on the part of a *fighting seaman*! It was a great mystery and puzzle; yet the man's evident gratitude for my attentions—it was annoying that

I could not demand a solution to the mystery from the gentlemen or officers, for it would not be politic to reveal an ignorance based on a pleasant preoccupation with a member of the Sex. I could not at once think how to go on. I returned to our lobby, proposing to go into the saloon and discover if I could by attending to casual conversations the source of Mr Colley's extreme gratitude and dignity. But as I entered the lobby Miss Brockle-bank hurried out of her hutch and detained me with a hand on my arm.

'Mr Talbot—Edmund!'

'How may I serve you, ma'am?'

Then throatily, contralto but pianissimo——

'A letter—Oh God! What shall I do?'

'Zenobia! Tell me all!'

Does your lordship detect a theatricality in my response? It was so indeed. We were at once borne along on a tide of melo-drama.

'Oh heavens—it, it is a *billet*—lost, lost!'

'But my dear,' said I, leaving the stage at once, 'I have written you nothing.'

Her magnificent but foolish bosom heaved.

'It was from Another!'

'Well,' I murmured to her, 'I refuse to be responsible for every gentleman in the ship! You should employ his offices, not mine. And so——'

I turned to leave but she held me by the arm.

'The note is wholly innocent but may be—might be miscon-strued—I may have dropped it—oh Edmund, you well know where!'

'I assure you,' said I, 'that while I rearranged my hutch where it had been disturbed by a certain exquisite occasion I should have noticed——'

'Please! Oh please!'

She gazed into my eyes with that look of absolute trust mingled with anguish which so improves a pair of orbs however lustrous. (But who am I to instruct your lordship, still surrounded as you are by adorers who gaze on what they would have but cannot obtain—by the way, is my flattery too gross? Remember you declared it most effective when seasoned with truth!)

Zenobia came close and murmured up at me.

'It must be in your cabin. Oh should Wheeler find it I am lost!'

The devil, thought I. If Wheeler finds it, *I* am lost or near enough—is she trying to implicate me?

'Say no more, Miss Brocklebank. I will go at once.'

I exited right—or should it be left? I have never been certain, where the theatre is concerned. Say then that I moved towards my spacious apartment on the larboard side of the vessel, opened the door, went in, shut it and began to search. I do not know anything more irritating than to be forced to search for an object in a confined space. All at once I was aware that there were two feet by mine. I glanced up.

'Go away, Wheeler! Go *away*!'

He went. After that I found the paper but only when I had given up looking for it. I was about to pour water into my canvas basin when what should I see in the centre of it but a sheet of paper, folded. I seized it at once and was about to return it to Zenobia's hutch when I was stopped by a thought. In the first place I had performed my ablutions earlier in the morning. The canvas basin had been emptied and the bunk remade.

Wheeler!

At once, I unfolded the note, then breathed again. The hand was uneducated.

DEAREST MOST ADORABLE WOMAN I CAN WATE NO LONGER! I
HAVE AT LAST DISCOVERED A PLACE AND NO ONE IS IN THE NO!
MY HART THUNDERS IN MY BOSSOM AS IT NEVER DID IN MY
FREQUENT HOURS OF PERIL! ONLY ACQUAINT ME WITH THE TIME
AND I WILL CONDUCT YOU TO OUR HEVEN!
YOUR SAILOR HERO

Good God, thought I, this is Lord Nelson raised to a higher power of the ridiculous! She is having an attack of the *Emmas* and has infected this Unknown Sailor Hero with her own style of it! I fell into a state of complete confusion. Mr Colley, all dignity—now this note—Summers with Prettiman's blunderbuss that was really Brocklebank's—I began to laugh, then shouted for Wheeler.

'Wheeler, you have been busy in my cabin. What should I do without you?'

He bowed but said nothing.

'I am pleased with your attentiveness. Here is a half-guinea for you. You are sometimes forgetful though, are you not?'

The man's eyes did not flicker towards the canvas bowl.

'Thank you, Mr Talbot, sir. You may rely on me in every way sir.'

He withdrew. I examined the note again. It was not Deverel's, obviously, for the illiteracy was not that of a gentleman. I wondered what I should do.

Then—really, at some later date I must amuse myself by seeing how the thing would fit into a farce—I saw how the theatre would provide a means whereby I might rid myself of Zenobia and the parson together—I had but to drop the note in his cabin, pretend to discover it—Is not this note addressed to Miss Brocklebank sir? And you a minister of religion! Confess, you dog, and let us congratulate you on your success with your inamorata!

It was at this point that I caught myself up in astonishment and irritation. Here was I, who considered myself an honourable and responsible man, contemplating an action which was not merely criminal but despicable! How did that come about? You see I hide nothing. Sitting on the edge of my bunk I examined the train that had led me to such gross thoughts and found its original in the dramatic nature of Zenobia's appeal—straight back to farce and melodrama—in a word, to the theatre! Be it proclaimed in all the schools

Plato was right!

I rose, went to the next hutch, knocked. She opened, I handed her the note and came away.

(Ω)

Omega, omega, omega. The last scene surely! Nothing more can happen—unless it be fire, shipwreck, the violence of the enemy or a miracle! Even in this last case, I am sure the Almighty would appear theatrically as a *Deus ex Machina*! Even if I refuse to disgrace myself by it, I cannot, it seems, prevent the whole ship from indulging in theatricals! I myself should come before you now, wearing the cloak of a messenger in a play—why not your Racine—forgive me the 'Your' but I cannot think of him as otherwise——

Or may I stay with the Greeks? It is a play. Is it a farce or a tragedy? Does not a tragedy depend on the dignity of the protagonist? Must he not be great to fall greatly? A farce, then, for the man appears now a sort of Punchinello. His fall is in social terms. Death does not come into it. He will not put out his eyes or be pursued by the Furies—he has committed no crime, broken no law—unless our egregious tyrant has a few in reserve for the unwary.

After I had rid myself of the *billet* I went to the afterdeck for air, then to the quarterdeck. Captain Anderson was not there, but Deverel had the watch together with our ancient midshipman Mr Davies, who in bright sunlight looks more decayed than ever. I saluted Deverel and returned to the afterdeck, meaning to have some kind of exchange with Mr Prettiman who still patrols in all his madness. (I am becoming more and more convinced that the man cannot conceivably be any danger to the state. No one would heed him. Nevertheless, I thought it my duty to keep an acquaintance with him.) He paid no attention to my approach. He was staring down into the waist. My gaze followed his.

What was my astonishment to see the back view of Mr Colley appear from beneath the afterdeck and proceed towards the people's part of the vessel! This in itself was astonishing enough, for he crossed the white line at the mainmast which delimits their approach to us unless by invitation or for duty. But what was

even more astonishing was that Colley was dressed in a positive
delirium of ecclesiastical finery! That surplice, gown, hood, wig,
cap looked quite simply silly under our vertical sun! He moved
forward at a solemn pace as he might in a cathedral. The people
who were lounging in the sun stood at once and, I thought, with
a somewhat sheepish air. Mr Colley disappeared from my sight
under the break of the fo'castle. This, then, was what he had
spoken of with Summers. The people must have had their rum—
and indeed now I recollected that I had heard the pipe and the cry
of 'Up Spirits!' earlier on without paying any attention to a sound
that by now had become so familiar. The movement of the vessel
was easy, the air hot. The people themselves were indulged with
a holiday or what Summers calls a 'Make and Mend'. I stood on
the after-deck for a while, hardly attending to Mr Prettiman's
diatribe on what he called this survival of barbaric finery, for I
was waiting with some curiosity to see the parson come out
again! I could not think that he proposed to conduct a full service!
But the sight of a parson not so much walking into such a place
as processing into it—for there had been about him that movement, that air, which would suppose a choir, a handful of canons
and a dean at least—this sight I say at once amused and impressed
me. I understood his mistake. He lacked the natural authority of a
gentleman and had absurdly overdone the dignity of his calling.
He was now advancing on the lower orders in all the majesty of
the Church Triumphant—or should it be the Church Militant? I
was moved at this picture in little of one of the elements that have
brought English—and dare I say British—Society to the state of
perfection it now enjoys. Here before me was the Church; there,
aft of me and seated in his cabin was the State in the person of
Captain Anderson. Which whip I wondered would prove to be
the more effective? The cat-o'-nine-tails, only too material in its
red serge bag and at the disposal of the captain, though I have
not known him order its use; or the notional, the *Platonic Idea* of a
whip, the threat of hell fire? For I had no doubt (from the dig-
nified and outraged appearance of the man before the captain)
that the people had subjected Mr Colley to some slight, real or
imagined. I should not have been too surprised had I heard the
fo'castle to resound with wails of repentance or screams of terror.
For a time—I do not know how long—I waited to see what
would happen and concluded that nothing would happen at all! I
returned to my cabin, where I continued with the *warm* paragraphs

which I trust you will have enjoyed. I broke off from that employment at a noise.

Can your lordship guess what the noise was? No sir, not even you! (I hope to come by practice to subtler forms of flattery.)

The first sound I heard from the fo'castle was applause! It was not the sort of applause that will follow an *aria* and perhaps interrupt the business of an opera for whole minutes together. This was not hysteria, the audience was not beside itself. Nor were the people throwing roses—or guineas, as I once saw some young bloods try to into the bosom of the Fantalini! They were, my *social* ears told me, doing what was proper, the done thing. They applauded much as I for my part have applauded in the Sheldonian among my fellows when some respectable foreigner has been awarded an honorary degree by the university. I went out on deck quickly, but there was now silence after that first round of applause. I thought I could just hear the reverend gentleman speaking. I had half a mind to advance on the scene, conceal myself by the break of the fo'castle and listen. But then I reflected on the number of sermons I had heard in my life and the likely number to come. Our voyage, so wretched in many ways, has nevertheless been an almost complete holiday from them! I decided to wait, therefore, until our newly triumphant Colley should have persuaded our captain that our ancient vessel needed a sermon or, worse, a formal series of them. There even floated before my thoughtful eyes the image of, say, *Colley's Sermons* or even *Colley on Life's Voyage*, and I decided in advance not to be a subscriber.

I was about to return from where I stood in the gently moving shadow of some sail or other when I heard, incredulously, a burst of applause, warmer this time and spontaneous. I do not have to point out to your lordship the rarity of the occasions on which a parson is applauded in full fig or as what young Mr Taylor describes as 'Dressed over all'. Groans and tears, exclamations of remorse and pious ejaculations he may look for if his sermon be touched with any kind of *enthusiasm*: silence and covert yawns will be his reward if he is content to be a dull, respectable fellow! But the applause I was hearing from the fo'castle was more proper for an entertainment! It was as if Colley were an acrobat or juggler. This second round of applause sounded as if (having earned the first one by keeping six dinner plates in the air at once) he now had

added a billiard cue stood on his forehead with a chamber pot
revolving on the top of it!

Now my curiosity was really roused and I was about to go
forrard when Deverel descended from his watch and at once,
with what I can only call deliberate meaning, began to discuss La
Brocklebank! I felt myself detected and was at once a little flat-
tered as any young fellow might be and a little apprehensive,
when I imagined the possible consequences of my connection
with her. She herself I saw standing on the starboard side of the
afterdeck and being lectured by Mr Prettiman. I drew Deverel
with me into the lobby, where we fenced a little. We spoke of the
lady with some freedom and it crossed my mind that during my
indisposition Deverel might have had more success than he cared
to admit, though he hinted at it. We may both be in the same
basket. Heavens above! But though a naval officer he is a gentleman, and however things turn out we shall not give each other
away. We drank a *tot* in the passenger saloon, he had gone about
his business and I was returning to my hutch when I was stopped
in my tracks by a great noise from the fo'castle and the most
unexpected noise of all—a positive crash of laughter! I was quite
overcome by the thought of Mr Colley as a wit and concluded at
once that he had left them to themselves and they were, like
schoolboys, amusing themselves with a mocking pantomime of
the master, who has rebuked then left them. I went up to the
afterdeck for a better view, then to the quarterdeck, but could see
no one on the fo'castle except the man stationed there as a lookout.
They were all inside, all gathered. Colley had said something, I
thought, and is now in his hutch, changing out of his *barbaric
finery*. But word had flown round the ship. The afterdeck was
filling below me with ladies and gentlemen and officers. Those
who dared had stationed themselves by me at the forrard rail of
the quarterdeck. The theatrical image that had haunted my mind
and coloured my speculations in the earlier events now seemed to
embrace the whole vessel. For one dizzy moment I wondered if
our officers were out in the expectation of mutiny! But Deverel
would have known, and he had said nothing. Yet everyone was
looking forward to the great, unknown part of the ship where the
people were indulging in whatever sport was afoot. We were
spectators and there, interruptedly seen beyond the boats on the
boom and the huge cylinder of the mainmast, was the stage. The
break of the fo'castle rose like the side of the house, yet furnished

with two ladders and two entrances, one on either side, that were provokingly like a stage—provoking, since a performance could not be guaranteed and our strange expectations were likely to be disappointed. I was never made so aware of the distance between the disorder of real life in its multifarious action, partial exhibition, irritating concealments and the stage simulacra that I had once taken as a fair representation of it! I did not care to ask what was going on and could not think how to find out unless I was willing to show an unbecoming degree of curiosity. Of course your lordship's favourite would have brought forward the heroine and her confidante—mine would have added the stage instruction *Enter two sailors*. Yet all I could hear was amusement growing in the fo'castle and something the same among our passengers, not to say officers. I waited on the event, and unexpectedly it came! Two ship's boys—not Young Gentlemen—shot out of the larboard doorway of the fo'castle, crossed out of sight behind the mainmast, then shot as suddenly into the starboard entrance! I was reflecting on the abject nature of the sermon that could be the occasion of such general and prolonged hilarity when I became aware of Captain Anderson, who also stood by the forward rail of the quarterdeck and stared forward inscrutably. Mr Summers, the first lieutenant, came racing up the ladder, his every movement conveying anxiety and haste. He went straight to Captain Anderson.

'Well, Mr Summers?'

'I beg you will allow me to take charge, sir.'

'We must not interfere with the church, Mr Summers.'

'Sir—the men, sir!'

'Well, sir?'

'They are in drink, sir!'

'Then see they are punished for it, Mr Summers.'

Captain Anderson turned away from Mr Summers and for the first time appeared to notice me. He called out across the deck.

'Good day, Mr Talbot! I trust you are enjoying our progress?'

I replied that I was, couching my rejoinder in words I have forgotten, for I was preoccupied by the extraordinary change in the captain. The face with which he is accustomed to await the approach of his fellow men may be said to be welcoming as the door of a gaol. He has, too, a way of projecting his under-jaw and lowering the sullen mass of his face on it, all the while staring up from under his brows, that I conceive to be positively terrifying to his inferiors. But today there was in his face and indeed in his speech a kind of gaiety!

But Lieutenant Summers had spoken again.

'At least allow me—look at that, sir!'

He was pointing. I turned.

Has your lordship ever reflected on the quaintness of the tradition that signalizes our attainment of learning by hanging a medieval hood round our necks and clapping a plasterer's board on our heads? (Should not the chancellor have a silver gilt hod carried before him? But I digress.) Two figures had appeared at the larboard entry. They were now *processing* across the deck to the starboard one. Perhaps the striking of the ship's bell and the surely sarcastic cry of 'All's well!' persuaded me that these figures were those in some fantastic clock. The foremost of the figures wore a black hood edged with fur, and wore it not hung down his back but up and over his head as we see in illuminated manuscripts from the age of Chaucer. It was up and round his face and held by one hand close under the chin in the fashion that I believe ladies would describe as a tippet. The other hand was on the hip with elbow akimbo. The creature crossed the deck with an exaggeratedly mincing parody of the female gait. The second figure wore—apart from the loose garments of canvas which are the people's common wear—a mortar-board of decidedly battered appearance. It followed the first figure in shambling pursuit. As the two of them disappeared into the fo'castle there was another crash of laughter, then a cheer.

Dare I say what from its subtlety your lordship may well consider to be retrospective wisdom? This play-acting was not directed only inwards towards the fo'castle. It was aimed *aft* at us! Have you not seen an actor consciously throw a soliloquy outwards and upwards to the gallery and even into one corner of it? These two figures that had paraded before us had cast their portrayal of human weakness and folly directly *aft* to where their betters were assembled! If your lordship has any concept of the speed with which scandal spreads in a ship you will the more readily credit the immediacy—no, the instantaneity—with which news of the business in the fo'castle, whatever it was, now flashed through the ship. The people, the men, the crew—they had purposes of their own! They were astir! We were united, I believe, in our awareness of the threat to social stability that might at any moment arise among the common sailors and emigrants! It was

horseplay and insolence at liberty in the fo'castle. Mr Colley and
Captain Anderson were at fault—the one for being the occasion
of such insolence, the other for allowing it. During a whole
generation (granted the glory attendant on our successful arms)
the civilized world has had cause to lament the results of indisci-
pline among the Gallic Race. They will hardly recover, I believe.
I began to descend from the quarterdeck in disgust with a bare
acknowledgement of salutations on every side. Mr Prettiman now
stood with Miss Granham on the afterdeck. He might well, I
thought bitterly enough, have an ocular demonstration of the
results of the liberty he advocated! Captain Anderson had left the
quarterdeck to Summers, who still stared forward with a tense
face as if he expected the appearance of the enemy or Leviathan
or the sea serpent. I was about to descend to the waist when Mr
Cumbershum appeared from our lobby. I paused, wondering
whether to interrogate him; but while I did so, young Tommy
Taylor positively burst out of the fo'castle of all places and came
racing aft. Cumbershum grabbed him.

'More decorum about the deck, young fellow!'

'Sir—I must see the first lieutenant, sir—it's true as God's my
judge!'

'Swearing are you again, you little sod?'

'It's the parson, sir, I told you it was!'

'Mr Colley to you, sir, and damn your impudence for a squeaking little bugger!'

'It's true, sir, it's true! Mr Colley's there in the fo'castle as
drunk as the butcher's boots!'

'Get below, sir, or I'll masthead you!'

Mr Taylor disappeared. My own astonishment was complete at
finding the parson had been present in the fo'castle during all the
various noises that had resounded thence—had been there while
yet there was play-acting and the clock-figures mountebanking
for our instruction. I no longer thought of retiring to my hutch.
For now not merely the afterdeck and quarterdeck were crowded.
Those persons who were sufficiently active had climbed into the
lower parts of the mizzen shrouds while below me, the waist—
the pit, I suppose in theatrical terms—had yet more spectators.
What was curious was that round me on the afterdeck, the ladies
no less than the gentlemen were in, or exhibited a condition of,
shocked cheerfulness. They would, it seemed, have been glad to
be assured the news was not true—would rather be assured—

were desperately sorry if it *was* true—would not for the wide
world have had such a thing happen—and if, against all probab-
ility, no, possibility, it *was* true, why never, never, never—Only
Miss Granham descended with a set face from the afterdeck,
turned and vanished into the lobby. Mr Prettiman with his gun
stared from her to the fo'castle and back again. Then he hastened
after her. But other than this severe pair the afterdeck was full of
whispering and nodding animation fitted more for the retiring
room at an assembly than the deck of a man-of-war. Below me
Mr Brocklebank leaned heavily on his stick with the women
nodding their bonnets at him on either side. Cumbershum stood
by them, silent. It was at some point in this period of expectancy
that the silence became general so that the gentle noises of the
ship—sea noises against her planks, the soft touch of the wind
fingering her rigging—became audible. In the silence, and as if
produced by it, my ears—*our* ears—detected the distant sound of
a man's voice. It sang. We knew at once it must be Mr Colley. He
sang and his voice was meagre as his appearance. The tune and
the words were well enough known. It might be heard in an
alehouse or a drawing room. I cannot tell where Mr Colley learnt
it.

'*Where have you been all the day, Billy Boy?*'

Then there followed a short silence, after which he broke into
a different song that I did not know. The words must have been
warm, I think, country matters perhaps, for there was laughter to
back them. A peasant, born to stone-gathering and bird-scaring,
might have picked them up under the hedge where the workers
pause at noon.

When I go over the scene in my mind I am at a loss to account
for our feeling that Colley's misdemeanour would be rounded
out to the fullness of the event. I had been vexed earlier to see
how little the stage of the fo'castle was to be relied on for conveying to us the shape and dimensions of this drama! Yet now I
too waited. Your lordship might demand with reason, 'Have you
never heard of a drunken parson before?' I can only reply that I
had indeed heard of one but had not yet seen one. Moreover,
there are times and places.

The singing stopped. There began to be laughter again, applause, then a clamour of shouts and jeers. It seemed after a while
that we were indeed to be cheated of the event—which was
hardly to be borne, seeing how much in sickness, danger and

boredom we had paid for our seats. However, it was at this
critical juncture that Captain Anderson ascended from his cabin
to the quarterdeck, took his place at the forrard rail of it and
surveyed the theatre and audience. His face was as severe as Miss
Granham's. He spoke sharply to Mr Deverel, who now had the
watch, informing him (in a voice which seemed to make the fact
directly attributable to some negligence on Mr Deverel's part)
that *the parson was still there*. He then took a turn or two round his
side of the quarterdeck, came back to the rail, stopped by it, and
spoke to Mr Deverel more cheerfully.

'Mr Deverel. Be good enough to have the parson informed he
must now return to his cabin.'

I believe not another muscle stirred in the ship as Mr Deverel
repeated the order to Mr Willis, who saluted and went forward
with all eyes on his back. Our astonished ears heard Mr Colley
address him with a string of endearments that would have—and
perhaps *did*—make La Brocklebank blush like a paeony. The
young gentleman came stumbling out of the fo'castle and ran back
sniggering. But in truth none among us paid him much attention.
For now, like some pigmy Polyphemus, like whatever is at once
strange and disgusting, the parson appeared in the lefthand doorway of the fo'castle. His ecclesiastical garment had gone and the
marks of his degree. His wig had gone—his very breeches, stockings and shoes had been taken from him. Some charitable soul
had in pity, I supposed, supplied him with one of the loose
canvas garments that the common people wear about the ship;
and this because of his diminutive stature was sufficient to cover
his loins. He was not alone. A young stalwart had him in charge.
This fellow was supporting Mr Colley, whose head lay back on
the man's breast. As the curious pair came uncertainly past the
mainmast, Mr Colley pushed back so that they stopped. It was
evident that his mind had become only lightly linked to his
understanding. He appeared to be in a state of extreme and sunny
enjoyment. His eyes moved indifferently, as if taking no print of
what they saw. Surely his frame was not one that could afford
him any pleasure! His skull now the wig no longer covered it was
seen to be small and narrow. His legs had no calves; but dame
Nature in a frivolous mood had furnished him with great feet and
knots of knees that betrayed their peasant origin. He was muttering some nonsense of *fol de rol* or the like. Then, as if seeing his
audience for the first time, he heaved himself away from his

assistant, stood on splayed feet and flung out his arms as if to embrace us all.

'Joy! Joy! Joy!'

Then his face became thoughtful. He turned to his right, walked slowly and carefully to the bulwark and pissed against it. What a shrieking and covering of faces there was from the ladies, what growls from us! Mr Colley turned back to us and opened his mouth. Not even the captain could have caused a more immediate silence.

Mr Colley raised his right hand and spoke, though slurredly.

'The blessing of God the Father Almighty, God the Son and God the Holy Ghost be with you and remain with you always.'

Then there was a commotion I can tell you! If the man's uncommonly public micturation had shocked the ladies, to be blessed by a drunk man in a canvas shirt caused screams, hasty retreats and, I am told, one *évanouissement*! It was no more than seconds after this that the servant, Phillips, and Mr Summers, the first lieutenant, lugged the poor fool out of sight while the seaman who had helped him aft stood and stared after them. When Colley was out of sight the man looked up at the quarterdeck, touched his forelock and went back to the fo'castle.

On the whole I think the audience was well enough satisfied. Next to the ladies Captain Anderson seemed to be the principal beneficiary of Colley's performance. He became positively sociable with the ladies, voluntarily breaking away from his sacred side of the quarterdeck and bidding them welcome. Though he firmly but courteously declined to discuss *l'affaire Colley*, there was a lightness about his step and indeed a light in his eye that I had supposed occasioned in a naval officer only by the imminence of battle! What animation had possessed the other officers passed away quickly enough. They must have seen enough drunkenness and been part of enough to see this as no more than an event in a long history. And what was the sight of Colley's urine to naval gentlemen who had perhaps seen decks smeared with the viscera and streaming with the blood of their late companions? I returned to my hutch, determined to give you as full and vivid an account of the episode as was in my power. Yet even while I was busy leading up to the events the further events of his fall raced past me. While I was yet describing the strange noises from the fo'castle, I heard the sound of a door opened clumsily on the other side of the lobby. I jumped up and stared (by means of my *louvre* or spyhole) across it. Lo, Colley came out of his cabin! He held a sheet of paper in his hand and he still smiled that smile of aery contentment and joy. He went in this joyous distraction in the direction of the necessary offices on that side of the ship. Evidently he still dwelt in a land of faery which would vanish presently and leave him—

Well. Where will it leave him? He is quite unpractised in the management of spiritous liquors. I imagined his distress on coming to himself and I started to laugh—then changed my mind. The closeness of my cabin became a positive fetor.

This is the fifty-first day of our voyage, I think; and then again perhaps it is not. I have lost interest in the calendar and almost lost it in the voyage too. We have our shipboard calendar of events which are trivial enough. Nothing has happened since Colley entertained us. He is much condemned. Captain Anderson continues benign. Colley himself has not been out of his hutch in the four days which have passed since his drunkenness. No one but the servant has seen him if you except me on the occasion when he took his own paper to the loo! Enough of him.

What might amuse you more is the kind of *country dance* we young fellows have been performing round La Brocklebank. I have not yet identified her *Sailor Hero* but am sure that Deverel has had to do with her. I taxed him with it and drew an admission from him. We agreed that a man might well suffer shipwreck on *that* coast and have decided to stand shoulder to shoulder in mutual defence. A mixed metaphor, my lord, so you can see how dull I find myself. To resume. We both think that at the moment she is inclined to Cumbershum. I owned that this was a relief to me and Deverel agreed. We had feared, both of us, to be in the same difficulty over our common *inamorata*. You will remember that I had some hare-brained scheme, since Colley was so clearly *épris* with her, of having a MUCH ADO ABOUT NOTHING and bringing this Beatrice and Benedict into a mountain of affection for each other! I told Deverel this, at which he was silent for a while, then burst out laughing. I was about to inform him plainly that I took exception to his conduct when he asked my pardon in the most graceful way. But, said he, the coincidence was past the wit of man to invent and he would share the jest with me if I would give him my word to say nothing of what he told me. We were interrupted at this point and I do not know what the jest is, but you shall have it when I do.

I have been remiss and let a few days go by without attention to the journal. I have felt a lethargy. There has been little to do but walk the deck, drink with anyone who will, walk the deck again, perhaps speaking to this passenger or that. I believe I did not tell you that when 'Mrs Brocklebank' issued from the cabin she proved to be if anything younger than her daughter! I have avoided both her and the fair Zenobia, who *glows* in this heat so as almost to turn a man's stomach! Cumbershum is not so delicate. The boredom of the voyage in these hot and next to windless latitudes has increased the consumption of strong spirits among us. I had thought to give you a full list of our passengers but have given up. They would not interest you. Let them remain κωφὰ πρόσωπα. What is of some interest however is the behaviour—or the lack of it—of Colley. The fact is that since the fellow's fall he has not left his cabin. Phillips the servant goes in occasionally and I believe that Mr Summers has visited him, I suppose thinking it part of a first lieutenant's duty. A lustreless fellow like Colley might well feel some diffidence at coming again among ladies and gentlemen. The ladies are particularly strict on him. For my own part, the fact that Captain Anderson *rode the man hard*, in Deverel's phrase, is sufficient to temper any inclination I might have absolutely to reject Colley as a human being!

Deverel and I agree that Brocklebank is or has been the keeper of both the doxies. I had known that the world of art is not to be judged by the accepted standards of morality but would prefer him to set up his brothel in another place. However, they have two hutches, one for the 'parents' and one for the 'daughter', so he does at least make a tiny gesture towards preserving appearances. Appearances are preserved and everyone is happy, even Miss Granham. As for Mr Prettiman, I suppose he notices nothing. Long live illusion, say I. Let us export it to our colonies with all the other benefits of civilization!

60

I have just come from the passenger saloon, where I have sat for a long time with Summers. The conversation is worth recording, though I have an uneasy feeling that it tells against me. I am bound to say that Summers is the person of all in this ship who does His Majesty's Service the most credit. Deverel is naturally more the gentleman but not assiduous in his duties. As for the others—they may be dismissed *en masse*. The difference had been in my mind and I did, in a way I now fear he may have found offensive, discuss the desirability of men being elevated above their first station in life. It was thoughtless of me and Summers replied with some bitterness.

'Mr Talbot, sir, I do not know how to say this or indeed whether I should—but you yourself made it plain in a way that put the matter beyond misunderstanding, that a man's original is branded on his forehead, never to be removed.'

'Come, Mr Summers—I did not so!'

'Do you not remember?'

'Remember what?'

He was silent for a while. Then——

'I understand. It is plain when I see it from your point of view. Why should you remember?'

'Remember *what*, sir?'

Again he was silent. Then he looked away and seemed to be reading the words of the following sentence off the bulkhead.

'"Well, Summers, allow me to congratulate you on imitating to perfection the manners and speech of a somewhat higher station in life than the one you was born to."'

Now it was my turn to be silent. What he said was true. Your lordship may, if you choose, turn back in this very journal and find the words there. I have done so myself, and re-read the account of that first meeting. I believe Summers does not give me credit for the state of bewilderment and embarrassment in which I had then found myself, but the words, the very words, are there!

'I ask your pardon, Mr Summers. It was—insufferable.'

'But true, sir,' said Summers, bitterly. 'In our country for all her greatness there is one thing she cannot do and that is translate a person wholly out of one class into another. Perfect translation from one language into another is impossible. Class is the British language.'

'Come, sir,' said I, 'will you not believe me? Perfect translation from one language to another is possible and I could give you an example of it. So is perfect translation from class to class.'

'*Imitating* to perfection——'

'Perfect in this, that you are a gentleman.'

Summers flushed red and his face only slowly resumed its wonted bronze. It was high time we moved our ground.

'Yet you see, my dear fellow, we have at least one example among us where the translation is not a success!'

'I must suppose you to refer to Mr Colley. It was my purpose to raise that subject.'

'The man has stepped out of his station without any merit to support the elevation.'

'I do not see how his conduct can be traced to his original for we do not know what it was.'

'Come. It appears in his physique, his speech and above all in what I can only call his habit of subordination. I swear he has got out of the peasantry by a kind of greasy obsequiousness. Now for example—Bates, the brandy, please!—I can myself drink brandy as long as you please and I issue a guarantee that no man and particularly no lady will see in me the kind of behaviour by which Mr Colley has amused us and affronted them. Colley, plied, as we must suppose, with spirits there in the fo'castle, had neither the strength to refuse it nor the breeding which would have enabled him to resist its more destructive effects.'

'This wisdom should be put in a book.'

'Laugh if you will, sir. Today I must not be offended with you.'

'But there is another matter and I had intended to raise it. We have no physician and the man is mortally sick.'

'How can that be? He is young and suffering from no more than over-indulgence in liquor.'

'Still? I have talked with the servant. I have entered the cabin and seen for myself. In many years of service neither Phillips nor

I have seen anything like it. The bed is filthy, yet the man, though he breathes every now and then, does not stir in it. His face is pressed down and hidden. He lies on his stomach, one hand above his head and clutched into the bolster, the other clutching an old ringbolt left in the timber.'

'I marvel you can eat after it.'

'Oh that! I tried to turn him over.'

'Tried? You must have succeeded. You have three times his strength.'

'Not in these circumstances.'

'I own, Mr Summers, that I have not observed much intemperance in Colley's line of life. But the story goes that the Senior Tutor at my own college, having dined too well before a service, rose from his seat, staggered to the lectern, slumped, holding on to the brass eagle and was heard to mutter, "I should have been down had it not been for this bleeding Dodo." But I daresay you never heard the story.'

Mr Summers shook his head.

'I have been much abroad,' he replied gravely. 'The event made little noise in that part of the Service where I then was.'

'A hit, a palpable hit! But depend on it, young Colley will lift up his head.'

Summers stared into his untouched glass.

'He has a strange power. It is almost as if the Newtonian Force is affected. The hand that holds the ring-bolt might be made of steel. He lies, dinted into his bunk, drawn down into it as if made of lead.'

'There he must stay then.'

'Is that all, Mr Talbot? Are you as indifferent to the man's fate as others are?'

'I am not an officer in this ship!'

'The more able to help, sir.'

'How?'

'I may speak to you freely, may I not? Well then—how has the man been treated?'

'He was at first an object of one man's specific dislike, then an object of general indifference that was leading to contempt even before his latest—escapade.'

Summers turned and stared out of the great stern window for a while. Then he looked back at me.

'What I say now could well ruin me if I have misjudged your character.'

'Character? *My* character? You have examined my character? You set yourself up——'

'Forgive me—nothing is further from my mind than offending you and if I did not believe the case desperate——'

'What case, for God's sake?'

'We know your birth, your prospective position—why—men—and women—will flatter you in the hope or expectation of gaining the governor's ear——'

'Good God—Mr Summers!'

'Wait, wait! Understand me, Mr Talbot—I do not complain!'

'You sound uncommonly like a man complaining, sir!'

I had half-risen from my seat; but Summers stretched out his hand in a gesture of such simple—'supplication' I suppose I must call it—that I sat down again.

'Proceed then, if you must!'

'I do not speak in my own behalf.'

For a while we were both silent. Then Summers swallowed, deeply as if there had been a real drink in his mouth and that no small one.

'Sir, you have used your birth and your prospective position to get for yourself an unusual degree of attention and comfort—I do not complain—dare not! Who am I to question the customs of our society or indeed, the laws of nature? In a sentence, you have exercised the privileges of your position. I am asking you to shoulder its responsibilities.'

During—it may be—half a minute; for what is time in a ship, or to revert to that strange metaphor of existence that came to me so strongly during Mr Colley's exhibition, what is time in a theatre? During that time, however long or short, I passed through number-less emotions—rage I think, confusion, irritation, amusement and an embarrassment for which I was most annoyed, seeing that I had only now discovered the seriousness of Mr Colley's condition.

'That was a notable impertinence, Mr Summers!'

As my vision cleared I saw that the man had a positive pallor under his brown skin.

'Let me think, man! Steward! Another brandy here!'

Bates brought it at the run for I must have ordered it in a more than usually peremptory voice. I did not drink at once but sat and stared into my glass.

The trouble was that in everything the man had said, he was right!

After a while, he spoke again.

'A visit from you, sir, to such a man——'

'I? Go in that stinking hole?'

'There is a phrase that suits your situation, sir. It is *Noblesse oblige.*'

'Oh be damned to your French, Summers! But I tell you this and make what you choose of it! I believe in fair play!'

'That I am prepared to accept.'

'You? That is profoundly generous of you, sir!'

Then we were silent again. It must have been in a harsh enough voice that I spoke at last.

'Well, Mr Summers, you were right, were you not? I have been remiss. But those who administer correction out of school must not expect to be thanked for it.'

'I fear not.'

This was too much.

'Fear nothing, man! How mean, how vindictive, how small do you think I am? Your precious career is safe enough from me. I do not care to be lumped in with the enemy!'

At this moment, Deverel came in with Brocklebank and some others so that the conversation perforce became general. As soon as possible I took my brandy back to my hutch and sat there, thinking what to do. I called Wheeler and told him to send Phillips to me. He had the insolence to ask me what I wanted the man for and I sent him about his business in no uncertain terms. Phillips came soon enough.

'Phillips, I shall pay a call on Mr Colley. I do not wish to be offended by the sights and smells of a sick-room. Be good enough to clean up the place and, as far as you can, the bunk. Let me know when it is done.'

I thought for a moment he would demur but he changed his mind and withdrew. Wheeler stuck his head in again but I had plenty of rage left over and told him if he was so idle he might as well go across and lend Phillips a hand. This removed him at once. It must have been a full hour before Phillips tapped on my door and said he had done *what he could*. I rewarded him, then fearing the worst went across the lobby attended by Phillips but with Wheeler hovering as if expecting a half-guinea for allowing Phillips the use of me. These fellows are as bad as parsons over

fees for christenings, weddings and funerals! They were disposed
to mount guard at the door of Mr Colley's cabin but I told them
to be off and watch till they disappeared. I then went in.

Colley's hutch was a mirror image of mine. Phillips, if he had
not rid it completely of stench, had done the next best thing by
covering it with some pungent but not unpleasantly aromatic
odour. Colley lay as Summers had said. One hand still clutched
what both Falconer and Summers agreed was a ringbolt in the
side of the ship. His scrubby head was pressed into the bolster,
the face turned away. I stood by the bunk and was at a loss. I had
little experience of visiting the sick.

'Mr Colley!'

There was no reply. I tried again.

'Mr Colley, sir. Some days ago I desired further acquaintance
with you. But you have not appeared. This was too bad, sir. May
I not expect your company on deck today?'

That was handsome enough, I thought in all conscience. I was
so certain of success in raising the man's spirits that a fleeting
awareness of the boredom I should experience in his company
passed through my mind and took some edge off my determination to rouse him. I backed away.

'Well sir, if not today, then when you are ready! I will await
you. Pray call on me!'

Was that not a foolish thing to say? It was an open invitation
to the man to pester me as much as he would. I backed to the
door and turned in time to see Wheeler and Phillips vanish. I
looked round the cabin. It contained even less than mine. The
shelf held a Bible, a prayer book, and a dirty, dog-eared volume,
purchased I imagine at third hand and clumsily rebound in brown
paper, which proved to be *Classes Plantarum*. The others were
works of devotion—Baxter's *Saints Everlasting Rest*, and the like.
There was a pile of manuscript on the flap of the table. I closed
the door and went back to my hutch again.

Scarce had I got my own door open when I found Summers
following me close. He had, it appeared, watched my movements.
I motioned him inside.

'Well Mr Talbot?'

'I got no response from him. However, I visited him as you
saw and I did what I could. I have, I believe, discharged those
responsibilities you were so kind as to bring to my notice. I can
do no more.'

To my astonishment he raised a glass of brandy to his lips. He had carried it concealed or at least unnoticed—for who would look for such a thing in the hands of so temperate a man?

'Summers—my dear Summers! You have taken to drink!'

That he had not indeed was seen only too clearly when he choked and coughed at the first taste of the liquid.

'You need more practice, man! Join Deverel and me some time!'

He drank again, then breathed deeply.

'Mr Talbot, you said that today you could not be angry with me. You jested but it was the word of a gentleman. Now I am to come at you again.'

'I am weary of the whole subject.'

'I assure you, Mr Talbot, this is my last.'

I turned my canvas chair round and sank into it.

'Say what you have to say, then.'

'Who is responsible for the man's state?'

'Colley? Devil take it! Himself! Let us not mince round the truth like a pair of church spinsters! You are going to spread the responsibility, are you not? You will include the captain and I agree—who else?—Cumbershum? Deverel? Yourself? The starboard watch? The world?'

'I will be plain, sir. The best medicine for Mr Colley would be a gentle visit from the captain of whom he stands in such awe. The only man among us with sufficient influence to bring the captain to such an action, is yourself.'

'Then devil take it again, for I shall not!'

'You said I would "Spread the responsibility". Let me do so now. *You* are the man most responsible——'

'Christ in his heaven, Summers, you are the——'

'Wait! Wait!'

'Are you drunk?'

'I said I would be plain. I will stand shot, sir, though my career is now in far more danger from you than it ever was from the French! They, after all, could do no more than kill or maim me— but you——'

'You *are* drunk—you must be!'

'Had you not in a bold and thoughtless way outfaced our captain on his own quarterdeck—had you not made use of your rank and prospects and connections to strike a blow at the very foundations of his authority, all this might not have happened.

He is brusque and he detests the clergy, he makes no secret of it. But had you not acted as you did at that time, he would never in the very next few minutes have crushed Colley with his anger and continued to humiliate *him* because he could not humiliate *you*.'

'If Colley had had the sense to read Anderson's Standing Orders——'

'You are a passenger as he is. Did you read them?'

Through my anger I thought back. It was true to some extent—no, wholly true. On my first day Wheeler had murmured something about them—they were to be found outside my cabin and at a suitable opportunity I should——

'*Did* you read them, Mr Talbot?'

'No.'

Has your lordship ever come across the odd fact that to be seated rather than erect induces or at least tends towards a state of calm? I cannot say that my anger was sinking away but it was stayed. As if he, too, wished us both to be calm, Summers sat on the edge of my bunk, thus looking slightly down at me. Our relative positions seemed to make the *didactic* inevitable.

'The captain's Standing Orders would seem to you as brusque as he is, sir. But the fact is they are wholly necessary. Those applying to passengers lie under the same necessity, the same urgency, as the rest.'

'Very well, very well!'

'You have not seen a ship at a moment of crisis, sir. A ship may be taken flat aback and sunk all in a few moments. Ignorant passengers, stumbling in the way, delaying a necessary order or making it inaudible——'

'You have said enough.'

'I hope so.'

'You are certain I am responsible for nothing else that has gone awry? Perhaps Mrs East's miscarriage?'

'If our captain could be induced to befriend a sick man——'

'Tell me, Summers—why are you so curious about Colley?'

He finished his drink and stood up.

'Fair play, *noblesse oblige*. My education is not like yours, sir, it has been strictly practical. But I know a term under which both phrases might be—what is the word?—subsumed. I hope you will find it.'

With that, he went quickly out of my hutch and away somewhere, leaving me in a fine mixture of emotions! Anger, yes, embarrassment, yes—but also a kind of rueful amusement at having been taught two lessons in one day by the same schoolmaster! I damned him for a busybody, then half undamned him again, for he is a likeable fellow, common or not. What the devil had he to do with *my* duty?

Was that the word? An odd fellow indeed! Truly as good a translation as yours, my lord! All those countless leagues from one end of a British ship to the other! To hear him give orders about the deck—and then to meet him over a glass—he can pass between one sentence and the next from all the jargoning of the Tarpaulin language to the plain exchanges which take place between gentlemen. Now the heat was out of my blood I could see how he had thought himself professionally at risk in speaking so to me and I laughed a little ruefully again. We may characterize him in our theatrical terms as—enter a Good Man!

Well, thought I to myself, there is this in common between Good Men and children—we must never disappoint them! Only half of the confounded business had been attended to. I had visited the sick—now I must try my influence in adjusting matters between Colley and our gloomy captain. I own the prospect daunted me a little. I returned to the passenger saloon and brandy and in the evening, to tell the truth, found myself in no condition to exercise judgement. I think this was deliberate and an endeavour to postpone what I knew must be a difficult interview. At last I went with what must have been a stately gait to my bunk and have some recollection of Wheeler assisting me into it. I was bosky indeed and fell into a profound sleep to wake later with the headache and some queasiness. When I tried my repeater I found it was yet early in the morning. Mr Brocklebank was snoring. There were noises coming from the hutch next to mine from which I inferred that the fair Zenobia was busy with yet another lover or, it may be, client. Had *she*, I wondered, also wanted to reach the governor's ear? Should I one day find myself approached by her to get an official portrait of the governor executed by Mr Brocklebank? It was a sour consideration for the early hours that stemmed straight from Summers's frankness. I damned him all over again. The air in my hutch was thick, so I threw on my great coat, scuffed my feet into slippers and felt my way out on deck. Here there was light enough to make out the difference between the ship, the sea, and the sky but no more. I remembered my resolution to speak with the captain on Colley's behalf with positive revulsion. What had seemed a boring duty when I was elevated with drink now presented itself as downright unpleasant. I called to mind that the captain was said to take a constitutional on the quarterdeck at dawn, but such a time and place was too early for our interview.

Nevertheless, the early morning air, unhealthy as it may have been, seemed in a curious way to alleviate the headache, the queasiness and even my slight uneasiness at the prospect of the interview. I therefore set myself to marching to and fro between the break of the afterdeck and the mainmast. While I did so, I tried to see all round the situation. We had yet more months of sea travel before us in the captain's company. I neither liked nor esteemed Captain Anderson nor was able to think of him as anything but a petty tyrant. Endeavour—it could be no more— to assist the wretched Colley could not but exacerbate the dislike that lay just beyond the bounds of the unacknowledged truce between us. The captain accepted my position as your lordship's godson, *et cetera*. I accepted his as a captain of one of His Majesty's ships. The limit of his powers in respect of passengers was obscure; and so was the limit of my possible influence with his superiors! Like dogs cautious of each other's strength we stepped high and round each other. And now I was to try to influence his behaviour towards a contemptible member of the profession he hated! I was thus, unless I was very careful, in danger of putting myself under an obligation to him. The thought was not to be borne. At one time and another in my long contemplation I believe I uttered a deal of oaths! Indeed, I had half a mind to abandon the whole project.

However, the damp but soft air of these latitudes, no matter what the subsequent effect on one's health, is certainly to be recommended as an antidote to an aching head and sour stomach! As I came more and more to myself I found it more and more in my power to exercise judgement and contemplate action. Those ambitious of attaining to statecraft or whose birth renders the exercise of it inevitable would do well to face the trials of a voyage such as ours! It was, I remember, very clearly in my mind how your lordship's benevolence had got for me not only some years of employment in a new and unformed society but had also ensured that the preliminary voyage should give me time for reflection and the exercise of my not inconsiderable powers of thought. I decided I must proceed on the principle of the use of *least force*. What would move Captain Anderson to do as I wished? Would there be anything more powerful with him than self-interest? That wretched little man, Mr Colley! But there was no doubt about it. Whether it was, as Summers said, *my* fault in part or not, there was no doubt he had been persecuted. That he was a fool and had made a cake of himself was neither here nor there. Deverel, little Tommy Taylor, Summers himself—they all implied that Captain Anderson for no matter what reason had deliberately made the man's life intolerable to him. The devil was in it if I could find any word to sum up both Summers's phrase of '*Noblesse Oblige*' and mine of 'Fair Play' other than 'Justice'. There's a large and schoolbook word to run directly on like a rock in mid-ocean! There was a kind of terror in it too since it had moved out of school and the university onto the planks of a warship—which is to say the planks of a tyranny in little! What about *my* career?

Yet I was warmed by Summers's belief in my ability and more by his confident appeal to my sense of justice. What creatures we are! Here was I, who only a few weeks before had thought highly of myself because my mother wept to see me go, now warming my hands at the small fire of a lieutenant's approval!

However, at last I saw how to go on.

61

Well! I returned to my hutch, washed, shaved, and dressed with care. I took my morning draught in the saloon and then drew myself up as before *a regular stitcher*. I did not enjoy the prospect of the interview, I can tell you! For if I had established my position in the ship, it was even more evident that the captain had established his! He was indeed our moghool. To remove my foreboding I went very briskly to the quarterdeck, positively bounding up the ladders. Captain Anderson, the wind now being on the starboard quarter, was standing there and facing into it. This is his privilege; and is said by seamen to rise from the arcane suggestion that 'Danger lies to windward' though in the next breath they will assure you that the most dangerous thing in the world is 'a lee shore'. The first, I suppose, refers to a possible enemy ship, the second to reefs and suchlike natural hazards. Yet I have, I believe, a more penetrating suggestion to make as to the origin of the captain's privilege. Whatever sector of the ship is to windward is almost free from the stench she carries everywhere with her. I do not mean the stink of urine and ordure but that pervasive stench from the carcass of the ship herself and her rotten bilge of gravel and sand. Perhaps more modern ships with their iron ballast may smell more sweetly; but captains, I dare say, in this Noah's service will continue to walk the windward side even if ships should run clean out of wind and take to rowing. The tyrant must live as free of stink as possible.

I find that without conscious intention I have delayed this description as I had dallied over my draught. I live again those moments when I drew myself together for the jump!

Well then, I stationed myself on the opposite side of the quarterdeck, affecting to take no notice of the man other than to salute him casually with a lifted finger. My hope was that his recent gaiety and elevation of spirits would lead him to address me first. My judgement was correct. His new air of satisfaction was indeed apparent, for when he saw me he came across, his yellow teeth showing.

'A fine day for you, Mr Talbot!'

'Indeed it is, sir. Do we make as much progress as is common in these latitudes?'

'I doubt that we shall achieve more than an average of a knot over the next day or two.'

'Twenty-four sea miles a day.'

'Just so, sir. Warships are generally slower in their advance than most people suppose.'

'Well sir, I must confess to finding these latitudes more agreeable than any I have experienced. Could we but tow the British Isles to this part of the world, how many of our social problems would be solved! The mango would fall in our mouths.'

'You have a quaint fancy there, sir. Do you mean to include Ireland?'

'No sir. I would offer her to the United States of America, sir.'

'Let them have the first refusal, eh, Mr Talbot?'

'Hibernia would lie snugly enough alongside New England. We should see what we should see!'

'It would remove half a watch of my crew at a blow.'

'Well worth the loss, sir. What a noble prospect the ocean is under a low sun! Only when the sun is high does the sea seem to lack that indefinable air of Painted Art which we are able to observe at sunrise and sunset.'

'I am so accustomed to the sight that I do not see it. Indeed, I am grateful—if the phrase is not meaningless in the circumstances—to the oceans for another quality.'

'And that is?'

'Their power of isolating a man from his fellows.'

'Of isolating a captain, sir. The rest of humanity at sea must live only too much herded. The effect on them is not of the best. Circe's task must not have been hindered, to say the least, by the profession of her victims!'

Directly I had said this I realized how cutting it might sound. But I saw by the blankness of the captain's face, then its frown, that he was trying to remember what had happened to any ship of that name.

'Herded?'

'Packed together, I ought to have said. But how balmy the air is! I declare it seems almost insupportable that I must descend again and busy myself with my journal.'

Captain Anderson checked at the word 'journal' as if he had trodden on a stone. I affected not to notice but continued cheerfully.

'It is partly an amusement, captain, and partly a duty. It is, I suppose, what you would call a "log".'

'You must find little to record in such a situation as this.'

'Indeed, sir, you are mistaken. I have not time nor paper sufficient to record all the interesting events and personages of the voyage together with my own observations on them. Look— there is Mr Prettiman! A personage for you! His opinions are notorious, are they not?'

But Captain Anderson was still staring at me.

'Personages?'

'You must know,' said I laughing, 'that had I not his lordship's direct instructions to me I should still have been scribbling. It is my ambition to out-Gibbon Mr Gibbon and this gift to a godfather falls conveniently.'

Our tyrant was pleased to smile, but quiveringly, like a man who knows that to have a tooth pulled is less painful than to have the exquisite torturer left in.

'We may all be famous, then,' said he. 'I had not looked for it.'

'That is for the future. You must know, sir, that to the unhappiness of us all, his lordship has found himself temporarily vexed by the gout. It is my hope that in such a disagreeable situation, a frank, though private account of my travels and of the society in which I find myself may afford him some diversion.'

Captain Anderson took an abrupt turn up and down the deck, then stood directly before me.

'The officers of the ship in which you travel must bulk large in such an account.'

'They are objects of a landsman's interest and curiosity.'

'The captain particularly so?'

'You sir? I had not considered that. But you are, after all, the king or emperor of our floating society with prerogatives of justice and mercy. Yes. I suppose you do bulk large in my journal and will continue to do so.'

Captain Anderson turned on his heel and marched away. He kept his back to me and stared up wind. I saw that his head was sunk again, his hands clasped behind his back. I supposed that his jaw must be projecting once more as a foundation on which to sink the sullenness of his face. There was no doubt at all of the effect of my words, either on him or on *me*! For I found myself quivering as the first lieutenant had quivered when he dared to beard Mr Edmund Talbot! I spoke, I know not what, to Cumbershum, who had the watch. He was discomforted, for it was clean against the tyrant's Standing Orders and I saw, out of the corner of my eye, how the captain's hands tightened on each other behind his back. It was not a situation that should be prolonged. I bade the lieutenant good day and descended from the quarterdeck. I was glad enough to get back into my hutch, where I found of all things that my hands still had a tendency to tremble! I sat, therefore, getting my breath back and allowing my pulse to slow.

At length I began to consider the captain once more and try to predict his possible course of action. Does not the operation of a *statist* lie wholly in his power to affect the future of other people; and is not that power founded directly on his ability to predict their behaviour? Here, thought I, was the chance to observe the success or failure of my prentice hand! How would the man respond to the hint I had given him? It was not a subtle one; but then, I thought, from the directness of his questions that he was a simple creature at bottom. It was possible that he had not noticed the suggestiveness of my mentioning Mr Prettiman and his extreme beliefs! Yet I felt certain that mention of my journal would force him to look back over the whole length of the voyage and consider what sort of figure he might cut in an account of it. Sooner or later he would stub his toe over the Colley affair and remember how he had treated the man. He must see that however I myself had provoked him, nevertheless, by indulging his animosity against Colley, he had been cruel and unjust.

How would he behave then? How had I behaved when Summers had revealed to me my portion of responsibility in the affair? I tried out a scene or two for our floating theatre. I pictured Anderson descending from the quarterdeck and walking in the lobby casually, so as not to seem interested in the man. He might well stand consulting his own fading Orders, written out in a fair and clerkly hand. Then at a convenient moment, no one being by—oh no! he would have to let it be seen so that I should record it in my journal!—he would march into the hutch where Colley lay, shut the door, sit by the bunk and chat till they were a couple of bosoms. Why, Anderson might well stand in for an archbishop or even His Majesty! How could Colley not be roused by such amiable condescension? The captain would confess that he himself had committed just such a folly a year or two before——

I could not imagine it, that is the plain truth. The conceit remained artificial. Such behaviour was beyond Anderson. He might, he might just come down and gentle Colley somewhat, admitting his own brusqueness but saying it was habitual in a captain of a ship. More likely he would come down but only to assure himself that Colley was lying in his bunk, prone and still and not to be roused by a jesting exordium. But then, he might not even come down. Who was I to dip into the nature of the man, cast the very waters of his soul and by that chirurgeonly experiment declare how his injustice would run its course? I sat before this journal, upbraiding myself for my folly in my attempt to play the politician and manipulator of his fellow men! I had to own that my knowledge of the springs of human action was still in the egg. Nor does a powerful intellect do more than assist in the matter. Something more there must be, some distillation of experience, before a man can judge the outcome in circumstances of such quantity, proliferation and confusion.

And then, *then* can your lordship guess? I have saved the sweet to the last! He did come down. Before my very eyes he came down as if my prediction had drawn him down like some fabulous spell! I am a wizard, am I not? Admit me to be a prentice-wizard at least! I had said he would come down and come down he did! Through my louvre I saw him come down, abrupt and grim, to take his stand in the centre of the lobby. He stared at one hutch after another, turning on his heel, and I was only just in time to pull my face away from the spyhole before his louring gaze swept over it with an effect I could almost swear like the heat from a burning coal! When I risked peeping again—for somehow it seemed positively dangerous that the man should know I had seen him—he had his back to me. He stepped to the door of Colley's hutch and for a long minute stared through it. I saw how one fist beat into the palm of the other hand behind his back. Then he swung impatiently to his left with a movement that seemed to cry out—*I'll be damned if I will!* He stumped to the ladder and disappeared. A few seconds later I heard his firm step pass along the deck above my head.

This was a modified triumph, was it not? I had said he would come down and he had come down. But where I had pictured him endeavouring to comfort poor Colley he had shown himself either too heartless or too little politic to bring himself to do so. The nearer he had come to dissimulating his bile the higher it had risen in his throat. Yet now I had some grounds for confidence. His knowledge of the existence of this very journal would not let him be. It will be like a splinter under the nail. He would come down again——

Wrong again, Talbot! Learn another lesson, my boy! You fell at that fence! Never again must you lose yourself in the complacent contemplation of a first success! Captain Anderson did not come down. He sent a messenger. I was just writing the sentence about the splinter when there came a knock at the door and who should appear but Mr Summers! I bade him enter, sanded my page—imperfectly as you can see—closed and locked my journal, stood up and indicated my chair. He declined it, perched himself on the edge of my bunk, laid his cocked hat on it and looked thoughtfully at my journal.

'Locked, too!'

I said nothing but looked him in the eye, smiling slightly. He nodded as if he understood—which indeed I think he did.

'Mr Talbot, it cannot be allowed to continue.'

'My journal, you mean?'

He brushed the jest aside.

'I have looked in on the man by the captain's orders.'

'Colley? I looked in on him myself. I agreed to, you remember.'

'The man's reason is at stake.'

'All for a little drink. Is there still no change?'

'Phillips swears he has not moved for three days.'

I made a perhaps unnecessarily blasphemous rejoinder. Summers took no notice of it.

'I repeat, the man is losing his wits.'

'It does indeed seem so.'

'I am to do what I can, by the captain's orders, and you are to assist me.'

'I?'

'Well. You are not ordered to assist me but I am ordered to invite your assistance and profit by your advice.'

'Upon my soul, the man is flattering me! Do you know, Summers, I was advised myself to practice the art? I little thought to find myself the object of such an exercise!'

'Captain Anderson feels that you have a social experience and awareness that may make your advice of value.'

I laughed heartily and Summers joined in.

'Come Summers! Captain Anderson never said that!'

'No, sir. Not precisely.'

'Not precisely indeed! I tell you what, Summers——'

I stopped myself in time. There were many things I felt like saying. I could have told him that Captain Anderson's sudden concern for Mr Colley began not at any moment of appeal by me but at the moment when he heard that I kept a journal intended for influential eyes. I could have given my opinion that the captain cared nothing for Colley's wits but sought cunningly enough to involve me in the events and so obscure the issue or at the very least soften what might well be your lordship's acerbity and contempt. But I am learning, am I not? Before the words reached my tongue I understood how dangerous they might be to Summers—and even to me.

'Well, Mr Summers, I will do what I can.'

'I was sure you would agree. You are co-opted among us ignorant tars as the civil power. What is to be done?'

'Here we have a parson who—but come, should we not have co-opted Miss Granham? She is the daughter of a canon and might be presumed to know best how to handle the clergy!'

'Be serious, sir and leave her to Mr Prettiman.'

'No! It cannot be! Minerva herself?'

'Mr Colley must claim all our attention.'

'Well then. Here we have a clergyman who—made too much of a beast of himself and refines desperately upon it.'

Summers regarded me closely, and I may say curiously.

'You know what a beast he made of himself?'

'Man! I saw him! We all saw him, including the ladies! Indeed, I tell you, Summers, I saw something more than the rest!'

'You interest me deeply.'

'It is of little enough moment. But some few hours after his exhibition I saw him wander through the lobby towards the *bog*, a sheet of paper in his hand and for what it is worth a most extraordinary smile on that ugly mug of his.'

'What did the smile suggest to you?'

'He was silly drunk.'

Summers nodded towards the forward part of the vessel.

'And there? In the fo'castle?'

'How can we tell?'

'We might ask.'

'Is that wise, Summers? Was not the play-acting of the common people—forgive me!—directed not to themselves but to those in authority over them? Should you not avoid reminding them of it?'

'It is the man's wits, sir. Something must be risked. Who set him on? Beside the common people there are the emigrants, decent as far as I have met them. *They* have no wish to mock at authority. Yet they must know as much as anyone.'

Suddenly I remembered the poor girl and her emaciated face where a shadow lived and was, as it were, feeding where it inhabited. She must have had Colley's beastliness exhibited before her at a time when she had a right to expect a far different appearance from a clergyman!

'But this is terrible, Summers! The man should be——'

'What is past cannot be helped, sir. But I say again it is the man's wits that stand in danger. For God's sake, make one more effort to rouse him from his, his—lethargy!'

'Very well. For the second time, then. Come.'

I went briskly and, followed by Summers across the lobby, opened the door of the hutch and stood inside. It was true enough. The man lay as he had lain before; and indeed seemed if anything even stiller. The hand that had clutched the ringbolt had relaxed and lay with the fingers hooked through it but without any evidence of muscular tension.

Behind me, Summers spoke gently.

'Here is Mr Talbot, Mr Colley, come to see you.'

I must own to a mixture of confusion and strong distaste for the whole business which rendered me even more than usually incapable of finding the right kind of encouragement for the wretched man. His situation and the odour, the stench, emanating I suppose from his unwashed person was nauseous. It must have been, you will agree, pretty *strong* to contend with and overcome the general stench of the ship to which I was still not entirely habituated! However, Summers evidently credited me with an ability which I did not possess for he stood away from me, nodding at the same time as if to indicate that the affair was now in my hands.

I cleared my throat.

'Well Mr Colley, this is an unfortunate business but believe me, sir, you are refining too much on it. Uncontrolled drunkenness and its consequences is an experience every man ought to have at least once in his life or how is he to understand the experience of others? As for your relieving nature on the deck—do but consider what those decks have seen! And in the peaceful counties of our own far-off land—Mr Colley I have been brought to see, by the good offices of Mr Summers, that I am in however distant a way partly responsible for your predicament. Had I not enraged our captain—but there! I shall confess, sir, that a number of young fellows, ranged at upper-storey windows, did once, at a given signal, make water on an unpopular and bosky tutor who was passing below! Now what was the upshot of that shocking affair? Why nothing, sir! The man held out his hand, stared frowning into the evening sky, then opened his umbrella! I swear to you, sir, that some of those same young fellows will one day be bishops! In a day or two we shall all laugh at your comical interlude together! You are bound for Sydney Cove I believe and thence to Van Diemen's Land. Good Lord, Mr Colley, from what I have heard they are more likely to greet you drunk than sober. What you need now is a dram, then as much ale as your stomach can hold. Depend upon it, you will soon see things differently.'

There was no response. I glanced enquiringly at Summers but he was looking down at the blanket, his lips pressed together. I spread my hands in a gesture of defeat and left the cabin. Summers followed me.

'Well, Summers?'

'Mr Colley is willing himself to death.'

'Come!'

'I have known it happen among savage peoples. They are able to lie down and die.'

I gestured him into my hutch and we sat side by side on the bunk. A thought occurred to me.

'Was he perhaps an enthusiast? It may be that he is taking his religion too much to heart—come now, Mr Summers! There is nothing to laugh at in the matter! Or are you so disobliging as to find my remark itself a subject for your hilarity?'

Summers dropped his hands from his face, smiling.

'God forbid, sir! It is pain enough to have been shot at by an

enemy without the additional hazard of presenting oneself as a
mark to—dare I say—one's friends. Believe me properly sensible
of my privilege in being admitted to a degree of intimacy with
your noble godfather's genteel godson. But you are right in one
thing. As far as poor Colley is concerned there is nothing to
laugh at. Either his wits are gone or he knows nothing of his own
religion.'

'He is a parson!'

'The uniform does not make the man, sir. He is in despair I
believe. Sir, I take it upon myself as a Christian—as a humble
follower at however great a distance—to aver that a Christian
cannot despair!'

'My words were trivial then.'

'They were what you could say. But of course they never
reached him.'

'You felt that?'

'Did not you?'

I toyed with the thought that perhaps someone of Colley's
own class, a man from among the ship's people but unspoilt by
education or such modest preferment as had come his way, might
well find a means to approach him. But after the words that
Summers and I had exchanged on a previous occasion I felt a new
delicacy in broaching such a subject with him. He broke the
silence.

'We have neither priest nor doctor.'

'Brocklebank owned to having been a medical student for the
best part of a year.'

'Did he so? Should we call him in?'

'God forbid—he does so prose! He described his turning
from doctoring to painting as "deserting Aesculapius for the
Muse".'

'I shall enquire among our people forrard.'

'For a doctor?'

'For some information as to what happened.'

'Man, we *saw* what happened!'

'I mean in the fo'castle or below it, rather than on deck.'

'He was made beastly drunk.'

I found that Summers was peering at me closely.

'And that was all?'

'All?'

'I see. Well, sir, I shall report back to the captain.'

'Tell him I shall continue to consider how we may devise some method of bringing the wretched fellow to his senses.'

'I will do so; and must thank you for your assistance.'

Summers left and I was alone with my thoughts and this journal. It was so strange to think that a young fellow not much above my years or Deverel's and certainly not as old as Cumbershum should have so strong an instinct for self-destruction! Why, Aristotle or no, half an hour of La Brocklebank—even Prettiman and Miss Granham—and *there*, thought I, is a situation I must get acquainted with for a number of reasons, the least of them entertainment: and then——

What do you suppose was the thought that came into my mind? It was of the pile of manuscript that had lain on the flap of Colley's table! I had not noticed the flap or the papers when Summers and I entered the cabin; but now, by the incomprehensible faculties of the human mind I, as it were, entered the cabin *again* and surveying the scene I had just left, I saw in my mind that the writing-flap was empty! There is a subject for a savant's investigation! How can a man's mind go back and see what he saw not? But so it was.

Well. Captain Anderson had co-opted me. He should find out, I thought, what sort of overseer he had brought into the business!

I went quickly to Colley's cabin. He lay as before. Only when I was inside the hutch did I return to a *kind* at least of apprehension. I intended the man nothing but good and I was acting on the captain's behalf; yet there was in my mind an unease. I felt it as the effect of the captain's rule. A tyrant turns the slightest departure from his will into a crime; and I was at the least contemplating bringing him to book for his mistreatment of Mr Colley. I looked quickly round the cabin. The ink and pens and sander were still there, as were the shelves with their books of devotion at the foot of the bed. It seemed there was a limit to their efficacy! I leaned over the man himself.

It was then that I perceived without seeing—I knew, but had no real means of knowing——

There had been a time when he had awakened in physical anguish which had quickly passed into a mental one. He lay like that in deepening pain, deepening consciousness, widening memory, his whole being turning more and more from the world till he could desire nothing but death. Phillips could not rouse him nor even Summers. Only I—my words after all had touched something. When I left him after that first visit, glad enough to be gone, he had leapt from his bunk in some *new* agony! Then, in a passion of self-disgust he had swept his papers from the table. Like a child he had seized the whole and had jammed them into a convenient crack as if it would stay unsearched till doom's day! Of course. There was, between the bunk and the side of the vessel a space, just as in my own hutch, into which a man might thrust his hand as I then did in Colley's. They encountered paper and I drew out a crumpled mass of sheets all written, some cross-written, and all, I was certain, material evidence against our tyrant in the case of Colley versus Anderson! I put the papers quickly into the bosom of my coat, came out—unseen I pray God!—and hurried to my cabin. There I thrust the mass of papers into my own writing-case and locked it as if I were concealing the spoils of a burglary! After that I sat and began to write all this in my journal as if seeking, in a familiar action, some legal security! Is that not comic?

Wheeler came to my cabin.

'Sir, I have a message, sir. The captain requests that you give him the pleasure of your company at dinner in an hour's time.'

'My compliments to the captain and I accept with pleasure.'

What a day this has been. I commenced it with some cheerfulness and I end it with—but you will wish to know all! It seems so long ago that the affair was misty and my own endeavours to pierce the mist so complacant, so self-satisfied——

Well. As Summers said, I am partly to blame. So are we all in one degree or another; but none of us, I think, in the same measure as our tyrant! Let me take you with me my lord, step by step. I promise you—no, not entertainment but at the very least a kind of generous indignation and the exercise not of my, but *your* judgement.

I changed and dismissed Wheeler only to find his place taken by Summers, who looked positively elegant.

'Good God, Summers, are you also bidden to the feast?'

'I am to share that pleasure"

'It is an innovation, for sure.'

'Oldmeadow makes a fourth.'

I took out my repeater.

'It still wants more than ten minutes. What is etiquette for such a visit on shipboard?'

'Where the captain is concerned, on the last stroke of the bell.'

'In that case I shall disappoint his expectations and arrive early. He anticipates, I believe, knowing me, that I shall arrive late.'

My entry into Captain Anderson's stateroom was as ceremonious as an admiral could wish. The cabin, or room, rather, though not as large as the passengers' saloon or even the saloon where the lieutenants *messed*, was yet of palatial dimensions when compared with our meagre individual quarters. Some of the ship's full width was paired off on either side for the captain's own sleeping quarters, his closet, his personal galley, and another small cabin where I suppose an admiral would have conducted the business of a fleet. As in the lieutenants' wardroom and the passenger saloon, the rear wall, or in Tarpaulin language *the after bulkhead*, was one vast, leaded window by means of which something like a third of the horizon might be seen. Yet part of this window was obscured in a way that at first I could scarcely credit. Part of the obscuration was the captain, who called out as soon as I appeared in what I can only call a holiday voice.

'Come in, Mr Talbot, come in! I must apologize for not greeting you at the threshold! You have caught me in my garden.'

It was so indeed. The obscuration to the great window was a row of climbing plants, each twisting itself round a bamboo that rose from the darkness near the deck where I divined the flower pots were. Standing a little to one side I could see that Captain Anderson was serving each plant into its flower pot with water from a small watering can with a long spout. The can was the sort of flimsy trifle you might find a lady using in the orangery—not indeed, to serve the trees in their enormous vats, but some quaintness of Dame Nature's own ingenuity. The morose captain might be thought to befit such a picture ill; but as he turned I saw to my astonishment that he was looking positively amiable, as if I were a lady come to visit him.

'I did not know that you had a private paradise, captain.'

The captain smiled! Yes, positively, he smiled!

'Do but think, Mr Talbot, this flowering plant that I am tending, still innocent and unfallen, may have been one with which Eve garlanded herself on the first day of her creation.'

'Would that not presuppose a loss of innocence, captain, precursor to the fig leaves?'

'It might be so. How acute you are, Mr Talbot.'

'We were being fanciful, were we not?'

'I was speaking my mind. The plant is called the Garland Plant. The ancients, I am told, crowned themselves with it. The flower, when it appears, is agreeably perfumed and waxen white.'

'We might be Grecians then and crown ourselves for the feast.'

'I do not think the custom suited to the English. But do you see I have three of the plants? Two of them I actually raised from seed!'

'Is that a task as difficult as your triumphant tone would imply?'

Captain Anderson laughed happily. His chin was up, his cheeks creased, twin sparks in his little eyes.

'Sir Joseph Banks said it was impossible! "Anderson," he said, "take cuttings, man! You might as well throw the seeds overboard!" But I have persevered and in the end I had a box of them—seedlings, I mean—enough to supply a Lord Mayor's banquet, if—to follow your fancy—they should ever require their aldermen to be garlanded. But there! It is not to be imagined. Garlands would be as out of place as in the painted hall at Greenwich. Serve Mr Talbot. What will you drink, sir? There is much to hand, though I take no more than an occasional glass myself.'

'Wine for me, sir.'

'Hawkins, the claret if you please! This geranium you see, Mr Talbot, has some disease of the leaf. I have dusted it with flowers of sulphur but to no effect. I shall lose it no doubt. But then, sir, he who gardens at sea must accustom himself to loss. On my first voyage in command I lost my whole collection.'

'Through the violence of the enemy?'

'No sir, through the uncommon nature of the weather which held us for whole weeks without either wind or rain. I could not have served water to my plants. There would have been mutiny. I see the loss of this one plant as no great matter.'

'Besides, you may exchange it for another at Sydney Cove.'

'Why must you——'

He turned away and stowed the waterpot in a box down by the plants. When he turned back I saw the creases in his cheeks again and the sparks in his eyes.

'We are a long way and a long time from our destination, Mr Talbot.'

'You speak as though you do not anticipate our arrival there with pleasure.'

The sparks and creases vanished.

'You are young, sir. You cannot understand the pleasures of, no, the necessity of solitude to some natures. I would not care if the voyage lasted for ever!'

'But surely a man is connected to the land, to society, to a family——'

'Family? Family?' said the captain with a kind of violence. 'Why should a man not do without a family? What is there about a family, pray?'

'A man is not a, a garland plant, Captain, to fertilize his own seed!'

There was a long pause in which Hawkins, the captain's servant, brought us the claret. Captain Anderson made a token gesture towards his face with half a glass of wine.

'At least I may remind myself how remarkable the flora will be at the Antipodes!'

'So you may replenish your stock.'

His face was gay again.

'Many of Nature's inventions in that region have never been brought back to Europe.'

I saw now there was a way, if not to Captain Anderson's heart, at least to his approval. I had a sudden thought, one worthy of a *romancier*, that perhaps the stormy or sullen face with which he was wont to leave his paradise was that of the expelled Adam. While I was considering this and my glass of claret, Summers and Oldmeadow entered the stateroom together.

'Come in, gentlemen,' cried the captain. 'What will you take, Mr Oldmeadow? As you see, Mr Talbot is content with wine— the same for you, sir?'

Oldmeadow cawed into his collar and declared he would be agreeable to a little dry sherry. Hawkins brought a broad-bottomed decanter and poured first for Summers, as knowing already what he would drink, then for Oldmeadow.

'Summers,' said the captain, 'I had meant to ask you. How does your patient?'

'Still the same, sir. Mr Talbot was good enough to comply with your request. But his words had no more effect than mine.'

'It is a sad business,' said the captain. He stared directly at me. 'I shall enter in the ship's log that the patient—for such I believe we must consider him—has been visited by you, Mr Summers, and by you, Mr Talbot.'

It was now that I began to understand Captain Anderson's purpose in getting us into his cabin and his clumsy way about the business of Colley. Instead of waiting till the wine and talk had worked on us he had introduced the subject at once and far too abruptly. It was time I thought of myself!

'You must remember, sir,' said I, 'that if the wretched man is to be considered a patient, my opinion is valueless. I have no medical knowledge whatsoever. Why, you would do better to consult Mr Brocklebank!'

'Brocklebank? Who is Brocklebank?'

'The artistic gentleman with the port-wine face and female entourage. But I jested. He told me he had begun to study medicine but had given it up.'

'He has some medical experience, then?'

'No, no! I jested. The man is—what is the man, Summers? I doubt he could take a pulse!'

'Nevertheless—Brocklebank you said? Hawkins, find Mr Brocklebank and ask him to be good enough to come and see me at once.'

I saw it all—saw the entry in the log—*visited by a gentleman of some medical experience!* He was crude but cunning, was the captain! He was, as Deverel would say, 'keeping his yardarm free.' Observe how he is forcing me to report to your lordship in my journal that he has taken every care of the man, had him visited by his officers, by me, and by a gentleman *of some medical experience!*

No one said anything for a while. We three guests stared into our glasses as if rendered solemn by a reminder of the sick. But it could not have been more than two minutes before Hawkins returned to say that Mr Brocklebank would be happy to wait on the captain.

'We will sit down, then,' said the captain. 'Mr Talbot on my right—Mr Oldmeadow here, sir! Summers, will you take the bottom of the table? Why, this is delightfully domestic! Have you room enough, gentlemen? Summers has plenty of course. But we must allow him free passage to the door in case one of ten thousand affairs takes him from us about the ship's business.'

Oldmeadow remarked that the soup was excellent. Summers, who was eating his with the dexterity acquired in a dozen fo'castles, remarked that much nonsense was talked about Navy food.

'You may depend upon it,' he said, 'where food has to be ordered, gathered, stored and served out by the thousands of ton there will be cause of complaint here and there. But in the main, British seamen eat better at sea than they do ashore.'

'Bravo!' I cried. 'Summers, you should be on the government benches!'

'A glass of wine with you, Mr Summers,' said the captain. 'What is the phrase? "No heel taps"? A glass with all you gentlemen! But to return—Summers, what do you say to the story of the cheese clapped on the main as a mastcapping? What of the snuff-boxes carved out of beef?'

I saw out of the corner of my eye how the captain did no more than sniff the bouquet of his wine, then set the glass down. I determined to humour him if only to see round his schemes.

'Summers, I must hear you answer the captain. What of the snuff-boxes and mastcheeses——'

'Mastcappings——'

'What of the bones we hear are served to our gallant tars with no more than a dried shred of meat adhering?'

Summers smiled.

'I fancy you will sample the cheese, sir; and I believe the captain is about to surprise you with bones.'

'Indeed I am,' said the captain. 'Hawkins, have them brought in.'

'Good God,' I cried, 'marrow bones!'

'Bessie, I suppose,' said Oldmeadow. 'A very profitable beast.'

I bowed to the captain.

'We are overwhelmed, sir. Lucullus could do no better.'

'I am endeavouring to supply you with material for your journal, Mr Talbot.'

'I give you my word, sir, the *menu* shall be preserved for the remotest posterity together with a memorial of the captain's hospitality!'

Hawkins bent to the captain.

'The gentleman is at the door, sir.'

'Brocklebank? I will take him for a moment into the office if you will excuse me, gentlemen.'

Now there occurred a scene of farce. Brocklebank had not remained at the door but was inside it and advancing. Either he had mistaken the captain's message for such an invitation as had been issued to me, or he was tipsy, or both. Summers had pushed back his chair and stood up. As if the first lieutenant had been a footman, Brocklebank sank into it.

'Thankee, thankee. Marrow bones! How the devil did you know, sir? I don't doubt one of my gals told you. Confusion to the French!'

He drained Summers's glass at a draught. He had a voice like some fruit which combines the qualities—if there be such a fruit—of peach and plum. He stuck his little finger in his ear, bored for a moment, inspected the result on the end of it while no one said anything. The servant was at a loss. Brocklebank caught a clearer sight to Summers and beamed at him.

'You too, Summers? Sit down, man!'

Captain Anderson, with what for him was rare tact, broke in.

'Yes, Summers, pull up that chair over there and dine with us.'

Summers sat at a corner of the table. He was breathing quickly as if he had run a race. I wondered whether he was thinking what Deverel thought and had confided to me in his, or perhaps I ought to say *our*, cups—*No, Talbot, this is not a happy ship.*

Oldmeadow turned to me.

'There was mention of a journal, Talbot. There is a devil of a lot of writing among you government people.'

'You have advanced me, sir. But it is true. The offices are paved with paper.'

The captain pretended to drink, then set the glass down.

'You might well think a ship is ballasted with paper. We record almost everything somewhere or another, from the midshipman's logs right up to the ship's log kept by myself.'

'In my case I find there is hardly time to record the events of a day before the next two or three are upon me.'

'How do you select?'

'Salient facts, of course—such trifles as may amuse the leisure of my godfather.'

'I hope,' said the captain heavily, 'that you will record our sense of obligation to his lordship for affording us your company.'

'I shall do so.'

Hawkins filled Brocklebank's glass. It was for the third time.

'Mr, er, Brocklebank,' said the captain, 'may we profit from your medical experience?'

'My what, sir?'

'Talbot—Mr Talbot here,' said the captain in a vexed voice, 'Mr Talbot——'

'What the devil is wrong with him? Good God! I assure you that Zenobia, dear, warm-hearted gal——'

'I myself,' said I swiftly, 'have nothing to do with the present matter. Our captain refers to Colley.'

'The parson is it? Good God! I assure you it doesn't matter to me at my time of life. Let them enjoy themselves I said—on board I said it—or did I?'

Mr Brocklebank hiccupped. A thin streak of wine ran down his chin. His eyes wandered.

'We need your medical experience,' said the captain, his growls only just below the surface, but in what for him was a conciliatory tone. 'We have none ourselves and look to you——'

'I have none either,' said Mr Brocklebank. 'Garçon, another glass!'

'Mr Talbot said——'

'I looked round you see but I said, Wilmot, I said, this anatomy is not for you. No indeed, you have not the stomach for it. In fact as I said at the time, I abandoned Aesculapius for the Muse. Have I not said so to you, Mr Talbot?'

'You have so, sir. On at least two occasions. I have no doubt the captain will accept your excuses.'

'No, no,' said the captain irritably. 'However little the gentleman's experience, we must profit by it.'

'Profit,' said Mr Brocklebank. 'There is more profit in the Muse than in the other thing. I should be a rich man now had not the warmth of my constitution, an attachment more than usually firm to the Sex and the opportunities for excess forced on my nature by the shocking corruption of English Society——'

'I could not abide doctoring,' said Oldmeadow. 'All those corpses, good God!'

'Just so, sir. I prefer to keep reminders of mortality at arm's length. Did you know I was first in the field after the death of Lord Nelson with a lithograph portraying the happy occasion?'

'You were not present!'

'Arm's length, sir. Neither was any other artist. I must admit to you freely that I believed at the time that Lord Nelson had expired on deck.'

'Brocklebank,' cried I, 'I have seen it! There is a copy on the wall in the tap of the Dog and Gun! How the devil did that whole crowd of young officers contrive to be kneeling round Lord Nelson in attitudes of sorrow and devotion at the hottest moment of the action?'

Another thin trickle of wine ran down the man's chin.

'You are confusing art with actuality, sir.'

'It looked plain silly to me, sir.'

'It has sold very well indeed, Mr Talbot. I cannot conceal from you that without the continued popularity of that work I should be in Queer Street. It has at the very least allowed me to take a passage to, to wherever we are going, the name escapes me. And imagine, sir, Lord Nelson died down below in some stinking part of the bilges, I believe, with nothing to see him by but a ship's lantern. Who in the devil is going to make a picture of that?'

'Rembrandt perhaps.'

'Ah. Rembrandt. Yes, well. At least Mr Talbot you must admire the dexterity of my management of smoke.'

'Take me with you, sir.'

'Smoke is the very devil. Did you not see it when Summers fired my gun? With broadsides a naval battle is nothing but a London Particular. So your true craftsman must tuck it away to where it does not obtrude—obtrude——'

'Like a clown.'

'Obtrude——'

'And interrupt some necessary business of the action.'

'Obtrude—Captain, you don't drink.'

The captain made another gesture with his glass, then looked round at the other three of his guests in angry frustration. But Brocklebank, his elbows now on either side of the marrow bone intended for Summers, droned on.

'I have always maintained that smoke properly handled can be of ma-material assistance. You are approached by some captain who has had the good fortune to fall in with the enemy and get off again. He comes to me as they did, after my lithograph. He has, for example, in company with another frigate and a small sloop—encountered the French and a battle has ensued—I beg your pardon! As the epitaph says, "Wherever you be let your wind go free for holding mine was the death of me." Now I ask you to imagine what would happen—and indeed my good friend, Fuseli, you know, the Shield of Achilles, and—well. Imagine!'

I drank impatiently and turned to the captain.

'I think, sir, that Mr Brocklebank——'

It was of no avail and the man drooled again without noticing.

'Imagine—who pays me? If they *all* pay there can be no smoke at all! Yet they must all be seen to be hotly engaged, the devil take it! They come to blows, you know!'

'Mr Brocklebank,' said the captain fretfully, 'Mr Brocklebank——'

'Give me one single captain who has been successful and got his K! *Then* there will be no argument!'

'No,' said Oldmeadow, cawing into his collar, 'no indeed!'

Mr Brocklebank eyed him truculently.

'You doubt my word, sir? Do you, because if you do, sir——'

'I sir? Good God no, sir!'

'He will say, "Brocklebank," he will say. "I don't give a tuppenny damn for me own part, but me mother, me wife and me fifteen gals require a picture of me ship at the height of the action!" You follow? Now after I have been furnished with a copy of the gazette and had the battle described to me in minutest detail he goes off in the happy delusion that he knows what a naval battle looks like!'

The captain raised his glass. This time he emptied it at a gulp. He addressed Brocklebank in a voice which would have scared Mr Taylor from one end of the ship to the other if not farther.

'I for my part, sir, should be of his opinion!'

Mr Brocklebank, to indicate the degree of his own cleverness, tried to lay a finger cunningly on the side of his nose but missed it.

'You are wrong, sir. Were I to rely on verisimilitude—but no. Do you suppose that my client, who has paid a deposit—for you see he may be off and lose his head in a moment———'

Summers stood up.

'I am called for, sir.'

The captain, with perhaps the only glimmer of wit I have found in him, laughed aloud.

'You are fortunate, Mr Summers!'

Brocklebank noticed nothing. Indeed, I believe if we had all left him he would have continued his monologue.

'Now do you suppose the accompanying frigate is to be portrayed with an equal degree of animation? She has paid nothing! That is where smoke comes in. By the time I have done my layout she will have just fired and the smoke will have risen up round her; and as for the sloop, which will have been in the hands of some obscure lieutenant, it will be lucky to appear at all. My client's ship on the other hand will be belching more fire than smoke and will be being attacked by all the enemy at once.'

'I could almost wish,' said I, 'that the French would afford us an opportunity for invoking the good offices of your brush.'

'There's no hope of that,' said the captain glumly, 'no hope at all.'

Perhaps his tone affected Mr Brocklebank, who went through one of those extraordinarily swift transitions which are common enough among the inebriated from cheerfulness to melancholy.

'But that is never the end of it. Your client will return and the first thing he will say is that *Corinna* or *Erato* never carried her foremast stepped as far forrard as that and what is that block doing on the main brace? Why, my most successful client—apart from the late Lord Nelson if I may so describe him—as a client I mean—was even foolish enough to object to some trifling injuries I had inflicted on the accompanying frigate. He swore she had never lost her topmast, her fore topmast I think he said, for she was scarcely in cannon shot. Then he said I had shown no damage in the region of the quarterdeck of his ship, which was not accurate. He forced me to beat two gunports into one there and carry away a great deal of the rail. Then he said, "Could you not dash me in there, Brocklebank? I distinctly remember standin' just by the broken rail, encouragin' the crew and indicatin' the enemy by wavin' me sword towards them." What could I do? The client is always right, it is the artist's first axiom. "The figure will be very small, Sir Sammel," said I. "That is of no consequence,' said he. "You may exaggerate me a little." I bowed to him. "If I do that, Sir Sammel," said I, "it will reduce your frigate to a sloop by contrast." He took a turn or two up and down my studio for all the world like our captain here on the quarterdeck. "Well," said he at last, "you must dash me in small, then. They will know me by me cocked hat and me epaulettes. It's of no consequence to me, Mr Brocklebank, but me good lady and me gals insist on it."'

'Sir Sammel,' said the captain. 'You did say "Sir Sammel"?'

'I did. Do we move on to brandy?'

'Sir Sammel. I know him. Knew him.'

'Tell us all, Captain,' said I, hoping to stem the flow. 'A shipmate?'

'I was the lieutenant commanding the sloop,' said the captain moodily, 'but I have not seen the picture.'

'Captain! I positively must have a description of this,' said I. 'We landsmen are avid, you know, for that sort of thing!'

'Good God, the shloop! I have met the sh—the other sh—the lieutenant. Captain, you must be portrayed. We will waft away the sh—the smoke and show you in the thick of it!'

'Why so he was,' said I. 'Can we believe him anywhere else? You were in the thick of it, were you not?'

Captain Anderson positively snarled.

'The thick of the battle? In a sloop? Against frigates? But Captain—Sir Sammel I suppose I must say—must have thought me a young fool for he called me that, bawling through his speaking trumpet, "Get to hell out of this, you young fool, or I'll have you broke!"'

I raised my glass to the captain.

'I drink to you, sir. But no blind eye? No deaf ear?'

'Garçon, where is the brandy? I must limn you, Captain, at a much reduced fee. Your future career——'

Captain Anderson was crouched at the table's head as if to spring. Both fists were clenched on it and his glass had fallen and smashed. If he had snarled before, this time he positively roared.

'Career? Don't you understand, you damned fool? The war is nigh over and done with and we are for the beach, every man jack of us!'

There was a prolonged silence in which even Brocklebank seemed to find that something unusual had happened to him. His head sank, then jerked up and he looked round vacantly. Then his eyes focused. One by one, we turned.

Summers stood in the doorway.

'Sir. I have been with Mr Colley, sir. It is my belief the man is dead.'

Slowly, each of us rose, coming, I suppose, from a moment of furious inhospitality to another realization. I looked at the captain's face. The red suffusion of his anger had sunk away. He was inscrutable. I saw in his face neither concern, relief, sorrow nor triumph. He might have been made of the same material as the figurehead.

He was the first to speak.

'Gentlemen. This sorry affair must end our, our meeting.'

'Of course, sir.'

'Hawkins. Have this gentleman escorted to his cabin. Mr Talbot. Mr Oldmeadow. Be good enough to view the body with Mr Summers to confirm his opinion. I myself will do so. I fear the man's intemperance has destroyed him.'

'Intemperance, sir? A single, unlucky indulgence?'

'What do you mean, Mr Talbot?'

'You will enter it so in the log?'

Visibly, the captain controlled himself.

'That is something for me to consider in my own time, Mr Talbot.'

I bowed and said nothing. Oldmeadow and I withdrew and Brocklebank was half-carried and half-dragged behind us. The captain followed the little group that surrounded the monstrous soak. It seemed that every passenger in the ship, or at least the after part of it, was congregated in the lobby and staring silently at the door of Colley's cabin. Many of the crew who were not on duty, and most of the emigrants, were gathered at the white line drawn across the deck and were staring at us in equal silence. I suppose there must have been some noise from the wind and the passage of the ship through the water but I, at least, was not conscious of it. The other passengers made way for us. Wheeler was standing on guard at the door of the cabin, his white puffs of hair, his bald pate and *lighted* face—I can find no other description for his expression of understanding all the ways and woes of the world—gave him an air of positive saintliness. When he saw the captain he bowed with the unction of an undertaker or indeed as if the mantle of poor, obsequious Colley had fallen on him. Though the work should have gone to Phillips, it was Wheeler who opened the door, then stood to one side. The captain went in. He stayed for no more than a moment, came out, motioned me to enter, then strode to the ladder and up to his own quarters. I went into the cabin with no great willingness, I can assure you! The poor man still clutched the ringbolt—still lay with his face pressed against the bolster, but the blanket had been turned back and revealed his cheek and neck. I put three hesitant fingers on his cheek and whipped them back as if they had been burned. I did not choose, indeed I did not need, to lean down and listen for the man's breathing. I came out to Colley's silent congregation and nodded to Mr Oldmeadow who went in, licking pale lips. He too came out quickly.

Summers turned to me.

'Well, Mr Talbot?'

'No living thing could be as cold.'

Mr Oldmeadow turned up his eyes and slid gently down the bulkhead until he was sitting on the deck. Wheeler, with an expression of holy understanding, thrust the gallant officer's head between his knees. But now, of all inappropriate beings, who should appear but Silenus? Brocklebank, perhaps a little recovered or perhaps in some extraordinary trance of drunkenness, reeled out of his cabin and shook off the two women who were trying to restrain him. The other ladies shrieked and then went silent, caught between the two sorts of occasion. The man wore nothing but a shirt. He thrust, weaving and staggering, into Colley's cabin and shoved Summers aside with a force that made the first lieutenant reel.

'I know you all,' he shouted, 'all, all! I am an artist! The man is

not dead but shleepeth! He is in a low fever and may be recovered
by drink——'

I grabbed the man and pulled him away. Summers was there,
too. We were mixed with Wheeler and stumbling round Oldmeadow—but really, death is death and if *that* is not to be treated
with some seriousness—somehow we got him out into the lobby,
where the ladies and gentlemen were silent again. There are some
situations for which no reaction is suitable—perhaps the only one
would have been for them all to retire. Somehow we got him
back to the door of his hutch, he meanwhile mouthing about
spirits and *low fever*. His women waited, silent, appalled. I was
muttering in my turn.

'Come now, my good fellow, back to your bunk!'

'A low fever——'

'What the devil is a low fever? Now go in—go *in*, I say! Mrs
Brocklebank—Miss Brocklebank, I appeal to you—for heaven's
sake——'

They did help and got the door shut on him. I turned away,
just as Captain Anderson came down the ladder and into the
lobby again.

'Well gentlemen?'

I answered both for Oldmeadow and myself.

'To the best of my belief, Captain Anderson, Mr Colley is dead.'

He fixed me with his little eyes.

'I heard mention of "a low fever", did I not?'

Summers came out, closing the door of Colley's cabin behind
him. It was an act of curious decency. He stood, looking from the
captain to me and back again. I spoke unwillingly—but what else
could I say?

'It was a remark made by Mr Brocklebank who is, I fear, not
wholly himself.'

I swear the captain's cheeks creased and the twin sparks came
back. He looked round the crowd of witnesses.

'Nevertheless, Mr Brocklebank has had some medical experience!'

Before I could expostulate he had spoken again and with the
tyrannical accents of his service.

'Mr Summers. See that the customary arrangements are made.'

'Aye, aye, sir.'

The captain turned and retired briskly. Summers continued in
much the same accents as his captain.

'Mr Willis!'

'Sir!'

'Bring aft the sailmaker and his mate and three or four able-bodied men. You may take what men of the off-duty watch are under punishment.'

'Aye, aye, sir.'

Here was none of the pretended melancholy our professional undertakers have as their stock-in-trade! Mr Willis departed *for-rard* at a run. The first lieutenant then addressed the assembled passengers in his customary mild accents.

'Ladies and gentlemen, you will not wish to witness what follows. May I request that the lobby be cleared? The air of the afterdeck is to be recommended.'

Slowly the lobby cleared until Summers and I were left together with the servants. The door of Brocklebank's hutch opened and the man stood there grotesquely naked. He spoke with ludicrous solemnity.

'Gentlemen. A low fever is the opposite of a high fever. I bid you good day.'

He was tugged backwards and reeled. The door was shut upon him. Summers then turned to me.

'You, Mr Talbot?'

'I have the captain's request still to comply with, have I not?'

'I fancy it has ended with the poor man's death.'

'We talked of *noblesse oblige* and fair play. I found myself translating the words by a single one.'

'Which is?'

'Justice.'

Summers appeared to consider. 'You have decided who is to appear at the bar?'

'Have not you?'

'I? The powers of a captain—besides, sir, I have no patron.'

'Do not be so certain, Mr Summers.'

He looked at me for a moment in bewilderment. Then he caught his breath. 'I——?'

But men of the crew were trotting aft towards us. Summers glanced at them, then back at me.

'May I recommend the afterdeck?'

'A glass of brandy is more appropriate.'

I went into the passenger saloon and found Oldmeadow slumped there in a seat under the great stern window, an empty glass in his hand. He was breathing deeply and perspiring profusely. But colour was back in his cheeks. He muttered to me.

'Damned silly thing to do. Don't know what came over me.'

'Is this how you behave on a stricken field, Oldmeadow? No, forgive me! I am not myself either. The dead, you see, lying in that attitude as I had so recently seen him—why even then he might have been—but now, stiff and hard as—where the devil is that steward? Steward! Brandy here and some more for Mr Oldmeadow!'

'I know what you mean, Talbot. The truth is I have never seen a stricken field nor heard a shot fired in anger except once when my adversary missed me by a yard. How silent the ship has become!'

I glanced through the saloon door. The party of men was crowding into Colley's cabin. I shut the door and turned back to Oldmeadow.

'All will be done soon. Oldmeadow—are our feelings unnatural?'

'I wear the King's uniform yet I have never before seen a dead body except the occasional tarred object in chains. This has quite overcome me—touching it I mean. I am Cornish, you see.'

'With such a name?'

'We are not all Tre, Pol and Pen. Lord, how her timbers grind. Is there a change in her motion?'

'It cannot be.'

'Talbot, do you suppose——'

'What, sir?'

'Nothing.'

We sat for a while and I attended more to the spreading warmth of the brandy through my veins than anything else. Presently Summers came in. Behind him I glimpsed a party of men bearing a covered object away along the deck. Summers himself had not yet recovered from a slight degree of pallor.

'Brandy for you, Summers?'

He shook his head. Oldmeadow got to his feet.

'The afterdeck and a breath of air for me, I think. Damned silly of me it was. Just damned silly.'

Presently Summers and I were alone.

'Mr Talbot,' he said, in a low tone, 'you mentioned justice.'

'Well, sir?'

'You have a journal.'

'And——?'

'Just that.'

He nodded meaningly at me, got up, and left. I stayed where I was, thinking to myself how little he understood me after all. He did not know that I had already used that same journal—nor that I planned this plain account to lie before one in whose judgement and integrity——

My lord, you was pleased to advise me to practise the art of flattery. But how can I continue to *try it on* a personage who will infallibly detect the endeavour? Let me be disobedient to you if only in this, and flatter you no more!

Well then, I have accused the captain of an abuse of power; and I have let stand on the page Summers's own suggestion that I myself was to some extent responsible for it. I do not know what more the name of justice can demand of me. The night is far advanced—and it is only *now* as I write these words that I remember the *Colley Manuscript* in which there may be even plainer evidence of your godson's culpability and our captain's cruelty! I will glance through what the poor devil wrote and then get me to bed.

I have done so oh God, and could almost wish I had not. Poor, poor Colley, poor Robert James Colley! Billy Rogers, Summers firing the gun, Deverel and Cumbershum, Anderson, minatory, cruel Anderson! If there is justice in the world—but you may see by the state of my writing how the thing has worked on me—and I—I!

There is light filtering through my louvre. It is far advanced towards morning then. What am I to do? I cannot give Colley's letter, this unbegun, unfinished letter, cannot give his letter to the captain, though *that* for sure, legalistical as it might sound, is what I ought to do. But what then? It would go overboard, be suppressed, Colley would have died of a *low fever* and that would be all. My part would disappear with it. Do I refine too much? For Anderson is captain and will have chapter and verse, justifications for everything he has done. Nor can I take Summers into my confidence. His precious *career* is at stake. He would be bound to say that though I was perhaps right to appropriate the letter I have no business to suppress it.

Well, I do not suppress it. I take the only way towards justice—

natural justice I mean, rather than that of the captain or the law courts—and lay the evidence in your lordship's hands. He says he is 'For the beach.' If you believe as I do that he went beyond discipline into tyranny then a word from you in the right quarter will keep him there.

And I? I am writ down plainer in this record than I intended, to be sure! What I thought was behaviour consonant with my position——

Very well, then. I, too.

Why Edmund, Edmund! This is methodistical folly! Did you not believe you were a man of less sensibility than intelligence? Did you not feel, no, *believe*, that your blithely accepted system of morality for men in general owed less to feeling than to the operations of the intellect? Here is more of what you will wish to tear and not exhibit! But I have read and written all night and may be forgiven for a little lightheadedness. Nothing is real and I am already in a half-dream. I will get glue and fix the letter in here. It shall become another part of the *Talbot Manuscript*.

His sister must never know. It is another reason for not show-ing the letter. He died of a low fever—why, that poor girl there forrard will die of one like enough before we are done. Did I say glue? There must be some about. A hoof of Bessie. Wheeler will know, omniscient, ubiquitous Wheeler. And I must keep all locked away. This journal has become deadly as a loaded gun.

The first page, or it may be two pages, are gone. I saw them, or it, in his hand when he walked, in a trance of drunkenness, walked, head up and with a smile as if already in heaven——

Then at some time after he had fallen into a drunken slumber, he woke—slowly perhaps. There was, it may be, a blank time when he knew not who or what he was—then the time of re-membering the Reverend Robert James Colley.

No. I do not care to imagine it. I visited him that first time— Did my words bring to his mind all that he had lost? Self-esteem? His fellows' respect? *My* friendship? *My* patronage? Then, *then* in that agony he grabbed the letter, crumpled it, thrust it away as he would have thrust his memory away had it been possible—away, deep down beneath the bunk, unable to bear the thought of it——

My imagination is false. For sure he willed himself to death, but not for that, not for any of that, not for a casual, a single—— Had he committed murder—or being what he was——!

It is a madness, absurdity. What women are there at *that* end of the ship for him?

And I? I might have saved him had I thought less of my own consequence and less of the danger of being bored!

Oh those judicious opinions, those interesting observations, those sparks of wit with which I once proposed to entertain your lordship! Here instead is a plain description of Anderson's *commissions* and my own—omissions.

Your lordship may now read:

so I have drawn a veil over what have been the most trying and unedifying of my experiences. My prolonged nausea has rendered those first hours and days a little less distinct in my memory, nor would I attempt to describe to you in any detail the foul air, lurching brutalities, the wantonness, the casual blasphemies to which a passenger in such a ship is exposed even if he is a clergyman! But now I am sufficiently recovered from my nausea to be able to hold a pen, I cannot refrain from harking back for a moment to my first appearance on the vessel. Having escaped the clutches of a horde of *nameless creatures* on the foreshore and having been conveyed out to our noble vessel in a most expensive manner; having then been lifted to the deck in a kind of sling—somewhat like but more elaborate than the swing hung from the beech beyond the styes—I found myself facing a young officer who carried a spyglass under his arm.

Instead of addressing me as one gentleman out to address another he turned to one of his followers and made the following observation.

'Oh G——, a parson! That will send old Rumble-guts flying into the foretop!'

This was but a sample of what I was to suffer. I will not detail the rest, for it is now many days, my dear sister, since we bade farewell to the shores of Old Albion. Though I am strong enough to sit at the little flap which serves me as *priedieu*, desk, table and lectern I am still not secure enough to venture further. My first duty must be, of course (after those of my calling) to make myself known to our gallant captain, who lives and has his being some two storeys, or decks as I must now call them, above us. I hope he will agree to have this letter put on a ship proceeding in a contrary direction so you may have the earliest news of me. As I write this, Phillips (my *servant!*) has been in my small cabin with a little broth and advised me against a premature visit to Captain Anderson. He says I should get up my strength a little, take some

food in the passenger saloon as a change from having it here—
what I could *retain* of it!—and exercise myself in the lobby or
further out in that large space of deck which he calls the *waist* and
which lies about the tallest of our masts.

Though unable to eat I *have* been out, and oh, my dear sister,
how remiss I have been to repine at my lot! It is an earthly, nay,
an oceanic paradise! The sunlight is warm and like a natural
benediction. The sea is brilliant as the tails of Juno's birds (I
mean the peacock) that parade the terraces of Manston Place! (Do
not omit to show any little attention that may be possible in that
quarter, I must remind you.) Enjoyment of such a scene is as
good a medicine as a man could wish for when enhanced by that
portion of the scriptures appointed for the day. There was a sail
appeared briefly on the horizon and I offered up a brief prayer for
our safety subject always to HIS Will. However, I took my temper
from the behaviour of our officers and men, though of course in
the love and care of OUR SAVIOUR I have a far securer *anchor* than
any appertaining to the vessel! Dare I confess to you that as the
strange sail sank below the horizon—she had never appeared
wholly above it—I caught myself day-dreaming that she had
attacked us and that I performed some deed of daring not, indeed,
fitted for an ordained minister of the Church but even as when a
boy, I dreamed sometimes of winning fame and fortune at the
side of England's Hero! The sin was venial and quickly acknowledged and repented. Our heroes surrounded me on all sides and
it is to them that I ought to minister!

Well, then, I could almost wish a battle for *their* sakes! They go
about their tasks, their bronzed and manly forms unclothed to
the waist, their abundant locks gathered in a queue, their nether
garments closely fitted but flared about the ankles like the nostrils
of a stallion. They disport themselves casually a hundred feet up
in the air. Do not, I beg you, believe the tales spread by vicious
and un-Christian men, of their brutal treatment! I have neither
heard nor seen a flogging. Nothing more drastic has occurred
than a judicious correction applied to the proper portion of a
young gentleman who would have suffered as much and borne it as
stoically at school.

I must give you some idea of the shape of the little society in
which we must live together for I know not how many months.
We, the gentry as it were, have our castle in the backward or after
part of the vessel. At the other end of the waist, under a wall

pierced by two entrances and furnished with stairs or, as they still call them, *ladders*, are the quarters of our Jolly Tars and the other inferior sort of passenger—the emigrants, and so forth. Above that again is the deck of the fo'castle and the quite astonishing world of the bowsprit! You will have been accustomed, as I was, to thinking of a bowsprit (remember Mr Wembury's ship-in-a-bottle!) as a stick projecting from the front end of a ship. Nay then, I must now inform you that a bowsprit is a whole mast, only laid more nearly to the horizontal than the others. It has *yards* and *mastcapping*, *sidestays* and even *halyards*! More than that, as the other masts may be likened to huge trees among the limbs and branches of which our fellows climb, so the bowsprit is a kind of road, steep in truth but one on which they run or walk. It is more than three feet in diameter. The masts, those other 'sticks', are of such a thickness! Not the greatest beech from Saker's Wood has enough mass to supply such monsters. When I remember that some action of the enemy, or, even more appalling, some act of Nature may break or twist them off as you might twist the leaves off a carrot, I fall into a kind of terror. Indeed it was not a terror for my own safety! It was, it is, a terror at the majesty of this huge engine of war, then by a curious extension of the feeling, a kind of awe at the nature of the beings whose joy and duty it is to control such an invention in the service of their GOD and their King. Does not Sophocles (a Greek Tragedian) have some such thought in the chorus to his Philoctetes? But I digress.

The air is warm and sometimes hot, the sun lays such a lively hand on us! We must beware of him lest he strike us down! I am conscious even as I sit here at my *desk* of a warmness about my cheeks that has been occasioned by his rays! The sky this morning was of a dense blue, yet no brighter nor denser than the white-flecked blue of the broad ocean. I could almost rejoice in that powerful circling which the point of the bowsprit, *our* bowsprit, ceaselessly described above the sharp line of the horizon!

Next day.
I am indeed stronger and more able to eat. Phillips says that soon all will be well with me. Yet the weather is somewhat changed. Where yesterday there was a blueness and brightness, there is today little or no wind and the sea is covered with a white haze. The bowsprit—which in earlier days had brought on attack after

attack of nausea if I was so rash as to fix my attention on it—
stands still. Indeed, the aspect of our little world has changed at
least three times since our Dear Country sank—nay, appeared to
sink—into the waves! Where, I ask myself, are the woods and
fertile fields, the flowers, the grey stone church in which you and
I have worshipped all our lives, that churchyard in which our
dear parents—nay, the earthly remains of our dear parents, who
have surely received their reward in heaven—where, I ask, are all
the familiar scenes that were for both of us the substance of our
lives? The human mind is inadequate to such a situation. I tell
myself there is some material reality which joins the place where I
am to the place where I was, even as a road joins Upper and
Nether Compton. The intellect assents but the *heart* can find no
certainty in it. In reproof I tell myself that OUR LORD is here as
much as there; or rather that here and there may be the same
place in HIS EYES!

I have been on deck again. The white mist seemed denser, yet
hot. Our people are dimly to be seen. The ship is utterly stopped,
her sails hanging down. My footsteps sounded unnaturally loud
and I did not care to hear them. I saw no passengers about the
deck. There is no creak from all our wood and when I ventured
to look over the side I saw not a ripple, not a bubble in the water.

Well! I am myself again—but only just!

I had not been out in the hot vapour for more than a few
minutes when a thunderbolt of blinding white dropped out of the
mist on our right hand and struck into the sea. The clap came
with the sight and left my ears ringing. Before I had time to turn
and run, more claps came one on the other and rain fell—I had
almost said in rivers! But truly it seemed they were the waters
over the earth! Huge drops leapt back a yard off the deck. Between
where I had stood by the rail and the lobby was but a few yards,
yet I was drenched before I got under cover. I disrobed as far as
decency permits, then sat at this letter but not a little shaken. For
the last quarter of an hour—would that I had a timepiece!—the
awful bolts have dropped and the rain cascaded.

Now the storm is grumbling away into the distance. The sun is
lighting what it can reach of our lobby. A light breeze has set us
groaning, washing and bubbling on our way. I say the sun has
appeared; but only to set.

What has remained with me apart from a lively memory of my

apprehensions is not only a sense of HIS AWFULNESS and a sense of the majesty of HIS creation. It is a sense of the splendour of our vessel rather than her triviality and minuteness! It is as if I think of her as a separate world, a universe in little in which we must pass our lives and receive our reward or punishment. I trust the thought is not impious! It is a strange thought and a strong one!

It is with me still for, the breeze dying away, I ventured forth again. It is night now. I cannot tell you how high against the stars her great masts seem, how huge yet airy her sails, nor how far down from her deck the night-glittering surface of the waters. I remained motionless by the rail for I know not how long. While I was yet there, the last disturbance left by the breeze passed away so that the glitter, that image of the starry heavens, gave place to a flatness and blackness, a nothing! All was mystery. It terrified me and I turned away to find myself staring into the half-seen face of Mr Smiles, the sailing master. Phillips tells me that Mr Smiles, under the captain, is responsible for the navigation of our vessel.

'Mr Smiles—tell me how deep these waters are!'

He is a strange man, as I know already. He is given to long thought, constant observation. He is aptly named, too, for he has a kind of smiling remoteness which sets him apart from his fellow men.

'Who can say, Mr Colley?'

I laughed uneasily. He came closer and peered into my face. He is smaller even than I, and you know I am by no means a tall man.

'These waters may be more than a mile deep—two miles— who can say? We might sound at such a depth but commonly we do not. There is not the necessity.'

'More than a mile!'

I was almost overcome with faintness. Here we are, suspended between the land below the waters and the sky like a nut on a branch or a leaf on a pond! I cannot convey to you, my dear sister, my sense of horror, or shall I say, my sense of our being living souls in this place where surely, I thought, no man ought to be!

I wrote that last night by the light of a most expensive candle. You know how frugal I must be. Yet I am forced in on myself and must be indulged in a light if nothing else. It is in circumstances such as these present that a man (even if he make the fullest use of the consolations of religion that are available to his individual nature), that a man, I say, requires human companionship. Yet the ladies and gentlemen at this end of the ship do not respond with any cheerful alacrity to my greetings. I had thought at first that they were, as the saying is, 'shy of a parson'. I pressed Phillips again and again as to the meaning of this. Perhaps I should not have done so! He need not be privy to social divisions that are no concern of his. But he did mutter it was thought among the common people that a parson in a ship was like a woman in a fishing boat—a kind of natural bringer of bad luck. This low and reprehensible superstition cannot apply to our ladies and gentlemen. It is no kind of explanation. It seemed to me yesterday that I might have a clue as to their indefinable *indifference* to me. We have with us the celebrated, or let me say, the *notorious* free thinker, Mr Prettiman, that friend of Republicans and Jacobins! He is regarded by most, I think, with dislike. He is short and stocky. He has a bald head surrounded by a wild halo—dear me, how unfortunate my choice of words has been— a wild fringe of brown hair that grows from beneath his ears and round the back of his neck. He is a man of violent and eccentric movements that spring, we must suppose, from some well of his indignations. Our young ladies avoid him and the only one who will give him countenance is a Miss Granham, a lady of sufficient years and, I am sure, firmness of principle to afford her security even in the heat of his opinions. There is also a young lady, a Miss Brocklebank, of outstanding beauty, of whom—I say no more or you will think me arch. I believe she, at least, does not look on your brother unkindly! But she is much occupied with the indisposition of her mother, who suffers even more than I from *mal de mer*.

I have left to the last a description of a young gentleman whom I trust and pray will become my friend as the voyage advances. He is a member of the aristocracy, with all the consideration and nobility of bearing that such birth implies. I have made so bold as to salute him on a number of occasions and he has responded graciously. His example may do much among the other passengers.

This morning I have been out on deck again. A breeze had sprung up during the night and helped us on our way but now it has fallen calm again. Our sails hang down and there is a vaporous dimness everywhere, even at noon. Once more and with that same terrifying instantaneity came flashes of lightning in the mist that were awful in their fury! I fled to my cabin with such a sense of our peril from these warring elements, such a return of my sense of our suspension over this liquid profundity, that I could scarce get my hands together in prayer. However, little by little I came to myself and to peace though all outside was turmoil. I reminded myself, as I should have done before, that one good soul, one good deed, good thought, and more, one touch of Heaven's Grace was greater than all these boundless miles of rolling vapour and wetness, this intimidating vastness, this louring majesty! Indeed, I thought, though with some hesitation, that perhaps bad men in their ignorant deaths may find here the awfulness in which they must dwell by reason of their depravity. You see, my dear sister, that the strangeness of our surroundings, the weakness consequent on my prolonged nausea and a natural diffidence that has led me too readily to *shrink into my shell* has produced in me something not unlike a temporary disordering of the intellects! I found myself thinking of a seabird crying as one of those lost souls to whom I have alluded! I thanked GOD humbly that I had been allowed to detect this fantasy in myself before it became a belief.

I have roused myself from my lethargy. I have seen at least one possible reason for the indifference with which I feel myself treated. I have not made myself known to our captain and this may well have been thought a slight upon him! I am determined to undo this misapprehension as soon as possible. I shall approach him and express my sincere regret for the lack of Sabbath observance that my indisposition has occasioned in the ship, for she carries no chaplain. I must and will eradicate from my mind the ungenerous suspicion that on reaching or *joining* the ship I received less courtesy from the officers than is due to my cloth. Our Stout-hearted Defenders cannot, I am sure, be of such a sort. I will walk a little on deck now in preparation before readying myself to visit the captain. You remember my old diffidence at approaching the face of Authority and will feel for me!

I have been into the waist again and spoken once more with our sailing master. He was standing on the left-hand side of the vessel and staring with his particular intentness at the horizon; or rather, where the horizon ought to have been.

'Good morning, Mr Smiles! I should be happier if this vapour were to clear away!'

He smiled at me with that same mysterious remoteness.

'Very well, sir. I will see what can be done.'

I laughed at the quip. His good humour restored me completely to myself. So that I might *exorcise* those curious feelings of the strangeness of the world I went to the side of the vessel and leaned against the railings (the bulwarks as they are called) and looked down where the timbers of our enormous vessel bulge out past her closed gunports. Her slight progress made a tiny ripple in that sea which I made myself inspect coldly, as it were. My sense of its depth—but how am I to say this? I have seen many a millpond or corner of a river seem as deep! Nor was there a spot or speck in it where our ship divided it, a closing furrow in the poet Homer's 'Unfurrowed ocean'. Yet I found myself facing a new puzzle—and one that would not have presented itself to the poet! (You must know that Homer is commonly supposed to have been blind.) How then can water added to water produce an opacity? What impediment to the vision can colourlessness and transparency spread before us? Do we not see clear through glass or diamond or crystal? Do we not see the sun and moon and those fainter luminaries (I mean the stars) through unmeasured heights of pendant atmosphere? Yet here, what was glittering and black at night, grey under the racing clouds of awful tempest, now began little by little to turn blue and green under the sun that at last broke through the vapour!

Why should I, a cleric, a man of GOD, one acquainted with the robust if mistaken intellects of this and the preceding century and able to see them for what they are—why, I say, should the material nature of the globe so interest, so trouble and excite me? *They that go down to the sea in ships!* I cannot think of our Dear Country without finding myself looking not over the horizon (in my imagination, of course) but trying to calculate that segment of water and earth and *terrible deep rock* that I must suppose myself to stare through in order to look in your direction and that of our—let me say *our*—village! I must ask Mr Smiles, who will be well enough acquainted with the angles and appropriate mathematics of the case, as to the precise number of degrees it is necessary to look beneath the horizon! How immeasurably strange it will be at the Antipodes to stare (near enough I think) at the buckles of my shoes and suppose you—forgive me, I am off in a fantasy again! Do but think that there the very stars will be unfamiliar and the moon stood on her head!

Enough of fantasy! I will go now and make myself known to our captain! Perhaps I may have some opportunity of entertaining him with the idle fancies I have alluded to above.

———————

I have approached Captain Anderson and will narrate the plain facts to you if I can. My fingers are almost nerveless and will scarcely allow me to hold the pen. You may deduce that from the quality of this handwriting.

Well then, I attended to my clothes with more than usual care, came out of my cabin and ascended the flights of stairs to that highest deck where the captain commonly stations himself. At the front end of this deck and rather below it are the wheel and compass. Captain Anderson and the first lieutenant, Mr Summers, were staring together at the compass. I saw the moment was unpropitious and waited for a while. At last the two gentlemen finished their conversation. The captain turned away and walked to the very back end of the vessel and I followed him, thinking this my opportunity. But no sooner had he reached the rail at the back than he turned round again. As I was following closely I had to leap sideways in what must have appeared a manner hardly consonant with the dignity of my sacred office. Scarcely had I recovered my balance when he *growled* at me as if I had been at fault rather than he. I uttered a word or two of introduction which he dismissed with a grunt. He then made a remark which he did not trouble to modify with any show of civility.

'Passengers come to the quarterdeck by invitation. I am not accustomed to these interruptions in my walk, sir. Go forrard if you please and keep to looard.

'Looard, captain?'

I found myself drawn forcibly sideways. A young gentleman was pulling me to the wheel whence he led me—I complying—to the opposite side of the ship to where Captain Anderson was. He positively hissed in my ear. That side of the deck, whichever it may be, from which the wind blows is reserved to the captain. I had therefore made a mistake but could not see how I was at fault but by an ignorance natural in a gentleman who had never been at sea before. Yet I am deeply suspicious that the surliness of the captain towards me is not to be explained so readily. Is it perhaps sectarianism? If so, as a humble servant of the Church of England—the Catholic Church of England—which spreads its arms so wide in the charitable embrace of sinners, I cannot but deplore such divisive stubbornness! Or if it is not sectarianism but a social contempt, the situation is as serious—nay, *almost* as serious! I am a clergyman, bound for an honourable if humble situation at the Antipodes. The captain has no more business to look big on me—and indeed less business—than the canons of the Close or those clergy I have met *twice* at my Lord Bishop's table! I have determined therefore to emerge more frequently from my obscurity and exhibit my cloth to this gentleman and the passengers in general so that even if they do not respect *me* they may respect *it*! I may surely hope for some support from the young gentleman, Mr Edmund Talbot, from Miss Brocklebank and Miss Granham—It is evident I must return to the captain, offer him my sincere apologies for my inadvertent trespass, then raise the question of Sabbath Observance. I would beg to offer Communion to the ladies and gentlemen—and of course to the common people who should desire it. There is, I fear, only too plainly room for much improvement in the conduct of affairs aboard the vessel. There is (for example) a daily ceremony of which I had heard and would now wish to prevent—for you know how paternally severe my Lord Bishop has been in his condemnation of drunkenness among the lower orders! Yet here it is only too true! The people are indeed given strong drink regularly! A further reason for instituting worship must be the opportunities it will afford for animadverting on the subject! I shall return to the captain and proceed by a process of mollification. I must indeed be all things to all men.

I have attempted to be so and have failed abjectly, humiliatingly. It was, as I wrote before, in my mind to ascend to the captain's deck, apologize for my previous trespass, beg his permission to use it and then raise the question of regular worship. I can scarcely bring myself to recount the truly awful scene that followed on my well-meant attempt to bring myself to the familiar notice of the officers and gentlemen. As soon as I had written the foregoing paragraph I went up to the lower part of the quarter-deck where one of the lieutenants stood by the two men at the wheel. I lifted my hat to him and made an amiable comment.

'We are now in finer weather, sir.'

The lieutenant ignored me. But this was not the worst of it. There came a kind of growling roar from the back rail of the ship.

'Mr Colley! Mr Colley! Come here, sir!'

This was not the kind of invitation I had looked for. I liked neither the tone nor the words. But they were nothing to what followed as I approached the captain.

'Mr Colley! Do you wish to subvert all my officers?'

'Subvert, sir?'

'It was my word, sir!'

'There is some mistake——'

'It is yours then, sir. Are you aware of the powers of a captain in his own ship?'

'They are rightly extensive. But as an ordained minister——'

'You are a passenger, sir, neither more nor less. What is more, you are not behaving as decent as the rest——'

'Sir!'

'You are a nuisance, sir. You was put aboard this ship without a note to me. There is more courtesy shown me about a bale or a keg, sir. Then I did you the credit to suppose you could read——'

'Read, Captain Anderson? Of course I can read!'

'But despite my plainly written orders, no sooner had you recovered from your sickness than you have twice approached and exasperated my officers——'

'I know nothing of this, have read nothing——'

'They are my Standing Orders, sir, a paper prominently displayed near your quarters and those of the other passengers.'

'My attention was not drawn——'

'Stuff and nonsense, sir. You have a servant and the orders are there.'

'My attention——'

'Your ignorance is no excuse. If you wish to have the same freedom as the other passengers enjoy in the after part of the vessel—or do you wish not to live among ladies and gentlemen, sir? Go—examine the paper!'

'It is my right——'

'Read it, sir. And when you have read it, get it by heart.'

'How, sir! Will you treat me like a schoolboy?'

'I will treat you like a schoolboy if I choose, sir, or I will put you in irons if I choose or have you flogged at the gratings if I choose or have you hanged at the yardarm if I choose——'

'Sir! Sir!'

'Do you doubt my authority?'

I saw it all now. Like my poor young friend Josh—you remember Josh—Captain Anderson was mad. Josh was always well enough in his wits except when frogs were in question. *Then* his mania was clear for all to hear, and later, alas, for all to see. Now here was Captain Anderson, well enough for the most part, but by some unfortunate chance fixing on me in his mania for an object to be humiliated—as indeed I was. I could do nothing but humour him for there was, mad or no, that in his enraged demeanour which convinced me he was capable of carrying out at least some of his threats. I answered him as lightly as possible but in a voice, I fear, sadly tremulous.

'I will indulge you in this, Captain Anderson.'

'You will carry out my orders.'

I turned away and withdrew silently. Directly I was out of his presence I found my body bathed in perspiration yet strangely cold, though my face, by some contrast, was as strangely hot. I discovered in myself a deep unwillingness to meet any eye, any face. As for my own eyes—I was weeping! I wish I could say they were tears of manly wrath but the truth is they were tears of shame. On shore a man is punished at the last by the Crown. At sea the man is punished by the captain who is visibly present as the Crown is not. At sea a person's manhood suffers. It is a kind of contest—is that not strange? So that men—but I wander in my narrative. Suffice it to say that I found, nay, groped my way back to the neighbourhood of my cabin. When my eyes had cleared and I had come to myself a little I searched for the captain's written Orders. They were indeed displayed on a wall near the cabins! Now I did remember too that during the convulsions of my sickness Phillips had talked to me about *Orders* and even *the captain's Orders*; but only those who have suffered as I can understand how slight an impression the words had made on my fainting spirits. But here they were. It was unfortunate, to say the least. I had, by the most severe standards, been remiss. The Orders were displayed in a case. The glass was somewhat blurred on the inside by a condensation of atmospheric water. But I was able to read the writing, the material part of which I copy here.

Passengers are in no case to speak to officers who are executing some duty about the ship. In no case are they to address the officer of the watch during his hours of duty unless expressly enjoined to do so by him.

I saw now what a hideous situation I was in. The officer of the watch, I reasoned, must have been the first lieutenant, who had been with the captain, and at my *second* attempt the lieutenant who had stood by the men at the wheel. My fault was quite inadvertent but none the less real. Even though the manner of Captain Anderson to me had not been and perhaps never would be that of one gentleman to another, yet some form of apology was due to him and through him to those other officers whom I might have hindered in the execution of their duty. Then too, forbearance must be in the very nature of my calling. I therefore easily and quickly committed the essential words to memory and returned at once to the raised decks which are included in the seaman's term 'Quarterdeck'. The wind was increased somewhat. Captain Anderson paced up and down the side, Lieutenant Summers talked to another lieutenant by the wheel, where two of the ship's people guided our huge vessel creaming over the billows. Mr Summers pointed to some rope or other in the vast complication of the rigging. A young gentleman who stood behind the lieutenants touched his hat and skipped nimbly down the stairs by which I had ascended. I approached the captain's back and waited for him to turn.

Captain Anderson walked through me!

I could almost wish that he had in truth done so—yet the hyperbole is not inapt. He must have been very deep in thought. He struck me on the shoulder with his swinging arm and then his chest struck me in the face so that I went reeling and ended by measuring my length on the white-scrubbed planking of the deck!

I got my breath back with difficulty. My head was resounding from a concussive encounter with the wood. Indeed, for a moment it appeared that not one but two captains were staring down at me. It was some time before I realized that I was being addressed.

'Get up, sir! Get up at once! Is there no end to your impertinent folly?'

I was scrabbling on the deck for my hat and wig. I had little enough breath for a rejoinder.

'Captain Anderson—you asked me——'

'I asked nothing of you, sir. I gave you an order.'

'My apology——'

'I did not ask for an apology. We are not on land but at sea. Your apology is a matter of indifference to me——'

'Nevertheless——'

There was, I thought, and indeed was frighted by the thought, a kind of stare in his eyes, a suffusion of blood in all his countenance that made me believe he might well assault me physically. One of his fists was raised and I own that I crouched away a few steps without replying. But then he struck the fist into the other palm.

'Am I to be outfaced again and again on my own deck by every ignorant landsman who cares to walk there? Am I? Tell me, sir!'

'My apology—was intended——'

'I am more concerned with your person, sir, which is more apparent to me than your mind and which has formed the habit of being in the wrong place at the wrong time—repeat your lesson, sir!'

My face felt swollen. It must have been as deeply suffused as his. I perspired more and more freely. My head still rang. The lieutenants were studiously and carefully examining the horizon. The two seamen at the wheel might have been cast in bronze. I believe I gave a shuddering sob. The words I had learned so recently and easily went clean out of my head. I could see but dimly through my tears. The captain grumbled, perhaps a thought—indeed I hope so—a thought less fiercely.

'Come, sir. Repeat your lesson!'

'A period for recollection. A period——'

'Very well. Come back when you can do it. Do you understand?'

I must have made some reply, for he concluded the interview with his hectoring roar.

'Well, sir—what are you waiting for?'

I did not so much go to my cabin as flee to it. As I approached the second flight of stairs I saw Mr Talbot and the two young gentlemen he had with him—three more witnesses to my humiliation!—hurry out of sight into the lobby. I fell down the stairs, the ladders as I suppose I must call them, hurried into my cabin and flung myself down by my bunk. I was shaking all over, my teeth were chattering. I could hardly breathe. Indeed I believe, nay, I confess that I should have fallen into a fit, a syncope, a seizure or the like—something at all events that would have ended my life, or reason at least, had I not heard young Mr Talbot outside the cabin speak in a firm voice to one of the young gentlemen. He said something like—Come, young midshipman, one *gentleman* does not take pleasure in the persecution of another! At that my tears burst forth freely but with what I may call a healing freedom! God bless Mr Talbot! There is one *true* gentleman in this ship and I pray that before we reach our destination I may call him *Friend* and tell him how much his true consideration has meant to me! Indeed, I now knelt, rather than crouched by my bunk and gave thanks for his consideration and understanding—for his noble charity! I prayed for us both. Only then was I able to sit at this table and consider my situation with something like a rational coolness.

However I turned the thing over and over, I saw one thing clearly enough. As soon as I saw it I came near to falling into a panic all over again. There was—there *is* no doubt—I am the object of a particular animosity on the part of the captain! It was with a thrill of something approaching terror that I re-created in my imagination that moment when he had, as I expressed it, 'walked through me'. For I saw now that it was not an accident. His arm, when it struck me, moved not after the common manner in walking but continued its swing with an unnatural momentum—augmented immediately after by the blow from his chest that ensured my fall. I knew, or my person knew, by some extraordinary faculty, that Captain Anderson had deliberately struck me down! He is an enemy to religion—it can only be that! Oh what a spotted soul!

My tears had cleansed my mind. They had exhausted but not defeated me. I thought first of my cloth. He had tried to dishonour that; but I told myself, *that* only I could do. Nor could he dishonour me as a common fellow-being since I had committed no fault, no sin but the venial one of omitting to read his Orders! For that, my sickness was more to blame than I! It is true I had been foolish and was perhaps an object of scorn and amusement to the officers and the other gentlemen with the exception of Mr Talbot. But then—and I said this in all humility—so would my Master have been! At that I began to understand that the situation, harsh and unjust as it might seem, was a lesson to me. He puts down the mighty and exalteth the humble and meek. Humble I was of necessity before all the brutal powers which are inherent in absolute command. Meek, therefore, it behoved me to be. My dear sister——

Yet this is strange. Already what I have written would be too painful for your—for her—eyes. It must be amended, altered, softened; and yet——

If not to my sister than to whom? To THEE? Can it be that like THY saints of old (particularly Saint Augustine) I am addressing THEE, OH MOST MERCIFUL SAVIOUR?

I have prayed long. That thought had flung me to my knees—was at once a pain and a consolation to me. Yet I was able to put it away at last as too high for me! To have—oh, indeed, not touched the hem of those garments—but to have glanced for a moment towards THOSE FEET—restored me to a clearer view of myself and of my situation. I sat, then, and reflected.

I concluded at last that it would be proper to do either of two things. Item: never to return to the quarterdeck, but for the remainder of our passage hold myself aloof from it with dignity; the other: to go to the quarterdeck, repeat Captain Anderson's Orders to him and to as many gentlemen as might be present, add some such cool remark as 'And now, Captain Anderson, I will trouble you no further,' then withdraw, absolutely declining to use that part of the vessel in any circumstances whatever—unless perhaps Captain Anderson himself should condescend (which I did not believe) to offer me an apology. I spent some time emending and refining my farewell speech to him. But at last I was driven to the consideration that he might not afford me the opportunity of uttering it. He is a master of the brutal and quelling rejoinder. Better then to pursue the first course and give him no further cause or opportunity to insult me.

I must own to a great feeling of relief at reaching this decision. With the aid of PROVIDENCE I might contrive to avoid him until the end of our voyage. However, my first duty, as a Christian, was to forgive him, monster as he was. I was able to do this but not without recourse to much prayer and some contemplation of the awful fate that awaited him when he should find himself at last before the THRONE. There, I knew him for my brother, was his keeper, and prayed for us both.

That done, to trifle for a moment with profane literature, like

some Robinson Crusoe, I set to and considered what part of the
vessel remained to me as my—as I expressed it—my *kingdom!* It
comprised my cabin, the corridor or lobby outside it, the passenger saloon, where I might take such sustenance as I was bold
enough to in the presence of the other ladies and gentlemen who
had been all witnesses of my humiliation. There were too the
necessary offices on this side of the vessel and the deck, or *waist*
as Phillips calls it, as far as the white line at the main mast which
separates us from the common people, be they either seamen or
emigrants. That deck was to be for my airing in fine weather.
There I might meet the better disposed of the gentlemen—and
ladies too! There—for I knew he used it—I should further and
deepen my friendship with Mr Talbot. Of course, in wet and
windy weather I must be content with the lobby and my cabin. I
saw that even if I were to be confined to these areas I might still
pass the months ahead without too much discomfort and avoid
what is most to be feared, a melancholy leading on to madness.
All would be well.

This was a decision and a discovery that gave me more earthly
pleasure, I believe, than anything I have experienced since parting
from those scenes so dear to me. Immediately I went out and
paced round my island—my *kingdom!*—in the meantime reflecting
on all those who would have welcomed such an expansion of
their territory as the attainment of liberty—I mean those who in
the course of history have found themselves imprisoned for a just
cause. Though I have, so to speak, abdicated from that part of
the vessel which ought to be the prerogative of my cloth and
consequent station in our society, the waist is in some ways to be
preferred to the quarterdeck! Indeed I have seen Mr Talbot not
merely walk to the white line, but cross it and go among the
common people in a generous and democratic freedom!

Since writing those last words I have furthered my acquaintance
with Mr Talbot! It was he of all people who did in fact search me
out! He is a true friend to religion! He came to my cabin and
begged me in the most friendly and open manner to favour the
ship's people in the evening with a short address! I did so in the
passenger saloon. I cannot pretend that many of the *gentry*, as I
may call them, paid much attention to what they heard and only
one of the officers was present. I therefore addressed myself
particularly to those hearts I thought readily open to the message

I have to give—to a young lady of great piety and beauty and to Mr Talbot himself, whose devotion does credit not only to him in person but through him to his whole order. Would that the gentry and Nobility of England were all imbued with a like spirit!

———————

It must be the influence of Captain Anderson; or perhaps they ignore me from a refinement of manners, a delicacy of feeling— but though I salute our ladies and gentlemen from the waist when I see them up there on the quarterdeck, they seldom acknowledge the salutation! Yet now, truth to tell, and for the past three days there has been nothing to salute—no waist to walk on since it is awash with sea water. I find myself not sick as I was before—I am become a proper sailor! Mr Talbot, however, is sick indeed. I asked Phillips what was the matter and the man replied with an evident sarcasm—*belike it was summat he ate!* I did dare to cross the lobby softly and knock, but there was no reply. Daring still further I lifted the latch and entered. The young man lay asleep, a week's beard on his lips and chin and cheeks—I scarce dare put down here the impression his slumbering countenance made on me—it was as the face of ONE who suffered for us all—and as I bent over him in some irresistible compulsion I do not deceive myself but there was the sweet aroma of holiness itself upon his breath! I did not think myself worthy of his lips but pressed my own reverently on the one hand that lay outside the coverlet. Such is the power of goodness that I withdrew as from an altar!

The weather has cleared again. Once more I take my walks in the waist and the ladies and gentlemen theirs on the quarterdeck. Yet I find myself a good sailor and was about in the open before other people!

The air in my cabin is hot and humid. Indeed, we are approaching the hottest region of the world. Here I sit at my writing-flap in shirt and unmentionables and indite this letter, if letter it be, which is in some sort my only friend. I must confess to a shyness still before the ladies since the captain gave me my great *set-down*. Mr Talbot, I hear, improves and has been visible for some days, but with a diffidence before my cloth and indeed it may be with some desire to spare me embarrassment, he holds aloof.

Since writing that, I have walked again in the waist. It is now a mild and sheltered place. Walking there I have come to the opinion of our brave sailors which landsmen have ever held of them! I have observed these common people closely. These are the good fellows whose duty it is to steer our ship, to haul on the ropes and do strange things with our sails in positions which must surely be perilous, so high they go! Their service is a continual round and necessary, I must suppose, to the progress of the vessel. They are for ever cleaning and scraping and painting. They create marvellous structures from the very substance of rope itself! I had not known what can be done with rope! I had seen here and there on land ingenuities of wood-carving in imitation of rope; here I saw rope carved into the imitation of wood! Some of the people do indeed carve in wood or in the shells of coconuts or in bone or perhaps ivory. Some are making the models of ships such as we see displayed in the windows of shops or inns or alehouses near seaports. They seem to be people of infinite ingenuity.

All this I watch with complacency from far off in the shelter of the wooden wall with its stairways that lead up to where the *privileged* passengers live. Up there is silence, or the low murmur of conversation or the harsh sound of a shouted order. But forward, beyond the white line, the people work and sing and keep time to the fiddle when they play—for like children, they play, dancing innocently to the sound of the fiddle. It is as if the childhood of the world were upon them. All this has thrown me into some perplexity. The ship is crowded at the front end. There is a small group of soldiers in uniform, there are a few emigrants, the women seeming common as the men. But when I ignore all but the ship's people, I find *them* objects of astonishment to me. They cannot, for the most part, read or write. They know nothing of what our officers know. But these fine, manly fellows have a complete—what shall I call it? 'Civilization' it is not, for they have no city. Society it might be, save that in some ways they are *joined* to the superior officers, and there are classes of men between the one and the other—warrant officers they are called!—and there appear to be grades of authority among the sailors themselves. What are they then, these beings at once so free and so dependent? They are *seamen*, and I begin to understand the word. You may observe them when they are released from duty to stand with arms linked or placed about each other's shoulders. They sleep sometimes on the scrubbed planking of the deck, one it may be, with his head pillowed on another's breast! The innocent pleasures of friendship—in which I, alas, have as *yet* so little experience—the joy of kindly association or even that bond between two persons which, Holy Writ directs us, passes the love of women, must be the cement that holds their company together. It has indeed seemed to me from what I have jestingly represented as 'my kingdom' that the life of the front end of the vessel is sometimes to be preferred to the vicious system of control which obtains *aft of the mizzen* or even *aft of the main!* (The precision of these two phrases I owe to my servant Phillips.) Alas that my calling and the degree in society consequent on it should set me so firmly where I no longer desire to be!

We have had a spell of bad weather—not very bad, but sufficient to keep most of our ladies in their cabins. Mr Talbot keeps his. My servant assures me that the young man is not seasick, yet I have heard strange sounds emanating from behind his locked door. I had the temerity to offer my services and was both disconcerted and concerned to wring from the poor young gentleman the admission that he was wrestling with his soul in prayer! Far, far be it from me to blame him—no, no, I would not do so! But the sounds were those of *enthusiasm!* I much fear that the young man for all his rank has fallen victim to one of the extremer systems against which our Church has set her face! I must and will help him! but that can only be when he is himself again and moves among us with his customed ease. These attacks of a too passionate devotion are to be feared more than the fevers to which the inhabitants of these climes are subject. He is a layman; and it shall be my pleasant duty to bring him back to that decent moderation in religion which is, if I may coin a phrase, the genius of the Church of England!

He has reappeared; and avoids me, perhaps in an embarrassment at having been detected at his too protracted devotions; I will let him be for the moment and pray for him while we move day by day, I hope, towards a mutual understanding. I saluted him from far off this morning as he walked on the quarterdeck but he affected to take no notice. Noble young man! He who has been so ready to help others will not deign, on his own behalf, to ask for help!

This morning in the waist I have been spectator once again of that ceremony which moves me with a mixture of grief and admiration. A barrel is set on the deck. The seamen stand in line and each is given successively a mug of liquid from the barrel which he drains off after exclaiming, 'The King! GOD bless him!' I would His Majesty could have seen it. I know of course that the liquid is the devil's brew and I do not swerve one jot or tittle from my previous opinion that strong drink should be prohibited from use by the lower orders. For sure, ale is enough and too much—but let them have it!

Yet here, *here* on the bounding main, under the hot sun and with a whole company of bronzed young fellows bared to the waist—their hands and feet hard with honest and dangerous toil—their stern yet open faces weathered by the storms of every ocean, their luxuriant curls fluttering from their foreheads in the breeze—*here*, if there was no overthrowing of my opinion, there was at least a modification and mitigation of it. Watching one young fellow in particular, a narrow-waisted, slim-hipped yet broad-shouldered *Child of Neptune*, I felt that some of what was malignant in the potion was cancelled by where and who was concerned with it. For it was as if these beings, these young men, or some of them at least and one of them in particular, were of the giant breed. I called to mind the legend of Talos, the man of bronze whose artificial frame was filled with liquid fire. It seemed to me that such an evidently fiery liquid as the one (it is *rum*) which a mistaken benevolence and paternalism provides for the sea-service was the proper *ichor* (this was the blood of the Grecian Gods, supposedly) for beings of such semi-divinity, of such truly heroic proportions! Here and there among them the marks of the discipline were evident and they bore these parallel scars with indifference and even pride! Some, I verily believe, saw them as marks of distinction! Some, and that not a few, bore on their frames the scars of unquestioned honour—scars of the cutlass, pistol, grape or splinter. None were maimed; or if they were, it was in such a minor degree, a finger, eye or ear perhaps, that the blemish hung on them like a medal. There was one whom I called in my mind my own particular hero! He had nought but four or five white scratches on the left side of his open and amiable countenance as if like Hercules he had struggled with a wild beast! (Hercules, you know, was fabled to have wrestled with the Nemaean Lion.) His feet were bare and his nether limbs—*my* young hero I refer to, rather than the legendary one! His nether garments clung to his lower limbs as if moulded there. I was much taken with the manly grace with which he tossed off his mug of liquor and returned the empty vessel to the top of the barrel. I had an odd fancy. I remembered to have read somewhere in the history of the union that when Mary, Queen of Scots, first came into her kingdom she was entertained at a feast. It was recorded that her throat was so slender and her skin so white that as she swallowed wine the ruby richness of the liquid was visible through it to the onlookers! This scene had always exercised a powerful influence over my infant spirits! It was only now that I remembered with what childish pleasure I had supposed my future spouse would exhibit some such particular comeliness of person— in addition of course to the more necessary beauties of mind and spirit. But now, with Mr Talbot shy of me, I found myself, in my *kingdom* of lobby, cabin and waist, unexpectedly dethroned and a new monarch elevated there! For this young man of bronze with his flaming ichor—and as he drank the liquor down it seemed to me that I heard a furnace roar and with my inward eye saw the fire burst forth—it seemed to me with my *outer* eye that he could be no other than the king! I abdicated freely and yearned to kneel before him. My whole heart went out in a passionate longing to bring this young man to OUR SAVIOUR, first and surely richest fruit of the harvest I am sent forth to garner! After he retired from the barrel, my eye followed him without my volition. But he went where I, alas, could not go. He ran out along that fourth mast laid more nearly horizontal, the bowsprit I mean, with its complication of ropes and tackles and chains and booms and sails. I was reminded of the old oak in which you and I were wont to climb. But he (the king) ran out there or up there and stood at the tip of the very thinnest spar and looked down into the sea. His whole body moved easily to counter our slight motion. Only his shoulder leaned against a rope, so that he lounged as he might against a tree! Then he turned, ran back a few paces and *lay down* on the surface of the thicker part of the bowsprit as securely as I might in my bed! Surely there is nothing so splendidly free as a young fellow in the branches of one of His Majesty's *travelling trees*, as I may call them! Or forests, even! There lay the king, then, crowned with curls—but I grow fanciful.

We are in the doldrums. Mr Talbot still avoids me. He has been wandering round the ship and descending into her very bowels as

if searching for some private place where, perhaps, he may
continue his devotions without hindrance. I fear sadly that my
approach was untimely and did more damage than good. I pray
for him. What can I do more?

We are motionless. The sea is polished. There is no sky but
only a hot whiteness that descends like a curtain on every side,
dropping, as it were, even below the horizon and so diminishing the circle of the ocean that is visible to us. The circle itself
is of a light and luminescent blue. Now and then some sea
creature will shatter the surface and the silence by leaping
through it. Yet even when nothing leaps there is a constant
shuddering, random twitches and vibrations of the surface, as
if the water were not only the home and haunt of all sea creatures but the skin of a living thing, a creature vaster than
Leviathan. The heat and dampness combined would be quite
inconceivable to one who had never left that pleasant valley
which was our home. Our own motionlessness—and this I believe you will not find mentioned in the accounts of sea voy-
ages—has increased the effluvias that rise from the waters
immediately round us. Yesterday morning there was a slight
breeze but we were soon still again. All our people are silent,
so that the striking of the ship's bell is a loud and startling
sound. Today the effluvias became intolerable from the necessary soiling of the water round us. The boats were hoisted out
from the *boom* and the ship towed a little way from the odious
place; but now if we do not get any wind it will all be to do
again. In my cabin I sit or lie in shirt and breeches and even
so find the air hardly to be borne. Our ladies and gentlemen
keep their cabin in a like case, lying abed I think, in hope that
the weather and the place may pass. Only Mr Talbot roams as
if he can find no peace—poor young man! May GOD be with
him and keep him! I have approached him once but he bowed
slightly and distantly. The time is not yet.

———————

How next to impossible is the exercise of virtue! It requires a
constant watchfulness, constant guard—oh my dear sister, how
much must you and I and every Christian soul rely at every
moment on the operation of Grace! There has been an altercation!
It was not, as you might expect, among the poor people in the

front of the ship but here among the gentlemen, nay, among the very officers themselves!

It was thus. I was sitting at my writing-flap and recutting a quill when I heard a scuffle outside in the lobby, then voices, soft at first but raised later.

'You dog, Deverel! I saw you come from the cabin!'

'What are you about then, Cumbershum, for your part, you rogue!'

'Give it to me, sir! By G—— I will have it!'

'And unopened at either end—— You sly dog, Cumbershum, I'll read it, I swear I will!'

The scuffle became noisy. I was in shirt and breeches, my shoes under the bunk, my stockings hung over it, my wig on a convenient nail. The language became so much more blasphemous and filthy that I could not let the occasion pass. Not thinking of my appearance I got up quickly and rushed out of the cabin, to find the two officers struggling violently for possession of a missive. I cried out.

'Gentlemen! Gentlemen!'

I seized the nearest to me by the shoulder. They stopped the fight and turned to me.

'Who the devil is this, Cumbershum?'

'It's the parson, I think. Be off, sir, about your own business!'

'I am about my business, my friends, and exhort you in a spirit of Christian Charity to cease this unseemly behaviour, this unseemly language, and make up your quarrel!'

Lieutenant Deverel stood looking down at me with his mouth open.

'Well by thunder!'

The gentleman addressed as Cumbershum—another lieutenant—stuck his forefinger so violently towards my face that had I not recoiled, it would have entered my eye.

'Who in the name of all that's wonderful gave you permission to preach in this ship?'

'Yes, Cumbershum, you have a point.'

'Leave this to me, Deverel. Now, parson, if that's what you are, show us your authority.'

'Authority?'

'D——n it man, I mean your commission!'

'Commission!'

'Licence they call it, Cumbershum, old fellow, licence to preach. Right parson—show us your licence!'

I was taken aback, nay, confounded. The truth is, and I record it here for you to pass to any young clergyman about to embark on such a voyage, I had deposited the licence from my Lord Bishop with other private papers—not, as I supposed, needed on the voyage—in my trunk, which had been lowered somewhere into the bowels of the vessel. I attempted to explain this briefly to the officers but Mr Deverel interrupted me.

'Be off with you, sir, or I shall take you before the captain!'

I must confess that this threat sent me hurrying back into my cabin with some considerable trepidation. For a moment or two I wondered whether I had not after all succeeded in abating their mutual wrath, for I heard them both laughing loudly as they walked away. But I concluded that such heedless—I will not call them more—such heedless spirits were far more likely to be laughing at the *sartorial* mistake I had made and the result of the interview with which they had threatened me. It was clear that I had been at fault in allowing myself a public appearance less *explicit* than that sanctioned by custom and required by decorum. I began hurriedly to dress, not forgetting my bands, though my throat in the heat felt them as an unfortunate constriction. I regretted that my gown and hood were packed or, should I say, *stowed* away with my other impedimenta. At length, then, clothed in at least some of the visible marks of the dignity and authority of my calling, I issued forth from my cabin. But of course the two lieutenants were nowhere to be seen.

But already, in this equatorial part of the globe, after being fully dressed for no more than a moment or two I was bathed in perspiration. I walked out into the waist but felt no relief from the heat. I returned to the lobby and my cabin determined to be more comfortable yet not knowing what to do. I could be, without the sartorial adornment of my calling, mistaken for an emigrant! I was debarred from intercourse with the ladies and gentlemen and had been given no opportunity other than that first one of addressing the common people. Yet to endure the heat and moisture in a garb appropriate to the English countryside seemed impossible. On an impulse derived, I fear, less from Christian practice than from my reading of the classical authors, I opened the Sacred Book and before I was well aware of what I was doing I had employed the moment in a kind of *Sortes Virgilianae*, or consultation of the oracle, a process I had always thought to be questionable even when employed by the holiest servants of the

Lord. The words my eyes fell on were II Chronicles viii. 7–8. 'The Hittites, and the Amorites, and the Perizzites, and the Hivites, and the Jebusites which were not of Israel'—words which in the next moment I had applied to Captain Anderson and Lieutenants Deverel and Cumbershum, then flung myself on my knees and implored forgiveness!

I record this trivial offence merely to show the oddities of behaviour, the perplexities of the understanding, in a word, the *strangeness* of this life in this strange part of the world among strange people and in this strange construction of English oak which both transports and imprisons me! (I am aware, of course, of the amusing 'paranomasia' in the word 'transport' and hope the perusal of it will afford you some entertainment!)

To resume. After a period at my devotions I considered what I had better do in order to avoid any future mistake as to my *sanctified* identity. I divested myself once more of all but shirt and breeches, and thus divested, I employed the small mirror which I have for use when shaving to examine my appearance. This was a process of some difficulty. Do you remember the knothole in the barn through which in our childish way we were wont to keep watch for Jonathan or our poor, sainted mother, or his lordship's bailiff, Mr Jolly? Do you remember, moreover, how when we were tired of waiting, we would see by moving our heads how much of the exterior world we could spy through the knot? Then we would pretend to be seized of all we saw, from Seven Acre right up to the top of the hill? In such a manner did I contort myself before the mirror and the mirror before me! But here I am—if indeed this letter should ever be sent—instructing a member of the Fair Sex in the employment of a mirror and the art of, dare I call it, 'Self-admiration'? In my own case, of course, I use the word in its original sense of surprise and wonder rather than self-satisfaction! There was much to wonder at in what I saw but little to approve. I had not fully understood before how harshly the sun can deal with the male countenance that is exposed to its more nearly vertical rays.

My hair, as you know, is of a light but indeterminate hue. I now saw that your cropping of it on the day before our parting— due surely to our mutual distress—had been sadly uneven. This unevenness seems to have been accentuated rather than dimin- ished by the passage of time so that my head presented an appear- ance not unlike a patch of ill-reaped stubble. Since I had not been able to shave during my first *nausea* (the word indeed derives from the Greek word for a ship!) and had feared to do so in the later period when the ship was in violent motion—and at last have been dilatory, fearing the pain I should inflict on my sun-scorched skin, the lower part of my face was covered with bristles. They were not long, since my beard is of slow growth—but of varying hue. Between these two *crop-yielding areas*, as I may call them, of scalp and beard, king Sol had exerted his full sway. What is sometimes called a widow's peak of rosy skin delineated the exact extent to which my wig had covered my forehead. Below that line the forehead was plum-coloured and in one place burst with the heat. Below that again, my nose and cheeks appeared red as on fire! I saw at once that I had deceived myself entirely if I supposed that appearing in shirt and breeches and in this *guise* I should exert the authority inhering in my profession. Nay—are these not of all people those who judge a man by his uniform? My 'uniform,' as I must in all humility call it, must be sober black with the pure whiteness of bleached linen and bleached hair, the adornments of the Spiritual Man. To the offi-cers and people of this ship, a clergyman without his bands and wig would be of no more account than a beggar.

True, it was the sudden sound of an altercation and the desire to do good that had drawn me forth from my seclusion, but I was to blame. I drew in my breath with something like fear as I envisaged the appearance I must have presented to them—with a bare head, unshaven, sunblotched, unclothed! It was with con-fusion and shame that I remembered the words addressed to me individually at my ordination—words I must ever hold sacred because of the occasion and the saintly divine who spake them—'Avoid scrupulosity, Colley, and always present a decent appear-ance.' Was *this* that I now saw in the mirror of my imagination the figure of a labourer in that country where 'the fields are white to harvest'? Among those with whom I now dwell, a respectable appearance is not merely a *desideratum* but a *sine qua non*. (I mean, my dear, not merely desirable but necessary.) I determined at once to take more care. When I walked in what I had thought of as my kingdom, I would not only be a man of GOD—I would be *seen* to be a man of GOD!

Things are a little better. Lieutenant Summers came and begged the favour of a word with me. I answered him through the door, begging him not to enter as I was not yet prepared in clothes or visage for an interview. He assented, but in a low voice as if afraid that others would hear. He asked my pardon for the fact that there had been no more services in the passenger saloon. He had repeatedly *sounded* the passengers and had met with indifference. I asked him if he had asked Mr Talbot and he replied after a pause that Mr Talbot had been much occupied with his own affairs. But he, Mr Summers, thought that there might be a chance of what he called a *small gathering* on the next Sabbath. I found myself declaring through the door with a passion quite unlike my usual even temper——

'This is a Godless vessel!'

Mr Summers made no reply so I made a further remark.

'It is the influence of a certain person!'

At this I heard Mr Summers change his position outside the door as if he had suddenly looked round him. Then he whispered to me.

'Do not, I beg you, Mr Colley, entertain such thoughts! A small gathering, sir—a hymn or two, a reading and a benediction——'

I took the opportunity to point out that a morning service in the waist would be far more appropriate; but Lieutenant Summers replied with what I believe to be a degree of embarrassment that *it could not be*. He then withdrew. However, it is a small victory for religion. Nay—who knows when that heart of awful flint may be brought to yield as yield at last it must?

I have discovered the name of my Young Hero. He is one Billy Rogers, a sad scamp, I fear, whose boyish heart has not yet been touched with Grace. I shall try to make an opportunity of speaking with him.

I have passed the last hour in *shaving!* It was indeed painful and I cannot say that the result justifies the labour. However, it is done.

I heard an unwonted noise and went into the lobby. As I did so, I felt the deck tilt under me—though very slightly—but alas! The few days of almost total calm have unfitted me for the motion and I have lost the 'sea legs' I thought I had acquired! I was forced to retire precipitately to my cabin and bunk. There I was better placed and could feel that we have some wind, favourable, light and easy. We are moving on our way again; and though I did not at once care to trust to my legs I felt that elevation of the spirits which must come to any traveller when after some let or hindrance he discovers himself to be on the move towards his destination.

A day's rest lies in that line I have drawn above these words! I have been out and about, though keeping as much as possible away from the passengers and the people. I must re-introduce myself to them, as it were, by degrees until they see not a bare-headed clown but a man of God. The people work about the ship, some hauling on this rope, others *casting off* or slackening that one with a more cheerful readiness than is their wont. The sound of our progress through the water is much more clearly audible! Even I, landsman that I am and must remain, am sensible of a kind of lightness in the vesel as if she too were not inanimate but a partaker in the general gaiety! The people earlier were everywhere to be seen climbing among her limbs and branches. I mean, of course, that vast paraphernalia which allows all the winds of heaven to advance us towards the desired haven. We steer south, ever south, with the continent of Africa on our left hand but hugely distant. Our people have added even more area to the sails by attaching small *yards* (poles, you would call them) from which is suspended lighter material beyond the outer edge of our usual *suit!* (You will detect the degree to which by a careful attention to the conversations going on round me I have become imbued with the language of navigation!) This new area of sail increases our speed, and, indeed, I have just heard one young gentleman cry to another—I omit an unfortunate expletive— 'How the old lady lifts up her p-tt-c--ts and makes a run for it!' Perhaps these additional areas are to be called 'p-tt-c--ts' in nauti-cal parlance; for you cannot imagine with what impropriety the people and even the officers name the various pieces of equipment about the vessel! This continues even in the presence of a clergy-man and the ladies, as if the seamen concerned were wholly unconscious of what they have said.

Once again a day has passed between two paragraphs! The wind has dropped and my trifling indisposition with it. I have dressed, nay, even shaved once more and moved for a while into the waist. I should endeavour, I think, to define for you the position in which I find myself vis-à-vis the other gentlemen, not to say ladies. Since the captain inflicted a public humiliation on me I have been only too aware that of all the passengers I am in the most peculiar position. I do not know how to describe it, for my opinion of how I am regarded alters from day to day and from hour to hour! Were it not for my servant Phillips and the first lieutenant Mr Summers, I believe I should speak to no one; for poor Mr Talbot has been either indisposed or restlessly moving towards what I can only suppose to be a crisis of faith, in which it would be my duty and profound pleasure to help him, but he avoids me. He will not inflict his troubles on any one! Now as for the rest of the passengers and officers, I do sometimes suspect that, influenced by the attitude of Captain Anderson, they disregard me and my sacred office with a frivolous indifference. Then in the next moment I suppose it to be a kind of delicacy of feeling not always to be found among our countrymen that prevents them forcing any attention on me. Perhaps—and I only say perhaps—there is an inclination among them to let me be and make belief that no one has noticed anything! The ladies, of course, I cannot expect to approach me and I should think the less of any one who did so. But this (since I have still limited my movements to the area that I called, jestingly, my *kingdom*) has by now resulted in a degree of isolation which I have suffered in more than I should have supposed. Yet all this must change! I am determined! If either indifference or delicacy prevents them from addressing me, then I must be bold and address *them!*

I have been again into the waist. The ladies and gentlemen, or those who were not in their cabins, were parading on the quarterdeck where I must not go. I did bow to them from far off to show how much I desire some familiar intercourse but the distance was too great and they did not notice me. It must have been the poor light and the distance. It could have been nothing else. The ship is motionless, her sails hanging vertically down and creased like aged cheeks. As I turned from surveying the strange parade on the quarterdeck—for here, in this field of water everything is strange—and faced the forward part of the ship I saw something strange and new. The people are fastening what I at first took to be an awning before the fo'castle—*before*, I mean, from where I stood below the stairs leading up to the quarterdeck—and at first I thought this must be a shelter to keep off the sun. But the sun is dropping low and, as we have eaten our animals, the pens had been broken up, so the shelter would protect nothing. Then again, the material of which the 'awning' is composed seems unnecessarily heavy for such a purpose. It is stretched across the deck at the height of the bulwarks from which it is suspended, or stretched, rather, by ropes. The seamen call the material 'tarpaulin' if I am not mistaken; so the phrase 'Honest Tar' here finds its original.

After I had written those words I resumed my wig and coat (they shall never see me other than properly dressed again) and went back to the waist. Of all the strangenesses of this place at the world's end surely the change in our ship at this moment is the strangest! There is silence, broken only by bursts of laughter. The people, with every indication of enjoyment, are lowering buckets over the side on ropes that run through pulleys or *blocks*, as we call them here. They heave up sea water—which must, I fear, be most impure since we have been stationary for some hours—and spill it into the tarpaulin, which is now bellied down by the weight. There seems no way in which this can help our progress; the more so as certain of the people (my Young Hero among them, I am afraid) have, so to say, relieved nature into what is none other than a container rather than awning. This, in a ship, where by the propinquity of the ocean, such arrangements are made as might well be thought preferable to those our fallen state makes necessary on land! I was disgusted by the sight and was returning to my cabin when I was involved in a strange occurrence! Phillips came towards me hastily and was about to speak when a voice spoke or rather shouted at him from a dim part of the lobby.

'Silence, Phillips, you dog!'

The man looked from me into the shadows from which none other than Mr Cumbershum emerged and stared him down. Phillips retired and Cumbershum stood looking at me. I did not and do not like the man. He is another Anderson I think, or will be should he ever attain to captaincy! I went hastily into my cabin. I took off my coat, wig and bands and composed myself to prayer. Hardly had I begun when there came a timid knocking at the door. I opened it to find Phillips there again. He began to whisper.

'Mr Colley, sir, I beg you——'

'Phillips, you dog! Get below or I'll have you at the grating!'

I stared round in astonishment. It was Cumbershum again and Deverel with him. Yet at first I only recognized them by Cumbershum's voice and Deverel's air of unquestioned elegance, for they too were without hat or coat. They saw me, who had promised myself never to be seen so, and they burst out laughing. Indeed, their laughter had something maniacal about it. I saw they were both to some degree in drink. They concealed from me objects which they held in their hands and they bowed to me as I entered my cabin with a ceremony I could not think sincere. Deverel is a gentleman! He cannot, sure, intend to harm me!

The ship is extraordinarily quiet. A few minutes ago I heard the rustling steps of the remainder of our passengers go through the lobby, mount the stairs and pass over my head. There is no doubt about it. The people at this end of the ship are gathered on the quarterdeck. Only *I* am excluded from them!

I have been out again, stole out into the strange light for all my resolutions about dress. The lobby was silent. Only a confused murmur came from Mr Talbot's cabin. I had a great mind to go to him and beg his protection; but knew that he was at private prayer. I stole out of the lobby into the waist. What I saw as I stood, petrified as it were, will be stamped on my mind till my dying day. *Our* end of the ship—the two raised portions at the back—was crowded with passengers and officers, all silent and all staring forward over my head. Well might they stare! There never was such a sight. No pen, no pencil, not that of the greatest artist in history could give any idea of it. Our huge ship was motionless and her sails still hung down. On her right hand the red sun was setting and on her left the full moon was rising, the one directly across from the other. The two vast luminaries seemed to stare at each other and each to modify the other's light. On land this spectacle could never be so evident because of the interposition of hills or trees or houses, but here we see down from our motionless vessel on all sides to the very edge of the world. Here plainly to be seen were the very scales of GOD.

The scales tilted, the double light faded and we were wrought of ivory and ebony by the moon. The people moved about forward and hung lanterns by the dozen from the rigging, so that I saw now that they had erected something like a bishop's *cathedra* beyond the ungainly paunch of tarpaulin. I began to understand. I began to tremble. I was alone! Yes, in that vast ship with her numberless souls I was alone in a place where on a sudden I feared the Justice of GOD unmitigated by HIS Mercy! On a sudden I dreaded both GOD and man! I stumbled back to my cabin and have endeavoured to pray.

I can scarcely hold this pen. I *must* and *will* recover my composure. What a man does defiles him, not what is done by others—— My shame, though it burn, has been inflicted on me.

I had completed my devotions, but sadly out of a state of recollection. I had divested myself of my garments, all except my shirt, when there came a thunderous knocking at the cabin door. I was already, not to refine upon it, fearful. The thunderous blows on the door completed my confusion. Though I had speculated on the horrid ceremonies of which I might be the victim, I thought then of shipwreck, fire, collision or the violence of the enemy. I cried out, I believe.

'What is it? What is it?'

To this a voice answered, loud as the knocking.

'Open this door!'

I answered in great haste, nay, panic.

'No, no, I am unclothed—but what is it?'

There was a very brief pause, then the voice answered me dreadfully.

'Robert James Colley, you are come into judgement!'

These words, so unexpected and terrible, threw me into utter confusion. Even though I knew that the voice was a human voice I felt a positive contraction of the heart and know how violently I must have clutched my hands together in that region, for there is a contusion over my ribs and I have bled. I cried out in answer to the awful summons.

'No, no, I am not in any way ready, I mean I am un-clothed——'

To this the same unearthly voice and in even more terrible accents uttered the following reply.

'Robert James Colley, you are called to appear before the throne.'

These words—and yet *part* of my mind knew them for the foolery they were—nevertheless completely inhibited my breathing. I made for the door to shoot the bolt but as I did so the door burst open. Two huge figures with heads of nightmare, great eyes and mouths, black mouths full of a mess of fangs drove down at me. A cloth was thrust over my head. I was seized and hurried away by irresistible force, my feet not able to find the deck except every now and then. I am, I know, not a man of quick thought or instant apprehension. For a few moments I believe I was rendered totally insensible, only to be brought to myself again by the sound of yelling and jeering and positively demonic laughter. *Some* touch of presence of mind, however, as I was borne along all too securely muffled, made me cry out 'Help! Help!' and briefly supplicate MY SAVIOUR.

The cloth was wrenched off and I could see clearly—all too clearly—in the light of the lanterns. The foredeck was full of the people and the edge of it lined with figures of nightmare akin to those who had hurried me away. He who sat on the throne was bearded and crowned with flame and bore a huge fork with three prongs in his right hand. Twisting my neck as the cloth came off I could see the after end of the ship, *my rightful place*, was thronged with *spectators*! But there were too few lanterns about the quarterdeck for me to see clearly, nor had I more than a moment to look for a friend, for I was absolutely at the disposal of my captors. Now I had more time to understand my situation and the cruelty of the 'jest', some of my fear was swallowed up in shame at appearing before the ladies and gentlemen, not to refine upon it, half-naked. I, who had thought never to appear but in the ornaments of the Spiritual Man! I attempted to make a smiling appeal for some covering as if I consented to and took part in the jest but all went too fast. I was made to kneel before the 'throne' with much wrenching and buffeting, which took away any breath I had contrived to retain. Before I could make myself heard, a question was put to me of such grossness that I will not remember it, much less write it down. Yet as I opened my mouth to protest, it was at once filled with such nauseous stuff I gag and am like to vomit remembering it. For some time, I cannot tell how long, this operation was repeated; and when I would not open my mouth the stuff was smeared over my face. The questions, one after another, were of such a nature that I cannot write any of them down. Nor could they have been contrived by any but the most depraved of souls. Yet each was greeted with a storm of cheering and that terrible British sound which has ever daunted the foe; and then it came to me, was forced in upon my soul the awful truth—*I was the foe!*

It could not be so, of course. They were, it may be, hot with the devil's brew—they were led astray—it could not be so! But in the confusion and—to me—horror of the situation the thought that froze the very blood in my veins was only this—*I was the foe!*

To such an excess may the common people be led by the example of those who should guide them to better things! At last the leader of their revels deigned to address me.

'You are a low, filthy fellow and must be shampoo'd.'

Here was more pain and nausea and hindrance to my breathing, so that I was in desperate fear all the time that I should die there and then, victim of their cruel sport. Just when I thought my end was come I was projected backwards with extreme violence into the paunch of filthy water. Now here was more of what was strange and terrible to me. I had not harmed them. They had had their sport, their will with me. Yet now as I struggled each time to get out of the wallowing, slippery paunch, I heard what the poor victims of the French Terror must have heard in their last moments and oh!—it is crueller than death, it must be—it must be so, nothing, *nothing* that men can do to each other can be compared with that snarling, lustful, storming appetite——

By now I had abandoned hope of life and was endeavouring blindly to fit myself for my end—as it were *betwixt the saddle and the ground*—when I was aware of repeated shouts from the quarter-deck and then the sound of a tremendous explosion. There was comparative silence in which a voice shouted a command. The hands that had been thrusting me down and in now lifted me up and out. I fell upon the deck and lay there. There was a pause in which I began to crawl away in a trail of filth. But there came another shouted order. Hands lifted me up and bore me to my cabin. Someone shut the door. Later—I do not know how much later—the door opened again and some Christian soul placed a bucket of hot water by me. It may have been Phillips but I do not know. I will not describe the contrivances by which I succeeded in getting myself comparatively clean. Far off I could hear that the devils—no, no, I will not call them that—the *people* of the forward part of the ship had resumed their sport with other victims. But the sounds of merriment were jovial rather than bestial. It was a bitter draught to swallow! I do not suppose that in any other ship they have ever had a 'parson' to play with. No, no, I will *not* be bitter, I will forgive. They are my brothers even if they feel not so—even if *I* feel not so! As for the gentlemen—no, I will not be bitter; and it is true that one among them, Mr Summers perhaps, or Mr Talbot it may be, did intervene and effect an interruption to their brutal sport even if late in it!

I fell into an exhausted sleep, only to experience most fearful nightmares of judgement and hell. They waked me, praise be to GOD! For had they continued, my reason would have been overthrown.

I have prayed since then and prayed long. After prayer and in a state of proper recollection I have thought.

I believe I have come some way to being myself again. I see without any disguise *what happened*. There is much health in that phrase *what happened*. To clear away the, as it were, undergrowth of my own feelings, my terror, my disgust, my indignation, clears a path by which I have come to exercise a proper judgement. I am a victim at several removes of the displeasure that Captain Anderson has evinced towards me since our first meeting. Such a *farce* as was enacted yesterday could not take place without his approval or at least his tacit consent. Deverel and Cumbershum were his agents. I see that my shame—except in the article of outraged modesty—is quite unreal and does my understanding little credit. Whatever I had *said*—and I have begged my SAVIOUR's forgiveness for it—what I *felt* more nearly was the opinion of the ladies and gentlemen in regard to me. I was indeed more sinned against than sinning but must put my own house in order, and learn all over again—but there is no end to that lesson!—to forgive! What, I remind myself, have the servants of the LORD been promised in this world? If it must be so, let persecution be my lot hencefoward. I am not alone.

I have prayed again and with much fervour and risen from my knees at last, I am persuaded, a humbler and a better man. I have been brought to see that the insult to *me* was as nothing and no more than an invitation to turn the other cheek!

Yet there remains the insult offered not to me, but through me to ONE whose NAME is often in their mouths though seldom, I fear, in their thoughts! The true insult is to my cloth and through it to the Great Army of which I am the last and littlest soldier. MY MASTER HIMSELF has been insulted and though HE may—as I am persuaded HE will—forgive it, I have a duty to deliver a rebuke rather than suffer *that* in silence!

Not for ourselves, O LORD, but for THEE!

I slept again more peacefully after writing those words and woke to find the ship running easily before a moderate wind. The air, I thought, was a little cooler. With a start of fear which I had some difficulty in controlling I remembered the events of the previous evening. But then the *interior* events of my fervent prayer returned to me with great force and I got down from my bunk or I may say, leapt down from it, with joy as I felt my own renewed certainties of the Great Truths of the Christian Religion! My devotions were, you must believe, far, far more prolonged than usual!

After I rose from my knees I took my morning draught, then set myself once more to shave carefully. My hair would have benefited from your ministrations! (But you shall never read this! The situation becomes increasingly paradoxical—I may at some time *censor* what I have written!) I dressed with equal care, bands, wig, hat. I directed the servant to show me where my trunk was *stowed* and after some argument was able to descend to it in the gloomy interior parts of the ship. I took out my Hood and Square and extracted his lordship's licence which I put in the tail-pocket of my coat. Now I had—not *my* but MY MASTER's quarrel just, I was able to view a meeting with anyone in the ship as an encounter no more to be feared than—well, as you know, I once spoke with a highwayman! I climbed, therefore, to the upper portion of the quarterdeck with a firm step and beyond it to the raised platform at its back or after end, where Captain Anderson was commonly to be seen. I stood and looked about me. The wind was on the starboard quarter and brisk. Captain Anderson walked up and down. Mr Talbot with one or two other gentlemen stood by the rail and he touched the brim of his beaver and moved forward. I was gratified at this evidence of his wish to befriend me, but for the moment I merely bowed and passed on. I went across the deck and stood directly in Captain Anderson's path, taking off my hat as I did so. He did not *walk through me*, as I expressed it, on this occasion. He stopped and stared, opened his mouth, then shut it again.

The following exchange then took place.

'Captain Anderson, I desire to speak with you.'

He paused for a moment or two. Then——

'Well, sir. You may do so.'

I proceeded in calm and measured accents.

'Captain Anderson. Your people have done my office wrong. You yourself have done it wrong.'

The hectic appeared in his cheek and passed away. He lifted his chin at me, then sank it again. He spoke, or rather muttered, in reply.

'I know it, Mr Colley.'

'You confess as much, sir?'

He muttered again.

'It was never meant—the affair got out of hand. You have been ill-used, sir.'

I answered him serenely.

'Captain Anderson, after this confession of your fault I forgive you freely. But there were, I believe, and I am content to suppose they were acting not so much under your orders as by force of your example, there were other officers involved and not merely the commoner sort of people. *Theirs* was perhaps the most outrageous insult to my cloth! I believe I know them, sir, disguised as they were. Not for my sake, but for their own, they must admit the fault.'

Captain Anderson took a rapid turn up and down the deck. He came back and stood with his hands clasped behind him. He stared down at me, I was astonished to see, not merely with the highest colouring but with rage! Is it not strange? He had confessed his fault yet mention of his officers threw him back into a state which is, I fear, only too customary with him. He spoke angrily.

'You will have it all, then.'

'I defend MY MASTER's Honour as you would defend the King's.'

For a while neither of us said anything. The bell was struck and the members of one watch changed places with another. Mr Summers, together with Mr Willis, took over from Mr Smiles and young Mr Taylor. The change was, as usual, ceremonious. Then Captain Anderson looked back at me.

'I will speak to the officers concerned. Are you now satisfied?'

'Let them come to me, sir, and they shall receive my forgiveness as freely as I have given it to you. But there is another thing——'

Here I must tell you that the captain uttered an imprecation of a positively blasphemous nature. However, I employed the wisdom of the serpent as well as the meekness of the dove and affected at *this* time to take no notice! It was not the moment to rebuke a naval officer for the use of an imprecation. That, I already told myself, should come later!

I proceeded.

'There are also the poor, ignorant people in the front end of the ship. I must visit them and bring them to repentance.'

'Are you mad?'

'Indeed no, sir.'

'Have you no care for what further mockery may be inflicted on you?'

'You have your uniform, Captain Anderson, and I have mine. I shall approach them in that garb, those *ornaments* of the Spiritual Man!'

'Uniform!'

'You do not understand, sir? I shall go to them in those garments which my long studies and ordination enjoin on me. I do not wear them here, sir. You know me for what I am.'

'I do indeed, sir.'

'I thank you, sir. Have I your permission then, to go forward and address them?'

Captain Anderson walked across the planking and expectorated into the sea. He answered me without turning.

'Do as you please.'

I bowed to his back, then turned away myself. As I came to the first stair Lieutenant Summers laid a hand on my sleeve.

'Mr Colley!'

'Well, my friend?'

'Mr Colley, I beg you to consider what you are about!' Here his voice sank to a whisper. 'Had I not discharged Mr Prettiman's weapon over the side and so startled them all, there is no knowing how far the affair might have gone. I beg you, sir—let me assemble them under the eyes of their officers! Some of them are violent men—one of the emigrants——'

'Come, Mr Summers. I shall appear to them in the raiment in which I might conduct a service. They will recognize that raiment, sir, and respect it.'

'At least wait until after they have been given their rum. Believe me, sir, I know whereof I speak! It will render them more amiable, calmer—more receptive, sir, to what you have to say to them—— I beg you, sir! Otherwise, contempt, indifference—and who knows what else——?'

'And the lesson would go unheeded, you think, the opportunity lost?'

'Indeed, sir!'

I considered for a moment.

'Very well, Mr Summers. I will wait until later in the morning. I have some writing in the meantime which I wish to do.'

I bowed to him and went on. Now Mr Talbot stepped forward again. He asked in the most agreeable manner to be admitted to a familiar degree of friendship with me. He is indeed a young man who does credit to his station! If privilege were always in the hands of such as he—indeed, it is not out of the question that at some future date—but I run on!

I had scarcely settled myself to this writing in my cabin when there came a knock at the door. It was the lieutenants, Mr Deverel and Mr Cumbershum, my two *devils* of the previous night! I looked my severest on them, for indeed they deserved a little chastisement before getting forgiveness. Mr Cumbershum said little but Mr Deverel much. He owned freely that they had been mistook and that he had been a little in drink, like his companion. He had not thought I would take the business so much to heart but the people were accustomed to such sport when crossing the equator, only he regretted that they had misinterpreted the captain's general permission. In fine, he requested me to treat the whole thing as a jest that had got out of hand. Had I then worn such apparel as I was now suited in, no one would have attempted—in fact the d-v-l was in it if they had meant any harm and now hoped I would forget the whole business.

I paused for a while as if cogitating, though I knew already what I would do. It was no moment at which to admit my own sense of unworthiness at having appeared before our people in a garb that was less than fitting. Indeed, these were the sort of men who needed a *uniform*—both one to wear, and one to look up to!

I spoke at last.

'I forgive you freely, gentlemen, as I am enjoined to do by MY MASTER. Go, and sin no more.'

On that, I shut the cabin door. Outside it, I heard one of them, Mr Deveral, I think, give a low, but prolonged whistle. Then as their steps receded I heard Mr Cumbershum speak for the first time since the interview began.

'I wonder who the d-v-l his Master is? D'you think he's *in* with the d-mned Chaplain to the Fleet?'

Then they had departed. I own I felt at peace for the first time for many, many days. All was now to be well. I saw that little by little I might set about my work, not merely among the common people but later, among the officers and gentry who would not be, could not be now so insensible to the WORD as had appeared! Why—even the captain himself had shown some small signs— and the power of Grace is infinite. Before assuming my canonicals I went out into the waist and stood there, free at last—why, no doubt now the captain would revoke his first harsh prohibition to me of the quarterdeck! I gazed down into the water, the blue, the green, the purple, the snowy, sliding foam! I saw with a new feeling of security the long, green weed that wavers under the water from our wooden sides. There was, it seemed too, a peculiar richness in the columns of our rounded sails. Now is the time; and after due preparation I shall go forward and rebuke these unruly but truly lovable children of OUR MAKER! It seemed to me then—it still seems so—that I was and am consumed by a great love of all things, the sea, the ship, the sky, the gentlemen and the people and of course OUR REDEEMER above all! Here at last is the happiest outcome of all my distress and difficulty! ALL THINGS PRAISE HIM!

As your lordship knows, Colley wrote no more. After death—nothing. There must be nothing! The only consolation I have myself over the whole business is that I can ensure that his poor sister will never know the truth of it. Drunken Brocklebank may roar in his cabin, 'Who killed cock Colley?' but *she* shall never know what weakness killed him, nor whose hands—mine among them—struck him down.

When I was roused by Wheeler from a too brief and uneasy sleep, I found that the first part of the morning was to be passed in an enquiry. I was to sit, with Summers and the captain. Upon my objecting that the body should—in these hot latitudes—be buried first of all, Wheeler said nothing. It is plain that the captain means to cloak his and our persecutions of the man under a garment of proper, official proceedings! We sat, then, behind the table in the captain's cabin and the witnesses were paraded. The servant who had attended Colley told us no more than we knew. Young Mr Taylor, hardly subdued by the man's death but in a proper awe of the captain, repeated that he had seen Mr Colley agree to taste of the rum in a spirit of something or other, he could not recollect quite what—On my suggesting that the word might be 'reconciliation' he accepted it. What was Mr Taylor doing there, forrard? (This from Mr Summers.) Mr Tommy Taylor was inspecting the stowage of the cables with a view to having the cable to the bower anchor rousted out and walked end-for-end. This splendid jargon satisfied the naval gentlemen, who nodded together as if they had been spoken to in plain English. But what was Mr Taylor doing, in that case, out of the cable locker? Mr Taylor had finished his inspection and was coming up to report and had stayed for a while, never having seen a parson in that state before. And then? (This from the captain.) Mr Taylor had 'proceeded aft, sir, to inform Mr Summers' but had been '*given a bottle* by Mr Cumbershum before I could do so.'

The captain nodded and Mr Taylor retired with what looked like relief. I turned to Summers.

'A bottle, Summers? What the devil did they want with a bottle?'

The captain growled.

'A bottle is a rebuke, sir. Let us get on.'

The next witness was one East, a respectable emigrant, husband to the poor girl whose emaciated face had so struck me. He could read and write. Yes, he had seen Mr Colley and knew the reverend gentleman by sight. He had not seen him during the 'badger bag', as the sailors called it, but he had heard tell. Perhaps we had been told how poorly his wife was and he was in near enough constant attendance on her, himself and Mrs Roustabout taking turns, though near her own time. He had only glimpsed Mr Colley among the seamen, did not think he had said much before taking a cup with them. The applause and laughter we had heard? That was after the few words the gentleman had spoken when he was being social with the sailors. The growls and anger? He knew nothing about that. He only knew the sailors took the gentleman away with them, down where the young gentleman had been among the ropes. He had had to look after his wife, knew nothing more. He hoped we gentlemen would think it no disrespect but that was all anyone knew except the sailors who had the reverend gentleman in charge.

He was allowed to withdraw. I gave it as my opinion that the only man who might enlighten us would be the fellow who had brought or carried him back to us in his drunken stupor. I said that he might know how much Colley drank and who had given it to him or forced it on him. Captain Anderson agreed and said that he had ordered the man to attend. He then addressed us in not much above a whisper:

'My *informant* advises me this is the witness we should press.'

It was my turn.

'I believe,' I said, and braced myself—'we are doing what you gentlemen would call "making heavy weather of it"'! The man was made drunk. There are some men, as we now know to our cost, whose timidity is such that they are wounded almost to death by another's anger and whose conscience is so tender they will die of what, let us say, Mr Brocklebank would accept as a peccadillo, if that! Come, gentlemen! Could we not confess that his intemperance killed him but that our general indifference to his welfare was likely enough the cause of it!'

This was bold, was it not? I was telling our tyrant that he and I together—But he was regarding me with astonishment.

'Indifference, sir?'

'Intemperance, sir,' said Summers, quickly, 'let us leave it at that.'

'One moment, Summers. Mr Talbot. I pass over your odd phrase, "our general indifference". But do you not understand? Do you think that a single bout of drinking——'

'But you yourself said, sir—let us include all under a *low fever!*'

'That *was* yesterday! Sir, I tell you. It is likely enough that the man, helplessly drunk, suffered a criminal assault by one, or God knows how many men, and the absolute humiliation of it killed him!'

'Good God!'

This was a kind of convulsion of the understanding. I do not know that I thought anything at all for minutes together. I, as it were, *came to*, to hear the captain talking.

'No, Mr Summers. I will have no concealment. Nor will I tolerate frivolous accusations which touch me myself in my conduct of the ship and in my attitude to the passengers in her.'

Summers was red in the face. 'I have made a submission, sir. I beg your pardon if you find it beyond the line of my duty.'

'Very well, Mr Summers. Let us get on.'

'But captain,' said I, 'no man will admit to *that!*'

'You are young, Mr Talbot. You cannot guess what channels of information there are in a ship such as this, even though her present commission has been of such a short duration.'

'Channels? Your informant?'

'I would prefer us to get on,' said the captain heavily. 'Let the man come in.'

Summers himself went out and fetched Rogers. It was the man who had brought Colley back to us. I have seldom seen a more splendid young fellow. He was naked to the waist and of a build that one day might be over-corpulent. But now he could stand as a model to Michelangelo! His huge chest and columnar neck were of a deep brown hue, as was his broadly handsome face save where it was scarred by some parallel scratches of a lighter tone. Captain Anderson turned to me.

'Summers tells me you have claimed some skill in cross-examination.'

'Did he? Did I?'

Your lordship will observe that I was by no means at my best in all this sorry episode. Captain Anderson positively beamed at me.

'Your witness, sir.'

This I had not bargained for. However, there was no help for it.

'Now, my good man. Your name, if you please!'

'Billy Rogers, my lord. Foretop man.'

I accepted the honorific. May it be an omen!

'We want information from you, Rogers. We want to know in precise detail what happened when the gentleman came among you the other day.'

'What gentleman, my lord?'

'The parson. The reverend Mr Colley, who is now dead.'

Rogers stood in the full light of the great window. I thought to myself that I had never seen a face of such wide-eyed candour.

'He took a drop too much, my lord, was overcome, like.'

It was time to *go about*, as we nautical fellows say.

'How came you by those scars on your face?'

'A wench, my lord.'

'She must have been a wild cat, then.'

'Nigh on, my lord.'

'You will have your way, whether or no?'

'My lord?'

'You would overcome her disinclination for her own good?'

'I don't know about all that, my lord. All I know is she had what was left of my pay in her other hand and would have been through the door like a pistol shot if I had not took a firm hold of her.'

Captain Anderson beamed sideways at me.

'With your permission, my lord——'

Devil take it, the man was laughing at me!

'Now, Rogers. Never mind the women. What about the men?'

'Sir?'

'Mr Colley suffered an outrage there in the fo'castle. Who did it?'

The man's face was without any expression at all. The captain pressed him.

'Come, Rogers. Would it surprise you to know that you your-self are suspected of this particular kind of beastliness?'

The man's whole stance had altered. He was a little crouched now, one foot drawn a few inches behind the other. He had clenched his fists. He looked fom one to the other of us quickly, as if trying to see in each face what degree of peril confronted him. I saw that he took us for *enemies*!

'I know nothing, Captain sir, nothing at all!'

'It may not have anything to do with you, my man. But you will know who it was.'

'Who was who, sir?'

'Why, the one or many among you who inflicted a criminal assault on the gentleman so that he died of it!'

'I know nothing—nothing at all!'

I had got my wits back.

'Come, Rogers. You were the one man we saw with him. In default of any other evidence your name must head the list of suspects. What did you sailors do?'

I have never seen a face of more well-simulated astonishment.

'What did *we* do, my lord?'

'Doubtless you have witnesses to testify to your innocence. If you are innocent then help us to bring the criminals to book.'

He said nothing, but still stood at bay. I took up the questioning again.

'I mean, my good man, you can either tell us who did it, or at the very least you can furnish us with a list of the people you suspect or know to be suspected of this particular form of, of, interest, of assault.'

Captain Anderson jerked up his chin.

'Buggery, Rogers, that's what he means. Buggery.'

He looked down, shuffled some papers before him and dipped his pen in the ink. The silence prolonged itself into our ex-pectancy. The captain himself broke it at last with a sound of angry impatience.

'Come along, man! We cannot sit here all day!'

There was another pause. Rogers turned his body rather than his head to us, one after the other. Then he looked straight at the captain.

'Aye aye, sir.'

It was only then that there was a change in the man's face. He thrust his upper lip down, then as if in an experimental manner tried the texture of his lower lip judiciously with his white teeth.

'Shall I begin with the officers, sir?'

It was of the utmost importance that I should not move. The slightest flicker of my eye towards either Summers or the captain, the slightest contraction of a muscle would have seemed a fatal accusation. I had absolute faith in them both as far as this accusation of *beastliness* was concerned. As for the two officers themselves, doubtless they also had a mutual faith, yet they too did not dare risk any movement. We were waxworks. Rogers was waxworks too.

It had to be the captain who made the first move and he knew it. He laid his pen down beside the papers and spoke gravely.

'Very well, Rogers. That will be all. You may return to your duties.'

The colour came and went in the man's face. He let out his breath in a prolonged gasp. He knuckled his forehead, began to smile, turned and went away out of the cabin. I cannot say how long the three of us sat without word or movement. For my part, it was something as simple and ordinary as the fear of doing or saying the wrong thing; yet the 'wrong thing' would be, so to speak, raised to a higher power, to such a power as to be fearful and desperate. I felt in the long moments of our silence as if I could not allow myself to think at all, otherwise my face might redden and the perspiration begin to creep down my cheeks. I made by a most conscious effort my mind as nearly blank as might be and waited on the event. For surely of the three of us it was least my part to speak. Rogers had caught us in a mantrap. Can your lordship understand how already touches of suspicion came to life in my mind whether I would or no and flitted from the name of this gentleman to that?

Captain Anderson rescued us from our catalepsy. He did not move but spoke as if to himself.

'Witnesses, enquiries, accusations, lies, more lies, courts-martial—the man has it in his power to ruin us all if he be brazen enough, as I doubt not he is, for it would be a hanging matter. Such accusations cannot be disproved. Whatever the upshot, something would stick.'

He turned to Summers.

'And there, Mr Summers, ends our investigation. Have we other informants?'

'I believe no, sir. Touch pitch——'

'Just so. Mr Talbot?'

'I am all at sea, sir! But it is true enough. The man was at bay and brought out his last weapon; false witness, amounting to blackmail.'

'In fact,' said Summers, smiling at last, 'Mr Talbot is the only one of us to have profited. He had at least a temporary elevation to the peerage!'

'I have returned to earth, sir—though since I was addressed as "my lord" by Captain Anderson, who can conduct marriages and funerals——'

'Ah yes. Funerals. You will drink, gentlemen? Call Hawkins in, Summers, will you? I must thank you, Mr Talbot, for your assistance.'

'Of little use I fear, sir.'

The captain was himself again. He beamed.

'A low fever then. Sherry?'

'Thank you, sir. But is everything concluded? We still do not know what happened. You mentioned informants——'

'This is a good sherry,' said the captain brusquely. 'I believe, Mr Summers, you are averse to drinking at this time of the day and you will wish to oversee the various arrangements for the unfortunate man's committal to the deep. Your health, Mr Talbot. You will be willing to sign, or rather counter-sign, a report?'

I thought for a while.

'I have no official standing in this ship.'

'Oh, come, Mr Talbot!'

I thought again.

'I will make a statement and sign that.'

Captain Anderson looked sideways up at me from under his thick brows and nodded without saying anything. I drained my glass.

'You mentioned informants, Captain Anderson——'

But he was frowning at me.

'Did I, sir? I think not!'

'You asked Mr Summers——'

'Who replied there were none,' said Captain Anderson loudly. 'None at all, Mr Talbot, not a man jack among them! Do you understand, sir? No one has come sneaking to me—no one. You can go, Hawkins!'

I set down my glass and Hawkins took it away. The captain watched him leave the stateroom, then turned to me again.

'Servants have ears, Mr Talbot!'

'Why certainly, sir! I am very sure my fellow Wheeler has.'

The captain smiled grimly.

'Wheeler! Oh yes indeed! *That* man must have ears and eyes all over him——'

'Well then, until the sad ceremony of this afternoon I shall return to my journal.'

'Ah, the journal. Do not forget to include in it, Mr Talbot, that whatever may be said of the passengers, as far as the people and my officers are concerned this is a *happy* ship!'

At three o'clock we were all assembled in the waist. There was a guard, composed of Oldmeadow's soldiers, with flintlocks, or whatever their ungainly weapons are called. Oldmeadow himself was in full dress and unblooded sword, as were the ship's officers. Even our young gentlemen wore their dirks and expressions of piety. We passengers were dressed as sombrely as possible. The seamen were drawn up by watches, and were as presentable as their varied garments permit. Portly Mr Brocklebank was erect but yellow and drawn from potations that would have reduced Mr Colley to a ghost. As I inspected the man I thought that Brocklebank would have gone through the whole of Colley's ordeal and fall with no more than a bellyache and a sore head. Such are the varied fabrics of the human tapestry that surrounds me! Our ladies, who must surely have had such an occasion in their minds when they fitted themselves for the voyage, were in mourning—even Brocklebank's two doxies, who supported him on either side. Mr Prettiman was present at this *superstitious ritual* by the side of Miss Granham, who had led him there. What is all his militant Atheism and Republicanism when pitted against this daughter of a canon of Exeter Cathedral? I made a note as I saw him fretting and barely contained at her side, that *she* was the one of the two with whom I must speak and to whom I must convey the kind of delicate admonition I had intended for our notorious Freethinker!

You will observe that I have recovered somewhat from the effect of reading Colley's letter. A man cannot be forever brooding on what is past nor on the tenuous connection between his own unwitting conduct and someone else's deliberately criminal behaviour! Indeed, I have to own that this ceremonious naval occasion was one of great interest to me! One seldom attends a

funeral in such, dare I call them, exotic surroundings! Not only
was the ceremony strange, but all the time—or some of it at
least—our actors conducted their dialogue in Tarpaulin language.
You know how I delight in that! You will already have noted
some particularly impenetrable specimens as, for instance, mention of a *badger bag*—does not Servius (I believe it was he) declare
there are half a dozen cruxes in the *Aeneid* which will never be
solved, either by emendation or inspiration or any method
attempted by scholarship? Well then, I shall entertain you with a
few more *naval cruxes*.

The ship's bell was struck, muffled. A party of sailors appeared,
bearing the body on a plank and under the union flag. It was
placed with its feet towards the starboard, or honourable side, by
which admirals and bodies and suchlike rarities make their exits.
It was a longer body than I had expected but have since been told
that two of our few remaining cannon balls were attached to the
feet. Captain Anderson, glittering with bullion, stood by it. I
have also been told since, that he and all the other officers were
much exercised as to the precise nature of the ceremonies to be
observed when, as young Mr Taylor expressed it, 'piping a sky
pilot over the side'.

Almost all our sails were *clewed up* and we were what the
Marine Dictionary calls, technically speaking—and when does it
not—*hove to*, which ought to mean we were stationary in the
water. Yet the spirit of farce (speaking perfectly exquisite Tarpaulin) attended Colley to his end. No sooner was the plank laid
on the deck than I heard Mr Summers mutter to Mr Deverel:

'Depend upon it, Deverel, without you aft the driver a hand-
span she will make a sternboard.'

Hardly had he said this when there came a heavy and rhythmical
thudding from the ship's hull under waters as if *Davey Jones* was
serving notice or perhaps getting hungry. Deverel shouted orders
of the *warrarroohoowassst!* variety, the seamen leapt, while Captain
Anderson, a prayerbook clutched like a grenade, turned on Lieutenant Summers.

'Mr *Summers*! Will you have the sternpost out of her?'

Summers said nothing but the thudding ceased. Captain
Anderson's tone sank to a grumble.

'The pintles are loose as a pensioner's teeth.'

Summers nodded in reply.

'I know it, sir. But until she's rehung——'

'The sooner we're off the wind the better. God curse that drunken superintendant!'

He stared moodily down at the union flag, then up at the sails which, as if willing to debate with him, boomed back. They could have done no better than the preceding dialogue. Was it not superb?

At last the captain glanced round him and positively started, as if seeing us for the first time. I wish I could say that he *started like a guilty thing upon a fearful summons* but he did not. He started like a man in the smallest degree remiss who has absentmindedly forgotten that he has a body to get rid of. He opened the book and grunted a sour invitation to us to pray—and so on. Certainly he was anxious enough to get the thing over, for I have never heard a service read so fast. The ladies scarce had time to get out their handkerchiefs (tribute of a tear) and we gentlemen stared for a moment as usual into our beavers, but then, reminded that this unusual ceremony was too good to miss, all looked up again. I hoped that Oldmeadow's men would fire a volley but he has since told me that owing to some difference of opinion between the Admiralty and the War Office, they have neither flints nor powder. However, they presented arms in approximate unison and the officers flourished their swords. I wonder—was all this proper for a parson? I do not know, neither do they. A fife shrilled out and someone rattled on a muffled drum, a kind of overture, or postlude should I call it, or would *envoi* be a better word?

You will observe, my lord, that *Richard is himself again*—or shall we say that I have recovered from a period of fruitless and *perhaps* unwarranted regret?

And yet—at the last (when Captain Anderson's grumbling voice invited us to contemplate that time when there shall be no more sea) six men shrilled out a call on the bosun's pipe. Now, your lordship may never have heard these pipes so I must inform you that they have just as much music in them as the yowling of cats on heat! And yet and yet and *yet*! Their very harsh and shrill unmusicality, their burst of high sound leading to a long descent that died away through an uneasy and prolonged fluttering into silence, seemed to voice something beyond words, religion, philosophy. It was the simple voice of Life mourning Death.

I had scarcely time to feel a touch of complacency at the directness of my own emotions when the plank was lifted and tilted.

The mortal remains of the Reverend Robert James Colley shot
from under the union flag and entered the water with a single
loud phut! as if he had been the most experienced of divers and
had made a habit of rehearsing his own funeral, so expertly was it
done. Of course the cannon balls assisted. This subsidiary use of
their mass was after all in keeping with their general nature. So
the remains of Colley dropping *deeper than did ever plummet sound*
were to be thought of as now finding the solid base of all. (At
these necessarily ritualistic moments of life, if you cannot use the
prayer book, have recourse to Shakespeare! Nothing else will
do.)

Now you might think that there was then a moment or two of
silent tribute before the mourners left the churchyard. Not a bit
of it! Captain Anderson shut his book, the pipes shrilled again,
this time with a kind of temporal urgency. Captain Anderson
nodded to Lieutenant Cumbershum, who touched his hat and
roared:

'Leeeoonnawwll!'

Our obedient vessel started to turn as she moved forward and
lumbered clumsily towards her original course. The ceremonially
ordered ranks broke up, the people climbed everywhere into the
rigging to spread our full suit of sails and add the stun's'ls to
them again. Captain Anderson marched off, grenade, I mean
prayerbook in hand, back to his cabin, I suppose to make an
entry in his journal. A young gentleman scrawled on the traverse
board and all things were as they had been. I returned to my
cabin to consider what statement I should write out and sign. It
must be such as will cause his sister least pain. It shall be a *low
fever*, as the captain wishes. I must conceal from him that I have
already laid a trail of gunpowder to where your lordship may
ignite it. God, what a world of conflict, of birth, death, procrea-
tion, betrothals, marriages for all I know, there is to be found in
this extraordinary ship!

$$(\&)$$

There! I think the ampersand gives a touch of eccentricity, does it not? None of your dates, or letters of the alphabet, or presumed *day of the voyage*! I might have headed this section 'addenda' but that would have been dull—far too, too dull! For we have come to an end, there is nothing more to be said. I mean—there is, of course, there is the daily record, but my journal, I found on looking back through it, had insensibly turned to the record of a drama—Colley's drama. Now the poor man's drama is done and he stands there, how many miles down, on his cannon balls, alone, as Mr Coleridge says, all, all alone. It seems a different sort of *bathos* (your lordship, as Colley might say, will note the amusing 'paranomasia') to return to the small change of day to day with no drama in it, but there are yet some pages left between the rich bindings of your lordship's gift to me, and I *have* tried to stretch the burial out, in the hope that what might be called *The Fall and Lamentable End of Robert James Colley together with a Brief Account of his Thalassian Obsequies* would extend right to the last page. All was of no avail. His was a real life and a real death and no more to be fitted into a given book than a misshapen foot into a given boot. Of course my journal will continue beyond this volume— but in a book obtained for me by Phillips from the purser and not to be locked. Which reminds me how trivial the explanation of men's fear and silence concerning the purser proved to be. Phillips told me, for he is more open than Wheeler. All the officers, including the captain, owe the purser money! Phillips calls him *the pusser*.

Which reminds me again—I employed Phillips because no matter how I shouted, I could not rouse Wheeler. He is being sought now.

He *was* being sought. Summers has just told me. The man has disappeared. He has fallen overboard. Wheeler! He has gone like a dream, with his puffs of white hair, and his shining baldness, his *sanctified* smile, his complete knowledge of everything that goes on in a ship, his paregoric, and his willingness to obtain for a gentleman anything in the wide, wide world, provided the gentleman pays for it! Wheeler, as the captain put it, *all over ears and eyes*! I shall miss the man, for I cannot hope for as great a share in the services of Phillips. Already I have had to pull off my own boots, though Summers, who was present in my cabin at the time, was good enough to help. Two deaths in only a few days!

'At least,' said I to Summers with meaning, 'no one can accuse me of having a hand in *this* death, can they?'

He was too breathless to reply. He sat back on his heels, then stood up and watched me pull on my embroidered slippers.

'Life is a formless business, Summers. Literature is much amiss in forcing a form on it!'

'Not so, sir, for there are both death and birth aboard. Pat Roundabout——'

'Roundabout? I thought it was "Roustabout"!'

'You may use either indifferently. But she is delivered of a daughter to be named after the ship.'

'Poor, poor child! But that was the mooing I heard then, like Bessie when she broke her leg?'

'It was, sir. I go now to see how they do.'

So he left me, these blank pages still unfilled. News, then, news! What news? There *is* more to be recorded but germane to the captain, not Colley. It should have been fitted in much earlier—at Act Four or even Three. Now it must come limping after the drama, like the satyr play after the tragic trilogy. It is not a *dénouement* so much as a pale illumination. Captain Anderson's detestation of the clergy! You remember. Well now, perhaps, you and I *do* know all.

Hist, as they say—let me bolt my hutch door!

Well then—Deverel told me. He has begun to drink heavily— heavily that is in comparison with what he did before, since he has always been intemperate. It seems that Captain Anderson— fearful not only of my journal but also of the other passengers who *now* with the exception of steely Miss Granham believe 'Poor Colley' was mistreated—Anderson, I say, rebuked the two men, Cumbershum and Deverel, savagely for their part in the affair. This meant little to Cumbershum, who is made of wood. But Deverel, by the laws of the service, is denied the satisfaction of a gentleman. He broods and drinks. Then last night, deep in drink, he came to my hutch and in the dark hours and a muttered,

slurred voice gave me what he called necessary observations on
the captain's history for my journal. Yet he was not so drunk as
to be unaware of danger. Picture us then, by the light of my
candle, seated side by side on the bunk, Deverel whispering
viciously into my ear as my head was inclined to his lips. There
was, it appears, and there is, a noble family—not I believe more
than distantly known to your lordship—and their land marches
with the Deverels'. They, Summers would say, have used the
privilege of their position and neglected its responsibilities. The
father of the present young lord had in keeping a lady of great
sweetness of disposition, much beauty, little understanding and,
as it proved, some fertility. The use of privilege is sometimes
expensive. Lord L—— (this is perfect Richardson, is it not?'
found himself in need of a fortune, and that instantly. The fortune
was found but her family in a positively Wesleyan access of
righteousness insisted on the dismissal of the sweet lady, against
whom nothing could be urged save lack of a few words spoke
over her by a parson. Catastrophe threatened. The dangers of her
position struck some sparks from the sweet lady, the fortune
hung in the balance! At this moment, as Deverel whispered in my
ear, Providence intervened and the incumbent of one of the three
livings that lay in the family's gift was killed in the hunting field!
The heir's tutor, a dull sort of fellow, accepted of the living and
the sweet lady and what Deverel called her curst cargo together.
The lord got his fortune, the lady a husband and the Reverend
Anderson a living, a wife and an heir *gratis*. In due course the boy
was sent to sea, where the casual interest of his real father was
sufficient to elevate him in the service. But now the old lord is
dead and the young one has no cause to love his bastard half-
brother!

All this by an unsteady candle light, querulous remarks in his
sleep from Mr Prettiman, with snores and farts from Mr Brocklebank in the other direction. Oh that cry from the deck above
us——

'Eight bells and all's well!'

Deverel, at this witching hour, put his arm about me with
drunken familiarity and revealed why he had spoken so. This
history was the *jest* he had meant to tell me. At Sydney Cove, or
the Cape of Good Hope, should we put in there, Deverel intends—or the drink in him intends—to resign his commission,

call the captain out and shoot him dead! 'For,' said he in a louder voice and with his shaking right hand lifted, 'I can knock a crow off a steeple with one barker!' Hugging and patting me and calling me his *good Edmund* he informed me I was to act for him when the time came; and if, *if* by some luck of the devil, he himself was taken off, why the information was to be put fully in my famous journal—

I had much ado to get him taken to his cabin without rousing the whole ship. But here is news indeed! So *that* is why a certain captain so detests a parson! It would surely be more reasonable in him to detest a lord! Yet there is no doubt about it. Anderson has been wronged by a lord—or by a parson—or by life—Good God! I do not care to find excuses for Anderson!

Nor do I care as much for Deverel as I did. It was a misjudgement on my part to esteem him. He, perhaps, illustrates the last decline of a noble family as Mr Summers might illustrate the original of one! My wits are all to seek. I found myself thinking that had I been so much the victim of a lord's gallantry I would have become a *Jacobin*! I? Edmund Talbot?

It was then that I remembered my own half-formed intention to bring Zenobia and Robert James Colley together to rid myself of a possible embarrassment. It was so like Deverel's *jest* I came near to detesting myself. When I realized how he and I had talked, and how he must have thought me like-minded with the 'Noble family' my face grew hot with shame. Where will all this end?

However, one birth does not equal two deaths. There is a general dullness among us, for say what you will, a burial at sea, however frivolously I treat it, cannot be called a laughing matter. Nor will Wheeler's disappearance lighten the air among the passengers.

Two days have passed since I diffidently forbore to ask Summers to help me on with my slippers! The officers have not been idle. Summers—as if this were a Company ship rather than a man of war—has determined we shall not have too much time left hanging on our hands. We have determined that the after end of the ship shall present the forrard end with a *play*! A *committee* has been formed *with the captain's sanction*! This has thrown me will-he, nill-he, into the company of Miss Granham! It has been an edifying experience. I found that this woman, this handsome, cultivated maiden lady, holds views which would freeze the blood of the average citizen in his veins! She does *literally* make no distinction between the uniform worn by our officers, the woad with which our unpolished ancestors were said to paint themselves and the tattooing rife in the South Seas and perhaps on the mainland of Australia! Worse—from the point of view of society—she, daughter of a canon, makes no distinction between the Indian's Medicine Man, the Siberian Shaman, and a Popish priest in his vestments! When I expostulated that she bid fair to include our own clergy she would only admit them to be less offensive because they made themselves less readily distinguishable from other gentlemen. I was so staggered by this conversation I could make no reply to her and only discovered the reason for the awful candour with which she spoke when (before dinner in the passenger saloon) it was announced that she and Mr Prettiman are *officially* engaged! In the unexpected security of her *fiançailles* the lady feels free to say anything! But with what an eye she has seen us! I blush to remember the many things I have said in her presence which must have seemed like the childishness of the schoolroom.

However, the announcement has cheered everyone up. You may imagine the public felicitations and the private comments! I myself sincerely hope that Captain Anderson, gloomiest of Hymens, will marry them aboard so that we may have a complete collection of all the ceremonies that accompany the forked creature from the cradle to the grave. The pair seem attached—they have fallen in love *after their fashion*! Deverel introduced the only solemn note. He declared it was a great shame the man Colley had died, otherwise the knot might be tied there and then by a parson. At this, there was a general silence. Miss Granham, who had furnished your humble servant with her views on priests in general might, I felt, have said nothing. But instead, she came out with a quite astonishing statement.

'He was a truly degraded man.'

'Come, ma'am,' said I, '*de mortuis* and all that! A single unlucky indulgence—The man was harmless enough!'

'Harmless,' cried Prettiman with a kind of bounce, 'a priest harmless?'

'I was not referring to drink,' said Miss Granham in her steeliest voice, 'but to vice in another form.'

'Come, ma'am—I cannot believe—as a lady you cannot——'

'*You*, sir,' cried Mr Prettiman, '*you* to doubt a lady's word?'

'No, no! Of course not! Nothing——'

'Let it be, dear Mr Prettiman, I beg of you.'

'No, ma'am, I cannot let it go. Mr Talbot has seen fit to doubt your word and I will have an apology——'

'Why,' said I laughing, 'you have it, ma'am, unreservedly! I never intended——'

'We learnt of his vicious habits accidentally,' said Mr Prettiman. 'A priest! It was two sailors who were descending one of the rope ladders from the mast to the side of the vessel. Miss Granham and I—it was dark—we had retired to the shelter of that confusion of ropes at the foot of the ladder——'

'Chain, ratlines—Summers, enlighten us!'

'It is no matter, sir. You will remember, Miss Granham, we were discussing the inevitability of the process by which true liberty must lead to true equality and thence to—but that is no matter, neither. The sailors were unaware of our presence so that without meaning to, we heard all!'

'Smoking is bad enough, Mr Talbot, but at least gentlemen go no further!'

'My dear Miss Granham!'

'It is as savage a custom, sir, as any known among coloured peoples!'

Oldmeadow addressed her in tones of complete incredulity. 'By Jove, ma'am—you cannot mean the fellow chewed tobacco!'

There was a roar of laughter from passengers and officers alike. Summers, who is not given to idle laughter, joined in.

'It is true,' said he, when there was less noise. 'On one of my earlier visits I saw a large bunch of leaf tobacco hung from the deckhead. It was spoilt by mildew and I threw it overboard.'

'But Summers,' said I. 'I saw no tobacco! And that kind of man——'

'I assure you, sir. It was before you visited him.'

'Nevertheless, I find it almost impossible to believe!'

'You shall have the facts,' said Prettiman with his usual choler. 'Long study, a natural aptitude and a necessary habit of defence have made me expert in the recollection of casual speech, sir. You shall have the words the sailors spoke *as* they were spoken!'

Summers lifted both hands in expostulation.

'No, no—spare us, I beg you! It is of little moment after all!'

'Little moment, sir, when a lady's word—it cannot be allowed to pass, sir. One of these sailors said to the other as they descended side by side—"Billy Rogers was laughing like a bilge pump when he come away from the captain's cabin. He went into the heads and I sat by him. Billy said he'd knowed most things in his time but he had never thought to get a chew off a parson!"'

The triumphant but fierce look on Mr Prettiman's face, his flying hair and the instant decline of his educated voice into a precise imitation of a ruffian sort threw our audience into whoops. This disconcerted the philosopher even more and he stared round him wildly. Was anything ever more absurd? I believe it was this diverting circumstance which marked a change in our general feelings. Without the source of it being evident there strengthened among us the determination to get on with our play! Perhaps it was Mr Prettiman's genius for comedy—oh, unquestionably we must have him for our comic! But what might have been high words between the social philosopher and your humble servant passed off into the much pleasanter business of discussing *what* we should act and *who* should produce and *who* should do this and that!

Afterwards I went out to take my usual constitutional in the waist; and lo! there by the break of the fo'castle was 'Miss Zenobia' in earnest conversation with Billy Rogers! Plainly, he is her *Sailor Hero* who can '*Wate no longer*'. With what kindred spirit did he concoct his misspelt but elaborate billet-doux? Well, if he attempts to come aft and visit her in her hutch I will see him flogged for it.

Mr Prettiman and Miss Granham walked in the waist too but on the opposite side of the deck, talking with animation. Miss Granham said (I heard her and believe she intended me to hear) that *as he knew* they should aim first at supporting those parts of the administration that might be supposed still uncorrupted. Mr Prettiman trotted beside her—she is taller than he—nodding with vehemence at the austere yet penetrating power of her intellect. They will influence each other—for I believe they are as sincerely attached as such extraordinary characters can be. But oh yes, Miss Granham, I shall not keep an eye on him—I shall keep an eye on you! I watched them pass on over the white line that separates the social orders and stand right up in the bows, talking to East and that poor, pale girl, his wife. Then they returned and came straight to where I stood in the shade of an awning we have stretched from the starboard shrouds. To my astonishment, Miss Granham

explained that they had been *consulting with Mr East*! He is, it
seems, a craftsman and has to do with the setting of type! I do not
doubt that they have in view his future employment. However, I
did not allow them to see what an interest I took in the matter
and turned the conversation back to the question of what play we
should show the people. Mr Prettiman proved to be as indifferent
to that as to so much of the common life he is allegedly concerned
with in his philosophy! He dismissed Shakespeare as a writer who
made too little comment on the evils of society! I asked, reasonably enough, what society consisted in other than human beings
only to find that the man did not understand me—or rather, that
there was a screen between his unquestionably powerful intellect
and the perceptions of common sense. He began to orate but was
deflected skilfully by Miss Granham, who declared that the play
Faust by the German author Goethe would have been suitable—

'But,' said she, 'the genius of one language cannot be translated
into another.'

'I beg your pardon, ma'am?'

'I mean,' said she, patiently, as to one of her *young gentlemen*,
'you cannot translate a work of genius entirely from one language
to another!'

'Come now, ma'am,' said I, laughing, 'here at least I may claim
to speak with authority! My godfather has translated Racine entire
into English verse; and in the opinion of connoisseurs it equals
and at some points surpasses the original!'

The pair stopped, turned and stared at me as one. Mr Prettiman
spoke with his usual febrile energy.

'Then I would have you know, sir, that it must be unique!'

I bowed to him.

'Sir,' said I, 'it is!'

With that and a bow to Miss Granham I took myself off. I
scored, did I not? But really—they are a provokingly opinionated
pair! Yet if they are provoking and comic to *me* I doubt not that
they are intimidating to others! While I was writing this I heard
them pass my hutch on the way to the passenger saloon and
listened as Miss Granham *cut up* some unfortunate character.

'Let us hope he learns in time, then!'

'Despite the disadvantage of his birth and upbringing, ma'am,
he is not without wit.'

'I grant you,' said she, 'he always tries to give a comic turn to
the conversation and indeed one cannot help finding his laughter

at his own jests infectious. But as for his opinions in general—
Gothic is the only word to be applied to them!'

With that they passed out of earshot. They cannot mean Deverel, surely—for though he has some pretension to wit, his birth
and upbringing are of the highest order, however little he may
have profited from them. Summers is the more likely candidate.

I do not know how to write this. The chain would seem too thin,
the links individually too weak—yet something within me insists
they *are* links and all joined, so that I now understand what
happened to pitiable, clownish Colley! It was night, I was
heated and restless, yet my mind is in a fever—a *low* fever
indeed!—went back over the whole affair and would not let me
be. It seemed as if certain sentences, phrases, situations were
brought successively before me—and these, as it were, glowed
with a significance that was by turns farcical, gross and tragic.

Summers must have guessed. There *was* no leaf-tobacco! He
was trying to protect the memory of the dead man!

Rogers in the enquiry with a face of well-simulated astonishment—'What did *we* do, my lord?' Was that astonishment well-
simulated? Suppose the splendid animal was telling the naked,
the physical truth! Then Colley in his letter—*what a man does
defiles him, not what is done by others*—Colley in his letter, infatuated
with the 'king of my island' and longing to kneel before him—
Colley in the cable locker, drunk for the first time in his life and
not understanding his condition and in a state of mad exube-
rance—Rogers owning in the heads that he had knowed most
things in his life but had never thought *to get a chew off a parson*!
Oh, doubtless the man consented, jeeringly, and encouraged the
ridiculous, schoolboy trick—even so, not Rogers but Colley
committed the *fellatio* that the poor fool was to die of when he
remembered it.

Poor, poor Colley! Forced back towards his own kind, made
an equatorial fool of—deserted, abandoned by me who could
have saved him—overcome by kindness and a gill or two of the
intoxicant——

I cannot feel even a pharisaical complacency in being the only
gentleman not to witness his ducking. Far better had I seen it so
as to protest at that childish savagery! Then my offer of friendship
might have been sincere rather than——

I shall write a letter to Miss Colley. It will be lies from begin-

ning to end. I shall describe my growing friendship with her
brother. I shall describe my admiration for him. I shall recount all
the days of his *low fever* and my grief at his death.

A letter that contains everything but a shred of truth! How is
that for a start to a career in the service of my King and Country?

I believe I may contrive to increase the small store of money
that will be returned to her.

It is the last page of your journal, my lord, last page of the
'ampersand'! I have just now turned over the pages, ruefully
enough. Wit? Acute observations? Entertainment? Why—it has
become, perhaps, some kind of sea-story but a sea-story with
never a tempest, no shipwreck, no sinking, no rescue at sea, no
sight nor sound of an enemy, no thundering broadsides, heroism,
prizes, gallant defences and heroic attacks! Only one gun fired
and that a blunderbuss!

What a thing he stumbled over in himself! Racine declares—
but let me quote your own words to you.

> *Lo! where toils Virtue up th'Olympian fteep——*
> *With like fmall fteps doth Vice t'wards Hades creep!*

True indeed, and how should it be not? It is the smallness of
those steps that enables the Brocklebanks of this world to survive,
to attain a deboshed and saturated finality which disgusts everyone but themselves! Yet not so Colley. He was the exception.
Just as his iron-shod heels shot him rattling down the steps of the
ladders from the quarterdeck and afterdeck to the waist; even so a
gill or two of the *fiery ichor* brought him from the heights of
complacent austerity to what his sobering mind must have felt as
the lowest hell of self-degradation. In the not too ample volume
of man's knowledge of Man, let this sentence be inserted. Men
can die of shame.

The book is filled all but a finger's breadth. I shall lock it, wrap
it and sew it unhandily in sailcloth and thrust it away in the
locked drawer. With lack of sleep and too much understanding I
grow a little crazy, I think, like all men at sea who live too close
to each other and too close thereby to all that is monstrous under
the sun and moon.